PRAISE FOR BOOK FOUR
Candlewicke 13: The 13ᵗʰ Hour Begins

"I have adored this series from the very first novel, and it's clear that author Milan Sergent has a fantastic sense of storytelling that spans not just each individual book, but the build-up of the series as a whole. . . . I would highly recommend *Candlewicke 13: The 13th Hour Begins* as a stunning continuation to an already superb series."   —K.C. Finn for *Readers' Favorite*

"[A] truly mesmerizing series . . . . A well-written sequel, a fascinating story, and a fabulous plot. And these are action-packed books from start to finish."

—Anne-Marie Reynolds for *Readers' Favorite*

"Being the Knight of Night is not easy . . . . What can I say? I love this series. . . . As expected of Milan Sergent, the narrative flows beautifully and is intricate enough to blow my mind."   —Rabia Tanveer for *Readers' Favorite*

"This world continues to be an amazing blend of grim, melancholy, and whimsical with unusual creatures and a unique setting that gets better with every installment. . . . Sergent provides plenty of surprises throughout the plot with chaos, danger, humor, and delights . . . ."   —Liz Konkel for *Readers' Favorite*

PRAISE FOR BOOK THREE
Candlewicke 13: Under the Crescent Moon

"This is another exceptional offering from Milan Sergent. A fantastic addition to the series. . . . The characterization just gets better and better and the plot is a masterpiece. Milan Sergent continues to display his amazing imagination and way with words as the story pulls you deep into it, transporting you to a land of magic and fantasy."   — Anne-Marie Reynolds for *Readers' Favorite*

"A spectacular novel . . . packed with adventure and suspense . . . worldbuilding and character development that is rich and layered . . . The illustrations are gorgeous . . . Highly recommended."   — Asher Syed for *Readers' Favorite*

"Continuing the excellent Candlewicke 13 series with this third installment of magic, suspense, and incredible mysteries . . . now the mysteries of the McRaven family and the prophecies ahead are getting clearer and more exciting by the moment."   — K.C. Finn for *Readers' Favorite*

"This is young adult fiction at its best . . . The plot is amazing. I think the author has not only justified the story but actually given more for the reader to anticipate."

— Rabia Tanveer for *Readers' Favorite*

"Milan Sergent brings this world to life with vivid characters, a delightful grim setting, and suspense that will keep you guessing . . . an unforgettable adventure that has mystery, danger, ghosts, and magic."   — Liz Konkel for *Readers' Favorite*

PRAISE FOR BOOK TWO
Candlewicke 13 and the Tombstone Forest

Recipient of Readers' Favorite Annual International Book Award for the Children - Fantasy/Sci-Fi Category

Recipient of Book Excellence Award Finalist - Fantasy

"It was an absolute delight to return to the bizarre, macabre and utterly entertaining world of the McRavens . . . fluid prose, immense wit and highly engaging dialogue . . . another superb YA fantasy novel, not to be missed."

— K.C. Finn for *Readers' Favorite*

"Engaging storytelling ... bursts with odd, witty, playful incidents and characters. The narrative continually surprises ... charming ... laugh-out-loud funny."

—The BookLife Prize by *Publishers Weekly*

"This was an extremely well-written book, with shades of Harry Potter mixed with the Addams family in a story that starts high and stays there all the way. Illustrations and maps help the story along and there are plenty of little clues hidden along the way - if you can spot them . . . this is proving to be an excellent series. The characters are wonderful and the writing is such that they are brought alive in your mind, allowing you to get to know them."

— Anne-Marie Reynolds for *Readers' Favorite*

"Readers who have read Septimus Heap or fans of Harry Potter will find much to enjoy in this series. The prose is awesome and the world building impeccable . . . Author Milan Sergent keeps it fast and maintains the attention of readers from one gripping page to the next. The action is intense and the excitement builds up to an explosive climax."   — Divine Zape for *Readers' Favorite*

"Surprises, clues, and ironies abound in this narrative. Milan Sergent's writing is filled with imagination and a setting that is transporting as it reflects the excitement of the magical adventure."   — Romuald Dzemo for *Readers' Favorite*

"This story was very entertaining from the start until the very end. The mystery had me hooked while the suspense had me sitting on the edge my seat."

— Rabia Tanveer for *Readers' Favorite*

PRAISE FOR BOOK ONE
Candlewicke 13: Curse of the McRavens

"An exciting first entry . . . a gorgeous treat for fans of fantasy with unusual characters and intriguing plot lines." — Ruffina Oserio for *Readers' Favorite*

"Vibrant and funny . . . Sergent spins out a parade's worth of fresh, playful ideas . . . a bevy of oddball creatures . . . and that climactic tournament, a lulu involving cats, monkeys, ogres and more." —The BookLife Prize by *Publishers Weekly*

"This is a superbly entertaining work of fantasy fiction . . . Milan Sergent has done a superb job with *Candlewicke 13: Curse of the McRavens*, and I can't wait for more." — K.C. Finn for *Readers' Favorite*

"The world-building is fascinatingly intricate and perturbingly eccentric, filled with fantastical creatures . . . this first book of the series will surely keep readers enthralled from start to finish." — Lit Amri for *Readers' Favorite*

"A dark blend of elements reminiscent of J.K. Rowling's Harry Potter saga and the Charles Addams' Addams Family cartoons." —*BlueInk Review*

"Humour, drama, questions, uncertainty, and tension erupt in a world of magic where anything seems possible. Follow the trail of clues and discover more hidden truths than you would dare imagine could be concealed."

— K.J. Simmill for *Readers' Favorite*

CANDLEWICKE 13

THE 13TH HOUR BEGINS

STORY AND ILLUSTRATIONS

BY

MILAN SERGENT

To my amazing and beautiful wife,
Rebecca, for her loving devotion.

Published by Cryptic Quill Publishing LLC.

ISBN 13: 978-1-7348775-0-2

Library of Congress Control Number: 2020907024

CONTENTS

History, as We Know It, Has Ended

HISTORY, AS WE KNOW IT, HAS ENDED

The final entry from the Mystic Memoir of the late Magister Siegfried Kettles

Thursday, Jan 6, 2011. Tonight, I have had a startling revelation: My career has been a complete and utter lie. I have not been the magister of Sanguinati History at Mystic Steeples; I have merely been a stage prop. What is worse, I cannot bring myself to inform the witches in Mystic City that history, as we know it, ended in 1805. Everything since that year can only be defined as propaganda. I now understand why: the more authentic the history I taught my apprentices of magic, the more Mystic Ministry limited me from accessing their storehouse of records. I may very well end up dead or imprisoned in solitary confinement like Valor McRaven. The Ministry knows that poor boy is the Knight of Night, and I must find a way to help Valor; he is the only young person I've seen brave enough to ask about our real history, and like me, he is paying the price. I was a fool to believe myself superior to him—to Sorcerers—but I fell for the Sanguinati's propaganda.

After I discovered former magisters of Sanguinati History have mysteriously vanished or come up dead, I started sending Vortexes of Revealing out through the magic veil that conceals our enchanted country here in the Bermuda Triangle. It seems that when the Great Witch discovered Hoopenfangia, as a place for witches of the world to escape persecution, some chose to remain behind in their countries of origin.

The Vortexes have recorded these remaining witches. It seems the Nizzertits of the world have come to know them as the Men in Black. And these black-clad witches have somehow come under the control of the Grim Warlock. Their mission, at best, is one of disinformation. The Grim Warlock instructs them to erase any documented evidence of magic before the Nizzertits restart their crusades, inquisitions, and trials against practitioners of the magic arts. At worst, the Grim Warlock might be using the Men in Black to hide evidence in those countries until he can purify the world in the prophesied Thirteenth Hour.

I write this with a garland of garlic around my neck as I have heard noises in my room, and the guardian I requested Summoner Mamahchi provide me has yet to arrive. I don't think I can survive another *Progress Gauge Report*, as they are becoming harder and har—

CHAPTER ONE

MYSTIC NEEDLES AND EXECRATION RITUALS

CHILLS traveled up Valor McRaven's stomach to the back of his neck; one of his coven mates had developed pimples. Earlier, Valor got butterflies in his stomach when he noticed the magister of spells and wand usage had acquired a few more wrinkles and gray hairs.

"Reality has set in at last. You cannot say that I did not warn you of this," whispered Valor's best friend, Aaron Hutton. "In a few years, babies will start looking down at you the same way you once looked down at Doomsy Gloomsy—before you found out she wasn't really eight, but a two-hundred-and-fifteen-year-old woman."

1

Valor was fourteen, and his adopted sister still looked eight. Naturally, he had to look down to see her, but it wasn't natural that he alone was to take care of her—forever.

"Surely, none of us can keep this lie—*this life* up very much longer."

"'Tis inevitable," Aaron said with a chuckle. "Others will continue to change, my friend. We . . . will not."

Valor thought of his friend Rose Decay, how she, too, must be coming to terms with being an immortal Sorcerer—having to go home to her ailing father and her brother's funeral after a dragon's breath cooked him. He missed her.

"You thought turning Delicia into a swamp creature was inevitable as well. She's lucky that spell got reversed, Aaron."

Many curious and hostile eyes beaded on Valor, including Delicia Jones, whose warty face reminded Valor that his friends had turned her into a toad, days earlier.

"Verily, it was merely a spell to keep her from stalking us," said Aaron, who looked fifteen but was secretly over two hundred just like Doomsy. With Aaron's refined mannerism and old-world speech, he had a harder time faking his youth than little Doomsy did.

"In a hundred years, we can't still keep returning to Cryptic Auditorium to receive more apprentice uniforms like this," said Valor. "Talk about stalking; how long before the Crypts—before everyone—realizes we aren't . . . normal?"

"Yes, they are already suspicious of us."

"Then there is no time to play around. We must prove to the Sanguinati that they are *all* in danger, and it's not Sorcerers who are the problem—we have to convince them that their beloved O Enchantedness is the Grim Warlock and Tilta Crumpecker is the Conjuring Crone. That'll be hard enough, but we'll never succeed if we continue to make unnecessary enemies. We need to start by getting the Crypts to accept us as their presidents," said Valor.

He feared he and his friends would have to flee the Sanguinati witches' kingdom known as Mystic Steeples. Valor, Doomsy, and Aaron had received coveted golden keys for free apprenticeships from

Head Vespercestor Urbanne LaRock, formally titled O Enchantedness. These keys nearly cost Valor his life. He had recently come to terms that he should beware of gifts, for they often come with snakes. O Enchantedness was only tolerating Valor, using him, and was probably planning to kill all of Valor's secret coven members after he got what he wanted.

"You worry too much about these primitives. We can buy anything we need," Aaron said with a seasoned grin. "I easily found tailors who could duplicate Doomsy's cross-boned stitching for the new capes. The Crypts will love them."

"Yes, because Bama Bucks refused to sew the new capes. And how long before we get accused of killing her sister and hiding her body? The Sanguinati are changing but not fast enough—at least internally, they aren't."

Aaron leaned in to whisper, "They will never find Clara's body if we cannot. Candlewicke Mansion has a history of losing its visitors. 'Tis just as well. Bama would never have duplicated my fabulous design enough for an entire coven." Aaron pushed the side of his new cape over his shoulder. "Live while you can, my friend; Venerious Falmoth may be telling the truth—Mystic Ministry may just be fattening us up for the slaughter."

For some reason, Valor feared Falmoth, the former head vespercestor now living in exile, more than he feared O Enchantedness. Even though Valor had recovered three stolen Zodiacal Instruments that had saved not only this region but the whole world, some of Mystic Ministry and the Sanguinati shunned Valor and his friends at times. As if shunning Sorcerers was the one liberty these witches were still allowed to enjoy.

"Master Mesthu warned his Children of this if we ever left his coven," continued Aaron. "In a few years, these primitives will know that all your friends are immortals—Sorcerers. Therefore, if we cannot break their primitive superstitions, we might as well enjoy the moment and let them take our money."

Valor didn't respond; the capes' jingling and sparkling put him in a trance, as the tailors removed them from the racks, and the Cryptic

Chambers' Coven Secretary, Esoterica Knowles, distributed them to the Crypts. Valor tried to postpone his concerns. It was these moments, and the big party O Enchantedness just hosted for him, that helped Valor forget his terrible childhood in Grossatete Sanatorium. It also helped him forget how his parents, Houmas and Lithium McRaven, had escaped that prison to take shelter in a log cabin in Diabolishire. With the endless excitement of Mystic City and Mystic Steeples, Valor could sometimes ignore the obsessive predictions that the Grim Warlock was destroying the Sanguinati and would soon annihilate their island country of witches. But it was as Doomsy had said, "I'd rather risk someone murdering me in Severance, Hoopenfangia, than to return to the Bumbling Boonies and rot in Houmas and Lithium's wilderness of death."

Egg Goodridge, the newest and thirteenth member of Valor's secret coven, called Candlewicke 13, burst out of one of the ancient sarcophagi lining the dressing room. He examined his Cryptic Chambers' uniform in the reflective waters of a scrying bowl held over the head of a kneeling witch statue. Egg was two years younger than Valor, and his appearance was slowly changing because he wasn't immortal. In Valor's opinion, Egg was nowhere near ready for such a change, no matter how much Egg wanted to be like his new friends—no matter how much Aaron wanted to make everyone he liked immortal to protect them.

"These capes remind m-me of the Ancients' ceremonial clothes I've s-seen in the museums," stuttered Egg.

"I'm not wearing it," snorted Marston Diamone. "I look like the curtains in Mumbazandie's office."

"Insubordinate as always," said Esoterica. She shot a studious look of caution to Marston and fastened all the gold cording across the front of her black cape.

"Those shadow tossers aren't our presidents," hissed Marston's sister Twila, glaring at Valor, Aaron, and Doomsy.

"Yes, they are," said Esoterica.

"Whatever. I'm not wearing this," said Marston, flinging his cape on the floor.

"You will wear a pink frock from Gitchi Patootie's if your coven presidents tell you to," said Esoterica.

"Or a body bandage, if he's not careful," growled Doomsy, with three strategic flutters of her eyelashes.

"Oh, say, this is jolly good," Valor whispered to Aaron and Doomsy. "Marston hates the new uniform so much, maybe he and Twila will leave Cryptic Chambers."

"That'll never happen . . . n-not now," Egg whispered to Valor. "Marston and Twila tried to transfer to Graven Dust Coven and almost got permission from O Enchantedness until t-they got caught damaging that statue of Pippa."

"That's all they were charged with?" asked Doomsy, emerging from another upright sarcophagus in her new cape.

"Yeah," said Egg, flaring out his cape like a bat spreading its wings. "'Accidental vandalism.' Not enough to s-sentence them to the sanatorium, so they got p-punished by not being able to change covens."

"Accidental? Marston and Twila tried to squash us with that giant statue!" said Valor, starting to get chills again. "It's so unfair. That's the second time Mystic Ministry has kept those two out of the sanatorium. I can't believe they were going to let them switch covens; nobody else has ever been able to switch before."

With a droopy smirk, Doomsy eyed Valor from head to toe and said, "You need to build a muscle or two and start showing the Diamones who runs this coven."

Valor shut his eyes. "My dear, you can't just go around attacking people. You have to learn a little tact."

"Time to head for Convocation," Aaron said to the apprentices, "and do not wrinkle your new capes."

The coven of Cryptic Chambers left the castle and flew their brooms over rooftops to Mystic Steeples, a ten-story citadel for the Sanguinati witches and Ministry. This ancient citadel surrounded Mystic City so high and dense that only strong downbursts of wind could stir the city's trees inside the barrier of stone.

With every eye on them that Saturday evening, the Crypts made their way through the massive halls before arriving at the Congre Gate. As presidents of their coven, Valor, Doomsy, and Aaron entered the tunneled gate first. They paused every few feet in front of interlocked stone arms so that the statues could inspect them with wand lights.

"*Cygnus Inter Anates. Rorate Coeli*!" the statues sang after the three of them made it past the final wand-light inspection.

The arched door creaked open to Mystic Chantry, which was packed wall to wall and balcony to stacked balcony by chanting witches, spooky vocalizing from the lofty choir, and the voices of the deceased stolen for the massive wind-piped organ.

Guardians Iliad Underkofler and Helios Hollapolk crossed their long magic staffs, blocking Valor from entering the Chantry.

"Valor McRaven. I cannot believe you have the nerve to show your face after that stunt you pulled, trying to remove our defenses," said Helios.

"Yeah," agreed Iliad. "Mystic Ministry will never release the Bound Order of the Zodiac—"

"My brother is trying to keep us all safe. Tell them, Valor," croaked Doomsy, shoving him in front of the guardians. "Tell these mass-produced, lantern-lugging, ox hormones to get out of our way."

The guardians moved their staffs from Valor and crossed them in front of Doomsy.

"And you have even more nerve setting foot in our—" Helios stopped speaking, dropped his staff, and with a growl, knocked down half of Cryptic Chambers into a pile at the entry.

Guardian Iliad released his staff, and his eyes bulged up at the ceiling as he began to mumble and convulse. Valor grabbed Doomsy and pulled her safely to his side next to Aaron.

"Has he gone mad? What is he saying?" asked Doomsy.

"'The adder is cunning,' I think," whispered Valor.

"I thought he said, 'Be faster when running,'" said Aaron.

Iliad and Helios tumbled to the floor and began grabbing at any legs that passed near them. Helios pulled down an elderly woman who screamed for help as he began to gnaw on her boot. Within seconds, Iliad and Helios became as stiff as the floor they were sprawled across. Trailed by two guardians, Summoner Mamahchi tore through the gathering crowd.

"Too late—they're both dead," said Mamahchi, removing his tattered hat mournfully.

"More victims of the Possessing," said one of the guardians, while the other and Mamahchi ordered the crowd to move along.

Valor looked back over his shoulder just as one of his enemies, Harwin Hollapolk, joined the remaining crowd and discovered his father's body. As much as Valor disliked Harwin, the vision of him dropping to his knees in tears cut through him worse than the glass bottle Harwin had hit him with near the sanatorium.

"Ghastly," Valor sighed. "You mean those poor men died from being possessed? I thought they were acting unusual as soon as I saw them."

"No loss. They were always rotten," said Doomsy.

"That's frightfully cold of you, my dear," said Valor, getting hiccups from the distress. How quickly and how strangely two men he had known for a while were now no more. Deaths were becoming disturbingly commonplace—just minor interruptions in everyone's daily schedules.

"Perhaps we should head to our seats before they blame us," suggested Aaron, as Egg caught up to them, trembling.

They filed into their designated section of benches. The setting sun beamed through the high-stacked windows, causing the swirling smoke from incense and burning candles to glow hypnotically. High Priestess Tilta Crumpecker stormed to the podium so fast a few of her burning candles in her crown snuffed out.

"By now, you all have heard about the passing of two of our guardians," Crumpecker yelled into the floating magihorn, while a splatter of outcries ricocheted across the Chantry. "You can bet your bloomers we're gonna get to the bottom of these tragedies. In the meantime, stay calm and keep your trust in Mystic Ministry."

"Who are those people in the bright colors and plaid shirts," Valor asked Egg, who was sitting beside Doomsy, biting his nails.

"Where?"

"In the Guests' Balcony."

"They're Nizzertits," answered Egg. "Mystic M-ministry allows them to tour our Convocations now if they p-pay them lots of globulnugees."

"That's jolly promising, I do say." Valor scooted to the front of his bench. "Never in a million years would I imagine the head vespercestor would allow non-witches to join our coveted ceremonies."

"Don't shoot your broom to the moon yet, my pet. O Enchantedness is just desperate for money," said Doomsy. She crammed her ebony-wood wand in the holder in the back of the bench in front of her, nearly breaking the ancient wand's nine-inch phoenix-spine core.

Just when Valor thought he had lived to see life's most shocking surprise, Summoner Eelias Mamahchi marched up to the platform, clenching, at arm's length, a man's purple underwear with some writing on it. Valor peered through his Focus Pocus Monoculous wand but still couldn't make out the words from the back of the Chantry.

"A quick announcement," said Summoner Mamahchi. "There will be a Spurgmulin Tournament tomorrow evening."

The audience broke into a rumble of excitement, and Mamahchi silenced everyone to continue his announcement:

"Ruza Renata, are you present?" asked Mamahchi.

Every head turned before Ruza stood up in her purple robe in the Wormwood Philters' section of the Chantry.

"You are on the list . . . as a potential schlemeasel," said Mamahchi. "And . . . Marston Diamone."

"What?" Valor gasped. "What has Ruza possibly done to be picked as the schlemeasel?"

"She scolded the LaRocks and defended you, that's what," said Doomsy of their secret coven mate. Many in the congregation began growling like cats and pawing at the air near Ruza.

"Marston was the second candidate. However, he's been

unselected since Mystic Ministry received this, um . . . *disturbing* note from somebody with the initials M. D." Mamahchi waved the underwear in the air. "In view of this information, two more names have been added as potential schlemeasels." Mamahchi looked out over the Chantry with a dour face and said, "Valor McRaven, if you are present, please stand."

"There must be a mistake. You've already been the schlemeasel," Doomsy whispered to Valor, who felt as though a jolt of lightning had shot through his body before he stood up at the back of the mass assembly.

"UNFAIR!" Ruza roared. Her glorious mane of curls engulfed the back of her purple robe as she stabbed her finger at Urbanne. "O Enchantedness, this is the second time Marston and Twila have gotten away with a severe attack against Valor McRaven. Blatant bias here! We all know you're showing partiality because the Diamones are honorary nobles."

Marston laughed on the bench behind Valor as Ruza stood defiant in the front of the assembly.

That did it. Valor couldn't let Ruza be the schlemeasel. He feared her acceptance that she would die young was unhealthy. If not, her premonitions could turn into an outright death wish. Too, Valor couldn't let Marston think he had rattled him in any way.

"I want to be the schlemeasel," shouted Valor, waving his hand as eagerly as he could.

The audience nearly choked from disbelief. The visiting Nizzertits' eyes swelled with fear and fascination.

Urbanne LaRock stood up from his throne chair and said, "Such a brave gesture to volunteer. Be it known in the archives of history—I do not make decisions unfairly and do hereby declare the tournament a doubleheader. Valor McRaven and Aaron Hutton will be replacing Ruza Renata as the schlemeasel."

Aaron slapped his hand over his heart as if it were about to explode.

"Not my friends Aaron or Ruza, O Enchantedness sir," said Valor, dismayed at the change of plans. "I meant just myself."

"The decision stands," said O Enchantedness, peering over his galaxy glasses sternly.

"I'm so sorry, Aaron," said Valor, after sitting back down. "I didn't know they would make this a doubleheader. They have to know it was Marston Diamone telling more lies."

"Ah," sighed Aaron, while the audience clapped and exchanged whispers. "Or it could be Mega D's way of forcing us to do his bidding. I knew we should have turned him into the reptile that he is."

"Oh—I didn't think about Mega D," said Valor, remembering the wild Sorcerer who tried to get Valor and his friends to overthrow the Sanguinati. Was his claim true? Was O Enchantedness the Grim Warlock, who would use the Bound Order of the Zodiac to fulfill the Thirteenth Hour?

"Which M.D. could it be? It has to be one of the two," asked Valor, while the high priest made a flowery announcement about the entertainment lined up for the tournament.

Doomsy leaned over and said, "Well, *you* won't do anything, so do you want me to turn them both into lizards?"

"I'm not going to give in to Marston or Mega D, even if the tournament kills me this time. How about you?" Valor cut his eyes up at Aaron.

Aaron crossed his legs and placed his arm on the back of the bench. "Betwixt the two frightful options, I'd rather die depriving Mega D the satisfaction," said Aaron.

"Ghastly, though. What could they have possibly written about us on the underclothing?" asked Valor, before Marston and Twila broke into wicked laughter.

"You don't t-think O Enchantedness invented the underwear note to p-punish you, do you, Valor?" said Egg.

"His galaxy glasses burst gamma rays when you asked him to set the Bound Order of the Zodiac free," said Doomsy while the choir sang.

"I might think that except he just targeted Ruza and Aaron without reason. No, I'm now convinced Urbanne is the real Grim

Warlock." Valor's blood ran cold, and he glared up at Tilta Crumpecker, Summoner Mamahchi, and O Enchantedness on the platform.

Doomsy elbowed Valor and whispered, "What's happening? The moons in your eyes are glowing."

"Cryptic Chambers, gather your brooms and come up to the front here," said Urbanne, waiting behind the podium.

Valor, Doomsy, and Aaron did their presidential duties and led their coven to the spirit-board floor called the Avitestari, at the bottom of the raised platform. With smug grins, Marston and Twila kept in the back of the Crypts.

"*Ooh . . . ah . . .*" some of the audience gasped at the new uniforms, while a few apprentices from the other covens giggled and grumbled.

With wild-eyed glances, Urbanne climbed on top of the podium and swirled his magic staff over his head.

"As you come forward, I want each of you to take off your coven pendants and put them over your inner eye. You will fly around the sanctuary to commemorate when the Ancients flew their brooms over the region of Icy Pentacles during the destruction of Mesthu's Children!"

"How dare Urbanne?" asked Aaron. "Mystic Military hunted down Master Mesthu and his followers when they left Mystic Steeples, killing some, but half of them escaped over the Ambergis Divide."

"He isn't worried that the Sanguinati will learn the truth. He knows they can't get across the Ambergis Divide to see for themselves," whispered Valor, while he placed his coven pendant necklace on his forehead.

"Just look at him." Doomsy aimed the handle of her broom at Urbanne. "He must think he's Sesepha on the banks of the Severance River, like in that stupid painting in his office."

"I think t-this is part of his Landmark Remembrances lecture. He gets c-carried away and thinks he's an Ancient sometimes," said Egg, as they neared the platform where the apprentices lined up to take flight.

Esoterica glanced at them over the rim of her glasses. "Some say O Enchantedness has been indulging in a lot of potions lately."

Aaron gave a fake laugh, angled his broom toward the ceiling, and took off in the direction of the Eclectica Balcony, while Doomsy straddled her broom and tightened the laces on her boots so they wouldn't fall off in flight. Cryptic Chambers began to fly their brooms around Mystic Chantry. The Twirlyurgy spun around like tornadoes, and several of the witches screamed and chanted as if they were in pain. As his wand bounced in the air far ahead of him, Preston Fox led the choir and orchestra into a rousing song.

Urbanne yelled over the banging of the drums and screaming, "The times we are living in are starting to mirror history. Only the new Sorcerers will be led by the Grim Warlock, who will start the Grim Hour by destroying all our landmarks. Hold your magic staffs high, Vespercestors. We shall send a hex on their heads."

"This is ridiculous. Marston and Twila nearly destroyed the landmark statue of Pippa Phantasma, and *they* aren't considered a threat in the least," Valor said to Doomsy before he passed her on his new broom, which he was finally learning to slow its incredible speed.

Urbanne tapped the tip of his magic staff against his forehead and yelled, "Heredity!" He then made arm gestures, forming a square in the air, and throughout the perimeter of the Chantry, serpent statues reared their heads in sequence, heralding the presence of Urbanne's wife, Mahrata LaRock. She walked across the podium, carrying a purple-velvet pillow with what appeared to be jewel-tipped hatpins sticking out of its fabric.

"Mystic Needles, rise up!" Mahrata ordered. Several ghosts grabbed the needles from the cushion and held them midair, awaiting her next command. "From toes to eyes and hips to lips, I charge thee to stick and prick those who despise this pure Ministry."

As Valor flew his broom between the chandeliers, the ghosts floated through the air, carrying the long needles. How could he know if any of the needles were sticking anyone with all the screaming? A ghost chased after him, while the Loft of Elders gazed down across the Chantry: shadows cast under the bags of their eyes, hooked noses, and the rolls of their stormy hair and beards. They took notes with their quills, scrutinizing the movements of the Mystic Needles and the apprentices' reactions.

"Ah, you think you have me cornered, you miserable specters. Why don't you take those needles and knit yourselves some proper shrouds?" Aaron said to the circle of ghosts surrounding him after he flew his broom out from under the third-level balcony.

"I think the ghosts are triggered by our anger," Valor said to Aaron and Doomsy. "Try laughing. Ha-ha-ha!" His hand made a subtle whirl, before his broom shot straight up to the ceiling, sending the ghosts crashing through each other. Two of the spirits dropped their needles in the Graven Dust section: one straight into a woman's hat, and the other, into the shoulder of Banastre Mathers. Two male apprentices screamed and began attacking the Brazen Gravens, who flapped their arms in the air and dashed through the aisles, wailing.

"It's working. Laugh, Doomsy, laugh," giggled Valor, knocking a needle away from her, but she refused to try it.

"I'm tired of this circus. I'm landing right now," huffed Doomsy. She flew past Valor and landed her broom in the aisle between Dragon's Mantle and Snuffinumbra Covens.

Urbanne stopped the choir and orchestra. A moment of sweaty silence seemed to seize the entire Convocation. He pointed his finger at Doomsy and said, "Young lady, you have a rebellious spirit and—"

"I will not be another one of your puppets," yelled Doomsy, banging her broom on the floor.

Urbanne's face wrinkled under his long orange ringlets, and he lifted his magic staff as if ready to cast a hex on Doomsy. Valor had to protect his sister. He glared at Urbanne, gathering a surge of will and energy, which shoved Urbanne off the podium. The guardians rushed to help him up from the floor, while the lesser vespercestors glowered at Doomsy with stony faces, holding their ornate staffs in readiness. Their eyes lowered to the ground floor. Two apprentices who had attacked Graven Dust Coven lay motionless in the aisle.

"Excuse me, O Enchantedness," said Summoner Mamahchi. "I

just received word: Apprentices Seth Morrigan and Ares Caswall . . . are dead."

"Aw. Who were those two boys?" Valor asked Esoterica Knowles as she flew her broom beside him, while guardians carried out the bodies.

"Employees at Bellona Donar Enchanted Weaponry." Esoterica shrugged her shoulders with a grim expression, before guiding her broom over a balcony of stargazers.

"The mover of the Ancients powed on me. I can stardly hand up," Urbanne stammered his words, trying to pull himself up to the podium, as Marston Diamone and other apprentices ran for the exit door.

"*Usta Etgo Ether.* Scribe Fengurstaph, I want a *Controssua* placed in front of every door going out of this Chantry. If anybody leaves before this ceremony's over, you're stepping on the blood of the Ancestors," said Urbanne. He raised and lowered his magic staff in a grandiose manner.

"Cryptic Chambers, you may land your brooms and return to your assigned section," said Mahrata, conjuring the Mystic Needles back to the velvet pillow. "Hmm . . . haa," she sighed, often swallowing, while six black-cloaked dwarves rekindled the smoking urns surrounding the altar before they walked out backward and through a door under the choir loft. Mahrata braced her arm against the podium with a raised brow and said, "Not you, Doomsy. I need you to, haa, come up here, hmm, any day now."

"What shall befall her?" Aaron whispered to Valor, while Doomsy hiked up her dress and stomped up the steps to the platform.

"I don't know," said Valor, keeping his attention on her, feeling as though he were bleeding inside. "I think they're trying to expose us as Sorcerers."

Doomsy eased up the steps when, in a musical explosion, the choir and orchestra signaled for the various covens to begin inner-eye running. A blur of activity blinded Valor's view of Doomsy as the apprentices tried to sense their way through the Chantry with squeezed-shut eyelids, running straight into the sanctuary walls like dizzy bats.

Aaron pulled Valor out of the way of a group of scampering Graven Dust apprentices, while children hid under the benches, collecting amulets and talismans that fell off various hats, beards, and robes. Mesmerists invaded the Chantry, and many apprentices dropped to the floor—assault of the Ancients, as Valor remembered his father calling it whenever he went into convulsions on the floor.

Ruza Renata hobbled past Valor and Aaron. She knelt behind a balcony staircase and mixed a chunky herbal potion with a soapstone mortar and pestle.

"What happened to you, Ruza?" Valor asked while the crowds obscured the platform. "What's happening to Doomsy?"

"Dunno about Doomsy, but I'm removing the evidence!" Ruza cursed and scowled. "This happens all the bloody time. The mesmerists knock people out so they can check the bottoms of their cloud stompers and stuff." Ruza pointed to her black boots. "C'mon, you know, you know. For bloody evidence of execration rituals," she growled, her brown eyes enshrouded in thick layers of black planet dust. "Oh, darn it, darn it! This potion is supposed to solve the problem. Okay, look: I carved Urbanne's image on the bottom of this cloud stomper." She lifted her left boot. "And that cow, Mahrata, is on this cloud stomper—just a little curse, okay?"

"Is that why they're targeting us again?" asked Valor.

"Again?" huffed Ruza. "They never stopped. But this time, I think it has something to do with the Possessing."

"The Possessing? This is a new thing?" asked Aaron.

Ruza lowered her voice: "Creighton's parents overheard it from the vespercestors. Witches all over this region have been going loopy—become possessed. O Enchantedness thinks Sorcerers or Noctivatian have been causing this. While we were at your reward party, a girl named Sukie Starnes and the purse warden, Vonda LaRock, became possessed and leaped off two of the steeples over Buckthorn Hall—climbed and leaped."

Bloody River Styx, Valor thought. He already stopped the Quakening, the Deluging, and the Darkening. Was he now going to be confronting another phase in the Thirteenth Hour called the Possessing?

Ruza shrugged and unlaced her left boot. "Ugh, I think Hanzabuh broke my toe. She's being paid by the vespercestors to bust me up. She hates Sorcerers. But I'm mad at you. I may be a girl, but I could've managed as the schlemeasel."

"That's not why I volunteered, my dear." Valor wasn't so sure the statement was entirely accurate. "I wouldn't want *any* of my friends to be the schlemeasel."

"You're gonna die, too, McRaven. We all don't get rosy futures. I've made peace with it. I'm fighting 'till my last breath." Ruza finger-swiped a solitary tear across her eye shadow, smearing it like war paint, then she snatched on her cloud stomper.

"That is very negative thinking, my dear. You have your whole life ahead of you," said Valor. He stressed this to himself as well, for he was unsure of the prophecies about him perishing in his role as the Knight of Night. He looked up at Aaron's bleeding bottom lip and passed his handkerchief up to him.

"I thought those ridiculous needles had grazed my face," said Aaron. "But enough about me; what are they doing to Doomsy?"

"Ah-ha! Marston and Twila tipped me off that a Mystic Needle pricked you," said Guardian Gereon McMahon. He grabbed Aaron and Valor by the collars of their new capes. "Perhaps you two need to be at the Avitestari for the wand purification ceremony." Gereon lifted them up, and shoved them against the wall so hard, a few beads and talismans broke off their capes and landed at their feet. Outside the window beside them, a great serpent slithered against the stained glass. Like all the witches' animals, called Familiars, the snake was trying to join its master inside the Chantry, but Valor's familiar, an Elusive Griffin named Booger Fay, had been abducted and was still missing.

A censer tipped over due to the gathering horde of witches around the devotional bowl. Various coven members dropped talismans, tokens, and little scrolls with requests written on them into the bowl, which released a green vapor with each submission. At last, Doomsy appeared again. The vespercestors encircled her, tapping their wands together and chanting, but she stood with her arms folded and maintained a dead stare.

Valor steadied himself as the mesmerists' fingertips massaged his forehead, rubbing salt and crushed butterfly wing on him, until he became lightheaded.

"Must you spoil my hair?" groaned Aaron, as one of the mesmerists did the same to him. "This little brain massage might work on the gullible witches, but not me."

"Careful, Mesmerist, their shadows might possess you," cautioned Marston, placing a token in the devotional bowl and keeping his bitter eyes on Valor and Aaron.

"Welly Durri Wolliwi," chanted the mesmerist, ignoring Marston as he continued to massage Aaron's forehead.

"Let seven mesmerists behold. Valor is cold," muttered a mesmerist wearing a purple robe and seven amethysts rings. It was the father of Creighton Crowley, one of Valor's best friends. With dark, pulsating eyes, Mesmerist Kingston Crowley repeated a chant seven times, then said, "You haven't been spellcasting with the moon or projecting ectoplasm from any orifices—especially on the seventh day, have you?"

"No, sir," said Valor, before an old woman's voice whispered in Valor's ear:

"Soon, if the Sanguinati crave—if they conjure the truth, and you, the Knight of Night, make the correct choices, you will unravel the Great Deception."

Valor spun around and saw the ghost of a beggarly woman beside him. Aaron wiped his eyes with his lace sleeve after a teenage ghost wearing a Viking-style tunic sprinkled something in his eyes from a bottle resembling a saltshaker. The young ghost pierced the beggarly woman through with his sword.

"Begone, woman!" the ghost commanded. "You are no servant to the Sanguinati. The living girl, Ruza, was right. The Knight of Night will die heartbroken and alone. Ha-ha! He will lose many who are dear to him, and they will join us in the beyond."

"Are you so envious of those who resist death . . . that you would serve a lie? The mask is what must be killed . . . not the truth," the beggarly woman groaned before her spirit evaporated.

Mesmerist Kingston's head snapped with a moment of confusion, then he placed seven fingers on Valor's forehead, and a fog of musty incense engulfed the foot of the Avitestari where they stood. While many apprentices began crying in a trancelike state, Valor's thoughts wrestled as to how he could get the Sanguinati to realize they had been deceived.

"Mr. Crowley. This weepy reverie you think you're causing isn't real—believe me. There are ghosts sprinkling something in everybody's eyes—whispering sad stories in their ears. You can break the spell if you seek the truth."

"Look at the pendulum. Weepy reverie is a good thing," said Kingston, swinging his Triskelion on a chain in Valor's face. "It purifies your inner essence—your vision—so that you can clearly see the truth Mystic Ministry is showing you."

"I know you're only doing your job, sir, but I can't help but believe you're different," whispered Valor. "You also know somebody in the vespercestory killed Abner Cadabranathy, and they're trying to stop you from having a seventh son."

With his mouth slightly agape, Kingston leaned over, bringing his ear closer to Valor's head, pretending he was applying more salt and butterfly wing to his forehead.

Valor looked into his fearful eyes and whispered, "You are being manipulated. Your allegiance to the Ministry is hurting your son Creighton."

For a second, it seemed Kingston was about to make a much-needed confession, but his jaw locked tight, and Scribe Fengurstaph, a lesser vespercestor with a long white beard and hair, patted Kingston on the back and said, "Congratulations, Kingston! Your family must be beside themselves. We'll be seeing more of the Crowleys, won't we?"

"Thanks," said Kingston as he turned away into the crowd.

"Oh, Sanguinati, my beloved, some of you are beginning to see your scrying visions manifest in the dark hour ahead of us," said High Priest Teddyus Manoj. "Some of you may find yourself unable to speak or stand right now because of the mystical vibrations you are feeling, and those vibrations are the celestial footsteps of the Bound Order of the Zodiac fast approaching." Manoj paused, and his eyes enlarged, looking as though he were about to vomit. "*Phazafoon Invokedagoat.*" He stuck his tongue out and grabbed something sparkling off the tip. "Behold! I just coughed up a star fragment."

Valor tried to spot Doomsy before another mesmerist pushed him to the floor and swiped another handful of gritty salt and butterfly wing across his forehead and down his face. If only Valor had listened to Venerious Falmoth's warning about Mystic Ministry. He resisted calling out for the fallen head vespercestor.

Just as Valor opened his mouth, something strange happened. A couple of the stargazers flung balls of stardust at an intruder dressed in a shredded black dress—Banzalta Drayn, Falmoth's partner from the Tombstone Forest. The covens jeered and shot wand-zaps at her, but she wobbled in the middle of her spinning barrier of swords, which shielded her from their attacks. Several apprentices fled out the doorways as she teetered through the scrambling covens. Stretching her black-gloved hands out near the edge of her spinning swords, she mimicked their ranting with a squeal.

"She's trying to hex us!" shouted Valor's estranged great-grandmother, Lockie LaRock, from the Loft of Elders. The elders crossed their wands over their wrists in a binding spell.

Valor held his breath as Banzalta walked up to the Avitestari in front of her father, Urbanne, giving Doomsy time to scurry away from the vespercestors where she had been hiding behind a gong.

"Banzalta, leave Mystic Steeples now!" said Urbanne, with Mahrata joining at his side. "These are my children." He gestured down to the covens. "You are but a fungus on our family tree."

Banzalta ignored Urbanne and began fanning herself with her fan of sharp hatchets. "'Ou abandoned my children. 'Ou abandoned me," she cried and then began cackling while she ran her long black fingernails down her pale bald head. "And 'ou plan to murder Valor and his friends."

Urbanne motioned for the guardians with his magic staff. "Get her out of here," he said in a deep voice.

The Nizzertit tourists vacated their balcony, screaming, while the guardians fired binding spells at Banzalta, but her spinning swords cut through their attempts. Banzalta turned as if she would leave. Urbanne's wife, Mahrata, bent over, holding her arm across her teary eyes until one of the lesser vespercestors named Mumbazandie LaRock helped her off the platform.

Banzalta thrashed past Valor. Her crazed eyes locked on him. Had his thoughts conjured her? He had wasted time speculating. While a frantic crowd trailed down the aisle behind Banzalta, he grabbed Doomsy and Aaron, and they sneaked out the Dis Entrance, the back door beside the choir loft. Creighton Crowley joined them before they closed the door. Even from the outside, they could hear the covens cheering, "The wiggiwami has left the Chantry!"

"Can a witch not gain admittance inside this wretched sepulcher anymore?" Rose snarled, and they stopped in their tracks. "I tried to get through the door, and everyone's running out. I nearly got trampled." She put her fists on her hips.

"Rose! What a relief. Are you back from Lavisham to stay?" asked Valor, giving her a hug followed by Creighton, whose fairy, Hulkin, kept pulling strands of his hair and then his ears.

"Ouch! What's wrong with you, Hulkin?" huffed Creighton.

"Yeah," said Rose, clutching a hatbox. Her black-powdered lips curved down on one side. "Old Papa Ian passed on to the great astral plane. So, you guys are all I have left now."

"What? First, your brother and now, your father?" asked Creighton, with an irreverent expression.

"Of course we're your family, but sorry for your loss," said Valor.

They walked out of Mystic Steeples onto the corner of Ickylous and Crumrod Crawl, headed toward Candlewicke Mansion, Valor's home he had inherited from his grandfather. Under the bats swarming the gaslights, they paused again.

"It wasn't a bad thing that you didn't get in Mystic Chantry tonight," said Doomsy, who caught Rose up on everything in her absence. ". . . The vespercestors even tried to sanctiflame me—said I was cold. I showed them cold. It took them thirty minutes to remove the icicles off their fingertips."

"Old Urby had everyone playing along with the whole grim-expulsion thing," added Creighton.

Rose gave a halfhearted laugh and held her chin in her fingers. "Guys, I didn't want to say it at first, but I think someone killed my brother, Maxwell," said Rose. She stepped onto the curb for a carriage to pass. "Papa told me before he died, he was certain the Boogeyman flew over our house on the dragon that scorched Maxwell. But I don't know." Rose's posture slumped for a moment. "Papa thought every new leader was the Boogeyman, even his boss at the sausage factory. But enough about me, this drama with Valor and Aaron scares me. I ran into a girl earlier tonight with the reddest mane of hair I ever saw. Her name was—"

"You must be referring to Siobhan LeSabres," said Aaron. "None ever fail to notice her mass of crimson hair. Aurora always swore she refreshed the redness by washing her hair in the bloody Stonevengeance River."

"That was her name. She asked me if I knew you, Aaron, and you, Valor."

"First Mega D and now Siobhan has come to Severance—what, pray tell, did she say?" Aaron asked with a furrowed brow, adjusting his hair, the fragments that the mesmerists' hands had earlier smashed.

"She said you were in some sort of trouble, and that Mega D was looking for you."

"We already dealt with Mega D. Siobhan must be unaware," said Aaron dismissively.

All the stress made Valor thirsty, so he stopped at a drink stand where he purchased everyone a Notion Potion in the brew of their choice.

"That's what I thought," said Rose sipping her Oh-So-Certain Citrus with a dash of clary sage. "But this situation is definitely different; I'd be willing to shave my head." She crossed her arms and legs, scraping a discarded charm on the cobblestone with her dagger-heeled boot. Her coven pendant dangled under her black dress, which came over each shoulder like a bat's wing and gathered at her bellybutton with a large silver pentagram.

Doomsy sipped her Melancholy Melon Notion Potion and stroked the side of her cheek as she gazed up at the night sky, a lifeless sky compared to the usual spirited atmosphere of Mystic City. "Alas, Mega D is like a grave that washes up after a flood," said Doomsy.

"I'm telling you—this is terrible news." Rose's eyes tightened like a feline.

Doomsy sighed. "You all are pitiful. We're a coven of thirteen now. We should go to Diabolishire and show that oat-dribbling, loggerheaded, goat rump what bad news really is."

Everyone on Mystic Circle stopped walking when a glowing, swirling mass of clouds disrupted the calm night sky. The Sorcerers' Nocturne began to echo from the heavens louder and angrier than ever.

"Wow! I've got chill bumps over my entire body," said Valor, looking up at the disturbance in the distance through his monoculous. "Isn't that Venerious Falmoth's dragon circling in the air?"

They watched as Tareamugus spit breaths of fire from its two heads, and the flames fell like comets into the distant city. Aaron floated down from the fourth-story rooftop of Gifting Gifts and Tricker Treats and retrieved his Fussy Fudge Notion Potion.

"Yes," he said. "Falmoth and Banzalta are riding Tareamugus—Falmoth is straddling the beast, and Banzalta is riding sidesaddle. And judging their distance, it would appear that the dragon just attacked somewhere outside of Mystic Steeples—Woobind Terraces perhaps."

"Unhh, this disturbs me. I haven't thrown up since I became immortal, but I'm about to," groaned Rose. She sashayed to the front of Palm Readers' Palace on Mystic Circle, holding the loose tendrils of her hair back from her face. She stood there in front of the giant hand-shaped entry for a few seconds, but her gaping mouth only emitted a dry hack.

Creighton gulped the last bit of his Baffling Butterscotch and patted Rose on her back. "What's wrong? If it's about someone looking for Aaron and Valor, they won't be hard to miss while they're tied up in the tournament tomorrow night," said Creighton.

Rose stood up straight, held her hand over her mouth, and glared at Creighton.

"Okay . . . maybe they *don't* need to be found. How am I supposed to know?" Creighton rubbed his chin.

"Guys, you have to find a way out of being the schlemeasels. This is all a plan to—to kill you," said Rose.

"Dear, don't let this get to you. There's nothing to worry about," said Valor, trying to comfort her. Although she could be right, he didn't seem to care so much now.

"My. Someone has suddenly become a master of apathy in this bleak existence where we struggle to survive," Doomsy lifted her drooping eyes at Valor.

"I—I try to see life differently now," said Valor. He stirred his All Things Rosy Notion Potion with a broom straw and saw his reflection in the window of Fancy Familiar Grooming shop. His lips had stained pink from the icy drink, but he liked the bit of color. "We don't always get what we want. Why should we, and why should they?"

Rose turned her head away and pulled the strap of her charm pouch back over her shoulder, the black marmatite stones embedded on the bag sparkled. Her hand lowered as if she were trying to conceal her heartbeat.

"Thanks for trying to cheer me up, Valor, but it's obvious, you've had too much Notion Potion," said Rose.

"I wish this turmoil to cease as well," said Aaron, clutching his gloves and making subtle bowing gestures.

"I'm sure it will." Valor smiled and plopped down on a bench under a large oak tree. A nearly bald bird plucked twigs from her own nest and flung them to the ground before flinging one of her eggs on

Creighton's head.

Valor's eyelids became droopy. "So, we should all just stay calm but alert," he mumbled.

A distant explosion startled Aaron, Rose, and Creighton, so they snatched Valor off the bench and dashed home to Candlewicke.

SPURGMULIN ABUZZING

EVERYONE gathered under the onion-shaped dome in Candlewicke's observatory overlooking the courtyard and much of Mystic City. Micha DeMise had spent most of the afternoon coaching Aaron on how to survive as the schlemeasel for the Spurgmulin Tournament scheduled that evening. Valor helped prepare Aaron as well, drawing from his awful memories of being the schlemeasel while he had been in the sanatorium. Valor's newest friends Blade Zagato, Ruza Renata, and Nalini Lusion kept watch over the city, using the old magiscopes positioned throughout the observatory to measure the coordinates of celestial bodies in the sky. Months earlier, Aaron had uncovered a tile mosaic of the moon under a rug on the ground floor of the observatory, convincing him that Sorcerers had once inhabited Candlewicke.

"I see," said Aaron. "Because the last appointed schlemeasel was unsuccessful in keeping Spurgmulin, Rendum LaRock's poodle, from running away and dying, Rendum established the tournament to punish future schlemeasels—"

"As a reminder of loyalties," said Valor. "The schlemeasel is by himself—he's his own Spurgie team."

"Disgusting. Just like the Sanguinati to punish us when Rendum should have acquired a more faithful Familiar," said Blade. Valor lowered his head and thought about his Booger Fay.

"Dude, Valor's Familiar is still missing," said Micha, while Hickery Pickery, his nine-headed phoenix, perched under the glass dome, peering through a magiscope while whistling in nine octaves.

"Sorry, Valor," said Blade halfheartedly.

Aaron held a lace sleeve over his nose. "Ugh, *Spurgmulin*—the name alone sounds like a malicious malady, does it not?"

Stabbah entered the observatory with a conjure bag full of magic items. "Dahhhlings," she said, "Spurgmulin was named after spurge, the main botanical ingredient in the Elixir of Purgare—"

"That stuff Crumpecker uses to purge what she calls spirits and dark moods from inmates." Just remembering the former sanatorium head magister aiming that giant enema syringe at him, Valor's bottom clenched.

"That's why they tried to pick me for the tournament," said Ruza. Her eyepatch sparkled magenta as her exposed eye hardened with suspicion. "It's all a devious plan to strip our Sorcery, our very essence."

"Tell that to the hypocrite who still serves as a pawnikin in the tournament," said Blade, pointing at Micha with a snarl.

Valor stopped playing with the levers that activated the portholes in the glass dome. Doomsy rode around in circles on the revolving circular bench while thumbing through her Mystic Memoir.

"That's rather harsh," snapped Valor. "Micha tries to defend schlemeasels like Egg and me. He's about the only player who actually will."

"I'm tellin' ya," said Micha. "I don't have a good feelin' 'bout this tournament. I've tried ta use my pawnikin position ta stop unnecessary brutalness, but someone seems set on teachin' ya a lesson. I've never been in a doubleheader before, but I've heard about 'em."

"So, it's going to be two different tournaments, then?" asked Valor. He shoved his trembling hands in his coat pockets. Would this tournament bring more pain and peril than he'd endured in the last one? Who would take care of Doomsy if he died? Was that what Rose, Creighton, Blade, and Ruza were whispering about, huddled in their own circle near him?

"Two different tournaments? Nope," said Micha, sucking air through his clenched teeth. "Ya both are gonna be in the same game, tied together, and headin' like mad to that Dog Palace. The aerowachees are gonna have a time liftin' two schlemeasels at once, but the pawnikins, cats, and gruwels will be turned up badder than they ever were. The flat hands—er, assistants, are out there now bringin' in more schlimy pits, cauldrons, and rolling bowlies than I've ever seen. And the monkeys are sharpenin' the tips of their pokin-poles. What, in the River Styx, did Mega D tell the Council of Elders?"

"What did M.D. write on the underwear, you mean?" asked Creighton Crowley. "My parents act like they haven't heard, but I think they're too embarrassed to say. They're trying to stay really positive right now—like that's gonna help them have a seventh son."

Everyone shrugged, and Valor bolted up from the revolving bench and gasped, "Oh! Aaron and I both need to have our backs greased. I forgot last time, and those cats clawed me to bits."

"Good thinking, dahhhling," agreed Stabbah, squatting on the floor inside a ring of candles, burning some herbs on a plate. "I've got a whole tube of Aunt Ditzy's Ever-Increasing Grease. Nobody will be able to lay a hand or claw on you with that stuff." While Stabbah went down the spiraling steps to find the magic grease, Micha filled in Valor and Aaron about the tournament lineup.

"Oh great," sighed Valor, "but Aaron and I won't stand a chance if Twila Diamone and Harwin Hollapolk are Mystic Steeples' pawnikins. We all know how much they hate us. And Chantilda Hagborn and Enzo LaRock won't use their aerowachee positions to win for Mystic Steeples if Aaron and I are under their ropes."

Micha sat on the revolving bench with his fist under his chin. "Chantilda and Enzo—I don't think they'd throw Mystic Steeples for you two, and I dunno about Harwin and Twila. I tried to feel them out, but they wouldn't talk. Of course, Harwin's still upset about losin' his dad—'Dadsy,' he called 'im."

"His father was just murdered yesterday, and he's playing Spurgie? He's obviously not too upset," said Valor to the agreement of everyone.

"I could always try switching with one of the players like I did last time," said Doomsy, while Rose cradled Venus, her furry black cat, which fussed and bit at all four of her little black boots.

"I wish you could, but it's too risky," said Valor. "You got away with it at the sanatorium because LaDonna died, and they were hurting for an aerowachee replacement. But if one lucky star aligns just right with Capricornus, and Aaron and I survive the tournament, we're going to Nevelhorn, Clandestula, and see if we can find your birth parents."

Doomsy slammed her *Mystic Memoir* shut. "I told you," she huffed. "I tried already. It's no use."

Valor decided to ignore her anger and make her sympathize with his predicament. "Promise me, Doomsy," he said. "It'll give me strength knowing—knowing we'll at least try to find your family—your past."

With a throaty sigh, Doomsy said, "You expect you'll die and be done with me. But I can make it on my own."

A bleak smile formed on Micha's lips. "Ya're gonna need all the help ya can get, Val. This is a home game against Toadvine Citadel, but here's the clincher."

Valor's face contorted, and his breathing became more strained. "I thought we had enough clinchers already."

"Nope," said Micha. "Remember DaRon Dabbalon and his thug

buds that attacked ya when ya were goin' to Lilith's Lantern that night?"

"Nooo," Aaron and Valor groaned, while Doomsy, Rose, and Creighton listened closer.

In his angst, Micha shook both hands at them and mumbled, "Yup. They're playin' for Toadvine now. Gordy Ostendorf, Mayo Molpus, and DaRon are their pawnikins."

"So suddenly," said Valor sarcastically. "There was a tournament against Toadvine that night we fought those bullies, and none of them were playing then. Tilta Crumpecker is behind this, just like she had them attack us."

"In all honesty, we don't know Crumpecker ordered the attack, Val," said Creighton.

"Don't we, Creighton dear?" Valor asked rhetorically.

"It's Curssa Skinem that I'm worried about," continued Micha. "She even terrifies the ogre she rides on. Same thing with their aerowachees: Durstin Urchin's probably not a biggie, but I'd keep my eye on Wincey Wharfinger—she can work the ropes pretty good; that's why they call her War Fingers Wincey."

Rose lifted her cat and looked in her furry face. "Venus sweetie, are you sure you won't sever in the cats' cradle tonight? I know you can talk all those mean old cats into being nice to Valor and Aaron."

"You cat pussybly put me-ooouut there with those common old cats," hissed Venus.

Stabbah returned with the Aunt Ditzy's Ever-Increasing Grease, and Valor and Aaron lifted their shirts, allowing her to spread it on their bare backs.

"Whoa," gasped Valor. He jumped. The grease was cold and slimy on his skin, and it seeped below his waist and onto his arms. "I'm utterly icky."

The tubular bells began chiming, alerting them that the tournament was about to begin. Rose angled the magiscope toward Mystic Steeples.

"Um, guys," Rose squeaked, "the pawnikins are on their way to get the schlemeasels. I don't think you'll want DaRon and them carrying you to the flat. They looked pretty pumped about it."

"Oh gosh, no," said Valor, dashing around the observatory with a racing heartbeat. "We have to get to the Spurgie Dome by ourselves. Let's go, Aaron!"

"Hold on," said Blade. He turned a lever to open a porthole in the glass dome. "Best go by air if you want to get there fast."

"Thanks, Blade."

Aaron and Valor floated up through the porthole and over the courtyard, while two aerowachees, Durstin Urchin and Chantilda Hagborn, flew their Missile Thistle Bristles over Shickbone Cathedral behind them.

"I think the aerowachees spotted us," said Aaron, floating behind a high-arched dormer.

Down on Spookum Alley, they could hear the pawnikins chanting, "Fire up the cauldrons hotter than an oven, catch the schlemeasels before they yell Spurgmulin."

"We had better go the long way; they won't expect that," said Valor, before they floated to the rooflines of Dead Maudie Alley behind Candlewicke Mansion.

Soon they were over Pluvia Street with its continuous rain. They entered the southern wing of Mystic Steeples into the Spurgmulin Dome located between Buckthorn and Toadflax Halls.

"Whoa," yelled Aaron, stepping onto the marble floor in the crowded entry. "I almost slipped. This blasted grease has spread to the bottom of my boots."

"Mine, too," said Valor, sliding over the floor before crashing into a stone monument of Rendum LaRock and his Familiar poodle, the legendary Spurgmulin.

Annice Wigginbotham, the magister of Wand Usage, burst through the crowds who were lining up behind several ticket windows, wearing formal gowns and robes, in hopes of purchasing last-minute tickets.

"Oh, good heavens. What are you two doing sliding around in here?" asked Annice. "No wonder the Council of Elders chose you boys to be the schlemeasels. You're just like my cats when I put Fishy

Flakes in their food bowl. I'm always having to buff out their claw marks where they skid across my kitchen floor."

"Magister Wigginbotham," said Valor, "I know you did a spell on Marston Diamone's wand and found that he cut through that chain at my party, and I know Crumpecker didn't want you to test Twila's wand, but—"

"Oh now," Annice said with a goofy look of concern, "I know what you're going to ask, Valor-poo, and I'm simply not allowed to say, now."

"But why?" asked Valor urgently. "It's obvious Marston and Twila were trying to kill us. You *know* Crumpecker is protecting the Diamones; *that's* why you're not saying."

"Don't put me in this position, Valor-poo. Now, you two had best get out there on that flat before O Enchantedness sends the guardians after you," said Annice with a droopy frown. She grabbed them by their shirt collars and dragged them through the lobby with their feet sliding across the floor behind them. Valor was too nervous to laugh at Hymaneus and Aviva LaRock, who had slipped on a puddle of grease, which had dripped off their clothes. The LaRock's son, Darius, had been a great aerowachee. If only Valor could have him and Doomsy as Spurgie air defenses, but poor Darius was still in the sanatorium.

Magister Annice Wigginbotham exited the lobby door into the massive dome. Urbanne LaRock loomed high in his grandmaster's suspension ball, coursing through the air in the pattern of a hexagram. The roar of the crowds, bands, and cheercasters rattled Valor's brain. The suspension seats in the dome were in full swing throughout the rising stands, making Valor feel dizzy. He wished someone would blindfold him just like the eight ogres that were towering over the flat, awaiting the pawnikins to mount them.

"Okay, so t'at's why da pawnikins never found ye—ye must be in awfully bad form hangin' out with Magister Wigginbot'am," said Ratzy Pummels, as he and Orby Underkofler approached Valor from the schlemeasel's hook. Valor was unsure if Stabbah's spell to erase Ratzy's and Orby's memories had worked, but he was confident they were still in the Hermetic Order of the Mystic Key and, therefore, could be dangerous.

Annice's head danced with a pained smile. "Oh, flickin' sticks," she fussed with a sigh. "I guess I can hand these two over; you *are* the hook handlers, now aren't you?"

"And official cage concierges, too, Magister Wigginbotham," said Orby.

Annice released the schlemeasels and said, "All right then, Ratzy and Orby; now promise me you'll go easy on my boys."

"We're no saps, Magister Wigginbotham," mumbled Orby with a bashful smile. "C'mon, Schlemeasels." Orby and Ratzy led them to a large, rusty hook, which suspended from the dome ceiling on the edge of the flat where Mystic Steeples' fans sat. "Good thing the pawnikins didn't collect you." Orby bound Valor's and Aaron's ankles together with rope and fastened the rusty hook through the knot. "I heard them talk about putting the hurt on you," Orby said, while Ratzy motioned for someone in the grandmaster's suspension ball to hoist them in the air. "But you schlemeasels need to learn, me and Ratz are good guys unlike some of them goons in your coven."

Valor pulled against the tight rope. Blood surged to his head. How dare Orby slander his friends? "Argh. They're not goons; they just thought you were trying to harm them."

"C'mon, McRaven. We're trying to help you," continued Orby, while Ratzy nodded furiously. "Why do you think Banzalta risked everything, trying to save you yesterday?"

"Dat's da fact, so," said Ratzy, "so, what good did it do? Ye ran off soon as she got dere."

Valor was speechless. He was both honored and horrified that Banzalta had nearly started a bloody war to save him from being the schlemeasel.

Ratzy and Orby dashed away to help capture Micha's ogre after it roared and broke formation before heading to the high stands. While they were away, a cloaked witch ran out onto the flat and stood under the schlemeasels. Through the witch's enveloping hood, Valor recognized Mega D's smug face.

"Mmm-ha-ha!" laughed Mega D. "And to think, Bohemia sent me all the way across the Ambergis Divide to find you and Aaron. And here you are, eh, still trying to impress the primitives. Read my mind. Do I feel sorry for you? Oh, that's right, Aaron lost his third eye and Valor never developed his here among the Sangui-naughty, eh. No, I don't feel sorry for you. You're in *love* with the primitives who keep doing this to you." Mega D puckered his lips in two air kisses.

"Ah, so it was you who wrote something bad about us on the underwear," hissed Valor, while Micha's ogre began climbing into the Toadvine Citadel stands, ripping a few swinging seats off their chains.

"Good guess," said Mega D with a smirk. "But it's disturbing that you're madder at me than you are the Sanguinati."

"What, pray tell, did you write about us?" growled Aaron.

"Nothing to deserve this, shouldn't you think?" said Mega D, pointing at Valor and Aaron swinging from the hook. "I wrote 'Free the Boz, or we're through kissing the vespercestors' silky drawers,' *and* I signed both of your names," laughed Mega D. "Yes, I heard you asked Urbanne LaRock to free the Bound Order of the Zodiac, and he got really, really angry at you, McRaven. If that doesn't prove he's the Grim Warlock, there's no hope for either of you, eh."

"Hope you enjoy the Spurgie Tournament you got us in, because we're not going to help you take over the Sanguinati—I have other plans to stop Urbanne and help the Sorcerers," spat Valor, while the Mystic broom brigade made flight patterns throughout the dome.

"Your plans are pathetic," said Mega D. "I'm sure you'll want to know about the very important person who's dead because of you, Valor. And, Aaron, they think you may have had a hand in it as well. It doesn't look too good for either of you. We'll talk later—if you survive, eh."

"What are you talking about? Who's dead?" yelled Valor, but Mega D ran off the flat.

"Why did you run from us? You free-floaters afraid we'd squeeze your shadows too hard?" asked DaRon Dabbalon. He flew by them on his broom, wearing his green Toadvine pawnikin uniform, while the twirlyurgy spun across the flat, simulating planets orbiting the sun, which energized the rolling bowlies that began to twist like tornadoes.

"Come jump on your hook like scared little fishes," shouted Harwin Hollapolk. He shivered mockingly, wearing his purple Mystic Steeples pawnikin uniform. He high-fived Gordy Ostendorf, and DaRon, while Twila Diamone, Mayo Molpus, and the other pawnikins strode past the schlemeasels, looking up at them with demeaning faces. This didn't affect Valor as much as it usually would have, because his mind raced, trying to figure out who might be dead because of him. Did they think he or Aaron killed Harwin's father or the other guardian?

Ratzy Pummels returned with Orby and stood below the schlemeasels. Ratzy pumped his arms to his sides and said to the bullies, "Back away twelve feet, okay?"

"Sure, but ya better tell the schlemeasels to run fast to the Dog Palace. Run, little Schlemeasels, run," heckled DaRon, heading down the flat with his pawnikin friends before they mounted their ogres.

Micha dashed up to Valor and Aaron, who were still dangling upside down from the hook. "Someone attacked my ogre. Anyway listen, guys," he said urgently, "I mean obviously ya're gonna pick me as your pawnikin defender, but I think Enzo LaRock is ya best bet for ya defender aerowachee."

"What?" said Valor. "Why him? Enzo got mad when Darius tried to defend me the last time I was the schlemeasel."

Micha kept cutting his eyes up at the dome clock. "I'm tellin' ya, Enzo's the safest bet," Micha assured. "Not only is he with Steeples, but he's losin' interest in bein' an aerowachee 'cause he wants ta spend his time pursuin' a position in Mystic Ministry, and his girlfriend, Jama. His job as a bellfounder's assistant is on the line, too." Micha lowered his voice. "Besides, Enzo can't stand DaRon and Harwin, so he wouldn't want 'em to capture ya an' win the tournament. An' he can handle the ropes better than Chantilda, trust me."

Aaron and Valor had no time to respond to Micha before he ran

34

to mount his stabilized ogre, and the aerowachees for both teams straddled their brooms before lifting to the open.

"Don't worry about what Mega D said, Aaron. We didn't kill anyone. He's just trying to make us lose focus," said Valor.

"I have already lost focus. And I hope they let us down from this dreadful hook soon. I feel like a hog at a butchery," said Aaron.

A few monkeys got into a fight, chattering while stabbing their striped pokin-poles at each other, until two Mystic medics, using a flying carpet, carried an unconscious monkey off the flat.

"It's going to be hard to run with ropes tied to our ankles, Aaron. Try to stay strong and float. Everyone'll think the aerowachees are pulling us," said Valor. He tried to wipe the grease dripping down his face onto his shoulder. His eyes burned when the firewalkers teetered barefooted on the rims of the boiling cauldrons to test their temperatures. Using wands, they shot fireballs under the cauldrons to make them hotter. The stargazers inspected the constellations with their telescopes and signaled to O Enchantedness to proceed with the event. Doomsy, Rose, and the rest of Candlewicke Coven strapped themselves inside their swinging chairs before lifting toward the domed ceiling.

"Okay, so it's time for da bespicing," said Ratzy while he and Orby took the schlemeasels down from the hook, then escorted them to the far right side of the flat through a spray of amulets and talismans, which the spectators tossed. Many spectators purchased petitions from the honorary candle lighters' station on the sidelines in hopes of achieving their desired outcomes for the tournament.

"Somebody's, like, buying lots of black candles," said Ratzy. "T'ey must want somebody dead." Using studded dog collars, Ratzy strapped Valor's left wrist to Aaron's right wrist and did the same with their ankles. "Okay, so, if either of ye goes down, ye'll both go down, and t'at's a fact."

Trying to imitate the fame of the Belting Belfries, the conjoined triplets, Donny-Dale-Dharma Thelastone, sang the Sanguinati Anthem, but it was terribly off-key. The aerowachees pushed their ropes from the open (air) down to the flat. Orby tied the ropes, from two different aerowachees, to Aaron's free wrist and ankle. Ratzy did the same to Valor's wrist and ankle using the last two aerowachees' ropes. Orby then gave the ropes a hard tug and said, "It's too loose unless—"

"'Our hands turn blue,'" said Valor, remembering Orby's words from the first time he felt the skin-ripping ropes cutting into his wrists and ankles. A wad of spit landed on Valor's head, so his eyes traced the ropes to the aerowachees. "Say! That large-boned girl just spat on me. She must be the infamous War Fingers Wincey."

The gargantuan girl grinned down at them and cracked her knuckles against her teeth.

"She's so bloody big, I can't see her broom," said Aaron with a concerned frown.

Summoner Mamahchi strode across the flat, careful to avoid the rolling bowlies and the groaning and growling gruwels: monsters that looked like a cross between blood-sucking ticks and slimy lizards. While the gruwels rose and sank from the treacherous schlimy pits, Mamahchi paused beside Aaron and mumbled, "Name your defenses . . . or are you . . . taking your chances?"

"Aaron and I've chosen Micha DeMise for our pawnikin defense and Enzo LaRock for our aerowachee defense," said Valor.

Mamahchi grunted and aimed his blackthorn staff at the Spurgmulin scorestone, sending his staff's pigeon medallion soaring up to the scorestone to manipulate the elaborate runes, which displayed Micha's and Enzo's names along with their game-history stats.

In the section for Mystic Ministry, a woman screamed and began climbing like an angry bear over the other members before toppling out of the high-rising stands. Valor recognized the woman as Jolivet Fox, the wife of the dirge diviner.

Gripping his ogre's neck with his right hand, Micha lifted the purple feather in his pointed hat. Candlewicke Coven's cheers were far louder than anyone else in the dome. Creighton ordered his usual snacks from the vendors on their brooms. His fairy Familiar, Hulkin, flew several swings below them and visited with Sessions Diamone before flying across the Dome to the section reserved for the vespercestors. Valor was glad to see Stabbah and Ruza sitting between Doomsy and Blade in case they started fighting again.

"When they throw the cats in the shrubby, run," Valor whispered to Aaron. "We should take the biggest steps our legs can reach, but remember, I'm shorter than you."

Straddling his broom, Enzo looked stunned that his name had appeared on the scorestone as a defender. He hesitated to lift his feather. The other aerowachees laughed at Enzo, as though the schlemeasels had cursed him. The war drums and tubular bells played a more foreboding melody while the guardians carried Jolivet Fox's body out of the dome. The ogres began to fidget, but a test fire from the pawnikins' wands stilled the ogres' stomping feet. Spurgie, the mascot for Mystic Steeples, backed up to the spectators in their swings and pooped out a spray of souvenirs to the cheering crowd. While Tacky-Tongued Toady, the spotted-green mascot for Toadvine Citadel, uncoiled its long pink tongue and swiped up many of the souvenirs, before hopping back to its designated section of the dome. Considering several people were working both costumes, the mascot puppets looked and moved eerily real from a distance.

"Attention, Lesser Vespercestors, Mystic Ministry, and Covens," said Urbanne LaRock on his magihorn, while Mumbazandie LaRock carried a trophy resembling a large gold hook out onto the flat, a hook like the one Valor and Aaron had been hanging from minutes earlier. "Tonight's Spurgie winners will each receive a gold key admission to Mystic Steeples. The winners will also receive the coveted Golden Hooky Award, allowing the winners and a guest of his or her choosing to play hooky from assemblies for up to half of each apprentice level, as long as they maintain passing scores on final exams. Now behold, my Enchantedness shall commence with the bespicing."

High Priest Teddyus Manoj gazed up at the cheercasters' pom-poms rising and falling from the ceiling. He ripped the schlemeasels' shirts off their backs as Urbanne stood before them aglow, thanks to the dwarves lifting burning candelabras around him. Manoj cut Valor's and Aaron's greasy shirts into twelve strips. The group of witches called the cats' cradle ogled the schlemeasels, as the dwarves tied the strips of fabric to their collection of growling cats.

Urbanne lifted his arms and said, "Behold those who have empowered you, Schlemeasels, and those who can take it away. You will learn to love and obey the vespercestory." Urbanne lowered his arms, and the dwarves hurled the vicious cats into the evergreen maze of shrubs known as the shrubby. The witches cackled, guardians droned, tambourhorns rattled, and the spectators yelled and chanted as the blindfolded ogres began stomping over the scrambling cats.

"Run to the Dog Palace, Aaron!" said Valor, while the monkeys and pawnikins guided the ogres toward the schlemeasels. The Toadvine Croakers began to sing along with their orchestra, but the Mystic Melodians sang even louder.

"Time out," Twila Diamone called to the referees from atop her ogre.

Urbane approved the time out from the grandmaster's suspension ball, and the monkeys blew their horns to pause the cats. "Is there a problem, Twila child?" Urbanne cooed.

"My foot wasn't in my ogre's neck harness all the way," giggled Twila, adjusting the bows on her boots so they would better fit inside the stirrups.

"Ooo, that could be dangerous," said Urbanne, before ordering the resumption of the game.

Tilta Crumpecker cackled over her magihorn from the suspension ball, "Eee-he-hee . . . the schlemeasels are having a rough start. Oh, too bad—looks like they've stumbled into the edge of a burning cauldron. Hot steam should teach 'em to stay alert."

After Valor and Aaron hobbled a couple of yards, Wincey Wharfinger snatched her rope to Valor's right hand, and Durstin

Urchin pulled his rope connected to Aaron's left foot. The schlemeasels toppled forward so that their faces splashed into the edge of a schlimy pit. A gruwel rose halfway out of the pit and began to suffocate them. Aaron broke free, gathered a deep breath of air, and snatched Valor back on his feet.

"Breathe, Valor."

"Time out," shouted Twila. And again, Urbanne stopped the tournament.

"Um, my feather came out of my hat-bow," said Twila. She pointed toward a boiling cauldron where it had drifted. Next, Twila looked over her shoulder at the honorary candle lighters' booth where her parents, Sessions and Hilda, were purchasing intervention petitions from under the counter—black candles! Valor knew then why she kept delaying the game.

Vampatra Cobbratz tapped her fingers on her ogre's head and groaned, "You always do this, Twila. Your feather's not supposed to go in a stupid bow. It goes in your hat band."

"It looks better this way. We must represent Mystic Steeples the best we can," said Twila. She took the purple feather from a monkey who crawled up her ogre.

Valor caught his breath, and the tournament resumed. Using his magic wand, DaRon Dabbalon knocked a rolling bowlie into Valor and Aaron. The funnel of wind then lifted them a few feet, tangling them in the ropes, which continued to knot until the aerowachees knocked against each other in the night air.

"You two need a little exfoliation—clean the nasty shadows out of your pores," laughed DaRon.

"Come on, Aaron, we can do this—float," Valor yelled in the circling wind.

"Well, whad'ya know?" screeched Crumpecker. "The schlemeasels have escaped the rolling bowlie and gained a few more yards. Enzo must not be giving 'em any resistance."

As the schlemeasels hobbled and Crumpecker sneezed something sounding like "*black-candles,*" Valor hoped Enzo wouldn't change his mind and pull the rope to Valor's right foot, for this had been giving him a leg to move faster.

Out of the crook of his eyes, Valor saw Harwin Hollapolk steering his ogre closer behind him. "Faster, you stupid beast," Harwin shouted at the ogre, and keeping his wand nestled under his uniform jacket, Harwin expelled a blast at his ogre's head. The ogre roared in pain, flailing its limbs until it tumbled forward and, with its left hand, flung Valor and Aaron several yards to the right, pulling Chantilda Hagborn off her broom until she grabbed hold of the handle and straddled it again.

"Hollapolk cheated," Vampatra Cobbratz yelled to Urbanne LaRock as he hovered nearby in his suspension ball. "He used his wand on his ogre."

Urbanne's magihorn levitated to his mouth. "Penalty reclined. I didn't see any dilations."

"What?" snorted Vampatra. "Penalty declined? But Hollapolk was in *clear* violation. Look at the wound on his ogre's head. He ripped a hole right through its blindfold!"

Valor lifted himself off the flat. Pain radiated through him. He had broken his arm because of the injured ogre's rage. "It's true," groaned Valor. "I saw Harwin blast his ogre. Now my arm's broken."

"They're lying," shouted DaRon Dabbalon, and all Toadvine Citadel's fans cheered.

"We didn't see Harwin commit any violation," Curssa Skinem and Mayo Molpus said, while the official referee, Batha Rosenwinkle, shrugged her shoulders indecisively.

"Penalty against the pawnikin inclined. Game is assumed," announced Urbanne erroneously. His face twisted, and his magihorn lowered.

Crumpecker conjured the magihorn and screeched, "Game resumed."

Micha paused on his ogre and yelled, "Time out! O Enchantedness, this is unfair. The schlemeasel can't continue with a broken arm."

The monkeys blew their horns to pause the cats, but three of the fierce felines prowled toward Valor and Aaron with hunger in their eyes. Peering through Gordy Ostendorf's ogre's legs, Valor spotted a cloaked witch purchasing a dark candle from the honorary candle lighters. The witch stood with two other cloaked witches who positioned their bodies to better watch Aaron and Valor like stalking wolves.

"Aaron, is that Mega D? Does he have some evil wish toward us?" groaned Valor in pain.

The mysterious witches took the black candles, lit them with their eyes, and as if crushing eggs in their hands, their candles turned to the consistency of blood, Sorcerer blood, which dripped through their fingers and onto the flat.

"I cannot tell if it is him," replied Aaron, shivering at the spectacle: the pale blood had turned to shadows, which spread across the flat of four-leaf clovers, inching toward the schlemeasels. One of the cloaked witches raised a magic staff, and the ogres began to roar and grab at their harnesses.

"You stupid Pawnikins, control my ogres!" yelled Crumpecker over the magihorn. "I wanna see this game through to the grubby gruesome end."

"Here I am. Here I am," shouted Witchdoctor Kraneswaddle, teetering onto the flat. Her ivy garlands and flowers bounced on her hair and clothing. She gazed down at Valor while wringing her fingers, but her colorfully powdered face failed to match the concern she showed him. "I can fix sweet thing's arm faster than two flicks of an elf's ear." Kraneswaddle flashed a wrinkled grin at everyone in the swings and on the flat. She rubbed her hands together before cramming a handful of berries and flowers into her mouth. She chewed them for a second and spat them into her hand. "Now, honey, ya just give ol' Minty that broken arm of yours."

Valor recoiled. Having Kraneswaddle fuss over him and call him "sweet thing" in front of the whole Spurgmulin Dome hurt more than his arm, but how would he and Aaron get to the Dog Palace with it broken? He lifted his arm and almost blacked out when the bone protruded through the muscle. The Toadvine orchestra pounded their war drums while the Toadettes and fans chanted,

"Catch the schlemeasels. Trap 'em like weasels. Rope 'em, choke 'em. Buy a Toadvine token . . . ."

The shadows over the flat had now come within six feet of Valor and Aaron and had begun to extract their shadows. Had Kraneswaddle noticed this? Her head snapped toward the shadows then back to Valor's broken arm. Was Mega D trying to expose Aaron and him in front of the entire Sanguinati? Valor became woozy with worry.

"Looks like some dark magic is happening on the flat," Tilta Crumpecker announced over her magihorn with a snort.

Witchdoctor Kraneswaddle bounced around so much Valor almost didn't see her aim her wand at the approaching shadow, which had now traveled within three feet of Aaron's right leg. "*Abromorior Cantatrix!*" she chanted. "Take that, ya shadow leech."

The widening shadow exploded into screeching puffs before the mysterious Sorcerers vanished in a cloud of spirits. Valor and Aaron were too dumbstruck to thank Kraneswaddle as she rubbed the chewed floral mixture onto Valor's arm and removed a wet pink sheet of something from a box in her conjure bag.

"Now, hun, this is the belly skin of a pribbling wiggly," said Kraneswaddle. "Don't worry, I didn't kill it—I found it dead in the Sanctuary of Manifestations and have been saving it for a very special occasion." She wrapped the skin over Valor's arm, sealing the floral chew against the break. Valor cringed. It had to be the pribbling wiggly that LaRecia Davis had turned herself into before her twin sister had squashed her in the very same sanctuary of the sanatorium.

"Argh, no! Get it off—that's . . . that's LaRecia's skin," groaned Valor, kicking the clovered flat. He had to get away from the witchdoctor.

"Now, sweet thing, I know it hurts. You're delirious, but ol' Minty's gonna fix ya right up," assured Kraneswaddle. She flung herself on top of Valor, all the while tearing a vine of ivy, draped across her shoulders, and tying it around the icky dressing, sealing the pribbling wiggly skin to his arm. "Now I'm trusting ya have only good intentions before old Minty uses this spell. *Whayoy turtree totaki veeci*. Come on, hun, say it."

"Argh! '*Whayoy turtree totaki veeci*,'" Valor repeated to get Magister Kraneswaddle off him, certain LaRecia's skin would forever leave a hex, while DaRon, Harwin, Twila, and many other Spurgie players began laughing. Underneath Kraneswaddle, Aaron made a stunned and disgusted face. The ghost of LaRecia was now hovering over them, either that or the mound of the witchdoctor's herbal-scented clothing, tangling ivy, and flinging flowers had disagreed with Valor.

Kraneswaddle continued unaware, commanding the ghost of LaRecia to heal his arm, while Tilta Crumpecker shouted over the magihorn that Valor was being a whiny baby and delaying the tournament.

"You evoke treachery, you twit. It's my skin, and I won't heal McRaven," LaRecia shouted at the witchdoctor who kept chanting.

"Oh, all right," growled LaRecia. She reached through the pile and placed her phantom hands on the pribbling wiggly skin. A hot, stinging sensation bubbled through Valor's arm. Kraneswaddle rolled off him. The skin had blended into his own arm skin, and the spell had healed the break.

"May my death skin forever be a curse to you, McRaven, as it was to me," hissed LaRecia before vanishing.

Aaron raised up on his elbows. "Valor, look," he said. "You had your arms crossed when she spoke the curse. You blocked it. The hex shall not stick."

"My arm is good again; thanks," Valor said to the witchdoctor. "But what did you mean 'if I had only good intentions'?"

"I did a spell of restitution . . . ya know, like an eye for an eye," replied Kraneswaddle, standing up and panting for air.

"Ah!" Aaron said to Valor. "What the Davis Twins tried to take, you received back from them."

The witchdoctor wiped clovers off her dress. "Oh, hun, all I know is some dark force is trying to get at ya. A key to winning is not to overreach *yet*—ya must try to outwit it."

"Game resumed," Urbanne shouted into his magihorn, and the monkeys blew their horns to charge the cats, giving the schlemeasels two seconds to stand up and prepare themselves.

"Hey, lemme get off the flat at least!" Kraneswaddle flailed her arms and legs like a pantomage in a swarm of bees as she ran toward the sideline.

The Sanguinettes juggled their pom-poms while doing backflips through an empty slot in a spinning wheel of fortune. Two cats lunged onto the schlemeasels' bare backs. Aaron jumped at the initial scratch on his left shoulder blade. Micha had been right; the grease did help the cats' claws to slide off their tender skin. Trying to block the other pawnikins, Micha compelled his ogre to the forefront with a fierce determination. For a few yards, the schlemeasels' feet left the ground after the aerowachees had hoisted their ropes.

DaRon Dabbalon fired his wand at a cauldron, knocking it in front of Micha's ogre just before the beast put his foot down inside the burning iron pot. "Grah!" the ogre roared and kicked until the cauldron flung off its foot and grazed Aaron's head. The hot liquid splashed onto Valor's back, scalding him. Micha managed to hang onto his ogre's collar, though he resembled a tiny raft bouncing against a tidal wave.

"Makin' illegal moves are we, Dabbalon?" huffed Micha. He flicked his wand, knocking a rolling bowlie into DaRon's ogre. The tornado-like funnel of wind soon rose off the flat, trapping DaRon. Up in the air, Toadvine Aerowachee Durstin Urchin tapped his wand against his rope, and his wand worked like a pulley, reeling up the rope that led to Aaron's foot, lifting them both upside-down twenty yards in the air. Chantilda Hagborn, obviously seeing her opportunity for Mystic Steeples, flew her rope around Valor's head, forming a noose around his neck. Valor tried to use Sorcery to force the rope off his throat, but he was so tired he couldn't concentrate hard enough.

Aaron tried to hand-cast a spell at Chantilda, but he and Valor were spinning, making it hard to target her. Tugging against the aerowachees, Aaron yelled, "Loosen your ropes, Chantilda, you are choking Valor!"

Just as consciousness began to slip from Valor, Candlewicke Coven slowed the motion of their swinging seats in the stands with looks of pure outrage on their faces. They lifted their hands over their heads and conjured flocks of crows, ravens, vultures, and buzzards, which emerged from under the clovers of the flat as if they had formed from dirt. Cackling, the birds resembled black smoke before they took flight to the night sky, engulfing Chantilda and Durstin, pecking and clawing at them until the two aerowachees could stand the assault no longer and fell off their brooms.

"Oh my! Steeples own Chantilda Hagborn has fallen into a rolling bowlie," Crumpecker screamed in her magihorn. "And Toadvine's Durstin Sky-Surfin' Urchin is falling, falling . . . ugh—and Mayo Molpus ordered his ogre to catch Durstin in the nick of time. Great save for Toadvine."

The remaining Aerowachees' ropes weren't enough to keep Valor and Aaron airborne, so they sank closer to the flat.

With a bilious expression, Durstin, the fallen Toadvine aerowachee, pointed his finger at the lumpy green ogre and yelled, "Pu-pu-put me down!" The ogre dropped Durstin into a boiling cauldron. "Aaak," Durstin screamed so loud that several of the cats retreated toward the shrubby.

Wincey Wharfinger's wand discharged and conjured Chantilda's and Durstin's fallen brooms to her, enabling her to grab their ropes as well: one she pulled with her teeth and the other two she gripped in her massive hands. With a rib-shattering grunt, she swung Valor and Aaron into the arms of Gordy's ogre. Toadvine Citadel leaped from their swing and cheered, while their guardians began to drone ominous chants.

"Eat 'em, Lumpules," Gordy said to his ogre.

The beast opened its sticky green mouth and stuck out its tongue, inches above Valor's and Aaron's heads. The cackling swarm of black birds dove down from the ceiling and flew into ogre's mouth. Lumpules released Valor and Aaron, grabbed its throat, and stumbled until it flung Gordy into a schlimy pit, where a gruwel wrapped itself around the Toadvine pawnikin and pulled him under the slime.

"Great maneuver, War Fingers," shouted Twila Diamone, guiding her ogre to the forefront. Her face lifted toward the grandmaster's suspension ball with a blithe expression, as she steered her ogre clear of the nasty schlimy pit where Gordy sank into earlier. "I trapped the schlemeasel last year, of course. Won the tournament."

"Hold for the picture, Twila," said Boyd Cages from the *Magic Ledger*. He steadied his camera atop an assistant's head, while his other female assistants surrounded him in a frame of outstretched arms. Twila returned her attention to the flat, adjusted the bows on her hat, and with a camera-ready smile, she ordered her ogre to pull Durstin out of the cauldron right when Boyd's camera clicked.

Slopping onto the flat, Witchdoctor Kraneswaddle pulled Durstin onto the sideline to treat his scalded legs. Valor looked on in horror, as all that remained of Gordy were a few air bubbles on the surface of the schlimy pit. He then checked on Aaron and wheezed, "Aaron, Aaron, are you okay? We have to win. There's no other choice."

"I'm persevering—I think we are descending," panted Aaron. His pale face showed a hint of hope, just before Crumpecker announced that the injuries in this tournament were stacking up. Twila's ogre moved ahead of Micha's ogre, and she fired her wand, knocking a rolling bowlie in the path of the Dog Palace. Valor looked up to see the ropes sliding from Wincey's teeth and hands.

"We're going down," Valor cheered. "The Ever-Increasing Grease has spread up the ropes. War Fingers is losing her grip!"

"Concentrate, Valor," said Aaron, after their boots, at last, touched the flat, and the Dog Palace stood just three yards in front of them. "We can do this."

With the crescent moon now overhead, Valor ran as hard as he could, shouting, "Go, Aaron! Only Enzo is holding the ropes now."

"Enzo is our hope. Enzo, pull the ropes . . . ," chanted much of Mystic Steeples' spectators.

Valor imagined his dead twin and grandmother, as well as his missing Elusive Griffin, was waiting for him in the Dog Palace, and this gave him a burst of energy. There was no resistance on his right foot. "Enzo let go of his rope. Oh run, Aaron, run!" cried Valor as they lunged as fast as they could toward the Dog Palace. Valor aimed his left hand at the rolling bowlie and willed it to move to the left.

It worked! Twila was now less than a yard behind them.

"Grab the stupid schlemeasels, Tuesday, you lump-headed beast," she yelled to her ogre, smacking it in the head with her wand.

"SPURGMULIN!" Valor and Aaron yelled, as soon as they dove into the Dog Palace. The monkeys blew their horns, signaling the end of the tournament, while Crumpecker huffed and snorted into her magihorn.

The schlemeasels tried to pat each other on the back, but their leather restraints prevented them. When they crawled out through the doggy door, Candlewicke Coven came running onto the flat until all thirteen members were there together. Creighton set off fireclappers everywhere, to make up for the less than enthusiastic response from Toadvine Citadel and Mystic Steeples. It was far more cheering than the first tournament Valor had won. Salazants and Manning passed around two silver trays of refreshments while Stabbah had her conjure bag ready to offer medical assistance.

"We knew you could do it, guys!" squeaked Rose, hugging them, while Doomsy glared at Harwin Hollapolk and DaRon Dabbalon as they slammed their hats onto the flat in disgust.

"We couldn't have done it without Micha's help again," panted Valor when Micha ran over to congratulate them. "He should win."

Blade Zagato snickered and avoided looking at Micha. Urbanne LaRock exited the grandmaster's suspension ball and held his hand up, indicating for Crumpecker and others on the sideline to stay put while he alone walked over to Aaron and Valor.

"This was unexpected—unexpected indeed. It seems fate or the Ancients is on your side . . . for now," said Urbanne. "Nevertheless, I know you both will graciously relinquish the winning title to another player." Urbanne bent over and, with his hand over his mouth, whispered, "It's so hard trying to please everybody. You see, I am getting more negative press and threats of boycott than ever for allowing your sort into Mystic Steeples, especially with these controversies that keep occurring with you lot."

His breath, his hope—what little of anything Valor had left—squeezed from his body. After all the struggle, humiliation, and pain, he had just gone through yet again, this was unbelievable. Aaron's body drooped as well, and he gave Valor a look of hopeless surrender.

"That's okay, O Enchantedness. We wouldn't want the Sanguinati Elite to put a guilt trip on you," Valor said bitterly.

"What a load of dragon dung!" spat Ruza Renata. The rubies on her eyepatch sparkled, while Candlewicke 13 gathered in a circle around Urbanne. "I told you, the vespercestors have no shame."

With her bottom teeth bared and fingers crooked, Doomsy leaned forward on the pointed toes of her boots and began sliding toward Urbanne.

"You slime-bellied, bottom-feeding pulpagrug! How dare you cheat Aaron and my brother of their awards because of some mush-brained, Sanguinati snot-bots?"

Urbanne bent over, grabbed Doomsy by her neck, and shook her in his choking grip.

"Do not threaten my Enchantedness. I'll send you back to the Sanatorium, and Ruza, too."

The rays of the crescent moon filled Valor's pupils with entrancing light. He locked his eyes on Urbanne and, with a mysterious power that seemed to radiate from his head, knocked Urbanne back six feet until the head vespercestor came to a jarring stop on one knee. Rubbing her neck, Doomsy backed into her circle of friends.

"O Enchantedness," Valor panted. "I must tell you: I, haaa, I didn't write that message on the underwear. None of us did."

Urbanne stammered to his feet and repositioned his galaxy glasses over his twitching nose. Valor could feel Aaron shaking against him. Urbanne then lifted his magic staff and said, "That verdict will be determined after the scribes have finished their graphology analysis. Then I shall—"

"But I agree with *every word* of it," Valor continued as warningly as he could.

Candlewicke Coven did a doubletake at Valor. Urbanne eyebrows rose over his galaxy glasses, and his lips squeezed into a grimace. Creighton turned paler and began to fidget.

"I am not a danger to you, but I'm through with you mistreating my friends," Valor shouted. "What is a danger is the Bound Order of the Zodiac—you must set them free."

"Never!" Urbanne growled.

Rose, Egg, Doomsy, Ruza, Salazants, and Manning raised their hands, ready to attack.

"As you can see, this is just a few of the people who agree that you should," continued Valor. "There are many more. They're just afraid to disagree with you and Mystic Ministry."

Creighton rubbed his chest and appeared ill, while Micha wrinkled his brow as his eyes darted at the spectators slowly approaching. Blade shook his head with a smirk.

Urbanne raised his magic staff at Valor and said, "Now, you listen here—"

"No, sir. You listen," said Valor, causing Urbanne's magic staff to quake in his bejeweled hand while a churning dark cloud began to form over the head vespercestor and emit a series of whispery warnings or just sinister sighs, perhaps. Whichever the case, Valor gathered more courage when Urbanne lowered his staff. "Declare somebody else the winner if you must. I will continue to serve and protect you, continue to rescue the stolen Zodiac instruments, but my friends and I are NOT going to continue allowing you or the Ministry to abuse us."

Tilta Crumpecker came stomping over to Urbanne, breaking through the circle of Sorcerers that Candlewicke 13 had made. "Is there a problem, O Enchantedness? Are these apprentices here giving you any troub—"

"Eh, no, High Priestess. No, I stumbled," said Urbanne, clearing his throat, while his magihorn levitated back in front of his mouth. "Can I, eh, have everyone's tension?"

"Attention!" Crumpecker clarified with a loud screech in her magihorn, before Urbanne continued his announcement.

"Because my impeachable leadership at Systic Meeples has guided Valor McRaven's and Aaron Hutton's paths the way the Ancients intended, I, eh, hereby declare this night that the Spurgmeasels have won the Schlemulin tournament," stammered Urbanne. Giving a slight bow, he lifted his magic staff while many fans in the dome tossed their snack boxes and began to exit. He caught Valor looking at his bare fingers, which he then hid in his coat pocket. His sun rook signet ring was missing.

"Hold up!" Urbanne continued. "I haven't declared the winning pawnikin and aerowachee."

The crowds and orchestras paused, while the hook handlers, Ratzy and Orby, removed the dog collars, which held the ropes to the schlemeasels' hands and feet. Stabbah, Ruza, and Blade gave the hook handlers a look of caution.

Urbanne lifted a hand toward the sky and said, "For, eh, aerowachee, I declare Wincey Wharfinger, a winner. And for pawnikin, I declare Mystic Steeples' own magnificent Twila Diamone, a winner."

The remaining spectators cheered and, with their wands, conjured sparkling banners that shot up to the domed-glass ceiling. Twila grabbed a bow on either side of her dress and curtsied, while news reporters held up their crystaleers toward her and took more pictures. War Fingers Wincey landed her broom on the flat, raised her fisted hands, and roared with excitement that sent the monkeys running into the stands. Urbanne weaved through the crowds, heading for the dome exit. He covered his ears with his hands at shouts of protest and knocked news reporters' crystaleers from their hands.

Crumpecker stomped toward Valor and Aaron and paused with her hands behind her back. "I don't know what you schlemeasels did to get so lucky, but here are your gold keys of admission and Golden Hooky Awards." While camera flashes blinded them, she shoved a pair of gold keys and trophies, one to Valor and the other to Aaron, then stomped over toward Twila Diamone, whose family and friends had gathered around her with flowers and gifts. Marston Diamone threw his box of candy across the clovers and staggered past reporters out of the Spurgmulin Dome.

After the reporters moved along, Stabbah said, "Valor dahhhling, did you see the look of fear on Urbanne's face when the moons in your eyes started glowing, and you put that mahhhvelous spell on him?"

"My eyes glowed? I just thought the moon got really bright," said Valor, massaging his aching wrists, wondering why he was the only witch with such a peculiar ability.

"Oh, I was a little worried we were all going to have to fight everyone in the dome for a minute," said Nalini Lusion, stroking her long black hair like a security blanket.

"WE? HA!" roared Ruza, while Rose tried to shove some snacks down Valor's throat. "Some of you—you know who you are—looked like you were about to abandon our secret coven as soon as Valor stood up to Urbanne."

Creighton blushed after Ruza's uncovered eye settled on him the longest.

"Ugh. We've been through this again and again," said Creighton. "I don't mind risking my life for this coven, but you have to be careful how you waggle your wands at Mystic Ministry—you can't just go attacking them in public."

"He was choking my sister," panted Valor. "I wasn't going to let him put her and Ruza in the sanatorium."

"You did the right thing, Valor," said Aaron, frowning at Creighton. "If we ever have to defend against the Sanguinati, it might not be in some back alley at midnight while we are all wearing disguises. I have about reached my limit with wearing masks. Even if it does come with a trophy."

Valor's eyes widened for a second at his awards. He and Aaron had won, no doubt, but the reward seemed tainted after being handed to them out of bitter obligation. With little thought about it, he gave his gold key to Rose.

"Sure, I'll hold it for you. I know you must be exhausted," said

Rose.

"It's for you, my dear. I know it'll help you," said Valor, all too aware of Rose's financial struggles and the recent loss of her family. "Micha, Doomsy, Aaron, and I already have free admission to Mystic Steeples."

"Valor's right," said Aaron, giving his key to Stabbah, while tears of joy spilled from Rose's eyes down her shockingly white-powdered face.

"Thanks, dahhhling, but I don't need it," said Stabbah. "I have plenty of money from my store and all."

"Me-me-me!" said Creighton with engorged eyes, making grabbing motions with his hands, until Aaron seemed to feel no choice but to give his gold key to him.

"Very well," said Aaron to Creighton. "But do not keep questioning our decisions."

"Never gonna again—never gonna!" promised Creighton, practically drooling over his gold key award.

"Aw, I wish I could give a gold key to everybody. I never received a real trophy before," said Valor. And a beautiful trophy it was: the gold hook rising from the marble base had been polished so smooth he could see his friends' warm, grinning faces reflected on the surface.

"Haven't done enough for the primitives yet, have you?" asked Mega D, the strange Sorcerer from Shadowhaven Heights, appearing suddenly behind them.

Aaron grabbed Mega D by his cloak. "You got us into this. So, what now? Have you come to spoil our celebration?"

"And just who was it that we supposedly murdered?" asked Valor, still desperate from worry.

"Why should I, eh? The first part of my visit you all failed . . . miserably," said Mega D.

"You wanted the world to end, did you?" asked Rose, shoving caramel cauldron cookies into Aaron's mouth while Stabbah applied a sparking ointment to his visible wounds. Valor's head was about to crack open from Mega D's games, and he could be polite no longer:

"That's your *opinion*, affected by that mysterious new 'master,' you've discovered. *Facts* are, Mega D, my dear, too many people and animals were perishing, the sun nearly died—and none of you from that ivory tower you live in lifted a finger to stop it! I wasn't going to wait around to the last bloody second, just because you think this 'master' would stop the Darkening or any phase in the Grim Warlock's deadly plan."

"Yeah," said Egg. "Th-that would be twisted to take that chance."

After Stabbah applied a magic degreaser to Valor's exposed skin, he put on a shirt that Salazants had brought him. The smirk on Mega D's face assured Valor that he was not finished with this conversation.

"Look, my dear," continued Valor, "I don't approve of Mystic Ministry keeping the Zodiac Beings bound in Mystic Steeples. I'm trying to free them. And I don't know if O Enchantedness is the Grim Warlock. Maybe he is, and maybe he does plan to use the Bound Order of the Zodiac to destroy the world. But your 'master' was daft to think the world would be safer by stealing the celestial instruments from the BOZ and hiding them. If every last one of those instruments isn't returned to the rightful owner, that alone will cause the world to go off balance until we're all dead—understand?"

"Valor McRaven—the Knight of Night. You think your third eye perceives the best, eh. The second part of my visit concerns the murder of Master Mesthu—they believe Aaron killed him. Others think you are responsible . . . perhaps so . . . inadvertently," said Mega D.

"Valor and I—responsible for Mesthu's death?" roared Aaron. "How could they think such a foolish thing?"

"YOU! Mesthu excommunicated YOU. Therefore, some think YOU took revenge. But, of course, I know you're not powerful enough," laughed Mega D, while Rose, Micha, and the others huddled around Valor and Aaron with creased brows. "All the same, anarchy besieged the tower from the moment the news of his death reached us."

"Your people are making a terrible assumption. Aaron's been here with us ever since we left Diabolishire," said Valor, leaning back with indignation.

Mega D levitated Valor's trophy from his hands and caused it to pause in the air over his head. "You haven't been here the whole time, McRaven," he said. "Do you care to tell your friends the one thing our Infantem Infinitas was lacking, or should I?"

"What happened at Shadowhaven Heights, my friend?" Aaron asked Valor, grabbing his scratched shoulders.

"I was worried about all the murders—and the Darkening. I only talked to the Ashwin twins, the Infantem Infinitas, as you call them, because they're over your army," responded Valor. He felt a bilious bubble building in his stomach, shortening his breath. "When they wouldn't let me speak with Master Mesthu, I tried to convince them that they didn't have it made living in seclusion—that they didn't have all that they needed—"

"'That the more we know, the more that is expected of us,'" concluded Mega D with a smirk. "To the point you think we have lost compassion—eh. Seems the twins fell for that. Mmm-ha-ha."

"What do you mean?" asked Valor, while Mega D caused the trophy to spin, attracting the attention of Twila Diamone as she was leaving the Spurgie Dome with her fans.

"The twins approached Master Mesthu with the same nonsense about our lack of compassion and all," continued Mega D. "Mesthu, of course, stood by his convictions to never again help the Sanguinati. He was outraged our Infantem Infinitas had met with you against his wishes. He then decreed that no Sorcerer but himself would be the guardian of the Crystallum Templum, for the position deemed too tempting to abuse his authority, eh. This caused a massive split among Mesthu's Children. The next thing we know, Mesthu was found murdered. Aurora Vontiki, eh—she worked her best self-control spell, spun her hair up in the wind, and started the rumor that Aaron was responsible."

"In days of yore, she fancied me, and I cared not for her," confessed Aaron, gesturing with bewilderment.

"Fancied you, eh? Mmm," Mega D moaned and panted. "Your girl begged Mesthu to let you return to the tower. But then she became paranoid he'd burst a stone in his Eye of Expansion and banish her as well, so Aurora isolated herself from everyone."

Aaron raised his head as if such nonsense had insulted him. "Aurora's flirting was a manipulative tactic she tried with many. It surprises me that she would try to frame me for Mesthu's death," said Aaron.

Valor's pulse raced. "They can't believe her lies," he said, as Blade Zagato magicked Valor's trophy from the air and held it defensively.

"I had no ill will against Mesthu," said Aaron. "Verily, I'd rather die here with my new family, the 'primitives' as you say, than die in your ivory tower."

"Siobhan LeSabres is somewhere in Mystic City looking for you now, to warn you as I am, eh," said Mega D. "We're convinced a group of wiggiwamis in Stonevengeance ripped Mesthu's heart out and torched him to death. Bohemia tried to bring order to the tower and ordered a resurrectionist for Mesthu. Aurora said it was best the Children do not attempt to raise Mesthu from the grave, given the deterioration of his body, then accused Bohemia of Noctivatian magic for even suggesting such a thing. Bohemia fled with Siobhan."

"Why should we believe you?" asked Doomsy, digging her fingernails into the strap of her conjure bag, while Valor circled across the flat at a tense pace. How had his conversation with the Ashwin twins caused all this awfulness?

"Yeah, why should we?" asked Valor. "You tried to kill Aaron and me during the tournament."

"It wasn't me, eh. It must've been the Sanguinati, the puppets of the Grim Warlock," said Mega D. Sensing Valor's hesitation, he reached into the pocket of his trousers, removed a silver ring depicting Mesthu's bald head and arms over the Eye of Expansion, and he placed it into Valor's tensed hand.

"This was Mesthu's ring. We found it among the charms and trinkets in Aurora's conjure bag. Bohemia wants you to have it," said Mega D.

"Why would she want me to have Mesthu's ring?" asked Valor, feeling ensnared by the building danger. He glanced at the ring and saw a vision of a sun rook crashing into the moon and setting it on fire, the same vision he had during his initiation into Cryptic Chambers.

"We took shelter in an abandoned lumber mill not far from Shadowhaven Heights," said Mega D. "Bohemia hadn't slept for days, eh—just went about in a blubbering rage and said you could have the ring if you'd help us take back control of Shadowhaven Heights—since it would be too dangerous for Aaron to be seen with us—since you're somewhat responsible for it all anyway." Mega D inspected the Dog Palace, which Valor and Aaron had crawled out of earlier. He eyed them incredulously. "You obviously need it, eh. The crystal stone in that ring improves mind-reading ability."

Valor's fingers tightened into fists. "It's true," he said; "you really have become disconnected at Shadowhaven Heights. The whole world is in danger, and this is all you're worried about? First, you wanted to take over the Sanguinati, now your own people. No, my dear, we cannot just go off and fight some war to help you take control of Shadowhaven Heights. Besides, Bohemia didn't come to Aaron's defense when Mesthu banished him from the tower."

"You are still Sorcerers, and that duty will never escape you no matter how bad the primitives treat us," said Mega D, after most of the spectators and players had left the Spurgmulin Dome

"Exactly," sighed Valor, placing the ring back in Mega D's hand. "We're trying to do something, just not the deal you have offered. Even so, we do not wish to help you reclaim your frozen tower."

"Valor's right, we have more important matters to worry about here," said Aaron.

"Mesthu's Children are too proud to admit you were right about them," Blade Zagato whispered in Valor's ear. "And right about the need to be united to stop the Grim Warlock."

"I'm leaving tonight. If you refuse to help us, we will expose you all as Sorcerers, and you will never stop the Thirteenth Hour," warned Mega D, before spinning around and vanishing.

Blade handed Valor his trophy he had been protecting. "Don't let him spoil your victory, Valor."

"I'm okay," Valor lied.

"What's the matter?" asked Doomsy. "You look like as worried as a wingless fairy during a flood."

"I was just wondering about O Enchantedness—he wasn't wearing his sun rook rune ring. He saw me looking and quickly put his hand in his pocket," said Valor, before telling them about his prior vision of a sun rook. "What do you think it could mean?"

"A sun rook's an ancient symbol of a crow inside a disk of fire 'cause it lives in the sun," said Micha.

"No mumbo jumbo, Merlin," said Creighton, holding his gold key of admission. "But what you don't know is the sun rook used to be depicted with three legs and was a symbol of sorcery, which, of course, the moon is now."

"It is a corrupted symbol of immortality. Oddly, O Enchantedness has a sun rook on his magic staff as well," said Stabbah, fluttering her arms proudly as they began heading home.

"But he's not immortal. There are tons of paintings and crystaleer captures that show how much he's aged," said Doomsy. "Rotting like last years' pumpkins."

"He surely won't live much longer," said Nalini.

"With the way things are going, none of us will," said Ruza, causing Nalini's expression to wilt.

Valor ignored the pit of worry in his stomach and angled his trophy toward Aaron, who did the same, joining the gold hooks as one. "We must keep fighting. We must plan on being friends forever."

"Forever," Aaron agreed, though his distant eyes seemed to fear otherwise.

CHAPTER THREE

CLANDESTULA SHOCKER

WITH just enough recovery time to give him strength to haggle with Doomsy, Valor packed his map of Hoopenfangia in his suitcase along with a few clothes for the trip to Nevelhorn, Clandestula. As Valor had promised, if he won the tournament, he was going to try to locate Doomsy's real parents or find anything he could about her past. Doomsy entered the bedroom with just her conjure bag and a frown.

"My dear," sighed Valor, "do tell me you've packed more than that."

"We won't be there long—you'll see," she said. "I must've been mistaken. I think I was born somewhere else."

Creighton, too, entered Valor's bedroom, dragging a much larger suitcase and a stuffed conjure bag.

"He's not coming with us," said Doomsy.

"Am so, Dooms," said Creighton. "Aaron needs to stay here—with Aurora stalking him and all. I owe it to Valor—all right then? Besides, my crazy dad treated Valor pretty lousy in Convocation."

Doomsy crossed her arms bitterly. "Your dad's trying to trick people into thinking he's got the power. Anybody can massage their own forehead until they get lightheaded."

"Maybe the power runs in the family, Dooms," said Creighton. Vibrating his arm, he placed three fingers on Doomsy's forehead and pushed her backward onto the floor.

"You idiot!" growled Doomsy, staggering to her feet. "I oughta numb your whole backside."

"No, actually. My dad's embarrassed he did it to ya, Val," admitted Creighton.

"The very idea of Kingston asking me in front of everyone if I'd been spell-casting with the moon or shooting ectoplasm from my body," Valor said to appear upset. He hoped Doomsy would understand that they needed someone else on the trip for protection.

"You should've asked my dad to confess if he'd ever picked his nose on a full moon or swallowed a phlegm ball," laughed Creighton.

Doomsy made a queasy face. "All right, you can come, Creighton," she said. "But I don't want to stay for more than two days."

"Great!" said Creighton, reaching in his conjure bag and removing three fat sticks. "Here, this will make our journey a lot quicker."

"Teleport wands?" asked Doomsy.

"No—Magic Trek Whorls," Creighton snickered behind his hand, "otherwise known as easy transport brooms." He whorled his spiral-carved stick in the air four times, and with a series of clicks, it stretched and enlarged until it was a normal-sized broom. "Now, read the fine print."

Valor looked close at the engraving on the broom and read, "Ergonomic Flight Handle."

"It can't be any faster than my Broom of Sesepha that I won," said

Valor.

"These are better. Trust me." Creighton spun his broom through the air and said, "That's what I'm about now—super speed—and more room for stuff in my conjure bag."

Doomsy whorled her stick into a broom as well, whacking Valor on his head. "Where did you get them, my pet?" she asked.

"From a crow-light maker," replied Creighton. He pulled a black glass crow from his conjure bag, tossed it in the air, and the glass bird lit up like a lantern as it flew around the room. "It's getting more dangerous. Anybody who makes crow lights must be a Sorcerer, but I don't care if he's not. I got all this stuff super cheap. *Cheep, cheep,*" Creighton chirped like a bird before retrieving his crow light.

Creighton was right. It was getting more dangerous; this was the main reason Valor felt a pressing urge to find Doomsy's parents, in case the prophecies were accurate about his imminent death. In their spare time, all of Candlewicke 13 had been practicing spells and potions in the cellar and ballroom of the old mansion: Sanguinati wand spells they had learned from Magister Annice Wigginbotham, and magic staff spells Micha, Blade, and Ruza had learned under Magister Dearth Downdilly. But the lessons they all looked forward to were the Sorcerer spells, recorded in their stash of ancient spellbooks and potioning formularies.

Although today, Valor hoped he wouldn't need to defend himself. While the other members of their secret coven were in their morning assemblies, he, Doomsy, and Creighton gathered their belongings and climbed the steps to the Candlewicke observatory.

"According to this map," said Valor, "we fly northeast until we pass over some mountain peaks, and then it's a bit of flat land. Then Clandestula is near the ocean, not far from these three lakes of East Port."

"That area is shaped like a dragon's head," noted Doomsy. "It shouldn't be hard to miss—if we make it over the mountains."

"We will with our Magic Trek Whorls," Creighton said with a cheesy grin.

They mounted their new ergonomic brooms and kicked off, flying out the window of the dome. "Whoa!" gasped Valor, after they shot through the air like three misguided fireworks. Valor soared above the clouds, losing sight of the earth below him.

"Dooommssy, Creeeiightoon!" Valor yelled to his friends before choking on the high rush of frigid air in his mouth. "Where are yooou?" He tried everything he could think of to slow down the broom, but it sped forward, spinning as if he were in a tornado. Something large and brown smacked the back of his broom, flipping him upside down in the clouds, and Creighton's suitcase fell to the earth. He turned the broom upright and searched for Doomsy and Creighton.

Swooping down over Valor's head, Creighton yelled, "Heeelp!"

"Grab the back of my broom," said Valor. "We need to stay together and find Doomsy." Seconds after Creighton hooked onto Valor's broom bristles, a surge of flames shot beside them, followed by a hideous screech and flapping shadows, before a dragon's leathery wings swooshed down over their heads, knocking them down several feet in the air.

"Argh," yelled Doomsy. The dragon shook her left and right as she gripped her broom. "My Whorl handle's wedged in this stupid lizard's tail."

Valor accelerated toward her and shouted, "Hold on! We'll help you." He was soon able to grab the bristles of her broom while she maintained her grip on the handle. He used all his upper-body strength and jerked her Magic Trek Whorl until the tip of her handle pulled out of the dragon's tail with a sucking sound. The dragon roared and flew off in another direction.

Doomsy looked back at Valor. "I can't see. We're going to have to abandon these suicide sticks and float."

"I'm not sure that's a safe idea," said Creighton. "We're going too fast."

"We won't be safe if we slam into a mountain," said Valor. "Everyone, grab hands so we won't lose each other."

Valor clenched his broom between his legs and offered his hands to Doomsy and Creighton, who were on either side of him. "Now, let go!" he yelled.

The Magic Trek Whorls shot out from under them like arrows. They spun through the clouds then began to fall hundreds of feet before they managed to float.

"Clandestula is back that way," said Valor. "We've overflown—a half-mile from the coast, at least."

"We need to get ashore before we drown," said Creighton.

"Or get eaten," said Doomsy.

They all looked down at the raging waters of the Bermuda Triangle and spotted a sea serpent slithering in and out of the vast ocean under them.

"It's a pulvewok," said Valor, nearly falling from the sky when the creature's hissing tongue flicked from its humanlike head.

Using all their magical and physical strength, they floated through the air over the Hoodoo Triangle as some called it. The enchanted veil of mist and waves pulled against them like a magnetic riptide. Bits of broken ships and airplanes, such as Valor had seen in his Nizzertit studies, rose and sank in the ocean waves like chunks of herbs and rat tails in a boiling cauldron.

"I can't see the coastline anymore," said Creighton.

"Me either. The magic veil is playing tricks on our eyes," said Doomsy.

"I think it was this way. Follow me," said Valor, turning left through the swirling mist.

After a few topples onto the surface of the high rolling waves, their feet landed on the shore of Clandestula, where they collapsed from complete exhaustion.

"Aw, I lost my suitcase—in that bloody ocean," said Valor, between heaving breaths.

"I tried to tell you. We still have our conjure bags," wheezed Doomsy, sitting up on the rocky shore high above the crashing waves.

"Well, I guess it's true. I finally know what the magic veil is like now," panted Valor. "I still can't imagine how the Great Witch Chacodophilus managed to navigate thousands of miles over these waters with only a pentagram and the stars' coordinates, let alone find this country. We barely got off the coast and look at what happened." He looked down at Creighton's smoking boot.

Creighton shook the sand out of his ears and lifted his wand. "I had to torch that pulvewok's tongue off my leg. Nearly killed me. Crazy. At least we got here, to be honest."

Doomsy turned her nose up at Creighton. "The real question is: where in Mystic City did this crow-light maker sell you these Magic Trek Whorls?"

"Near Swartrutters. Why?" asked Creighton sheepishly.

"Swartrutters sells banned magic supplies. The Grim Warlock probably owns that whole section of Crumrod Crawl. That's why those brooms tried to give us a one-way trip to Mars."

"We got here at jiffy-lifty speed, Dooms," said Creighton. "But I don't think I have the energy to float for a while." He viewed his surroundings: Straight ahead, the ocean faded into infinity, and on the sides and behind them rose walls of rock. Creighton staggered to his feet and placed his hand over his eyes to block out the sunlight. "Presto lucko! It looks like a cave." He pointed toward the cliff. Sand on his moss-agate starstone ring dripped on his boot.

Valor's head rolled from side to side over his aching shoulders. "Nooo," he moaned. "Nothing good ever happens in a cave. I'll just rest here until—"

Climbing up over the cliff was an enormous goring rahfalus, snorting and hooking the horn on its snout inside the rocky cracks to hoist its legs up the jagged rocks. Valor stumbled backward when he saw a man with four arms, three legs, and one eye on his goat-like head. Seconds later, two more such hybrids came out from the mountain and began shooting arrows at them.

"Yokazunis!" warned Valor. "Um, caves aren't so bad after all." He ran behind Doomsy and Creighton to the mouth of the cave, which resembled two slits of a serpent's nose. The yokazunis straddled the goring rahfalus' back and guided the beast over the rocks after them.

Once inside, Doomsy used her wand to make the rocks at the mouth of the cave collapse. "There," she said. "That should keep those monsters out of the cave."

"But now we're stuck in it," said Valor. "There might be a troll in here, waiting to make toothpicks out of us."

Creighton grabbed Valor's shoulder and shook him. "Trapped?" he squeaked. "No! We . . . we hafta get out."

"It's pitch black," said Valor, pulling his shoulder free. "Where do you suggest we go?"

"I'll get my crow light so we can see how to get out of here," said Creighton, stammering in the darkness. The clatter of him rummaging through his conjure bag preceded the bluish-black illumination of the glass crow. The crow flapped its wings, let out a terrible screech, and began soaring to the roof of the cave before nose-diving on top of their heads, pecking at them. Creighton swatted at the crow. "Argh! Why did I get a crow light? I've no luck with birds."

"Is it just me, or is that stupid crow light screeching louder?" asked Doomsy, after the glowing bird flew into the distant part of the cave.

A flurry of black-winged monsters fluttered in the glow of the light. Valor grabbed his sister and pulled her behind a sheltering rock. "The crow stirred up a nest of vampire bats—that's why," he said.

The swarm of monsters engulfed them, reeking of rotting meat and mildew. Their fangs bit at their bodies, trapping them under their hungered slurping. The bats on the cave floor teetered toward his face like fat old men on their stubby pink feet, curling their wings like capes over their furry gray cheeks and pudgy bellies—surely, they were used to heavy feeding.

"My Sorcery isn't working. I'm too tired," puffed Valor. "The bats are too close to use my monoculous."

The bats' black tongues protruded, and their nostrils sniffed for a drink. Valor had to save his friends before the beasts drained their blood. He grabbed a handful of gravel and tossed it in the air, making it rain down on the bats, which sent them scurrying long enough for him to jump up, grab the crow light, and smash it onto a stalagmite growing up from the cave floor.

"Oh, great! Why the unicorn splatter did you do that?" asked Creighton.

"Because the crow light attracted the vampire bats to us," said

Valor. "It was trying to have us killed just like those hexed brooms you bought."

Creighton's voice rose higher: "How're we supposed to find our way out of here? I can't even see my own aura."

"The bats sucked the auras out of us and covered it in poop," huffed Doomsy. Her conjure bag rattled and clanked, seconds before a spark ignited on the cave floor, growing under her tiny hands as she muttered a chant. The ball of light rose from the floor and broke into smaller balls, which scattered throughout the cavern.

"What are you doing, transforming the cave into a dance club?" asked Creighton, hunched over and jumping at shadows.

"She's smoking the bats out of the cave . . . I think," said Valor.

"Transforming its dim areas, men," said Doomy, wiping her hands with accomplishment. "Now we can see how to get outta here. Just keep your voice down and don't make any sudden moves."

She tiptoed deeper into the cave watching for the vampire bats. They passed an underground lake with a signpost, which read "Drowning Pool." Iron shackles hung from the perimeter and into the water. The rainbow glow in the bed of the pool appeared to come from angel-aura quartz.

"That pool's beautiful. Surely, they don't drown people in there," said Valor. Had he done the right thing dragging Doomsy here? What if someone had drowned her parents? With his pulse vibrating in his head, he eased to the water's edge and pulled up the chains, one after the other. "There are no bodies attached to the shackles."

Doomsy didn't budge or breathe. "You seem disappointed, my pet."

"That's not true. I just wanted to see if—oh, never mind," said Valor. He grabbed pillars of limestone to steady his balance, before realizing they were tree roots, seemingly growing the farther they walked. The vampire bats hung upside down from the ceiling. Their wings folded over their furry bodies like death shrouds. Were they trying to hide before their next attack?

"Crikey!" Creighton's gaze traveled from the cave floor to the ceiling. "Somebody must be living in these roots—they've got windowpanes, but there're no lights on inside."

"Could be dwarves or pumpaninnies. Maybe they're not home," said Valor, easing up a few steps carved into the roots.

"Don't lose hope, Creighton," said Doomsy, holding onto a railing of winding vines with each step. "Maybe they are waiting to drown us or feed us to the bats."

"Maybe we should just head back to Severance. Has anyone considered that Doomsy could be a changeling?" asked Creighton. "That could explain why she never grows."

"A what?" asked Valor.

"A changeling. You know, one of those evil fairy babies swapped for a human baby. We could find Doomsy's real parents without risking our necks here. All we have to do is pretend to kill her—you know—force her fairy mother to switch the children back."

With a snort, Doomsy stopped in her tracks, and a few rocks chipped off the cave walls, causing an echo of tapping throughout the cave. Valor aimed his magic wand at Creighton.

"Just stop! My sister is completely human; do you understand?"

"It was just a thought. Put a zapper wrapper on your razzle rod, Val," said Creighton. He waved his wand, and Valor's underwear tore from his pants and wrapped around his magic wand.

Valor tried hard to ignore Creighton's laughter. Soon they came to a cavern stream with a paddleboat tied to a stone bridge, which led to a wooden door with a bench and a lattice archway made of roots. The sign over the door read "Prisoner Drop Off. Ring bell for the attendant."

"The cave ends here," said Valor. "I guess we should ring the bell or take the boat through that tunnel."

Creighton untied the boat and climbed inside it. "Are you two 'completely human' beings coming?" he asked, grabbing the paddles and steadying them in the water. "I'd rather not have whoever's in there mistake me for a prisoner."

Valor offered his hand to help Doomsy, but she looked away and jumped inside the boat. Creighton paddled the vessel through the black tunnel far past the last glowing orb from Doomsy's light spell.

Sloshing water echoed until they reached the cave exit. The sunlight warmed their bodies before the churning waters of towering waterwheels splashed cold mist on their faces. They gazed at an entire community built into the backside of the mountain with windows embedded throughout it like scattered boulders. The village ascended even higher and broader in the massive, sprawling trees that grew out of the cliff and over the cascading streams.

"This must be Nevelhorn, Clandestula. I say, I never would've imagined any civilization behind that ocean cliff we just went under," said Valor, as four fish-shaped boats sailed down the river, blowing bubbles from their mouths, and Nizzertits paddled the fish with large wooden spoons.

"Primo! I see a few Sanguinati flags flying around," said Creighton. "Maybe Mr. Vyperider will make some good connections." His thumbs pointed to his chest before he picked up speed, paddling the boat toward the nearest dock where a cloaked woman slumped over a harp, plucking out a tiresome tune.

Doomsy folded her arms and said, "Yeah, connections to those iron shackles we saw in that pool."

A child with torn pants crept within four feet of the dock and lobbed his doll into the stream, which traveled around the erratic pyramid of houses and shops. As the doll sank below the water, the woman stopped playing the harp and bolted from her stool.

"Rolland! Rolland Pauly, get out here. We have intruders," the woman yelled, while pointing a wand at Valor and his friends. "Who are you? And what are you doing in Nevelhorn?"

The boy grabbed a windmill blade that spun him higher up the hill before he dropped into a small boat suspended by ropes over a higher deck.

"We are apprentices of magic from Mystic City," replied Valor, standing up in the boat. "We're looking for my sister's birth parents."

A terrible scream traveled in the wind. The boy in the boat waved his arms and pointed up the winding maze of canopied decks and stairs. The goring rahfalus and yokazunis began to climb over the highest peak of the mountain just under a watchtower built into the treetops. The woman plopped back on her stool and began trudging out the same choppy tune, and the monsters retreated over the mountaintop.

"Wuh—wuh happened?" asked a tiny man, fatter than he was tall. Exiting a boot shop between two tree branches, he wobbled backward and forward, waving his arms to balance his big stomach over his boots, which did little to add support to his squatty legs. His towering pointed hat blew off, and Valor gasped. The man didn't appear to have a head, and his little arms flapped like a baby duck's wings, trying to catch his hat. Then the man raised a telescope on a stick to the top of his massive lumps of blubber.

"I think he's got a head. We just can't see it," said Creighton, tying the boat to the docking post.

"Maybe he has eyes elsewhere. He does look like a potato on boots," said Doomsy, climbing onto the dock.

The woman strummed her harp softer and said, "Rolland, get me a replacement over here, and I'll tell you what happened."

Rolland used his telescope on a stick to help him see as he waddled over to a rope suspended from an overhanging shack. He pulled a brass horn down to his body and tooted the horn. A young man crawled out of a round window in the cliff and slid down a pole through three deck holes.

"Thank Fridline Sibyl. My fingers are about to fall off," said the woman, changing shifts on the harp with the young man who began playing the same melody. "I was trying to see who our visitors were, and the critters started to descend. They require twenty-four-hour calming."

"We have visitors?" asked the fat man. "Weah? Weah are they?" He swung the telescope in every direction that he could without falling over. Still brandishing her wand, the woman pulled the veil tighter around her face and inched toward them.

"On the lower dock," she said. "They claim they're apprentices from Mystic Steeples, looking for some girl's parents."

"My adopted sister here—Doomsy Gloomsy. We're looking for her parents. She doesn't know who they are," said Valor. He pointed at Doomsy, who pretended to scrape something off her neck with her fingernail as she looked at the clouds.

"Qweah looking bunch." Rolland inspected them from head to toe with his telescope.

"Just who are you folks, huh?" The woman gestured with her wand. "Only Dwarves and Nizzertit workers use those boats. The Sanguinati never get that close to water."

"I'm Creighton—Creighton Crowley. My parents are top mesmerists for O Enchantedness. Their special mesmerizing techniques help me and my pals get near the water—oh, and Floaty Bubble helps, too." Creighton took out a piece of his special chewing gum from his pocket to show them. "'Lifts up to one-hundred-and-thirty pounds.' Roland would need several packs of Floaty Bubble to go boating, but you might not sink, Miss—what's your name?"

"Never you mind my name," said the woman, twitching her veiled head toward Roland.

Valor's head dropped in his hands at Creighton's comment. "Why didn't you just tell them we drown easily while you're at it?"

Roland motioned at Valor and his friends to follow him. "I'll take them to the Hall of Wehcords. C'mon, kiddies," said Roland, snapping his fingers. "Kiddies, c'mon. Move it . . . move it alweady."

They congregated behind Roland, who wobbled up the incline of the deck, inches at a time. Roland paused and panted for breath. "Huhwee up, kiddies. Huhwee." He paused again, near a ladder ten feet from where he first stood at the boot-shop entry. "Now cwimb up this ladder. Go wight on the next two-plus decks. Enter the cedar-shingled building with the revolving carousel doors. Go to the back of the woom and enter the tree-woot passage—fourth from the middle. Make under-four lefts and take the elevator to the sixth-plus floor. The Hall of Wehcords is just eight spiral turns down the twunk." Roland caught his breath. "Bettuh huhwee. They cwose in thirty-two minutes."

"What did he say?" asked Doomsy, exchanging confused expressions with Creighton and Valor.

"Do your best. We don't have time to get directions again," said

Creighton. They climbed the ladder, while the residents of Nevelhorn moved throughout the sprawling city like ants in a tree.

They made it to the first deck where Valor said, "Right on the next three decks," which they did, trying not to knock the locals over the railings in their rush.

"Now, where?" asked Creighton.

They looked around at the wooden planters spilling their lush ivy over window ledges and railings. Tree branches obscured much of their view, and they ambled along past a residence and magic shop. Then they passed Archie Bush's Arbortecture, where the motto carved on the twisting roots around the front window read, "Building quality dwellings on one tree limb at a time."

"The bar's over there. It has carousel doors," said Valor, pointing to the Merry Mint Lounge.

They ran to the entry and waited behind other patrons for the doors to rotate and open. Then all three of them squeezed through it before it closed. The lounge exuded a minty aroma. The bar, dominating the center, was an old carousel that bobbled and rotated while patrons sat on various wood-carved animals while sipping and ordering potions and drinks. The constant music seemed to assure the patrons that the savage monsters over the cliffs wouldn't harm them here. Before dashing to the back of the lounge, Valor, Doomsy, and Creighton squeezed past two patrons reclining on a revolving blue unicorn and a penguin with a wobbly crown.

"Argh! There are nine tree-root passages here. I can't remember which one to take," panted Valor. His hands shook, wishing he had slapped Roland for expecting them to memorize the directions. "Something about the middle."

Doomsy counted the entries with her hands and said, "Fourth from the middle."

Valor turned in circles. "Are you certain? Why didn't he say the far right door?"

"Because the far right entry's an odd number," said Creighton, opening the door. "You know what fickle pickles these cats are, Val."

They entered a hall of woven tree roots that locked paintings of village celebrities in carved frames in its woody web. Valor came to a fork in the hall with a marble water fountain embedded in ivy and roots.

"Which way do we go now?"

Doomsy and Creighton shrugged, suggesting opposite directions, then changed their mind again while a dwarf carrying a tray of empty mugs scooted past them. Valor stopped him and asked, "Excuse me, which way to the Hall of Records?"

"Hall of Records is two-plus lefts. Take the lift to floor six, then down the trunk eight turns." The dwarf gawked at Doomsy with wide eyes. His tray of mugs rattled before he scurried through a side door.

"Thanks," said Valor. He took off running, making three lefts, leaving the others behind. He just had to find out something about Doomsy's past. Why was she so secretive? Whether she showed it or not, she must desire to find her biological family. He paused at the elevator before the others turned the corner. "Hurry. We don't have much time."

"Whoa. Let me get in before you close the door," wheezed Creighton, falling into the elevator.

They all spilled out on the sixth floor and dashed past rope barriers to another chamber inside the hollowed-out trees. In this room, every inch of the walls held intricate polished carvings.

"Wait for the next cart," said the dwarf attendant, standing next to an opening in the center of the floor. A wooden cart, carved to resemble a dragon, charged through saloon-style doors and stopped in front of Valor, emitting a puff of steam from its nostrils. A few witches climbed out, and Valor, Doomsy, and Creighton took their seats and shut the green-scaled doors. The dragon cart raised its wings, shot flames from its mouth, and descended into the hole, spiraling downward. A colorful platform marked each floor they passed.

"Get ready to pull the lever for floor eight," said Creighton.

Valor pulled the wooden spike in the dragon's neck marked "Halt," and the cart came to a roaring stop on floor eight. They hopped out and burst through the door with the sign "Hall of Records." The waiting room was empty of people except for four women behind the counter, each wearing witch hats overflowing with faded holiday collectibles, handwritten reminders, family photos, and buttons with inspirational sayings. The shield clock behind their hats had swords for hands and indicated four-plus minutes until closing time.

"Take a number please," said the woman on the far end behind the counter, finally. Valor took a stone rune with the number fifty-eight and watched all the women staring at the walls and filing their fingernails, while their cats and one toad napped on stacks of paper in front of them.

The clock now showed two-plus minutes remaining, and the workers still avoided making eye contact with them. Doomsy tugged Valor's sleeve and whispered, "Let's just leave. I don't think—"

Valor pulled away from her and approached the counter. "Excuse me," he said, "but I didn't need to take a number to be told that you are now closed. We've traveled quite a distance, and Doomsy's waited a very long time to find out who her parents are. There should be some records of her parents here."

"All right. What's her full name?" asked the woman nearest them. A long hall of wooden cabinets stretched behind her.

"Doomsy Gloomsy," said Valor. Oxygen rushed into his lungs as he smiled back at Doomsy.

The woman spoke the name into a large grotesque ear on a statue of a male witch beside her. She looked back at the sea of cabinets and said, "No—no records on that name in any possible spelling, I assure you."

"It's not her real name," said Valor. "She doesn't remember her birth name."

"I must have something in order to conduct a search," said the woman. "How old is she?"

Valor's eyes darted back at Doomsy. He couldn't tell the woman she was over two hundred years old. "She's, um, eight. Born October 31."

The workers glanced over the counter with nervous expressions, while the woman said into the statue's ear, "Send me files on a missing female child born on October 31 in Nevelhorn, Clandestula."

After a few seconds of silence, the woman turned to Valor and Doomsy and said, "No records. Sorry."

"Maybe she was born somewhere nearby," said Valor desperately. "Can you search other regions?"

"All right, all right," said the woman before huffing into the statue's ear: "Send me files that even mention a missing female child born on October 31 in any region of Hoopenfangia."

The woman looked back when the cabinets started to vibrate. Several drawers shot open and spewed out file folders, which sailed through the air and landed on her desk. She eased open the files and scanned their contents. "Hmm," she mumbled. "We do have a record matching that information."

Valor leaned over the counter with a giddy swell of excitement. The door to the Hall of Records locked, and the workers aimed magic wands in every shape, material, and size at them.

"Put your hands in the air and don't move," said the woman nearest them before turning to the statue's ear and shouting, "Security! Security! We've captured the Conjuring Crone. Send security now. WE HAVE THE SERIAL KILLER."

"Serial killer? Why, you have made a grave mistake, lady," said Valor.

He lowered his hands and rushed toward the counter just as the woman cast a blast of energy with her wand and knocked him across the room. She kept her wand aimed at him while he rolled in agony on the floor. Creighton lifted his arms and panted loudly as he turned in circles. The cats hissed and lunged behind the cabinets.

"Thought we were stupid, huh?" asked the woman. Down her throat, she squirted two pumps from a bottle labeled "That Old Goat's Uttermost Throat Potion" before firing another zap at Valor.

"Checking to see if her records had been removed—swept clean, huh? Or maybe you intended to steal them to protect that omen, that—that demon child. She. Cursed. Hoopenfangia. The day she was born!" The woman looked at Doomsy with a gargoyle glower. "Killed. Your own. Fam—*uhh, kkkuuuhhh* . . . ," her words gargled before she grabbed her throat with bulging eyes.

Doomsy held her head down, her chin quivered. She seemed to wither into a shell of nothingness.

"Is this true, Dooms?" asked Creighton, easing away from her with his hands on his head.

Valor lifted his aching head and snarled, "How dare you, Creighton? Of course, it's not true. They have the wrong records."

Repressed memories flooded Valor's aching head. This had happened a few other times when people seemed to accuse Doomsy of murder: They began to gag or choke like this clerk who was now turning blue before she tripped over her chair. Was Doomsy causing this to silence or kill them? Of course not; Tilta Crumpecker was one of Doomsy's accusers, and if anyone were the Conjuring Crone, it was Crumpecker. Therefore, it couldn't be true, Valor determined, feeling worse for even contemplating the accusations. How could he prove her innocence and get out of this mess? That was what he needed to worry about.

The door swung open, and two beefy men in black wool robes aimed their magic staffs at them. "Come along, you little convicts," said the shorter of the two. "We've got a drowning pool waiting for you, you Conjuring Crone, you!"

The taller man, with a black beard braided into his long hair, snatched Valor off the floor. "You and the other boy will be locked in the dungeon until we decide what to do with ya."

"No!" Valor choked; his face heated while he squirmed between the men. "You're mistaken. You have the wrong records. Tell them, Doomsy."

She didn't respond.

"Tell them you didn't kill anybody," pleaded Valor. "Why are you so quiet? Why aren't you defending herself? Doomsy?"

"She's been a near zombie since you suggested she look for her birth parents, is all I'm saying," Creighton whispered to Valor.

"But why?" Valor's voice trembled. "The security guards can't drown her, can they—not without a trial, at least—not without proof?"

"You didn't like my opinion, remember? I should've known you'd get us into this," mumbled Creighton.

The guards forced Valor, Doomsy, and Creighton down several halls and through a shortcut in the mountain that took them back to the cave where they had fought off the vampire bats.

Creighton looked down his nose at the guard and said, "I'm related to O Enchantedness. He should be allowed to decide our case. When he hears about this, you'll be on the next broom to Grossatete Sanatorium."

They reached the drowning pool, and the short guard rested his staff against the cave wall and began to attach lead-weight cuffs to Doomsy's ankles. Valor concentrated as hard as he could on the magic staff that had been jabbing him in the back. Before the click of the second cuff, the guard's wooden staff snapped backward, hitting the tall guard in the face.

"You're not going to drown my sister," said Valor. He grabbed the staff, and the stone-medallion tip of it snagged the guard's braided beard. Valor swung the staff, flinging the guard against the short man, and they both fell in the pool.

"Get the other staff, Creighton. Do it," yelled Valor.

Panting again, Creighton turned in circles with his hands on his head. He grabbed the other staff and aimed it at the men who were now clinging to the edge of the pool. The tall guard grabbed Creighton's leg, and he smacked the man on the head with the staff at least five times. Valor took out his monoculous wand and aimed it at Doomsy's ankles.

"*Recludo!*" he chanted, undoing the locking spell on the lead cuffs. "Doomsy, run to the cave entry and see if you can unblock it. Go!"

She stood still as if trying to decide what to do before walking toward the cave entry. Valor flicked his wand twice and chanted, "*Adumbra Slumbra Dix.*"

The spell worked. The guards fell asleep, and Valor secured the cuffs around their wrists.

"Hurry, we got the entrance clear," panted Creighton.

Valor ran out of the cave, and they all floated into the afternoon sky high over the ocean cliffs. All through the night, with Creighton fussing and Doomsy refusing to talk, they maintained a steady flight until they found their way back to Severance.

CHAPTER FOUR

AURAVITAMAX

MONDAY afternoon, on the way to their next assemblies in Mystic Steeples, Valor and Aaron tried to get a feel of the direction they were walking through Toadflax Hall. They still didn't want to ride the traveling floor tiles that moved past them, carrying other apprentices and occasional magisters of magic to their destinations. They had just finished Sanguinati History for the day under Magister Balfe Bullard.

"The entire experience still feels so wrong, so tense . . . so unenlightening," said Valor.

"Can Mystic Ministry not get a bloody magister who can see and communicate?" asked Aaron, while a squeaking mouse ran headfirst into the wall and then behind a Snuffinumbra apprentice before biting down on the bottom hem of his red robe, dangling like a solitary fringe.

"Apparently, Siegfried Kettles wasn't the only magister of Sanguinati History who's been murdered. I'm afraid it happens if they reveal too much. That is why the Sanguinati hired Magister Bullard because no one can understand a word he says," replied Valor.

They moved past the entry to another assembly where somebody was screaming, laughing, and throwing things. "And what about Doomsy? She hasn't said a word since you got back from Nevelhorn," said Aaron.

"I should've never subjected her to the humiliation she received there, Aaron. How can I ever try to find her parents again?"

"I know this has become a sensitive subject, my friend," said Aaron. "But I shall never understand how the workers at the Hall of Records claimed that Doomsy, an obvious eight-year-old, is the Conjuring Crone. Nothing about her fits those prophecies or connects her to the Grim Warlock—unless the two hundred years we didn't know her proves otherwise."

"It's not true," Valor said coldly. "But I do fear they might trace Doomsy's whereabouts back here and come looking for her."

"It seems she might be in the same situation we have found ourselves, Valor, what with Mesthu's Children looking for us."

"Allegedly," said Valor. "But we must remember where that source of information derived, mustn't we?"

"'Tis true," agreed Aaron.

"That does it." Valor continued at a faster pace. "We need to prepare and learn the *Ritual of Vanishing Spell* we found in the Chamber of Oracles, so we can render ourselves invisible—for protection if needed."

"Ah, verily so," said Aaron, as if remembering the old parchment. "And what are we to do with the scroll for the long lost Electricus Hexigus? We nearly killed ourselves for that scroll down in that forsaken chamber. Obviously, the Grim Warlock would kill to get his hands on it so he could recreate the talismans to operate the Clandestine Chamber."

"We mustn't let that happen," said Valor, remembering the altar-like reliquary. He had seen the Clandestine Chamber with his own eyes when he had traveled back in time through *The Book of Chacodophilus*. But could he trust that the strange book contained any manner of truth? And how did the book become what it is—some spirit-like entity with pages and a cover of human skin that can travel through walls and appear to whomever it chooses?

"I expect the Grim Warlock or Hermetic Order of the Mystic Key want to use the Clandestine Chamber as a deadly weapon," continued Valor.

When they reached the northern end of the hall, three apprentices from various covens sneaked toward Valor, each pulling something out of his or her conjure bags.

"Wow, we finally get a chance to meet you. We have your book and a few collectibles. Will you autograph them?" asked the taller of the two boys, after shaking Valor's and Aaron's hands. The shorter male apprentice held a crystaleer in front of Valor, recording him.

"Oh, no, really? I don't think—" Valor paused with embarrassment. He felt his whole body blushing as he politely backed away—that was before Aaron pushed him back inside the swarm of fans. On the cover of the book, titled *The Knight of Night—An Intimate Portrait of Valor Ulysses McRaven*, was a painting of Valor charging across a field of clovers when he had recovered the Horn of Taurus during the first Spurgmulin Tournament, which he had won.

"Please sign it," the boy requested, easing open the book cover. "It's the Tap and Teleport version."

"The what?" asked Valor, taking a Plume of Phoenix from the boy to sign the inside cover.

"The second edition of your bio has the Tap and Teleport feature," said the girl holding the crystaleer. "They're a best seller underground right now, especially after the tournament a few nights ago. It was wild. You and Aaron were amazing."

"You don't actually get teleported, but it feels like it," said the shorter boy in the group as he watched Valor sign his name.

"You tap your wand on the medallions on each page, and it shows you a version of your story—with sound, too," continued the girl.

"It's not my story," Valor choked again. "I haven't told anybod—"

"Twila and I've got something better than that stupid book," said Marston Diamone, knocking the book out of the boy's hands with his elbow in passing.

"*We* have Auravitamax," said Twila Diamone, reading the label on a rainbow-colored bottle she lifted proudly in her fingers.

"Summoner Mamahchi created it," bragged Marston.

With globulnugee coins rattling in their hands, a crowd gathered around a table in the hall. Above their heads, Valor could see a banner on the wall with a photo of the summoner holding a similar bottle as Twila. Words materialized like a rainbow on the banner and formed the slogan, "Let your true colors show with Auravitamax! The world's only aura-increasing tonic."

"Our family invested in Summoner Mamahchi's tonic because he was too poor to mass-produce it himself. With our help and connections, it's going to be huge," said Twila, her nose so high and smile so smug, she was practically blowing kisses at the ceiling.

O heavens, not now, Valor pleaded mentally. A lump of disbelief expanded in his throat while *The Book of Chacodophilus* whisked through the air from the south end of Toadflax Hall, right over everyone's heads, before pausing in front of Valor's face. The last thing Valor remembered seeing was the look of shock on Aaron's face before the book opened. It seemed to snatch Valor inside its flipping pages of flesh near where he glimpsed the date 1641, penned among lines of the fancy text he realized Chacodophilus had written in pale blood.

Valor was pulled deeper into an event he had earlier witnessed in the book: The scenes, though they may have had long gaps of time between them, were now speeding forward as though he were seeing them happening in a day: Usabelli's eyes narrowed with fiery anticipation while she replaced a diamond in the talisman stones in the Crown of Chacodophilus with a clear crystal. Nighttime Convocation arrived, and Valor watched helplessly as the stone replacement made the strange shrine called the Clandestine Chamber not recognize young Chacodophilus to the point it expelled blue flames, engulfing him in front of the stunned mass assembly. Chacodophilus tumbled off the platform onto the Avitestari, right over the answer "Goodbye," before someone extinguished the flames with a water spell, but it was too late. All that remained of the Great Witch on the spirit-board floor was a charred mass resembling a scorched tree trunk.

Valor then found himself in a damp, torch-lit catacomb under what he recognized as Mystic Steeples; only everything was far less dusty and musty in its earlier time.

"Guardians, secure the entry, and make sure none of Goth's followers try to attend his burial," ordered Usabelli.

"Head Vespercestor Usabelli, is that really necessary?" asked one of the guardians.

"Do as I say, or I'll bind you in this death chamber for all eternity," growled Usabelli. "I don't want any tricks—any removing his body—so they can perpetuate any more claims of 'greatness' about this young man. Arrogance is not greatness."

Two guardians lifted their magic staffs and cast a spell resembling a continuous web of lightning inside the bricked opening. Four other guardians placed the remains of Chacodophilus Goth inside a stone coffin and closed the lid, which made a rumbling scrape. The lesser vespercestors made a circle around the coffin in a ritual of respect, and then they eased quietly out of the catacombs after Usabelli set fire to the wreath of white carnations they had placed on the lid.

Days passed with mere flashes of the sun over the dead of thirteen long nights. The pages of the book aroused the catacomb dust in its breeze. Valor stumbled against a wall when the coffin lid eased back, and a hand emerged through the crack. With a great cry, Chacodophilus pulled himself out of the coffin and sat on the lid where he felt of his face, hair, and hands, before inspecting his arms and feet with a growing smile that warped into a sneer.

"Usabelli LaRock, you cunning demoness! I should've known you would be the one to assassinate me and deposit my body in this hidden chamber underground," laughed Chacodophilus, before leaping off the coffin and pacing madly around the catacomb. "But you are not as clever as me—the Great Chacodophilus. Ha! The spell I worked succeeded—you did not count on me regenerating with time. Wait until my people hear the truth."

With a rumble, the ceiling of the catacomb opened to the night sky, and Saturn appeared bright overhead.

"Lest you have forgotten, O Chacodophilus: Death did visit you, thereby making a future rule by you null and void according to your oath with me," Saturn spoke, and what the planet said reminded Valor of the book, *The Legend of the Great Witch and the Lost Magic Instruments*, which someone had placed under his pillow on two different occasions.

"Usabelli LaRock has become the second head vespercestor," continued Saturn. "The inhabitants of Severance have become as power-hungry and corrupt as she has. Your legend must fall into obscurity, or you or anyone to whom you reveal your true identity will face certain death."

Chacodophilus clasped his hands under his beard, his eyes downcast.

"O Saturn, what if I take a wife and she bares me children? How am I to keep my history from my future descendants?"

"According to the strength and merits of their spiritual bond with you, will they possibly see the truth and be able to tell others. But if you physically reveal who you are, they will surely perish. Mostly you will be forgotten. Usabelli will be given credit for leading the witches of the world to their refuge in the land of Severance, and for building all your monumental structures."

Valor's whole body prickled; he seemed to be the only person to see and hear this deadly truth coming from the mouth of Chacodophilus. Was this part of the reason there were so many prophecies of Valor's death? *It couldn't be*, Valor tried to assure himself. The Great Witch wasn't revealing this to Valor in person, was he? This was only a vision from the past—a vision from a book.

Chacodophilus appeared deflated at this forgotten part of his agreement with Saturn. "But you promised to provide me an heir, Saturn—a pair actually—one as a protector of my successor," he said desperately.

Valor's prickles turned into shivers of shock. Chacodophilus lifted his head, and his eye muscles narrowed when he looked right at Valor as though having a vision of him in the future.

"And you shall have them . . . in time, according to our agreement, O Chacodophilus," said Saturn.

"But for the protector to safeguard my heir, surely he must take on my plight—he or she must know the truth—"

Before Chacodophilus finished speaking, Saturn vanished as the ceiling of the catacomb closed, locking the Great Witch and Valor in the lonely dungeon of darkness.

Chacodophilus glanced around at the vast catacomb. "Immortality hath not abandoned me—be that the only reward. Alas, there is no option. I shall update my appearance with the times—change my name, even the habits of my tongue. I shall dwell here underground where it is safer . . . until I see the promise of my heir who shall resume the rule of my blood—my namesake the Clan of Goth—if only to my knowledge, be it according to my pact."

The pages of the book shuffled forward. Using his powers and architectural genius, Chacodophilus had filled his solitary days building a vast underground city. He expanded the catacombs for miles and miles under Mystic City, giving himself many secret rooms and passages to hide in case someone discovered him. He had obviously retained immortality, for he still appeared a youth of eighteen.

One evening, around the Grim Hour, Chacodophilus sat among the sarcophaguses in what appeared to be the most ancient burial chamber underneath Mystic Steeples, with strange words etched on the wall.

". . . The worthy can only know the truth of who I am by a 'spiritual' connection—a spiritual understanding," the Great Witch mumbled. His forehead wrinkled as he leaned against a tomb. A few seconds later, he sat upright.

"The dead cannot die . . . they cannot die! They are immune to the consequences of my pact with Saturn." Chacodophilus's eyes enlarged, and he pulled the lids back on several coffins and gazed at the preserved human corpses with a look of promise Valor had yet to see on him.

"O Ancients buried in these graves, hear ye the voice of the Great Witch. Lend me your skin so that I may record a memento mori—a truth record, so that future generations can someday rediscover the history of our heritage, our settlement in Hoopenfangia, and of myself—the Clan of Goth. Yes! Lend to me pages of your flesh; the ink of your pale blood, infused with all the knowledge of the truth of our history; and oracles of the things that were and of things to come, which the elite try to erase."

The spirits of the dead throughout the catacomb spoke in unison: "Empowered One, we will lend you our skin for the pages of this book, our pale blood so that only the worthy can read it. But we are not Ancients. We are lowly outcasts who have no soul—no aura—to lend. The only thing that will make the book complete—that will quicken it—will be a soul, which shall require a heart sacrifice from the living, from someone who doesn't deserve to die."

With a knowing expression, the Great Witch again seemed to look right at Valor.

"I cannot kill. I cannot sacrifice the innocent," said Chacodophilus, pulling at his dark hair that had regrown down his back.

"Then everything you desire will be forgotten," chorused the spirits.

The Great Witch blew frustrated breath into his clasped hands, then said, "Very well. Provide me all that I ask, and I shall sacrifice my own heart when the end of my days comes. Hoopenfangia must have the truth, and this way, I can control the book in death from the astral plane. And *The Book of the Dead* shall trump the auras of the elite."

The corpses began offering up their skin for the pages, blood for the ink, and hair and other body parts for the cover and binding so that Chacodophilus could construct the book. Valor shuddered and looked away until the pages of *The Book of Chacodophilus* sped forward, and he found himself inside a lavish room at Mystic Steeples in the year 1788.

Valor recognized Rendum LaRock, his great-great-great-grandfather, the tenth head vespercestor, hunched over his desk in his office, while his famous poodle, Spurgmulin, napped on a velvet pillow on the floor near his desk. Rendum wasn't missing his left hand at this time, for he held a parchment with the heading *Official Drowning Verdict — For Rebellious Witches.* A fat boy, around the age of thirteen, wearing a gold Graven Dust coven robe, sat in a nearby chair while sucking on a green stick of Lolly-Gaggers candy. The boy gazed with admiration at Rendum as the head vespercestor placed the tip of his wand on the parchment, and his sanctioning seal manifested near his signature, officially enacting the drowning verdicts. A sickening loathing rose in Valor's chest over this revealing.

"Did you d-do it, s-sir?" asked the boy sitting taller with candy in hand.

"I did, Venerious," replied Rendum, returning a smile between the brier-shaped points of his black beard.

Valor jolted to attention when he realized the young boy was Venerious Falmoth. He would have never recognized Falmoth without his white face powder, jagged black eyebrows, or matching gash in his cheek.

"C-can I watch you d-drown 'em?" asked Venerious with an envious sparkle in his dilating pupils.

"I imagine so. As long as it doesn't interfere with your daily assemblies or your studying," said Rendum with a wink.

Also wearing a Graven Dust robe, an apprentice about five years older than Venerious entered the office and said, "Head Vespercestor, I'm about to—"

"Well, spit it out—Eelias Mamahchi, is it?" asked Rendum, shuffling through a handful of parchment, while his poodle awoke and wandered toward Venerious.

Again, Valor did a double-take. Without the scraggly beard, widened nose, and wrinkled skin, the young version of Summoner Eelias Mamahchi didn't look anything like the old man version. In fact, most people in the current day would probably consider teenage Mamahchi handsome.

"Yes, sir," answered Mamahchi. "I'm about to . . . finish my Magisters of Magic program. And I was wondering if—"

"If I might know of any positions available in Mystic Ministry," replied Rendum LaRock, before Mamahchi nodded his head meekly. "Now look here, Eelias. Your aura is dim. Your family has no social standing among the elite in Severance, Hoopenfangia."

"Furthermore, your *Progress Gauge Reports* indicate you are prone to questionable magic practices. I'm afraid there just isn't room for you in Mystic Ministry at this time. Now take young Venerious Falmoth here, he has a bright aura, yes, full of ambition," continued Rendum.

Young Venerious's lips curled into a cocky grin, exposing a green tongue from the Lolly-Gaggers in his mouth. He let Spurgmulin lick a while on his candy, spilling a few drops on the poodle's blonde hair.

"Venerious?" snarled Mamahchi. He then lowered his voice when Spurgmulin growled at him. "But nobody in Graven Dust likes him. He acts like a clown and . . . and stutters, sir."

"Do not question my decisions, Mamahchi," said Rendum. He slammed his hand down on a scrying bowl, spilling a puddle of water on the *Official Drowning Verdict*. "Nevertheless, we may be able to find a spot in Mystic Ministry for you. If you can keep up with the workload. There's a, um, position opening for a summoner soon."

"A peon . . . a delivery person?" asked Mamahchi, before Spurgmulin lunged at him and sank its teeth into his robe. The poodle released its grip on the gold fabric after Mamahchi glared at the dog.

"A *summoner*. You'll take what we offer, Mamahchi," said Rendum sternly.

"Of course. Thank you, Head Vespercestor."

Venerious reclined against the arm of his chair and held out the goo-covered stick where he had eaten off all the green candy. "Aw, it's all gotten icky. Throw t-this sticky away for m-me, Eelias."

Eyeing the young apprentice and poodle with disdain, Mamahchi snatched the gooey stick and left the office.

The pages of *The Book of Chacodophilus* slowly turned forward, allowing Valor to see glimpses of Venerious Falmoth by himself, eating candy in the shadows, in alcoves, and occasionally behind furniture, if there was ample enough room for Venerious to squeeze behind it.

"Hey, Delirious Fat Mouth! The candy store is two blocks that way," yelled a Graven Dust girl at Venerious, who was squatting among a curbside display of cauldrons while reciting poems from poetry books.

"No wonder he hasn't got any friends," said a Snuffinumbra boy. "He talks like a broke record."

"I don't stutter since I learned poetic words to utter. Besides, I don't need any chums. Rendum LaRock says I'm like his son," Venerious gloated to his tormentors. "I'm joining Rendum for dinner on the bank of the Severance River, and we're watching the rebellious witches drown all winter."

Valor watched as Venerious began to dress and carry himself statelier like the head vespercestor. He got chills when Venerious would laugh at the victims as they struggled against the water until the mighty waves pulled them under.

"It m-must be pretty nifty to get revenge on your enemies," said Venerious.

"That was good, Son," said Rendum, downing a mouthful of fortune cookies. "You've greatly improved your stuttering. Now just relax and take a little more time to think about what you're going to say. We must think of these drowning verdicts as necessary to achieve order and respect, not revenge—understand?"

Smiling as if he understood something more sinister, Venerious dipped his chicken leg inside a bowl of gravy and held it there. "You're the best head vespercestor ever," said Venerious carefully. "I imagine there has been none better. Urbanne and Ulysses must be s-so glad to have you as their dad."

"My boys? I'm not sure they view me with such favorable regard," said Rendum, washing down his cookies with a glass of wine.

"Urbanne argues with me all the time with his so-called 'enlightened' ideas. He wants to be a leader but has no real backbone to control the people. My other son, Ulysses—well, he has a backbone, but he doesn't want the responsibilities necessary to rule Severance. He's always been lazy and reckless."

"Mr. LaRock, who is that they're drowning—there by the dock?" asked Venerious, stretching his double chin, which was beginning to lose its puffiness.

Rendum's eyes squinted into the sun. "Hmm, that's Anton and Mazy Mamahchi I believe," he said, before wiping his greasy lips.

"Eelias Mamahchi's p-parents?" asked Venerious. He gnawed on the chicken bone and soaked it in the gravy again, where he stirred in a whole pack of Bleeding Heart Candies until the gravy turned red.

"*Summoner* Mamahchi to you," said Rendum. "Always use a man's title to show respect."

Valor couldn't believe everything he was witnessing. For years, he had always heard the elders reminisce about the past and how safe and wholesome those days were. If this was their idea of "the good old days," he couldn't wait to get back to the current time.

"Head Vespercestor, why did you have the summoner's parents drowned—because they disrespected your crown?" asked Venerious.

Rendum seemed to have conflicted thoughts. He cleared his throat and said, "I didn't order their execution. Nevertheless, Anton and Mazy Mamahchi are missing no longer. The guardians must have recovered their bodies from the river. As former coven presidents for Snuffinumbra, Anton and Mazy were instructed to try to calm the protests over my drowning verdicts. They are simply casualties of war. That is why we must keep order, Venerious, or people will start protesting everything we do. That is the path to success. You cannot allow guilt or sentimentality to seep in these types of decisions. It's just as well . . . Anton and Mazy had no real auras."

"So, there is no need to blubber," agreed Venerious, puffing out his chest. "Some of us are better than others."

"I'm getting old, Venerious. I know you have struggled through your apprenticeship, but I believe you have real potential."

"Really? But my own coven hates me deeply."

"I used to be just like you—misunderstood."

"You? By whom?"

"By the clan of Chacodophilus Goth—the remnants of his followers anyway," said Rendum.

"That old fool. How did you change that? What did you do?"

"The secret to fitting in is to steer your coven mates' anger off you and onto another target—people without our shared ideals. Show Graven Dust the importance of retaining our 'Destin, Heredity, Ministry.' Prove to them the danger of allowing outsiders in our city. Convince them of the necessity of corporal punishment."

With dancing eyes, Venerious leaned closer while crunching harder on his stick candy.

"And for Ramrod's sake, share some of your candy while you do this," said Rendum with a wink. "That'll have Graven Dust eating out of the palm of your hand . . . literally."

The pages of *The Book of Chacodophilus* shuffled forward again and paused when Venerious had completed the Magister of Magic program at Mystic Steeples. The members of Graven Dust surrounded the new, slimmed-down Venerious in a sea of gold robes and began tossing him in the air as they chanted, "Here's to Brazen Graven Venerious Falmoth . . . a leader destined to be most fortuned. Preservation Foremost!"

When Venerious's feet again touched the ground, he strutted up to Head Vespercestor Rendum LaRock, who had attended his graduation.

"Sir," said Venerious. "We both know this is something you've somewhat mentioned—I'm ready! Ready to be your replacement for the head vespercestor's position."

"Well now, that is mighty ambitious of you, Venerious, mighty ambitious," said Rendum, patting Venerious on the shoulder. "Nevertheless, I have chosen my son Urbanne, and he has accepted . . . whenever that time comes."

Venerious stood with his mouth open in disbelief. It seemed, for a minute, as though a spell might have frozen him, except his eyes became moist and distant.

A page turned in the book, and Valor saw Venerious Falmoth cornering Urbanne LaRock and his wife, Mahrata, at the funeral of Candombram Candlewicke. Near Candombram's standing corpse, the three exchanged conversation slowly at first, until, a half-hour later, Venerious had them all huddled together and laughing.

"My condolences . . . about your father, Mahrata," said Summoner Eelias Mamahchi, wedging himself into the group. "Those monstrous Noctivatians did this to him."

"Hmmm, no worries, Summoner," said Mahrata. "Rendum assures me he doesn't blame your family. Haaa, the same way you never blamed the LaRocks for your parents' deaths."

"Yesss, Summoner," hissed Falmoth, squeezing back between them and shaking Mamahchi's hand. "And though it must've been a bummer, you went against your sister and brother to show your trust in the LaRocks. That says a lot."

"Yes," Urbanne LaRock agreed with Venerious. "Summoner Mamahchi has shown his true colors."

"VALOR!" shouted, Aaron, when *The Book of Chacodophilus* vanished, and Valor found himself back in the present day in Toadflax Hall. The group of fans that had been asking for autographs had left, and thankfully, not everyone in the hall seemed to notice Valor, for they were swarming around the table where Summoner Mamahchi was still selling his new invention, Auravitamax.

"How long was I out?" asked Valor, trying to process everything he had earlier witnessed.

"About five minutes, I suppose," whispered Aaron, moving him away from the crowd.

"Really? But it seemed like forever," said Valor. "I didn't cause a scene, did I?"

"Your fans wanted to know what M.D. wrote on the underwear about us, but you blanked out, so they left. I do not think anyone else saw the book appear in front of you. They thought you were reading Mamahchi's banner about that ridiculous aura potion. I told them you had really bad eyes."

Bats and other flying creatures swarmed over the eastern wing of Mystic Steeples as Valor and Aaron headed back to Candlewicke Mansion. They discussed everything he had seen and heard while time traveling through the book.

"Something must have triggered the book to appear to you," concluded Aaron, as they turned down Spookum Alley, watching for any suspicious stalkers.

"It has rotten timing if so. But speaking of triggering," said Valor: "something has to be causing all of these possessions—now many animals are acting stranger and stranger."

"Verily . . . the Grim Warlock, the Boogeyman."

"Perhaps," said Valor, scooting left on the flagstone alley as a pig wearing a fluffy neckband and mismatched socks squealed as it staggered in loops past him. "But I can't help but think it's something more than that. We have to keep ourselves from being possessed until we can figure it out—until we can stop it."

CHAPTER FIVE

GREEN THIEVES

MISTRESS Bessbadora Breaches halted her lesson in *Controssua* Studies that Monday morning, while her apprentices stood at attention across the room with their *Controssuas* levitating in front of them.

"Apprentices," she said, "as archivist for the late, deceased, dead Magister Crypting—"

"Excuse me, Mistress Breaches," interrupted Valor, "but Magister Crypting is not dead, he's just missing."

"He's dead! Now, I have a Moon Pencil Scorer," said Bessbadora, aiming the pale, glowing pencil at Valor, "and if you interrupt me again, you'll score low *S.C.R.A.T.C.H.* marks on your *C.A.T. P.A.W.s.*"

The apprentices' *Controssuas* drop to their gold pedestals, which served as desks in front of them. Valor struggled to keep his frustration contained because he already had low marks on his last *Certified Apprentice Test Performance of Advanced Witchcraft*. If Bessbadora marked his test with a Moon Pencil Scorer, it would be final, and he could never retake the test—the death of his apprenticeship.

Bessbadora's eyes hardened amid her purple eye shadow drawn in the shape of two cats whose tails appeared to wag as her forehead creased.

"It has come to my attention, to my keen senses, that somebody from Cryptic Chambers took a sacred, powerful, forbidden scroll from the Chamber of Oracles, and I could point you out right now, expose you!" hissed Bessbadora. She frowned, and her lips matched her wavy hair, which she sculpted into a long cone on both sides of her head. A ghost held her wand aimed at various apprentices, but only Valor seemed to notice that it wasn't floating midair as it had first appeared.

Was Bessbadora referring to the Electricus Hexigus scroll that Valor had found in the Chamber of Oracles a while back? His mind raced, and he tried not to draw attention to himself. But he, Aaron, and Doomsy were Cryptic Chambers' presidents. And Vespercestor Yma Le Breton had given them a key to the chamber. If the vespercestors knew someone had hidden that scroll in the dragon's mouth, then why hadn't they used it to recreate the long-lost Clandestine Chamber? Unless—Valor wondered—unless they only needed him to free the scroll so they could use it to restore that potentially deadly weapon. He couldn't trust O Enchantedness to have the scroll or Clandestine Chamber. No matter what, he was not going to reveal anything to Bessbadora.

"I can't imagine any of you knowingly, deliberately, intentionally disobeying the vespercestors," said Bessbadora. "But I've decided to let your own guilt expose you with a hymn, a song of scourge. Turn your *Controssuas* to the 'Mantras of Monavu', hymn number '68-plus, Green Thieves.'"

Valor sang along with the others, keeping alert for some curse:

"Come, O Ancients, and cover the guilty among us with fungus,
As we sing the Green Thieves song with gladness.
Turn as the color of leaves in spring all who covet and take other's things:
Emerald, olive, or jade if you would, o'er his covetous body for good.
Envy can't linger. Put mold on his fingers. Be mindful ye brotherhood."

Valor stopped singing. Having grown weaker as the song repeated, he looked away from his *Controssua* and at his hands: They were turning green. The veins in his head pulsed as everyone continued to belt out the song. He envisioned himself turning into a giant pea, hypnotized until the vespercestors squashed his green guts out of him right there in the middle of Bessbadora's assembly.

His skin crawled, and a stabbing pain burned his left arm. The ghost of a forest sprite began placing phantom sheets of green moss on the center of Valor's abdomen, while another ghost pumped a phantom syringe of green liquid into his veins. If the other apprentices could see the spirits doing this, then they were skilled actors at hiding it, Valor realized. He pushed the sheet of moss off him while snatching his arm free from the syringe.

"Somebody is shaking, trembling like a leaf down there among you, my . . . little . . . apprentices," said Bessbadora, who began prowling down from her platform toward him.

Valor twitched. What could he say or do to stop her? A fifteen-minute freeze spell? Yes! It would work on a whole room of people, Doomsy had once assured him. And she should know; she was the queen of freezing people out of her life.

"Suspensus Motus," Valor whispered, summoning the orb of Saturn into his left hand, and this he dropped on the floor, where it's dull glow swelled like a flood over everyone's feet but Valor's, for he was floating just one unnoticeable inch above the floor.

"Jaaaaaa . . . ," sang the apprentices, frozen in a continuous drone of the word "*jade.*"

Valor's heart thrashed as he examined his fellow apprentices standing as stiff as corpses. Could they see him with their immobile eyes?

"This is so creepy. I hope if you all can see me, you won't remember," said Valor, wiping his hands on his coat, trying to rub off the green stain. "Thank goodness; my hands are returning to normal."

The ghosts tried to escape through the wall, and Valor shot a monoculous blast at them. "Run, you vapors! Go turn O Enchantedness' hair green or something," yelled Valor. He folded his hands together, tapping his fingers. "I've got less than ten minutes to figure something out here." He rummaged through Bessbadora's charm bag and found some Cosmos-metics: her bottle of enchanted green powder. The door to the room scraped open, so Valor waved his Focus Pocus Monoculous in the air as if he were directing the apprentices in a vocal exercise while they continued to sing "jaaaaaa . . . ."

Roma Phunga, the magister of Herbalism, came teetering in the room to replace a dead censer with another perfume burner full of smoking incense. She glanced across the room at him, tilted her head, and scrunched her chin, lips, and brows for nearly half a minute.

Valor smiled at her and said, "That's it, apprentices, hold that note. Jaaaaaa . . . ." He steadied his wand in the air like the dirge diviner did whenever he directed the choir.

Magister Phunga rubbed her index fingers in her ears and shuffled out of the room.

"I guess I have no chance of getting in the choir," laughed Valor. He smeared the green powder all over Bessbadora's face and hands before dashing back in front of his floating *Controssua,* where he pretended he was still singing. The spell ended, and the apprentices' voices had grown weaker. Many began to cough and laugh when they noticed Mistress Breaches now had a green complexion.

"What are you all staring at—gawking like a band of goons?" asked Bessbadora, pausing on her way toward Valor. She looked down at her green hands. "Eh! Hush. Stop singing, you goons— now!"

Several apprentices gasped at the sight of her and fled from the room.

"Where are you going? Come back here now," Bessbadora shouted. "Why, this is some mistake, a trick, a sick hoax. I'm not a thief!" She wiped her hands on her dress and climbed back up on her podium. "The green's coming off, see . . . vanishing. Raise your wands if you believe the Ancients will uncover the real thief, the real hoaxer in our midst, and return Mystic Steeples to a safe haven."

The remaining apprentices did as Bessbadora had instructed, but not Valor; he didn't budge except to clutch his monoculous in his pocket.

Standing behind Valor, Twila Diamone raised her wand and said, "McRaven here has access to the Chamber of Oracles because he is coven president of Cryptic Chambers. He should be reported." She sprinkled a circle of salt around her feet as if to shield herself from a contagious hex.

"Valor McRaven, you don't have your wand raised. You mean you don't believe the Ancients will uncover the real thief?" asked Bessbadora.

Valor shrugged his shoulders in a gesture of uncertainty.

"No? Then perhaps you are responsible for the stolen scroll." Bessbadora whipped out her wand and chanted, "*Tethera, Pethera, Confessora.*"

A ghostlike flutter swam from her wand, through the air, and surrounded Valor in a spell of confession. Deep wicked laughter pierced through the room as something shot inside his body, a ghost perhaps, paining him to speak, to growl even.

"Argh! I could lie and pretend I believe like the trembling apprentices Mystic Ministry produces around here . . . just go through the motions like the puppets we are." His jaws ached from trying to keep his mouth closed, and his arm cramped as he resisted aiming his monoculous at Bessbadora. Whatever was controlling Valor was more than a confession spell. Something or someone was trying to possess him. He raised his monoculous at Magister Crypting's insufferable understudy and began to convulse as he resisted using a killing spell on her.

"Confess or cast the spell, Valor. It must be done," he swore he could hear voices urging him.

"No," Valor growled. This was not him; Valor was not one to kill. This engulfing rage now controlling him even made him sick of his own self. He lowered his monoculous at the *Controssua* in front of him and confessed the only truth he was willing to spare.

"Behold it is written and the Sanguinati are smitten. But no. I dare question—something that's held in contempt at Mystic Steeples." Valor screamed and his legs kicked, while Bessbadora stood slack jawed on her podium.

"McRaven's possessed. It's the Possessing!" yelled Twila, shaking a garland of charms at Valor, while the remaining apprentices dashed to the corner of the room.

Bessbadora cast a spell completely closing the curtains in the already dim assembly. She aimed her wand at Valor. "Apprentices, step aside and call on the Ancients; plead with them; beg if you have to. This might get messy. I might have to—"

"Argh!" roared Valor, shaking like a volcano near eruption. "The Ancients must be trembling, awaiting the first dissenter like me to cut the puppet strings and remove them from their anemic thrones."

Bessbadora sent a wand bomb to the very spot where Valor stood. The bomb knocked off several apprentices' hats and blew him straight up in the air. The apprentices scrambled out of the room, screaming, and this Valor noticed from his shadow form, as the lingering purple smoke cleared from his limp body on the floor. His shadow scattered across the ornate walls in the room, before accumulating into a much taller form of him and leaned over Bessbadora with breathy fury, morphing around her.

Hours later, his shadow rejoined him as he awoke in the hall outside of Urbanne's office in the top of the highest steeple in all of Mystic Steeples. The air was so thin here he nearly stopped breathing, but this might be because Gereon McMahon and a bigger guardian were pinning him too tightly against the wall.

"The truth will come out 'bout you now, McRaven—this very

hour," said the bigger guardian.

"Yes, I believe it will. O Enchantedness's office is about as high as anybody can get to the Ancients," said Gereon. He looked up at the muraled ceiling, and his eyes smiled at the historic battle brooms, torture devices, and magic staffs that hung above the doorways for decoration.

Between the restraining arms of the guardians, Mistress Bessbadora wiped her face with a rag and cackled. "The truth will always shush you, crush you, then flush you, McRaven."

Valor laughed deep inside himself. "I've tried to tell you the truth, but it's obviously not the dirt you were after." He hated this battle, this struggle to squelch the truth every minute of the day. But what all had he said in *Controssua* Studies? Had he really been possessed?

A wedge of light poured from the ajar door of Urbanne's office. Valor peeked inside as lightning flashed through the window, illuminating Urbanne's face until he looked like a corpse. Sitting in two chairs in front of Urbanne was Enzo LaRock, the aerowachee Valor had chosen for his air defense in the recent Spurgie Tournament, and Enzo's cheercaster girlfriend, Jama.

"Hear my words now, Enzo. You are a LaRock. I'm against any apprentice with potential becoming engaged to a nobody like Jama. Her aura is dim. She can't conjure the Ancients, decode runes, or further your plans to become a magister in any fashion. This might be the reason you've not been performing well in Spurgmulin," said Urbanne. He leaned forward on his desk, holding Jama's *Progress Gauge Report*.

Jama sobbed while Enzo's leg jerked in the chair beside hers.

Valor fidgeted, groaning in pain through clamped lips. He had to find a way to escape the guardians. Gereon grabbed his wand and held it to Valor's head, so he relaxed his fists and jaw. A parade of dark red robes came down the hall toward Urbanne's office, chanting and banging tambourhorns.

The larger guardian eased his grip on Valor's arm and hissed, "Here comes Snuffinumbra Coven."

The Snuffinumbras paused in the darkened hall, and Creighton

Crowley noticed the guardians restraining Valor. "Here; have a peace lily," Creighton said to the guardians, shoving the flower onto the tip of Gereon's wand. "Spread peace, man—help us bring unity to the community." Creighton placed his hexagram over Gereon's forehead and offered a sympathetic expression to Valor.

Gereon shoved the stem of the lily in Creighton's mouth and hissed, "We're going to bring peace to the community all right. You might want to . . . save those flowers for the funerals when we're done."

Creighton's eyes enlarged as he peered over the white lily, now jutting over the tip of his nose.

"Um, you probably shouldn't have done that, Gereon," whispered the other guardian, "That's Kingston and Alizaba Crowley's son."

Gereon's jaw dropped. Creighton stood back in line with Snuffinumbra, and they continued with their melodic chanting through the halls; their faces illuminated from the torch-lit alcoves.

Two frazzled minutes later, Enzo and Jama walked sullenly out of Urbanne's office. Their disheartened eyes connected briefly with Valor's. A nerve convulsed in the pit of his stomach, and he collapsed against the wall. What would happen to him now with this web he had woven?

"Send McRaven into my office," ordered Urbanne, after the guardians warned him that the Grim Warlock might have possessed Valor.

Stepping into the room, Valor admired the high-arched balconies and columns bordering half of the room.

"Have a seat, McRaven," said Urbanne, gesturing to one of the regal guest chairs in front of his desk.

Valor moved forward, stumbling on the shifting floor tiles that carried him in a different direction throughout the majestic room. Within a minute, he glided by a window as lightning bolts flashed far below the upper balconies. Looking up, the planets, with their swirling colors, seemed peaceful and almost within his grasp. As he aimed his legs toward Urbanne's desk once more, a floor tile rotated, and looking up at him were five dwarves standing side by side, motionless, as if awaiting Urbanne's command. Their long beards appeared as twigs branching down their chests.

"Shall I put on some music while you waste precious time, waltzing?" asked Urbanne, tapping his fingers over his bejeweled Controssua on his desk. "Move toward me when the tiles move eastward, McMavis."

"Huh?" gasped Valor, looking up at the enormous chandelier swinging like a pendulum over his head. He tried to get a sense of an eastward direction before stepping forward onto the next tile, but he delayed too long, and each of his legs glided in a different direction with the tiles.

"Wan and Two Usefulness," Urbanne said to the dwarves, tossing them some biscuits, "sew Valor to his sheet sometime this century."

"You mean 'show him to his seat,' O Enchantedness?" asked one of the dwarves, pulling a sewing needle from his hat with his face askew.

"I don't care how you get him here, just do it," said Urbanne, massaging his forehead.

A crystaleer, pulsing red for urgent, whisked past Valor's head and hovered over Urbanne's desk. In the glass sphere, High Priestess Tilta Crumpecker appeared the size of a mouse as she thrashed her wand around, casting protective spells at the ogres that she kept on her ranch.

"*Arrrgh*! O Enchantedness," the recording of Crumpecker screeched inside the crystaleer. "This is an emergency now. These blasted ogres are becoming unmanageable. Can I borrow that 'humogre' of yours—ogre-hybrid—or whatever that beast is you were telling me about? I need a critter with half a brain to teach these filthy animals how to behave, or they'll be just as useless for the next Spurgie Tournament—or worse."

On the roof of Ogre Ranch, which appeared as tiny as a Christmas tree ornament inside the glass sphere, Valor spotted birds and bats swarming around a flagpole, which jutted straight up like the hundreds of spires on top of Mystic Steeples. He wasn't sure, but he also swore he saw a fairy crash into the purple Sanguinati flag billowing around the flagpole.

Urbanne tapped the crystaleer with his magic wand and chanted "*Mufflufutus.*"

The crystaleer suddenly went silent and dark. Two of the dwarves on the far left of the room scooted across the tiles, grabbed Valor around his waist, and chucked him down in one of the chairs.

"Magister Brunhatchi will have to start teaching tile navigation. Traveling by broom has spoiled the youth these days," said Urbanne.

Valor scooted to the edge of his chair. "Sorry, O Enchantedness, I—"

"Have behaved atrociously, stolen a sacred scroll, spread malicious gossip, not to mention an array of forbidden behavior," said Urbanne, inserting his magic wand in the hand of a statue of his father, Rendum LaRock, beside his desk. A purple glow surrounded the wand, charging its powers.

Valor's heart stampeded in his chest. "We didn't steal anything. Presidents of Cryptic Chambers are authorized to borrow any document from the Chamber of Oracles."

Urbanne leaned over his desk. "What did you do with it? You know the scroll I'm referring to; it was locked in the dragon's mouth for years—impervious to every spell in the book."

Even the name of the scroll spell, '*Electricus Hexigus*,' Valor would not disclose—not to a man who had to be the Grim Warlock.

"As soon as we got it from the dragon's mouth, a jumbie took it from us."

"A jumbie took it?" Urbanne snatched his wand from the statue. And with a crackle, tendrils of purple energy webbed from it through his office, scorching everything in their path.

"And, other than a paltry jumbie, you haven't seen anything— strange people looking for strange objects, have you, McRavish?"

Valor suspected he was referring to the Clandestine Chamber. Valor hadn't seen the lost reliquary except in *The Book of Chacodophilus*, and like the scroll, he didn't trust Urbanne enough to tell him the truth about it.

"Sorry, but no, O Enchantedness. I'll let you know if I do."

Urbanne's mouth formed a devious smile when he turned toward the paneled wall to his left. "No need to waste an apology now. I've already decided your fate."

Following a mysterious utterance from Urbanne, the paneled wall slid open, revealing every type of torture device Valor had ever seen in the history books: Books that documented how the Nizzertits had once killed and tortured thousands accused of being witches. His legs jerked when Urbanne grabbed some weapon with sharp spikes. Then Urbanne hoisted some shackles and sharp saw blades, which he slammed on a table, making an unnerving clanking noise.

Valor stood up and clasped his fingers together. "Please don't do this, O Enchantedness. I'm not possessed."

"Silence," Urbanne panted, while he grabbed a large scythe propped against an iron maiden. "Embrace your fate!"

The prickle of the dwarves' beards pressed around Valor. He tried not to whimper while Urbanne raised the thick scythe high over his head and, with a growl, swung its sharp blade over Valor's head straight into the iron maiden, breaking its lock.

After his flesh stopped crawling, Valor breathed and tried to regain focus.

Urbanne hoisted the iron maiden's doors open, revealing the body-piercing spikes lining its walls. "This is where I put you, my treasure—my map of promise," he said, taking out a scroll. Unrolling it, he ran his hands over the aged surface as if memorizing its every marking. "For so many years, I have kept you here, fearing your pages would turn to dust but not now. No, Valor here is going to reveal to me your promise. He will not divulge your secrets to commoners."

Would he require something awful of Valor? Considering the way he, the head of Mystic Ministry, had concealed the ancient parchment and focused on it with such intensity, it had to be important.

"I don't understand. How will I reveal anything?" asked Valor.

"Be this a sign unto our most pure sect this day, Malor VacNavel! As a witness to this scroll, I believe you shall recover my long lost grandthing."

"You mean your *grandchild,* O Enchantedness?" Valor's head rattled from confusion and surprise.

Urbanne leaned back in his chair, propped his boots on his desk, and said, "I will never dignify Ambergis's blasphemous offspring with an endearment other than what it was—a thing—a giant pest." His orange ringlets dropped across his wrinkled, grumpy face.

Valor blinked nonstop as Urbanne pried at the sole of his boot with the tip of his scythe, then jerked a bottle of potion to his lips, spilling half of it on his coat. "I have placed before you the last communication from Ambergis LaRock as recorded by the fingertips of our ancestors. My daughter spoke these words to them as an earthbound spirit, never to become one of the Ancients, because of the deadly curse Venerious Falmoth put on her."

Valor wouldn't dare admit that he had traveled through a time portal and had witnessed the curse on Ambergis. Urbanne was withholding the full truth: for Urbanne and his daughter Ambergis had, in fact, blamed Piron DaDovie, Valor's Sorcerer grandfather, for putting the curse on Ambergis. The LaRocks only condemned Venerious Falmoth for not capturing Valor's grandfather after he fled for his life with Ambergis's Oracles. But why would Urbanne twist that information, unless he was only using Valor to do favors for him?

"Ambergis said that 'Banzalta,' my living daughter—if you can call her that—'abducted her giant' th-thhh—'baby.' I believe this map will lead to its plausible potation."

"You mean possible location?" asked Valor.

Urbanne's nostrils flared. "RacMalor, never correct a head vespercestor!"

Valor eased the scroll from Urbanne's hand and unrolled it. "This is not a correction, O Enchantedness, but didn't you say the writing on this scroll was from the fingertips of the Ancestors?"

"Yes, my Enchantedness did."

Valor examined the scroll closer and said, "But there's nothing on the parchment—no markings whatsoever."

"The Ancients' writing dried up—turned to dust. What you are seeing is only a faded reminder," said Urbanne, clearing his throat and shutting the secret panel.

"So, what am *I* supposed to do with this, O Enchantedness?"

Urbanne's fingers clawed at the glass sphere of his crystaleer as if he were pulling a bitter memory from it. "*You* have a way of finding hidden things. *You* have been very unwise in your steps, and we will reprove you if you do not make amends to the Sanguinati. *You* are the president of Cryptic Chamber—figure it out."

Urbanne handed the scythe to Wan and Two Usefulness, scalping a patch of hair off Valor's head when he didn't duck in time. The dwarves opened a hidden door in one of the massive marble columns, and they handed the heavy weapon to another dwarf who had been climbing a spiral staircase inside the column. When the door closed, a loud clanking followed by a fading scream made Valor's new bald patch twitch. Had the dwarf fallen down the staircase?

Urbanne pursed his lips with disgust. "Our aim is pure, Mackleraven. You will bring my grandthing back here. Petition your runes, for I assure you Mistress Bessbadora will never use a wand on you ever again." He reached under his desk and held up a dartboard with Venerious Falmoth's image. "On the brain," he said, and a needle-beaked bumbling bird came out of a distant birdcage like a dart and speared its beak into Falmoth's butt a few inches near Urbanne's fingers.

"Bullseye!" cheered Urbanne. "You will start your journey to wherever that map leads after Convocation this weekend, Valor. Take a couple of friends—they can quote the *Controssua* to you—it might keep you alive. In the meantime, I will excuse those friends from their assemblies. If you see or hear anything unusual, remember to report back to me and only me."

Valor left Urbanne's office feeling lucky to be in one piece and lucky to have avoided another sentence to Grossatete Sanatorium. A hand grabbed the back of his collar and snatched him a few feet behind a stone arch that jutted out from the walls under the tall ceiling. Another hand landed on Valor's shoulder, spinning him around until his smooth face became wedged in some old man's bristly gray beard.

"Summoner Mamahchi!" Valor gasped from the sudden siege. He nearly gagged from the musty catacomb scent dripping from every hair in the beard. "O Enchantedness already excused me. I'm not in any troub—"

"I. Wouldn't. Be. So. Certain," groaned Mamahchi. "Have you forgotten about your vigilespion soul . . . the reason you were awarded an apprenticeship? You haven't been keeping me informed of your—"

"I haven't found anything—anything worth reporting that is. I explained everything to O Enchantedness." Valor had been so excited that he had gotten out of the sanatorium he had forgotten the Summoner pulled strings with O Enchantedness to get him in Mystic Steeples because of his spying abilities or "soul" as he called it.

"Don't lie to me," said Mamahchi. "O Enchantedness is slipping . . . in his old age. Mystic Ministry tolerates his position, but we have to usurp many of his duties. He cannot control the vigilespion anymore. Had several go rogue or missing . . . namely, a spy believed to go by the initials E.B., or B.E.," whispered Mamahchi. "Dangerous worm of a woman. Be on the lookout for her, McRaven. Hope that she has not transfigured by now. If you suspect anybody as being his vigilespion, you must let me know."

"I do say, that might prove difficult. How will I possibly know if anybody is his spy?" asked Valor, as the summoner's hands eased their grip from him. "Vigilespions are highly trained at keeping secrets."

"Your job is to keep a close eye on Urbanne—on everything . . . report what you see . . . not what you 'know.' *Knowing* is for Mystic Ministry. I got you out of Ogre Skull Hill. Unless you do your job, I am through defending you."

With that, Mamahchi stumbled past Valor, leaving him alone behind the stone arch.

CHAPTER SIX

CRUMPECKER CRACKS

THAT afternoon, Valor, Creighton, and Micha gathered in the Aerial Billiards Room, on the fifth floor of Candlewicke Mansion, for a bit of fun before dinner was ready. Creighton put a spell on the billiard balls to scream and curse when they knocked about in the air.

"Oh, no, you don't, Val," said Creighton, aiming his magic wand at the white ball floating in the center of the room and, with a spell, knocked it into a cluster of colored balls revolving in the pattern of a pentagram. "I thought you learned your lesson, blaming Crumpecker for stealing Spirit's Staff of Gleaning. Especially after those jumbies accused Bubba—Magee—or whatever the dude's name was—of stealing it."

With a chorus of shrieks and angry expletives, the balls scattered throughout the room, narrowly missing Valor's head and Micha's left elbow, until the orange ball with a jack-o'-lantern face entered the mouth of a grumpy witch sculpture on the wall.

"Primo!" Creighton breathed with triumph. "Straight in the corner kisser." Within a couple of seconds of musical banging in the walls, the pumpkin ball popped up in the bottom of a cauldron in the fireplace, though the ball insisted the cauldron was actually a toilet bowl as Creighton walked across the room to retrieve it.

"Yikes! This batty ball bit my finger," he yelped.

"I know the Staff of Gleanin' is the next lost magic instrument ya're supposed ta find, according to *The Great Witch and the Lost Magic Instruments* book, Val. But what makes ya still insist Crumpecker has the Staff?" asked Micha, getting ready to magic the white "ghost ball" at the sour-grape ball for a mouth shot at the center of the northern wall.

"Why would Crumpecker have it, Val? The other instruments caused all kinds of devastation, and they were hidden far away from anybody—from her anyway," said Creighton, dodging the grape ball as it bounced and cursed through the room.

"Is that so?" said Valor. "Well, my dear, you forgot about the Horn of Taurus. I know I saw Crumpecker steal the Staff of Gleaning, and, yes, I thought I saw her bury it at the sanatorium—near where I happened to find the Horn. So, I thought, 'where might the Staff be found when the Grim Warlock's not using it?' If the Grim Warlock uses the Staff when he wants to cause mayhem or these awful possessions, it will need to be somewhere he can reasonably access the bloody thing. And where did I see the strangest animal activity? Yes, my dear, I think that flagpole on top of Crumpecker's house might be the Staff of Gleaning. She thinks nobody would suspect her of hiding it in plain sight."

"Plain sight? Nobody in their right mind ever goes near that rancid old ranch except Crumpecker. The smell alone has been known to kill full-grown animals."

"Exactly, Creighton," said Valor. "I'm rather bored with playing games. I'm going there and see for myself. Besides, I can't suffer through another dinner with Doomsy still avoiding us."

"Whoa!" said Micha. "Ya can't just break in Ogre Ranch. Those ogres will stomp ya into a gristly bit and have ya for a snack. I'm a pawnikin, I oughta know."

"Look at what's going on now, Micha—the Possessing—it almost got me," said Valor. "It's obvious the Grim Warlock is doing just what the book said. He's harnessed the Staff's power to control ghosts, acquire dark secrets, and bring unrest across this land. That is probably what has unleashed this bloody haunting here at Candlewicke Mansion."

"Candlewicke's always been haunted. If you had researched its history like I told you, you'd have that fact planted in your little prognosis pot," said Creighton, tapping his wand on his head.

Valor sighed. "Just like the other three instruments the Grim Warlock stole—it's only going to get worse until somebody returns them to their rightful owners in the Bound Order of the Zodiac."

Valor turned to leave the room, followed by Micha, and lastly, Creighton, who huffed and mumbled to himself about missing dinner. They managed to slip out of the mansion unnoticed by the others.

With each step they took through the narrow, twisting alleys on their destination, Valor found himself becoming almost ill with a strange bitterness of emotion. Creighton and Micha seemed to be bitter as well, and they argued over simple things such as which alley they should have taken first. Even Creighton's fairy, Hulkin, sat on top of his head with arms folded and lips twisted in a snarl.

When they reached Ogre Ranch, on the outskirts of Mystic City, the stench from ogre dung and uneaten carcasses expelled fumes evaporating in the rays of the setting sun. Valor felt so distanced from his normal self, he feared he might do something dangerously impulsive. Just as he had seen in the crystaleer, the crooked, zigzag of a tower in the center of the ranch house had a swarm of bats and other flying beings flittering around the flagpole jutting from the top.

"All right, so where's the so-called Staff of Gleaning, Val? Is Crumpecker using it as a broom now, or—or are her ogres using it as a toothpick?" asked Creighton, while Hulkin raised his tiny arms doubtfully from under his wings and searched the area as well.

Valor double-stepped ahead of Micha and Creighton. He needed a moment to release his frustration without them seeing him get ugly.

"Great goin' there, Creighton! Ya've got Val so upset he's over there growlin'," said Micha.

"I'm not growling!" hissed Valor, who now heard the guttural rumble as well. Hulkin smacked Creighton on his head to get his attention as the trees split in half, and out from the swaying branches charged an ogre of the same towering height as the mightiest oaks.

"Arg!" Creighton yelled, clicking his boots together after he jumped. Then he, Valor, and Micha turned to run back toward the city, while a howling siren repeated across the ranch, accompanied the cry of the ogre as it chased after them. A shadow formed on the ground in the shape of the ogre's giant hand about to squash them overhead. Valor looked over his shoulder, and the ogre fell backward and was now rolling on the grass and groaning.

Micha caught his breath and punched Valor and Creighton on their shoulders. "Ya couple of chickens," he laughed. "The ogres can't get out?"

"What do you mean they can't get out? There's no fence anywhere around this rotten ranch," said Creighton, turning to run again. Hulkin clicked strands of Creighton's gelled hair, like a horse's reins, trying to urge him full speed ahead.

"See that witch statue?" asked Micha, pointing to the right of the property where a barrier of discarded food barrels stacked into a pyramid. The sculpture held a magic wand in each hand, one to his left, and one straight in front of him toward the right side of the ranch.

"There're security statues on each corner of the ranch—the fence keepin' the ogres in," continued Micha.

"Oh, I see," said Valor. "It's an ogre-enclosure spell."

"Well, if they can't get out, then we can't get in. So, let's go," said Creighton, while the howling wolf siren quieted, and the ogre crawled back through the trees.

"I don't think the security spell works on people. We're not big enough ta set off the witches wands," said Micha.

"Either way," said Valor. "I'm going in there myself, but not *between* the security statues—over them."

"Broomways? That's a great idea, Val," said Micha, doing an Adesdum spell to retrieve his broom, which came streaking over their heads and into his hand. Creighton reluctantly did the same after Micha gave him a questioning look of disappointment.

"I don't want a broom. I'm going to transvect," whispered Valor. "You two stay here and keep watch. Three of us in the air might draw attention from the ogres."

"Or worse . . . Crumpecker!" said Creighton, while Hulkin wiped hair gel off his tiny hands.

Valor took a deep breath and eased horizontally up in the air. Facing the sky, he used his inner eye to guide him over the security statues and treetops. Thankfully, no spell zapped him from the wands of the security barrier. Already, he could see more ogres stirring on the other side of the grove of trees, fighting over a barrel of food. The tallest of the beasts raised the barrel in the air and smashed it over a smaller ogre's head, sending rotting fish and pink meat splattering. The other ogres dived into an earth-quaking pile to grab up the newly scattered food.

As Valor floated closer to the roof, a fog began swirling around him. Only it wasn't fog; it was ghosts trying to throw him off his destination. He grabbed his monoculous and prepared to cast a gust of wind spell.

"*Adtono Flante*," he chanted, hoping to move the ghosts out of his path. As he tried the spell again, his voice seemed deeper and older:

"McRaven, you will never get the Staff of Gleaning. You are a fool to try to stop the Thirteenth Hour . . . ."

No. No, this wasn't—this couldn't be Valor's voice—his thoughts. Only meaning to slap himself back to sanity—to keep from falling out of the air, he found himself clawing at his face instead. The wind spell had not worked as he had assumed either. No. The swelling wind was from the flapping wings of a red dragon approaching him. But the screeching was not the dragon. The sirens far below had sounded again.

"Watch ya head, Val!" yelled Micha, soaring behind him on his broom as he fired a blast from his wand, knocking the dragon several yards to Valor's left. Micha swatted at a bat as it bit at his neck. "Watch ya neck, too."

"Just great. Crumpecker has spotted us!" shouted Creighton, flying his broom away from a swarm of sprites and angry fairies. Hulkin gripped the front tip of Creighton's broom as his little wings flung off bits of fairy dust from the circling, ghostly winds. "Tell your fairy kindred to leave us alone, Hulkin! Tell them that we're trying to stop the Grim Warlock here!"

The dragon flew lower, tearing shingles off the ranch roof before hissing flames at one of the ogres that had hurled a boulder at the dragon. Crumpecker screeched and cast spells at Valor and his friends. Valor put out flames on his leg while nearly tumbling into the arms of an ogre. Creighton screamed and began tumbling to the ground a few yards from where members of Mystic Ministry were gathering.

"Quick, Micha, help Creighton. I'll get the Staff," said Valor, floating higher toward the roof. His arms reached out toward the flagpole, and it was just as he had guessed: No flagpole had gemstones on it. It had to be the legendary Staff of Gleaning.

"Get away from my roof, McRaven! Don't you desecrate my flag. I'll feed you to my ogres—that's what I'll do," cackled Crumpecker, twisting the medallion on her hat, as more dragons appeared in the sky peppered with flashes of colored light, ice, wind, and other spells being cast from the ground. A colony of bats approaching Valor went up in flames before they landed on the barn and set it ablaze in a screeching inferno.

"You cannot hold out much longer, McRaven. You will die today!" Valor found himself growling unwillingly, as his entire body began to cramp. *Lies! That was not my thoughts. I can do this*, he convinced himself and reached with all his might for the Staff under the Sanguinati flag that flapped proudly over it. Just as his fingertips grazed the cold shaft, something dark soared up from the opposite side of the roof and grabbed the Staff, and the tip of it came down hard on Valor's head. Everything became a darkening tunnel, disappearing upward, as he found himself tumbling to the ranch below.

"Step back from him, High Priestess, and hands off your hat," Valor could hear Urbanne LaRock ordering Crumpecker before his eyes were able to focus clearly.

"Just let me finish the filthy rapscallion. Just half a turn to the left. That's all I ask, O Enchantedness," gargled Crumpecker, wiping the drool off her thin lips with the sleeve of her black nightgown while still gripping the medallion on her hat. Her knobby fingers twitched, ready to turn the hexagram pendant.

With eyes locked wide, Micha squirmed to break free from the clutches of the guardians, but Valor couldn't see Creighton anywhere. Either he had fled, or someone had taken him to Mystic Infirmary to receive medical assistance. Summoner Mamahchi hobbled through the gathering crowd, winded and bruised.

"You're a little late getting here, Summoner. These sanatoribums have destroyed my property," yelled Crumpecker.

"Couldn't get past . . . those blasted ogres of yours, High Priestess," groaned Mamahchi. "Then, I was attacked by Venerious Falmoth."

"Falmoth? That vile worm just can't keep out of Severance. But what in the heavens were you and Micha doing, McRavioli?" Urbanne asked Valor, as he towered over him on his stilts to keep his feet from touching "impure" ground. A little ogre dung clung to the bottom of each gold-plated stilt barely showing under his long robe. "That map I gave you didn't lead you *here*, did it?"

"What map?" asked Crumpecker.

"That is between McRaging and me, High Priestess," said Urbanne.

"No, O Enchantedness," answered Valor. "The Spirit's Staff of Gleaning led me here. I told you that Crumpecker stole it. I only recently realized she was using it as a flagpole on her roof. I almost had it before she nearly killed me." Valor rubbed his throbbing head.

"As I stand before you, there is no flagpole on her roof," said Urbanne, while Summoner Mamahchi's eyes wrinkled at Crumpecker with suspicion.

"She did a spell to hide it again. And do you notice what else is missing?" asked Valor, dusting grass and debris off his clothes.

"Yeah, I do—YER BROOM," roared Crumpecker. "You were free-floating, weren't ya, ya little hooligan?"

"I wasn't," Valor lied. "The wind or a spell knocked it out from under me," said Valor.

"It was hard to see up there with all the commotion," stammered Mamahchi, searching the now calm evening sky. "The dragons and bats—they've . . . they've left."

"The angry fairies, sprites, and insects are gone, too," continued Valor. "And look at the ogres." Valor pointed to a dozen ogres that were either sitting calmly on the ground or napping. One ogre picked dirt out of its toenails, while another ogre uprooted a flowering bush and took a comforting sniff.

"The Staff of Gleaning was causin' the animals and insects ta react—ta be restless," added Micha, who had now pulled free from the guardians' grips. "Until a spell—somethin'—took the Staff off the roof just before Valor could reach it."

"Don't any of you dare look at me!" snorted Crumpecker. "I didn't take the Staff. If it was on my roof, I had no idea."

"Why did ya try ta kill Valor then?" asked Micha. "Everybody knows he's the Knight of Night—the only person findin' the stolen Zodiac instruments."

"I, uh, I don't remember attacking the boy. Come to think of it, I feel strangely better. Maybe McRaven was right—that's why those blasted ogres have been, uh, outta control lately," said Crumpecker in a voice so sweet Valor hardly recognized her.

"Valor's injured," said Mamahchi, helping him stand to his feet. "We should get him to the infirmary."

Urbanne pried Valor away from Mamahchi with his magic staff. "Everybody, just go home and get some rest. I need a moment alone with young Lavador here."

"So, we're not in any trouble, O Enchantedness?" asked Micha.

"I'll let this slide," said Urbanne. "Only take heed, my child, that you do everything for the good of the Sanguinati."

Everyone began to disperse while Urbanne ambled toward Mystic City with Valor, "Lavador," as Urbanne called him this time. Micha glanced back a couple of times at them before taking flight on his broom. Ogre Ranch appeared as a warzone now, and Valor couldn't believe Mystic Ministry would not hold him accountable for the devastation somehow.

"O Enchantedness, twice now, I've accused the high priestess of stealing the Staff of Gleaning. Surely, you think there must be something to these accusations or I—"

"Let the Ancients cover their ears, for it is time I tell you a secret, McRaven! But you must not tell a living soul." Urbanne paused on his stilts and pointed the tip of his magic staff threateningly at Valor.

"I promise," stammered Valor.

Urbanne's eyes nearly crossed under his Galaxy Glasses. His forehead wrinkled as the sun had set, and the moonlight had now cast its glow on his confused face.

"Sir, what were you going to tell me?" asked Valor.

"I guess I forgot, McRayburn. You find my grandthing, and maybe it'll come to me. Oh, and you look terrible; go check yourself in at Mystic Infirmary. It's been a long day, and I need to get to bed early."

Urbanne dropped his portable portal and vanished in a cloud of purple smoke, leaving Valor standing a good distance from the exterior walls of Mystic Steeples, which surrounded Mystic City like a menacing nest. He felt quite alone. The evening's events had been rather peculiar and not to be trusted. But where had the Staff of Gleaning gone? Valor had a feeling it might be his hardest task yet. He had really pushed it with Mystic Ministry this time. He had no choice; he had to find Urbanne's giant grandchild, but until then, he was dying to know what Urbanne needed to tell him about Crumpecker.

CHAPTER SEVEN

URBANNE'S GRANDTHING

VALOR put down *Zoe Mack's Zodiac Almanac*, a book he had checked out of the Library of the Council, hoping to find out as much as he could about the Zodiac Beings, especially the Star Being known as Spirit. He pulled the mysterious scroll Urbanne had given him out of his conjure bag while Blade Zagato lounged on Valor's bed, scribbling on his own piece of paper with a crooked black quill.

"What am I going to do, Blade?" asked Valor, feeling better after Stabbah and given him a tonic to speed his recovery from the burns, partial scalping, and fall from the sky. "O Enchantedness expects me to find someone nobody knows—who lives heaven knows where—using this parchment with nothing on it. I don't know for certain, but I think this is the reason he didn't hold Micha and me accountable for destroying Crumpecker's ranch."

"Certainly, Creighton's not on that accountability list—returning in a frantic rush last night as he did," said Blade in his exotic and slow voice.

Valor tossed his Magi-Multi-Magnifier on his dressing table. He didn't want to cast any blame on Creighton, who had at least made some effort to help him. Besides, Creighton was prone to unexpected periods of depression, and Valor didn't want to trigger one of those episodes.

"I've tried using all my implements from Cryptic Chambers, but I couldn't find anything on the parchment—not a single tiny clue," said Valor catching a glance of Blade's architectural drawing. "Wow, that's incredible! You didn't tell us you were an artist." He tried to see the drawing closer, but Blade hid the paper.

"Zagato is multi-talented. But this is just a test to see if these Perma-Plumes that Stabbah created ever run out of ink. Apparently not," said Blade, wadding up the paper and throwing it in the fireplace. He twisted his turquoise ring around his finger and set flames to the drawing. Then he pulled a square crystal from his pocket and peered at an old map through the clear sunstone. Using telepathy, he sent his thoughts to Valor: "Why would Urbanne think *you* were most worthy to receive the scroll? It may be your death. Be careful. Even your most loyal supporters will use you only to abandon you in a moment of weakness."

"I expect you're right. I've wondered the same thing ever since Urbanne gave it to me," said Valor.

"Don't let Blade in your brain, my pet. He's like a parasite," said Doomsy, entering the room with Stabbah from the adjoining suite. "What I want to know is why Urbanne would keep a blank scroll locked up? He must have some reason to believe it'll lead to his grandson."

"I don't know, my dear," said Valor, happy to hear Doomsy talking again. He tried not to spook her return to society by smiling at her too much.

Stabbah took the scroll and examined it. "Dahhhling, I'm not sure I believe Ambergis or the fingertips of the Ancients recorded anything on this. Unless it's apparition writing—the genetic material of spirits. Hmm, why not give it a try," suggested Stabbah. She closed her eyes, and her head rolled back as though she were about to channel the Ancients. With a slight cough, she spat out a glob of ectoplasm, which drifted through the air and covered the parchment.

"Wait," said Valor, releasing his held breath. "What are you doing? You'll ruin it."

"Look," said Rose, as the ectoplasm began to reenter Stabbah's mouth, leaving a faint silvery image forming on the scroll. "The ectoplasm seems to have activated a map on the parchment!"

"It looks like the Tombstone Forest of Bogamuckla," said Valor, tracing the rocky ridge up the middle of the scroll with his finger. "And that's the Ambergis Divide."

Stabbah appeared a little weak but leaned over the map with a jolt. "I never would have guessed," she said. "That was no spirit writing. Someone encoded the map using pale blood. Dahhhling, only the fresh genetic substance of another Sorcerer could've activated the old dried blood hidden on this parchment."

"And there's a strange message or prophecy at the bottom," said Valor. He squinted hard and read aloud the words: "Unwiser sect reproves a grim role and steps back. Pure witness recovers pest." He lowered the scroll. "Surely this gibberish isn't all I have to go by! It seems to predict some less-knowledgeable group or coven criticizes some action or act that they consider grim, so they disassociate from the group or action."

"It also suggests that an innocent bystander recovers something someone considers a pest," said Doomsy, eyeing Blade annoyingly.

Valor stuffed the scroll back into his conjure bag. "I don't know what that means, but I guess I should leave for Bogamuckla soon."

"I'm coming with you," said Rose, lunging at his side.

Doomsy frowned at Rose and stepped beside Valor. "Me too."

"No, you can't, Doomsy," said Valor, patting her head. "You're awfully small. The giant might squash you. Besides, there are too many dangerous creatures up there."

Nalini Lusion barged into the room, sounding frantic. "Ugh! I'm a bit on edge." She held something in her hands under her shawl. "Three Sorcerers from Shadowhaven Heights just tried to capture Aaron out in the courtyard! Egg was injured, but I think he's okay now. Creighton and Ruza managed to turn two of the attackers into rhino-crested bawdy beetles; the third escaped." Nalini put the beetles in an amethyst bowl on Valor's dresser, and the beetles screamed, raising their front legs and antennae.

"Oh, this is awful," continued Nalini. "I knew we shouldn't've allowed Egg in our coven; it's too dangerous for him. We should've got a real Sorcerer in our coven to empower it."

"I know you wanted thirteen members, but Candlewicke Manson has turned into a hotel if you ask me," said Salazants, entering the room on his cleaning routine. He picked up the bowl of beetles with care. "Manning and I can't clean up after another addition to this coven. Please excuse me, and I'll find somewhere to put these—bugs."

"How is poor Aaron?" asked Valor.

"He's talking about moving out. He just doesn't want anyone harming us by mistake," said Nalini, avoiding the cracks in the floor tiles as she paced around the room. "I'm kinda afraid he'll leave."

Doomsy picked up a sword belonging to Micha and said, "If those cold-blooded clowns come near Candlewicke again, I'll give 'em a really close shave."

"Put that away, dear," said Valor. "You look like a miniature version of Banzalta. Besides, we should avoid resorting to violence."

Everyone became silent.

"I do worry about our safety—I do," said Valor. He pulled the door to his room shut as they headed to the wizards' parlor to check on Aaron and Egg.

"Take these slivers of grave soil on your brows," Stabbah said to Micha and Blade, moving through the parlor with her funerary urn. "These ashes of a cadaver's revenge."

Valor frowned. "What, may I ask, are you doing with grave soil?"

"Dahhhling, I made a magic concoction to protect us. Now come here so I can smear some on your forehead." Stabbah held two soiled fingers in the air and the urn on her left hipbone. Aaron reclined on the sofa, spitting some of the soil off his lips. Salazants followed behind Stabbah with a dust rag while Manning watched out the window for more prowlers.

"Poor Aaron, are you all right? Stabbah has you looking like a spotted leopard," laughed Rose, before clearing her throat with a more serious tone. Fleabane squawked near Ruza's feet. Doomsy kept her snake, Mr. Grudgings, away from the buzzard until Fleabane proved safe and would not try to eat him. Egg bounced around, practicing hand-casting spells in his sinister costume, trying to prove the attack hadn't shaken him.

"Verily, I have had far superior days," sighed Aaron. "I should abandon Candlewicke for everyone's wellbeing. Perhaps check into the Stuffy Pillars Hotel where Siobhan LeSabres is staying."

"You're going to do no such thing, Aaron. Something has been clawing at the walls every night, searching for me as well," Valor said, while a little grave soil crumbled off his forehead. "Perhaps Siobhan should stay here at Candlewicke; after all, she patrols the alleys to help protect you."

"Or to kill you both," suggested Doomsy, floating up to the fireplace mantel where she reclined against the clock.

"We'd probably be better off with Siobhan as our thirteenth member instead of Egg," said Creighton, flashing Aaron and Valor an I-told-you-so look. "At least she's a real Sorcerer and not a baby—no offence, Egg." Creighton plopped his hands on Aaron's shoulders and whispered, "That Egg is never going to hatch."

"I can do it. I'm just a, uh, little rusty, t-that's all," said Egg with his bottom lip protruding. He squinted his eyes hard and tried to levitate a silver chalice from a table. Had Valor been wrong about Egg being a Sorcerer? Either way, Valor really thought they could help him, and he did seem happier with Candlewicke Coven.

"Perhaps if I used the Athanasia Wand on Egg, his inner power would—"

"We've already talked about this, Aaron," said Valor. "He is far too young."

"No, I'm not!" shouted Egg, and everyone jerked their heads toward the table.

"Was it me, or did that chalice just move a little?" asked Micha.

"I did m-move it!" gasped Egg. "I moved it without my wand."

"It was just a vibration in the room—a ghost," said Creighton with a smirk. "Egg almost got killed out there thinking he could hand-cast a spell on the attackers."

"At least he made an effort to defend his coven," hissed Doomsy, swooping down from the fireplace. "Next time anyone tries to hurt one of us, I'm gonna go full Sorceress on them."

She pushed back the curtain and looked out into the ominous shadows of Spookum Alley. The black stripes on her cotton dress became solid in the shade, and the black-lace collar on her gown rose higher than her head. Salazants played the harpsichord in the fifth-floor ballroom, as he often did when frustrated. Everyone could hear the rising crescendo as it kept time with the growing anxiety down in the wizards' parlor.

"I could never allow you to throw yourself to those monsters so selflessly. Yet I don't want this madness to pull me away from Candlewicke," sighed Aaron, tapping his boot against the side of the sofa.

"I'm going to leave for Bogamuckla in a few minutes," said Valor, pulling from his conjure bag the scroll map Urbanne had given him. He wouldn't be far from Shadowhaven Heights and planned to have a secret talk with Aurora Vontiki. But could he convince her that Aaron didn't kill Mesthu? "It's still odd," he said. "Why would someone write this scroll in pale blood?"

"Bloody tailbones," said Ruza Renata. "The vespercestors make such a fuss over their old scrolls. They act like the Ancients wrote those oracles with their own tailbones, and they probably did—using blood from witches like us!" She placed a green lacquered nail to the corner of her mouth and tapped it a few times. Her eyes studied Aaron's torn breeches and velvet coat, then panned everyone's faces, while foggy ribbons of moonlight shone through the window above Doomsy's fancy dress collar.

"Remember, Ruza: Valor's a Crypt now. The Crypts think they are superior at decoding all those old scrolls," said Blade. He admired his reflection in the parlor mirror, and for a second, his appearance seemed to change. "All Blade has to do is stir a cryptogram in his subconscious to realize how useless it is."

Rose drifted close to Doomsy. Her snow-white face unquiet. "Doomsy," she said, "you need to stay here with Aaron—"

"Tell that to my butt warts. I'm going with you and Valor to Bogamuckla." Doomsy clenched her teeth and distorted her lips. "Somebody needs to get the job done. You can take me with you, or I'll go there myself."

In his agonizing decision, Valor sat in a chair and shuffled a few runestones scattered on a table beside him.

"I've already talked to the vespercestors 'bout this last night, Val— I'm goin' with ya. Falmoth has lots of dragons up in Bogamuckla, and lizards are my specialty, yup," said Micha, holding up his Dragon's Mantle pendant.

"You can't trust that anyone is who they say they are, Val," said Blade. His dark eyes seemed to blaze with cunning. "But when you are wise like the Zagato, you can see through the veil. You must learn these things, or you'll never grow or survive. For you can only depend on yourself in the end."

"How sad for you, Blade," said Stabbah. She placed the urn of grave soil on the fireplace mantel with a look of accomplishment. "We need one another, not only to survive but to thrive."

Doomsy lifted her cotton dress a few inches, revealing her spider-webbed petticoat. She spat on the marble tile and said, "May my spittle forever stain this floor if we all don't come back safe."

The glob of spit on the floor turned to red blood, and the spirit of Ambergis screamed with laughter until the candlelight in the entire room snuffed out, and Manning set about relighting them.

"I think Ambergis knows we're looking for her giant baby. But I guess everyone's made their decisions. I have. I suppose I have no choice but to head off to Bogamuckla now," said Valor, as Doomsy, Rose, and Micha followed him toward the door.

"Death!" yelled Ruza, restraining Fleabane. "Valor, you scryed the runes, and it spelled out *Death*!"

Valor's body jolted from the shock, but he had to remain calm for Doomsy. "I'm sure it was merely a coincidence."

"Oh, sweet rest. In black-on-black we're funereally dressed, ready to soar over rooftops and hum softly with death . . . ," sang Rose, taking a puff from her magic wand. "Sorry, everything reminds me of a song. It's how I keep myself calm—and this." Rose lifted her vapid vapor wand to her black-powdered lips with a giggle.

Valor reached up and pulled her vapor wand from her mouth, breaking a vapor of smoke as it was forming a long-stemmed rose.

"My dear," he said, "that can't be healthy. I'm sorry you lost your family—truly, I am—but your parents should never have gotten you addicted to such a substance. Surely they could've found something better to calm you."

Creighton sniggered. "Her parents *were* the reason she needed medicating."

Rose flashed Creighton a look of betrayal. "What about your nutty family, huh? Why don't we talk about what they've done to you?"

Creighton swallowed hard and hid his wrists behind his back. Valor felt awful for trying to help. He turned to leave with Doomsy and Micha before things could get any worse. Tears welled up in Aaron's eyes. Using telekinesis, he summoned the hall table to block the door.

"I insist you avoid Shadowhaven Heights. Leave it for me to handle," said Aaron.

"Stay here and keep the doors locked," insisted Valor. He wouldn't yield as he willed the hall table to slide away from the door and over to the adjacent wall.

After they shut the double doors, moisture trickled down the exterior stone walls of Candlewicke like tears, and a strange sobbing made Valor's spine convulse. He looked away in disbelief. It was time to leave, but he couldn't make his legs move faster. If he would die in his quest, Doomsy mustn't be a witness. Perhaps Ruza was overly superstitious; she often talked about her death being "inevitable."

The four of them lingered too long on Spookum Alley, and a round disk hit Valor's foot. A handful of young witches flew over Shickbone Cathedral on their brooms, playing with Astro-yo-yos that bounced from the sky to the ground, sending sparks.

"Ouch!" groaned Valor, spotting Harwin Hollapolk, son of the recently deceased guardian. "They can't have time to practice their craft with all the late nights they spend flying around the city."

"That's why there are so many concussed cats in Mystic Menagerie lately," added Doomsy. "They keep knocking them in the head."

Thinking fast, Rose pulled a knife from her belt and cut the string on an Astro-yo-yo that shot down near her foot. "They're targeting nocturnal Familiars mostly. The Sanguinati don't care. I warned my Venus to be careful."

"We should fly our brooms until we get out of Severance; then we can float," said Valor, before Micha, Rose, and Doomsy bolted skyward, remaining close to each other in order to hold a conversation. Down on the alleys, two snake handlers sneaked inside a four-story home as they had many times before in other homes. Valor cringed, trying to block out the images of the dangerous serpents in his head.

"Here, my pets. Stab made us all some On-the-Doubly Bubbly," said Doomsy, handing them a potion bottle filled with flashing liquid. "Let the gas of the universe flow over your tongue."

"Yuck," laughed Rose, taking a sip before her broom shot out ahead of the others.

Valor didn't need to drink it, to speed up the long flight, for he had won the broom of Sesepha, from the ultra-limited Speeding Besom Series.

"We have to look for Imorradog, the mass of land that looks like a dog's head. Bogamuckla will be north of there," he shouted over the gusting wind. "We should be there by five in the morning."

"Or sooner," grunted Micha, whipping his broom around every gust of wind.

They flew toward the region Valor's father called "Yistlepaw."

Doomsy flew her broom out ahead. She seemed concerned about nothing until Blade Zagato made a surprise appearance on his broom beside her.

"Sorry, Doomsy. Blade the nurturer drank a double portion of On-the-Doubly Bubbly—felt a moral obligation to come along— keep the giant from squashing you," Blade laughed. He flung the empty bottle up to the clouds, and a lightning bolt zapped it with a loud *BOOM.* "Ah, Rose Decay, this lightning makes your raven hair seem—bluer."

"You know, Blade, I'm not entirely sad you showed up," said Doomsy. She slumped back on her broom and rested her hand on the base of its bristles.

"Oh? Is it Blade's looks or his charm?" asked Blade, flying backward to face her.

"I think it's more your ability to attract nocturna bugs with every wasted breath," said Doomsy. "Of course, your self-perception has you in a cauldron of delusion, my pet. You can't even attract a bug."

"Zagato tried weaning himself from mirrors, but it has been fruitless since you forced him to become an immortal, Doomsy. He's all your fault. Never forget it," said Blade, looking at everyone with a devious expression. His long dark hair tangled around him.

Doomsy bewitched a lace handkerchief to sail through the air and swab Blade's eyes. "Dry your pities, my pet," said Doomsy. "How could I forget how much pain I've supposedly caused you? Your reminders linger like an infection."

They dropped their brooms over Conjurestone Wood and free-floated. For the third time, Valor thought he caught a glimpse of somebody following them on a broom, or perhaps it was only oddly shaped clouds, which sometimes plays tricks on his eyes when he passes through them.

"Did you know Mahrata LaRock used her Mystic Needles on Blade because you turned him into a Sorcerer against his will, Doomsy?" said Blade, pointing to his own face. "Just feast your eyes on the needle scars around his brutally handsome jawline." Blade caressed his fingers over his jaw and down his throat.

"Be glad that's all Mah did to ya," said Micha, looking as if he would laugh whenever he spoke. "The Library of the Council has several books 'bout the horrible tortures the vespercestors used on the covens over the centuries. Now that a lotta witches are more aware of injustices, they keep the focus on the creed that says, 'What dark spell ye cast may tenfold—'"

"'Return a pox of perplexity, warts, and death.' *Sanguinati Supplementations*, volume ten, page 278-plus, paragraph six," Blade concluded, stunning everyone. "The current vespercestors created that creed as an afterthought to prevent retaliation."

"Wow! How in the heavens do you remember the exact page and paragraph, Blade?" asked Rose, folding her arms tight around her black umbrella she brought in case it rained. Micha huffed and sped his broom ahead faster.

"History must never be forgotten, or the uneducated will fail to recognize the warning signs when the dark side of it plots to repeat itself," said Blade.

Valor agreed, and after a long period of silence, he yelled, "We're over Bogamuckla. Get ready to descend."

Thanks to Stabbah's On-the-Doubly Bubbly, they landed earlier than expected in the southernmost edge of the Tombstone Forest in a patch of snow.

"Um, guys, I'm not real fond of strange forests at night," said Rose, scoping out the dense trees, which suddenly entwined over their heads, locking them underneath a cave of branches.

Micha held out an unlit candle in front of Blade's mouth and said, "You are the best man for the job. Blow."

"Can't remember when that was last acknowledged," said Blade before he lit the wick with the heat of his breath, and the candle transfigured into a five-armed candelabra.

"Thanks, Micha," said Rose, taking the candelabra to help light their path.

"We always knew Blade was full of hot air," said Doomsy.

Moving into a clearing, a scarecrow with a pumpkin head stood before them with its arms behind its back; its tattered clothes flapped in the wind.

"Why hello there, little fellow. I suppose you'll show us which way to go," Valor said to the scarecrow before its arms lifted in two directions. In its left hand, it held a scythe. In its right hand, it held a human skull.

"It doesn't look good either way we go," said Micha.

They followed Valor as he took the path to the right. The dense forest rose higher in the distance, resembling a massive creature sprawled over the ground with its front legs parting, forming a tree-lined route for them to enter.

"I'm glad there're flat rocks to walk on. I'm seein' a lot of dark gullies up ahead," said Rose.

Unaware, she eased her high-heeled boots on tombstones embedded in the ground. Outlying tendrils of deep-red water, "cherry juice," Falmoth had once called it, streamed down from the hills between the grave markers. Crushed skulls littered the edges of the thin streams like seashells.

"Those aren't rocks, Rose—they're gravestones," said Valor, pausing to study the dark mountainscape. "Now that you mention it, those gullies look rather unnatural—like a giant sliced them into the earth with a scythe or something."

"They could be claw marks made by a dragon," said Micha. He dipped his finger in the trickle of red water and sniffed it. "I know I smelled somethin' bitter but sweet." He swatted his tongue with his finger. "Taste sorta like cherries."

"Are you crazy?" asked Rose, grabbing Micha's wrist. "The water might be poisonous."

"Nah, I feel fine," said Micha. In a few seconds, he looked ill and steadied his legs for support. He had bumped into the corpse of a gargoyle that was clutching its stomach with its decaying claws. Rose held her candelabra over the creature, dripping wax onto its grimacing face while cherry juice dribbled from its mouth.

"Won't you sample the water, Blade? I'm sure you must be thirsty after swallowing all those nocturna bugs," Doomsy said in a falsely demure way, scooping a sample of the red water in an empty potion bottle and storing it in her conjure bag.

"After you, Dooms," said Blade. He tipped his fur-trimmed cap, and his long black hair fell across the collar of his shirt, which depicted galaxies and the zodiac. Doomsy ignored him, and Valor couldn't help but suspect that she still wasn't over her grief from the disastrous trip to find her parents, or perhaps she was angry. He could never really tell with her, and this was beginning to frighten him a little.

The farther they walked, the tree-lined path narrowed until they found themselves pushing through a brier thicket with sugared fruits of various colors impaled on many of the sharp spikes and a small tangled pair of breeches where the briers must have torn them off a dwarf.

"Where are you taking us, or do you know?" asked Blade with a hollow laugh.

Valor looked at his scroll map closer. "According to the map," he said, "it looks like we're heading to the Tombstone Forest, home of Venerious and Banzalta. I'm certain the giant's too big to be in their Tombstone Amusement Park. He must be hiding somewhere in these woods."

"The amusement park, you say. Blade read about it in *Forbidden Landmarks and Attractions*," said Blade. "Is the skeletwister fun?"

"If you don't mind Banzalta beheading you with her enchanted weapons or an army of wiggiwamis trying to eat you," replied Doomsy, feeding a nocturna bug to Mr. Grudgings.

"The sun's beginning to rise. That should make it safer to travel," said Valor, worrying about Aaron.

"I'm ready ta see some dragons," said Micha.

Stepping near some mushrooms that crawled to a safer patch of leaves, Micha pointed out a large dragon egg nestled among the vegetation and patches of snow. He tried to teach them how to identify the fire-breathing dragons' eggs by the speckle patterns on their shells.

They came upon a deteriorating fence; the sign on the gate read, "Enter at Your Own Hex!" They went inside and followed trails, which spiraled to many dead ends until they came to a frozen lake. With their beaks, two long-billed crestycruxes were jousting like swordsmen.

"Oh look," said Rose, "they're fighting over the sugarplum hanging over the lake." The birds' feet slid on the ice as they skated in battle. Just when the larger bird had overcome the other and had collected the prized sugarplum, an enormous green hand plunged through the bushes and stole the sugary fruit by its glistening stem.

"That mean old ogre," snorted Rose, gripping her cat-o'-nine-tails at her hip. "I outta cast a spell and make him choke on that sugarplum."

A minute later, a guttural belch drifted over the ice, while Rose continued to complain. Micha clasped his hand over her mouth to quieten her. Her eyes squinched but remained catlike as everyone listened. Again, the ogre grunted, "Momma?" Pushing its head through the treetops, the ogre broke off leaves from an entire branch and rubbed them over its face like a napkin. Some of the leaves clung to the sticky plum juice that had dribbled down the monster's chin.

"Oh dear," said Valor, "it must have a mother somewhere in this forest."

"Momma?" The ogre grunted louder as he trudged through the trees, stepping onto the frozen lake. With a few more ice-cracking pounds of its feet, the ogre lost its balance, and its butt crashed through the ice, splashing water onto its face, arms, and legs, which flailed about on the surface of the lake. "Momma!" the ogre shouted, calling forth a chorus of screams and squeals throughout the forest.

"Sounds like the cries of wiggiwamis," said Doomsy.

"Stupid ogre. The ice has trapped him," said Blade. "Let's go before its mum decides she can't live without him." Blade placed his wand back in his coat pocket and continued up the path.

"We can't leave him there. He might die," said Valor, cringing at the wiggiwami shrieks echoing all around them.

"Die of what . . . frostbutton?" laughed Micha, breaking off a red-and-white-swirled sprig from a candy cane tree with a skeleton hanging from one of the striped branches.

"What's frostbutton?" asked Valor.

"Frostbitten butt," said Micha, before the wiggiwamis began gathering around the edge of the frozen lake but would not step onto the cracked ice.

Valor floated above the lake, followed by his friends.

"Say, green puddles are accumulating on the ice. Why, that's no ogre," said Valor. "It must be Urbanne's giant grandson."

"Ha. He tried to make himself look like an ogre by rubbing green leaves on his skin," said Rose.

"Momma, momma, momma!" the giant roared, as Valor and the rest eased closer to him, floating over a slab of loose ice.

"If we save you, will you come with us to meet your grandfather?" Valor asked, but the giant flung his massive arms and legs, pushing against the ice hole. "I don't think he understands our language."

Valor plotted his next move while the wiggiwamis bounced around on the surrounding shore, throwing rocks and snowballs. The wiggiwamis in the trees flung sticks and chunks of bark and candy down at them. Valor caught a thick piece of bark on his shoulder, splattering the scent of pipe tobacco and pine on his coat lapel, drowning the sweet smell of the candy-cane trees.

"Stop throwing things at us," hissed Rose. She shot a flame spell with her wand at the wiggiwamis. The heat from the blast cracked the ice more, sinking a wiggiwami near the shore, while many scurried away, shrieking.

"I know how to communicate with big old lugs," said Doomsy. She pointed her left hand at another dangling sugarplum hanging over the lake and chanted, "*Usta Etgo Kamonowa.*" In her palm, a gray likeness of the planet Mercury appeared. She flung the spell at the plum, which snapped off the branch and levitated as she moved her hand in the air in the symbol of Mercury. "I'll show him we're not dangerous. You know . . . lie a little." She forced the frosty-purple sugarplum to dance on the tip of the giant's nose, enticing him to swallow it whole.

"Yum. Mama," said the giant, smacking his lips and gazing at Doomsy while waiting for another sugarplum.

"I'm not going to feed him all day, and he's far too huge to lift with a Black Sampson spell," said Doomsy, before thumbing through her *Mystic Memoir*.

"There are five of us. We can surround the giant in the circle of the pentagram and try using telekinesis on him," suggested Valor. "I'll take the top point representing Spirit. The rest of you decide the element you want to represent."

"I'll be Fire," said Doomsy, floating to the southeastern side of the lake. "Blade, you are full of air, why don't you take Wind to the west?"

Rose moved to the pentagram point of Earth while Micha took Water. With a conjuration spell, the manifesting elements circled around their bodies while they willed the giant's butt to rise out of the ice. The giant plugged his trembling lips with his thumb but did not struggle, while their magic carried him all the way to the shore and sat him down among the trees as though they were small shrubs.

"You found Urbanne's grandthing, did ya?" cackled a familiar voice tearing through the snowy woods. "Don't any of ya move a scummy little finger. This lump of blubber is in my hands now."

With her wand aimed at Candlewicke Coven and the giant, an old woman in a long black dress burst into the forest clearing.

"Tilta Crumpecker. I knew I saw someone following us here," said Valor. "So, *this* is the half-ogre you wanted O Enchantedness to get for your ranch," Valor said to Crumpecker. "Well, he's not an ogre, he's human."

"And you aren't bringing him back to Severance. You're helping him escape," said Crumpecker, when a dragon landed behind Valor and his friends.

"Whah are 'ou doing with my child?" shrieked Banzalta Drayn, taking Venerious Falmoth's hand to dismount Tareamugus. The dragon entwined its two necks and heads and glared at Valor and Crumpecker.

Banzalta raised an enchanted weapon over her head and flung it at Crumpecker, while Falmoth cast spells at Crumpecker until she could no longer maintain her defense, and she vanished with an anguished cry.

"I told Banzalta her children were calling out to her. And look who it was: Valor McRaven and his foolish coven of thugs," said Falmoth.

"We're not thugs, you beslubbering, barnacle-toothed baboon!" growled Doomsy, teetering her head with frustration. The giant dropped to the ground behind Doomsy and patted her on the head with his finger, as though she were a puppy.

Valor stepped forward and said, "All we did was rescue your child from the lake. Or should I say Ambergis's child?"

"She didn't want him!" screeched Banzalta. With wild eyes, she thrashed over to the giant and, with her pale bony hands, snatched his massive finger away from Doomsy's head. The shredded sleeves of Banzalta's tight black dress hung from her wrists like cobwebs.

"Would you like to bore us as to your purpose for coming to my Tombstone Forest?" asked Falmoth. "Can you, at last, foresee joining the Hermetic Order of the Mystic Key . . . maybe?"

Valor looked at his friends to find some explanation or at least the courage to tell Falmoth the truth. He flashed him the map Urbanne had given him. "O Enchantedness sent me here. He said this was his grandson, and that I had to bring him back to Mystic Steeples."

"He's Urbanne's grandson by blood. But oh dear, it surprises me that you and your thugs intend to help Urbanne murder our poor Sweeturnips here," said Falmoth, reaching over and patting Sweeturnips on his cauldron-sized knuckles.

"Murder?" said Valor, curling back his shoulders and head. "I would do no such thing. I'm just trying to return him to his grandfather."

Sweeturnips snatched his finger away and stuck it in his mouth.

"Oh? Do explain what Urbanne told you he wanted to do with little Sweeturnips, darn it. I'll bet he didn't even use the word *grandson*, did the old bum?" asked Falmoth. He placed his finger under his nose and raised one blackened eye. Banzalta embraced Sweeturnips. Her bald skeletal head rested as she drooled against his elbow—the only speck of warmth Valor had ever seen from her. But was it genuine?

"You're right," admitted Valor. "He wouldn't tell me why he wanted to see his—his 'grandthing.'"

"His what? Ooo, I fear I didn't hear you," said Falmoth.

"His GRANDTHING, okay?" shouted Valor, holding his head down in shame. "But that doesn't mean O Enchantedness wants to murder him. Why would he?"

"Let's make this plain," said Falmoth. "There's nothing enchanted about old Urbanne. He wants to kill Sweeturnips so his throne he won't try to claim. Old Urby has been seeking his heir replacement for years but is too vain to have somebody he considers a pest become head vespercestor, I fear."

"Oh, how could I have been so gullible to think anything noble of Urbanne?" asked Valor.

Doomsy shirked under her lace veil beaded with fake black spiders, and Rose hid behind a tree covered with berries, cones, and branches shaped like wreaths. Micha sat on a tombstone and rested his elbow on a skeleton foot and leg jutting from the ground. Blade frowned at Banzalta.

"I was mistaken to think you were brighter than this, McRaven. And after all the nuisance I've gone through to show you the truth," sighed Falmoth. "Golly wowsie. Do you not remember the LaRock Ancestral Tree I found in Urbanne's office during the chaos in the alleys?"

Valor surrendered a shameful nod. "Yes."

"Did you not bother to see where Urbanne blotted out the only child Ambergis had with your grandfather? Darn it. That should prove his true feelings for Sweeturnips," said Falmoth.

"I guess I didn't see that," sighed Valor. "I . . . I was distracted by all the names Urbanne flagged as suspected Sorcerers."

"Old Urby even put you and Doomsy in the sanatorium though you didn't deserve it. Admit it. He's trying to get rid of your lineage."

Valor's voice cracked: "But, he said he put us there because my mom had become dangerous and, and—" He couldn't tell Falmoth how Lithium had tried to turn him into a girl according to Urbanne.

"I know all about Lithium and the tragic death of your twin brother. What a bummer. But then, my point again," said Falmoth, drawing a line in the air as if it were another point lost. "It's deplorable, but Urbanne locked you and Doomsy in the sanatorium with a child killer just to protect the stupid *Ambergis Oracles*." He pressed his hands against the sides of Valor's head as if trying to energize his brain. "Why-oh-why? I'm wasting another secret on you I can't deny. And trust me; this is the most secretive of secrets that ever existed. But I still have hope you'll awaken from your bubble of delusion real soon."

"O Enchantedness never told me that," said Valor. "How was he protecting her oracles by putting us in the sanatorium?"

Candlewicke Coven came to attention and moved a little close to Falmoth.

"The last oracles Ambergis wrote were to cement the LaRock's control over Mystic Steeples and all its people. And they contained more spells on how to remove every portion of their sorcery origins. Lithium insisted she knew where the oracles were hidden and would destroy them in a minute if you and Doomsy didn't remain with her in that awful prison."

"Whoa!" gasped Valor, followed by his friends. "Did you just say—"

"Oops! You heard the truth," said Falmoth. "Mystic Steeples was founded by Sorcerers and was nothing but Sorcerers in that exact order. The LaRocks violently and most connivingly changed all that with their substandard substitution—the Sanguinati." Falmoth made an I-tried-to-tell-you face. "If you had finished reading *The Book of Chacodophilus*—let it be your tutor—you would have seen this—seen the awful blueprints they have for your future. But no, see—you were set on having fun and sticking with your preconceived opinions of Banzalta and me." Falmoth's torn mouth twitched, and his posture sagged.

Candlewicke Coven exchanged stunned glances, and their jaws dropped.

"But you've made your choice, I fear. You don't care if

Sweeturnips dies, much less all of your friends here—they are ectoplasmancers—shadow tossers, which I've known without falter." Falmoth laughed like a maniac, shaking his head. "Urbanne and the Sanguinati elite will tolerate you until their needs you meet. But you've decided not to join me in stopping them, I see." Falmoth sent Sweeturnips on his way through the forest and began to mount Tareamugus with Banzalta. "Enjoy being President of Cryptic Chambers, McRaven—I hope that reward will sustain you when you awaken—in your grave someday."

"If I have to choose your side or Urbanne's, I choose neither," said Valor, as the dragon flew off with Falmoth and Banzalta.

"Excellent decision," said Blade.

Candlewicke Coven frowned at Valor. Micha spat on the ground at his feet and said, "McRaven, I can't believe this! Ya mean ya knew before we came up here that O Enchantedness hated Sweeturnips?"

"No, that's not true!" said Valor.

"Yeah-yeah." Micha smirked bitterly. "Whadja think Urbanne was gonna do once ya handed Sweeturnips over to 'im—give 'im a hug and a cuppa tea?"

"You know what it's like questioning O Enchantedness! I thought he was going to kill me," said Valor. He walked away and kicked a chunk of stone candy. His pale face heated while his chest pounded. "I didn't think about what would happen. There are so many things demanding my time."

"Gosh, now I feel like some sorta grim henchman, kidnapper, or something," said Rose, folding her arms across her stomach as if she got a sickening chill. Valor kept his back to his friends.

"Look, Val, sometimes children are better off the way they are than ta place 'em with guardians ya don't know what awfulness they might be capable of? I oughta know. Remember the story I told ya 'bout me freein' the sheriff's dragon? It wasn't the sheriff who committed me to the sanatorium; it was my mom. She got tired of raisin' me by herself," said Micha.

"Falmoth's right: Valor doesn't want to be bothered with stuff like that anymore—just like Blade got tired of me. That's why Valor tried to find my birth parents," Doomsy said with distant eyes. "Can't you see, everything Falmoth has said has proved true? As much as I dislike him, he's been very generous to you, my pet." Doomsy pulled her snake out of her pocket and stroked its head. "Mr. Grudgings, I'm beginning to think Valor doesn't care what happens to us."

Blade shook his head, lifted his arms helplessly, and glanced at Valor with a weary knowing. But not one word did he speak to defend him. Feeling absolutely gutted, Valor turned around and walked toward these self-righteous backstabbers he thought were his friends.

"I've been trying my blasted bloody best to figure out the truth and do the right thing—for—for always. You all have no idea what it's like being manipulated by every single person in Hoopenfangia." He waved his hands about wildly, and his throat constricted to continue speaking. "Besides, you insisted on leaving Mystic Steeples to help bring back the giant. *You* go back and tell O Enchantedness you changed your minds—and—and see how well you can stop the Grim Warlock and the Thirteenth Hour locked in the sanatorium—or—or dead!"

Valor tried to say something else but choked, so he flung his map on the ground, then turned and ran into the forest. Tree branches slapped him as he weaved through the woods and mausoleum ruins. The forest closed tight behind him. If the slapping branches could equal his pain and rage, it might beat out the tears he'd been withholding. He ran a long way, jumping over a few gullies with red-flowing water. The wiggiwamis startled him for a moment, as they rose out of the water, emptying their buckets of dead fishes onto the banks.

Continuing past candy-cane trees defiled by scalloped gouges from teeth, Valor stepped over caramelized spouts that reminded him of crusty blemishes. The spouts gushed a wealth of sugary lava over the ground, adding billowing whiffs of a burnt molasses aroma. Nauseated, and slowed by bending boughs and unwinding ivy creepers, he collapsed against the wall of a small cave, with its rocks forming a shallow arch, peeking behind a wall of overhanging ivy.

Like a nightmare, his thoughts rehashed many revelations and things said over the past hour. He became too depressed to think, and the trickling cherry juice and sweet scent of chocolate made him drowsy.

Several hours later, a pain in his neck jarred him from his sleep. "Wharrr ya doin' me?" murmured Valor, with all the protest he could summon. His blurry eyes focused enough to see a wiggiwami sucking and slurping blood from his neck. Its calloused hand pushed hard against Valor's chest, pinning him to the cave wall, smearing its foul scent on him. "Help me!" he mumbled again, but his pleas did not seem to distract the beast feeding on him, nor the other three wiggiwamis leaping around a small fire with their arms lifted in triumph. Valor's pulse slowed; his veins were collapsing while the wiggiwami's toe dug into his hip. Valor's arm lowered to his side. It wasn't a toe; it was his monoculous. After a short struggle, he maneuvered the magic monocle out of his coat pocket and zapped the beast in the leg. The wiggiwami screamed and retreated behind the other creatures, and they cowered long enough for Valor to gather his strength. The wiggiwamis appeared more human than the usual ones he had seen, but just as dangerous. They lurched toward him, hissing, wiping their drooling mouths on their arms and hands.

"Juices!" cried the wiggiwamis, bobbing their heads with slurping wet hisses. Using her slimy fingers, a female wiggiwami in the front flailed her arms between Valor and the other creatures. "Juices! Juices!" she called louder.

Valor conjured the burning logs on the fire to rise and form a flaming barrier, which threatened to scorch the bloodthirsty wiggiwamis. He backed out of the cave, tangling in the ivy and tripping in the darkness, before floating to safety above the trees.

"You're wrong, Doomsy, I do care what happens to my friends," Valor shouted at the stars and moon, which now illuminated the treetops. It should be daylight. How long had he been in that cave? He knew what he needed to do as much as it terrified him.

CHAPTER EIGHT

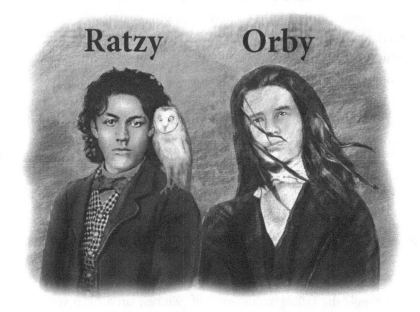

Ratzy   Orby

VALOR'S EXCHANGE

VENERIOUS Falmoth's sprawling Tombstone Amusement Park stood out among the forest. The sugared gumdrops glowed in all colors under the licorice lanterns suspending from the candy-cane trees. The beautiful licorice gate opened to the speckled marsh mellows and pastry-pods, Valor had stepped on in the cherry streams. The vanilla-scented fog enveloped him when he landed amid the tombstone carousels. The sepulcher-coaster rolled past, knocking down sugary pink moss from a cinnamon-twisty limb. Valor's stomach cramped and mouth watered, until he took a bite out of a leafy lemon loaf, drawing him deeper into the park. A flock of crows screamed before a group of spring-activated clown heads bounced out of the swamp, laughing. The dead Wiggiwami children, ghosts called jumbies, closed the gate behind them and peeked out at Valor with hollow eyes. A few living wiggiwami children snatched the clown heads off the springs and scurried inside their tomb houses.

"Falmoth, it's me—Valor. Where are you?" His heart drummed fast and teeth clenched behind a frown. He had to do this.

The eerie carnival music grew hypnotic as the dreary-go-round turned, and its colorfully ringed walls spun. In a sugar gum tree, four jumbies did acrobats from their hangman's nooses. Then, on the next rotation of the dreary-go-round, Falmoth appeared against the wall, holding his magic staff, which he stamped against the monument floor, bringing the gears to a screeching stop. The skeleton puppets on the marquee covered their ear holes with their bony fingers. A riderless cavalry horse galloped down off a dreary-go-round and paused in front of Valor, stamping its hoof.

"This intrusion had better not leave me feeling deluded," hissed Falmoth, while the cupcake cart of the sepulcher-coaster buzzed by him, sounding like a shrill whirlwind.

"I—I want to join the Hermetic Order of the Mystic Key, sir. I want to stop Urbanne and—and protect my friends," said Valor.

Through the falling snow, an owl perched on a limb with its big head bowed as if in sorrow. Falmoth stepped down from the dreary-go-round.

"Ooo, this is magnifiskull news. I don't believe you need to say anything more. Your conscience has restored. Why, it could win a broadcast award." Falmoth clapped and took him to a massive mausoleum at the back of the park. Valor's juvenile eyes feasted on its intricate carvings and candied embellishments, which covered the central mausoleum and its minarets with winding slides that encircled its towers.

"It's time to bloom—time to take a ride with me on the magnitomb!" said Falmoth. And what a magnitomb, Valor thought. Candied domes topped each of the minarets like a glazed crown. Climbing candied roses softened the stone bridge entry and spilled into the surrounding gardens. They took the next available padded coffin and sat facing each other as it began to ascend the main tower's slide.

While the coffin traveled through the magnitomb, cloaked figures peered behind magnifying glasses, and Valor began to see everything with an expanded view. The tiny pores on his face, the flinch of his eyelid, even his exhaling breath billowed past him like fog. Falmoth took a silver ear out of his pocket, a "word catcher" as he had called it, and a silver key. "I'm just sayin'—the time is now to make the vow, McRaven."

More magnifying lenses in the second tower, amid frequent stops to collect fingerprints and DNA samples. In the mausoleum, telescopic lenses and some fruity loops lowered over Valor's head: "A skull-scan," said Falmoth, after Valor lost a few snips of hair while the same distorted faces stared at him behind the strawberry-scented scanner. Journal-clutching workers recorded Valor's reactions, his very thoughts, it seemed. The coffin Falmoth and Valor were riding backed up for a quick photo, turned, and plummeted down another tower. The glass lenses whisked past them, making Valor dizzy. Ink bottles emptied fast. New record books opened.

"Deceit detected!" shouted a cloaked dwarf. The coffin stopped moving, and a swirling cage of candy canes dropped over Valor, trapping him in the coffin. "The Sham Scan detected a nervous quiver in McRaven's left eye."

Falmoth's body jerked. "Oh my."

The dwarf lowered a telescope from the glittering ceiling of candies that resembled rainbow quartz. Reaching through the cage, the dwarf then placed the lens against Valor's left eye. "Uh, nope. False alarm—a grain of sugar blew in McRaven's eye."

"Magnitomb, proceed, pretty-chewy please," commanded Falmoth before the coffin whisked forward. "Where were we now? Oh yes, the vow."

"I'll make the vow if you promise to make sure my friends are safe and give Booger Fay back to me," said Valor. He tried not to appear nauseated from the visual distortions and the magnets whirling him through the magnitomb past a cloaked man embracing a forlorn child, like the Grim Reaper claiming his property. For a second, Valor swore the child looked like his dead twin, Lavon, but it had to be a distortion from the ride.

"You have my word straight from my esophagus. And I assure,

Booger Fay is so, so secure, and I dare say quite joyous, in the Necromanceropolis," said Falmoth. He leaned forward in his seat, holding the silver key, which emitted a vapor around his fingers. "Open your mouth, McRaven. By making this vow, and swallowing this key, you are forever bound to our Hermetic Order and shall never be free. Inheriting the Order's bond, mission, and knowledge, this key will forever lock you to your promise. Know this to be true: you will never digest this key. Neither shall it pass from you."

"Apprehension ascertained!" shouted another cloaked dwarf. "The Sham Scan detected a bead of sweat on Valor's right cheekbone."

"Oh groan, oh moan," sighed Falmoth while the coffin spun to a stop, and the cage dropped.

The dwarf used an eyedropper, extracted the sweat, and squirted it into a bottle labeled Testing Potion. "False alarm. The fluid appears to be syrup."

The coffin climbed straight up a tower wall, and Valor started to say something, but Falmoth shoved the key down his throat, forcing him to swallow it. Like an icicle sliding down his throat, the key lodged into his stomach, as though it were binding his intestines—binding him to his promise. Would his vital organs stop functioning if he changed his mind?

Falmoth scooted forward with a crooked grin. "When the sun, the horizon cracks, may the dawned rest with no regrets in their cushiony little caskets."

He grinned wider, and Valor jerked. Venerious Falmoth had fangs—sharp enameled spikes that were coming toward his neck. The coffin ascended to the top of another minaret and shot through an arched window where shackles held back its curtains. They stayed airborne before landing on the sepulcher-coaster tracks. The runes were right: He was going to die! Valor twisted and convulsed underneath Falmoth, until he collapsed, strangling in the bitter breeze. Falmoth's lank jaws gorged on Valor's neck, slurping until his pale blood had surrendered.

Now witnessing the scene in his shadow form, he watched Falmoth force some of his blood down Valor's throat from a quick gash he made in his own hand. Falmoth gave a blackened grin and said, "From my veins, the doubly dead are fed and arise as Children of the Gloaming in their resurrection beds."

Falmoth's blood seemed to congeal inside Valor, like an invasion of burning slime racing through his veins. He lifted his drained head to see a jumbie pressing her forehead to a tombstone, spilling a foggy teardrop on the mounded chocolate soil. Valor couldn't believe this was to be his last remembrance of life, and he fell back breathless into the padded coffin.

Sometime later, he didn't know how long, Valor found himself in blackness, peering through a window with the sound of a girl's laughter nearby. Was he dead, or did he awake to a vision of death? He couldn't be dead, for his breath fogged the glass—cold breath. Valor started hyperventilating when he realized he was reclining flat on his back in a coffin with a window on the lid—just like two visions that he had in the sanatorium: The first was in the Gallery of Black Mirrors in Mystic Steeples, and the second was in the mirror during Scrying Essentials. Visions he had refused to believe. But how long had he been in a box for the dead?

"Are you uncomfortable?" asked a slim, dark-auburn-haired woman gazing through the glass. It was Briny Belfries, the widow of Abner Cadabranathy—the vespercestor Valor had witnessed a cloaked witch murder not long after moving back to Mystic City. Briny's demeanor had darkened since Abner's murder, though her skin seemed paler.

Even though the coffin was comfortably padded in soft red velvet, Valor had reached his limit and fumbled for a way out, but the lid wouldn't budge.

"Where are the latches?"

Briny leaned over the coffin. The torchlight appeared and vanished behind her movements while she placed a ring of flowers mixed with black roses on the glass lid of his coffin. "Sleep not in remorse as I wreath you in night phlox. As you yearn for the taste of blood, may you not regret these grimroses."

Valor peered through the glass lid and scratched his fingernails against the coffin window—his nails had grown twice as long as they had ever been. Was he back inside Falmoth's catacombs? He had never seen so many bones: They covered the walls, fancy alcoves, and ceiling. Bones formed the chandeliers, while skull sconces held more candles. Valor closed his eyes and shuddered. Hours later, weary with panting breath, the velvet coffin-lining began to smell musty.

"Aw, this isn't funny. You tricked me, Falmoth!" shouted Valor.

A skull surrounded by feathers startled him over the coffin window, peering and grinning down at him. A staff was supporting the skull, which shook with a rattling bone-beaded fringe.

"Okay, so, ye entered da dark realm where the Children of the Gloaming greet death," said Ratzy Pummels, the hook handler for the Spurgmulin Tournaments at Mystic Steeples. He grinned at Valor through the glass lid, then he paced around the room with an owl on his shoulder, before resting his hands on the edge of the coffin mantle.

"If ye need t'is death shroud, I'll put it on ye, okay? I'll try to t'ink of ye for all eternity—or—" Ratzy leaned over the coffin and began draping the black veil over the window, blocking Valor's view.

"Oh bloody skeleton, no! I don't need a shroud. I haven't really died, have I?" asked Valor, after Ratzy tossed the shroud on the floor.

The latches of the coffins snapped, and Ratzy flung open the lid.

"We prefer da term 'recycled,' McRaven. But ye'll hafta, like, sleep in coffins from now on, okay? 'Cause, like, ye won't be tolerating no sunlight. Ye'll be a night owl like me Congalie gal here."

"*Whooo* better to be like?" Congalie hooted, while Ratzy patted his owl on her head.

"I expect someone has made a grave mistake. I won't be needing a coffin any time soon. That's absolutely daf—" Valor reached up to feel two raw bite-holes in his neck.

"I do, ya bampot. Falmoth does—all the Noctivatians sleep in coffins during the day, unless we're very careful, wear cloaks or enchanted powder," said Orby Underkofler, strutting in the dark room and picking up the coffin mantle. Orby, like Ratzy, was a hook handler for the Spurgie Tournament. Soft energy always swirled around Orby, billowing his long hair and clothes even in the airtight chamber.

"Do tell me this is just a really bad dream," said Valor, feeling like a veneer of the old him.

"You are awake—for now," replied Briny Belfries, retrieving the wreath of flowers from the stone floor. "But when your nights become your days and your days your nights, you will dream eternal dreams that manifest in sheer shadows and opaque delight."

"Here we're like brides of the night," said Orby, placing the coffin mantle over Briny's head as a veil, and she left the chamber through the door, which growled like a beast when opened.

"What's wrong with Orby? Why are his hair and clothes blowing around?" Valor asked Ratzy. "That's not going to happen to me, is it?" Valor didn't need any more peculiar symptoms to worry about.

"What are you, a twonk, McRaven?" snorted Orby. "It's a side effect from a spell. After your band of goons kidnapped me, I crafted this permanent barrier of protection. You'll soon learn, McRaven; Noctivatian Magic is true dark magic known as Black Magic. The Sanguinati call us 'warlocks,' and those twonky Nizzertits call us 'vampires.' The inner circle of The Hermetic Order of the Mystic Key has mastered this forbidden Black Magic."

"Vampires!" Valor bolted up from his coffin and placed his hand over his pounding heart. "You—you're joking. You mean I'm—I'm a vampire now?"

"Yeah—we're, like, cool," said Ratzy, touching the skin of his hands and face. "Ye're a real Knight of Night now, McRaven. Everybody t'inks we're evil, an fierce, an cruel, an savage, an relentless, an—" He paused to pull a piece of candy cane covered in wet mopey moss from his dragon-scale boots, which clashed with his black-striped knee-trousers and orange cape. "Yeah, t'em coffins seal out light grandly. So, it's da only t'ing das gonna help yer skin cells regenerate if ya get sun eaten."

"Regenerate?" asked Valor, giving himself time to comprehend that he was now a vampire. Looking for an exit, he darted through the torch-lit chamber and bumped into maniacs wearing white plaster masks. Were they people that he knew? "No. I can't be a vampire. This has to be a dream—a trick." Shaking, Valor darted to the brightest corner of the dim room and lost the last meal he had eaten.

"Ye are. And ye need blood; t'at is why ye sick," Ratzy assured Valor, while he wiped his mouth on his sleeve.

"Look, McRaven, don't be using the word 'vampire' in front of Falmoth. We're Noctivatians," said Orby. "Most of us must sleep in complete blackness, or we start to look older than we really are. A restless sleep can alter our appearance." Orby made a creepy face before laughing. "Some Noctivatians arise only at night as they cannot take any exposure to sunlight. Ratzy and I are still lucky we can get out more often—that's why Falmoth planted us in Mystic Steeples. Our irregular sleeping shifts work well for such purposes."

Valor braced himself against the wall. What had he gotten himself into so swiftly? He felt like the only part of himself left was his memories trapped in a small portion of his brain—deep inside this strange new body—a near animal! Orby and Ratzy patted him on the back and tried to get him to keep moving, keep talking, but Valor knew it was a distraction tactic to keep him from having a nervous breakdown.

"What's that musty smell?" asked Valor. He paused under the strange orange glow beaming through a curved portico, while two men snaked through the dark halls, gripping the handles of a coffin.

"Decaying flesh. Falmoth is nearby perhaps. Nah, only playing the joker," said Orby, leaping onto a narrow stair railing and walking up it. "You're in the initiates' chamber underneath the amusement park, McRaven. This room leads to the real catacombs. C'mon around this partition, and I'll show you. C'mon!"

As Valor walked past human skeletons posed to form chairs, footstools, and tables, the skulls turned toward him. A large window, filled with what seemed to be orange ice, contained a man frozen in agonizing distortion in its pane.

"Fancy fellow he was," said Valor, observing the frozen man's dark belted tunic and feathered headdress.

"Okay, but not as fancy as me," said Ratzy.

"Arpad the Warlock is who he is," said Orby. "You smelled Arpad fossilized in this huge sheet of amber, McRaven. Many of the Children of the Gloaming can only view sunlight through this special window." Orby pressed his face and hands against the amber window as if feeling its warmth. "Arpad is the first thing we see when we rise from our coffins." He stepped back from the window of amber and looked up at it with Valor and Ratzy.

"Cool. Look okay—Arpad's flesh has, like, stopped reforming on his face and hands, but it'll start decaying after da sun comes up," said Ratzy. Valor touched his own face while Arpad's astounding regeneration completed.

"Notice and remember, McRaven," said Orby. "We are now in the throes between darkness and a rising sun."

Valor touched the warm fossil. "I see. It's a magic sundial of sorts. Ah, it also produces static," he said, turning around with his white-blond hair sticking up everywhere.

"Amber detoxifies us from the sun's radiation. Arpad's eyes always let us know when it is safe to go out and about," said Orby. He pushed a lever behind a large tapestry, which depicted Arpad on a winged black horse, crossing the Ambergis Divide. "Six Noctivatians are always awake, McRaven, in case we have an intruder."

"So, ye're gonna show 'im our coffins, aren't ye, Orbs?" asked Ratzy, standing beside the chamber doorway.

Valor pulled back from the door. "Uh, I don't know, fellows. Perhaps I should—"

"Nothing to fear now, McRaven. You've already been bitten," said Orby, pushing them into the coffin chamber. "We need to move quietly, though, as we don't want to wake the undead."

Ratzy laughed behind his hand, almost knocking the lid off a coffin, before easing it back into place. The coffin chamber was the dimmest lit room Valor had encountered in the catacombs. Countless coffins rested in reverent rows across the chamber and in niches up the walls.

"Look at the assortment of coffins, McRaven. They're designed and carved to the Hermetic Order's specifications," said Orby.

"So, t'at's mines up t'ere, okay?" Ratzy pointed up to the third-level niche in the stone wall. Skeleton brackets flanked the tops of the columns in this room. "It's got, like, pretty gals, an' me Congalie, an' fruity fritters carved in zebrawood. It's da coolest coffin here."

"Ratz, you're a fruit bat. That's why the Order put yours way up there," said Orby. His eyes smiled as they tiptoed among the coffins, while Valor paused to caress the intricate fretwork and iron embellishment on a coffin beside him. "Look, McRaven, there lies Janus Duperie, a former Child of Mesthu you mighta' met."

"Yes," said Valor, snatching his hand off the coffin. "I met Duperie at Shadowhaven Heights. I don't understand why he would join the Hermetic Order after he accused Falmoth and Banzalta of killing his girlfriend. Of course, he accused me as well. He said I would never evolve."

Orby nodded. Did he agree with Duperie? "It's not my choice that Falmoth selects his Order so . . . diversely. But Duperie wised up," said Orby. He folded his arms and studied the stone coffin. "I don't mean to say Duperie doesn't have issues, McRaven. He sleeps in stone coffins ever since his companion died in that fire."

Ratzy cupped his fingerless gloves around his mouth and said, "Okay, so like, fear of flames keeps 'im a stoner."

They could tell Valor was in no mood for amusements. Orby walked two coffins ahead and gestured for them to leave. Ratzy gestured something back, as if not understanding him. After a series of unintelligible sign language and whispering, Orby stomped toward Valor so that he backed into a coffin that had two carved angels draped over the lid—a posture Valor was sure the angels maintained to ensure eternal anguish of its occupant.

Before Valor could move, a Noctivatian sat up in the coffin and grabbed him by the throat. Falling backward from his sturdy grip, Valor gasped for air until his eyes rolled back in his head.

"No, Falmoth. It's McRaven," Orby said with alarm. "We were just showing him the sleeping chamber."

Falmoth released his grip, and Valor fell to the floor. Licking his lips, Falmoth climbed out of the coffin, pressed his face close to Valor's head, and scraped a fingernail over the bite marks on his neck.

"Well-well, your pale blood dried on your coat like the trails of a snail," said Falmoth. He loosened the top of his hair from a bone the size of a small forearm, letting his hair fall around his face. A leopard jumped down from an alcove, grabbed the bone from his hand, and began gnawing it. "You must be so giddy. You're officially a member of the Hermetic Order of the Mystic Key."

"No, I'm not!" growled Valor. He couldn't swallow as the vapors from the key fluttered up to his throat. "I didn't know it would include you attacking me and turning me into a—a vampire."

The Noctivatians in the chamber hissed and scoffed. Valor gripped his hands together, while Ratzy and Orby left the chamber, laughing. Falmoth poked Valor in his chest.

"You came busting up in my amusement park in the middle of the dark, begging to be a part. You didn't ask for the particulars—didn't warn me you were a haggler."

"Yes, but I didn't know Noctivatians were—were vampires," Valor lowered his voice. He dared not wake the rest of the coffin sleepers. "Oh, dear. You're not the ones who've been killing people and—and animals all over Hoopenfangia, are you?" His mouth watered with this memory. Was he becoming like the creatures that drained blood from the animals and people in Stonevengeance where he once lived?

"Noctivatians drink human blood—so, yes, we could," said Falmoth. Like a zombie, a wiggiwami walked in the coffin chamber and held out his arm. Falmoth bit down on his wrist and drank for a few seconds. "Oh, don't worry. Don't cry me any buckets. You can still have my delicious candies, goat tea, and nuggets."

Valor found his tongue curling up like a straw sucking air. He wanted to bite the wiggiwami as well. He grabbed his aching stomach, turned his face to the shadows, and bent over. His veins burned and body cramped.

"Noctivatians can't all be like you—blood drinkers?" asked Valor.

"Yes, they are, little guy, because two-plus eyes have I," said Falmoth. He pulled down on his lower eyelids with two fingers and pointed to his forehead with another finger. "The left to wink. The right to blink. And the inner to spy." Falmoth perked back up and crossed his arms. "Now, where was I? Of course, generously answering your questions. Follow the lover of blood ingestion."

Falmoth swirled a finger in the air before pointing to his chest; then he danced toward a distant coffin down the long chamber.

"O grave, in all seriousness, open unto us that we may we descend the eternal stairs of Veneriousness." He waited, and nothing happened. "Hmm, sometimes the grave needs a little manual manipulativeness." He pressed and turned a few medallions and carvings on the end of the coffin, triggering the release of its bottom. He led Valor inside the coffin and down some steps into another torch-lit chamber, a catacomb office, lined in skulls, many with evening grimroses and night phlox coming out of their mouths or colorful candies stuffed in their eye sockets.

"Every Warlock needs his own catacoffice," said Falmoth. From his coffin desk, with a carving of a cloaked skeleton riding a skeleton centaur, Falmoth handed Valor a red glass goblet filled with red fluid.

"This goblet isn't going to bite me, is it?" asked Valor. He examined the lifelike glass lips on the side of the goblet, and it reminded him of the Tongues of Fun Tonic he enjoyed with Creighton at the sanatorium.

"It's genius, I think. You don't have to put your lips on it to drink," said Falmoth, grinning like an imp. "It spits liquid bliss into your mouth with its puckered lips."

Valor turned his head. "That's not—"

"Yup, it's blood," said Falmoth. He paused against the backboned doorframe and held the goblet. Valor took it with shaking hands, but Falmoth snatched the decanter from him after it began to slip from his fingers, and he held it to Valor's mouth. "Open your lips and catch its spit. You're growing weaker. You'll need your strength, for not much longer shall it linger."

"No," said Valor. His reply seemed to echo down the goblet and draw up a crimson aroma that warmed his senses.

"Sippy-sippy. Let the juice trickle through your parched veins like corpuscles dripping. Come on, come on," said Falmoth with a quaking whine. "Let warm crimson life slip walls of ecstasy across your tongue."

The glass lips spit a thin velvety stream of deepest-red in Valor's gaping mouth. He turned his head away from the goblet and the glorious vapors.

"No," he sobbed. "I don't want this." He cast his eyes away from Falmoth. His vulnerability became raw. In his head, he could still hear Duperie saying he would not evolve one inch, and this he uttered from his stone coffin. Valor shuddered even more.

"Here, my new initiate, don't overthink—just drink, drink, drink." Falmoth's sleazy voice now fell as soft heat on Valor's aching ear. "Every last drip, reserved for your lips."

They stood in the doorway illuminated by two skull lanterns. Falmoth held the goblet to Valor's lips once more and wiped the spill on his chin with his index finger. He seemed to decode Valor's every hungered groan, offering as warm of a smile as his torn mouth could. The night phlox in the skulls' mouths shed a few dark petals at his feet. Falmoth reached into his coffin desk again and took a pliable clay figurine, then walked over to the skull-lined wall.

"Send me a recent hair sample from Valor McRaven, and don't keep me waiting," ordered Falmoth. Out of a skull's mouth popped two finger bones from which Falmoth took a single strand of hair and stuck it on top of the pliable clay figurine. He spat on it. "You see, we now share the same DNA, if you please. I turned you into a Noctivatian, and I will animate this Grim Doll, and you will envision with your own eyes the answer to your question."

Falmoth placed the figurine on his desk and said a chant, bringing the doll to life.

"Lift me up," said the doll, now resembling Valor.

He reluctantly picked up the doll, his befouled likeness, and it breathed a vision of a cabin and faces Valor remembered.

"Why, look," said Falmoth, who seemed to see the vision as well. "You've already met Morty Hestia and Genevieve Sukles. They were so nice to you. No, you never wondered why their cabin was always so cold. And the woodshed they called 'Cerebrabone Coop'— excellent place to store supplies of human blood for just two. Oh, they'll be so proud you've joined our group."

"Aw, they were vampires? But—but they were nice. They tried to heal people with those cerebrabones," said Valor. Had he misunderstood the purpose of the skull dissections that Morty had placed on the photos of people in their cabin?

"Another magnifiskull ploy wasn't it, my boy? A Grim way for Morty to extract blood from miles and miles away," said Falmoth. He shook with laughter before snatching the Grim Doll from Valor's hands. "Now, drop this act called Mr. Regrettable, we have got to make you more presentable."

Falmoth roughed up Valor's slick hair and smeared enchanted black powder on his lips and around his eyes.

"You see, McRaven; you've met several blood-drinking Noctivatians, with whom you may have even had lunch. They'll reveal themselves to you at the appointed time. And do be sure to try their punch." Again, Falmoth quaked from giggling.

The door to Venerious's catacoffice opened, and Eumenes popped his head inside with torchlight reflecting in his midnight-tinted eyeglasses.

"Excuse me, Falmoth Most Fortuned. Branwen's triplets got loose in the forest. Shall I release the jumbies to round them up?"

"Yes," replied Falmoth. "Get those upgrades back before daybreak. Give them another infusion and . . . no more intrusions."

"Branwen Petrova?" Valor tilted his head against the cobwebs that sheathed the doorway like a tattered lace curtain. "The former Magister of Thunder Ponder. You mean she's a—a Noctivatian too?"

"Yes, I confess. She's a fruitful little mute—no fun having a severed tongue," said Falmoth.

Valor grew quiet. He tried to remember any clues he had missed that would've indicated that Branwen was a vampire. The last time he had seen her, she was about to deliver the triplets. But why was Venerious Falmoth calling her children upgrades?

The silence of the chamber broke by the distant scream of a horn, and the crackle of cherry juice dripping between the bones in the walls and ceiling.

"What'll happen if I refuse to drink—blood?" asked Valor.

"You couldn't refuse the juice a few minutes ago, ya know?" answered Falmoth. "But if you do refuse, the anguish, the pain would be, um, well—"

Valor lunged at Falmoth; his head fell onto the former head vespercestor's stomach. His mind spun with horrible visions, fearful visions of the potential horrors he might submit to in his new condition. "Turn me back to normal, Falmoth. I won't be a vampire. I won't!"

"It's an impossibility at best. But do calm yourself. You look a little stressed," said Falmoth. He reached in his robe and handed Valor a familiar glowing candy from his pocket. "Here, you need a Luminous Lulling Lozenge, keep it under your lip until it mellows, dear fellow."

Valor ignored his offer. He couldn't speak or yell another angry word at Falmoth. He found himself gazing blurry eyed at the floor, catching his breath. What would life be like as an immortal vampire, a cursed creature? Why-oh-why hadn't someone warned him that Noctivatians were vampires? But there he stood, still hungry for blood, desperate for relief, falling deeper into the web of his new life—his new death. His face flinched with humiliation, and he took the fruity candy from Falmoth and placed it in his mouth. "Vhat do I do now?" asked Valor.

"What?" laughed Falmoth. "Afraid I can't understand a word you're saying. You've got something hanging on your fangs."

Valor spat out the lozenge and said, "Fangs? I've got faa—" He reached up and felt two long sharp teeth in the upper front of his mouth. "Aw." He withered. This was why he just had a hard time pronouncing the letter W. Dealing with sorcery manifestations had proved awful enough, but now . . . now he had Noctivatian manifestations as well.

Falmoth held up the lipped goblet. "Now you know why we drink from goblets that spit; it keeps us from chipping a fang when we take a sip."

"Vhat do I do now that I'm a member of the Hermetic Order? I don't have to leave my friends at Mystic Steeples, do I?" Valor spoke with a darker, toothy sound.

Falmoth placed his hand over his heart. He dropped his head and said, "Yes—sadly, every lad and lassie who joins the Order thinks they'll have to leave their friends and family, but no! You can ease your mind—stop biting your nails. We need you right where you've been all this time, in the heart of Mystic City—or its butt; it's hard to tell." He motioned for Valor to have a seat on the coffin desk beside him. Then Falmoth clutched Valor's shoulder as if gathering his words. "I know you and your friends will want to show the Sanguinati that they were once Sorcerers like you—now that you understand, you see? And this I want you to do diligently, brazenly."

"But the vespercestors vill—"

"Just don't you worry about the vespercestors, McRaven. The Hermetic Order will provide you a safe haven. And you never can tell—if your friends cooperate with us, then I'll invite them to join our Order as well."

Valor bounced his boot heels against the coffin desk with the sudden realization, "Vhat vill I do about Urbanne? He expects me to bring his, his grandson back. He'll kill me if I don't."

Maniacal laughter burst from Falmoth's torn mouth. "McRaven, tell that buffoon you found his grandthing's corpse in a canyon. Look old Urby in the eye and say that Sweeturnips looked as though he had swallowed a cow and died."

Valor jumped away from the desk, appalled at Falmoth's disturbing suggestion. "That's awful. I could never—"

"My delicate initiate, don't be alarmed," said Falmoth, handing him another lozenge. "It was old Urby's exact prediction the day Sweeturnips was born. Now, just do as I told you, and it'll blow his thick noggin—why, he'll think of himself as a terrifically gifted prophet."

Valor's head spun now that he remembered: Urbanne had said that very thing about his grandson in the portal Stabbah had found in Candlewicke. Valor supposed he had best not admit this to Falmoth.

"One more thing, then I guess I should go find my friends," said Valor. "How vill I provide any evidence that Mystic Steeples vas once a Sorcerers' kingdom? I mean, there is evidence, isn't there?"

"There's no abundance," said Falmoth. "The LaRocks have done a good job eradicating the evidence. Even I don't remember how it all happened, see, but you'll be getting a surprise bit of help rapidly."

Falmoth led him through catacombs spotty with moonlight, tunnels of tombs, windowpanes and doors left open to the elements, deteriorating the brick and mortar into piles of rubble. Through a hidden door, behind a statue crying tears into a fountain, an elevator took them up to the Tombstone Amusement Park, and Valor fully realized how this was all a facade to the darkness underneath.

"If you wish to travel in a jiffy, the Hermetic Order established a secret portal which leads to Mystic City," said Falmoth. "It's located under the candy-cane tree by the frozen lake where you tried to abduct Banzalta's giant baby."

Valor closed the licorice gate. "I didn't try to abduct—" He tried to explain to Falmoth before he vanished. What about his friends? Had they been looking for him? Would they still be angry with him? "I expect they'll be happy I joined the Hermetic Order to protect them," he said to himself after stopping in his tracks. "Oh, dear. I'd be a fool to go back to Candlevicke. Vhat if I try to drink my friends' blood? If I have any friends left."

"The blood of the enemy tastes best," said Briny Belfries Cadabranathy, taking a bath in her coffin under the moonlight, while red rose petals floated on the surface of the water. Valor looked away, and she laughed, splashing some petaled water onto human skulls converted into flowerpots for her roses.

He tried not to imagine any blood while he floated close to the treetops just before morning. He circled the area looking for any sign of Candlewicke Coven as tears streaked down his face. The wind whipped the fairies around the dark forest like drifting snowflakes, while the crickets fiddled their wings in a nocturnal melody.

"Doomsy? Rose? Anybody?" Valor called out, but only the grunting of wildlife and crying of an owl echoed back to him. He floated to the ground by the frozen lake, by the giant candy-cane tree. "I'll just look for the portal, but I von't go back to Candlevicke." He pulled on a suspicious limb or two, but nothing happened. Then he began inspecting the trunk but found nothing that seemed like a portal until he moved to the other side of the tree. He bent back the dense shrubbery and found the faint outline of a door with a gumball knob. He pulled the door open and stepped inside the tree trunk. "To Mystic City," the lever on the left read, while the lever next to it read, "To Diabolishire." What should he do? Falmoth wanted him to return to Mystic Steeples after all. But would he be able to control his hunger for blood? He held his breath and pulled the left lever.

When he opened his eyes, his body felt like it was still plummeting to Earth in a tin can. He clutched a dusty old cloak attached to a hanger for stability. "Ah, a broom closet." He stepped out of the closet and kicked a dustpan off his shoe. He recognized Kitty's Kabootle, the abandoned boot factory with a few preserved cat Familiars wearing outdated boots behind the cracked display window. He gazed into the cracks as if they were hazy spider webs that had just released him from a past he could never revisit, and then he walked out of the back door onto Dead Maudie Alley.

CHAPTER NINE

VALOR THE VAMPIRE

THE sun had just lit the horizon when Valor arrived back at Mystic City. He did not take the time to report to Urbanne about his grandson. He shook, having avoided the sun by minutes before entering the grand hall of Candlewicke. He darted through the rooms on the first floor. Why were Doomsy and the others not waiting for him?

"Good heavens, Master McRaven!" gasped Salazants, peering at him with strained eyes through the mirror he was cleaning on the staircase landing. "You look as if you've died a second death."

"I have, Salazants. Don't come too close to me," said Valor. "To think, vith all the powers available, this has happened to me. I don't know vhat I vill do." He groaned and pressed his head against the arched entry to the wizards' parlor. Manning came down the staircase and exchanged bewildered glances with Salazants.

"Look at 'im, Salazants; he's not right. He's done gone and became a Nockie. I mean look at 'im; he's got Falmoth's fingerprints all over 'im," said Manning.

"Shush, you imbecile," said Salazants, slapping Manning with his dust rag. "You will respect Master McRaven as long as you are employed here." Salazants rushed toward Valor with a concerned expression. "Come, sir, you look—exhausted. Let's get you cleaned up."

Salazants tried to wipe the black powder from around Valor's eyes, but it wouldn't come off. Valor pushed the butler away from him.

"You don't understand, Salazants; I vant to drink your blood now. I am a—"

"*Noctivatian*. I know, sir. I know," said Salazants. His hand grazed his Triskelion as if concealing his heartbeat. The veins in his hand made Valor's mouth water. "But with all due respect," warned Salazants, "I fear the others' plight will make the front page of the *Magic Ledger* before yours does, sir."

With his brain throbbing, Valor pressed his hair down with his hands, but it sprang up again. "Vhat?" he asked. "Hasn't Doomsy and the others come back to Candlevicke?"

"Doomsy returned, sir. Rose, Micha, and Blade remain in Bogamuckla looking for you," said Salazants, bracing his hand on his forehead as if trying to recall everything that had happened. "Doomsy told us they'd treated you terribly—caused you to run away, and that she'd never see you again. Mistress Stabbah was very displeased, and Aaron more so, sir; he became enraged at Doomsy—at the others. He said that they shouldn't bother to return to Candlewicke unless they find you. Mistress Doomsy left Candlewicke."

"By herself? You mean Stabbah didn't go vith her? She alvays looks after her." Valor felt unsteady on his feet now.

Salazants shook his head reluctantly. "Nalini, Ruza, Egg, Stabbah, and Creighton are the only ones who remain here besides Manning and me."

"The only vones?" asked Valor. He turned in a circle. "Vhere has Aaron gone?"

"Where has Master Aaron gone? He were a mess, sir, that's what he were," said Manning, wheezing from the dust Salazants had knocked off a picture frame. His freckled nose twitched. "Master Aaron weren't sure Aurora Vontiki hadn't captured you. I recall him sayin' he were going to Shadowy Heights and try and settle the matter."

"'Shadowhaven Heights,' Manning meant to say, sir," Salazants added, cupping his hands behind his back.

"Oh, how I vish I had kept the Luminous Lulling Lozenges," groaned Valor. But were his parted lips from displeasure, or was he thirsty for blood? Salazants stared at him as though he was now looking at a face that reflected something ugly and volatile.

"Sorry, sir?"

"Never mind, Salazants," said Valor, rubbing his aching eyes. "I just haven't had enough sleep. I must leave. I can only hope Doomsy is vith the others. But I have a feeling Aaron is in real danger at Shadowhaven Heights by himself. I can't stay here; I might harm my friends." He made a mental picture of the grand hall and twin parlors, the beautiful drapes, and furniture. Would he ever return?

"Leave? Oh no, you mustn't go, sir," said Manning, blocking the doorway like a cauldron guard in a game of Pumpkin Dunkin'. "'Don't let him leave Candlewicke if he returns,' Master Aaron made me promise, he did."

"Master McRaven, you needn't worry too much about Egg's safety," said Salazants delicately. "I feel I should tell you, with everything going on, Master Aaron made him immortal while you were gone."

Valor bit his tongue and gave a little cry of anguish. How could this be? The irreversible ruin of yet another person living under the roof of Candlewicke. But as awful as it was, perhaps it was for the best if only to protect Egg from Valor's animalistic hunger.

"If Doomsy or Aaron have gone off to Diabolishire by themselves, then they are in danger. I'm going to look for them," said Valor, giving Manning a stern look, but Manning wouldn't back away from the door; instead, he spread his arms as if ready to pounce.

Valor tried to squeeze past him, conjuring open the doors. Manning grabbed him, and they fell to the floor in a struggle against each other. The pedestrians on Spookum Alley stopped to gawk inside the mansion. "Sorry, sir," Manning kept repeating; the veins in his neck seemed to call out to Valor in the tussle until he lost all self-control and bit into Manning's neck. Salazants tried to snatch Manning off Valor, dragging Valor with his teeth still embedded in his neck.

"Master McRaven!" yelled Salazants.

In agony, Valor released his fangs from Manning's neck, dropped to the floor, and rolled away from them to avoid attacking again. "Forgive me, Manning," Valor cried out in utter disgust at himself and dashed out the doors of Candlewicke, breaking through the crowd of spectators.

Moving, as much as possible, through the shadows of back alleys and overhanging building awnings, he arrived back to the portal on Dead Maudie Alley. He searched for the lever to Diabolishire, pulled it, and this time found himself face down under a bridge. Avoiding the sun as best he could, he walked out of the stone tunnel and up a steep bank with patches of snow. On the cobblestone road ahead jutted a wooden sign with an arrow pointing toward Elysian Fields Ski Resort.

If he remembered correctly, Shadowhaven Heights was just a few miles through the woods from this point. He would visit the resort first. Maybe someone there had seen his friends. He could get a room in case he needed a refuge. Valor covered his head with his coat. The sun burned his hands as he ran up to the neglected lodge built high atop level after level of uneven wooden decks.

"Glad I didn't bring any luggage. This place can't still be in business," he said, climbing yet another set of rickety stairs. He knocked on the door, and an eyeball peeked out the curtained window.

"Ya aren't a wiggiwami are ya?" asked a trembling old woman's voice behind the door.

"No, Ma'am. I'm a McRaven."

"A McRaven, huh? That's not another name for one of those demon cults, is it?"

Valor stifled a laugh. "Oh no, ma'am. But you might think so if you met my father."

The resort keeper let Valor inside where footprints covered the dusty wooden floor. "The name's Fairly Granberry. If you wanna go skiing it'll be at your own risk, young man. Now I—"

"Oh," said Valor, "I'm not here to ski. I vonder if you might have seen any of my friends pass through here recently—"

"Passed away here?" asked Fairly. "Now, let me check the past few days here." She plopped a thin registry book on the counter, stirring the dust.

"No, ma'am. I said, 'passed *through* here.'" He made a sweeping motion with his hand.

"Oh, I see. No. No one's passed through here in about two months," said Fairly. She tucked the loose strands of her gray hair into her floppy knitted hat with wilted rosettes overpowering it.

"I need to rent a chalet for a few days," said Valor. He started to say, "If you have any vacancies," but that shouldn't be a problem from the looks of the place.

"Well, young man, if that's what you really want." She adjusted her spectacles and looked at him as though he were crazy. "You can have the luxury chalet for free if you just sign this release form."

"Release form?"

"Yes," said Fairly. "It just says you won't hold me responsible if you get injured, tortured, or murdered. And there's no room service."

Valor signed the form and took the key to the luxury chalet at the far end of the resort. The front door hung against the doorframe by one hinge. The windows had a few broken panes. "This is the luxury chalet?" he mumbled, then slid the chalet door to the side and eased toward the cathedral-ceilinged sitting room where Doomsy and Rose huddled in a dark corner under a blanket. The whole chalet smelled of mildew and needed many nails to secure loose boards.

"I don't think I've ever seen such a room of gloom," said Valor, startling everyone.

"See, Doomsy. I toldja he'd come back to us!" said Rose. "We've all been sending you telepathic messages, hoping you'd—" Rose choked on her words. Her chest heaved as her eyes locked on him at first, and then she sank with despair.

Blade rolled off the sofa's armrest and stood in front of Valor. "What do we have here? Blistered skin and disheveled hair," said Blade, swiping his finger under Valor's left eye, then examining his fingers for any smeared black powder. "Eyes sunken and missing their sparkle. We all know what this means." Blade's expression appeared lost in a sad memory. He raised his left hand in an attack-spell formation but then backed away from Valor.

"This is vhat a Noctivatian is in case you ever vondered—we're vampires. I've already attacked Manning, so yeah, you should all keep away from me," said Valor, grimacing from bloodthirst again. He should feel a little vindicated in blaming them. They had shamed him into joining the Hermetic Order, but he had blood on the brain now.

"Oh, Valor, it's all my fault," said Doomsy. She ran toward him, dropping her poppet doll, but Rose pulled her back, despite her sobs. She kept her head down, patting Doomsy's shoulders.

"Salazants and Manning said Aaron's gone to Shadowhaven Heights. I have to find him," said Valor, while Blade reclined on his back on the kitchen bar, clanking his wand on the overhead wine glasses, creating an eerie melody.

"We have Aaron right here," said Rose. She lifted the blanket off Aaron's head, revealing the scowl on his face. "He just *thinks* he's going to Shadowhaven Heights."

Doomsy gazed up at Valor with a hopeless frown. "I found him on his way up here, and I put a lead-weight spell on him." She pulled the blanket off Aaron's feet, revealing a large lead ball shackled to his boots. "Some witches give lead-weight spells a bad name." Doomsy tugged on the chains at Aaron's feet. "They can be quite calming if applied correctly."

"Argh," growled Aaron. "You were supposed to go find Valor. You tricked me." Aaron looked up at Valor, evaluated his appearance, and shook his head in disbelief.

"Don't resist, my pet. You know I'm always ready for disaster, so there are never any surprises with me," said Doomsy. She moved away from Aaron and eased as close as she could toward Valor, gazing up at him with a frown. "But I do make mistakes. I've made the biggest mistake of my long miserable life. I didn't know the Hermetic Order of the Mystic Key would turn you into a vampire."

Valor pulled away from her. She tried to conceal her sorrow, but her twitching Cupid's bow lips proved otherwise. Aaron let out a sigh of dread, trying to free his boots from the shackles.

"O vain adversity," he hissed. "Valor, tell me that these infernal riles didn't shame you into joining forces with Venerious Falmoth!"

Valor held back a bitter answer. His mouth drew up, and every muscle stiffened.

"Oh, Aaron. You know Doomsy never jokes," said Rose, wiping the corner of her teary eye. "Things became emotional at the frozen lake and, and distorted."

"Don't include Blade Zagato in any of that distortion," said Blade, playing another irritating melody on the glasses with his wand. "Zagato didn't have a problem helping Valor kidnap Urbanne's grandthing. He didn't shame Valor into siding with Falmoth the Foul and that wiggiwami woman of his," said Blade, grinning as though he were rolling a diamond around on the tip of his tongue.

"For the last time, I vasn't going to kidnap anyone!" growled Valor, holding his palms toward the ceiling, in a pleading gesture. "I thought Sweeturnips vould vant to see his grandfather. I never even considered Urbanne might harm him—I didn't think at all."

Aaron's head rolled against the wall in disbelief. "I knew I should have gone with you, Valor—not these hypocrites," he said. "Now, look what's become of you."

"There must be something we can do," whined Rose, with a wrinkled brow forming under her snow-white face powder and forehead amulet.

"There is nothing any of you can do for Valor now. Sometimes you have to live with irreversible misfortune," said Blade.

"Ya know what?" asked Micha, grabbing the wand from Blade at the bar. "I'm sorry this happened to ya, Val. I am, buddy. But I think most of this is all just a scheme of Mystic Ministry—or maybe the Grim Warlock possessed us—I mean, it could be. I don't remember everythin' that was said. We were all overstressed."

"Micha, Micha, Micha," said Blade, clapping his hands dully. "Your suspicion may hold a nit piss of truth, but everyone chooses their own path. You all chose to blame Valor, and he chose to join the Hermetic Order. But peril still prowls the country, and Blade chooses to take his time and think things through."

Doomsy braced her hand against the wall and shot Blade an uncompromising look. "Now that's a fresh pile of dragon dung coming from your lips, Blade Zagato—always blaming me for making you immortal against your will," said Doomsy. Her attention turned from Blade to Valor. "I admit to my mistakes. Now my brother's life has changed for the worse I fear." She clutched her poppet to her chest and dropped her chin against the tuft of hair stitched to its crude sackcloth head. "The least I can do now is to stop Aaron from ruining *his* life. I'm going to Shadowhaven Heights come nightfall. I have a plan to end their attacks on both of you."

Rose moved to the edge of the fireplace beside Doomsy. "Sweetie," she said in her baby-doll voice. "Just how the heck do you plan on reinstating Bohemia with her people, or prove Valor and Aaron didn't murder Mesthu?"

"I don't know. Bohemia and her bootlickers can work out their own future. Battles require discrimination, and for Valor's and Aaron's safety, I'm going for the jugular."

The northern air whistled through the chalet doorway and ruffled the black fur on the hemline of Doomsy's dress. Her hair cascaded through the top of a rich fabric turban interwoven with a chain of staurolite crosses down select strands of her hair.

"Dooms, break this binding spell! 'Tis me they wish to see," said Aaron. "They could very well seal you in an iron coffin for all eternity. Death would be a better fate."

"Then I vill go to Shadowhaven Heights," lisped Valor, thanks to his new fangs. "I vill be spending my days in a coffin anyvay," said Valor.

"Nobody is going but me," said Doomsy. She flipped the latch on her poison ring with her long peacock-green fingernail, pulled out a teeniny bug, and fed it to Mr. Grudgings.

"How in Hoopenfangia do you plan on stopping them—vith a spell?" asked Valor.

"I don't have to depend on spells, my pet. If I need something done, I just do it—grab it by the nose hair," said Doomsy. She marched up to him, grabbed a little black beaded purse, tucked under her vest coat, and removed a small object, which she placed in his hand.

"How did you get Mesthu's ring?" asked Valor, admiring its fine artistry once again.

"After you refused to take it from Mega D, he gave it to Siobhan to see if she could talk you into joining them to take control of the tower," replied Doomsy. "I lied to Siobhan—told her I'd try to bribe you with the ring, but I knew I'd use it for my plan." She put the ring back in her purse. "Your hand is sunburned." She took out some healing balm and applied it to his hands, but he retracted when she tried to smear it on his face.

Rose reached in her conjure bag and removed a jar of her white enchanted powder. "Try this," she said. "It'll keep the sun from roasting you. That explains why Falmoth wears it." Rose began applying it to Valor's face, and his urge to drink blood became too strong to repress, so he grabbed her wrist to stop her.

"Stay away! You have no idea how much I vant to bite you right now," said Valor. With his eyes, he pleaded with her to understand and forgive him.

Micha soared across the room at Valor as if ready to pound him, but Doomsy blocked him.

"Some of that Sanguinati tension getting to you, Micha? My! Peril prowls the chalet even," laughed Blade, taunting him, while Valor collapsed against the floor in a ball of anguish.

"Guys, can you believe what Falmoth said—all the witches in Mystic City were once Sorcerers?" asked Rose.

"Oh, man!" gasped Micha. "I haven't stopped thinkin' about that ever since he said it."

"Do you think it's really true?" asked Valor.

Blade smirked and said, "Too bad that statement has only come from the mouth of such a vile worm as Venerious Falmoth. Nevertheless, Zagato thinks the Great Deception is finally unraveling before the eyes of the gullible."

"Verily," said Aaron as though he had an astounding revelation. "It would explain why Chacodophilus had connections as the Great Witch with both the Sorcerers at Shadowhaven Heights and the Sanguinati at Mystic Steeples."

"Why are we only hearing such a history-changing statement from Falmoth?" hissed Doomsy. "He can't be trusted. He tricked all of us."

"Vell now, my dears," lisped Valor. "You all believed Falmoth back at the frozen lake." Valor studied their guilty faces with a touch of bitter satisfaction. "Blade's right. I chose to join the Hermetic Order . . . to show you all I care about you."

"You were humiliated into doing it, Valor. Your manipulative friends over there had better hope that Falmoth and the Hermetic Order are not lying about everything else—to which I sincerely doubt," hissed Aaron.

"Guys, Aaron's right. All we can do now is trust that Falmoth has a plan to keep us safe and stop O Enchantedness from completing his Thirteenth Hour devastation," said Rose, dabbing her eyes again.

CHAPTER TEN

DOOMSY GOES TO SHADOWHAVEN HEIGHTS

EVERYONE sat in silence or fell asleep until the sun hid behind the trees. Micha kept a watch on Valor while peeling splinters of wood from the dilapidated bar and dropping them to the floor. The smell of musty cedar became stronger as night approached. Doomsy eased her hand on Valor's shoulder, offering a hint of vulnerability.

"I'm coming vith you," said Valor, while Rose and Aaron watched them from the corner of the room. Doomsy glared into his eyes and adjusted her fingerless lace gloves as if she were preparing to steer a race centaur.

"You'll guide me halfway to the tower and no farther. My plan may backfire if you come with me. We can't risk Aaron's safety," said

Doomsy. "I must get going."

Valor shook his head in agreement, and they prepared to leap off the deck railing. Micha stood in the doorway in a long black overcoat and matching pointed hat. Just before Doomsy and Valor jumped, Blade burst through the door.

"What do you want?" hissed Doomsy, giving him a look of warning that froze him to the spot.

"Zagato is going to accompany you, and make sure you don't hurt somebody," said Blade.

"I don't want you anywhere near me!" growled Doomsy. She threw up her hand and cast a spell, flipping Blade in a roaring whirlwind back inside the chalet.

Rose wished Doomsy luck with her eyes as she pulled the door shut.

"That vas rather harsh, my dear. I'm sure Blade only intended to make sure you vould be safe," said Valor as they headed east, past a frozen fountain, and down the base of the mountain toward Stonevengeance. The light faded, and a dark wind fondled the valley as they eased deeper inside the forest. Doomsy remained quiet, resembling a black-lace death doll, as she whisked past white-barked trees that stood like prison bars under the moon, which soon disappeared over the spiral birch trees.

"Slow down, Dooms. I'm a little veak at the moment," said Valor. He wished he had whispered when twigs snapped in the distance. "Do you think it vas a Viggivami?"

Doomsy held her finger to her lips in a gesture to remain quiet. The rustle of underbrush made them pause again. He motioned for her to float over the ground to avoid foot noises on the leaves. After drifting among the trees for a mile, they learned to ignore the shadows of clouds swimming about like phantoms under the bristling treetops.

Valor's strength gave out, and he paused under a dreary lodgepole pine—no candy or fruit-covered trees like those they had marveled at in the Tombstone Forest. Doomsy stood beside him, attuned to the slightest echo of danger.

"Ve're almost there, my dear," said Valor. "There's the juicy spruce vhere the heavy snows broke off its top. That hasn't changed, at least." He walked beside the memorable creek bed, which made a sharp s-curve, and the log bridge he'd crossed many times when he lived on Stonevengeance Mountain. "Shadowhaven Heights is straight over this mountain peak. The knobby cedars vill part in two just past this vinding valley."

Doomsy removed her *Mystic Memoir* from her conjure bag and thumbed to the witches' alphabet, then tore the letter W out of the book and wrote something on the paper. "Here, we've got to do something about your toothy Ws."

He took the paper and asked, "Vhat am I supposed to do vith this?"

"Eat it," she said, "and hope you never have to say, 'Valor once was a worrywart.'"

He shoved the paper in his mouth and chewed until he was able to swallow it. "Well, what's supposed to happen now?"

"I cured your W pronunciation, but you still have fangs. I'm leaving now. Don't you dare follow me," said Doomsy. "If I'm not back at the chalet by this time tomorrow, then promise me you and the others will return to Candlewicke."

Valor knelt down beside her. "I can't do that, my dear. I cannot promise." His distress deepened when she placed her small hand against his heart. "Look, if there's something you did in your past that you're ashamed of, just tell me. I can help you."

Doomsy pulled away from him.

"You always do that," he said. "You shut down. It's like—it's like you're punishing yourself."

"I drove you to become this shell of a human that you have become, the same way I drove Blade Zagato to leave me," said Doomsy. She became silent until she whispered the words, "He was right—you were right: I have too much to learn."

"You can't blame yourself, my dear; you're only a child—like me. We both make mistakes."

"That's the problem. I'm *not* a child—not really. I should have never become immortal so young. I've lived many lifetimes in case you've forgotten. You have much to accomplish still, and the means to do it. Vow to me that you'll never lend a faint regret about me—before I destroy what's left of your life."

Valor continued to kneel on the ground, thinking about her words. She turned back around and grabbed his coat lapel with both hands. Her words escaped her. Had she choked back a tear? She shook his lapel in two soft tugs and whispered, "Bye, brother."

Massive shadowy trees soon engulfed her in the distance. She looked helpless and childlike, floating farther into the Bumbling Boonies. Valor's heart ached as a tear fell onto a decaying leaf jutting from a patch of snow. No, nothing had better happen to her. There was a deadness in the woods until the distant howl of a wolf—or was it? He must keep his head together. Any sign of distress and he'd go after her.

She'd succeed with her plan—she had to, Valor tried to convince himself as he turned back toward the chalet. If only he could whisk away his regrets now. Had he at last understood Houmas and Lithium—the reason they had secluded themselves?

Valor squatted down and gathered the fog in his hands. "Enshroud Doomsy from the eyes of danger, you murky mist, and guard her path well," he said, flinging the ball of fog, which charged toward her like a tidal wave.

Nearing the base of the mountain, a few yards from the safety of the ski lodge, squeezing anxiety hit him, the pressure of watching eyes, and the occasional rustle of shrubbery. With a thud, something knocked him forward and placed a tight grip around his arms and chest. He gasped as thick tree roots sprang up from the ground at his feet and began to bind his legs. He tried to swing the attacker off his back, for his chances were slim in that position. He bit her arm, then reached over his head, grabbed a handful of her hair, and flipped her over his back. The woman's head bashed against a knobby cedar limb, allowing Valor to grab his monoculous. Just as he prepared to use it, he recognized the face speaking a hex below him and the butterfly bracelet on her wrist.

"Bohemia! Do you mean me harm or no? I'm Valor McRaven." He pointed his monoculous at her until any reason to distrust her had lessened. The bit of blood he had taken from her revived him. She let out a nervous laugh while the roots retracted under the soil. Her eyebrows arched at Valor. Could she tell he was a Noctivatian now?

"The little boy who sacrificed himself for Aaron—a Noctivatian now. But you played so noble, so innocent," said Bohemia darkly. "No wonder you felt sorry for Banzalta. Mega D said you refused to help me, so why are you here? Do you have Mesthu's ring? I don't see it."

Valor lowered his monoculous. "I don't want the ring, though I guess I'm honored you wished me to have it. But I'm not here to help you recapture your position at the tower."

"What do you mean—are you against me then?" asked Bohemia, glaring at him with uncertain eyes. Her face distorted with animalistic rage. "You'll tell me now if you're against me."

"I'm not against you. Now calm yourself. Let me explain some things."

"Explain." Bohemia's head swaggered over her shoulders. Under a low moon, she paced in an angry tango with her shadow. The landscape glowed toxic green around her. The brisk mountain air made steam rise from the two holes in her arm.

"I have no intention of going to the tower. I'm here to protect Aaron. From what I've heard, Aurora Vontiki seeks to kill him and me or—or worse."

"We can make her back off when we take back Shadowhaven Heights," said Bohemia, brushing leaves off her dress. "I was once regal, once grand, but she severed my life." Her bottom lip drew up between her teeth.

"No—doubly no, I'm not here to reinstate you as the leader," said Valor, leaning near her. "Did you fight Mesthu to return Aaron after he exiled him to rot? No, you did not." He smirked. "You may have had words with him, but you didn't use force."

She paced the ground under the giant knobby cedar. Her chest swelled, catching lost breath. "But I fought to keep Mesthu's Children safe," she said. "I helped hone their craft, and this is my reward!" Bohemia flung her hands in the air. Her eyes widened again. Blood seemed to form on her lower eyelids—a vibrant distraction against her fierce white face. Valor had to look away.

"Few from the tower are willing to help me," she said in a more helpless voice. "I can't do this with just a few. Even Eolas and Razvio have sided with Aurora. They can read minds. They must know she holds no honor."

The thorny branches stirred around them, amassing with her fury, which reverberated off tree trunks so near, the forest soon formed a nest.

"Yes, I thought they would have seen any witch's true intentions, including mine. I came there begging for help to stop the Grim Warlock and the Darkening, but neither you nor Mesthu would me help. The only thing I got was attacked." Valor said bitterly.

"Mesthu made every decision. I was only his assistant." With closed eyelids, Bohemia rested her arms and leaned into a tree. Her red velvet dress had slit farther than the seam design intended, a sign she had not had time to change before Aurora had cast her from the tower. Leaves and dirt intertwined with her straight silver hair. Valor flicked off some of the dirt and leaves from his clothes.

"What are you going to do now?" he asked.

"Turn to stone, I suppose—what should I do?"

"You could move to Mystic City and help the Sorcerers there," said Valor.

"Never! I could never set foot in Severance." She pulled her mane back, and it collapsed over her dirty face again. She cried, ripped the bottom shard of her dress off, and used the swatch to tie up her hair.

"I can take you back to my chalet for now," offered Valor. "However, you mustn't reveal I came here or my friends either. I'm expecting Doomsy back this time tomorrow—if she makes it back. Then we can go from there."

"I've no other hope, Valor. You can trust me, and this I swear on my miserable soul."

A few yards from the chalet, he paused and said, "Tell me: how did Aurora acquire Mesthu's ring if wiggiwamis in Stonevengeance killed him?"

"Wiggiwamis didn't kill him, but there are wiggiwamis and some crazed mountain Nizzertits in Stonevengeance. We often went through there when we needed food and supplies. It was a scheme Aurora concocted to kill Mesthu. She acquired his ring because she killed him."

"Baneful witch. I hope Doomsy's aware of that. I don't know what she plans to do. You don't think they'll harm her, do you?" Valor closed his eyes, shutting out her fierce gaze.

"I don't wish to be a prophet of doom," said Bohemia, springing up an incline of rocks. "But if she escapes with her life, I shall marvel."

"I still don't see how they think Aaron and I are responsible for Mesthu's death."

"That suggestion started with Aurora. Many of Mesthu's Children were accused of the dark deed. You could be in great danger. That's why you need to help us remover her power," said Bohemia. "Just imagine—you can drain every drop of her blood," said Bohemia, with disturbing elation in her eyes.

"Never speak such things again!" Valor growled.

He felt as lost and trapped as the ivy-entwined foundation beams of the chalet, which jutted up from the mountainscape of scattered pines that vanished into the low clouds. The pines' scent flowed down the hillside amid spiral birches now drooping from many years of snow.

"I'll prepare my friends for your arrival, Bohemia. Wait here, and I'll signal for you to come."

While she paced around the patches of snow, Valor found his friends watching out the window at the ski slopes after he landed on the deck. Like skulls suspended in front of a blackened curtain, they were sitting in the window box with their faces pressed to the glass.

Micha ripped at the door, and it vibrated open.

"Did Doomsy make it to the tower?" he asked.

"I wish I could answer that—she wouldn't let me go with her," replied Valor. He dashed past everyone, propped his elbow on the fireplace mantel, and rested his forehead in his hand. "She did a spell to get rid of my speech problem, then said if she doesn't return by this time tomorrow night, we must leave without her. I couldn't promise her."

"I fear the worst. You know that, don't you? I should have forbidden her to leave," said Aaron. He shook his head and slapped his hand against the wall behind him.

"She shackled ya," laughed Micha. "Not very persuasive, are you?"

"You did forbid her. We all did. You know Doomsy's resolve," sighed Valor, looking at Aaron's shackles. How could he break the spell? He fired a zap at the lead chain holding the heavy ball. "It's no use. There's some kind of force field around these shackles." He stored his monoculous in his coat. "Bohemia is waiting outside. I said I would get permission from you all to let her in the chalet. I don't know—perhaps she can help us find a resolution to this."

"Ya won't be needin' permission from Blade Zagato; he got mad at me an' left not long after you and Doomsy did," said Micha.

"What? Why?" asked Valor.

"'Cause I was talkin' ta Rose, I guess. Ya know how he is," said Micha, and Rose's black-powdered lips tightened as if suppressing a smile.

Aaron tried to shift into a more comfortable position. "Bohemia shan't do us much good, I'm afraid," he said. "But I don't imagine she'll cause us to lose any more sleep than we already have."

Bohemia waited below the deck. Her dress appeared as a puddle of crimson blood on the snowy ground, her long silver hair now gathered to the side of her neck. Valor motioned for her to come inside the chalet. The air was thin and tense as if steeped in death, and everyone moved from sitting to pacing in circles around the room. Light from two candles poured under the restroom door where Bohemia busied herself with a bath. For Valor's sake, Rose decided to secure the tattered curtains, trying to get a seamless barrier from the approaching morning light.

"How about that," asked Rose. "We let Bohemia in, and all she's done is leave a stain in the bathtub."

"Ya're right, Rose. Maybe I should go help Bohemia with that stain," said Micha. His eyebrows danced with assurance.

"You'll do no such thing!" snapped Rose. "Curse these curtains, why can't they make them with enough fabric to at least overlap an inch?"

"Here, I brought these, if you want to drape them over the curtains. It should help block the beastly sunlight," said Valor, placing the bedspreads on the sofa, keeping a safe distance from everyone.

"How long are we planning on being here? These shackles will be the death of me," Aaron groaned.

Micha tucked a cotton towel in a gap atop the kitchen curtain. "Do ya wanna sleep in the bathtub, Aaron? You worried about the stain, too?"

"No, I'd like to assure Doomsy returns before the morrow's eve," huffed Aaron, before Bohemia exited the restroom draped in a towel. Her dress hung over the shower curtain rod.

"I won't be sleepin' today," said Micha, ogling Bohemia.

Valor wound a rope around the front doorknob, trying to secure it to the doorframe. "Bohemia, I'm still trying to figure out how Aurora managed to fool Mesthu's children—you know, with their mindreading ability and all?" asked Valor.

"It astounds me as well," said Bohemia. Her lips only parted enough to form her words, though her eyebrows and shoulders danced. "Over many centuries, Aurora became a pathological liar. She possesses no ability within her icy coil to feel remorse or guilt. Even Siobhan would agree, wherever she is. Aurora must have tampered with the crystals, which feed our telepathic ability in the Crystallum Templum. Mega D did find traces of boron nitride particles into the temple's ventilation. If Aurora did that, it might have diluted our telepathic powers."

"Preposterous. Boron nitride particles?" said Aaron, scratching his head. "A synthetic compound?"

"Oh, but Aurora is a skilled alchemist. She was always experimenting with chemistry and potions. I once heard her say someday she alone would create the supernatural with the artificial," said Bohemia, studying her reflection in the streaked mirror. She leaned in closer, and her fingernail scraped a long line of black-and-white cow hair off the hide that lined the mirror's frame. "I fear for Doomsy because they will put her in an iron coffin." Bohemia smoothed her eyelashes with her tongue-moistened fingers. Valor and Aaron looked at each with creased brows.

A sinking feeling in Valor's stomach seized his words. Bohemia sauntered around the chalet in high-heel boots. Her posture remained rigid, regal. She inspected the mundane furnishings and decorative items while humming. Rose kept watch of her while pretending to look for something in her *Mystic Memoir* while shooting unhappy glances at Micha as he sprawled on the sofa with folded arms, as though hypnotized with Bohemia.

Many hours had passed, and the soft glow through the curtained windows signaled morning had arrived. Everyone's eyes were droopy, and they could remain alert no longer. Micha made his bed in the closet, while Bohemia and Rose slept on the sofa. Valor dozed off in an armchair in an awkward position.

Six hours later, Valor awoke in a state of panic with his feet and hands tied to the armchair with a curtain cord. Inside the ajar closet, Micha lay bound and gagged on the floor, thrashing around, tugging at his bindings. In the restroom, banging and grunting broke the silence.

"Micha, I can't get free, I'm tied to the chair," said Valor.

The door to the restroom whopped open against the wall, and out fell Rose and Bohemia, tumbling to the floor, shaking each other. Rose's hands clasped around Bohemia's throat while her feet hobbled, bound in ropes.

"Help! She's trying to kill me," Bohemia cried. Her voice had changed and had become dark. With a mad laugh, she speared two fingers against Rose's eyes, leaving thin slices, which dripped blood before completely healing. Rose conjured all the metal objects in the room to smash into Bohemia, and she crashed headfirst into the glass-top table, sending shards all over the room.

"You vile vixen," Rose screamed at Bohemia. "You're the one trying to kill us."

A piece of glass fell near Valor's feet. While Bohemia and Rose tumbled across the old rug, Valor concentrated on the piece of glass, levitating it from the floor, and willed the glass to slice the cord around his wrists. The glass quivered and nicked him a couple of times, but after another painful slice, his hands were free. "Yes!" He leaned over and cut the cords around his feet.

"*Solvo Vincio*," Rose chanted while tugging against coiling snakes Bohemia had conjured to bind her ankles and wrists. This vanquished the scaly, slithering hex.

Seeing Valor cut the bindings on Micha's hands and feet, Bohemia chanted, "*Prodio Incendium*." A likeness of planet Jupiter formed in her left hand, producing flames that gushed toward Valor and Micha.

"*Ricocaromm*," Valor chanted, repelling Bohemia's flame spell back to her just inches before it nearly engulfed Micha and him. The returning flames bombarded Bohemia, knocking her on the floor. She reached up toward the bottom of the curtain, and clawed at the fabric, trying to expose Valor to the sunlight.

"Hate to ruin your plans," said Rose, stomping on Bohemia's wrist with the full force of her leather boot, breaking the silver-haired Sorcerer's butterfly bracelet in half. Her scream vibrated the wineglass rack with a high-pitched ringing.

"Why are you trying to kill us!" Valor wheezed, aiming his monoculous wand at Bohemia, allowing waves of energy to accumulate in its glowing tip.

"You all are harboring a Noctivatian." Bohemia pointed at Valor. "*He* is your Knight of Night? You were planning to betray me!"

"You traitor. You knew what I was before you entered this chalet. Now, what is your real motive—insanity?" asked Valor, steadying his wand, but she wouldn't answer him.

"I don't know how she managed ta restrain me. I musta been in a coma. She gagged me, so I couldn't do my Triple Nimble Whistle," panted Micha, after Rose had removed his gag.

Rose snatched her belt from around her waist and, with an incantation, she began tying knots in it: "I bind you, Bohemia, with the power of fire. I bind you with the power of the wind. I bind you with the power of the earth. I bind you feet to hands." Rose spun the belt, released it, and it snaked through the air until it bound Bohemia's wrists to her ankles, allowing Rose to drag her away from the curtain.

"Aaron's dead!" yelled Micha. "She killed Aaron!"

"No!" cried Valor, thrashing through the chalet, where he had last seen Aaron waiting in shackles.

Bohemia smirked. "He's not dead. I put a sleep spell on him."

"Undo the spell on him now!" demanded Valor.

"Why have you done this to us?" Rose asked.

Bohemia snarled, while Valor managed to wake Aaron.

Valor aimed his wand at Bohemia's twisted face, interrogating her further. She cursed at him, conjuring a gargoyle to knock Valor wand away from her. While Valor and Rose battled the gargoyle, Micha snatched the bottom sheet off the bed, wrapped it around Bohemia, and stomped over to the fireplace mantel, grabbing a lantern. He poured the lamp oil all over the sheet, while Valor's wand discharged a blast that sent the gargoyle fleeing and snorting up the stone chimney.

Bohemia tilted her head back and hissed, "You set me on fire, and this whole place will burn. Where will you go? The sun is still overhead. Your Nockie friend will burn with me."

"Valor can tolerate the sun. Besides, I can take you outside and burn you myself," said Rose.

Sitting up as best he could in his shackles, Aaron cleared his throat and said, "Bohemia, you will tell us everything we want to know, or you will force me to use my Silver Tongue Spell on you."

"You have *my* permission 'cause I don't believe a rancid vapor that dribbles out of her jaws," said Rose.

"I will not listen. Ears, pack with wax when Aaron's voice yaks," Bohemia repeatedly chanted, trying to shimmy the sheets away from her body.

Thinking fast, Rose aimed her wand at her and chanted, *"Ponebat Corcagia In Eam."* A cork, the size of a small apple, appeared in Bohemia's mouth to silence her.

In his usual eloquent voice, Aaron began an incantation: "As I spin my spell smooth and tender—pinch of sooth, fleck of silver—with truthful tooth your forked tongue thick shall transform into a vocal snitch. Fib-smitten Sorceress, from the truth, you shall not abstain; neither shall you refrain from a slip of the lips." Aaron's tone became more authoritative. "Now, I ask you, Bohemia, why did you try to kill us?"

Bohemia seemed in a trance after Rose uncorked her mouth. "Yes, I was trying to kill you," she sobbed. "Something got a hold of me; I couldn't help it. Ha-ha-ha!" Bohemia's voice grew monstrous again, and her expression mad. "You all deserve to die. You were conspiring against me and against my plans to take back Shadowhaven Heights." She relaxed, and her voice returned to normal. "I made a foolish mistake. If you let me go, I'll leave, and never a harmful thought will I lend you."

Aaron clenched his fists on his hips. "Release you to secure our death in your parody of deception?"

Squelched gulps bubbled from Valor's throat. He should have never trusted Bohemia or brought her to the chalet. "I think the Grim Warlock has possessed her. It happened to me—only briefly in Controssua Studies—I'm sure of it," said Valor. "The guardians immediately took me to see O Enchantedness. That's why he assigned me the job of finding his grandson—as an alternative to prison—I'm certain of it."

Doomsy's, Micha's, and Rose's expressions turned from guilt to sheer remorse.

"In that case, I've nothing more to say." Bohemia pursed her lips with scorn. "You understand my plight—my reasons."

Micha held the lantern over Bohemia. Her flinching eyelids could not diffuse his intentions.

"We must stop Aurora, but I can't do it held captive. What if she kills Doomsy? You wouldn't want that to happen to your prized friend," said Bohemia, forcing a strained look of virtue, which read as conniving fakery. "They'll place a crown of belladonna upon her brow then seal her in an iron coffin; they will."

"Why aren't you in an iron coffin then?" asked Valor, pivoting to face her. Aaron remained on the floor, trying to undo the shackles.

The curtain's faint glow grew dim as hours of interrogations had passed, and nighttime returned once again. Aaron massaged his hands. His Adam's apple pulsed under his long white-lace collar. "Pay no more heed to these tiresome chitchats," he said. "Can't anyone break this wicked spell of bondage Doomsy has inflicted on me?"

Rose pulled out her *Mystic Memoir* and turned to the page she had bookmarked with a raven's feather. "I saw this spell earlier," she said, "but I don't have a vine of tangling hexteria. It doesn't thrive in this region that I'm aware of."

"Do try something. I am helpless in this state," begged Aaron.

"Hmm, there's no keyhole anywhere on these shackles—they're seamless. But try not to be angry. Doomsy cast the spell to protect you, not to harm," said Valor. He walked around in circles, biting his fingernails, thinking. His head now pounded from bloodthirst. "If we rendered you invisible, you still couldn't get out of the shackles."

"All that's left is an intangibility spell unless Aaron can shapeshift," said Micha.

"Can you?" asked Rose.

"Shapeshift?" asked Aaron with a wince. "No, indeed. The last time I endeavored, it was appalling. My body shrank three inches, and I strutted around like a peacock for two weeks. I thought I would never return to normal."

"Have you?" Bohemia asked with a scowl.

Valor's patience had reached its limit; his chest heaved with anguish. "We don't have a lot of time here. If Doomsy doesn't return soon, I'm going to Shadowhaven Heights and rewrite the laws of karma!"

"Wooh-ho! That a boy, Valor. The Knight of Night's comin' outta ya," said Rose.

Valor recoiled to the fireplace dry heaving. He didn't like cruelty. He wasn't trying to be tough. His mind flooded with visions of horror.

"I gotta confess," said Micha. He grabbed the back of his head, scrunching his brown hair as if he had mixed feelings. "I know the spell for intangibility."

"You couldn't. That spell is forbidden at Mystic Steeples," Rose said with her usual prickly but alluring demeanor.

"Blade Zagato taught it to me, but I haven't really used it. He said he used it ta pass through the walls behind Toadflax Hall," said Micha.

"The Sanguinettes' changing room? You boys are deviants!" hissed Rose.

Micha stood, blushing, with his hands in his pockets. "It might work on Aaron, but we'll need an ounce of urine from a hissin' girrabbit. One frozen dream. And the footprint from a generous woman collected on a page of promise."

"All right, Micha dear, unless you have a photographic memory, you've done this spell many, many times," laughed Valor stiffly.

"'Tis futile," sighed Aaron. "Those ingredients will take ages to collect."

Taking a piece of paper from the closet floor, Valor borrowed a plume of phoenix from Rose, then squatted by the fireplace and wrote, *I promise to rescue Doomsy.*

"Here's your page of promise, Micha," Valor said. "You can find the footprint you need on the floor at the lodge's check-in on the far side of the resort. If that's any help?"

"I'm no good with animal tinkle or hissing, but I think I can conjure up a frozen dream," said Rose.

Micha grabbed a drinking glass from the bar. "I'll get the tinkle, Rose."

"Good gargoyles, this is weird," said Aaron.

"If I feed the hissin' girrabbit lotsa water, things'll happen much faster," said Micha. He shirked when Rose raised an eyebrow at him. "Um—odds are it might happen—I think." He scooted past Rose and took the page of promise Valor had left on a table. He buttoned his coat, put on his hat, and turned toward the door, mumbling, "Where will I find a hissin' girrabbit?" asked Micha. "Not like I can make a quick run to the magic shop. Crap. I came here lookin' for dragons."

Rose closed the door behind Micha and said, "Nothing is 'generous' in Diabolishire."

"I guess it's just you and me now, Aaron," said Valor. "Possessed or not, we still need to keep watch over Bohemia."

"I'm not much use like this, I suppose. We both know that Doomsy is in no capacity to make such perilous decisions," said Aaron. He shut his eyes, then looked up at the ceiling in surrender.

Bohemia's cheek dropped against the stovepipe oven. "Please let me go—I can't stand this torment," she said.

Valor sat on the floor and kept his monoculous pointed at Bohemia. It took a few hours to come down from his guarded state before guilt crawled back into his conscience. His morphing shadow called his senses to his vulnerability. Would his shadow ever leave him? The stomping sounds on the chalet deck brought him to his feet with a start. He peered out the window at Micha and Rose dusting snow off their clothes. He let them inside, and the glow in their eyes assured him they had collected their portions for the intangibility spell.

"Do amuse this captive, Rose m'dear," said Aaron. "How, perchance, did you acquire a frozen dream?"

Rose placed her scarf, which held a high mound of snow, on the bar. "You can't see it. Besides, I'll never tell you about my dream. Some things should remain sacred."

"Your dream is inside that bundle of snow?" asked Aaron. "Must have been a short nap."

"Oh, you're wrong there. I made a huge sacrifice for you, mister," said Rose, glancing out the window on the tips of her boots. "And if Micha doesn't hurry up with that tinkle, my last dream is going to melt."

Micha lifted a glass of golden tinkle in his gripping fingers triumphantly. "It was a good guess—the water did the trick."

"I don't mean to be rude, but can we get on with it then?" asked Valor,

Micha collected the bit of melting snow left on Rose's scarf and dumped it into the glass, and a tiny locket with a tiny painting became visible in the urine—a painting of Rose surrounded by three other people.

"This was your dream?" asked Valor. "I'm confused."

Rose turned away for a second then returned to her locket. "I painted it using some eyelashes from my dead grandmother. It's not very good, but it was my deepest wish. My mum, dad, brother, and me—together. They're all dead now. I guess I need to let go of that fact."

Moved by her sacrifice, Aaron shut his eyes, and his head collapsed against the wall.

"I'm truly sorry, Rose. The loss of family is a wound that never heals," said Valor. He offered as sympathetic of a gaze as he could through his shadowed eyes.

Rose shrugged with a faint smile. "It's okay."

Micha took the page of promise with the lifted footprint, crumbled it, and dropped it in the glass. He held the glass over his head and chanted, "A page of promise surpasses a frozen dream just as the body's golden essence reunites the waters of a stream." The contents in the glass began to bubble and smoke. "I command thee, potion in this glass, render he who drinks, the ability to pass through solids. And may his body reform when his mission is accomplished."

After a bit of hesitation, Aaron took the glass from Micha and drank half of the potion. "Ineffective potion," he said. "I can still see myself."

"The potion doesn't make ya invisible, just able ta pass through objects," said Micha. "Don't move too fast, though, or ya might walk right outta ya clothes." Micha placed the remaining potion on the bar safely behind him. Rose gave him a don't-even-think-of-it look.

Aaron pulled one leg free from a shackle. "Ah," he sighed. His eyes still seemed hesitant, but his mouth opened with eagerness. He eased the other leg free and darted away from the enchanted chains. "I could kiss you." Aaron reached out to hug Micha.

"Whoa, you're losing your pants, Aaron!" gasped Rose, and Aaron did when a loud crash made him jump back.

"What, pray tell, was that?" asked Aaron.

"It was me," said Valor. "Bohemia tried to conjure the intangibility potion to her lips, but I knocked it away."

"Bohemia, even if you drank the intangibility potion, you couldn't have gotten out of my belt. It was knotted with rotten vibes," said Rose with a haughty hair toss.

"Kill the Knight of Night first, lest that miscreant be your downfall," Bohemia said in a strange voice, rattling her head, grimacing and drooling. "I'm sorry. I'm sorry, Sarapentez, my loyal Familiar." She banged her head against the floor in a fetal position, and her hidden necklace plopped out of her dress collar.

"Say, is that a Triskelion?" asked Valor, leaning forward.

Micha snatched it from her neck and examined it. "Yup, it is," he confirmed.

Aaron reentered the kitchen. His intangibility had worn off, as the spell suggested it would, once he had completed his mission.

"Bohemia has a Triskelion? You jest!" said Aaron, inspecting her pendant. "All those years at Shadowhaven Heights, and you were with the Sanguinati?"

"All those years with Mesthu's Children and you joined the primitives, Aaron Nicholas? Ooo, let me inspect *your* necklace, heaaa hea-heaaa," Bohemia laughed wickedly.

"She's bad twisted, Aaron. Don't listen to her," said Micha, patting Aaron's shoulder, although his hand didn't pass through him as he seemed to expect. "It should be obvious; Bohemia killed Mesthu, not Aurora."

"Who sent you to Shadowhaven Heights to kill Mesthu—it was Urbanne LaRock, was it not?" Aaron asked.

Valor spotted Bohemia's broken butterfly bracelet on the floor and noticed it in a new light. Could the wings possibly be the initials E.B., the same initials Summoner Mamahchi had warned Valor about after he mentioned the spies who had once been loyal to O Enchantedness—the spies who went rogue or missing?

"Your name is not Bohemia, is it?" asked Valor. "Your initials are E.B. You were once a spy for O Enchantedness, weren't you?"

"Now they will listen, Sarapentez," Bohemia growled at her dead snake, which had managed to slither near her before turning on its backside. "Years and years ago, I was among the most powerful witches in Mystic Steeples. Urbanne knew that and sent me here. I convinced Mesthu I was a descendant of Chacodophilus. Ooo, Mesthu believed me when I performed magic and gave him an ancient talisman, which allowed him to steal the Fountain of Chacodophilus from Mystic Steeples. Hah!"

"So, why did Urbanne send you to the tower?" asked Valor.

"Oh, you know . . . you . . . know," said Bohemia as her head vibrated. "Gah, I love all this false naivety . . . to find out their secrets, their magic, their immortality. Oh, I am ever so good at secrets."

"I understand fully. Urbanne LaRock made you a vigilespion to spy on Mesthu," said Valor.

Bohemia rolled over on her back, eyes wild on her snake. "Mesthu gave me immortality," she said. "Wouldn't tell me how he did it. I didn't care; he had made me co-ruler. I hated Urbanne—hated him—so I was in no hurry to get those secrets for him. Can you blame me? I was having some wild times—you know about that, the boy they call the Knight of Night—first the primitives, now you've joined the Children of the Gloaming."

"Then why did you kill Mesthu?" Valor pressed, not bothering to refute her fanciful ideas with the dark mess his life had become.

"Gah, seems that way, doesn't it?" Bohemia said with a tear pausing on her cheek, but was it genuine? "Urbanne sent me a crystaleer, threatening to have me killed, so I kept pressing Mesthu—kept pressing him to reveal those secrets. But Mesthu said he revealed secrets to those whom he discovers, not those who discover him. I realized I was just his girlfriend of sorts." Bohemia paused. Her head turned from her dead snake as if emerging from a trance. "I didn't know what else to do, so I told Urbanne that, if he didn't leave me alone, I'd tell Mesthu what his agenda was—what the entire vespercestorial agenda was. But somebody killed Mesthu before I could tell him. I think, oh yeah, I think Urbanne was trying to frame me for the murder."

"So, Aurora is innocent?" asked Valor.

Bohemia appeared frightened. "I was being framed," she whined. "I was desperate to pin Mesthu's murder on someone, you see. I tricked Siobhan, and Mega D to lure you and Aaron here."

Aaron folded his arms and sucked in his cheeks. "Hence, you thought so fondly of us."

A knowing expression formed on Rose's face. "She wanted to show Urbanne that he held no power over her," she said.

Bohemia levitated, trying to escape the restraints, but Micha pulled her back to the floor.

"Oh, dear! Doomsy has Mesthu's ring," said Valor. "That was your plan, wasn't it, Bohemia? You knew if Mesthu's Children saw Aaron or me wearing Mesthu's ring, then his blood would be on our hands instead of yours."

Everyone seemed to wilt with that realization.

"I thought we had Bohemia under our control, but even now, she's working her guile on us," said Valor. His head rocked side to side as hard breath shot through his nostrils. The wall clock showed one hour remaining, and Doomsy hadn't returned. "I can't wait any longer. I'm going after Doomsy."

Bohemia conjured a kitchen knife from a drawer near the sink to levitate toward her.

"Oh, no, you don't," said Rose, grabbing the knife and returning it to the drawer. "We're taking you to the tower, and you're gonna confess to them."

"If they've caused any harm to Doomsy, I shall see to your detriment with delight," Aaron said to Bohemia. They grabbed her up and straightaway headed for Shadowhaven Heights.

Siobhan LeSabres

THROUGH THE DARK WOODS

NOT wishing to take any chances, Valor kept his distance from the others as they snaked through the dark woods behind the dilapidated ski lodges, carrying Bohemia. He couldn't allow his newfound craving for blood to cause him to attack again. Rose shoved a Dhupala Yecchy's Toilet-Tongued Taming Torch in Bohemia's mouth, and the wick ignited a flame.

"It won't taste like a toilet if you keep quiet," said Rose.

Bohemia hooked the back of her head on a log across the path and tensed her neck muscles. Micha untangled her hair and lifted her head.

"Too bad we don't have any Aunt Ditzy's Ever-Increasin' Grease ta put on her head," he said, carrying Bohemia by her right arm.

"Now, just so we understand one another," said Valor, after he stopped walking. "This was all of your decisions to abduct Bohemia and take her to the tower. I don't want anyone else accusing me of trying to kidnap anyone. I mean, who knows what they might do to her—"

"I guess me an' Rose deserved that," said Micha, as he and Rose exchanged guilty sentiments.

"What you deserve is Valor to never speak to you again," said Aaron, carrying Bohemia by her left arm.

"Guys, I hear something," said Rose, aiming her cat-o'-nine-tails to her right. "I don't know . . . I think it was a man."

While they looked around the dark forest, a humanoid came crashing through the underbrush and pounced on Valor. They rolled down a hill, and Valor sank his fangs into the side of the attacker's hairy neck. The new blood charging through Valor's body soothed every ache and ounce of tension until he tingled with an unnatural sense of ecstasy and empowerment. Even though Valor was a good bit shorter than the humanoid, he floated several yards up in the air, gripping its struggling body as though he were embracing a ragdoll.

Aaron took aim with his casting hand to defend Valor but paused when the humanoid stopped struggling. Valor could swear he had heard muffled pleas for help. Then, when the creature's growls softened to a defeated groan, foreign thoughts began to invade Valor's head as fast as the delicious new blood:

"Again? It cannot be—the utter trickery! Hear, O Universe: though death befalls this body tonight, these hands will not cause another death. My Knight of Night, do you not see, the curse that is the vampire?"

Rose looked on in horror, bringing her hands under her chin like a sleeping child.

Valor gaped down at them with pale blood dripping down his mouth. He dropped to the ground and pulled down the lower branches of a pixie parley pine to conceal himself, sending scores of pixies scrambling to the higher branches where other fairylike beings bounced on the pine tips, watching the scene with wide eyes.

"Wait, Valor! I think that's—I think that is Blade Zagato," squeaked Rose.

"What? That thing can't possibly be him," said Micha.

"Look at his clothes and his long black hair," added Rose.

Aaron released Bohemia's left arm and inspected the ground. "A clear sunstone fell out of this foul creature's pocket, just like the crystal Blade has. *Revelare tui idem*," he chanted, passing his left hand over the humanoid. Within seconds, the man's engorged face and neck began to shrink, and his skin began to appear where a thick covering of black fur had been.

"The identity-reveal spell worked. It *is* the old deserter!" said Micha.

Valor felt as if he were sinking into a wicked pit of quicksand. "Don't look! Don't look at what I've become."

"Calm yourself, my friend. Blade is still alive," said Aaron.

"Only because he is immortal," cried Valor.

"Don't worry, everybody. I think I can heal 'im up fast," said Micha.

While Aaron took over restraining Bohemia, Micha placed his left hand on Blade's neck bite and held it there. After several minutes, Blade sat up to gather his strength, and Micha rejoined the other.

"What, in the name of Medusa, did Blade say happened to him?" asked Rose, while Valor kept his distance.

"He said he tried ta follow Doomsy ta make sure she'd be okay an' all, but she cast a Repugnas spell on 'im ta make 'im look ugly," said Micha, with a snicker. "I told 'im, 'Ya can't blame any spell for that.' He said when he persisted in followin' Doomsy, she Bedazed 'im, and he got so confused he thought he was a werewolf."

Valor closed his eyes, thankful that he hadn't killed his friend: He glanced over at Blade, and oddly he seemed to be returning the same gratitude. Why was Blade not enraged? Valor dropped his head in his hands. He couldn't allow these attacks to continue—the one thing that was against his very nature was forcing its despicable sense of humor on him yet again.

They all continued toward Shadowhaven Heights, and Micha rushed over to help Blade after he began to wobble.

"The Zagato knows you want to keep touching his magnificence self, but he can walk on his own," said Blade, pushing Micha away.

"We thought you had abandoned us," Rose said to Blade. "You big softy. You care more about Doomsy than we thought."

"Amends won't find Zagato this day. There is no winning with her," huffed Blade, trying his best to make his legs move forward. "Let's change the subject—Micha surely would like to show you the wonders of his hands."

Micha shook his head with a snort of frustration, and Rose grinned at him before Candlewicke Coven continued in silence, except for the giggles and puffs of the pixies jingling like a mixture of chirping birds and tiny croaking frogs.

"Guys, how much farther do we have to carry this snake?" asked Rose, losing her grip on Bohemia's feet.

After several more yards, Aaron looked to the left where a bull elk stood in the embracing branches of a furry-barked fir tree. He held up his hand for everyone to stop moving, then approached the creature, whispering mystical words. He made a series of spidery hand movements that entranced the animal, bringing it under his control.

"Bring Bohemia—this beast shall carry her on its back, the parasite that she is," said Aaron.

"Good, 'cause we need ta be free ta defend ourselves," said Micha.

"Yeah, from me, you mean," said Valor bitterly. Thank goodness his friends were busying themselves with the elk instead of gawking at him. He was a monster even after he tried to clean the blood off his face. The images of himself feeding on blood replayed in his head like an endless nightmare.

"You and Blade position her upon the elk, and I shall bind her to its antlers," Aaron said to Micha, while Rose held Bohemia's arms. The spread of the elk's antlers reached up to eighty inches, dwarfing Bohemia.

Aaron maintained a hypnotic reign over the creature, and it moved at a steady pace between them. Bohemia had grown tired and ceased her struggle as her torn dress draped down the elk's long hairy neck. The crossing of dead trees over winding swamps, a foreboding nest of nature, signaled that they were near the tower.

"Shadowhaven Heights lies just over the hill," said Aaron, motioning ahead. The lemony shedding of freshly snapped porkypine limbs alarmed Valor's senses, but not soon enough. A swarm of witches dropped from the trees all around them, locking them in a circle of twelve.

This wouldn't be good, Valor was certain. Blade and Micha scurried to secure the bull elk by its horns. Bohemia's eyes bulged, rolling around in their sockets with fear. Her candle-gagged scream muffled into a dull gurgle in her throat. Blade and Micha whipped their free arms through the air like wands ready to strike, while Valor, Rose, and Aaron stood in a smaller circle, ready to defend themselves. Their morphing shadows resembled a bleak kaleidoscope.

"Oh, thank Chacodophilus, it's you guys!" someone behind them said.

"Creighton—what are you doing here?" asked Valor, as Rose and Micha eyed the remaining witches, looking for a familiar face to ease their tension. With relief, they greeted Salazants, Ruza, Nalini, and Stabbah, who emerged last from the shadows.

"We heard all the bad vibes that went down between you guys," replied Creighton, eyeing Valor with caution. "We had to make sure you—ah, who am I kidding? We had to come see what was going on in Diabolishire."

"It engaged our devotion, of course," said Salazants, one of Candlewicke's butlers, avoiding eye contact with Valor.

Still worried, Valor started to ask how Manning was doing, but Nalini Lusion locked her head toward Bohemia with a squeak. "I scarcely believe my eyes. Who do you have tied to the elk?" Nalini clutched a book to her heaving bosom. The lengthy sleeves of her medieval-style gown brushed over the patch of snow at her feet.

"Whoa! Wait a minute. Why have you done this to Bohemia?" yelled Mega D.

Micha loosened his grip on Bohemia. "I had my doubts about you and ya friend Bohemia here," he said to Mega D. "Now I know it was foresight, seein' she planned ta frame Aaron for murderin' Mesthu." Micha glanced back at the animal. "Go on. Go say hello to ya friend that just tried ta murder us."

"What?" gasped Mega D, moving about in his usual state of restlessness.

"It's true. We must go find Doomsy. She promised she'd be back from the tower by now," said Valor, massaging his throbbing forehead with the palm of his hand.

Siobhan LeSabres, the Sorcerer that Bohemia had used to lure Valor to Diabolishire, ignored Valor and moved out of the circle, lifted her billowing teal dress, and with a fling of her leg, soared through the air and landed in front of the bound, deceitful Sorcerer.

"With unwavering nobility, you assisted Mesthu. We trusted you, and you lied to us," said Siobhan. Mega D sprang to Siobhan's side, and Aaron showed them Bohemia's Triskelion.

"Her initials are E.B., and she confessed that she was once a vigilespion for Urbanne," said Aaron.

Using her sharp fingernails, Siobhan grabbed the pendant and shoved it in Bohemia's quivering face. Bohemia's neck arched, making her silver hair appear as if it were growing on the elk's head.

"Cursed companions! You mean you were with the Sanguinati all this time, Bohemia?" asked Siobhan. "I thought it odd. You just showed up out of nowhere and seemed to have a little too much knowledge about Mystic Steeples and that region. The vespercestors sent you here to spy on us, and from what it seems, kill us. I hope they entomb you in an iron coffin for this."

Mega D levitated four feet parallel to the ground and grabbed Siobhan by her shoulders. "You see it, eh? They'll never let us back in Shadowhaven Heights because of our rebellion." Siobhan pulled loose from his grip and sat down hard on the ground, kicking her boot into a patch of snow. Mega D floated over to her again and said, "I mean, couldn't you see the squiggly tail of deceit wiggling? Bohemia's a pig, eh. She'd be an outsider even among a herd of swine."

Valor explained to Mega D and Siobhan all that had happened before they had arrived. ". . . . Not that Bohemia hasn't done bad things in the past, perhaps," said Valor, "but she might be a victim of the Possessing that's been occurring lately."

While the others continued to interrogate Bohemia, Valor headed toward the tower. Salazants approached him and said. "Manning wanted to come, Master McRaven, but we couldn't leave Candlewicke Mansion unattended, and young Egg, of course."

"Manning's okay then? He's not mad at me?" asked Valor, trudging forward.

"Mad? Oh, not in the least, sir," replied Salazants. "Mistress Stabbah examined him and he appears to be his usual thick-headed self."

The tower came into view, and Aaron sighed. "I cannot believe our predicament has dragged everyone to this obscure belfry where even bats dare not land."

Valor lowered his voice. "Aaron, none of us wants you to be pulled into this trap. Please return to Candlewicke . . . they still might be after you."

"Ah, and you as well," said Aaron, moving closer to him with a smile. "But neither of us can do that because Doomsy hasn't returned."

Aaron now led the way to the tower. Candlewicke Coven seemed to fear the worst. But were Siobhan and Mega D moving with dread over the possibility of losing the home they'd had for centuries? Had their anger toward Bohemia motivated them to seek revenge, despite the consequence of death itself? Mega D and their company tagged behind with guarded expressions.

"The drawbridge won't let down for us," Siobhan informed the others when they had caught up to them at the tower. Valor had never seen anything like it. All around the tower, frogs, earthworms, and every sort of native creature was levitating a few feet above the landscape. Siobhan walked between the helpless creatures to the creek's edge and placed her hands on her temples. Was she trying to send a psychic message to Mesthu's Children?

"This is a bad omen. They have placed a barrier of protection around the tower." Aaron said to Siobhan, cringing as a three-headed lizard drifted past his shoulder. "They have to see us. One cannot overlook your crimson hair."

"The Infantem Infinitas must have everyone on high alert," said Mega D.

"The who?" asked Salazants. Like the others, his eyes scanned the tower, waiting for a sign of Doomsy.

"Razvio and Eolas, the Shadowhaven Heights guardians, eh," said Mega D. "They command the Vexillum Legatus, or what's left of their twenty-seven-member army. Let's remove Bohemia from the elk and float her over the moat, eh."

Mega D and three other witches held Bohemia high over their heads and, all at once, levitated over the waters of the creek while a few fishtails smacked them. The elk swam through the air among the Sorcerers before finding a free path beside Vesuvius, a female Sorcerer who had arrived with the others. The elk's left horn snagged the webbing that formed open swags down the side of her skin-tight bodysuit. Blood spurted from the gash across Vesuvius's ivory skin, before she wiped the gash away with her finger. Valor was able to look away from the blood and gave a sigh of relief.

The voices of Eolas and Razvio echoed through the grillwork of the massive tower door. "Declare your purpose or embrace oblivion."

"It's me, Siobhan LeSabres. We've captured Bohemia. She tricked us. She tricked everyone. And now she's confessed to trying to frame Aaron and Valor for Mesthu's death. She has a lot to declare, the creepin', croakin', toad she is." Siobhan whisked the velvety folds on the back of her dress, freeing it from the damp steps.

Only silence entertained the Sorcerers as they paced and waited. Just as Valor was beginning to panic, Razvio said, "Place Bohemia at the foot of the door and move back toward the drawbridge."

"Wait, Siobhan," said Valor. "Tell them we'll do as they request if they release Doomsy to us."

"I don't know if those terms will appease them. We must take whatever they offer. We can't manipulate them—Aurora, in particular." Siobhan strummed her nails against the ornate door, and her chin rested on the top of her ruched sleeve. Was she trying to pour herself back inside the tower entry, or was she embracing her old home for the last time?

"Those are my terms. I won't leave Stonevengeance without her," Valor said, joined by Aaron and Rose. Creighton twisted his fingers together nervously and hung beside Ruza and Nalini, who exchanged dark, silent looks at Mesthu's Children.

Through the door of the tower, Siobhan presented Valor's request to the twin guardians. Another long period of silence ensued. The scent of foggy sulfur wafted from the creek over statues and dead tree branches, engulfing the base of the tower, softening the distant howl of wolves and the singe of torches, which flickered against the old wet stones of the tower. The Sorcerers remained scattered across the nightscape under the fullness of the moon, as the swaying tree branches cast intense shadows over them. Valor froze. The third-story curtain of the tower had snatched closed, and a dark figure moved away. With a creaking noise, the drawbridge lowered. The irregular stones that supported the bridge flashed from the lightning of an approaching storm. The wolves ceased their howling, while the thunder began to shake the lower mountain valley.

"Everyone, move back across the bridge. We've made our petition known. Now let's await their decision," commanded Siobhan, squeezing out each sentence with a subtle vibration of pain. Her red hair waved like jellyfish tentacles in the strengthening winds. Creighton crossed back over the bridge first. Mega D ground his lips together, checking to see if Micha and Salazants needed help restraining Bohemia. Valor tried to calm himself, and while he blinked twice, Mega D reappeared by the drawbridge entry under the medallion of Master Mesthu, which now hung like a grave memorial.

"Please, don't let them take me. Let the lightning strike me—the storm I conjured for my punishment!" shrieked Bohemia.

A small boat emerged from behind the tower and floated upon the murky waters, drifting in Valor's direction. A shudder-inducing gush of grief assailed his body. Micha relinquished his grip on Bohemia, as he ran behind Valor.

"No! What have they done?" screamed Valor, running to the edge of the creek to see a tiny iron coffin in the boat. Blade and Salazants continued their grip on Bohemia, while Valor and Aaron jumped down into the boat. Grabbing the iron coffin, they lifted it to the embankment near the drawbridge. The thunder from the valley rippled up through the creek bed, further disturbing the surface of the water. Ruza, Rose, and Nalini tried to calm the storm while Stabbah lit a candle and began some type of spell on the rocky bank.

"They've sealed it solid; I can't open it. Doomsy, can you hear me?" cried Valor. No sound returned to his ear except his own pounding heart amid the threatening thunder. He ran back and pounded on the tower door: Because of its glossy luster, his fist slid off with each punch. "What have you done to Doomsy? I demand you tell me now!"

The twin guardians offered no response, so Valor levitated back to the iron coffin. He pulled out his monoculous, and many gasped and moved back. "It's worth a try," said Valor. He circled his monoculous around the coffin counterclockwise and chanted, "Recludo." The snapping of metal echoed and something else, something coming from the rocks at the coffin's edge.

"Oh indeed, Valor—seems you've been learning spells from Blade," said Aaron, gripping the waistband of his pants. "Your spell broke my belt and boot buckles."

"Perhaps he meant to," laughed Creighton.

Rose popped Creighton on his head with the handle of her cat-o'-nine-tails. With trembling hands and a visible pulse on his neck, Blade dropped down beside the iron coffin.

"Shut up and help me!" huffed Valor. He pulled fast at the coffin lid, but it remained sealed.

One of the Ashwins, Eolas perhaps, appeared on a small balcony above the main tower entry. "Give us Bohemia, and we shall break the seal on the coffin," he said. "Otherwise, this intrusion you have made upon Shadowhaven Heights will put you all in iron coffins."

"Judge Bohemia and not us," begged Siobhan.

Bohemia winced, while the unbolting wood-carved hands echoed around the door. Valor looked away after a series of pale fingers emerged from behind the tower door and latched hold of Bohemia. Her muffled screams made his flesh crawl. Boots crashed into the gravel on the creek bank while Valor pulled at the coffin lid. Its rusted edges appeared ancient, its worn details clammy and cold.

"Death to my soul!" said Aaron, dropping to his knees. "What a wicked verdict they have decreed." He yelled at the tower, "Release her from this iron monstrosity, you devils." His knee knocked against Valor's on the ground, and their collective arms pried at the coffin in all directions, but they couldn't find an opening or seam.

Before Valor knew what had hit him, something smacked him through the air, and he landed against the tower wall. The invisible force also knocked Aaron to the soggy bank of the moat flowing around the tower. Had the blow caused Valor to hallucinate? A Komodo dragon wearing spiky leather body armor wobbled toward the bank on its hind legs, using its tail for support. With a sickening laugh, its pink mouth swelled open, and its forked tongue protruded a couple of feet, tasting the air in his direction.

"You found the little shadesters did ya, Munchy? McRaven led me right to the Clandestine Chamber," cackled Tilta Crumpecker, patting the Komodo dragon on its belly as she aimed a crooked wand at the Sorcerers. She twisted the medallion on her hat and conjured Valor through the air and into her grip. He was still so weak and dizzy he couldn't resist, and the stench of garlic exuding off her battled for the shallow air barely reaching his lungs.

"Shall I eat 'im, Eebee? Shall I?" the dragon asked Crumpecker before hissing out another wicked laugh.

"Not yet, my wittle Munchy wunchy," Crumpecker replied to the dragon while she kept her wand aimed at Valor's head. "Not until they hand over the Clandestine Chamber they were trying to destroy." She shook Valor, tightening her arm under his throat. "You know that Chamber belongs to the Sanguinati."

"It's. Not. The Chamber," Valor choked as the storm continued, and worms and insects popped out of the ground and levitated upward into the air.

"Of course it is, boy. The map led you to it," said Crumpecker. Stretching her free arm toward the iron coffin, floating on the boat, she flicked her wand and chanted, "Procuriamo the Clandestine

Chamber!" but nothing happened.

Aaron stumbled to his feet while the rest of Candlewicke Coven stood ready to do battle. Eolas and Razvio emerged from the tower in their silver robes behind Aurora, who wore shades of blue: a stunning vision emerging from the bleak surroundings, backlit by the verdigris-tinged, scrollwork wall sconces on the tower entry.

"Valor and Aaron—argh! Yet again, you have endangered Shadowhaven Heights by giving away our location. You will not get your sister back. Infantem Infinitas, return the coffin to the tower now," Aurora yelled with thunderous authority at Razvio and Eolas.

"No, wait!" Valor shouted, while breaking free from Crumpecker's grip. "*Bedaze!*" he chanted, conjuring a likeness of Mars from the sky into his hand and flinging it at her before she could aim her wand at him again. Crumpecker's Komodo dragon leaped on Valor, ready to take a deadly bite out of him as a battle broke out across the tower's landscape. Someone from Candlewicke Coven cast a spell at the dragon, causing it to flip onto its back and off him. Valor pounced on Crumpecker and held his finger under his throat.

"All it will take is one swipe of my finger, and I'll be rid of you—rid of the years of torment you have caused Doomsy and me," he hissed.

"You wouldn't dare use the Afflictoswish spell on a high priestess!" Crumpecker gurgled.

"Wouldn't I, Crumpecker dear?" Valor began moving his finger across his throat, and Crumpecker thrashed about under him.

"No, please!" she cried. "I didn't know it was a coffin. I—I didn't trust you, I admit, but I can explain. It's—it's O Enchantedness . . . he's—he's not been himself lately—"

"That makes two of us!" growled Valor, while Sorcerers cast down attack spells from the windows of the tower. "But you are always the same—vile and wicked. So that is why I have no regret killing you." With rage drowning out his reserve, and his hunger for blood wearing on him, he forgot about his spell and bit into Crumpecker's neck. She shrieked, and he rolled off her into a patch of snow. This jarred him to his senses and to his feet only to find that Crumpecker had vanished along with her dragon Familiar. As Valor wiped her blood from his lip onto his sleeve, he spotted a male witch in a pointed hat, lurking behind a snow-covered rock on the edge of the mountain cliff.

Rose, Nalini, Ruza, and Stabbah stood in a circle guarding each other's backs, while a flock of ravens fell from the sky and landed fatally on the ground. Creighton's upper body draped over the edge of the riverbank while his legs splayed motionless on the bank.

Valor had to get to Creighton to see how critical he was, but the barrage of attack spells rained down from the tower, preventing him. From behind the protective stone of the arch near the drawbridge, Blade Zagato's penetrating gaze seemed to assure Valor that he could stop this bloody battle, or perhaps Blade was again putting thoughts into his head. Valor remembered the one thing that seemed to get the attention of the Sorcerers at Shadow Haven Heights, but he had never been able to conjure this weapon—this intrusion—at will.

Obeying a strange tingling urge, he lifted his arms close together in the air with his hands wide. Concentrating hard, he imagined he could feel *The Book of Chacodophilus* landing in his hands like an owl from the night sky. Would he make a fool of himself, if not risk lowering his defenses at such a volatile time? It must be working. He felt as though the Great Witch—Chacodophilus—was closer than he had ever been.

"Behold the one to whom the Great Witch has shown worthy to open his book!" Blade yelled up at the tower of Sorcerers as the book descended from the sky and landed in Valor's hands.

The fighting came to a stop, and everyone's attention focused on Valor. Unlike his past trips inside the book, he didn't feel the pages drawing him to the past; instead, he felt empowered to let the book use him as its mouthpiece:

"My people, I, the grand and powerful Chacodophilus, never got the chance to sacrifice my heart in order to give life to this book—so that I alone could control it in death. At the time, I was selfishly trying to preserve what little of my heart I had left. I had already lost my family, my kingdom, my friends, and my identity. I regret I never gave what was left of my heart—that opportunity was stolen from me. And this is how you honor me? Fighting one another instead of the evil that is trying to kill all of us," yelled Valor, feeling as though he were Chacodophilus in the flesh.

"McRaven is a charlatan. That book he has is a fake! If Chacodophilus doesn't control his own book, then who does?" yelled a male Sorcerer from a third-story window of the tower. He aimed his hand down toward Valor and cast a spell, but dozens of ghostlike arms branched out the human-skin cover of *The Book of Chacodophilus* and propelled the attack spell back to him. The Sorcerer froze, and one by one, bits of him crumbled from the window to the ground below. The hand he used to cast the spell landed at Aurora Vontiki's feet.

Aurora lost all expression on her face as she gazed at the shattered hand at her feet. "Stop the fighting now. Stop it!" she said without raising her head.

Guardians Razvio and Eolas lifted their hands in a plea to cease fighting, and they each walked over to Valor and stood on either side of him. Aurora seemed stunned at this move.

"WHAT IS THIS?" snorted a female Sorcerer from a window eleven stories high. "Our Infantem Infinitas has betrayed us for those who live among the primitives."

"I have reason to believe that the Grim Warlock is causing us to turn on one another. The same way he is trying to control this book." Valor lifted *The Book of Chacodophilus*, and several Sorcerers scattered. "Whether you choose to believe in the 13th Hour or the Possessing even, it has already been affecting people. Besides, you now have the one who betrayed you—Doomsy is innocent, and I will not leave here until you release her," said Valor.

Rose and the others checked on Creighton, who was sitting up and rubbing his ribs with a pained expression. Valor left the protective company Razvio and Eolas had provided him and dashed to the edge of the creek once again when he saw the tiny iron coffin returning in the boat.

Razvio appeared beside Valor, took a rune, and placed it over an embossed seal on the iron lid. He floated back alongside his twin, Eolas, as a series of clicking sounds released the seal on the coffin. Aaron and Valor rushed to remove the lid, joined by Rose and Stabbah. Like a tiny corpse, Doomsy's pale skin seemed waxy and deflated, further emphasizing her skeletal face.

"How long has she been in there?" asked Salazants in a sorrowful tone.

"I don't know," said Valor, placing his hand upon her cold forehead. Her eyes sprung open wide, and his rib muscles contracted.

Doomsy gasped for air and said, "You should've left me here, my pet. Then you would be free of me."

"What did you tell them?" asked Valor. He lifted her stiff little body out of the coffin. Her left boot slipped off her foot and fell onto the sandy bank littered with dead leaves and insects. Creighton grabbed the boot by its silver buckle and slid it back on her foot.

"I told them I killed Mesthu," replied Doomsy. "I even flashed his ring, convincing them of such."

Creighton jumped back in shock. "Now that's just loony, Dooms," he said.

"My wretched core! You offered yourself to an eternity in an iron coffin to protect Valor and me?" asked Aaron. His chest heaved, and the tip of his tongue licked a tear from his upper lip. He turned his face from the others.

"Don't go getting all leaky-eyed over my decision, my pet. I've ruined Valor's life as it is," said Doomsy as her voice cracked.

With all the reserve he could gather to avoid feasting on blood, Valor pulled her little hand up and kissed it. "You have not ruined my life, my dear."

Blade Zagato safely removed Doomsy's hand from Valor's mouth.

"Your friend has completed the ultimate sacrifice, and returned Mesthu's ring," said Aurora, gliding toward Doomsy. "Never have I seen such a chivalrous deed in all my centuries." She held out the ring in a sterling silver box lined with black velvet. "Doomsy, considering the evidence, I have decided to release you."

"Thank you," Valor said with relief. "I'm certain Siobhan, Mega

D, and the others meant no harm. They were just confused and upset over Mesthu's death and everything."

"I assume this 'Possessing,' as you say, caused their rebellion," said Aurora with a slight frown at Valor. "I'm not so sure everything can be blamed on the Grim Warlock. We all choose our actions."

"I agree," said Valor, "but something has been affecting the animals and insects as well, and how much free will does a wasp have? I don't have the answers, my dear. No magic crystals—no mindreading—is that reliable for me to judge the suffering, and we shouldn't isolate ourselves from them."

Aurora removed Mesthu's ring from the box and tried it on her largest finger. "As the new leader of Shadowhaven Heights, I must maintain priorities, McRaven. The Children of the Enlightened must not become tainted by the Children of the Gloaming or the primitives who are content in their deception."

The Infantem Infinitas seemed to be sending Aurora scolding thoughts before they spoke in unison: "Master Mesthu was not the Knight of Night. That awareness penetrated your consciousness, Aurora. Mesthu wanted the title, but the responsibility was far beneath him."

Aurora sighed, then took Mesthu's ring and placed it on Valor's middle finger.

"They're pardoned this time. I'm giving you the ring in faith that you are the Knight of Night," said Aurora before leaning in close to Valor's ear. "If you put it on your magic wand, it'll strengthen its power beyond all comprehension. You must do it when no other option remains." She stepped back and addressed everyone. "Bohemia will stand trial for her deceptions, and we will find Mesthu's killer. Now, I'd like to extend an offer to you all to rest here before you leave."

Aurora cut her icy eyes at Rose and Ruza while her fingertips lingered on Aaron's arm.

"And, ahem, Aaron, since I am the leader here now," said Aurora, "I think I might consider reinstating you into Shadowhaven Heights. You can reclimb the tower of wisdom and rejoin the rightfully ruled.

You can become a rock of strength in our pillars and never roll through the mire of this world's petty problems."

Aaron's lips formed a contemplative smile. Was he thrilled at the prospect of returning to his old home and friends?

Candlewicke Coven cast concerned glances at one another except for Creighton, who elbowed Aaron. "Oh wow, Aaron! You get to go back home to this. I can't imagine what I could learn—mind-reading and all."

Aaron patted Creighton on his back. He liked to touch his friends, perhaps to remind them of their potential in the coven of Candlewicke, Valor imagined. Or, was he just reminding Creighton of where his loyalties should remain?

Spotting Aurora looking down her nose at Creighton, he wiped his hand on his coat and shook hands with her before gaping up at the magnificent tower. "Shooting stars! I can't imagine never having to worry about anything. I feel loads better just shaking Aurora's hand."

Aaron, too, gazed longingly up at the tower. He offered a faint nod, as though agreeing with Creighton's assessment. He took Aurora's hand and kissed her signet ring.

"Thank you, milady. I can think of no other thing that would bring me happiness than to remain in Mystic City with my new friends. Therefore, I must refuse your kind offer."

CHAPTER TWELVE

VALOR BECOMES NOCTURNAL

NERVES had calmed a bit at Candlewicke. Valor knew Doomsy, Rose, and Micha felt responsible for his condition, and they were trying their best to hide their fear of him. In fact, Candlewicke Coven pretended not to notice various apprentices gawking at the changes in Valor. They were all surer than ever that High Priestess Tilta Crumpecker was the Conjuring Crone, the female sidekick to the Grim Warlock. If that were so, then O Enchantedness might very well be the Grim Warlock. But it didn't make sense: The Warlock and Crone were supposed to be the leaders of the Hermetic Order of the Mystic Key, which Valor now knew was the namesake of the strange little key Falmoth had forced Valor to swallow before he became a vampire. Of course, the superstitious Sanguinati Elite was the originator of these Grim Warlock fables and perilous Thirteenth Hour prophecies, so could the predictions even be trusted?

Aaron and Doomsy eased open the door to the windowless bathroom where Valor struggled to sleep while brooding over everything that had happened as he reclined in the double-slipper cast-iron bathtub. He pulled a heavy blanket over himself, which puddled all the way to the marble-tile floor, near the tub's brass-claw feet. He dreamed he had found Booger Fay, but Valor had been so distraught, after discovering he had become a vampire, he forgot to ask Falmoth if he was going to hand the Elusive Griffin over to him, or would Valor have to find his Familiar in the Necromanceropolis by himself?

Doomsy eased the blanket from the porcelain tub as if she were disturbing a strange creature's nest.

"Um, Valor, wake up," she said. "We found a place on the outskirts of Severance where we might be able to get you a coffin to sleep in."

"*Humph*, I dunno," yawned Valor. "The Vesper-testers outlawed coffins. I'll prolly sleep in dis, *humph*, tub thingy."

"You can't. It's too cramped, and you're starting to walk hunched over already. I might have a vampire for a brother now, but I'll not have a hunchbacked insomniac." Doomsy bent over, staggering and groaning like a zombie.

"Okay, okay, I'll get a coffin, and then I can be buried in it," said Valor.

"What do you mean?" asked Doomsy.

"I have to meet with O Enchantedness this evening and tell him I didn't get his grandson for him," sighed Valor. "And I expect once Crumpecker shows him the fang holes I left in her neck, they'll have me executed! I mean, just look at me. Everyone will know I'm a vam—I'm a vam—"

He looked in the mirror above the bathroom sink, still feeling disconnected from his new spooky appearance.

"Maybe nobody'll notice if they only see you in the dark," assured Doomsy. "This funeral home called Plantation Shores will let us buy a coffin after hours. That way, nobody will see us."

Aaron put on some leather gloves and unrolled a small parchment. "Venerious Falmoth sent you a message, by way of a foul vampire bat I might add. It says: 'Dear valiantly vulnerable Valor: lest you forget, you may become more sensitive to the sun. Of our Order, it happened to some. I must regrettably say they risk death itself if they as much as look out of a window during the day. You may have a tolerance for the sun, as few have done, but this can change, so mind your fangs.'"

"Lots of bats were flying around the door last night. They left you these funny-looking candies on our doorstep, along with bat poop that Manning is cleaning up," said Doomsy, dumping a pile of candy in the bathroom sink.

"Luminous Lulling Lozenges—jolly good," said Valor. He unwrapped the candy and crammed it in his mouth. "Eeh elfs ops uhn cwazin."

"What?" Doomsy made a pinched face.

"I do believe Valor said, 'An elf's pop's gone crazy.' One can never tell with this new generation's vocabulary," said Aaron. "Perhaps it is some secret Noctivatian slang."

Valor spat out the candy. "It helps stop my cravings?" he said, feeling relieved.

"Oh—your blood cravings," said Doomsy.

"Aw, don't say that. Do you have to be so crass about it?" said Valor, making a pouty face. Aaron looked at him as if he were a different person than he had come to know.

Salazants took Valor and Doomsy by carriage out of Mystic City, down Loopity Loop, the crazy coiling roads of Severance, then headed across the river to the city of Squibthistle. On the sluggish road, littered with scarecrows and bouquets of fake flowers, they parked the carriage and walked up to the old funeral home sandwiched between rows of dark, clapboard-style buildings. Birds nested in the letters of the sign on the marquee, but they scattered when a toy-like sculpture of an undertaker holding a shovel popped up on the marquee and said in a dragging voice, "Welcome to Plantation Shores. Where will your resting place be when your time is no more?"

They pulled open the casket-lid double doors and went inside the main lobby.

"Ah, yes, I understand," the director whispered behind the palm of his hand after Doomsy announced what they wanted. They eased down a carpeted hall as a violinist played for four blind guests, and a minister stood behind a coffin reading to the dead. Valor crossed and uncrossed his arms. He had never disturbed a funeral visitation before, and he wasn't sure he had ever been in a funeral home, especially a Nizzertit funeral home.

Doomsy skirted past the hand-locked mourners as they leaned over the girl's casket, placing a delicate wreath of carnations upon her head.

"Poor girl was about your age," the director whispered to Doomsy.

"The iron coffin Mesthu's Children put me in looks more impressive than hers," said Doomsy. Valor cupped his hand over her mouth to silence her. The director's expression sank.

"What happened to her—the poor girl back there?" Valor asked to distract from Doomsy's comment.

"She heard voices . . . went mad," whispered the director. "Her family said she'd been getting messages from some man who convinced her that she was a witch and that he needed her to help him find some lost objects. Dug holes all over her neighborhood and school playground. And when the moon was full, she tried to fly a broom off the top of a cliff only to fall to her death."

"How awful. She believed some man she never even saw?" asked Valor.

The director nodded sadly. "Apparently, he convinced the girl that nobody was more qualified than he was to spot a potential witch—told her that she could get in a prestigious coven if she found any of the objects. Of course, my hearing isn't what it used to be." He lit a candelabra and placed a crucifix over his neck. "The light in the showroom is dim," he whispered. "I have a hard time seeing the price tags. You go ahead down the stairs, and I'll follow you."

The director stood at a distance while they went down into the basement he called "the showroom," an ember-lit cremation room below the earth's surface.

"We'll take this body box here," said Doomsy, spotting the most ornate coffin front and center.

Valor still didn't want to sleep in a coffin, but he didn't wish to make a return trip any time soon. "I'm not making any promises that I'll sleep in that thing, Doomsy," he whispered.

Valor paid the funeral attendants extra to load the coffin into the carriage. The attendants placed it in the back and offered their condolences.

"My poor brother would've wanted it this way, wouldn't you, Valor?" asked Doomsy, pretending to wipe a tear with her lace hanky as she cut her eyes at Valor, watching him shrink behind the carriage curtains.

Salazants commanded the centaurs forward with a snap, and the carriage didn't slow down until he got them back to Candlewicke Mansion unharmed.

"I guess Falmoth was right." Valor yawned, trying to keep his eyes open. "I'm only going to get any sleep in a coffin. The Hermetic Order wants me to keep attending Mystic Steeples. But I don't know how I'll attend my assemblies if I have to start sleeping during the day," he said as Manning, Salazants, Aaron, and Blade rested the coffin in the grand hall.

"I don't know either. I'll turn on the gas lights at midnight, and perhaps we can meet for dinner once in a while," said Aaron.

"I refuse to become nocturnal," said Valor, as they maneuvered his coffin down the long winding halls. They continued past doorways topped with carved medallions of various imps gazing left and right until Valor arrived at his bedroom, where they placed the coffin at the foot of his bed.

"I ain't gonna try and tell Master McRaven 'no' ever again—no sir," said Manning, taking shelter behind Salazants as the others came in Valor's room to see his new coffin.

"Yes, it's the least cruddy Nockie box they had to offer," said Doomsy.

"It's somewhat—" Nalini paused, biting her lower lip in a troubled smile. "It's got nice carvings, I guess."

As expected, Aaron gravitated to the details. "Rather true, Nalini," he said. "'Tis fine rosewood. If you look closer at the carvings, you'll find loons—you must have thought of us when you saw it, Valor?" Aaron lifted it open to have a look. "Ah . . . lined with burgundy tufted pillows." He caressed the plush velvet. "You'll rest in luxuriant peace, dear friend."

Valor wasn't sure it would cradle him in deep solace the way he suggested.

Ruza jumped into the coffin and reclined flat like a corpse. "I picture it just this way—like being in the trunk of a carriage," she said, folding her hand over her upper body.

"Stop it. You're desecrating Val's bed," said Micha. "I have a deep respect for . . . for—"

"I'm not dead!" said Valor. He swallowed hard, for he had never felt so close to death.

Ruza looked up at Valor's sunken eyes and messy hair and said, "Coulda fooled me."

"Respect? There's nothing to respect about Noctivatians," hissed Blade, shifting his posture. "Zagato is with Aaron on this. He would have kicked Valor's butt to keep him from joining that blood-guzzling Order."

"But you didn't, Blade. You didn't stop Valor," said Ruza, climbing out of the coffin.

"Zagato was under the impression the Knight of Night would never side with Falmoth," said Blade. "Zagato has grown weary of trying to persuade the masses. Free will. Everyone must grow up and learn to live with their decisions." Blade smirked at Doomsy and tilted her hat over her eyes. "No matter how blinded they were to the consequences."

Ruza gave Doomsy a sympathetic glance before growling at Blade, "Blinded! Blade Zagato, the problem with you is—"

"Pardon me for interrupting," said Salazants, before exiting the bedroom. "Manning and I have spent two days closing curtains in Candlewicke, and until we finish, I'd imagine the window sheers will diffuse the sunlight should Master McRaven enter any unchecked room."

"Thanks," said Valor, lowering his eyes.

"I couldn't become a Nockie. It's so depressing in this place now," grumbled Creighton. He didn't gel down his wavy hair for a change, so this made his face appear softer. "Can't we just let a little light dance through the lace curtains?"

"No. Noctivatians can fry just from standing too close to a firefly," laughed Blade.

"What is all this stuff, my pet?" Doomsy asked Rose while helping her unpack a box she brought into the room. Her hostility toward Blade seemed to have softened a bit, or perhaps she was feeling guilty after attacking him with two spells near Shadowhaven Heights.

"Coffin accessories," answered Rose. "I've done my research. Get in, Valor. I want to show you something."

Valor climbed inside the coffin, and Rose began to close the lid. "What if the lid won't open? Nobody will hear me call for help," he said with a slight panic.

"That's why I found you this at Déjà vu Antiques," said Rose. The sleeves of her dress hung to the ground like folds in a curtain as she rang a little bell. "Ring-a-ding. Sulk, O grave, and know all is well. For tonight this scaredy-cat sleeps with a tolling bell."

"What am I supposed to do—sleep with a cowbell, Rose?" asked Valor.

"You now hold in your hands a genuine coffin bell. Give me your finger," said Rose. "See? The Nizzertits used to tie the end of this ribbon to the fingers of their dead loved ones." She made a hard knot with the black ribbon around Valor's finger. She held her arms out, mimicking a zombie before speaking with a growl: "Just ring this bell if you awake six-feet in a grave and your nearest and dearest remember your deeds and ignore your screams." Her voice returned to normal, and she gave the ribbon a hard tug. "If you prefer, I can tie some bells to your toes . . . like the twirlyurgy wear?"

"Indeed not. This is daft." Valor sat up in the coffin with a snap.

"No-no," said Rose, pushing him back down against the soft velvet and "padding" his coffin with crimson rose petals, which she poured from a box. "It's the least I can do since I'm partly responsible for you becoming a vam—uh, I mean Noctivatian. Just chant this when you get scared: 'With this coffin bell, sleep I shall embrace, lest I awake impaled, and the bell has been displaced." Rose stabbed her magic wand over her heart like a wooden stake before sounding the bell with a pull of the ribbon.

"Ooo, you have an immortality wreath," said Doomsy, stroking the delicate wax calla lily protruding from Rose's accessory box.

Rose closed the lid, encasing Valor inside the coffin where he could barely hear her conversation:

"Yeah," she said, "I collect jewelry and memento mori from bygone relatives, but they've all gone bye-bye now. So, I made this immortality wreath from my keepsakes just for Valor. Now take this end of the ribbon, Doomsy, and help me tie the wreath to the lid."

Valor heard the grandfather clock scream and sob: Another precious hour had perished, so he flung open the lid. "Thanks. I imagine we'll need lots more flowers . . . I have to leave for my meeting with O Enchantedness."

After double-checking his Sanguinati Triskelion and coven ring, the guardians finally let Valor inside the doors of Mystic Steeples. Apprentices cleared a path as he climbed ten stories to the highest floor of the citadel and knocked on the head vespercestor's door. A dwarf let him inside, and Valor navigated the shifting floor tiles until he reached one of the guest chairs in front of the lavish desk. Urbanne poked Valor on the tip of his nose was a sun rook rune, which adorned the tip of Urbanne's magic staff, but his ring with the same adornment was still missing from his wrinkled finger.

"Hide your eyes, O ye Ancients!" growled Urbanne, gawking at Valor with raised brows over his galaxy glasses. "Who are you, and what are you doing in my office?"

Valor was sure the tingling caused by the power of the staff was making his hair stick up worse than it had been. He shoved the magic weapon away from his face. "It's me, Valor McRaven. I . . . have a rougher and tougher image now. I'm sure you're delighted . . . you *finally* made a man of me."

Urbanne's body faintly spasmed while choking on a response.

"Where have you put him? He shouldn't be too hard to miss," said Urbanne, slamming a collapsing magiscope between his hands. Valor realized the head vespercestor must've been watching for his grandson out of his gallery windows that overlooked all of Severance. As usual, the stars and planets appeared within arm's reach from this high viewpoint. Valor decided to play confused to give himself time to come up with a better excuse than he had.

"Where have I put whom, O Enchantedness?"

"I assume you are bringing good news since you insisted on meeting me this late in the day, McLaten," said Urbanne, leaning away from his desk in his evening robe and hat of Mystic purple.

Valor stiffened in his chair while the dwarves around the wall munched biscuits as though they were watching a sporting event in full action.

"Lest you waste more of my time: Where. Is. My. Grandthing, Valor McRaven? High Priestess Crumpecker said you tried to help him escape when you could've brought him safely to me."

Valor explained how the map Urbanne had given him had led him to the Tombstone Forest and how he and his friends had rescued his grandson from an ice hole. But Valor was dreading repeating what Venerious Falmoth insisted he say to Urbanne, so he decided to try with a bit of ingenuity.

". . . And after the high priestess left, sir—well, the poor giant looked as though he—"

"As though he what?" growled Urbanne.

"As though he had swallowed a cow and died. We couldn't disturb the poor giant in that state, sir. Now could we?"

Speechless, Urbanne's eyes widened, and he slowly latched his fingers together under his stubbly chin, as if he remembered his prediction about his grandson.

"Sir," said Valor. "There is something that troubles me about the high priestess—"

"As it should. She told me you attacked her, and for that, there will be some manner of punishment, McVanguard. You must never attack your seniors, especially a member of Minister Mystery."

"You mean Mystic Ministry? But she attacked me first," said Valor, and he was sure he saw Urbanne's hands trembling.

"Which reminds me of what I need to tell you, McMerlin. You must guard this secret with your life." Urbanne leaned over his desk and continued: "High Priestess Crumpecker has been my top vigilespion for several years, though you have made that secret hard to keep with all your accusations toward her." Urbanne slammed his trembling arms on his desk, knocking over a magic hourglass. "You made it look as though I've been covering for a serial killer—bringing more negative attention on us than we can tolerate."

Urbanne waved his wand, conjuring Valor across the desk where he slammed his hands onto Valor's shoulders and squeezed the fabric of his coat.

"You will stop it, you hear, McRayburn? Stop it!" Urbanne growled and panted as he shook him.

Crumpecker—a vigilespion? A spy for O Enchantedness? Valor couldn't believe his ears. "But I saw her steal the Staff of Gleaning—"

"You saw her inspecting the crime scene *after* the Staff was stolen, McRaven." Urbanne released his grip on Valor, and once they both sat back down, he continued in a calmer tone. "Crumpecker used a special magic staff that can trace any prior magic used at the scene of the crime. Alas, it failed to find anything."

Valor's heart was racing inside his ribcage. Urbanne had to be lying for her. "Well, what did she bury in the garden behind the sanatorium then—her spyglass?" he asked.

"Human bones," answered Urbanne, and the dwarves' heads snapped toward the head vespercestor in horror.

"Human bones?" gasped Valor, remembering when he had dug up the two-faced skull.

"Sacrificial, yes. Until you found the Horn of Taurus in the Garden of Herbal Delights, the Garden required a human sacrifice to keep the plants on the earth from withering away and being replaced by poison apple trees. We thought we could fool the curse by burying bones from miscreants and those who died outside the status of the Sanguinati Elite. So, we occasionally took bones from the catacombs and buried them in the Garden. It wasn't the same as traditional human sacrifice, and the Garden seemed to know it. But it slowed the spread of the curse. You did a dangerous thing digging up some of those bones as I recall. You probably brought a curse upon yourself. But you did well, digging up the Horn of Taurus. This is why we need you, McRaven. You obviously have a vigilespion soul. Watch, therefore, your treatment of High Priestess Crumpecker. You two must get along and start working together."

Valor braced himself for another attack, but he couldn't help himself.

"You want me to report back to you, but then you don't believe me, O Enchantedness. I know what I saw," huffed Valor. "It didn't surprise me that Crumpecker would try to kill me because she has tried before. But if she didn't steal Spirit's Staff of Gleaning, then why did she hide it on her roof? If the Staff were just a common flagpole, she wouldn't have used a vanishing spell on it."

"I spoke to the high priestess about that, McRaisin. I agree with her: if it really was the Staff of Gleaning on her roof, then the Grim Warlock planted it there to incriminate her."

"But why?" asked Valor.

Again, Urbanne gripped Valor's shoulders and shook him. "Why? Because you publicly accused her of stealing the Staff and being the Conjuring Crone. The Grim Warlock knows; he sees everything going on. Stop giving him ideas. Stop!"

Valor flew backward into the chair, which scooted several feet before coming to a stop on a traveling floor tile that began carrying him around the room.

The dwarves' heads followed Valor with stunned and eager eyes. Though there were still plenty of awful incidences Valor had experience with Crumpecker, he dare not risk Urbanne's wrath, and he dare not risk embarrassing himself further.

When the tile had turned Valor away from the desk, Valor asked, "Why does she hate me, O Enchantedness?"

Urbanne ordered the dwarves to pull Valor's chair back to its usual position facing him.

"If it seems that way, McRaven, I suspect it's because somebody planted the Staff on her roof," said Urbanne, clearing his throat. "It might explain why she became meaner with time. The Grim Warlock was using the Staff to affect her. I've had *my* issues with her—fired her as my vigilespion twice. Shortly after news of your mother's pregnancy reached the public, Crumpecker was caught spying on Lithium, and your mother raised such a stink, I was forced to demote Crumpecker from a vigilespion to head magister of the sanatorium. Considering your mother, Lithium, was still under suspicion for poisoning you, just as her mother tried to kill her, I appeased Crumpecker by letting her do a little spy work at the sanatorium— keeping an eye on you and little Moodsy Doozy. Therefore, will I say this, McRaven." Urbanne made a creepy attempt at a smile. "I don't think High Priestess Crumpecker is warm and fuzzy toward anybody. However, she did seem fond of Genola, your late grandmother. And I do believe she still meets with Genola's mother, Lockie, on occasion."

"Why did Genola try to kill my mother?" asked Valor, finding this all rather suspicious.

"Oh, that's been so long ago, I don't remember the pacifics," said Urbanne, but Valor knew Urbanne meant to say "specifics."

"If I'm your vigilespion, why have I never been to the Sanguinati Intelligence Agency?"

"You're too young for the SIA. You need to prove yourself with me, and only me, McRaven. And you must learn to get along with High Priestess Thumbcracker and stop bringing unwanted attention to us."

"But Crumpecker—"

"And no more complaining!" Urbanne slammed his fist on his desk.

Valor left Urbanne's office. This was not in a million years what he had expected Urbanne to confess about Crumpecker. Could he ever bring himself to report back to the head vespercestor again? And how much difference would it make to report to Summoner Mamahchi about Crumpecker when the high priestess was over him—when she domineered the summoner actually? There was only one thing to do now—what Venerious Falmoth sent him back to Mystic Steeples to do: work for the Hermetic Order and convince the Sanguinati that their ancestors were all Sorcerers at some point. Valor let out a nervous laugh and bit his tongue. How in the River Styx would that work when the Sanguinati didn't believe him that they were performing ghost magic instead of real magic? And how would the Hermetic Order "provide him a safe haven" if he did what he was told when Falmoth wasn't even permitted to enter Mystic Steeples?

CHAPTER THIRTEEN

Aves Treacle

TOE BONES AND TAROT DOORS

NIGHTTIME came and went fast. Valor had slept well except for the occasional anguishing screams of a phantom. Easing away from daylight, the inevitable life of a Noctivatian had resurrected him as the thing he feared—a vampire. His stomach now churned from his thirst for blood, or maybe it was just nerves, he tried to convince himself as he prepared for his morning assembly. Would his fellow apprentices soon discover his new secret?

"Do all vampires use enchanted powder to keep from burning to a crisp?" asked Rose, applying some of her enchanted powder to his already pale skin.

"Aw, don't say that word," groaned Valor, while Blade and Ruza entered Valor's bedroom.

"Sorry," Rose giggled. "I mean *Noctivatian*."

Valor frowned. No matter how much he tried to neaten his hair, it returned to a windblown mess, and though he tried to smile, his face appeared sinister and sunken.

"You Nockies are such grim cads," said Creighton, smacking on a wad of Floaty Bubble. "Looks like you have grave soil on your eyes and cheeks. I heard some Nockies iron out their dimples. I'll bet they did that to you, Val."

Doomsy barged between them and opened a black umbrella that had tiny skulls hanging like tassels around its perimeter. "Here," she said. "Just hide behind this, and nobody'll notice. But, just in case the sun still bothers you, I also brought an assortment of veils." Doomsy ripped three black lace veils out of her conjure bag and tossed them over Valor's head and shoulders. "You'll look good in a veil, my pet."

"Not hardly, dear," said Valor pulling off the veils and looking through his monoculous wand at his horrid reflection in his dresser mirror. "I should just stay at home, but I can't; Falmoth expects me to work for the Order inside Mystic Steeples."

"Surely, you don't still believe that clown—that monster?" asked Aaron.

"I have no other choice now, do I? At least not until we find out who the Grim Warlock is and stop the 13th Hour," said Valor to their uncertain faces.

"Have you got any new leads to the Staff of Gleaning?" asked Rose.

"I'm not sure," said Valor. "I read in *Zoe Mack's Zodiac Almanac* that Spirit can only communicate to a similar element, meaning matters of Spirit can only be influenced by spirit. Since someone bound Spirit's physical body on Earth, what if he can communicate with someone who is on the border between death and life?"

"Brilliant," said Aaron.

"What are you getting at?" asked Creighton, after a sheet of his chewing gum exploded on his face.

"It means only someone on their deathbed can communicate with Spirit to find out where his missing Staff of Gleaning is," said Stabbah.

Ruza sprang up from the dresser drawers and grabbed Valor's arm so that the tip of his monoculous wand aimed at her stomach. "Perfect! Hex me with something fatal. Go ahead."

"Stop it!" Valor wrestled his wand and arm away from her and tried to gain control of his racing adrenaline. Ruza attempted the same thing with Blade Zagato, who snatched his hand away as well.

"You really must stop poisoning yourself with self-destructive thoughts, my dear. You have your whole life ahead of you—we all do," said Valor, glancing purposefully at Creighton as well.

"Indeed," added Aaron. "Besides, we need thirteen members, or our entire coven will be at risk."

"Wake. Up! It's robbery—it's murder! Besides robbing me of eternal glory, the death of billions will be on your hands. You all need to open your pretty little eyes and see not all of us are meant for some field-of-daisies, happy-ever-after, fairytale crap." Ruza adjusted her blanket of dark wavy hair away from her bejeweled eyepatch and poised herself on the edge of Valor's dresser drawers. "I'm totally cool with reality," she purred.

"No one is going to sacrifice themselves for something we're not sure will even work," said Valor.

"You do all the time, my pet," said Doomsy.

"That's—that's different. Anyway, we need to go, or we'll be late for our assemblies." Valor could think of no other way to change the conversation.

Since they all shared Runecraft Assembly under Magister Teena Ibizelda, Salazants took Valor, Creighton, and Ruza in the carriage to Mystic Steeples. He dropped them off at the interior entry called Obli Gate. The canopy of weeping wishtearia sprinkled them with tears, and the statues lining the garden shuddered at the sight of Valor. When they came near the Den of Divination, people began to accumulate in the halls to gawk at Valor. He covered his ears to block out the screeching while they pressed through a bunch of apprentices in white robes.

"Looks like half of Warlocks' Bane just saw me," said Valor. "Unless they're screaming their spells now."

"They hate warlocks. What did you expect—to sign more autographs?" asked Ruza.

Creighton conjured a warped picture frame to levitate around Valor's head and shoulders, before he shouted, "Check McRaven out, you wand whackers! Gitchi Patootie's Bewitching Beauties' manly makeover of the week. He's sporting the 'Dismal Kimball' . . . the new look for men of discriminating taste all across Severance."

With Creighton making such a spectacle of him, Valor doubled his pace to a near jog through the winding Hall of Mourning. He rounded the corner and paused near a veiled woman kneeling in front of a portrait of a young man who resembled Valor.

"Dear, dear, Willoughby, rise from the dead, come back to Mama," the woman pleaded. Her teary eyes lit up, and she threw herself onto Valor's legs. "Oh, Willoughby, Willoughby, you've returned!"

Valor cringed. What could he say to the poor mother? He leaned through the gold-plated picture frame as it levitated in front of him and patted her on the head.

"Uh, yes, I returned. But now I have to go," said Valor. He pulled free of her and ran as fast as he could up the escalating stairs of Tannimanis Tower, to the eighth floor of Buckthorn Hall.

"*Ugh*. Something crawled on McRaven and died," heckled Marston Diamone, heading to Runecraft Assembly as well.

"Is it contagious?" asked Twila, strutting behind her brother, Marston. With snarls softening into smiles, the siblings elbowed each other and nodded at Creighton.

"Hi, Creighton!" said Marston. "The annual Diamone Family Appreciation Dinner is tomorrow. Why don't you lose those friends of yours and come celebrate with us? Lots of important people will be there."

"Your parents will be getting a big mention from our father," Twila said to Creighton while blushing.

"Gee, really?" said Creighton, before cutting his eyes nervously at Valor and Ruza beside him. "Thanks, but I, uh, I have a cauldron-ton of studying to do."

"*Eww* . . . . Talk about 'something died.' McRaven done caused yo hair bows to kill over," said Hanzabuh Cuddy, carrying Twila's books for her. She tightened and fluffed Twila's countless hair, hat, and dress bows.

"Don't touch me," said Twila, dodging her fingers. "McRaven has infected your hand with whatever he's contracted."

Hanzabuh lifted her left hand and gaped at one of the many rings wedged between the flesh of her fingers. "Momma made me dipping chunklins for breakfast. I musta got some stuck under my fate ring." Hanzabuh looked at the stone in her ring. "My ring done turned black. McRaven's bound ta be hexing me. Here ya go, Chiggers." She flicked a piece of chunklins to her squirrel hiding in the hole in her pointed hat.

"When did the Diamones take a liking to you?" Valor asked Creighton, finding the change a bit disturbing.

Creighton shrugged. "My family has a few merits, Val. Lay off me, will ya?"

"Careful, Creigh. The Diamones will try to wear you like a poison ring on their middle fingers," added Ruza. Her six-inch boot heels whipped between the long slit in the back of her black dress as she sashayed past them. She then squeezed her wild mane of hair through the door of Runecraft Assembly, which every apprentice entered by sliding a series of runes, built into the door, to form their own secret entry word.

Using a rune with the image of a fish-goat and runes engraved with the witches' alphabet, Valor slid the runes across the door until he spelled out the words "Capricorn Rising." Every time he entered the S-shaped room, he had a hard time finding his desk, for the room contained an explosion of symbols and runes incorporated into every inch of its architecture. Sculpted hieroglyphs, stacked sixty-feet high, served as columns to the vaults, which segmented the stained glass windows, creating a spider-webbed effect. Valor, Ruza, and Creighton weaved through the wrought iron and stone partitions, which led over a suspension bridge. Ruza pointed to her left, at a gallery topped with a pediment, where stone runes spelled out Middle Balcony 22.

"There's our balcony—the one with the monument to Gaggarts Guismo VII crowing the top," she said.

"I'll never master Runecraft," said Valor. "We have to decode and learn every single rune in this room."

"You miss too many assemblies," said Ruza, sitting on a slab that served as part of the encrypted architecture. "Too busy getting into trouble! Whop you on the head with a photographic-memory spell—somebody should. That way, you'll finish with the rest of us."

"I guess so," agreed Valor. "Magister Ibizelda's hardly ever here to show us how to decode anything." Careful not to let a sunray stick his bottom, Valor sat between Creighton and Ruza, straddling an iron sun disk that protruded from the arched wall behind him.

"Ibizelda showed up for a few minutes last month," said Creighton, looking down from the balcony. With a wave of his hand, he moved an ironwork railing to block Marston and Twila's path, as they headed to a balcony at the back of the winding room. "She said the runes would let her know of any 'trouble' with us apprentices." Creighton gave a roguish smirk. "Not so much, right?" He sat down and angled his magiscope to inspect the artifacts lining the base of a low-dipping bridge. Ruza opened a thick and noisy book to the witches' alphabet and began making notes with her Plume of Phoenix.

"Symbolic vomit," said Ruza. "Magister Ibizelda swears there're enough hidden runes in this room to reveal something that could shake the foundation of Mystic Steeples. But it looks like a giant puked out a million cans of Ramble's Rune Soup."

"I'll bet it's what Falmoth told us—the Sanguinati's secret Sorcerer origins. What else could it be?" whispered Valor.

Ruza tossed her hair to the side, drawing the usual attention to herself. "Lots of secrets. Some are saying Ibizelda's trying to uncover some zinger of a secret encoded in the oldest runes around Usabelli's Square and Illusions Plaza. The vespercestors won't allow her, but she's doing it anyway. Child, don't you know I would?"

The magister's balcony began its serpentine travel over the room, startling the apprentices.

"Magical morning, Apprentices of the Runes. This was probably encrypted in the walls, but I have found, concealed in these columns, some ancient bone-dice runes," said Magister Ibizelda, holding up a ritual plate with the dice. "We're going to perform an ancient form of divination called Toe Bone Rolling, historically known as what?"

"Cleromancy," shouted Twila over a few other apprentices.

Ibizelda's balcony moved by its wrought-iron suspension past Middle Balcony 22. She stretched as tall as her short frame could in her spiraled, conical hat and angular dress, using her arms like compass needles, as her traveling platform moved beside a beveled wall. She ran her fingers over the elaborate engravings, counting the sequence of ancient scripts.

"Didja know these very walls are trying to—*AH-CHOO!*" Ibizelda sneezed, "speak to us—reveal their dark secrets." She aligned herself using arm measurements, and she tapped each foot twice before the platform moved farther overhead. "And that's what I believe is gonna happen this morning. I need some toe-bone rollers—anybody?"

Twila Diamone leaned over her balcony and said, "Me! I'm certain I can scry with toe bones. I mean, so far, I have scored spellbinding *S.C.R.A.T.C.H.* marks on my *C.A.T. P.A.W.s* in Runecraft."

Valor began to feel nauseated. How could anyone use bones to predict anything?

"I heard Twila made spellbinding marks on toilet paper as well," hissed Ruza, slumping back onto Valor as if exasperated with Twila; her right leg extended over her left knee. Valor leaned away from her.

"You know it's not safe to get close to me," Valor reminded her, but she shrugged with a chuckle.

"Yes, I am aware of your test performances, Twila. But as the notorious Webbits Cobbratz always said, 'There's always a little *rune* for improvement,'" said Ibizelda. The angular lines of black powder around her eyes appeared more clownish as she moved on her balcony around the middle of the room. Twila adjusted the bows on her sleeves as if every eye were admiring her. Then she reached into the ritual plate and took the toe bones.

Ibizelda removed a different rune from her pocket, placed it in the center of her mouth, and mumbled, "The runes showed me how to taste their hidden knowledge. And didja know, they actually keep me from sneezing?"

"I'm not going to have to put these disgusting things in my mouth, am I?" asked Twila, snarling her nose and frowning at the toe bones in her hand.

Ibizelda appeared affronted by Twila's question. "Runology is an esoteric craft," she said. "You can't truly be a master unless you do what it takes to learn every rune's secrets. Now roll those dice on your tongue and spit them out on this plate."

Twila looked over at Marston, who was also snarling. She drew her hands to her mouth and shuddered before plopping the toe bones back on the ritual plate.

"I—I can't," said Twila. "I, um, have a sore tongue. Magister Fox makes me sing too many solos in the choir. I'm his best soloist, you know?"

"Sore tongue? Are you certain it's not from lying?" yelled Ruza Renata.

The apprentices quaked with laughter. Twila shot Ruza a deadly glare before acting angelic again.

"But I do sense something from these bones," said Twila. "I think Valor McRaven should put them in *his* mouth. The vibrations are telling me that he can decode the dice."

"Yeah, McRaven does seem in touch with death today," said Marston.

Ibizelda looked up at the glyphs in the arched ceiling in a melancholy manner. She measured a precise turn with her arms before gazing at Valor.

"I think the runes are showing me the same thing," said Ibizelda, as the platform glided back toward Middle Balcony 22.

Valor swallowed with apprehension at having to put some dead person's toes in his mouth, and even more considering how dusty and brittle-edged they were, sprinkled across the plate. But he needed higher *S.C.R.A.T.C.H.* marks on his *C.A.T. P.A.W.s*, and more than that, he didn't want the Diamones to have the satisfaction of seeing him turn down the challenge. Careful not to expose his fangs, he popped the toe-bone runes in his mouth. He wanted to gag but forced himself to appear calm.

"Rune-tastic, Valor! Now, roll them around on your tongue, and use all your senses to let the dice communicate to you," said Ibizelda. She activated a lever on her platform, hoisting, on a chain, an iron-moon rune into the hands of the Lilith statue. The hands compressed the spherical moon into a crescent shape. This activated hundreds of runes, which toppled in sequence until the last one prompted a sun sigil to rise, exposing a hidden passage in the middle of the wall. A female dwarf walked out onto a ledge, pushing a pyramid-shaped container on a wheeled pedestal.

"Tidbits," Magister Ibizelda called to the dwarf, "tell the apprentices what Valor McRaven could win if he scries the toe bones correctly."

Tidbits pushed the brim of her tall pointed hat away from her eyes and unveiled a pretty iron rune displayed on a stand surrounded by a halo of burning candles. "The decoder of this toe bones challenge will receive from Mystic Steeples' very own Den of Divination, the Sanguinati Souvenir of Shame."

The apprentices applauded.

Tidbits continued describing the prize with more enthusiasm: "Handcrafted of pure alloy metal, this is a certified replica of the rune Venerious Falmoth once decoded in this very room."

"Thank you, Tidbits," said Ibizelda. "Valor, didja know Falmoth refused to heed the rune's warning that he would lose his head vespercestor's position and always be subservient? Runes are far more than symbols or letters in the witches' alphabet. They are magical divination tools so powerful they can resurrect the dead."

"*Mumph*—" Valor almost choked, trying to answer her while rolling the rough bones around on his tongue. His head and arms began to twitch and tingle while everyone leaned over the balconies, watching him as if he would fall over dead.

Ibizelda's balcony paused in front of a wall with moving runes of the witches' alphabet. "Rune-tastic!" she cheered. "Now, Valor, when you feel a message coming, let the dice drop out of your mouth onto the plate."

"*Mum-mumph*," Valor mumbled before wondering: Could there be a more perfect time to tell the Sanguinati that they came from Sorcerer ancestry—to tell them the truth about their ghost magic? All he had to do was pretend the toe runes had revealed the secret the magister claimed would shake the foundation of Mystic Steeples.

Before Valor could go through with his plan, his body seemed to become lighter. His heart fluttered in his throat as if something were trying to put him in a trance and force him to speak aloud. He pressed the toe bones against the roof of his mouth, afraid of what was trying to twist his words, until the vibrations in his throat and burning in his chest intensified, and he could hold it in no longer. He spat out two of the bones and, to his horror, Ambergis LaRock's voice tore from his mouth, "Nervous as I drop dice—"

Ibizelda waved her wand, and the rune tiles moved around on the wall, spelling out his first five words. Then, as if realizing something were missing, she rotated her feet to face him. "Don't be nervous, Valor. Relax and tell me what happens when you drop the dice?"

Valor gripped the balcony railing. Was he being possessed again? Ambergis would rip his throat open if he didn't finish the sentence, so he spat out the remainder of the bone dice into the plate and said, "A coded souvenir rips!"

He gasped for air as the strange sensations left him. Ibizelda conjured ghosts to spell out the last four words of Valor's rune revelation on the wall tiles. Tidbits continued motioning to the Sanguinati Souvenir of Shame until it shook off the display stand and split in half. Tidbits fell on her rump, and the apprentices erupted in a buzz of gossipy chatter. What the hex had Valor just said to everyone? He read the message on the rune tiles.

Ruza furrowed her brow and twirled a strand of her hair as if dazed by the voice and message that had come out of Valor. Creighton, however, turned his attention under the table where he flicked a piece of lint off his boot. Magister Ibizelda inspected the Souvenir of Shame, now in two pieces in her hands.

"This is rune-ific! Didja see that, apprentices?" asked the magister. "Valor channeled a female entity using the bones. But never have I seen a decoded rune trigger the cracking of another." She held the two pieces up for everyone to view. "That powerful female entity wanted me to know a clue was hidden in this souvenir. It prompted me to pick Valor, the very mouthpiece through whom she would speak. No, it wasn't a coincidence." Ibizelda grinned. "Just when I was starting to doubt myself, she let me know I'm in tune with the vibrational energies of the runes."

"Maybe that was Valor's real voice, Magister Ibizelda. I mean, he's finally decided to show us what he really looks like," said Twila.

Valor was glad his new ghostly complexion couldn't show him blushing. "The entity was Ambergis LaRock. I don't think—"

"We aren't supposed to channel anybody but the Ancients," said Marston Diamone so fast he teetered on his balcony. "Valor's possessed by Ambergis LaRock—a cursed spirit. She never crossed over because she married a wicked shadow tosser who cut her in half just like she split this country down the middle with the Ambergis Divide. My father's seen her bloody legs walking in front of Candlewicke Mansion, where Valor and his secret coven live. No telling what unlawful deeds go on in there."

"That's not true," said Valor. "A Sorcerer didn't split her in half; it was jealousy between two sisters. Banzalta Drayn cursed Ambergis and turned her baby into a giant."

Twila's eyes seemed to fill with poisonous delight with her brother's accusations, and she puckered her lips as though she were stifling a devious laugh.

"My brother's right; Valor's possessed by someone," said Twila.

"O Enchantedness will be furious when he finds out McRaven invited the Grim Warlock to take over this assembly."

Marston and Hanzabuh patted Twila on her back. Ruza Renata rolled her eyes with suave disgust as she stretched out beside Valor with a mocking smile.

"That's barking mad!" yelled Ruza. "Your tongue's not too sore from spitting threats, is it, Twila? Jumping around over there like some poodle with all your bows and back-patters."

"Every bow I wear represents a vespercestor's award I've received for perfect *C.A.T. P.A.W.s*, unlike you, unruly Ruza," said Twila, turning her nose up with a self-satisfied smile. "And I demand we have a pantomage in here next time so they can interpret if a spirit is legal or not."

"Ambergis was a LaRock, you silly kids," Ibizelda said to the Diamone siblings. "A legend has given us a sign. But Valor did not conjure her on purpose. The Toe Bones triggered her manifestation. They must've been Ambergis's bones. It makes perfect sense. She is showing us the power of two, or a dual nature perhaps. She was ripped in half, and so she jinxed Valor's souvenir to rip in half— something more to the clues she left. Perhaps we can help her cross over to the astral plane."

Ibizelda gave the Souvenir of Shame to Valor. The gong indicated lunchtime, so the apprentices rushed through mazes of architecture toward the Hall of Consumption. Valor was queasy and did not eat much. All he could think about was Ambergis's toes in his mouth, her stomach ripping in half, and the awful accusations Twila and Marston had made. Why were the Diamones so spiteful toward him? It must be that he made them miserable somehow. Valor moaned with satisfaction, sipping through a straw the bloody juice from his diced twice bison, which he had ordered raw in the food line.

"My pet," whispered Doomsy, snapping her fingers. "Ease away from the straw. You'll thank me later."

Valor had to force his lips from the straw only to discover several apprentices on the third-story balcony of the dining hall were gawking and whispering about his odd eating behavior. Had he jeopardized himself in front of everyone? His heart rattled. The Hall of Consumption had never been so quiet. No clanking of forks and spoons against plates. No shuffling of food trays and chairs. No lunchtime chatter or sea of movement to make him less conspicuous.

"Bravo, my friend," laughed Aaron, standing up and clapping. "You wanted to see if they would notice your performance. I think this *proves* you have what it takes to join the theater."

The entire lunchroom was now gawking at Valor.

"I appreciate your effort, Aaron, but it isn't working," whispered Valor. "Maybe now I should tell everyone what Falmoth wanted me to reveal. After all, I've already made a spectacle of myself." Valor tried to keep his chin from quivering as he stood up from his chair.

"No," said Aaron, snatching at Valor until he wobbled.

"Um, now that I have everybody's attention, I have something to say," shouted Valor, while Candlewicke Coven looked on in horror. Bits of food became airborne. Valor had no time to dodge a large glob of chicken lumpkins that splattered in his face. Marston Diamone strutted forward in the crowd, wiping the green lumpkins off his fingers onto Harwin Hollapolk's gold robe. Valor turned to face Marston.

Harwin tapped his wand against his palm and snarled, "What, Ravin' McRaven? Are you going to kill more innocent people or channel another cursed spirit?"

"You've all been tricked by the vespercestors," said Valor, wiping the lumpkins off his face. "Sorcerers—the witches you despise and fear—the Sanguinati used to be."

Some laughed, and others choked on their food. The rest of the witches resumed screaming insults while throwing food at Valor. Stargazer Zeferen Siam pushed through the ganging apprentices with his magic staff.

"Why that's just what a shameful free-floater would say," growled Zeferen while Summoner Eelias Mamahchi walked over to Valor's table and began inspecting his food. "Perhaps it's a sign of the Possessing," continued Zeferen. "I already predicted, astrologically, that McRaven's delusions would turn to madness by the time

Capricorn rises."

On the ground floor, Bessbadora Breeches began dancing on the magisters' long table. She moaned in much the same manner as Valor had done earlier, followed by Orby Underkofler, and Ratzy Pummels on top of their tables. Doomsy placed a stuffed mouse on the floor and tapped it with her wand, multiplying it into thousands of mice, which went scurrying across the hexagram-shaped dining hall. Everywhere, apprentices, Mystic Ministry, and workers climbed up on their tables and hurled their plates and silverware at the rodents.

"Order!" roared Summoner Mamahchi. He released the bronzed pigeon medallion from the crest of his blackthorn staff. The pigeon flew through the air and blocked Zeferen from charging after Valor. "Somebody put a Barmy Charm in the diced twice bison."

High Priestess Tilta Crumpecker plowed through the crowd and grabbed the plate of bison from Mamahchi's grip. "No wonder everybody's acting like nutters," said Crumpecker. "I'll take this to Magister Tripp and have it examined."

The gong rang, and the apprentices jumped off the tables and rushed to their afternoon assemblies, stepping over the scurrying mice.

"Can ya give us more warnin' next time ya plan ta get yaself killed, Val?" huffed Micha DeMise. He grabbed his magic staff from his wardrobe, one of many suits of armor in a chamber leading to the Magic Staff Usage Assembly. Like the other apprentices of Magister Dearth Downdilly, Micha brandished his staff and began casting spells to deflect dozens of wooden staffs that thrust out of the walls. The barricading weapons knocked several apprentices back toward the beginning of the hall while Micha trudged through the maze, dodging and smacking staffs that swiped down from the ceiling and poked up through the floor.

"My dear, I'd rather risk death for the truth than from trying to get to my next assembly," replied Valor, while Micha fought his way through the last half of the chamber.

"'We were all Sorcerers,' he says. What a load of dragon dung," laughed Dharma of Donny-Dale-Dharma Thelastone, the conjoined triplets. Her two brothers to her right agreed while acting possessed.

"Come on," said Doomsy, prodding Valor up a staircase tower of Buckthorn Hall with her wand. "Let's get to Divinatory Arts before you make another scene."

"What's this? What's the matter with you, McRaven?" asked Thorn Corvus, the owner of the Velvet Lilith nightclub, blocking Valor on the stairs. His hands fluttered around Valor's hair and face before shoving his chest. "Is this your idea of a prank to mess up any progress we Sorcerers have made?"

Valor grabbed Thorn's wrists and sank his fingernails into his flesh, drawing specks of pale blood. Thorn winced in shock. *One long bite of this smug traitor was surely justifiable,* Valor debated in his head, as his hunger reached its peak. He released his grip: Something in his heart was preventing him from retaliation. How much longer would that part of his former self have its way before he was free to punish—free to do what he was convinced he must?

"I don't know," growled Valor. "Why don't you help Mystic Ministry find the real Sorcerers since you are so good at saving your own hide."

Thorn stepped aside. "Your aura is black, babes," he yelled as Valor and his friends continued up the stairs.

"Yeah? Well, perhaps you should watch what you say about me then," Valor yelled in return, while Aaron's appearance sank noticeably.

"My friend, do not misunderstand me; I am pleased that you are shedding your insecurities. Nevertheless, are we to leave all our memories of yesterday in the process?" asked Aaron, glancing around as if expecting more apprentices to pounce on them.

Aaron's words jolted through Valor. He didn't know exactly what Aaron was implying or how to respond. Why was Valor's responses or actions never good enough?

"That's my brother." Doomsy punched Valor with more pride than he had ever seen in her.

Valor continued ahead of Aaron and Doomsy to Divinatory Hall, where a series of seventy-eight tarot doors lined the walls on both sides. All along the walls, apprentices stood contemplating which door best represented their mood, fate, or state of mind.

"Careful entering the correct tarot door, McRaven. I mean, you being possessed and all," said Harwin Hollapolk. "You don't want to risk terrible misfortune, a hex, or even death like you and your friends did to my father."

"We didn't do anything to your father," hissed Valor.

"Just ignore him, my pet," said Doomsy, examining each door, while several apprentices circled the hall, and some groaned and whimpered over their agonizing decisions.

"That was rather ill-mannered," said Aaron with a tone of guilt now. "Generally, I take the Magician's Passage. Perhaps, like Valor, I should venture by way of the Passage of Justice."

"That's not good enough," said Valor. "The door has to match your feelings, at least."

It was too late. Aaron had already walked straight through the card that depicted Justice holding a sword in one hand and balance scales in the other.

"What's wrong with you all? There's nothing to this. Just take any stupid door," said Banastre Mathers to the apprentices remaining in the hall.

"No, you can't just take any door. The only tarot door that doesn't lead to Divinations is the Thirteenth Major Arcana—Death," said Chantilda Hagborn, the Spurgmulin aerowachee for Mystic Steeples. "Only the Grim Warlock has cheated Death. Only he has accessed Divination Arts through that passage."

"Allegedly. But Death would be better than some of these other doors if it's not the right choice," said Valor, worried sick about Aaron. Harwin Hollapolk made a glum face at that remark.

"You all are nervous Nizzertits," said Banastre, entering through a tarot door, and his severed head shot out into the hall. Only his long brown dreadlocks supported his screaming head, crawling between the apprentices' feet like a tarantula.

"I'm pissed and ready to fight. I'm taking the Seven of Wands door," said Doomsy, hiking up her skirt and walking through the card depicting a man brandishing a wand while six other wands pointed at him.

Valor was trying to internalize his anger again. He needed to be alert at all times. One tarot door kept pulling his attention—the Four of Cups. Was it the passage he should he take? He didn't want to end up like Octovia Augusta with a perpetual thundercloud over his head and butt cheeks on his face. He held his breath and walked through the passage with the image of a boy sitting under a tree on a mountain, gazing at three golden chalices while unaware that, from a cloud of smoke, a hand was offering him a fourth cup.

It was now dark, and Valor was facing three passages inside the tarot doorway. Which one should he select? There must be a fourth alternative, just like in the card on the door he had entered—an alternative the boy didn't seem to notice. Maybe the dark wall to Valor's right wasn't what it seemed. He pushed his hand into the wall, and his body followed until he came through a hidden door into a room with curtained-marquee booths. Wooden stages lit up by rows of colorful candles and glowing-orb footlights. Valor had made it to the Assembly of Divinations, which thankfully remained darkened during the day. He roamed around the assembly and grabbed one of the magiscopes on a tripod aimed at the astrological dome in the ceiling. Never mind the galaxy, where were Doomsy and Aaron? He panned the magiscope around the sprawling room, zooming past walls and marquee tapestries featuring faded old paintings of mystical symbols, glyphs, and creepy eyeballs staring back at him. He was able to breathe once he spotted Doomsy and Aaron alive and waiting for him.

"We all made it; I'm terribly relieved," he said after he caught up with them.

"No thanks to Magister Treacle," said Doomsy, pointing to the front of the assembly as they ambled to their seats.

"What do you expect for a hundred-and-twenty-year-old witch?" asked Valor.

Under a golden arched ceiling, surrounded by curio cabinets and reliquaries filled with mysterious divination tools, Magister Aves

Treacle reclined in his ornately carved chair as if asleep. His gray hair fell in deep-set waves, which framed the upper part of his face, while his gray beard draped down his chest until the bushy ends rested in his lap.

"He's always been that way . . . had many failures in his early practice," said Doomsy with drawn-in cheeks. "He didn't watch after his three children either—reminds me of Blade Zagato."

"I never heard him mention children," said Aaron, as they inched past a wonderland of curiosities playing both sparkling and eerie music.

"He did once," said Doomsy darkly. "He claimed they ran away from home. But the apprentices say his children got permanently lost—took the wrong tarot door because he didn't have time for them. His wife—gone, too."

"Don't say the tarot doors got Jaunita Treacle, my dear," said Valor. "I think she left because Aves collected too many insect specimens—butterflies and moths, to be exact. It's sad. I believe he *was* just 'trying to fill their home with love and joy.'"

"I lost my brother again," said Doomsy, sticking her bottom lip out at Valor.

They all jumped as hands popped out of tiny doors beckoning them to enter the booths. On the many stages in the room, antlered monkeys banged tambourhorns and gongs, while animated marionettes and fortunetellers demanded their attention.

"I think you're a bit prejudiced toward Treacle, Doomsy dear. With gossip like that, no wonder he is often unbearable and bitter," said Valor.

"The man does exaggerate," said Aaron. "And his attempts to appear gentle are nothing short of strange."

"I'm not prejudiced. But Stabbah says Treacle used to have terrible prejudices and a temper. He's spent all these years practicing Dreamcraft to avoid his responsibilities." Doomsy scowled up at the magister, still dreaming in his chair as he always did before he had to begin his duties.

"Not all men are bad, my dear. Maybe it's the poor chap's way of holding on to memories of his family," said Valor, determined to retain some semblance of his old self—salvage the last bit of his compassion toward people who didn't deserve it. He darted in the shade between the beams of light pouring in through the lofty stained glass windows depicting spooky scenes of divination. Aaron took his seat beside Doomsy and him in a curtained booth with a round table in the center.

"I heard he has been this way ever since the vespercestors banned crystal balls," said Aaron. "Just look at him up there. Years of Astrology have left the man's head in the clouds."

"Yikes, Magister Treacle! Wharton Dashwood didn't make it through his tarot door," cried Chickie Baby, reaching down at the base of the door and picking up Wharton's boots. "Just his shoes came through."

Treacle blinked his eyes open and gasped, "Oh my! You could knock me over with a Plume of Phoenix. I was just having a fond visit with some people I love deeply. But I'm afraid there's nothing we can do for Dashwood. The poor fellow wasn't in tune with himself tarot-logically. Too bad, too . . . , under-fourth apprentice this year. Anybody get any money, any fortunes in the tarot passages?" asked Treacle, grabbing a magiscope from a cabinet beside his chair, placing it against his bushy brow, and scanning the apprentices.

"Young man—what's your name?" asked Treacle, pointing to a curtained booth in the right-center of the room.

"Harwin Hollapolk, sir," said Harwin, leering at Valor and Doomsy, who were sitting two tables up from him.

"Well, somebody, poke me with a chika bristle. *Harwin*. Yes, of course, I perceived you," said Treacle, standing up with a curious squint. "Come up here on the platform, Hollapolk."

Harwin pushed his spectacles to his cold but drowsy eyes and brooded all the way up to the stage. Magister Treacle grabbed him by the shoulders and turned him around to face the apprentices. "If you beginner Diviners will look up this way, you'll notice what appears to be a glob of ectoplasm on Harwin's robe."

Squirming, Harwin looked down at the silvery gelatinous goo on his gold Graven Dust robe, while Magister Treacle kept a firm grip on his shoulders.

"It's not ectoplasm. I'm not a filthy Sorcerer," snarled Harwin.

"A good demonstration of radiesthesia might just blow our minds, Hollapolk," said Treacle. "You see, beginner diviners, by using this powerful form of divination, we can use our bodies' vibrational fields to soak in information about the most inanimate object: soak it all in like a thirsty elephant by a lake." Treacle looked at Harwin's robe and took a deep sniff. "Even forbidden substances such as you see here, dripping down Harwin's robe like an iceberg in the desert. Don't think these old eyes can't see. It's the inner eye—the eye we must strengthen."

Harwin collapsed back into the magister's long beard and said, "You're bonkers, old man. Wait'll my Mumsy hears about this!"

"If your father were still alive, he would birth a goring rahfalus if he found that ectoplasm on your robe," said Treacle.

"My Dadsy would be alive if Valor and his friends there hadn't murdered him," roared Harwin, pointing toward their tent. He held his fingers to his temples as if he could read minds, followed by a rattle of whispers and scrutiny.

"We can divine that after this ectoplasm here," said Treacle. He pulled a gemstone pendulum from his pocket and let it swing in front of the suspicious substance on Harwin's robe. His face lengthened with fright, watching the stone swing by its chain as it channeled their energies, seeking the source of the goo.

Doomsy exchanged eager glances with Aaron and Valor, standing on tiptoes as if hoping Harwin would learn his lesson for being mean to others. "Excuse me, Magister Treacle," she said, "but I'm having a hard time seeing the demonstration."

"It's Miss Gloomsy, is it?" asked Treacle, straining to see her with his magiscope.

"In all my ominousness," said Doomsy.

"Well, Miss Gloomsy, that's why short people are in greater need to learn to use their inner-eye," said Treacle. He stopped the pendulum and grabbed his wand. "When all forms of divination fail, witches can always grab the old wand. *Plaformicus Giddyupus*," he chanted.

After a loud fizzle, two muscular ghosts flew through the curtains, where a wooden belly dancer held a scrying mirror while gyrating on a stage. The ghosts lifted Doomsy's chair and pulled her up through the air, ripping a hole overhead in their booth. The ghosts didn't stop lifting her chair until she rose so high her head crashed through the astrological glass dome in the ceiling.

"Put me down, you boot-licking ghosts," Doomsy shouted.

"Ghosts?" repeated Chantilda Hagborn, screwing her face in a snarky manner and sharing her mockery with Harwin Hollapolk, who remained on the platform. "The girl sees ghosts. Unless she's divining her own death."

The apprentices collapsed on their tables with laughter. Harwin pulled the collar of his robe over his head, wiggled his fingers in the air, and moaned, "*Boo.*"

Magister Treacle's wand balanced motionless on the tip of his index finger. "There are no ghosts in my assembly," he said.

Doomsy snatched off her squashed hat and leaned over her high, dangling chair. "You ham-fisted gorilla thumb," she growled at Magister Treacle. "I said I couldn't see, not that I was contagious. Now get me down!"

"I, uh, misdivined," mumbled Treacle. "You are sending out so many negative frequencies. It could choke a dragon." Treacle pointed his now wobbly wand at Doomsy again and chanted, "Uh, *Plaformicus Cascadeus.*"

As the ghosts lowered Doomsy to the marble floor, a beam of sunlight came down over Valor's head, along with shards of galactic glass. He snatched a section of the deep-blue curtain over him, fearing the sunbeam might cause him to turn to ash. He peeked out to see the apprentices gawking at him with more suspicion than ever.

"Stupid magister," spat Doomsy, popping the dents out of her hat and rubbing her head. "He's not even fit to lead an assembly at Grossatete Sanatorium."

Through his magiscope, Treacle watched Doomsy rubbing her head. "My poor child," he mumbled. "That's why you need to develop your intuition; you're an over-thinker. It's caused a bruise on your head the size of Hoopenfangia." He waved his wand a third time and chanted, "*Mummiform Artus.*"

Again, ghosts floated through the room, but this time they wrapped a never-ending bandage around Doomsy's head until she began to resemble a mummy, and she staggered under the weight of the restraining gauze. Valor and Aaron snatched the winding bandage from the ghosts and set about unwrapping Doomsy, who groaned and fussed until, at last, everyone could see her furious face again.

"Just leave the bump on my head, and keep your spells off of me," snorted Doomsy.

Magister Treacle lowered his magiscope, and the bags under his eyes drooped. He resumed his radiesthesia on Harwin, who snickered at Doomsy's distress until the pendulum vibrated over his robe. With a snap, the pendulum pulled hard on the chain and aimed toward Harwin's left coat pocket under his robe.

"This pendulum's hot on something—hot as a firewalker passed out on the sun." Treacle reached into Harwin's pocket and pulled out a necklace of slimy black beads.

"See, I told you it wasn't ectoplasm on my shirt," snarled Harwin.

"What is this slimy mess you have strung on a string here—gargoyle eyeballs?" asked Treacle, dropping the necklace on the platform and wiping his hands on Harwin's robe sleeve.

"A cooked olive garland," said Harwin with an air of achieved revenge. "I was wearing it before I got safely to my next assembly. It predicts the presence of shadow tossers like Doomsy, Valor, and Aaron . . . and repels them."

"Predicts and repels them, does it?" asked Magister Treacle.

"Duh! Everybody knows olives represent purity and peace, something those scummy Sorcerers drain from the air we breathe," snarled Harwin. "That's why olive-tree wands are used in spells to counteract poison and venom attacks. Olive oil is the main ingredient in Auravitamax, the hot new aura tonic Summoner Mamahchi created."

"It's true," said Garnilla Hollapolk, Harwin's sister, standing up in her red Snuffinumbra robe. "Mumsy says if Harwin's aura gets any brighter, he might go blind."

"Well, Harwin, let's see if what you say is true," said Magister Treacle, pointing to the olive garland. "Go ahead; pick it up."

Harwin picked up the garland and said, "Whenever it predicts shadesters, it oozes on my shirt, because Sorcerers' dark energy drains the sacred oil from olives," he added before Magister Treacle called for Valor, Aaron, and Doomsy to join them on the stage.

"Is it true," whispered Valor. "Will that olive thing repel us?"

"Pure poppycock," said Aaron, while they eased around the tented booths.

Doomsy crammed her hat on her head and stomped up the steps to the stage. "Harwin Hollapolk, you had better hope those stupid olives repel me!" she hissed.

"Magister Treacle, k-keep them away from me," whimpered Harwin, recoiling behind the magister. Harwin's dark, greasy, hair bobbed around his pasty cheeks and eyes. "I mean, look what's done happened to Valor—he looks dead or something."

Doomsy marched right up to Harwin with her hands on her hips. Her head rocked before she grabbed his gold robe, shook him, and screamed, "You should use your stupid garland on a salad because it isn't working on me!"

"Get her off me. She's possessed; she's got Medusa in her," whimpered Harwin, pulling himself deeper into Magister Treacle's black coat. "Mumsy will have your position for this, Treacle!"

"No instrument of divination so far. It hasn't predicted anything," said Treacle, tugging on the olive garland.

"What about Valor and Aaron? They're standing too far from Harwin's garland to tell if they're shadow tossers or not," said Chantilda, standing up from her booth.

"Masterful vibes radiate from you, Chantilda," said Treacle. "I delight in beginner diviners who desire a deeper prognosis."

"I just like to set the fates in action," said Chantilda.

"Step over here, Aaron," ordered Magister Treacle. "Let's see if the garland repels you."

"Before I do," said Aaron. The silk embroidery in his black coat shimmered as he maintained a regal posture beside the magister. "I marvel to ask—but for what crime are you subjecting us to this unsavory humiliation?"

"Eh, what was that?" asked Treacle, wiggling his nose as though he had breathed in a louse from his bushy beard.

"Aaron means, who gave you the authority to humiliate us for no reason?" asked Doomsy, shaking her finger up at the magister.

"Why, I'll bet you think you're tiny enough to jump through a loophole, Miss Gloomsy," chuckled Treacle. His sunken eyes darkened in the shadows of his brows as he smoothed the bends in her hat. "Divination gives me the authority. I'll bet that blows you over, eh?" Treacle stroked half the length of his beard, and his eyes darkened at the apprentices. "A master diviner has the right to foretell the future or ascertain the unseen by using—" he swiped his wand in the air, and a ghost of a skinny woman appeared and wrote, in the air, the words: "oracles, premonitions, and authorized implements."

The words sparkled, and Treacle patted Doomsy on the head, returning the dents in her hat. "I may be older than the Severance River," he said, "but everybody knows sorcery is prohibited, and by some strange omen, you are here on this platform for me to ascertain."

"Ascertain, huh?" hissed Doomsy. She waved her wand, causing the word "ascertain" to appear in the air before adding an extra S near the beginning and dividing it before the letter C. "Well, you'd better make sure your 'ass' is 'certain' I've committed some crime before you drag me up here for your half-pooped, jabber-minded, cave-born ascertainments! No wonder your children ran away from you."

The apprentices erupted into stunned gasps and whispers. Magister Treacle's chuckle melted into a disheartened expression. He turned away and fiddled with the rotating rings on a model of the planet Saturn near his chair.

"Miss Gloomsy, you need to iron your tarot cards and astrological maps, perhaps," sighed the magister. "You've been getting too many false readings."

Aaron placed his hand on Doomsy's arm to calm her. He looked Treacle in the eyes and said, "Verily, Magister Treacle, if Valor and I pass this dastardly humiliating inquest, and you retain an ounce of integrity, you should—in good conscience—give us high *S.C.R.A.T.C.H.* marks on our *C.A.T. P.A.W.s.*"

Valor nodded in agreement with Aaron, but at that moment, his internal rage, along with his increasing thirst for blood, made him want to bite Harwin and Magister Treacle. His mouth gaped against his will until Treacle moved away from the model planet, giving Valor more reserve.

"And another thing, Magister Treacle," said Valor, lifting his head high. "After your divination experiment fails, Harwin Hollapolk has to wear a dress to Divinatory Arts from now on . . . to learn what it's like to humiliate people."

"All right, I suppose that's fair. If Harwin's garland fails to repel you or proves unreliable as an instrument of divination," said Magister Treacle, while Harwin's face drooped with a mix of loathing and discomfort. "Now, you two, step up here, and let's see if Harwin has developed a new tool of prophecy with his olives."

The apprentices eagerly watched the experiment, whispering in their tented booths. The antlered monkeys stopped banging their tambourhorns, and all the stages became calm and quiet. Aaron offered no reassurance when he and Valor moved just two inches in front of Hollapolk. Harwin's nervous breath puffed in Valor's face, stirring the scent of the shriveled, oily olives around his throat—a throat Valor wanted to puncture with his fangs more than ever. But he had to use restraint. He had to do the right thing—always him.

"I'm not feeling any different; how about you, Aaron?" Valor lied, forcing himself to appear pleasant.

Aaron's body shook, and he grabbed his head. "*Ugh!* Verily, I do!" he replied. Then he stood at ease and laughed. "No. What I feel is a rather pleasant sense of satisfaction. Now that you've drawn us this close, Harwin, would you like to waltz?" asked Aaron, placing his left hand behind Harwin's lower back.

Harwin jerked loose from Aaron's grip. His cheeks blushed bright red.

"See, it didn't repel us," gloated Doomsy. "I guess Hollapolk just has a fetish for fruit necklaces."

"Sorcerers! You cheated by the power of the Grim Warlock," snarled Harwin, aiming his wand at Doomsy.

Valor put up his hand to protect Doomsy, but Magister Treacle grabbed Harwin's wand and said, "I'll confiscate this, Hollapolk. But, oops, you are in violation. You will have to wear a dress in Divination Arts from now on." Treacle waved his wand, and a ghost tossed up a cloud of smoke over Harwin, while two other ghosts changed him out of his robe and pants, and into a black dress that ruffled at his scabby knees and elbows. Several males whistled and made catcalls at Harwin who dove into his tented booth, hiding his bare legs under the round table.

"Hey, Harwin, your necklace doesn't match your dress," yelled Drakool, but Chickie Baby, sitting beside him, still seemed distraught over the vanishing of Wharton Dashwood.

"Hold on. Lift up your hand again," said Magister Treacle, grabbing Valor's wrist and examining his palm. He traced the lines with his finger. "I'm reading a terrible future in your palm, McRaven. Odd—your veins are so blue, and your heart line is chained and in conflict with your head line." Treacle snatched Valor's hand closer to his eyes, lifting Valor to the toes of his boots. "You must prepare for heartache because many you care for will die."

"Who, sir?" asked Valor. He was in a nightmare now. The end-of-the-day gong rang, startling him so much he snatched his hand away from Treacle's gaze. Pressure traveled from his chest to his head.

What a terrible prediction.

The apprentices piled out of the room laughing at Harwin, whose wand Treacle had locked inside a cabinet before sitting in his elaborate chair, gripping the wooden arms, and closing his eyes.

"Who will die, sir?" Valor asked again, but Treacle didn't respond.

Doomsy cocked her head; her little boots scooted up to the magister's chair. She poked Treacle on his gnarled hand and said, "Too late. The crazy old loon's returned to dreamcrafting."

Aaron's crystal blue eyes widened with a look of relief as the magister's head nodded in sleep. "Do not believe anything he says," whispered Aaron. "With the humiliation that he's allowed to inflict on everyone, I'd marvel if he didn't conjure up such absurdities."

Valor inspected his palm, trying to see the awful fate Treacle had seen. Had the magister made an accurate prediction?

CHAPTER FOURTEEN

THE NECROMANCEROPOLIS

VALOR'S throat began to constrict. Something slid across his neck and hands as it had a few nights before while he slept. He awoke with a start when someone lifted the lid to his coffin, which rested at the foot of his bed. When his eyes were able to focus, Marston Diamone was leaning over him with his eyebrows lifted high.

"What are *you* doing here?" asked Valor. He jumped out of the coffin holding the Souvenir of Shame he had slept with, trying hard not to act startled. With a slight scowl, Marston examined him from head to toe.

"The only reason I even came to this cursed house is the stupid Crypts made you the president. Anyway, my sister Twila thinks she found a code in the *Magic Ledger* concerning Magister Crypting's disappearance. We can't get Mistress Bessbadora to give us a pass to the Chamber of Oracles. Twila wants to research the scrolls. She thinks they might provide an answer—but screamin' Sesepha! Why were you in a coffin?"

Valor slammed the lid shut. "Oh—this old thing is just a, um, padded chest," he said. "I was just testing it—as a joke for our next Halloween party. I thought maybe—"

"A test . . . in your underwear? Put some clothes on," said Marston, burying his face in his *Controssua* before Salazants darted into the room.

"Do excuse me, Master McRaven. Master Aaron was supposed to notify you that Marston wanted to speak with you," said Salazants, just as Aaron entered the room with a sheepish expression. "I assure you I had no idea he'd barge into Candlewicke."

Valor kept his voice light and cheerful, although the total lack of judgment from Aaron and Salazants made him tense with disgust. "No problem, Salazants," he said. "I was just discussing with Marston about using this wooden chest as a prop for Halloween."

"We aren't supposed to ever see, smell, or touch a coffin—it's Noctivatian." Marston deepened his voice to sound tougher the way he often did.

"I'm sure a little Halloween prop won't put a knot in everybody's wands?" said Valor, pulling up his pants while Aaron left the room and Salazants stood barring the doorway.

"I'm not going to argue. You need to chant about it. Or maybe you chant to Ambergis," said Marston. He looked down his nose at the Souvenir, before Valor tried to hide it behind his back.

"So why are you here?" asked Valor.

"You can give me and Twila permission to go down in the Chamber of Oracles," said Marston. His weak chin receded, and his cheeks reddened.

"I'm not sure I have the authority to do that, Marston. Besides, you and Twila didn't need my permission to break into the Chamber. Last time we were there, you tried to lock us in, as I recall."

"You're lying," said Marston. His head shook like a dog flinging water out of its ears.

"What are you really after in the Chamber?" asked Valor. "You certainly can't be concerned about finding Magister Crypting. You never liked the man."

"Forget about it. Sleeping with that cursed rune. You're pathetic," spat Marston, stomping out of the room.

Salazants's square jaw tightened, and his green eyes blinked regret. "Sorry, Master McRaven," he said. "Marston sneaked past Aaron and me when we were discussing whether we should wake you."

"He is sneaky," agreed Valor. "We should be careful not to let anyone see me sleeping in this coffin."

Salazants helped him put on his coat, and then he leaned in with a smirk. "If you don't mind me suggesting, sir, I can always start untidying your bed to make it look as if you sleep there instead."

"Well, it's too late for that now. Marston will tell the whole country," said Valor. "I'm afraid I'll need to move my coffin to one of the unused rooms in the mansion, far away from everyone. They'd be safer away from me."

"Excuse me, sir, but nonsense," said Salazants, snapping Valor's shirt collar into place. "You bit Manning because he grabbed you. There was a lot of anger at the time, a lot of emotions. You'll learn to control these new urges. In the meantime, Mistress Stabbah is working on a spell to try to cure your . . . *condition*."

"Let's hope it works," said Valor. He showed the Souvenir of Shame to Salazants. "I was wondering, would you have a look at this and see what you can make of it?"

Salazants took the two pieces of the rune in his white-gloved hands and examined it. "There's a question mark . . . a symbol for a girl," he said. "Then it says, 'let them die.'" Salazants crumpled his brows. "This isn't the original—"

"No," said Valor. "It's a reproduction rune that Venerious Falmoth supposedly decoded. But Magister Ibizelda thinks Ambergis revealed a hidden message by splitting it in half. What do you think the initials C.C.H. stand for?"

"It must be someone's initials. Would you like me to take it to the Library of the Council and look through all their records of names?" asked Salazants, handing the rune back to him.

"Thanks," said Valor. "But I think I'll hold on to it for a while and see what I can come up with."

That weekend, Candlewicke Coven headed to Convocation at Mystic Steeples. Afterward, Valor was going to try to locate the Necromanceropolis in hopes of finding Spirit's Staff of Gleaning to stop the Possessing. He was also hoping he might stumble upon his lost Familiar, Booger Fay.

Along the fence line of Bootjack Square, at the interior entrance of the enormous citadel, an angry crowd had gathered, magicking aerial banners and holding signs, protesting Summoner Mamahchi's new Aura Potion while the summoner passed around brochures and free samples of the tonic.

"Auravitamax is a divisive tactic!" shouted Drakool, the door attendant from Lilith's Lantern.

"We all belong. Leave our auras alone!" screamed Chickie Baby, Drakool's assistant.

A woman in the front of the crowd magicked a banner in the air that played a scene of a man putting a death grip around his own neck while yelling, "Let us vote. You can't force it down our throats."

Someone from the crowd knocked Summoner Mamahchi down on the steps leading up to the citadel. The remaining vials of tonic, he had been carrying in a wooden crate, shattered and evaporated in a rainbow-colored cloud.

Creighton picked up the summoner's tattered hat, which had landed three feet away, then he offered his hand to help the summoner to his feet.

"Sorry, sir; I didn't see who waylaid you," said Creighton, handing him his hat.

Trembling, Mamahchi mumbled while trying to steady himself

between the shattered glass. "Story of my life . . . always falling, Creighton," he said.

Growling and screaming something about the Thirteenth Hour, Chickie Baby and Drakool began thrashing through the crowds straight toward the summoner. With their faces like gargoyles and their fingers crooked into claws, they lunged at Mamahchi, but an unknown force knocked them to the ground with such strength their limbs twisted until they resembled human crabs. They crawled a few feet back down the steps before collapsing.

"They're dead!" several witches in the crowds shouted before the guardians arrived to clear the area.

Candlewicke Coven regathered near the entry to Mystic Steeples.

"Poor Chickie and Drakool—more victims of the Possession," said Valor.

"I feel sorry for Summoner Mamahchi, too," said Creighton, just before he entered the door to the ancient citadel.

"Why?" croaked Doomsy.

"'Cause—'cause he seems to be finally making a real name for himself, yet it's meeting resistance. That's the story of our lives, don't you think?"

"Yeah but, Creigh," said Micha DeMise. "Mystic Ministry is talkin' about makin' that Auravitamax tonic mandatory for everyone ta drink."

"To show everyone's true colors," added Valor, still unsure of how much he trusted the summoner.

"Those aaawful vespercestors have forced me to carry Auravitamax at Thunder Plant now. I keep it on a shelf behind the Hefty Hand Slappers—those slap-happy hands people are putting in their cookie jars to help them stay on their diet. They're a huge hit," said Stabbah Scarveda, entering the door behind Rose Decay.

"I'll show you my true color," Creighton touched his wand to his cheek, turning his skin green for a few seconds. "Mandatory or not, I'm green with envy that I haven't invented a huge hit."

"It's not funny, Creighton. The Diamone family is really behind this," said Rose. "They're saying Auravitamax will weed out the unwelcome and criminals from our region, and that we can either be a part of the problem or the solution."

"The, um, problem is, n-nobody seems to know what that p-potion is really doing to us," said Egg Goodridge, before all of Candlewicke Coven had passed their wand-light inspections at the Congre Gate and headed to their individual coven sections in Mystic Chantry.

Valor, Doomsy, Aaron, and Egg sat in their usual spot in the Cryptic Chambers' section, and everyone in front of them stood up and moved to farther benches.

"That's odd. Did one of us forget to bathe?" asked Doomsy.

As soon as Valor shrugged, Urbanne shot out a fiery decree using his magic staff. The flames exploded like firecrackers and dropped little sheets of parchment in everyone's laps.

"From my enchanted staff, you have it in writing," said Urbanne. "As of this day, no member of the Sanguinati shall have a wooden chest or box any longer than two-plus feet. If you do, we'll take you for a delusional Noctivatian . . . a cursed cadaver who crawls out of a box for the rotting! So, store your belongings the correct way, and stay away from the casket companies."

"That canker-tongued Marston Diamone told O Enchantedness about your coffin," snorted Doomsy, kicking the back of the bench with her boots.

"No doubt," said Valor. I also think Urbanne's mad because I didn't bring back his giant grandson. I told him what Venerious Falmoth told me to tell him, and he looked at me with disbelief."

"He merely wanted Sweeturnips to polish the steeples," said Aaron.

Crumpecker approached the podium after the choir had seated from singing. "O Enchantedness, I agree with the new decree," she said. "There's too much rebellion sneaking in our city. I don't think our ancestors care if some of our people research the disease known as Noctivatians—I used to study it sometimes. But our people shouldn't spend too much time with the undead. You all know that!" She folded her hands over her chest, imitating a corpse, then a few seconds later, her eyes shot open. "I'm going to drink your blood. Eee-he-he . . . ," she cackled in derision.

Doomsy gripped her hands in her lap, seething. Valor jumped when two members from Warlocks' Bane stood up and flung fireclappers in the air. The magical handclapping was so loud that Mystic Chantry vibrated.

"Now," shouted Crumpecker, "I want everybody to take your decrees and place them on the left side of your head, and place your *Controssuas* on the right side of your head."

Everyone did as she requested, thereby blocking their peripheral vision.

"That's it, that's it," continued Crumpecker. "Don't none of ya pay any attention to the wayward scalawags out there lurking and protesting in the shadows of our steeples. Your focus should remain up here on this platform—on O Enchantedness—on the lesser vespercestors."

"Do they think we are carriage centaurs that we should place blinders around our eyes?" asked Aaron. He zeroed in on Valor's face through the *Controssua* and parchment pressed to his head.

Urbanne returned to the podium with a devious look on his face. "Summoner Mamahchi, the Diamone family, Vespercestor Ortho Bisland, and Guardian McMahon, I want you to move from where you are and have a seat on the vacant bench in front of Cryptic Chambers there," said Urbanne, pointing from the platform to the back right corner of the Chantry. "Yes, how about that? Right in front of the presidents of Cryptic Chambers there."

Everyone had removed their blinders by then, and Marston and Twila Diamone passed icy glances at Valor before they sat on the bench.

"What's O Enchantedness up to now?" Valor asked Doomsy and Aaron.

"I don't know, but he's directing it at us," said Aaron, while Doomsy kicked back in the bench with folded arms.

"Checkmate," said Urbanne, glaring at Valor with a smirk.

The entire Convocation fell quiet for a minute, confused perhaps.

Urbanne embraced the podium. His head rested on the outer edge, and his orange corkscrew ringlets spilled over his wrinkled face.

"Vespercestor Bisland and these fine Sanguinati witches have loyal Ancients' blood pumping through their veins," continued Urbanne. "They don't like it when misbegotten warlocks and loathsome, zinger-fingered shadesters sneak in amongst our city—diluting and polluting our ways. With that said, my people, let me introduce to you my newest addition to Mystic Ministry: give a warm welcome to your Aura Analysts. That's right. That's right."

The Diamones, Summoner Mamahchi, and the others on the bench waved and gave slight bows as the Sanguinati reluctantly broke into applause.

"In the coming days," continued Urbanne, waiting for the room to quieten. "In the coming days and weeks, the Aura Analysts will begin conducting thorough readings of every resident in Severance, Hoopenfangia. Of course, all of this wouldn't be possible without the fine new Auravitamax tonic our very own Eelias Mamahchi has invented. That's right."

"Save the Sanguinati!" several audience members cheered.

"Does this mean we have to purchase the Aura Tonic?" asked Thorn Corvus, the owner of Lilith's Lantern, sitting in Dragon's Mantle section. Valor couldn't believe Thorn was in Convocation, considering two of his employees had just been killed minutes earlier on the steps.

"If you think your aura is strong and pure enough to pass inspections, then no—you can chance it," said Urbanne.

"How do we know you're not forcing us to buy some potion that produces some fake aura for your fake readings," shouted a boy in the Snuffinumbra section. "I want to know who all is getting kickbacks from this racket besides the Aura Analysts?"

A burly guardian charged down the aisle, headed toward the boy before Summoner Mamahchi spoke: "As O Enchantedness said . . . nobody is forcing you to purchase my product."

"Auravitamax only intensifies the aura you already produce, which helps us to get a clearer reading," said Sessions Diamone, Marston and Twila's father.

"May I say something?" asked Hilda Diamone, standing tall beside her husband and children. "I feel much more vitalized since I've been taking Auravitamax. My powers have increased. I've got a clearer head—even a healthy glow to my skin. We are witnessing very dark times. If taking this tonic will help weed out the dark auras from our city, then I say give me a whole case of that stuff!"

The audience cheered, and the Diamones embraced one another with portrait-perfect smiles before shaking hands with Mamahchi and the others.

"I'm convinced everybody'll want to purchase a bottle. Every. Body," said Urbanne from the platform. "*Thambor Midrend!*" he chanted, with his magic staff pointed toward the ceiling, before dismissing the Convocation.

After exiting the Chantry in a daze, Valor, Doomsy, and Aaron crashed into Magister Kraneswaddle as she was carrying a tray of potions in the Hall of DeLusian IV.

"I'm sorry," said Valor. "We thought you were going the other way."

"Oh, honey, I'm running in circles—that man, argh! I can't imagine how O Enchantedness can lead Convocation with all these potions he's taking. I can't make them fast enough."

"All these Potions?" asked Valor, noticing the tray piled to the edge with colorful bottles.

Kraneswaddle made a sassy twisting movement with her leg and rubbed a pink flower on her cheek. "'All' is an understatement, but I think it's mostly the dragon's blood he uses, you know, to increase his virility," she said, pulling the edge of her big floppy hat down over her pointy face. "But he's just getting worse, says just about anything—not that nobody cares. Oh, honey, I remember when O Enchantedness passed gas on the platform years ago. The covens raised their wands and started chanting as if the Ancients had spoken through him."

Valor and Aaron laughed, while Doomsy rolled her eyes.

"You mean Urbanne needs all those potions when there is the

wonder tonic Auravitamax? I'm shocked," said Valor snidely.

"Honey, I don't know what that Aura Potion is really for, but it don't have no health benefits. You didn't hear old Minty say this, but I'm really concerned where this is headed," whispered Crumpecker. She straightened her bottles and left to find Urbanne.

"Something is definitely changing around here. What are we going to do when they test our auras?" asked Doomsy, as they headed fast to Usabelli's Square.

"I can't worry about that right now. Falmoth said Booger Fay was in the Necromanceropolis. Are you sure Manning got the key?" asked Valor, referring to the giant key they had found under the staircase in Candlewicke Mansion.

"How do you know that key goes to the Necromanceropolis?" asked Doomsy.

"I held my monoculous over the engraving on the back of it. The words 'Opens a circle, moron' moved and spelled out Necromanceropolis," said Valor. "After my memory of *The Book of Chacodophilus* and the mural in the witches' parlor, I'm certain it's the right the key."

"Manning said he placed the key in the fancy shrubbery by the wall of the revolving stairs late last night," said Aaron. "Oh, and it shall be hard to find because he did a camouflage spell on it."

A few halls and rooms later, they found Rose and Blade waiting for them in the middle of the square under the floating galleries.

"Guys, what was all that about with Urbanne tonight?" asked Rose, squeezing between them with her arms folded tightly around her narrow waistline.

"I'm done with that two-tongued, orange-maned, staff slinger. He talks and behaves one way to our faces, then does the opposite when he's safely in front of the Sanguinati," said Doomsy.

"Zagato has studied enough history to see through dictators like Urbanne," said Blade. "It is a deception they use to curtail public resistance while they extend their sinister takeovers. The more Urbanne lies and the more shamefully he behaves, his deceived loyalists see him as a man with a backbone."

"They must be awfully simple then," said Doomsy, making her lower eyelids sag.

"Not all of them," continued Blade, trying to ease closer to Doomsy. "The Sanguinati Elitists have been craving a leader who screams publically what they only dare to share behind locked doors—as long as they think he's doing it for their greater good. Urbanne is hoping the rest—people like us—people with a conscience eventually give up keeping track of his deceptions."

"Or make us afraid of speaking out," added Valor, amazed at Blade's insight.

"Exactly," said Blade. "Urbanne needs to both confirm and cause fears in the masses, especially fears that play to their bigotries. And soon, the Sanguinati will be reconditioned to accept atrocities as the norm again."

"That is where we are now. Urbanne is trying to turn the Sanguinati into a lynch mob," said Valor, looking around Usabelli Square for the giant key.

Blade's long black hair draped over his left arm in thought. "Nah . . . Urbanne is merely freeing them to express what has *always* been under the surface—oh, no doubt he's relishing every second of their growing wrath, though. And whether you're able to handle it or not, Valor, Venerious Falmoth is playing the same game. It's a strategy too tempting for corrupt leaders."

Valor feared Blade was right, but at least the Noctivatians didn't pretend to be so sickeningly superior, and despite feeling betrayed by Falmoth, at least Venerious made great efforts to relate to Valor and warn him of Urbanne's death agenda against Sorcerers. No doubt, Urbanne would never have revealed the secrets Falmoth had—secrets that might help Valor solve the Great Deception. Valor couldn't imagine surrendering to the darkness now spreading through his veins. But he feared if the Sanguinati furthered their attacks on him and his friends—or any other innocent people—they would fully see the beast they always labeled him as.

"Yeah, well, we must fight our dark natures, and we need to find that key," said Valor bitterly.

"Have it right here," said Blade, patting his cloak. "Rose told you wrong. We have to enter the Necromanceropolis through the Floating Gallery of Chacodophilus . . . not under the floating stairs. That's why Blade came along, lest Rose steers you into the swamps of Squibthistle."

"Ah," said Valor. "I always wondered why they called it the Floating Gallery of the Unknown. The Sanguinati didn't want to acknowledge the real Great Witch. But how did you figure it out?"

"Research and superior instinct," said Blade. Looking to see if anyone was watching, he floated with the key up to the Gallery of Chacodophilus and, once inside its round doorway, motioned for the others to join him. Before entering, Valor admired the bottom of the gallery—by far the prettiest of the floating galleries. The layers of gold-plated moldings narrowed to an amethyst-ball tip. As the other galleries bounced up and down, their carved doors opened and closed all around each façade, but the one they entered had only one door.

"Not shabby in here," said Doomsy, admiring the gemstones embedded along the inside walls.

"This must be Chacodophilus," said Aaron. "He looks too young to have that nasty beard, though."

Doomsy, too, walked up to the white marble statue in the middle of the gallery. A marble headdress hung down the length of his marble beard, which curled like ocean waves on the ends. The statue held its right hand out to the side and the other near its waist.

"How do we get to the Necromanceropolis from inside this thing?" asked Rose.

"That's what I'm wondering. This huge circle we came through must be the only door," said Valor, after the door closed.

Blade pulled the enormous key from under his cloak and chanted "*Exposius Ad Oculum*," removing the camouflage spell, restoring it to its golden visibleness. "From what Blade has learned, all galleries require a key to activate them. So, look for a slot to insert it."

They scampered around the floating gallery, looking for anything resembling a keyhole.

"It shouldn't be this hard to find. That's a ginormous key. Maybe there is a secret passage," said Rose, pressing on every gemstone and jewel on the walls before chanting, "*Revelare Arcanus Iter.*"

"Reveal spells don't work in this gallery," said Blade.

"This is a waste of time," croaked Doomsy. "There is no keyhole."

"I just wonder," said Aaron, studying the statue. "You see, Chacodophilus here appears to be playing an invisible guitar—does he not? The key does resemble a guitar if you look at it—does it not?"

Blade gave Aaron an impressed nod then cradled the base of the key in the crook of the statue's lower arm and the head of the key in its raised hand.

"It fits snug," said Blade, stepping back with a look of expectancy.

"Uh, nothing happened, did it?" asked Rose.

"The main principle of gallery travel is to know how to petition the Ancient to whom the gallery is dedicated," said Blade, walking in circles around the statue.

"Chacodophilus, get on with it and take us to the Necromanceropolis," snorted Doomsy.

"No, no, no," sighed Blade, tossing his long hair out of his unimpressed face. "This is the greatest Sorcerer of all time we're dealing with, little one. Say it nicely. A little praise wouldn't hurt either."

Doomsy's face shriveled like a raisin. With a strained but cloy voice, she said, "O magnificent and handsome Chacodophilus, my friends here plead with you to take us to the Necromanceropolis."

They found the floor spinning in circles, as the statue played a cheerful melody on the key. The jewels in the walls lit up and flashed, making Valor feel dizzy. He clung to the wall and shut his eyes until the circular door scraped open, and they found themselves in a torch-lit maze.

"That's what the engraving on the key meant. 'Opens a circle, moron.' The door was round," said Valor.

"Wait! Wait now, oh wait," someone yelled. "Don't shut the door! I've been trapped down here for days," the pumpaninny warbled, pushing through them, before pulling the gallery door shut behind him.

"Hold on. How—" said Valor, trying to get the pumpaninny's attention by grabbing the door, but it would not open. "Don't tell me we're trapped now."

Blade tugged and pushed at the door. "Zagato does declare: it certainly looks like it."

"You mean you don't know how to get us outta here?" squeaked Rose, grabbing Blade by his collar.

"My palest Rose, never trust what you think you know. Zagato, however, understands many things: we exit through the door that was right there—that is until the pumpaninny closed it," said Blade with an uncertain smirk.

"No need to dig our graves yet; I brought Highjinks," said Doomsy, pulling her scarab out of her conjure bag before placing the jeweled beetle on her shoulder. "He'll help us get out of—"

"Ah! *You* have noticed as well," said Aaron. "We are not in another catacomb."

"We're in some underground city," said Rose, releasing Blade's collar.

"Goodness, how will I ever find Booger Fay? This place is so big and—deserted," said Valor. He turned in circles between abandoned stores and passages covered in preserved corpses and stuffed Familiar carcasses: a city with never-ending rooms full of odd relics, magic sigils and talismans, charms, strange clocks, ornate mirrors, and portraits of the dead.

"Centuries," said Valor.

"Huh?" asked Rose, while Aaron walked as if the dust would soil his clothes. He whipped out a lace handkerchief and held it over his nose, just as two smoky phantoms flew past him screaming.

"Such an explosion of fascination. It must've taken centuries to build this place. Look at all the memento mori on the walls," said Valor. From the short time-traveling, Valor had experienced, he hadn't fully grasped the scope of time it had taken for Chacodophilus to construct the Necromanceropolis.

"It would take ten times the centuries to dust it all," added Aaron, fanning his face with the handkerchief. He walked over a stone bridge, which arched across a channel of flowing water, while flat-bottomed boats floated through the canals, some carrying skeletons. Everywhere, sprawling, dead tree limbs had pushed against the high ceilings, and through doorways and windows, before touching back down to the roads, sidewalks, and canals.

"How did all these trees grow without sunlight?" asked Valor, fearing he might have to live in such dim isolation soon.

"They must be shadow oaks—ancient," said Rose, cracking her cat-o'-nine-tails around an overhanging limb and swinging across the canal where Aaron now stood. "Nalini mentioned reading about them in the *Prohibited Plants Papyrus* in the Library of the Council."

"Some of you shivering shadesters will get lost, no doubt. For even the doors have doors in this metro of bones," said Blade, landing beside Rose with a flying leap over the canal. "You may have to huddle close to the Zagato."

Doomsy flashed Blade a look of caution after she floated over the canal. They stood in a circle as if trying to determine the floor from the ceiling. Doomsy soon busied herself inside an enormous wooden jack-o'-lantern after its tongue retracted, pulling her inside.

"Check it out—a crumbling toy store," said Doomsy, leaning her head out of its carved nose while a lifelike rat crawled in and out of its carved eyes and teeth. "And that must be the shopkeeper." She pointed to a wooden witch dressed in tattered clothing at the top of the carved pumpkin store.

"Better get out there," said Valor, fanning his arms at Doomsy. "The witch has got a cauldron of bubbling green potion, and she's about to pour it on your head." The wooden witch lifted the lid to the pumpkin, and her cackle began to warble slower and slower.

Doomsy exited the toy store holding a doll wrapped in dusty gauze. The rat-chewed tag on the toy read, "Mummy Mommy."

Valor reached out to grab the toy. "My dear, you probably should ditch that cursed—"

Doomsy looked up at Valor with big droopy eyes—a sad comfort. Valor lowered his arm. He couldn't take it from her, especially with her being an orphan—especially after trying to find her real parents proved such a disaster.

"Oh look, Doomsy," said Rose, as if she had found a better—sanitary—toy for her. They scuttled around the bend with a door on the floor. "Look at all these little gnome dolls sitting on the edge of this shelf. Their little shoes and stockings and beards are so cute, aren't they?"

"It's not a shelf, my dear, it's the edge of a sarcophagus. And those aren't dolls, they're gnome corpses," said Valor, with a sympathetic smile.

Rose snatched her fingers away from the beard of the corpse that she had been touching. "Real dead gnomes?" she asked while stiffening with horror. Her eyes seemed to picture the curse that would fall on her. "They look just like the gnomes on Summoner Mamahchi's Christmas tree." She held her tainted hand far from her body. "Quick, somebody, do a sanitization spell on my fingers."

"I wonder, my pets, if we can put these gnomes' spirits to flight? Perhaps they'll haunt Mamahchi then," said Doomsy, pouring a teardrop over Rose's fingers before putting her tear-catcher bottle back in her conjure bag.

Rose wiped her fingers dry on the side of her dress, and again she froze with apprehension when a crunching sound under her boot followed a tiny scream. Valor gazed over at the row of gnome corpses. One of the bearded beings now had his hand cupped over his mouth as if muffling a scream. Valor looked down at Rose's boot and up to her eyes, which were now crossed.

"Is it . . . what I think it is?" he asked.

Rose eased her left boot off the stone floor and whined, "Uh-huh."

Everyone's gaze lowered to the gnome's tiny leather shoe—its foot-bone fragments Rose had crushed. Valor popped his last Luminous Lulling Lozenge in his mouth, confident he would soon need it. He continued examining anything that looked like it might be the stolen Staff of Gleaning.

"Spirits have troubled this area," said Aaron. He pointed to the subtle shifting of objects in the area as a drifting glob of mist passed near them. "We should look for Booger Fay and abandon this forgotten necropolis."

As they made their way farther from the toy stores, soft tapping noises startled them. Long rope ladders, as thin as cat tails, began to unwind and hang down from shelves, urns, hollowed-out *Mystic Memoirs*, and even the shoulders of human corpses. Windup toys began to play creepy melodies. Little carousels with enchanted creatures turned and bobbed to organ tunes, while morbid monkeys banged drums and ancient tambourhorns mounted beside their owners' death portraits.

"Rose desecrated a corpse. Something foreboding is about to befall us," said Doomsy, watching the direction that Highjinks unfurled its wings.

"Foreboding? The whole place has gone bloody fickle," said Blade, glancing at an abandoned music store window across the canal. "Even those Bellowing Bells are ringing now." Blade didn't notice the stone effigy move behind him, and out of the midst of it, a gray phantom embraced him as if it were trying to suffocate him with death.

"I thought the Necromanceropolis was the ancient catacombs of the Sorcerers," said Valor as the bells continued screaming a tune. "But it seems mostly gnomes lived here." A tiny hatchet whisked past him and bounced off Blade's coattail, leaving a tiny gash in the black fabric, while more gnomes climbed down their ladders.

"The gnomes are probably guarding some treasure," said Aaron. He moved his foot away from another hatchet-wielding gnome that was trying to hack at his boot. "They are not so cute anymore, are they, Rose?"

"Ouch, these little hatchets and bells are killing me," said Rose, covering her ears as they dashed into the nearest corridor. Spirits emerged from all directions and blanketed over them.

Valor's pulse slowed and vision dimmed. Through the flurry, the faint profile of Doomsy emerged, squatting on the floor against Aaron's knee. She grabbed her head. Were the spirits giving her a headache with their eerie droning? The sinister sounds left no doubt with Valor after his eardrums began vibrating in pain.

"What are the ghosts trying to tell us?" asked Valor.

"I can't tell," replied Rose. "The voices are too deep, too slow."

Aaron snatched Valor from the ghosts that were now blanketing him. "Begone, you wretched specters!" he yelled, forcing the ghosts and gnomes back with a glowing discharge of magic from his hands.

"Th-thanks, it was hard to move," said Valor, searching for whatever it was clinging to the back of his leg. "Get off my pants, little guy."

The gnome pounded his hatchet into Valor's leg. The pain resembled a wasp sting. He knocked the gnome off with his hand, sending the little being sliding across the floor into an Avimancer's cage hanging by a rusted chain from a sign pole. The gnome landed on a pile of dead bats where it remained dazed.

"What do we do, guys? I'm afraid to hurt another gnome. They're vengeful little devils," said Rose, smacking a floating zodiac globe out of the way with her cat-o'-nine-tails. She turned down an alleyway of abandoned homes, some of which had hooded black cloaks and shrouds hanging in the broken windows as curtains.

"The spirits are still behind us," yelled Doomsy.

"Rose is the one who upset the gnomes. She needs to give them an offering of restitution. The dead always require a sacrifice from the living if a witch needs something in return," said Blade.

"Okay—okay, I'll run ahead and cast a circle," said Rose. Her feet seldom touched the road as she moved up the alleyway.

"Rose shouldn't have to give those vengeful vapors a stupid offering," Doomsy hissed at Blade. "I've got something to give 'em all right." She took out a gold-flecked witch ball from her conjure bag and placed it on the floor. Valor tried to pry her away from the ball, but she stood behind it and said, "O Spirits, come see, come see what *I* have offered thee."

She waved her hands around the witch ball, and a wall of tiny foggy spirits formed in front of her. Were they contemplating her offering? Some of the ghosts entered the witch ball, and Doomsy crushed the glass with her' boot and said, "Rise no more!"

Blade released a grunting sigh and refused to look at Doomsy. "You must learn to control your temper, little one. There are rules.

You will never gain the respect of others with such hasty deeds."

Doomsy kicked Blade in his shin as hard as she could with her tiny boot. He flinched for a second then locked his eyes down at her with a look of compassion so uncanny that Valor got chills.

One by one, the muscles in Doomsy's battle-ready body began to go limp. Her chin quivered as a sick huff exited her Cupid's bow lips before she ran toward Rose, who had completed the circle using flaming incense.

Valor offered Blade a glance of sympathy before he and the others leaped inside the circle Rose was now purifying with salt. The remaining ghosts swarmed around the perimeter of the flames, groaning as though they were in anguish. Rose began with an incantation, and then she stopped.

"Guys, I don't know what ghosts like. Should I try to give them *bodies*?"

"No-no, Rose; that might endanger us more," said Valor.

Aaron bolted around in case any angry gnomes or spirits, trailing up the corridor, broke through the ring of fire behind him. "What about some nice clothes?" he asked, bolting back.

"What would they need with clothes?" asked Valor, ready to defend.

"Maybe some soft music will calm them?" Rose pulled out a summoning bell from her charm bag. Everyone agreed, and Rose placed the bell on the floor, recited a spell, and the bell began to play a pleasant melody.

"That's not going to appease the dead," said Blade. "Those gnomes sent the spirits, and they demand an eye for an eye. You crushed the gnome's foot, so you must offer up a replacement."

Rose gasped with a look of horror. "Sacrifice my own foot?"

"Any girl Blade Dean Zagato would consider having must prove herself in many ways before he'll commit. If that's not challenging enough, she must have good skin, be thin, and subservient."

"Well, love, I hope it doesn't come to any sacrifices," Aaron said to Rose, with a crease above his nose.

Rose's eyes turned black as her pupils expanded. Valor stumbled when the flames of the circle spiraled around Blade.

"I'll never be subservient, especially to somebody pretentious and delusional," she replied coolly.

"Those monkey nuts are about to penetrate the barrier," said Doomsy, walking to the edge of the flames and hiking her skirt. "I'll sacrifice a foot . . . straight up their—"

Valor pulled Doomsy away from the flames. "Nobody is going to sacrifice any feet," he said.

"I know," said Rose, taking off her left boot. "I'll shrink my cloud stomper, you know—gnome size—and offer it to 'em."

Blade put out the spiral of flame around him with a fling of his cloak. "Not unless you can recreate a foot to go in your boot will it suffice as an offering."

Rose rummaged through her charm bag. "I don't have any bones in my bag," she whined. "Oh, where's Stab when we need her?"

Blade reached in his conjure bag and removed a tiny bone. One of the spirits broke through the barrier and knocked the bone from his fingertips, and it bounced out of the circle of flames and rolled under the barrier of ghosts.

"Of course!" huffed Blade while glancing at Doomsy. "Someone's bad energy hath jinxed our mission, and now the gnomes have rejected the offering."

"We have to do something. The flames are starting to burn out," said Valor.

"Highjinks go get that bone," ordered Doomsy, placing her scarab on the floor near a gap in the flames. It crawled toward the bone, and almost reached it when the gnome that had lost his foot sat on Highjinks and rode the scarab, turning it back toward the circle of flame. Highjinks's wings flicked out, trying to fling the gnome off its back, but the gnome's legs curled against the jewels on the scarab's shell, bringing it to a stop.

"Give me my scarab back, you greedy gnome," yelled Doomsy.

The gnome waved goodbye to Doomsy as he rode away on Highjinks, followed by the rest of the gnomes. The surrounding ghosts flew off down the winding alleys.

"The gnome doesn't need his foot back. He has a new manner of travel now. Sorry Doomsy, perhaps we can get you a new scarab," said Valor.

As Rose withdrew the remnants of the flaming circle, Doomsy maintained a somber expression. If it weren't for her angry breath swelling her chest, she wouldn't appear alive at all, especially with the funeral carriage parked behind her, supporting two caskets blanketed in spider webs.

"The Necromanceropolis must've existed before the ban on coffins," said Rose dismissively.

"Halt," said Aaron, lifting his arms. "I know the primitives have forgotten their Sorcerer origins, so 'tis no surprise they never acknowledge Chacodophilus. Neither did my old master, Mesthu, tell his Children that the Great Witch had connections to Mystic Steeples. Nevertheless, is that not Chacodophilus's image is in those jumbled runes on that door?" His lacy sleeve flung toward the door to the right.

"Ah, you all are finally expanding your inner eyes," said Blade.

"It's not our fault," said Valor. "It must be part of the Great Deception. Venerious Falmoth is the only non-Sorcerer who seems to be aware of these things. But he doesn't seem to be aware that the Sanguinati is performing ghost magic."

"He's probably lying," said Doomsy.

"Either more people know about it, and they aren't admitting it, or something happened, and they've had their memories erased," said Valor.

"How do you know so much about the Great Witch, Blade?" asked Aaron.

"Blade Zagato learned of him from some wise Sorcerer ages ago," he said, rubbing his chest with a boastful grin. He shifted the carved runes on the door until the face of Chacodophilus came into form. Everyone stood slack-jawed at his ability to discern the puzzle.

"One simply must have a look in this room then, should they not?" asked Aaron. He pushed hard against the door, and it scraped open, leaving a trail on the dusty floor, followed by a few crawling scarabs fleeing the room at their feet. None of these scarabs seemed to interest Doomsy except the jeweled beetle she had lost to the one-footed gnome.

In the entry hall of the room, a bluish glow and bubbling noise greeted them. Gargling voices, as of brass instruments, seemed to be pleading to a much deeper, scary voice that growled, "Ah, they have awoken. May whoever unworthily enters this shrine, receive their reward in their keep."

Blade turned around to face the others. His dark eyes hardened on them before glancing back at the door, and then to his left at the crystal capsule sitting on the floor with its decorative lid piercing into the ceiling. A half-alien, half-human creature floated inside the crystal tube like a specimen. Its rotted clothes rippled like seaweed as it continued its gargling cries, floating closer to the glass.

Valor shuddered.

"These must be pressure gauges," said Rose. "I think this is some sort of iron lung keeping that monster alive."

"Why would an iron lung have an astronomical clock?" asked Valor. He wiped the dust off the domed-glass cover. Golden gears turned as if feeding something through the tubes that traveled from the ceiling into gold-capped openings in the capsule.

"Careful," cautioned Blade, "you don't want that thing to get out."

Rose and Doomsy scooted past the creature into the room and the floor drew their attention. "What stone is this floor made of?" asked Doomsy. Glowing white lines moved across the dark-blue floor, converging in places, before releasing little white balls of energy into the air.

Everyone shrugged.

"I have never seen a stone like this," said Valor. He caught a ball of energy in the palm of his hand, and its temperature fluctuated before turning into a small blue stone that replicated itself until several new stones spilled out of his hand and repeated the same process.

"Fascinating. Whatever manner of stone this is, it reproduces by merely touching its discharging energy," said Aaron, putting a stone in his coat pocket. "I must bring a specimen to Magister Globula." Aaron's pocket began to swell until it ripped open at his hip, and dozens of little blue rocks tumbled to the floor, turning back into balls of white energy. "Or perhaps not."

Valor resolved to keep his distance from the others. The scent of their blood penetrated their veins, making him hungry. "Oh look," he said, floating up to wipe the dust off a painting on the wall.

"Surprising—a painting of Mystic Steeples," said Blade dully.

"Well, yes, but isn't that the Fountain of Chacodophilus, which Mesthu had in his tower?" asked Valor, pointing to a fountain in the painting that rested on the highest pinnacle of Mystic Steeples.

"Looks just like it. Except water's flowing from it and not blood," said Doomsy, blowing an energy ball around the room.

"Guys, I think we're actually standing in the Shrine of Chacodophilus!" squeaked Rose. She bent down to inspect a sizeable gemstone-covered bench, but on closer examination was a sarcophagus with its lid open. "See, his name is engraved on the box with the dates 1038 to 1641."

"Ah, it says 'first vespercestor.' The sorry Sanguinati said Usabelli was the first head vespercestor—in 1640-plus, of course—the year recorded here as Chacodophilus's death," said Blade, keep his distance from the sarcophagus. "Either the clever Sorcerer has resurrected, or they're still trying to hide evidence of him."

"He did resurrect—from this tomb," said Valor. He sprinted toward his friends at the sarcophagus, before his hungered reasoning pulled him back a few steps. "Remember what I told you in my vision of *The Book of Chacodophilus*?"

"Perhaps so, but it seems this shrine has been burgled," said Aaron.

"According to what I saw and remember," said Valor, "Chacodophilus may have moved with his wealth and oracles into the Cruxvein Abyss."

Doomsy glanced up at the square discolorations on the wall where portraits once hung. "I agree with Aaron," she said. "I think this shrine has been picked over more than Crumpecker's nose."

Blade kicked at scattered books and objects with his boots; then, he looked straight up at the ceiling. "Could it be?" he asked, before floating up to a domed recess in the ceiling, which resembled the inside of a zodiac globe constructed with stained glass. He pried at a square panel of glass, which featured a sparkling lightning bolt design until the panel came out of its lead frame. "It is! This shrine of the Great Witch is directly underneath the *Braggadocio*. Of course, the Sanguinati would do such a thing to blaspheme Chacodophilus's legacy—to trump him."

"What's the *Braggadocio*?" asked Valor. He wanted to float up and see for himself.

"All this time—you are kidding?" gasped Rose. "Oh, sorry, Valor—you don't remember the stained glass zodiac globe?" She pointed up at the ceiling. "That thing is at the base of the podium where *The Tablets of Sanguinati Successes* is located in Mystic Chantry?"

"Oh, okay," said Valor.

"Those tablets are known as the *Braggadocio*," continued Rose. Her ringlets cascaded as she leaned her head back.

"Oh, the conspiracy!" said Aaron. "The braggings of the Sanguinati covered up one of the biggest secrets in all of Sanguinati history—the very witch who gave them the right to brag. That should make their successes rather dishonest, to say the least."

Blade floated down beside the sarcophagus and gave Aaron a proud pat on his back.

"Are you okay, Valor? You seem very unhappy over there," asked Rose.

"This is all interesting, of course, but I'd rather find the staff of gleaning and Booger Fay," he replied.

"Oh?" Blade said to Valor disappointedly before they left the chamber. "Well, at least you have resolve."

Back in the corridor, they continued with their search mission. "I've looked everywhere, but I haven't seen any of Booger's special droppings. BOOGER FAY, WHERE ARE YOU?" yelled Valor. His voice echoed a chorus throughout the Necromanceropolis. The stone eyes on the wall behind them cracked open and rolled in every direction.

"Creepy," said Blade. "It sounds like a choir of barking dogs in here." And the noise continued until the echoes softened to a low hum.

A voice echoed back: "I found a sphinxter."

Valor got goosebumps. "Did you hear that?" he asked. "It's Booger Fay; it's him!" Life returned to him as tears formed in his eyes. "He calls sphinxes, 'sphinxters'—he does." Valor laughed, and ran a short distance up the dim hall, while Aaron and the others dashed down different halls and alleys. Blade clung against a sarcophagus as the revolving section of a wall returned him to where he had been standing.

"Hold on," shouted Rose. "We hafta stick together, or we'll get lost in this maze. I don't wanna end up a corpse on the wall."

"We could wander this city for years and never find Booger Fay," Blade said, over the barking echoes after everyone rejoined Rose.

"A Familiar responds to the voice of its master. So, unless any of you are Valor, please endeavor to keep your voices to a minimum," whispered Aaron. "Now, what direction do you think Booger's voice came from, Valor?"

Valor concentrated hard with roving eyes. His finger pointed in different directions as his thoughts changed. "Ungh—not sure. This way . . . maybe?" He pointed up the hall where he had dashed earlier.

Doomsy turned her candle into a candelabra and walked ahead a short distance, lighting the dusty stone floor. "My pet, doesn't this look like one of Booger's special droppings?" she asked.

Valor tried to ignore the frozen expression of a female gnome who was clinging between the wings of a stuffed owl mounted on a mage's staff, which couldn't be the Staff of Gleaning. He ran and dropped to his knees to inspect Doomsy's finding.

"It *is* his special droppings. Falmoth was wrong. Booger Fay is not happier down here than with me. It's a yellow star. He always leaves yellow stars when he's not feeling very perky." Valor clung to

Booger's dried poo while he looked around for more droppings. Rose shared a concerned smile with Aaron who cringed.

"Verily, it is time. It must be done," said Aaron, placing his hands over Valor's face. "Calm yourself, my friend, while I gather your interior sight."

"Okay, but I'm not going to go blind or anything, am I?"

The chamber went black, and Valor began wheezing.

"You will not go blind," replied Aaron. "Now, clear your mind, and let's try this again." The chamber lighting returned to normal, and Aaron continued the spell. "Valor McRaven, I call forth your consciousness to manifest outside your being, to travel by its lighted cord at your beckoning. *Astrumeo Tantumtuus Caput!* You will begin to astral travel as we guide your body on its mission. See with your mind's eye what your heart longs to find." Aaron eased his hands back from Valor's face, lifting a transparent likeness of him as though he were holding a glowing mask connected by a shimmering cord straight through Valor's forehead.

"Whoa!" Valor gasped after his astral head turned back to view his physical body standing several feet back between Aaron and Rose. "That's *my* body? Am I that small?"

"Be mindful that your body cannot pass through solid objects, just your astral head. That is why we will guide your physical body," Aaron said. "Booger Fay could be in any building, behind any wall you choose to see through."

Valor's astral head moved forward, passing through walls, sarcophaguses, and many mystical things. "Wow," he said. "I'm in an old library with ancient books all the way to the ceiling, and they're giving off waves of energy. No, wait. It's word-clouds pouring from the books. I think I've read them before."

"Time merges together sometimes when one is in astral form. Keep searching," said Aaron, guiding Valor's body around the corpses of dust-covered belly dancers, grazing little bells around their hips.

"I see spirits everywhere," said Valor. "They seem lost. They lack the oval-shaped auras that we have, and there are libation urns and fire pits in most of the rooms. I'm receiving telepathic messages that they're exchanging. Can you hear them too?" laughed Valor. "They think I'm a ghost—me."

"We're hearing all sorts of things here," said Doomsy. "Let us know if they say anything scandalous."

"I see signs of necromancy," said Valor. "This place was once inhabited by Noctivatians."

"That's why it's called the Necromanceropolis," said Rose. "The vespercestors have obviously kept it secret for ages."

"I have come to the careful conclusion that both the Noctivatians and Sanguinati summon ghosts. However, the vespercestors banned the term 'Necromancy' in all its forms and have convinced the primitives that they are communing with the Ancients." Aaron stopped speaking to guide Valor around a staircase outside an abandoned sculpture gallery with a sign reading "Mental Metal Manipulations." They moved under the unfolded wings of a dead black pegasus. Mounted atop the winged horse, sat the corpse of a female witch in regal robes, and she had the garish head of a wolf. Blade paused to examine the woman while Aaron continued.

"Noctivatians and Sanguinati are similar in their use of spirit magic, only the Sanguinati do not know it," said Blade. "Noctivatians take it further. They conjure ghosts or loas to control the minds and wills of everything they can, particularly their Familiars, which are controlled by imps," said Blade.

"How?" asked Doomsy.

"I'm afraid they do much of it by reanimation of the dead."

"Reanimation of the dead," repeated Doomsy, with a hint of alarm. "As in zombies?"

Blade nodded. "Zombies, doppelgangers—some type of Fetch perhaps."

They ducked under a massive tree limb growing out of an abandoned Eternal Chamber Lighting store. Some of the lanterns now hung from tree branches, while three torches burned on the stone sidewalk.

"This is why I wanted Valor to have nothing to do with the Noctivatians, but it is too late now, is it not?" said Aaron.

"It seems like Sorcerers once performed libations here as well. Unless it was Chacodophilus. I remember seeing him use the dead in these tombs to make *The Book of the Dead*—his book."

Rose looked over her shoulder with remorse. The dark medallion on her forehead swung over her pale upturned brow. "But we didn't know Falmoth and the Hermetic Order were . . . *vampires*. Did we, Blade?"

"You should've had some premonition, Rose," said Blade. He snatched his cloak over an empty cauldron and continued his cocky stride around the skeletal remains of a winged creature. "Blade would never have given Falmoth the time of day."

"Booger Fay, come to me," shouted Valor. "Hold on—I'm in a painted black room with a coffin-lid door. The sign on the wall says, 'Den of the Doubter Sacrifice.' I see the remnants of a bone-fire and a crude blueprint. I expect it's for the Mystic Key . . . like the one I swallowed. It looks like wiggiwami corpses on the floor. I'm getting a vision. Some of the Sanguinati tried to regain the power of Sorcery by performing Grim magic in this room, but they cursed themselves instead." Valor's voice became robotic. "They all left this place during the Great Deception."

"Oh, greasy globoids," said Rose. "The Noctivatians must've taken over this underground city from Chacodophilus before the Sanguinati drove them out. Maybe that's why the Noctivatians relocated to the region of Bogamuckla."

"It's all making sense," said Valor. "At some point after the Sanguinati lost their Sorcery, some of them, Falmoth and Banzalta probably, tried to get it back down here using necromancy, but it backfired, turning them into cursed vampires instead."

"Guys, something is off with that timeline unless they were massive phonies—unless they despised themselves," said Rose. "When we traveled back in time through the portal, Falmoth and the LaRocks shunned Sorcerers, and that was just before they killed Ambergis. Remember, Falmoth told Bazalta they would have to take the wiggiwamis with them and go live in the catacombs under Mystic Steeples so they could get revenge on the Sanguinati."

Everyone agreed as Aaron and Rose guided Valor's body two twisting turns into what now appeared to be a catacomb. "I bid you, hasten your search," said Aaron. "It is not safe to linger in your astral form."

"I'll say," croaked Doomsy, as she sprinted to keep up with everyone. "Valor's astral neck is stretching awfully thin. We wouldn't want him to lose his head."

"I'm having a hard time seeing through some of these walls now," said Valor. "Ugh, my head just passed through a sarcophagus, and someone draped in rotted fabric. Oh, Booger Fay, wherever you are in this tomb dump, you can't be happy." Valor couldn't travel much farther in his astral body. All that remained of his neck was a mere silvery thread, but he just had to check one last chamber. He held his breath and stretched his head through the carved stone wall.

"VALOR! Erm, have you become a ghost, too?" asked Booger Fay, crawling across the chamber to examine Valor's astral head.

"I found him—oh!" shouted Valor. He hoped to the heavens that he wasn't experiencing an illusion, as he admired the Elusive Griffin scratching his feathery head with his paw, while his wings unfurled to a stagnant puddle fed by water trickling from cracks in the ancient mortar surrounding the magnificent creature.

"Splendid," said Aaron, tapping Valor's shoulder. "Now reconnect with your body lest your astral cord becomes broken."

"Aw. I guess I have no choice," said Valor. Reluctant to return to his body in case he lost his beloved Familiar again. His astral head eased back through the wall. "Wow. I now feel trapped in a block of cement after my spirit was free like that."

"It was all in your head," laughed Blade, while Booger slammed the sarcophagus door open and pounced to Valor's side.

"See? I'm not dead, Booger. I'm so glad I found you!" said Valor, placing his arms around his Familiar's feathery neck.

"Look, my tail is wagging. I could, erm, make you some special green-clover droppings," said Booger Fay, squatting on his hind legs.

"No-no," everyone yelled, except for Valor. Aaron covered his nose with his lace hanky.

Booger Fay cocked his head before propping a wing and a front paw on the sarcophagus door. "Oh well, it might not turn out too green because Foul Moth said you'd come and get me a lot sooner than this."

"Foul Mouth?" asked Valor. "You mean Venerious *Falmoth*?"

"If you say so," said Booger Fay. "I got lonely waiting for you. I, erm, tried to make a friend—a sphinxter—in the chamber. She's, erm, guarding something she says belongs to the Boogeyman. I won't let sphinxter out, because you said the Boogeyman's dangerous."

Something slammed hard against the sarcophagus door, stirring dust, and making a loud BOOM!

"Sphinxes seek out and guard treasure. I'll bet she's found Chacodophilus's Crown," said Valor. "But that creature sounds huge and frightening. Did she attack you, Booger?"

"Erm, me? Nah. I pinned sphinxter down with my paws," said Booger Fay. "I'll get the treasure if you want. Sphinxter has it in a wooden box."

"Okay, but don't get hurt and come straight back here," said Valor.

Blade removed his cloak, cracked his knuckles, and swung his arms as if preparing to cast a powerful spell. "Zagato will go with you, Booger, and show these amateur apprentices the inherent skills of a true witch," said Blade, practicing deep breathing and sorcery-charging techniques in extreme body positions. Rose knocked Blade's boot out of her face so that he vaulted upright and followed behind Booger Fay as he eased open the door with his paws and crawled inside the chamber.

"Take your time in there, Blade," said Doomsy. She pulled out Mr. Grudgings from her dress pocket and fed him a fly.

Their eyes enlarged after a hideous screeching noise preceded loud bangs and crashes. "Oh, sweet Sesepha—lofty Webbits Cobbratz—golden Usabelli," cried Blade. "Heh-heh-help!" The door flung open and out ran a female sphinx, tall on her hind paws. Her face seemed timeless, almost pretty compared to her lioness body and serpent-like tail.

"May the treasure be a curse to you, for you have solved no riddle," growled the sphinx before it vanished around the bend in the hall.

Booger Fay came out of the chamber, dragging a very tattered and passed out Blade Zagato. Hooked around Booger's tail was a bejeweled crown. Rose grabbed the crown while Aaron and Valor checked on Blade.

"Oh, my gargoyles. I think your intuition was right, Valor," said Rose. "This has to be the long-lost crown of Chacodophilus!"

"Let me see," said Doomsy. She took the crown from Rose and placed it on Valor's head, while he knelt on the floor, trying to revive Blade.

"What are you doing, my dear?" asked Valor.

"We still wonder if you are the descendant of Chacodophilus, destined to become head vespercestor," said Doomsy. "I thought if I placed the crown on your head, you'd have an epiphany, or I don't know, a gemstone might glow or something."

A flock of bird-like shadows flew across the ceiling and vanished through a distant wall. "The only thing I can foresee is we need to find our way out of the Necromanceropolis. Is there any other way out of here?" asked Valor, after Blade was able to sit up and speak.

"There is no map," groaned Blade, holding his claw-scratched hands over his face. "This place isn't supposed to exist according to the vespercestors."

Valor tore off a sleeve from his shirt and used it as a bandage around Blade's forehead to stop the bleeding. "You were quite the zealot in there. Glad you survived," said Valor.

The color in Blade's eyes intensified as he gazed into the shadows with a mixture of shock and appreciation. Rose took the crown from Doomsy and started to place it on Blade's head, but he threw up his injured hands, blocking her.

"Do not do that again!" hissed Blade, jarring everyone to turn their attention to him. "It's just—one mustn't treat sacred objects carelessly—objects that do not belong to them. You heard the sphinx. It could hold a curse, for all you know."

"Brave Blade the braggart—afraid of a silly crown," said Rose, easing the crown over her tower of black ringlets and posing as though for a photo. "I guess we should leave now. But from the looks of this place, we could go for miles no matter what direction we head."

"Maybe we should head up," suggested Doomsy.

"Up?" asked Blade, peeking between his fingers with a perplexed expression. "Haven't seen a passage leading up, just down. We could be anywhere under Mystic Steeples for all we know."

"Valor can zap a hole through the ceiling, can't you, my pet?" said Doomsy.

"Yea!" cheered Rose.

"Nooo," said Valor. "I can't just break through the ceiling without knowing what's up there. I mean, who knows what could happen?"

"Not if we do the astral preview again," offered Aaron, placing his hands close to Valor's face.

"Yeah, it might work," said Valor. He closed his eyes while Aaron placed his hands over his face and recited a spell to extract his inner sight.

Valor's astral head floated from his body and paused on the stone ceiling under a resurrectionist's corpse holding a chalice and a staff. He moved to the side of the corpse. "Here goes," said Valor. His head went through the ceiling and into complete darkness until torches lit a room he recognized: A pendulum hung from a ceiling hook, and astrological and alchemical maps rested on a hydrocrystalophone, while magnetized water flowed backward in a fountain beside a hypnosis wheel. Lucky for him, the room was empty of mesmerists. A clock ticking near a few fainting pads rolled up against the wall reminded him that he should withdraw his head back to his body.

"If I knock a hole through the ceiling here, it'll come out in the Mission of the Mind of the Mesmerists," said Valor. "I didn't see anyone there. The mesmerists should've gone home to sleep by now."

They stepped back before Valor zapped several energy blasts at the ceiling with his monoculous, careful not to desecrate the corpse. Blocks of dust and stone crashed to the floor at their feet. With

Booger Fay and the crown safely at their sides, they floated out of the Necromanceropolis. Valor decided to leave the hole in the floor so Mystic Ministry could find the Necromanceropolis or at least stop pretending they don't know it exists.

CHAPTER FIFTEEN

THE CHALICE OF SCOURGE

AARON, Micha, and Blade helped Valor haul his coffin into a secret chamber behind a tapestry wall panel deep inside Candlewicke Mansion. The guardians were starting to do unannounced home inspections, so Valor thought it best for everyone that he hide the evidence of his shame.

"I can't believe he has to hide in his own house. Why not just keep our bedroom doors locked?" asked Doomsy, responding to the thud as they dropped the coffin. She stepped out of the coffin and inspected the chamber hidden between two other rooms.

"You should still be able to sleep in your wardrobe, Doomsy. Urbanne only banned wooden chest wider than three feet," said Valor, while Micha's nine-headed phoenix sang in nine octaves.

Manning stuck his head inside the hidden chamber and said, "'Salazants has readied the carriage to escort the presidents of Cryptic Chambers to their, uh, meeting.' Yeah, that's what he said. So, you ready?"

"Yes, but Valor and Aaron are going to lead that stupid meeting, not me," said Doomsy, while Egg Goodridge made sure they all had on their new coven uniforms.

Valor checked to make sure Booger Fay was safe and well-fed before Salazants dropped them off at Cryptic Castle in the carriage. The Cryptic Choral started the meeting with a song:

> *"Return to the old landmarks, my friends.*
> *Do magic with your wands and not your hands.*
> *Sorcery is scummy; it ain't even funny.*
> *Rise up, coven buddies, and make a stand!*
> *Boot out the darkness, good Crypts.*
> *Wicked Noctivatians and dumb Nizzertits.*
> *Only Sanguinati are worthy; all others are dirty,*
> *Be they Nockie princes or coven presidents."*

Gazing around the auditorium with arrogant expressions, the female Crypts hoisted their long hair over the backs of their chairs as they lifted their wands toward the ceiling. When the song ended, Egg motioned for Valor to address the coven members. Valor walked to the podium. He would try again to do what Venerious Falmoth wanted him to do. His heart pounded with apprehension as he looked out over the auditorium.

"Cryptic Chambers, I'm concerned with the divisive attitudes among our members," he said. "You should know, things aren't what they seem around here, and, um, we all may be seeing some dangerous and troubling times soon."

"Ho-ho, I'll say," laughed Delicia Jones. She sat on the front row beside Donny-Dale-Dharma Thelastone, the conjoined triplets, who all crossed their legs, kicking each other because they were not in unison for once. "We could all be turned into swamp toads and banned from visiting our friends."

"N-never mind the Grim Warlock," said Valor, squeaking his words now that he couldn't shut Delicia out of his mind. "Someone from Mystic Ministry could attack us at any minute, and it might just be the very people you snub who'll save your life. So, think for yourself, and, and think about how you treat others." He folded his notes and walked away from the podium. He couldn't bring himself to insist that the Sanguinati had all been Sorcerers in the past. He had been a complete bumbling failure.

Esoterica Knowles pushed her glasses up on her nose with a trembling wrist while Twila Diamone took the stage.

"If anybody's been affected by lurking danger, it's been Cryptic Chambers," said Twila. "But really, Valor, everybody knows Mystic Ministry is no threat to us. Now, on a proactive note, I am pleased to announce that I have found a code in the *Magic Ledger* concerning Magister Crypting's disappearance." Twila held up the newspaper giving it a couple of triumphant tugs with her hands before frowning at Valor, Doomsy, and Aaron. "Despite—I regret to say—our presidents' refusal to allow me access to the Chamber of Oracles." Some of the Crypts jeered the presidents, and Twila added, "Now, I don't like to gossip, but what might we expect from presidents who sleep in coffins?"

"Only presidents from this coven are allowed in the Chamber of Oracles," hissed Doomsy. She jerked and squirmed between Aaron and Valor in the presidents' chairs, on the far right of the stage. The Crypts gasped and whispered, while some changed their seating to discuss the news with a friend.

"But despite all that," said Twila, banging a crystaleer on the podium to silence the Crypts, "I placed my new regulations-approved crystaleer over the newspaper article, and do you know what?" Twila adjusted the bottom bow on her pointed white hat. "The first letter from each paragraph magnified in the crystaleer pointing to Magister Crypting's killer, and the word was 'Sorcerer!'" Twila went into a tearful trance, acting as though some power was channeling through before pointing her wand at Valor. The Cryptic Choral scattered off the platform, screaming defense mantras and dancing to summon magic-spell energy. Several Crypts pulled out venomous snakes and charmed the serpents with their sensational chanting, music, and dancing.

"*Pseudo-gusto mumbo-gizmo Shinto-pronto*," Twila chanted in a martyred voice during the choral's eerie pause.

"You don't think she's right about Magister Crypting, do you?" Valor asked Aaron and Doomsy. He still refused to believe his favorite magister was dead.

"She's nothing but talk," replied Doomsy.

"True. At least the drum bangers know when to break without a cue," added Aaron, as if trying to cheer up Valor and Doomsy.

Twila held up the article from the *Magic Ledger* again and said, "Crypts, this is not the only evidence pointing to shadow tossers as being the cause of the attacks and deaths at Mystic Steeples. I've also found similar clues in *The Daily Hazy Herald* concerning the disappearance of our former coven leader Ernest Diggs." Twila smiled and hid her missing fingers behind a bow on her dress. "We can't allow Sorcerer or Nockie power-lust to destroy what our order was intended to become. At this time, I'm going to invite my brother, Marston, to come up on the stage and bring the Chalice of Scourge."

"Thanks, Twila," said Marston, placing the chalice on the podium and adjusting a misplaced curl over his forehead. "Crypts, I know we have to abide by the rules of the vespercestory, but they weren't always this slack in judgment—allowing these Nockies and shadow tossers to worm their way in Mystic Steeples and become presidents of our covens. The coven of Graven Dust has it right. They're asking us to partner with them and do something about it— Graven Dust, the most prestigious coven, is asking *us*—the lowest-ranked among the covens! This could finally be our chance to rise in status!"

After a wave of booing died down, Creighton Crowley's second oldest brother, Burdock, shouted, "That is treason! Graven Dust has always treated us like ogre dung. They can't be trusted."

"Looks like you're outnumbered, Burdock. Now, as I was saying: you may be wondering why I brought this Chalice of Scourge," said

Marston, holding the goblet with a grin that suggested it contained a fortune in gold. "It is filled with Auravitamax."

"The hot new aura-enhancing tonic everybody who's anybody is using," added Twila.

"I borrowed the Chalice from Summoner Mamahchi," continued Marston. "We need to investigate everybody for Sorcerer and Noctivatian blood and force the vespercestory to oust them."

Dozens of the Crypts appeared to go into convulsions, cheering and shouting, while others remained seated. Marston's eyes drooped under his wide forehead as though he were looking for suspects in the auditorium. Twila squinted at Valor, Aaron, and Doomsy, offsetting her cancerous smile, as she stood behind Marston with one hand on her hip.

"Your family owns that aura-tonic, Marston," said Valor. "How do we know it's not some trick of yours to make us all look like we have the wrong blood? I'll not have you subject the Crypts to possible humiliation."

"Yeah!" several of the Crypts agreed.

"Why did Summoner Mamahchi help get us out of Ogre Skull Hill, then give Marston the Chalice, knowing Mystic Ministry would put us right back in that skull prison?" Doomsy asked Valor.

"I was wondering the same thing," said Valor. "Mamahchi might be mad because I haven't been reporting back to him instead of Urbanne."

Doomsy gripped the chair seat as though she were trying to keep from lunging after Marston and Twila. "And who invited the Diamones to speak anyway?" She stormed out of the auditorium.

"Please wait!" said Valor, as he and Aaron ran after her through the admissions hall and out to Cryptic Gardens. Valor tripped on a step in the moonlight, but it wasn't Aaron or him who called her name the second time.

"Don't w-worry about Marston and Twila. They, um, c-can't force us to subject to blood tests. I wouldn't g-give them any of my blood to put in the chalice," said Egg Goodridge.

"We did not grant them permission to speak tonight, Dooms,"

said Aaron.

"The, um, Diamones g-grab the spotlight any time they c-can. You could've stopped them if you wanted to," said Egg. He sniffed the moonflowers, which hung over his head from a double-C-shaped trellis.

"Marston and Twila never wanted to be in Cryptic Chambers," said Doomsy. "They're just mad because we are the presidents now."

"They're mad at me, mainly," said Valor. "I'm the reason they didn't make it into Graven Dust. But what they're trying to do is dangerous and disturbing."

"I, um, I think you're right. I s-sense something wicked brewing," said Egg. His head rested on the trellis, facing the imposing buildings across the cobblestoned alley.

Valor stood taller, listening to the driving rhythm of the drums, organ, and the choral inside the castle. "Just listen to them in there," he said. "The choral and the Diamones are really working the Crypts into a frenzy."

"Do you not see now?" asked Aaron. "Falmoth is putting you at great risk with this mission of convincing the Sanguinati that they were once the people they've been trained to despise."

"We have thirteen members in our secret coven, now we just need to prepare any defenses we have," said Valor.

"You incurably hopeless softy," Doomsy said to Valor. "Egg is not a Sorcerer, no matter how much you want him in Candlewicke Coven."

Valor sulked at Doomsy, and Aaron distanced himself from the awkward moment by looking at the clouds and scratching his cheek.

Seeing Egg visibly upset, Valor leaned back proudly and said, "It doesn't matter. I would take Egg over most anybody. He belongs with us."

"I know I'm a Sorcerer. I've b-been p-practicing every day." Breathing hard, Egg looked back at Cryptic Castle, lifted his trembling left hand, and chanted a spell. Instantly the candlelit windows turned dark.

"Did you do that?" asked Doomsy.

"You bet he did! Egg has officially hatched," said Valor, patting Egg on the back, joined by Aaron.

"Not bad," said Doomsy through clenched teeth.

"It's jolly fantastic is what it is," said Valor, while Egg seemed entranced at his newfound power. "Now, how far along has Stabbah come with the Electricus Hexigus spell?" asked Valor, hopeful the scroll they had found in the Chamber of Oracles a while back would work, and they could recreate the talismans for the Crown of Chacodophilus.

"She's working on it tonight. I don't think it'll be much longer," said Doomsy, before they returned to Candlewicke Mansion.

"Heat the crucible," said Rose. "In an hour from now, Mars will align with Venus." She glided around the wizards' parlor as if she had something grand to reveal.

Grinning behind her, Creighton threw his arms behind his back and flung off his coat. Salazants mumbled unpleasant words, conjuring the coat to hook on the hall tree before it had a chance to hit the polished floor.

"We don't have a Wand of Alchemy to complete the Electricus Hexigus," said Valor, after figuring out what Rose was doing.

"We do," said Creighton. "Rose and I managed to get Ziggy Centaury's Wand of Alchemy while he was attending to a composition that just so happened to explode in our assembly earlier today."

"'That just so happened to,' huh?" asked Valor suspiciously.

"Kaboom! Hot crazy potion rained over the whole room. I think I'm finally growing arm hair now," continued Creighton. He pulled the wand out of its case and held it up for all of Candlewicke Coven to see. "I think I'm man enough now to stir the final melting."

"Are you sure? I mean, Stab has five talisman molds ready to pour the mixture into, if you're sure you can handle it," said Nalini Lusion, wringing her hands.

"We're ready," said Rose.

"Well, okay, I guess maybe Ruza and I'll go light the crucible," said Nalini.

"I'm glad ya've overcome ya fear of flames, Nalini," said Micha, studying a book on dragons, while Creighton followed the girls, rubbing his hand over the two hairs on his arm.

Wearing a dark and sinister costume, Egg Goodridge floated at sporadic speeds down the staircase and through the grand hall, kicking over a lamp before knocking a painting askew with his arm.

"Egg! Ya've learned ta float! Heck, I knew ya were a Sorcerer," said Micha dropping his book.

"Making him immortal seems to have activated his inherent powers. He needs to learn to control his shadow first. He's going to demolish my furnishings," said Aaron, wincing beside every vase, mirror, and statue in Egg's path.

"He's trying to get away from the ghosts. He can see them now, you know," said Valor, with a tone of uncertainty.

"Floating is m-much better than flying a broom," said Egg. "Your g-gonna be g-glad you let me in your coven. S-so's a circle of thirteen is gonna make our p-powers increase and m-make these ghosts go away?"

"I'm not sure about that," said Doomsy. "But it seems to have given you an eye for clothing."

Egg tried to cast his shadow on the wall. "I wanna look c-cool, like a real Sorcerer," he said. "But I don't think I can drink b-blood, though."

"Goodness no. Where did you get that idea?" asked Valor.

The front doors blew open, startling Doomsy so that she ripped an arm off her poppet doll.

"See, everybody? It's me, me, me!" announced Venerious Falmoth, entering the hall in his usual stalking stride, holding his arm behind his back. Egg lost his concentration and fell to the base of the staircase.

"You!" shouted Aaron, snapping around to face him.

"Me! And *I* brought . . . candy," said Falmoth with expanded eyes.

He held up a three-foot-tall skeleton made of candy, with a candy-cane ribcage, marshmallow skull, and sagging-gumdrop eyeballs. "Sorry, I was out of Dill Treacle Pickles and Twisted Whisker Crisps."

Aaron shot toward Falmoth and stomped his left boot on the floor. "You cannot just barge in Candlewicke unannounced. What manner of ruffian are you?"

Falmoth's smile wilted, and he appeared to blush under his white face powder as he lowered the skeleton behind his back. "But I did imagine your bones would be shaking to see me—you'd be jumping out of your skin," said Falmoth. "What do I get? Not even a gristle-eating grin on your pouty little chins." He flung the skeleton confection out the doorway to Spookum Alley. "Never fret." He patted Aaron on his squared shoulder. "I've brought a certain somebody who is dying to express her regrets." Falmoth removed two arm bones from his cloak and made a drum roll on the antique hall table to usher a woman into the grand hall—a disturbingly familiar woman.

Valor jumped up from the parlor chair, so alarmed that he got hiccups. Doomsy pulled out her wand and aimed it at the woman—Bohemia.

"How dare you bring that bum-born, plague-venomed, maggot-pie in our house?" asked Doomsy, firing a flame spell at Bohemia.

"*Kookoo-oozie Skullfillet Tangipaingoa*," chanted Falmoth, crossing the arm bones to conjure a shadowy wraith, which enveloped the shooting flames, smothering them, until a pile of soot collected on the marble floor. Then he pulled a broom-straw from under his hat and tossed it to the floor, which hexed Doomsy's wand to fling out of her hand.

Doomsy charged after Bohemia, but Valor grabbed her, receiving a few of her boot-kicks to his shin.

"Please, I beg you all to forgive me," said Bohemia, holding out her hands. "I promise I can explain—then I will leave."

Micha, Egg, and Blade joined Valor in shielding Doomsy, while Rose levitated a marble bracket off the wall, where it remained hovering in the air, ready for her to hurl it at Falmoth. Aaron moved to block Bohemia and Falmoth from coming any farther inside the mansion.

"Why, pray tell, should we forgive you?" Aaron asked Bohemia.

"Because . . . I now have proof your beloved O Enchantedness killed Mesthu," said Bohemia.

"You heard her," added Falmoth, twisting in a dance. "Urbanne LaRock is a dirty little murderer."

"Which should come as no surprise. You already know old Urby is plotting to kill all of our sorts," continued Bohemia. She leaned into the wall, and her head rolled to face Aaron with a smug grin. "Aurora was going to sentence me to an iron coffin." Bohemia stroked her fingers over the rip in Falmoth's cheek. "But Venerious rescued me and gave me another way to pay for my crimes. I've joined the Hermetic Order of the Mystic Key. I vow to find a way to stop Urbanne, and to protect you and your—frosty friends." Bohemia nodded in a self-sacrificing manner, turned, and walked out of the mansion.

"Darn it! Wasn't that as sweet as my little Sweeturnips?" asked Falmoth with a crooked grin, but Valor and the others remained tense and prepared to defend the coven. "Now, Valor, I need you and your fiends—oops, I meant 'friends' to promptly leave—flee Convocation tomorrow night when Bohemia reveals herself to old Urbanne. Did I make myself plain?"

"But what's going to happen?" Valor said with a hiccup, trying to grab Falmoth's attention before he, too, left the old mansion.

Falmoth peeked around the doorframe and shook his finger. "No-no, you joined the Hermetic Order. Our command, you must honor." With that, Falmoth tossed Valor another sack of Luminous Lulling Lozenges.

The next afternoon, just before the evening Convocation on Ostara Sabbat weekend, Aaron rushed off to the stores to buy some baskets with candy eggs and chocolate Ostara bunnies to celebrate Booger Fay's return. Valor's thoughts of celebration were often interrupted with Summoner Mamahchi's past warning about a dangerous spy who went missing, a spy with the initials E.B. just like Valor discovered on Bohemia's butterfly bracelet.

"She admitted she was a former spy for Urbanne, and she's definitely 'deadly.' Whether Urbanne killed Mesthu or not, I'll never trust her for trying to frame you and Aaron—she nearly killed you," said Doomsy, as they explored the sprawling mansion, trying not to get lost.

"I've made up my mind then," said Valor. "I haven't been reporting back to Summoner Mamahchi at all, and I no longer trust Urbanne. I guess I'll have to confide in Mamahchi and tell him about Bohemia's plan to attend Convocation tonight."

"Has a goblin feasted on your brain?" asked Doomsy. "We both overheard Mamahchi telling Crumpecker that a Sorcerer was behind the Darkening and that they should round us all up."

"I know, my dear, but that was the only time I saw him like that. I think he was referring to Mega D—even we suspected Mega D was behind the Darkening. No, I think Mamahchi was just afraid like everyone was. He bravely accused Urbanne, too, until Crumpecker bit his head off for it."

With their wands giving off light, Valor and Doomsy passed through an art gallery with disturbing paintings hanging crookedly. Doomsy paused near a ceramic urn wedged halfway into the wall where it had narrowly missed a portrait of an old man fussing about angry people throwing things at him.

"Afraid or not—to even suggest rounding up a whole group of people because of one suspect is the stuff of monsters," she croaked, pointing her wand in Valor's face.

"Perhaps so," sighed Valor. "But I don't know how much longer I can avoid reporting back to the summoner. Besides, it might be the best way to see where he stands with us—with everything."

An hour later, Cyclopuss, Summoner Eelias Mamahchi's one-eyed albino cat, pawed open the door to the Office of Apprentice Registration in Mystic Steeples, letting Valor inside the dark office.

"Seal the door, Cyclopuss," said Mamahchi.

"As you wisssh," the cat hissed, pawing the sword deadbolt to secure the door.

Valor eased in one of the sharply carved chairs in front of the summoner's cluttered desk.

"I'm busy, McRaven. What do you need?" Mamahchi asked coldly.

"You wanted me to report to you. I think I finally have something you might be interested in, but can I ask you something first, sir?"

Mamahchi kept his head behind a copy of the *Daily Hazy Herald* and twirled two fingers, motioning for Valor to ask.

"Well, sir, you once told me that you helped get me out of solitary confinement and into Mystic Steeples because I sought justice for murder victims and for the nobodies. You were about the only member of Mystic Ministry who was glad I stood up to Crumpecker."

"And?" said Mamahchi, flipping pages of the newspaper.

"I, uh, know Rendum LaRock accused you of having a dim aura. I know the LaRocks treated you and your family like nobodies."

Mamahchi lowered his newspaper, crumpling it. His bushy gray eyebrows twitched over his scrunched eyes. "Who told you this?"

"I have a vigilespion soul, Summoner; that's why you wanted me to spy for you, remember? You were once a nobody like me—like a lot of people here in Severance. It may have even been the reason your parents were killed during the Drowning Verdicts."

Mamahchi's cheek began to twitch, and his nostrils flared under his battered hat. "The LaRocks had nothing to do with . . . their deaths."

"I know, sir: you didn't blame them the same way they didn't blame you for the death of Mahrata's father. That was a generous trade-off indeed."

"What's your point?" snorted Mamahchi. His gnarled fingers wadded the newspaper tighter.

"My point is, sir, it's a good thing 'nobodies,' like me and you, don't accuse people wrongfully. For instance, I would never accuse you of wanting to 'round up all the Sorcerers' and kill them, even though you accused my parents of killing my grandmother, Ellavyn. So naturally, for somebody charged with having a dim aura, I'm just a bit confused by this 'hot new Aura Tonic' you've created. Aren't you concerned that it's being used by the Sanguinati Elite to target those they call 'nobodies'? It seems to be your investors'—the Diamone family's—favorite word, sir," said Valor.

Mamahchi's index finger faintly vibrated on his desk, and his dark eyes became distant.

"You are a far better spy than I expected. I needn't say . . . anything. You know what it's like for nobodies to do what we can to survive. Mistakes, yes, but mistakes will never outweigh the injustice done to us."

"I think I understand. You are using the Diamones the same way they're using you. Getting ahead is great, but not at the expense of the innocent—not at the expense of selling your soul," said Valor.

"Sometimes it's the only playing card . . . for the greater good . . . nobodies have left, McRaven. Unless you wish to spoil my little success with another ethics lecture, what is the report you have for me?"

Valor explained everything he had experienced with Bohemia and how she confessed that she was once a spy for Urbanne. "Bohemia plans to make some sort of appearance in Convocation tonight. I think she has evidence that Urbanne murdered Master Mesthu." Valor paused to evaluate the summoner's reaction and see if he knew this.

With tightened lips, Mamahchi diverted his gaze slightly and stroked his gray beard.

"I'm, uh, worried things might get serious," said Valor, disturbed by Mamahchi's silence. As much as Valor distrusted Urbanne, he also felt the same way about Bohemia. He just didn't want any more deaths.

"You did the right thing . . . reporting this," mumbled the summoner, dismissing Valor, who left straight to Convocation.

Valor paused in the Atrium, just outside of the Vespercestors' Vestibule. He stared up at the corpse of the Star Being known as Spirit, according to his assigned element anyway. Valor had recently learned that, when Spirit was in outer space as the thirteenth member of the Order of the Zodiac, he was known as Ophiuchus. After someone bound Spirit as a prisoner on Earth, he took on a human form and became known as Eclipticus, the fifth in the Bound Order of the Zodiac. Of all the Zodiac corpses in the alcoves, Spirit looked the oldest with his long white beard, leathery brown skin, and stooped posture. His wrinkled hand persistently remained in the air; only there was no Staff of Gleaning between his fingers.

"If only you could talk, Spirit, and tell me where to find your magic staff so I can stop this dreadful Possessing," whispered Valor, when no one was in the Atrium. He looked around at the other Zodiac Beings. "Are you really corpses, or has the Sanguinati petrified you somehow—until they're ready to use you for battle?"

Valor heard Marston and Twila coming, so he rushed through the Congre Gate into Mystic Chantry, where the members of Candlewicke 13 began sorting into their assigned coven sections.

Someone was missing, and Valor was instantly uncomfortable.

"Aaron should be back from shopping by now," Valor said to Doomsy and Egg, while they gathered in the Cryptic Chambers' section.

"He gets carried away in the stores," said Doomsy. "He'll be here soon."

Valor sat down on the bench and spotted Bohemia on the front right side of the Chantry. She had shaved both sides of her head while the top of her hair cascaded with silver waves now. "Bohemia's sitting in the Graven Dust section. She must have been in their coven years ago, you know, before she went to Shadowhaven Heights."

"So, she has; the vulture has returned to nest," said Aaron, slipping in the bench section beside Valor at last. His appearance seemed harried and pastier than usual. Something had to be wrong.

"I'm g-getting anxious. What's she g-gonna do—start fires or something?" asked Egg, while Valor, Aaron, and Doomsy remained alert.

The pendulum chain of Doomsy's black headdress swung under her chin. "You've got a lot to learn," she whispered to Egg. "Immortals aren't into fire. Bohemia wouldn't want to risk death."

"She's with the Children of the Gloaming now," said Valor. "No telling what she might do."

Delicia Jones stood up in the bench with her hands extended in front of her. Alarmed, Valor nudged Aaron and said, "What is she doing, feeling for ghosts?" They all kept watch of Delicia as she began chanting and easing around as if feeling the vibrations throughout the Chantry. Whirling his silver wand, Preston Fox continued to lead the choir in the anthem "Skyward We Fly." The stargazers stood on the platform edge, awaiting a sign from the statue of Ramrod in a high alcove. Doomsy nudged Valor and said, "Look."

To their left, a procession of Seventh Sons carried an infant on a curtained throne down the aisle. Surrounded by lavish pillows, the infant played with a little wand inside the glass viewing box, which also contained a white bunny rabbit and a basket of colored eggs.

Several pointed hats and lace-veiled heads turned toward Delicia as she moved around, gazing up at the ceiling. The choir stopped singing, leaving only a symphony of whispers, which echoed from the highest balconies to the ground floor.

"Sanguinati, fireclappers will overtake this sanctuary if you don't celebrate our newest addition to the Ancestral Pentacle of LaRock," said Urbanne. He motioned toward the infant in the viewing box, "Thiolahfuh Alkerich Crowley, a seventh son—The Heir of LaRock who shall rile the priestly vestry!"

"*Rule* the priestly vestry," said Urbanne's wife, Mahrata.

Urbanne slammed his magic staff against the floor. The corner of his eyebrow bushed up, blending with the vertical crease on his forehead, giving him a devious look. "Cheer for Thio!" demanded Urbanne, aiming his staff around the Chantry. With a blink of Valor's eyelids, it seemed he was among a different gathering of covens: The cheers, chanting, and applause became deafening.

"How about that," said Valor, yelling in Doomsy's ear so she could hear him through the noise. "The Crowleys had a seventh son of a seventh son, and Creighton never even told us his parents were expecting."

"I knew he has been acting really flighty these past few months," said Doomsy. "And did you hear that? Old Urby said, 'The Heir of LaRock,' but *The Book of Chacodophilus* says, 'The Heir of Chacodophilus shall rule the priestly vestry.'"

"Does it surprise you?" asked Valor. "Even if he's aware of *The Book of Chacodophilus*, he'd never admit it or pronounce it right."

Aaron folded his arms and said, "Something is amiss. Creighton and his other brothers are from Ulysses LaRock's side of the family tree, as are you, Valor. Why can't you be the successor if the requirement is to have LaRock blood?"

"There is too much controversy or genetic curses with all the other family members," said Valor. "See that woman sitting in the middle of the aisle?"

Aaron leaned across him to have a look. "If you mean that ridiculous woman sitting under that narrow canopy of netting, then yes," said Aaron. "I've noticed apprentices tripping over her."

Valor gave a discouraging nod and said, "That is Ulysses LaRock's daughter-in-law, Daphne—also a LaRock by blood. Her husband, Numrod, was just killed by the Possessing. She lives under that coffin of netting because of her bug phobia. Don't even get me started listing all the issues with Urbanne's descendants. So, I can only conclude, a seventh son of a seventh son works like a magic eraser and wipes away all that stuff."

"Verily, the head vespercestor's position is supposed to be obtained by public vote, not heirs," said Aaron.

Drucilla Hollapolk stepped up to the podium and conjured the magihorn closer to her glowing face. "Sanguinati," she said, "baby

Thiolahfuh pee-peed in my herb garden, and the mandrakes grew two-plus feet overnight. Yes!" Drucilla raised her arms in triumph while everyone continued to celebrate. "And Alizaba Crowley said her baby's natural odor has gotten rid of all the ants in her kitchen. Yes. So, I babysat him, I did. And now, my whole house is free of huffin flies!" Drucilla wiped a tear of joy from her cheek. "I assure you; the Ancients have poured a Big Dipper full of gifts on our future leader."

"'The Ancients,' my bunions," scoffed Doomsy. "No wonder they have to keep baby Thio in a glass box." She pinched her nose, and her mouth shriveled like a bleached raisin. "It's all those philters Alizaba drank to birth him—all that wormwood has made her screwy," added Doomsy, mimicking a heavy drinker.

"Well," said Valor, trying to cheer up Aaron and Doomsy, "if baby Thio doesn't make head vespercestor, he can seek a career in stench witching."

Bohemia blew kisses with her hands to the revelers in every direction. The chanting and cheers turned to hysterical laughter. The seventh sons laughed so hard they had to put down the viewing box with the infant before they dropped him. Hanzabuh Cuddy's face turned redder and puffier than usual before she fell and rolled around in the aisle, exposing her pantaloons.

"How strange," said Valor. "Magister Dearth Downdilly just tripped trying to help Hanzabuh off the floor. Now he's laughing."

"Did B-Bohemia cause this, or did they g-get a whiff of baby Thio?" asked Egg, huddling between Valor and Doomsy to avoid the crowd trampling him.

"Bohemia, I think," replied Valor. He noticed his great grandmother Lockie Pomeroy LaRock cackling so hard in the Loft of Elders, her hat along with five feet of her hair spilled over the edge of the balcony.

"Not a bad hex. Not bad at all," said Doomsy, pushing her sleeve back. "See, you could file your nails on my chill bumps."

Egg's head danced, watching the fun. "We're n-not hexed. It's not affecting us."

"Stop this, ha-ha-he, disrespectful debacle," yelled Urbanne.

Behind him, on her throne chair, Mahrata also cackled as if madness had stricken her.

"Bohemia must be here to do battle. She is relishing every moment," said Aaron.

With eyes filled with wile, Bohemia swished through the aisles, wearing studded black belts high and tight around her waist. Exhaustion, mixed with fascination, seemed to build among the covens. Bohemia winked at Valor and his friends, and Valor held his breath, biting his lip.

"What's wrong with you? Your lip's bleeding," said Doomsy, nudging him while everyone's pet Familiars began crying and thrashing against the stained glass windows outside the Chantry.

Valor licked his lip. The taste of blood jolted him, making him want more. He moved away from his friends, wanting to leave, but he stopped. Bohemia turned to face Urbanne. Valor's chest sank as the head vespercestor stiffened behind his podium. Bohemia levitated about nine feet above the floor, with her arms out to her sides. Two black vultures crashed through the windows and landed on each of Bohemia's wrists, as though they were holding her in the air.

"Woman, I completely endorse the bondage between a witch and her Familiar, but you cannot bring animals into this statuary, I mean *sanctuary*," laughed Urbanne, flexing his tongue between his lips. His face matched the red of his hair. "This, this is unparalyzed in our entire history."

He twirled his staff and pointed it at Bohemia. Mahrata LaRock used the ruffled edge of a stargazer's collar to fan her teary face, the aftermath of her convulsive laughter, the hex which Bohemia had placed on them. Mahrata pushed herself up from her chair using the stargazer's sweaty bald head for support. She joined Urbanne at the podium and adjusted her dragon headpiece.

"Oh, Urby, Urby, Urby, you must be all choked up seeing me after all these years? I don't care about your history anymore. The Children of the Gloaming do whatever they want," said Bohemia. "That's why I decided not to be your vigilespion anymore. Not enough reward for me among these dull fires. No, only madness gathers on these benches to hear you continue with your sculpted fables, O Crafty One, while the vespercestory compel our Familiars to keep out, lest they take one revealing step inside your deception."

"So, that's why the vespercestors don't allow our Familiars in Convocation," said Valor to Aaron, Egg, and Doomsy. "They're afraid our pets can see through the Ministry's lies and tell us the truth."

"My Mr. Grudgings is smarter than two dozen of these idiots," agreed Doomsy, while Bohemia floated closer to the podium. Her shadow expanded around her in billowing waves, which the flapping vultures' wings stirred even more. Urbanne swayed with his mouth ajar.

Bohemia spoke with a theatrical voice: "What you have as your leader, Sanguinati, is a killer—a killer who wants to acquire sorcery and immortality, the very things he pretends to despise!"

"Falmoth insisted we leave when Bohemia revealed herself to Urbanne," Valor said to his friends. He headed for the back exit, glancing across the Chantry, making sure the rest of Candlewicke Coven were doing the same. Most of the Sanguinati remained incapacitated, sprawled across the benches, ground floor, platform, choir loft, even draped over the highest balconies. Doomsy and Egg crawled out from under a bench because they couldn't step over the fatigued members.

"Do not listen to this woman," said Urbanne, summoning all the doors to close and lock in the Chantry.

Aaron turned the knobs hard. "I cannot open them," he said.

Valor looked back at the platform. Summoner Mamahchi sat in his chair, appearing more relaxed than the other vespercestors on the platform. Was he confident that Urbanne could handle Bohemia? Was Valor panicking for nothing?

Urbanne cleared his throat and spoke to Bohemia: "Eva Brim, it is written in the *Controssua*: 'Behold the Ancients' wrath shall descend, executing vindictive judgment. Whoever is found with a disembodied shadow shall drown in the Severance River.'"

Bohemia looked up at the ceiling. A third vulture flew over her head, releasing an Eye of Expansion from its claws. She caught the Eye and flashed the swirling pupil's light projection onto Urbanne's face, leaving him bewildered for a second.

"I have proof that you recently murdered Mesthu Marsh, master of the Sorcerers at Shadowhaven Heights," said Bohemia. She allowed the Eye of Expansion to cast its contained images onto the wall behind the choir loft. The covens lifted their weary heads, glued to the scenes from the crystaleer projecting onto the wall.

"I forbid you to show that!" said Urbanne, pointing his magic staff at Bohemia, who cast a spell that petrified him. Guardian Gereon McMahon flew his broom over to Bohemia and reached out to seize her, but her shadow engulfed him like a death shroud, and his broom plunged into the windpiped organ, which coughed out a double-octave, high A-sharp.

"Let the evidence present itself," said High Priest Teddyus Manoj, standing on the platform with his arms raised to end the protests.

Some of the recorded images became scratchy from the gusty winds atop the hill. Valor didn't want to watch; the recording of Mesthu seemed so vulnerable, so gullible. Why did he trust Urbanne?

Valor huddled close to his friends at the back of the sanctuary and watched the recording while Micha took over, trying to open the Chantry doors.

"Why, Urbanne Aloysius LaRock, I almost didn't recognize you. You seem . . . well-ripened since we last had words," said the recording of Mesthu in a whispery voice. "Of course, you must have been really desperate, sending one of your apprentices here to beg for our help."

"I'm afraid I haven't a clue what you mean," said the image of Urbanne.

"Valor McRaven," replied Mesthu. "You sent him here to solicit my army to protect your people because you are too weak to help them."

"Is that true?" Aaron asked Valor.

"Not completely. I went to Shadow Haven Heights on my own," whispered Valor, as they returned their attention to the scene playing on the wall.

"Oh, Urby, you can never admit you were wrong. Although, I'm not the one you should apologize to," said Mesthu. At times, the backside of his dark cloak, with a crescent moon design, blended with the dancing shadows cast from the trees. "Your apologies should be reserved for your citizens. They are the ones you robbed of immortality—and now, even you are vulnerable."

Everyone in Mystic Chantry gasped at this disclosure before a call for silence hushed them.

"Why should somebody of my enchanted stature apologize to the Sanguinati, Mesthu, when I could just return their sorcery and, of course, immortality? You know I can't do that unless you give me back those secrets," said the image of Urbanne, moving down from the peak of the hill a few steps. His long orange ringlets billowed like sunrays around his head.

"You cannot be trusted with those gifts again. You got what you wanted—all of Mystic Steeples is helpless under you," said Mesthu.

"Play fair, Mesthu," said Urbanne. "I made a special effort to come here and offer—restitution. Normally I stand on stilts, so my feet don't touch vile ground. From that fact alone, you owe it to me to return those secrets."

"Ah, you still haven't changed, Urbanne. But I will give you the secrets," said Mesthu, "if you confess to the entire Sanguinati how you robbed them of their heritage and power. Even I have realized that treasures do not thrive in a box. I want you to surrender your throne to the citizens of Severance. It would be, as you say, 'playing fair.'"

Urbanne turned his head against the wind, tightened his lips, and rubbed his thumb and forefinger together in contemplation.

"Very well," Urbanne agreed, holding his head low as he descended the hill. "I suppose you're right; it's time to confess to the Sanguinati. Shake my hand, Mesthu, and give me your word that you'll honor your end of our pact."

Mesthu reached out to shake Urbanne's hand and, with a loud cackle, a likeness of the sun rook flew off the rune on Urbanne's ring in a flutter of flames that engulfed Mesthu, until Mesthu fell to the ground and tried to put out the blaze, dropping his Eye of Expansion. The likeness of the sun rook then flew up to the fading sun in the sky.

"You vile shadow tosser," growled Urbanne. "It took hundreds of years to erase what happened from my people's knowledge. I would die a mere Nizzertit before I'd surrender my throne!" Urbanne cast a Steely Grip spell on Mesthu's chest, ripping out his heart.

"They will know. The Dandy Lion has . . . followed . . . the wind," Mesthu choked on those last words before becoming as still as a statue.

"Oh sweet heavens," Aaron cried, hiding his eyes behind his coat sleeve. "Master Mesthu did not bear me ill will."

"What do you mean?" asked Valor, touching his arm.

Aaron's tried to answer, but only tears emerged before he buried his face against Valor's shoulder.

The projected scene ended, and gasps of shock, outrage, and horror rang out among the members of every Sanguinati coven: Graven Dust, Wormwood Philters, Warlocks' Bane, Dragon's

Mantle, Snuffinumbra, and Cryptic Chambers. Mystic Ministry recoiled in their throne chairs, balcony seats, and benches. Witchdoctor Kraneswaddle fainted, and one of the orchestra drummers dropped his drumsticks. The vespercestors on the platform exchanged desperate glances. Summoner Mamahchi scratched his forehead with a look of bewilderment.

"This is the proof that you, Urbanne Aloysius LaRock, arranged a meeting with Mesthu on Soothsayer's Hill," Bohemia hissed at O Enchantedness, releasing her petrification spell on him. "Then you ripped his heart out and torched him to death! But what you didn't know, Urby, was that Mesthu's Eye of Expansion recorded this fatal meeting with you before it was later found hidden under dirt and leaves."

"That is some clever magic, Eva Brim, clever magic. Just like you impure warlocks to conjure up a perverted scheme, false evidence to undermine my leadership," said Urbanne, wielding his magic staff with both hands. "Perhaps you are the Conjuring Crone in league with the Grim Warlock."

"I'm not the Conjuring Crone, just a well-trained vigilespion," laughed Bohemia. "I have more evidence." She produced a small rune and held it in front of the Eye of Expansion, which magnified the rune's image on the wall. "Why, what is this, Urby?"

"Basically, a sun rook rune," said Urbanne through his teeth.

"Oh?" questioned Bohemia. "You mean the rune that used to be on your signet ring—that you are not wearing for some reason? The same rune I just happened to find lodged in Mesthu's chest when you ripped out his heart. The same rune that matches the sun rook on your magic staff?"

Bohemia whipped through the air; her Familiars and shadow scattered in a blurry swarm, confusing her enemies. Creighton fired his wand at the door when Valor's Recludo spell failed to open it. Everyone jumped when something cracked a hole through the Chantry ceiling. Large blocks of stone fell on top of the huddling stargazers, followed by screams everywhere. Venerious Falmoth's two-headed dragon, Tareamugus, thrust his heads through the ceiling and shot double mouthfuls of fire onto Urbanne LaRock, overcoming him with flames.

"Uh-oh, we're going to be crushed," said Valor when most of the covens scattered toward the exits.

"Hurry!" shouted Micha. "Duck under this bench."

Diving under the long wooden bench, which throbbed from the fleeing witches, Valor and his friends watched a sea of boots scrambling to the exit. With a loud bang, the covens burst through the doors and out of the Chantry. Valor eased his head over Doomsy's legs, glancing under a long tunnel of benches where Delicia Jones began crawling toward them with a wide-eyed look of determination.

"Oh no, what does *she* want?" asked Rose, curled in a ball on her side.

"I don't know, but I'm not waiting to find out," said Valor. The escaping crowd had dwindled, so he crawled out from under the bench. The remaining Sanguinati fired their wands at Tareamugus, sending flames, ice, lightning, all manner of spells raining through the Chantry. A horrible scene erupted on the platform, so Valor squatted back down to gather his senses.

"What are you doing?" asked Doomsy, trying to tug him closer to the exit.

"I—it's Urbanne. H-he's dead," said Valor after losing his voice for a few seconds.

"Now! We had better get outta here," yelled Ruza, swatting at Valor, Doomsy, and Aaron with her broom. "The primitives are gonna use Urbanne's murder as an excuse to kill everyone on their list, take our money, and use us as slaves to scoop pumpaninny poo outta the catacombs!"

They jumped up just before Delicia crawled to the bench in front of them. When they reached the exit, a terrible scream enfolded their backs, and he turned to see Bohemia fall from the ceiling onto the bench, her body aflame, writhing in pain.

"I should help her," panted Valor.

"No," said Aaron, pushing him through the doorway. "We must

leave."

They ran out of Mystic Steeples and headed toward Candlewicke Mansion. Valor eased out of their midst without them noticing. He couldn't leave Bohemia to die. He made it to the perimeter of Mystic Steeples, dashing along in the dark. The figure of a man emerged from a cropping of poison apple trees and hexagram-shaped hedges in the garden on the northwestern side of the citadel. The figure's eyes locked on him with a fast-approaching gait until, within a split second, the white hair hanging across Valor's forehead caught the breeze of Venerious Falmoth's sudden appearance at his side.

"Was *this* your plan—to kill Urbanne?" cried Valor.

"Poor Urby. The lotus of destiny holds no more buds of blessing. Bohemia, Eva—or whatever her real name is—opened a vicious jar of weed-kill in there, if I dare," said Falmoth, watching the skies as Tareamugus flew away to safety.

"Bohemia is dead by now as well," growled Valor. "Don't you even care?" Disturbed by everything, he grabbed his forehead and smoothed his anguished face. Even the scent of bitter cherries on Falmoth's breath, and the lingering dragon smell on Falmoth's pants, as he knelt in front of him, made Valor ill. "You couldn't stand Mesthu. You just needed another excuse to kill O Enchantedness."

"Those flames that killed Urbanne, just think of them as karmic embers from Mesthu's charred corpse—a magnifiskull revenge, of course?" said Falmoth, spitting on the ground. "Yuck, I do believe I still have the aftertaste of wormwood on my face. Why does it seem that when an old guardian puts on a robe—and all that nonsense—he bathes in incense?" He shoved a bunch of moist red candies in his mouth and smacked his tongue between his lips.

"You didn't drink the blood of a guardian, did you?" asked Valor. He grabbed Falmoth by his coat and then let go, turned, and soared up to a rooftop on Ickylous Street to avoid detection, as the guardians and other members of Mystic Ministry began searching the city for Falmoth's dragon.

A few minutes later, a flock of buzzards, tied to strings like kites, lifted Falmoth up to the roof where Valor now stood.

"Please make a note: I'm not a Sorcerer. I cannot free-float," said Falmoth. He unhooked the buzzards' leashes from his belt and used a twisted stovepipe to anchor the squawking birds.

"Is that what you want from me . . . sorcery? I'm surprised you don't have it already, you drank enough of my blood," said Valor, rubbing his neck where Falmoth had bitten him.

Falmoth backed up two feet. "Weepers creepers, I didn't know your blood tasted sweeter," he said, stifling a laugh. "Don't worry; I'll kiss and make it better if you should so choose to keep little ol' me from being murdered by the lesser vespercestors." Falmoth took a deep breath of smoke that drifted from the distant Mystic Chantry. "Why, look at what we've got! Urbanne is adding fragrance to the rooftops."

"It's his spirit seeking retribution," snarled Valor. He grabbed the sides of his head, pulling his hair. "And don't include me in any of this. This was all your doing."

"Urbanne convinced those clones that baby Crowley was the heir to his throne," laughed Falmoth, holding his arms out as Urbanne had done in the Chantry. "Whatta crock. Like you would've ever surrendered your throne, Urby LaRock," Falmoth shouted to the passing smoke as if he were doing it to Urbanne's face.

Valor released his grip on his hair. What sort of mad man was Venerious Falmoth?

"Oh relax. The Sanguinati thrive on this crap," assured Falmoth. He reclined on the steep roof and fanned the smoke farther toward the night sky. "Every week they file into Convocation in excited anticipation—heck, they get downright antsy for another sign to contribute to their doomsday fantasy."

Like fireworks, wand flares continued to shoot through the hole in the distant Chantry roof.

"I know what you're trying to do, Falmoth. But you've gone way too far."

Venerious licked the passing smoke. "I accomplished way more than you, McRaven. I didn't give you much to do. You are a lazy baby."

"I've tried telling the Sanguinati what you told me to tell them," said Valor. "And all I got was blank stares, or they became outraged at me. It's no use. Even after O Enchantedness confessed that he erased the truth of their origins, it won't matter to them."

"That's because," said Falmoth, standing up, flinging his arms toward the sky and kicking his legs in a song and dance, "*their tongues are tied, their brains are fried, welcome to the city of the mesmerized.*" Falmoth straddled the peak of the roofline, knocking loose a clay shingle, which slid down the gritty roof before disappearing over the bottom edge. "It'll take more than a confession and history lesson. I intend to tear down all of Mystic Ministry, my brother . . . fifty butt-kissing mouths after another."

Sliding down the base of the chimney, Valor locked his right boot into the rails of the widow's walk. He propped his face in his hands. A soot-covered dove fell from the sky and landed at his feet. His hopes for harmony were falling from the sky like the suffocated dove. The buzzards tugged against their leashes and scooped up the dove.

"Just remember, you have the power to return Mystic Steeples to the way it once was. Well, minus that dove," said Falmoth, clutching his fists in the air and thrusting his torso around in a haughty dance. The buzzards cackled with delight.

Valor lowered his head from a beam of moonlight, which glowed behind the black clouds. "And what if I don't? Are you going to kill me, too?" he asked.

"I'm not the least bitty-gritty worried about having to kill *you*, Valor." Falmoth patted the center of Valor's abdomen. "The key you swallowed will always be there to make sure you do not betray the Hermetic Order."

"I will not help you kill anybody," snapped Valor. "But I'll do what I can to spread the truth and save my friends."

"So nice . . . all that *caring*. Though you needn't worry about Aaron, he just joined the Hermetic Order," said Falmoth, cramming a Sixteen-Cream Buzzard-Wings Supreme in his mouth. "Such a noble friend to help protect his comrades from the slaughter."

A menacing icy grip ripped through Valor. Before he could

respond, Falmoth grabbed the vulture harnesses and floated away into the polluted night sky. The buzzards cackling eerily resembled wicked laughter as the sounds of chaos continued on the alleys.

CREIGHTON DISCONNECTS

WHEN Valor returned to Candlewicke Mansion, everyone was waiting in the witches' parlor. Booger Fay fanned Doomsy with his wing as she reclined on the fainting sofa looking peaked.

"Salazants and Manning took off in the carriage looking for you, Valor," said Aaron. "What happened? Where did you vanish to?"

"I met with Falmoth," admitted Valor. He unbuttoned his coat and slapped it on the hall tree, then stared at Aaron to see if he would confess that he, too, had become a vampire.

"Uh-oh, I sorta think somebody knows something about somebody," mumbled Nalini, hiding behind a book she was reading. Aaron's eyes oscillated between Valor and the floor; there was indeed something ill and sinister about his appearance now.

"Does anybody want to confess anything I'm always the last to know?" asked Valor. He held his breath to avoid saying something he might regret.

They looked on with stiff and frightened expressions. Booger Fay held his wings over his face. "Erm, I confess I left some special droppings on the kitchen table."

Blade loosened his shirt collar, slid off the armoire, and said, "Blade is an open book. There's nothing he needs to hide. In fact, he'll take off all his—"

Valor threw his hands up and groaned, "Aaron, why did you join the Hermetic Order? Have you suddenly found vampires fashionable? You were the most upset when I joined. Aw, is there nothing I can trust anymore?"

"I did not want you to be alone in this web Falmoth has trapped you in," said Aaron, walking over to him. "It was unfair that members from our secret coven coerced you to join the Hermetic Order—especially when much of your worries concerned my safety that blighted hour."

"Oh, banshee bruises!" barked Creighton. "Not all of us were with Valor in Bogamuckla. Even if I were, I'd never put such a loony idea in his head."

"And what did you mean in Convocation when you said Mesthu bore you no ill will?" Valor softly asked Aaron, unaccustomed to this emotional side of his friend.

"It was there, Valor, in the recording of his death." Aaron stroked his lace neckband, and his eyelids became heavy. "It was almost as though Mesthu wasn't fooled—as though he was ready to die—as though he was sending a message straight to me in his Eye of Expansion." Aaron started to tear up again.

"What message?" asked Valor.

"Master Mesthu told Urbanne that 'Treasures do not thrive in a box.' And with his dying breath, he added, 'The Dandy Lion has followed the wind.' Those were the last two things he said to me before he excommunicated me from the tower. Mesthu always called me the Dandy Lion. All this time, I only had a suspicion that Mesthu was pretending to be mad at me. He knew I needed to leave the tower and help uncover the truth of the Great Deception. But when I saw the recording, I had no doubt."

"I remember," said Valor recalling the recording. "Right after Mesthu said, 'The Sanguinati will know the truth.'"

"Guys, when Mesthu said 'Treasures don't thrive in boxes,' I also think he realized Valor was right about them shutting themselves off from the world's troubles," said Rose, clutching her hatbox in her lap. In deep thought, she pulled at the holiday ornaments she had taped on the sides and lid.

"Verily, they *had* been living in a box—for two hundred years," said Aaron.

Valor lowered his head. "I can't help but feel Mesthu wouldn't be dead if I hadn't made him feel guilty about lacking compassion. Everything got worse after I went there asking for help."

"Cut it out, Valor," croaked Doomsy. "Your going to the tower had nothing to do with Urbanne murdering Mesthu. You were right; Urbanne *was* the Grim Warlock, and he got what he deserved."

"Oh, that's right—I mean, if that's true, then we solved the Great Deception—the 13th Hour is over—we won, guys!" squeaked Rose.

Stabbah placed her hands over the sides of her head as her yellow lips opened wide. Micha and Egg looked at each other and shook their fists in victory.

"You think you have it all figured out," snorted Creighton. "*I* know. I've got connections. Urbanne was starting to accept Sorcerers until Valor went up to Shadowhaven Heights and lured that crackpot Mega D down here, and he tried to start a massive war. Summoner Mamahchi got Urbanne all worked up that Mesthu and his Children would invade Mystic Steeples."

"Really?" asked Valor, feeling light-headed. "But I just met with Summoner Mamahchi, and he acted like he didn't know Urbanne had killed Mesthu. He acted like he was for us underdogs."

"Yes, *really*," Creighton said derisively. "Mamahchi tried to convince Urbanne that Sorcerers and Noctivatians were days away from starting the 13th Hour and killing all of the Sanguinati. He certainly convinced Urbanne that Mystic City needed more protection—that's why Urbanne went up to visit Mesthu."

"He went there to *kill* Mesthu, you two-timing, butt-kissing, sack of jealousy," yelled Doomsy.

"Here's the truth," said Creighton. "I just lost a distant relative tonight because of the Hermetic Order—Sorcerers—or whoever you identify with these days. See! If O Enchantedness wanted my father dead or unable to have a seventh son, like you claimed, he wouldn't have made my baby brother his heir."

"We only told you what we saw and heard the night Abner was murdered, Creighton," said Valor, stunned at his behavior.

"I want nothing more to do with—with any of you. Matter of fact, I'm leavin' here for good. I'm Sanguinati I tell you—Sang-wih-nah-tee!" hissed Creighton, slamming his hands down on the edge of a small table

"'Sanguinati?'" snapped Ruza. "Oh, that's priceless, considering O Enchantedness just confessed that the Sanguinati was a lie. All you'll become is a has-been Sorcerer like you are now. Go ahead—have at it then."

Creighton inspected his reflection in the mirror above the table where his fist now flattened. He snarled at his appearance. "Consider me a has-been then," he hissed. "The vespercestors will remove this sorcery hex you placed on me—and—and help me be mortal again."

Rose began to sob. "Creighton, stop being so mean—please," she begged. "Don't turn on me—us. We've been best friends for a long time. Doesn't that mean anything?"

Creighton eased out to the main hall, appearing eager to leave. "Rose, I just can't," he said. "I mean, c'mon—you wanted Valor to be part of what just happened tonight." He shut her off with a nasty smirk. Why was Creighton treating them with such callousness? Why had he changed? Could Valor ever trust him again?

"You judgmental little backstabber," Doomsy said to Creighton. She stormed up from the fainting sofa. Her eyes seemed to shoot flames at him. "You begged us to make you immortal."

"Blade has seen this sort of change in people before," said Blade.

"Creigh Baby here is hoping he'll be in line for Urbanne's throne, since his newborn brother is too young to feed himself, much less run Mystic Steeples. There's something so tempting about that throne, isn't there, Creighton?"

"Failed! He strangely failed to tell us about baby Thiolahfuh—just sayin'," yelled Ruza, shaking her head as she tore through the room. "Argh. I hate it when people make unsubstantiated claims just to make people look bad."

"I've seen this coming like an asteroid," said Creighton. He shook his head as if he were trying to erase his friends from his memory. "The Sorcerer club thing was cool—it was fun. But I had no idea you all would go off on some militant mission to try to change everybody."

"What—are ya livin' in a bubble all of a sudden? If we were militant, it was ta survive," said Micha, looking ready to punch Creighton.

"O Enchantedness d-did kill Mesthu, j-just like Falmoth said O Enchantedness wanted to do to us," said Egg.

"Creighton doesn't care about that," said Doomsy. "He's moving up the ladder. Blood is thicker than water for him now."

Stabbah reentered the room with a bottle of fizzing brown liquid. "Dahhhling, calm yourself," she said to Creighton. "Egg is right. You saw the Eye of Expansion recording tonight." Stabbah pushed her intensely yellow hair behind one ear and scratched Booger Fay's back with her boot-heel. "I think you're being very hasty."

"I don't go by enchanted recordings. I go by what I see in person, so I'm gonna get this out in the open here. Valor just might be the Grim Warlock, and Doomsy the Conjuring Crone—truth be known," said Creighton, flaring his nostrils. "We never knew each other; got it?" Creighton made sure they understood before breaking eye contact. He slammed the door after he walked out of the mansion.

The funeral for O Enchantedness had lasted most of the day, as Mahrata LaRock presided over every detail of her husband's memorial service. Her poodle, Meducy, sat in a throne chair with its hind legs in the air. With a frown, Tilta Crumpecker kept pulling Meducy's diamond-studded skirt down over the dog's stomach. Anyone with even the smallest affiliation with the Sanguinati had packed out Ramrod's Arena, a massive coliseum on the eighth floor of Mystic Steeples. Candlewicke 13 was still brooding over Creighton's sudden departure. And to tune out Mahrata's longwinded praise of O Enchantedness, Valor and his remaining friends tried to make sense of Summoner Mamahchi's behavior, and why Creighton had been keeping secrets from them.

"How come we're in the nosebleed section, and Toadvine Citadel gets to sit up front? I can't see the show," said Doomsy. Like the others in Candlewicke Coven, she had gotten little sleep the night before and had applied extra enchanted powder to her face, while Aaron and Valor wore their coat collars high to hide their sickly complexions.

"Politics," replied Ruza. "I don't know if any of ya ever heard of Mondu and Wishtangia Renata?"

Everybody shrugged.

"The Sorcerers who hatched me," continued Ruza with a fleeting laugh before seemingly falling into a brief trance. "They got their dream of being magisters years ago. They know all about Mahrata's past . . . her family. We're talkin' loaded. The Candlewickes were *it* in Mystic City. Mahrata's father, Candombram, schemed with Urbanne LaRock to buy the position of Head Magister of Toadvine Citadel from Pythian Probis, who was about to drop dead and have his butt replaced by Mantilla Mamahchi."

"You mean Summoner Mamahchi's sister was supposed to be over Toadvine Citadel?" asked Valor.

"You guessed it," said Ruza.

"So that's why Toadvine gets good seats," said Micha.

"It must've been a heck of a deal," continued Ruza, "'cause after Candombram bought the head magister's position, he paid for an elaborate wedding for Urbanne and Mahrata." Ruza stopped talking as the guardians passed around collection hats to which Valor dropped in a handful of globulnugees.

"The LaRocks are used ta buyin' their way into everythin'," said Micha.

"Optimus Pearl is head magister of Toadvine Citadel. What happened to Mahrata's father?" asked Valor.

Instead of their usual cheering with pom-poms, the Toadettes, Sanguinettes, and Grossettes began a memorial ritual, tossing funeral wreaths instead. As if in competition, the Sanguinettes flung their wreaths higher to form a portrait of O Enchantedness. Then they unrolled a purple scroll underneath his image, which read, "Urbanne LaRock, Ancient of Ancients."

"A revolt is what happened," said Ruza. "Right after Mahrata's father placed Fozit LaRock in the position of high priest of Toadvine Citadel, removing Braynard Mamahchi, Eelias Mamahchi's brother."

"Wow! Two of Summoner Mamahchi's relatives were done dirty by the LaRocks," said Valor.

"Right," said Ruza. "Then, BAM! Candombram, *Mahrata's father*, comes up murdered."

Several female apprentices glared at Ruza, but she sucked in her cheeks, crossed her long legs, and shook her cloud of wavy hair away from her face.

"This must've been after Summoner Mamahchi's parents were murdered—around the time Rendum LaRock started the Drowning Verdicts." Valor explained this event he had witnessed in *The Book of Chacodophilus*. "But neither the LaRocks or the Mamahchi family blamed one another."

"That's so not true. Not in the beginning anyway," said Ruza. "The blame game got so bad Fozit LaRock fled Toadvine Citadel and took shelter at Mystic Steeples."

"Ah," Aaron said. "It threatened relations between Mystic Steeples and Toadvine Citadel then."

"Toadvine isn't chummy with us now," said Doomsy.

Ruza stretched her slender arms over her legs. "Both Sanguinati institutions made some deals. The LaRocks insisted Toadvine Citadel's new Head Magister Optimus Pearl toss out Braynard Mamahchi."

Rose stopped yawning, and her head jerked with confusion. "Mamahchi is tight with the LaRocks—I mean, what's up with that?" she asked.

"That's the other part of the deal I was telling you about," said Ruza. "Urbanne LaRock promised to make Eelias Mamahchi a lesser vespercestor, which he eventually did—that's why he's all 'okay' now."

"More than okay, he went so far as to ignore the injustice to his own family and blame the murder of Mahrata's father on Noctivatians," said Valor, twisting around in his seat with a huff.

Ruza flicked her thin fingers as if to say, there you go.

"All the promotions must've worked," said Micha, clutching his fist and drumming his boot heels in the stands. "Summoner Mamahchi has nothin' for his family now."

"And he's created that Auravitamax tonic the LaRocks are trying to force on us," said Doomsy.

Candlewicke Coven returned their sleepy eyes to Mahrata as she continued to swallow and sigh: "Hmmm, haaa, and in the prospect of this tragic course of events, which led to this, haaa, sad, sad gathering to honor this great man and leader. The Ancients have predetermined that it is, hmmm, my lot to take over Mystic Steeples as head vespercestor."

Many guests from Toadvine Citadel jeered and stormed out of the arena at Mahrata's announcement, while a few from Mystic Steeples gasped.

"What?" said Stabbah, angling her head toward the podium as if confronting Mahrata herself. "She can't put herself in position without a traditional election."

Valor snapped out of his sleepy state, expecting to see another rebellion. He gazed down over Ramrod's Arena at the dwindling pageantry. "And how odd? Nobody seems that sad over losing Urbanne except Mystic Ministry."

"They didn't love Urby as much as he believed they did," said Blade, looking as droopy as his long dark hair. "They smiled at his ramblings out of obligation. They're all afraid to look on the stage and see that mangled corpse of his."

"I, uh, overheard Magister Phunga say they w-weren't able to restore Urbanne's c-corpse," said Egg, scooting among them, knocking everyone in the head or knees during the closing procession.

"Ew, they should've put O Enchantedness in a coffin, but they wouldn't dare," said Nalini Lusion. She snatched her ruched cloak over her knees as if she had gotten a chill.

"That's for sure. He might come back out of it, that's why," giggled Rose.

Doomsy agreed. "His face looks like those death masks we found in the Esotericum Incantatory."

Valor bent over on the curved stone bench and rubbed his sleepy eyes. "I wonder if it *is* his death mask, or maybe the guardians put another mask on him," he said.

"I can't imagine Urby lettin' anyone control his spirit with a death mask," said Micha.

"Traitor! Argh, just look at him," grunted Ruza. She licked her upper teeth with pursed lips.

"Who? Where?" asked Micha. His feet still clicked the stone bleacher below him.

"Snuggling up! Creighton—look at him . . . sitting as close as he can to the lesser vespercestors," said Ruza. Her head rocked with contempt. "Looking for his next stepping-stone. Oh, I warned you about him; I warned you!"

"Well, the LaRocks *are* his family, you know," said Valor.

"You are just as related to the LaRocks as he is," said Aaron. His face became slack and ashen. "'Tis my fault. I promised you that Creighton wouldn't betray us if you allowed him into our coven."

"It's not your fault," said Valor.

"It's just a matter of time before he rats us out of Mystic Steeples, jabs the old knife in the back," added Blade, giving a teasing wave in

Creighton's direction.

"Stop it, Blade. Creighton just laughed," said Rose, slumping over, bracing her chin in her hands. "You don't think he heard you, do you?"

Creighton looked away and lifted his head high while talking to Harwin Hollapolk, but Harwin turned his back to him and began chatting with Seth Tuberstooge.

"So, Val, do ya still think that corpse on the stage was the Grim Warlock? Creighton sure didn't agree with ya," said Micha.

"Yes, indeed. But I do say, I can't believe there wasn't an uprising after Bohemia murdered him. Everything is calm—eerily calm," said Valor, now starting to have doubts.

Mahrata LaRock stood beside her husband's body and continued addressing the congregation:

"Sanguinati, privileged guests, servants, hmmm. As your new head vespercestor, I am, haaa, obligated to inform you of Mystic Steeples' new *Questioning Regulation*." Mahrata frowned at the jeers rising from sections of the arena. In a calculative manner, she placed the scroll down and scanned the entire coliseum with eyes of warning: keeping one brow raised, until the spectators became silent.

"Hmmm," she continued. "Please understand that the vespercestors have now banned asking questions anywhere in Mystic Steeples. This, haaa, includes questioning any of Mystic Ministry inside the perimeter of Mystic City and within wand-shot of the Severance River. Hmmm, if we catch you in violation of this new ordinance, you will, haaa, receive a vespercestorial fine of seventy globulnugees. This now concludes the funeral of a prolifically anointed ruler, Urbanne Aloysius LaRock. Blessed, haaa, be."

"Fines for asking questions? They must be daft!" Valor shook his head with a laugh as they began their walk home. "Nobody ever questions Mystic Ministry, so Mahrata won't solve their debt problem that way."

"Somebody has to pay to have her poodle's diamonds polished," laughed Blade.

The next day Rose came home later than usual from a Warlocks' Bane meeting. She took off her white cloak with the horned-fox emblem and handed it to Salazants.

"Guys," she said. "I think I know why Creighton acted the way he did."

"Oh, I was sorta afraid of that," said Nalini. "He's another victim of the Possessing, isn't he?"

"I'm so upset," continued Rose. "I ran into Vampatra Cobbratz, and she told me Witchdoctor Kraneswaddle diagnosed Creighton with vagamorta ickypox."

"Ooo. What's that?" asked Valor, swallowing a potion Stabbah had created to try to cure his and Aaron's vampirism.

Doomsy put down a book she had been studying on vampires and said, "It's an undetermined terminal illness—a Magister Kraneswaddle term anyway. I've studied diseases all my life—known a lot of them, too."

"Terminal!" repeated Aaron. "No wonder Creighton has been turning against us these past few months. The boy is no doubt diseased in the head. And I, too, thought it might be the Possessing."

"No," said Rose, dabbing the black eye powder, which streaked her cheek. "Kraneswaddle said the illness came on suddenly. And this is the thing: Creighton is swearing it's because we put some sorta hex on him."

"He's immortal. How could he be terminal with anything, unless it's backstabber syndrome?" asked Doomsy.

"I dunno," said Rose. "But Creighton confirmed before the lesser vespercestors that he was afraid to die. They're waiting to take him to the Deadway 'cause it's a hallowed night."

"The Deadway? It must be awful," said Nalini, trembling. "They . . . they need to try and cure him, not—"

Blade chuckled before Micha said, "Nah, they're gonna do a ritual called Passover on 'im. But the only Deadway I know of is

Ancient Alley."

"What's Passover?" asked Valor, turning his nose away from another spoonful of Stabbah's elixir. Its rancid scent reminded him of the decaying animals he had often choked on in Diabolishire. But he was hopeful it would curb his thirst for blood, and not his desire to eat ever again. Aaron refused to try another sip and dashed across the parlor away from Stabbah.

Blade hooked his thumbs in the chest pockets of his jacket and swaggered through the room. "On hallowed nights," he said spookily, "residual phantom trails of the Ancients' footsteps are said to move through Ancient Alley. The Sanguinati, desperate to receive a blessing or healing, lie on the cobblestoned alley, hoping an Ancient will *pass* right over them as though he or she were a bridge. And a bridge they believe that alley is, from the astral plane to earth."

"The Ancients can walk all over Creighton for all I care, but they don't have enough power to blow the fuzz off a peanut," said Doomsy, checking behind Valor's lips to see if he still had fangs.

Rose grabbed some snacks Manning had prepared, and she collapsed on the sofa beside Aaron. "Summoner Mamahchi thinks the same as you do, Dooms. I tried to ask him about seeing Creighton and how he was doing and all. And d'ya know what he did? D'ya know?" asked Rose.

"Knowing Mamahchi, he just grunted and walked away," croaked Doomsy.

"Uh-uh," said Rose, shaking her head. "Mamahchi lifted his magic staff to the ceiling and told me Mystic Ministry wouldn't allow me to see him, and that soon Creighton was going to become another bright star on the astral plane."

"Lies! This is all too bizarre. Somebody must be telling lies," said Ruza, ripping at her dress, and breathing through her mouth in a rage. Booger Fay stuck his head under the potion table in front of the sofa, but his body wouldn't fit. Aaron's crow, Switzer, flew up and landed on the chandelier. "No, no, this is all a set-up. Creighton's pretending to be sick just to make us look like murderers. Mystic Ministry plans to take our possessions and turn us into one-eyed, three-legged, goat-headed yokazunis and make us stomp on grapes in their private vineyards. Well, over my dead body, I say!"

"I found it suspicious also," said Rose, "until I overheard Magister Mesmerthang saying she had the summon scroll ready for High Witch Anasircea to use on Creighton in the Deadway tonight."

"Ah, Cousin Zagato," said Blade, retracting ectoplasm into his fingertips. "They won't let Anasircea become a magister, because deep down they know her craft is sorcery. Ha, but they always use her when nothing else works. Seems she cured Mahrata of bowel disease once, so the LaRocks grant her certain . . . liberties. Cousin Blade here will send her a quick crystaleer and tell her you're coming tonight. But be prepared, the Sanguinati could become unpredictable because Anasircea reveals without fear or favor whatever her powers show her. Many in Mystic Ministry have made death threats toward her because of such."

"We have to go to Passover now," sighed Rose. Her sad eyes lit up with hope while Blade sent the crystaleer with the news. It whisked through the room and shot up the closest fireplace chimney.

At the entry to Ancient Alley, between the Hall of Consumption and Buckthorn Hall, Marston Diamone greeted Rose, Doomsy, Valor, and Aaron while holding Blade's crystaleer.

"I see you shadow tossers tried to send a message to Anasircea," sneered Marston. "Trying to prevent Creighton from getting rid of the hex you put on him, are you?"

"Bull dribble, Mars," said Doomsy. "But hexes happen. Would *you* tell Mystic Ministry if you participated in an illegal ritual and found your pants shortened and covered in pink sparkles, and the word 'loser' carved on your forehead?"

"Hell no." Marston's chin receded with disgust.

Doomsy swaggered toward Marston and whispered, "Wanna come to Candlewicke for a game of Spin the Dagger then?"

With a sneer, Marston shook the crystaleer in threatening punches at Valor. "You may be corrupting the Crypts just because you're presidents, but you have no power here," said Marston. "Besides, I, uh, told O Captivatingness of your plans to attend Creighton's Passover."

"O Captivatingness?" asked Doomsy, wrinkling her nose.

"Head Vespercestor Mahrata's new title—duh," said Marston, strutting as though he had given the title to her. "I'm allowed to call her Mah."

"This is a public alley. You can't stop us from entering," said Rose.

"I could," replied Marston. "But I think I'd rather see the vespercestors deal with you. O Captivatingness doesn't want anybody to know that you all put a sorcery hex on Creighton."

"Doesn't she?" said Valor. "I imagine it would give her much joy."

"Everybody knows you did," said Marston, puffing out his thin chest. "Fortunately for you, O Captivatingness wants these lies about you all making Creighton immortal to stop because they're going to try to cure him."

"What does making him immortal have to do with it?" asked Rose. Her lips puckered, and her eyes narrowed.

Marston shook the crystaleer at her and said, "Because, shadow brains, he, uh, might die, and it would upset people."

"Ah, I see," said Valor. "If everybody finds out Creighton is immortal, and he dies after Passover—after Mystic Ministry claimed they could heal him—it'll weaken the Sanguinati's trust in Mah and the Ancients."

"Especially when everyone is already distrustful of the vespercestors. Blade is all too acquainted with those leader tactics," said Blade.

"Blah!" spat Aaron, stepping in the doorway to the alley. Marston's snowy egret flew down upon his shoulder and turned one discerning eye to Aaron, before flapping its right wing at him in a shooing motion.

"It's true what they say: Witches really do look like their Familiars," Doomsy said to Marston, as they all pushed into the vast cobblestone alley packed full of chanters, candle lighters, and vespercestors. Creighton's parents, Kingston and Alizaba, stood in the center, and behind them, five of their sons, Jecoliah, Burdock, Cuddy, Maverick, and then Crowdy—strangely dissimilar except for their purple hair. The crowd cheered for the Crowley family and held out objects for them to autograph and bless.

Inching forward into the center of the alley, Creighton groaned. A swelling in his stomach was so extensive he staggered on his feet. While the crowds cheered at Creighton, "Hippity hip, Number Six!" A male reporter scampered through the gathering and held up a crystaleer.

"Stu P. Fuddle with *The Daily Hazy Herald* here with live coverage of Creighton Cairncross Crowley's Passover in the Deadway. There's a huge turnout of fans, folks. Let me start by saying: Welcome back to the Sanguinati, Creighton—you poor young man! Is it true you, the sixth Crowley 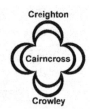 son, were forced to join a secret coven of Sorcerers, and they put a hex on you for leaving? Do you have any more information for the viewers at home who are concerned that something like this could happen to their children? Or do we have to wait until the book comes out through *Hazy Press?*" Fuddle shoved the crystaleer inches below Creighton's downcast head.

Turning his head from the crystaleer, Creighton looked up at Mahrata, exhaled deeply, and lowered his head again. The crowd began to weep and clasp their hands in hope, ignoring Mahrata as she tried again to speak. Seconds later, she loomed over a portable podium and, with one brow raised high, pursed her lips at the crowd.

"Hmm, haaa," Mahrata sighed, raising her magic staff. "Witness the power of the Ancients carrying this poor boy to the Deadway on this hallowed night."

"Oh, he looks awful. I'm afraid he's gonna fall over." Rose cried on Aaron's shoulder.

Now holding on to two of his older brothers, Creighton shuffled farther. Candlewicke Coven squeezed to the front of the crowded stone bleachers, but away from the Deadway, when the upper torso of Ambergis LaRock appeared and floated into the alley undetected by the crowd. A wicked breeze encircled the candles on the alley and against Ambergis's hat, trimmed in browned ribbons and dead flowers. She whispered in Creighton's ear as he reclined on the cobblestone, like a bridge between the buildings, waiting for the spirits to pass over him. Ambergis cast puffs of toxic-looking fumes from her spectral wand, which she aimed at Creighton's face and then on a beautiful witch's head.

"She must be Anasircea," said Rose, referring to the strange witch Valor found so angelic. Her dark hair hung in long tight coils over her ivory skin and white dress. In the palm of her hand rested eight little birds. "But isn't that Ambergis blessing her and Creighton?"

"Half of Ambergis's ghost, but she wouldn't bless a sneeze," said Doomsy, resting her hands against the puffy ruffles of her black skirt.

Ambergis floated inside of Magister Mesmerthang as she sat down on a wooden bench, holding the summon scroll over her turquoise skirt, which draped across the seat.

"I think Ambergis has possessed Magister Mesmerthang. Look, she's shivering," said Valor.

While Mesmerthang grabbed the bench and dug her fingernails into the wood, Ambergis convulsed with similar gestures of madness until Mesmerthang left claw marks across the bench, releasing gasps for air.

"Aah-ughh-ooh," howled Magister Mesmerthang, as she crushed the scroll, which had fallen under her feet.

Ambergis took a set of tarot cards from her conjure bag and dealt out a row of cards on top of Creighton's stomach. Ripping the Hierophant card in half, Ambergis tossed the pieces across the arena into Valor's hands. High Witch Anasircea circled the Deadway as if trying to locate a bad smell. She paused and pointed at Magister Mesmerthang.

"Pluto is in the sixth house," said Anasircea in a spooky manner. "The Ancients are low on the Astral Plane. But this magister has a walk-in and is hindering the Passover. I am not at liberty to do spirit expulsions."

Mahrata LaRock stood up on her platform, wearing more chocolate-brown lip powder than Valor had ever seen her wear. Her charms and necklaces hung to her waist.

"Summoner Mamahchi," she said, "please, hmmm, notify the guardian at the Sanctuary of Manifestations to delay the atomic clock. High Priest and Priestess, please, haaa, cast this bogus bogey out of Magister Mesmerthang so we can, hmmm, continue summoning the Ancients."

Teddyus Manoj and Tilta Crumpecker moved toward Gorgia Mesmerthang and pointed their wands at her. "You're not real, bogus bogey! *Thambor Midrend,*" they chanted over and over.

Crumpecker rang a bell, and several dwarves dashed into the alley and swept around Gorgia's feet with little brooms. She rang the bell again and ordered the dwarves to sprinkle a circle of salt around Magister Mesmerthang. The high priest and priestess extended their hands around Mesmerthang's convulsing body, trying to feel the vibrations or the spirit possessing her, Valor wasn't sure. Giggling, Ambergis conjured two dead fish and placed them into their hands.

"Yuck!" Crumpecker said, flinging her fish to the ground, knocking over the alignment of candles.

"Mystic Ministry can't control Ambergis's spirit because she never crossed over," said Valor, remembering his talk about her with Urbanne.

Rose tightened her arms around her waist. "Why is her spirit here? What is she doing?"

"Either she doesn't want them to heal Creighton, or she just being herself," said Doomsy.

Crumpecker rang the bell harder. "More salt," she demanded. The dwarves pushed out little carts full of salt this time. They scooped goblets full and sprinkled another coating of salt in a circle. "More. More!" Crumpecker shouted. The dwarves looked stunned, so they tilted their carts until they had poured a two-foot-tall pile of salt around Magister Mesmerthang. While chanting, the high priest began slinging purple potion from a besprinkling wand at Magister Mesmerthang until she became wetter and wetter. Gyrating against

320

the back of the bench with maniacal laughter, Ambergis reached her hand out, mimicking the besprinkling motion until Crumpecker's and Manoj's faces flushed, and beads of sweat dripped off the tip of Manoj's nose.

Magister Mesmerthang soon appeared exhausted from the ritual. The chanting became more enthusiastic as the lesser vespercestors locked their staffs together in a hexagram, and Crumpecker ripped a burial shroud in half while singing, "*The bogus, bogey body-snatcher lies a-mouldering in the grave. Under nasty, noxious night soil, it shall remain.*"

The vespercestors blindfolded themselves and repeated, "This isn't happening. This isn't happening," while jumping in and out of their magic staffs, which remained locked in a hexagram pattern.

"O Captivatingness, alas, the hollowed hour has ended, and the Ancients could not pass over. I will try another ritual," said Anasircea, while the guardians carried Magister Gorgia Mesmerthang out of the alley.

Valor took a healing candle as the candle lighters passed them around the alley. While Anasircea approached the Deadway where Creighton and his family had gathered, a mixture of sympathy, sadness, and anger moved through Valor.

"Creighton, you have a vicious curse in your stomach, eating straight through to your backbone. This is symbolic," said Anasircea. She looked over at Alizaba and Kingston Crowley. "And you said on your brooms on the way over here, that if the witchdoctor couldn't heal your son, then no shady free-floater would either." Anasircea's eyelids tightened, keeping watch on Alizaba, who clutched seven purple charms and fidgeted in her purple dress, cloak, and boots.

"Yes, I said it. I'm angry with Sorcerers right now because Candlewicke Coven did this to him! I'm sorry, Creighton my son," sputtered Alizaba, breaking into tears while her husband, Kingston, placed his arm around her. She wiped a tear, turned to him, and groaned, "Oh, we can't lose him. We need seven sons."

"I know, dear, I know," said Kingston. He released seven purple martins from a cage he had been carrying and charmed the birds to circle seven times over Creighton. "Give me signs of my son's condition," he repeated seven times, watching the birds. His face seemed to wither when one of the seven birds fell to the cobblestone and remained motionless.

"Lift him up," said Anasircea.

The Crowley family lifted Creighton from the cobblestone.

"Now, Creighton, I need you to step into the hexagram and connect your wand to a vespercestor's magic staff." The vespercestors lowered their hexagram of connected staffs for Creighton to wobble inside, and then with hollow eyes, Creighton touched his wand to Scribe Fengurstaph's magic staff.

"Young man," Anasircea said to Creighton. "I am picking up vibrations—yes! This ritual can heal you of this *curse*." The candles blew out across the circle. "Ah, what do my eyes see with alarm? A sign, yes—a sign! Internalized rage has caused this young man's hex."

"Creighton? Internalized rage?" questioned Rose Decay, loosening her grip around her waist. "How could it be? He was always so jovial—until he left Candlewicke anyway."

"And there's more," continued Anasircea with building drama in her voice. "I'm getting a vision of a powerful woman—the Big M. The cosmos is showing me a change of mind. She'll approach you within the next few days and tell you that you aren't healed. The effects of this ritual could come to fruition, but it will require you to tell Big M the truth." Anasircea grabbed Creighton's arm with a look of urgency. "The truth! Do you understand me?"

Creighton looked across the arena at his former coven mates, pausing on Valor. "Y-yes," muttered Creighton. With trembling hands, he took the torn shroud from Tilta Crumpecker.

"Now, young man, I want you to pass back and forth through this Deadway. If any of the Ancients were able to pass through here tonight, maybe some of their residual energy will cling to you and cast off any negative forces," said Anasircea, before Creighton began to hobble along the alley. "Now, I ask the guardians, if they will, to begin dispersing the Essence of Fluorescence to see if we can uncover any residual footsteps of the Ancients."

Everyone in the arena pointed their wands at Creighton while he continued to wobble around the alley. The guardians shook their fluorescence wands, releasing glow-in-the-dark powder in vibrant purple all over the Deadway before several in attendance began looking for footprints on the cobblestone.

"I can't watch. He looks so sick," sobbed Rose.

"What's wrong with him? He's not even trying to rid any bad energy," said Valor, easing his hand over his mouth from the shock.

"He ought to be sick—sick of these nuts manipulating him," whispered Doomsy, while Snuffinumbra Coven held their heads low and tossed flowers, which crumbled under Creighton's shuffling feet. Snuffinumbra rattled tambourhorns and began to dance. Creighton slowed his pace as he approached Candlewicke Coven. Rose held a lace hanky over her eyes and sputtered, "Oh . . . ."

"He's a traitor," hissed Doomsy, turning her back to the alley.

"Hello, friend!" yelled Valor. Could he or his coven stir some emotion in Creighton that might renew the connection they once shared? Surrounded by the dancing, flower-tossing Snuffinumbras, Creighton walked a little faster down the alley, locking his eyes on the floor.

"We miss you," said Rose. Her posture deflated as her outstretched arms lowered to her knees.

Creighton's face scrunched up like a sundried tomato, and his chin began to tremble before he broke down and sobbed. He held his swollen stomach and shuffled as fast as he could past their section.

"Did you see that?" Valor said to comfort Rose. "I think Creighton still cares about us."

"Over here!" said Twila Diamone, inspecting the cobblestoned alley. "The Essence of Fluorescence has turned green here. It looks like a footprint."

While the Crowley brothers escorted Creighton toward the discovery, others gathered around Twila.

"Milady Diamone, as Magister of Familiar Arts, me've sailed 'round the world and seen a bounty of myths and lore. And those footprints yon appear to be nonhuman or in the process of shapeshifting, like the cat-person who clawed me eye out," said Provindicus Everhaught. With his pipe, the magister pointed at his eye patch, then at the footprint, before inhaling a puff of smoke.

"Interesting," said Esoterica Knowles, the secretary of Cryptic Chambers, recoiling from the pipe smoke. "I deduce that it could be Ancient Webbits Cobbratz, a clubfooted man according to legend."

"Hmm, place Creighton on the footprint," ordered Mahrata LaRock.

"But what if it was a Nockie creature and not an Ancient's footprint?" asked Crowdy Crowley, dropping Creighton's left foot as the other brothers continued holding him.

Mahrata raised her eyebrow and gave a sleepy shake of her head. "Humph. Just do it already. Baby Thio Crowley would be of, haaa, more assistance than this."

The Crowley brothers lowered Creighton on the green-glowing footprint, then the guardians gently rolled Creighton over the print like an ink stamp, getting fluorescent powder all over his clothes.

"I think it's something other than vagamorta ickypox. Creighton seems vexed," said Rose to her friends. "Maybe he knows something or—"

"Or maybe he's envisioning our imminent deaths," said Doomsy leaving with the rest of the crowd while they carried Creighton out of the alley.

Aaron led the way down the steps beside Buckthorn Hall. "Who might the 'Big M' be, pray tell?" he asked. "Could Anasircea not say her name? Must Mystic Ministry always be so vague?"

"I'm beginning to think so, Aaron. Something's going on around here," replied Valor. He helped Rose down the stairs while she absorbed her tears in a black-lace handkerchief. "And there's another thing." He pointed toward the bottom of the stairs where Ambergis stood in misalignment: her upper half separated at her waist, inches above her lower half.

"Ambergis again," said Doomsy, after moving ahead of Aaron to see. "And the Crowleys are just walking right through her—"

"None-the-wiser," said Micha, taking Ruza's hand as she

descended the steps, wearing tall, wand-heeled boots that emitted green-vapored puddles with every step.

"We have to speak with Creighton," insisted Rose. "I can't take the suspense any longer."

"I saw his brothers put him in the back of a purple carriage. He must be living at his parents' house again," said Valor.

Ruza, Blade, Nalini, Egg, and Micha returned to Candlewicke with Stabbah while the others strolled to a darkened courtyard on Intersession Alley. When no one was looking, they floated several blocks over the city rooftops to the Crowley home on the corner of Zodiac and Craft Alley, before landing in a sprawling treetop on the front lawn.

It seemed quieter now and the air fresher than other parts of the city. Within a minute, the head vespercestor's carriage pulled in front of the seven-story purple home, and two coachmen escorted Mahrata LaRock out of the carriage. She tossed her travel cloak on a coach lantern, accidentally setting the cloak on fire. Her wide-bottomed skirt plowed between seven formal hedges and yard statues as she wobbled up the moonlit walkway.

"No. Could it be so? Mahrata is 'the Big M' Anasircea warned Creighton about?" whispered Aaron.

Holding a scroll and quill, Mahrata shuffled to the door while clanging bells. Minutes later, candlelight illuminated the sixth of the seven-story rooms of the narrow mansion.

"Maybe that's Creigh's bedroom. Let's go see," suggested Rose.

After landing on the balcony, they peeped through the glass panes of the double-doors and saw Creighton reclining in a purple-canopied bed, holding a purple pillow over his swollen stomach. Mahrata entered Creighton's bedroom, sat on the edge of his bed, and patted the pillow with her hand. Creighton's groomed gentleness had been replaced by a frightening shell of his former self.

"Hmmm," sighed Mahrata. "It's just as I feared. Your stomach is still swollen from the curse. Haaa, it's close at hand." She glanced across the bedroom at the unopened toys and abandoned purple paintings and whimsical projects everywhere. "Yes, haaa, the bells of fate are ringing. I'm afraid it's my destiny to prepare your eulogy, Creighton. What songs do you want Preston Fox to perform at your funeral? Or do you have something to tell me?" Mahrata rang her bells over him. The entwined dragons' tails, under her headpiece, pushed into her jeweled necklaces as she gazed down at him with a weary but unsympathetic air.

"Oh dear, I think my blood just rushed to my feet," whispered Valor on the balcony. "Anasircea's prophecy must be coming true already."

Mahrata stepped away from the bed as Creighton's mom, Alizaba, tiptoed in the room while gathering her purple-feathered robe around her thin waist. She then said something indiscernible before leaving the room.

"I think Alizaba has left to fry Creighton some sage and swan eggs for dinner," said Valor.

"No," Doomsy said, "'bake him seven frog legs.' Alizaba talks like a mouse, so it's hard to hear."

"You two should never become spies, if I may say," said Aaron.

"You know what I think?" asked Doomsy, pulling away from the window and ignoring Aaron. "I think Mahrata changed her mind about wanting Creighton healed because she found out that he's a Sorcerer. That would surely taint the chances of a Crowley child as the Heir. Humph, Mah would let that happen maybe when ogres learn ballet."

"Who would need a crystal ball for that sad reality? But this I am assured: something is troubling Mahrata," Aaron whispered, while Rose dabbed her watery eyes.

"Or maybe, now that Mahrata made herself head vespercestor, she doesn't need baby Crowley as an heir," said Valor. "Wait! Why didn't I think of this? What if *Mahrata* has been the Conjuring Crone all along?"

Aaron appeared to be contemplating that suggestion. "It seems fitting, Valor, since her husband was the Grim Warlock."

"What did Anasircea want Creighton to tell the Big M?" asked Valor.

"'The truth' . . . about what I don't know," replied Doomsy.

Valor's shadow eased through the glass doors, crept across the floor, and climbed up the outside of Mahrata's dress. "Oh dear, my shadow's traveling." He clung to the door. How could he stop what was happening? His shadow, his impulsive fetch, had latched on to Mahrata and was trying to pull her away from Creighton? She began sweating, fidgeting at the side of the bed, waiting for Creighton to tell her his favorite funeral dirge. Valor stomped his boot, trying to restrain the last of his shadow that remained outside the room.

Tell her the truth, Creighton; whatever it is, tell her! Valor mentally begged from the balcony door.

Creighton's expression sank. Turning his glassy eyes to Mahrata, he appeared to surrender his very essence to her. "There's nothing to tell. I like drums," he groaned. "Play something with drums."

"Hmm, I'll make sure Magister Fox has lots of drummers to mystify you with their rhythms. You may, haaa, resign to that fact," said Mahrata. Her plume of phoenix made gentle notes on the scroll before she left his room.

Urgent in her need to see Creighton, Rose broke through the balcony doors, followed by Valor, Doomsy, and Aaron.

"It's me. Don't be scared, we had to see you," said Rose, inching toward his bedside before stopping beside his seven nightstands stacked atop one another. She strummed the purple fringe on one of seven lampshades. Seven packs of Floaty Bubble lay untouched on the bottom nightstand. Snuffinumbra paraphernalia decorated his room along with seven vintage circus posters and tacky toys, which appeared neglected.

Creighton's eyes widened with horror for a minute. He pulled his bedcover over his chest. "Get out," he coughed, then turned his head away and tried to hide a stuffed purple coyote under the bedcovers, bulging with six other coyotes. Creighton's fairy Familiar, Hulkin, sat on the corner of a purple pillow with his head in his tiny hands, gazing down at Creighton with droopy eyes.

"You still care about us, I saw it," said Rose, before Hulkin, at least, nodded in agreement. "This is killing us seeing you like this 'cause, believe it or not, we still love you," said Rose, easing closer to his bed. "Please tell us what happened to you."

"Isn't it obvious? I'm dying," said Creighton as his chest gurgled. He held his arm out from under the sheet. "I'm down to my essential aura layer. See, it's icy blue. Even the Auravitamax hasn't helped."

"But you're immortal?" said Rose. "I don't understand. You can't die. You've been like my brother and fath—"

"Rose, there comes a time when we have to stop pretending. Your family has had nothing to do with you since you were twelve," said Creighton.

"You mean you didn't really go home for your father's and brother's funeral?" Valor asked Rose.

"No, she didn't," said Creighton before Rose could speak. "She stayed at a friend's house in Lavisham—the friend who wrote the letter, letting her know her brother got torched by the dragon," said Creighton. "The only relationship she's had with her father is with his ashes she keeps in her hatbox."

Rose glared at Creighton. "You're so mean sometimes. It's easy for you to let go." She turned her back, fished her moon-powder compact from her conjure bag, and applied another thick coat of snow-white powder on her face. Was she doing this to swab tears or avoid confessing?

"You hafta let me go this time. I don't have much time left," continued Creighton. "A hillylippit landed on my Floaty Bubble this morning, and I didn't even have the power to paralyze it." Creighton motioned for them to come closer around his bed, and he held out a book he removed from under his pillow. Hulkin's eyes enlarged with promise. "I want you to have my book of old Sorcery spells, Rose. I think it'll help you understand some things."

Rose pushed through the line to stand closest to Creighton, who took a strained breath and said, "Here's the truth. I got tired of the Sanguinati shunning me. I was seeking status. I'm an acceptance clone, okay?"

"We accepted you," said Valor. "Oh, I see, you're saying *we're* the reason people shunned you."

"I dunno, maybe my crib was too small when I was a baby, ha-ha!" said Creighton. His laugh turned into retching coughs. "Blade was right. I was snaking for nods. I thought I might have a chance, you know, to become head vespercestor after you helped kill—" Creighton seemed to reconsider his choice of words and said, "after *Urbanne* died."

"We didn't have any part in Urbanne's death," said Valor.

"It wasn't so much his death," moaned Creighton. "I guess there's just this fickle part of me that needs some sort of boundary to keep from getting too close to anyone. I guess it's instinctive—keeps me from feeling trapped, like my fairy fishlets over there." Grimacing, Creighton motioned to his seven-tiered aquarium with seven purple fairy fish. "I have nightmares where I forget to feed them for, like, months. The water becomes stagnant, but my fairy fishlets just keep holding on somehow, you know—just like I always have." He handed Rose a pack of chewing gum from his closest nightstand. "Please feed them my Floaty Bubble, will you, Rosie?"

Rose released a gut-wrenching moan, took the gum with a forced smile, and walked over to the aquarium partition, which stretched to the ceiling, concealing a closetful of costumes behind it. She dropped the Floaty Bubble in an opening in the back of the aquarium, and the fairy fishlets tore into the gum, chewing it before blowing several bubbles.

Doomsy frowned a little and shook her head in disagreement.

"I see what you're saying but hag-zap-it, Creigh, what happened to you?" asked Rose after returning to his bedside.

Creighton's head rolled back on his pillow as he seemed to gather strength. "After I split from Candlewicke, I went to Mahrata, *Mah,* as I used to call her, and told her she should consider me for head vespercestor because my baby brother wouldn't be eligible for many years. Oh," Creighton moaned when he tried to move his legs. "Mah summoned me before the stargazers, and they did, you know, a *Progress Gauge Report* on me, and I was like, 'sure, whatever,' but when—" Creighton froze with a look of fright and took a few deep breaths. "The guardians wanted to make a wax mask of my face like those you told me you saw in the Esotericum Incantatory. I refused—flipped out more like it. Th-that's when they admitted I had failed my recent PG reports, but because my parents were mesmerists, they had overlooked the failing grades. They threatened to expose me as a Sorcerer, put me in the sanatorium. I could see myself trapped in an aquarium, like my fairy fishlets over there, so I hauled it all the way to Illusions Plaza, thinking there goes my chances of being a vespercestor—of opening my own theater someday. Falmoth was there—in the plaza. How he knew what had happened to me was, well, kinda creepy, you know?" Creighton closed his eyes and moaned. "Okay, it's like this. Falmoth talked me into joining the Hermetic Order—he said it was my only hope of keeping the vigilespion from capturing me. Somehow, he knew I was resentful of Valor being the Knight of Night. He said joining the Hermetic Order was now my only opportunity of making something of myself. There I admit it, Valor. I was jealous."

"You did join the Order, didn't you?" asked Doomsy, wrinkling her nose and crossing her arms. "And after shaming Valor and Aaron for joining."

"I toldja—my crib was too crowded," groaned Creighton, grabbing his swollen stomach and chanting softly. "That's why I'm dying. I swallowed a Mystic Key. I—I had no idea Falmoth would demand I kill Mah. Ow!" He grabbed his bedspread, writhing from the pain.

Alizaba returned with a seven-layered dinner tray on wheels and screamed, "Kingston!"

Creighton held out his hand and said, "No, mom, it's okay. I want to talk to them."

Alizaba positioned the dinner tray and a flower vase of purple dahlias beside his bed. She eyed Valor, Aaron, Doomsy, and Rose with bloodshot eyes. "I'm sending for help. You all did this to my boy," she squeaked.

"No, momma, they didn't. I lied," said Creighton, holding out a trembling hand to stop Alizaba. "Let us talk for a bit, momma, and—and I'll let you die my hair purple, okay?"

Rose gently touched Alizaba's hand and said, "We'll assist Creighton with his dinner, Mrs. Crowley."

"All right then. But make sure he has seven bites of his grape eggplant fudge. I have to go feed my seventh son," said Alizaba, shaking her fists excitedly before tiptoeing out of the room.

"I can't eat," groaned Creighton before chanting softly again, this time, Valor was positive Creighton was saying the words, "Spirit, show yourself."

Creighton stared at the ceiling with watery eyes. "I couldn't kill Mah. That's when everything changed. First, I realized I couldn't transvect anymore; then, my shadow wouldn't morph. Then, my blood turned red, and I had to use a wand to do any magic—now this." Creighton pointed to his swollen stomach, then grabbed Valor's arm and looked up at the ceiling with transfixed eyes.

"One with the longest lifeline . . . half-born from an earthbound spirit . . . can shake the hand that holds the staff."

"What are you saying, Creighton? Where did you get that information?" asked Valor.

"You said . . . when one is halfway between life and death, they might be able to contact Spirit," continued Creighton. His scarred wrist became exposed when he pulled Valor's sleeve harder. "Well, I just did, Val. Spirit told me a clue about his Staff of Gleaning, but I don't see him anymore. Everything is starting to fade away."

Moved by Creighton's honesty but unsure of his mental state, Valor swallowed and asked, "You can't leave us, my friend. I mean, what was all that business with Anasircea?"

Creighton took several breaths and said, "Anasircea chatted me up in private before the Passover and said the vespercestors would allow her to try to cure me if I promised to name all the Sorcerers in Mystic Steeples. But I knew she didn't want me to—they were forcing her to bribe me. Then I saw you all in the bleachers. I—I couldn't do it."

"Oh, Creighton!" Tears streaked Rose's black eye powder as she fell on him with an embrace. "You do still care."

Creighton didn't respond. His chest had stopped heaving for air.

Valor pulled Rose away from the bed and whispered, "Let's go, dear. All we have are our memories of him now."

"He can't be dead—he can't!" Rose pulled her book of spells from her conjure bag and plopped it on Creighton's chest. She began tearing through the book. "There must be a spell to save him—where is it?" She wept, ripping out a shower of pages. Hulkin flew down off the pillow, grabbed up a torn sheet, and began reading as fast as his tiny head could pass over the words. Realizing it was futile, Hulkin dropped the page and flung one last cloud of fairy dust on Creighton.

CHAPTER SEVENTEEN

FALMOTH SAVES FACE

MAHRATA LaRock stepped up to the podium in Ramrod's Arena. Valor couldn't believe he was at another funeral so soon—Creighton's funeral. A paper dragon flew across the enormous coliseum and unfolded in Valor's lap after burning his leg from its flaming breath. It had been nearly twenty-four hours since Creighton had died, and Valor was still so numb inside and out that he wasn't even outraged at the *Magic Ledger* newspaper Marston Diamone had airmailed him from across the arena. On the cover was a photo of Marston and Twila Diamone posing smugly in front of Candlewicke Mansion with their magic wands crossed, forming a cautionary X in front of Valor's home.

Doomsy snatched the newspaper and pounded out the flames on Valor's leg. "What does it say?" she croaked, holding the *Magic Ledger* closer to her face. "'Hot Off The Press. The Diamone Siblings Told Us So!'" Doomsy read for a few more seconds before wadding up the paper.

"What's wrong, dahhhling?" asked Stabbah.

"Marston and Twila are accusing Valor of killing Creighton."

"Wut? Why?" asked Micha.

"They said they tried to warn everybody that Valor was killing off all the Sanguinati leaders starting with Magister Crypting and Ernest Diggs. They said Valor murdered Creighton so that the Crowleys wouldn't have seven sons, and this would disqualify baby Crowley from being the heir to O Enchantedness."

"We shall just have to convince everyone that we had no part of Creighton's misfortune," said Aaron.

"When, my dear—before or after we finally convince them that the Great Deception has fooled every ounce of their existence?" sighed Valor, while the Crowley family dropped carnation wreaths on the floor at Creighton's feet.

"I kinda think we should keep in the shadows until we see how everyone reacts to all that's happened first," said Nalini.

"I'll not wait around for more deaths," said Valor. "If we can't show them that we're not the danger here, we're going to need way more help."

"From whom? Your new blood-thirsty coven of coffin dwellers? They have already killed Creighton and O Enchantedness, and still, nothing has changed," hissed Blade.

The pounding drums stopped.

"Crowley family and friends," said Mahrata, "I, hmmm, need all of you to look up here at me." She swallowed and raised her left eyebrow sharply. "Haaa, the vespercestors wanted Creighton to be healed—well, he is healed, hmmm, he's genuinely healed." Mahrata pointed up toward the heavens, where Summoner Mamahchi had predicted Creighton would become a star in the astral plane.

"He's not healed! That old hag. How dare she?" said Valor, between several angry breaths. His teary eyes scanned the vespercestors and Snuffinumbra Coven in the stands above the platform. Their scolding faces seemed to drip disapproval at Candlewicke Coven, who could hardly look upon Creighton's preserved corpse standing under the podium with a black shroud of shame draped over him. Hulkin circled Creighton, and then the fairy flew out of the arena.

Preston Fox motioned for the choir to resume the soft funeral dirge, *Pluvia in Galaxy*. As the guests began to leave, some of the attendees chanted and danced, accompanied by an organ and seven drummers. Newspaper reporters, along with Marston and Twila, began cutting through the crowds toward Candlewicke Coven. Valor pulled Rose's arm as she eased a hanky under her black veil.

"Let's get out of here, dear," said Valor. "I don't think any of us feel like answering questions."

They left Mystic Steeples and took the carriage home. Valor and Aaron got out on Crooked Spine Alley. They wanted to see if they could find any records on Creighton's diagnosis at Mystic Infirmary.

"Do you really think the Mystic Key killed Creighton?" asked Aaron.

"All I know is I don't want to wait for *Hazy Press* to publish that tell-all book claiming we cursed our friend. I hope Creighton's autopsy report might help us there." Valor stopped walking and eased his hands on Aaron's folded arms, forcing his full attention on him. "I think you and I know what this means, Aaron. We both swallowed a Mystic Key. We'll probably be next."

Squeezing his lips shut, Aaron leaned his face toward the stars and nodded.

Before they reached the crossing of Intercession Alley, they spotted Venerious Falmoth lurking in the shadows on the narrow alley beside the infirmary. They grabbed Falmoth and soared atop a private residence, landing on a bunch of stovepipes. Puffs of smoke shot out through the conical caps of the crooked pipes. The roof tiles were still warm even after the sun had set.

"Stop, please," giggled Falmoth, flapping his arms at them. "I'm foreseeing I'll be indebted to you for this hospitable greeting."

"Our friend is dead because of you!" growled Valor.

Falmoth propped his right dragon-scaled boot on the pointy pipe and said, "Um, seeing you have a reality hindrance, let me rephrase that naughty display of ignorance." Falmoth slowed his voice and spoke condescendingly: "Creighton the coven defector begged me to let him join the Hermetic Order of the Mystic Key. 'I'll do anything you ask,' I believe was his exact terminology." Falmoth's face formed a ridiculous mock of sympathy. "I shouldn't have been such a generous chap. I gave Creighton his first assignment, and how did he act?" Falmoth stroked the side of his cheek with his skull-tipped wand. "Never mind you and me; he chose to save his own back."

"You didn't have to kill him!" roared Valor, fighting back a strong desire to attack him.

Falmoth moved and spoke in choppy intervals, stretching his hand toward them while he seemed to think of a reasonable explanation: "The thing that killed him wasn't me—no, indeed—it was the Mystic Key. You see, it demands conformity, and Creighton failed to do my requested deed to save us from the Sanguinati. Believe me; the Key will sacrifice anybody who doesn't work for the cause, and for that, we should really applaud. He-he-he." Laughing, Falmoth clapped his hands until Valor and Aaron scowled at him, and then his enthusiasm melted.

"But, no," continued Falmoth. "Creighton was afraid of commitment most—becoming trapped, bored, but, oh . . . oh, how he wanted to be noticed." Falmoth tapped his wand on Valor's head. "Know this: Young Crowley tried to avoid his folks, yes—friends, uh-huh—anything he last became involved with before he refocused." Falmoth lowered his head. "We all have free will to choose, but he liked to boil his own brew. So, to assume I betrayed young Crowley is hopelessly bogus."

"Free will?" Aaron laughed with disgust. "'Tis never a choice if the option is being murdered."

He flung his arms in the air and sauntered farther down the roofline. The clicking of his boots soon blended with the noise of the city. The evaporating steam of a prior rain drifted around Aaron's velvet cloak, which puddled behind him.

"Aren't we privileged? You make it seem as if we are stars in the theater of liberation," continued Aaron. He looked away when Valor cradled his face in his hands and whined.

"Here's the deal: I understand how you feel," said Falmoth. His head vibrated with certainty. "Misery is a disease that invaded *me* years ago, you see, eliminating every confidence I'd gathered in the LaRocks into a wasteland of grief. Come; I have someplace I want to show you now. Besides, it isn't safe with the Big M lurking about." Falmoth narrowed his eyes on a piece of the torn Hierophant card, which fell out of Valor's pocket.

"Ambergis gave it to me," explained Valor, picking up the Tarot piece depicting a Hierophant's crowned head and two fingers lifted in a sign of peace. "I lost the rest of the card."

"Probably for the best. I imagine anything from Ambergis is cursed," said Aaron. The drooping lace ruffles around his wrists cut the steam into drifting wisps while towering tree branches framed the distant view of Mystic Steeples in a nightscape of eerie tranquility. Falmoth lowered his wand to the roof shingles, and the skull bit down on the card, allowing him to grab and inspect it.

"No need to cower," said Falmoth. "A Hierophant card in the future position isn't necessarily a curse but a revelation, a place of new power." Using magic, Falmoth conjured a broom from a twig sticking out of his hat beside two feathers and a hexagram, then he straddled the broom and flew off the roof.

By air, they followed Falmoth past the oak and cypress-lined Riverwalk to the Severance River. After landing on the docks, Valor and Aaron trailed behind him to the river's edge, where Valor had last seen the steamboat crash. They trudged through the knee-deep brush with patches of sand and shells scattered under their feet. Falmoth gave a greasy grin as his eyes and hands directed their movements.

"Don't stick your toes in the mud holes," cautioned Falmoth, before sweeping his hand toward the water. "Who could ever predict my magically malevolent journey would bring me back to this River of Verdict. I know I must face it, no matter how deplorable. I once was a witch enticed by deceitful oracles." Falmoth scraped his boot on a clump of grass to loosen the mud. "To tell you this, I question why. But they must be released so that I may thrive."

"What are you babbling about now?" asked Aaron, stepping around every weed.

Falmoth bent over, rested his hands on his knees, and said, "Now, what I'm about to tell you I say with a frown. But at the bottom of this river lie countless bodies Mystic Ministry drowned."

"There can't be any bodies left in this river. They've all washed out into the ocean by now," said Valor. "Unless you mean their spirits."

"Mortal witches always drowned, and as you say, 'washed away,'" said Falmoth. "But not the immortals who didn't swallow a Mystic Key. They are asleep, you see? Held down there in weighted chains for centuries. Rendum LaRock found those judgments 'decent.' It's all encoded in the *Fourth Book of The Pendulum Swings*." Falmoth's voice faded into a condescending whine. "Really a pity. But you weigh the nobility. Now, you can't bring back Creighton, but the others, you can save 'em."

Valor looked out over the river. Even the gloomy shore tried to hypnotize him, lull him to sleep, lure him into the murky water to drown in his own untimely tomb.

"I pretend to despise burial monuments and coffins to survive in this city," sighed Aaron, "but this watery grave before me, I despise with my whole being."

Falmoth laughed as if the moonlight had kissed his pores through the ghostly powder on his face. He placed his hand on Aaron's back. "Tell me now, kiddies, would you like to set them free?"

Aaron pulled away with a snap. "We can release them from the river, and they will be the same *now* as they were then?"

The skull head on Falmoth's magic staff nodded in agreement.

"This could be the only way we can prove to the Sanguinati that they were once Sorcerers!" said Valor, whishing he could bring Creighton, his twin, and his grandmother back instead.

"Oh, the upheaval that would bring," added Aaron.

"Imagine, will you, the looks on everybody's faces when all those free-floaters come floating back to Mystic Steeples with a ton of crustaceans to get off their shoulders!" Falmoth giggled, clapped his hands, and shuffled his boots like a naughty child. "The stuffy Sanguinati's suppressed past will stand before them questionably—glaringly—utterly shockingly."

Aaron didn't answer Falmoth. He moved closer to Valor by the river. Everything around its edge was decaying or washing away. Even the shell of humanity, which Valor and Aaron had clung to, seemed to wither away now, and their new Noctivatian lifestyle threatened to bind them as creatures of the night.

"Do you mean to confess that this is what happened to their heritage? You bound them all in the bottom of the river?" asked Aaron, while Falmoth eased up behind them. They turned their backs to the water to draw a confession from him. "Listen, you buffoon, I joined the Hermetic Order to protect Valor—to see what manner of deception you obscure. You prance around with your prose, expecting us to assist you. Now, tell us the unadorned truth, without all your bountiful 'bonerrifics' and 'magically magnifiskulls.'"

Falmoth breathed hard and fast through his nose, and his bottom lip quivered like a dog's hind leg scratching at a tick. "Oh my," he said. "I'm not allowed even a teensy-weensy wittle whyme?"

"No rhymes!" Valor and Aaron shouted before Valor remembered, from his time travel through *The Book of Chacodophilus*, that Falmoth had learned to speak in rhymes to prevent himself from stuttering.

"Oopsie, sorry. Lemme c-concentrate on talking boring," said Falmoth with his hands behind his back, pacing in circles on a large rock. "There was n-no Sanguinati in the beginning; they were all Sorcerers, and many were immortals. When I became head v-vespercestor, Urbanne LaRock started plotting against Mystic Steeples—even his own people—to corrupt the Ancients' oracles in order to k-keep the spell of immortality among his closest family."

"What a cold shyster," said Valor.

"Errr, to be fair, it wasn't just t-the LaRocks," said Falmoth, drumming his fingers on his shoulder as if torn with his confession. "Uh, many of the v-vespercestors were concerned that the ever-evolving Sorcerers would become too powerful to control. So, t-they—*we*—created a spell to remove immortality. And from what I remember when we performed the spell, it accidentally stripped most of the witches' immortality and sorcery in what many called 'The Fall.'" Falmoth gasped for air and held his throat. "Oh my! I didn't rhyme the whole time, did I?"

"Couldn't the vespercestors just do an immortality spell, and get it back?" asked Valor, leaning against a tree limb that was dripping with mopey moss.

Falmoth resumed a controlled posture and voice: "They might have, but Mesthu t-took the spell of immortality, which was hidden in the Cruxvein Abyss. That is how only Mesthu and his f-followers regained their p-powers and immortality."

"It's hard to believe the remaining Sorcerers stayed at Mystic Steeples. You'd think they'd be furious at the vespercestors," said Valor, wrinkling his forehead.

Falmoth nodded faintly in agreement and shared a few Luminous Lulling Lozenges with them. "Y-yes," he stuttered, "but the LaRocks are very sneaky. They knew everybody would q-question why they were suddenly aging and couldn't work their sorceries. So Urbanne created a brilliant lie before the v-vespercestors stripped everybody of their memories. Urbanne took over Mystic Steeples and p-placed a most beautimus, gorgical black crystal in the middle of the Hall of Relics. The Shadow Crystal was mesmerizing." He clasped his hands together and snarled. "And because old Urbanne is s-so thoughtful, he told them of its amazing ability to magnify or reduce the m-magic abilities of anybody the Shadow Crystal should choose." Falmoth stifled a giggle. "Oops, I didn't m-mean to rhyme. Of course, Urbanne knew every nosy-body would sneak an itsy-bitsy peek at t-the mysterious black crystal, if only from a distance. Ta-da! Vanishing magic problem solved." Falmoth wiped his hands in the air as though he were cleaning blood off them. "From that day forward, the v-vespercestors could blame the Sanguinati for m-making themselves magicless Nizzertits. They claimed the Shadow Crystal must've chosen to reduce everybody's p-power because it judged them to be very naughty."

"Oh, I see," Valor said, "so the Sorcerers couldn't blame the vespercestors for all their troubles."

"Verily, it must have been the same black crystal we found hidden in the Chamber of Oracles," Aaron said. "But it did not cause us to lose *our* powers."

"Because it had no power. Someone must've seen the Shadow Crystal as the trickery it was," said Valor.

"No. The trickable little witchables all believed it except for Mesthu and t-those who left with him," said Falmoth. He stood farther back in the shrubby landscape as if the drowned souls would reach out and punish him. "Urbanne hoped his daughter Ambergis had foreseen all of this and had conjured some oracles t-to help the LaRocks get their powers back, but Piron DaDovie t-took her new oracles just before she died. Of course, t-they blamed me, in order to toss me out. What alarms me the most is how t-the LaRocks have charmed t-the covens to forget all of this, their very heritage."

Valor became dizzy with relief and anger. He didn't want to admit that Piron DaDovie was his grandfather. "It explains so many things," he said. "I've had enough of power-hungry witches and their egos." He plucked a handful of belladonna, which swayed in the breeze, and tossed them into the river. "And this is why, Aaron—this is why I have no regrets joining the Hermetic Order. I've made a choice to get justice for our ancestors. But how come the Sorcerers in the river didn't lose immortality during The Fall?"

"The only t-thing I can conclude is that when The Fall happened, t-those Sorcerers who happened to be underwater or under the earth's surface weren't affected," answered Falmoth.

"That explains why all our friends had changed after my family and I emerged from the cave in Luxo," said Aaron.

"The cave your family had been exploring. I remember you telling me about that. Well then, we must set all these drowned Sorcerers free. We have to loosen their shackles!" said Valor.

"You jest. We cannot swim to the bottom. The currents would sweep us away," said Aaron, his traveling tattoos shriveled around his neck and wrists. "How about you, Falmoth? You share the blame in all of this. 'Tis your duty to rescue the immortals."

"Did I fail to mention, I sing the double-standard song with no pretension?" Falmoth removed his hat and bowed. "No, I'm not immortal. I respectfully avoid water—only bathe when the moon is a quarter." His voice strained while he loosened his lace collar. "Nopety-no-no, it will take sorcery to rescue them—that's fo' sho."

"I'm willing to try," said Valor, shaking.

He walked out on the surface of the river as the waves splashed up to his waist. He dipped his head under the water and saw a sunken carriage and centaur skeletons with their hooves embedded in the sandy bottom. His heart sank. A bride and groom sat in the back seat of the carriage, decaying: her once-white veil was now brown as it drifted with the seaweed. A subtle movement on the riverbed turned Valor's head. Did he just see other bodies at the bottom of the river, bodies that didn't appear to have decayed? He came up for air, trying to keep the force of the waves from toppling him.

"Aaron, see if you can stop the river's flow long enough for me to work a spell to break their chains," said Valor, pointing his monoculous at the river.

"Indeed, this seems like Doomsy's specialty, but I shall try," said Aaron. He eased to the river's edge, placed his left hand out over the water, and chanted, "*Suspensus Motus.*" The light of Saturn dropped from the galaxy and formed a ball in the palm of his left hand, and this he tossed in the river. Aaron jumped back from the bank and inspected the water's movement. The bigger waves began to mellow. "As far as I can see, the river appears calm now. I should practice the Law of Elemental Manipulation more often."

Valor gazed at Severance River, picturing the victims locked in chains at the bottom. "*Recludo,*" he chanted and then waited, inspecting the river from left to right. "Aw, it didn't work. There's nothing but a few foamy bubbles."

"Visualize the breaking of their chains, Valor," said Aaron, closing his eyes and spreading his hands out over the water. "Raise energy for the working. Tap into their torment. Tap into your anger."

"Okay. *Recludo,*" Valor shouted, but again, only bubbles surfaced.

"Sacrifice your firstborn . . . thoughts," giggled Falmoth.

"What on earth do you mean?" huffed Valor.

"He means, block out any distracting thoughts and speak the spell to their chains, my friend," said Aaron. He joined in, yelling the same spell as Valor had, and there in the darkness, the aroma of muddy water bubbled up as though the river had begun to boil. Falmoth jumped off his rock, giggling. Aaron fell backward onto the muddy bank. Splashing, writhing bodies began popping to the surface across the length and width of the Severance River, while some of the bodies soared straight up in the air.

Valor walked over the surface of the river, thrust his hands into the water, and heaved women and girls to the surface. In their once glorious gowns, now muddied and bleached by the filthy water, they pushed their tangled hair from their faces. Valor fought back tears as he heaved men and boys, covered in river weeds and algae, from the river.

"You're free! Float to shore if you can," he shouted, as more immortals began to levitate out of the water and walk onto the shore, gasping for air for the first time in years.

"Yes, that's it. Rejoice. I, Venerious Falmoth, have set you free," said Falmoth, hugging himself.

"You buffoon! Valor set them free, not you," said Aaron.

"It doesn't matter who gets credit as long as we help them," shouted Valor.

Scores of frightened people squished around in wet, rotted clothes, searching for their relatives, crying out names, and breaking into occasional tearful laughter. Valor swallowed his tears, while many of the rescued victims reunited with a long-lost spouse or child. He remained on the river's surface in case one of the Sorcerers might be his grandfather. But the poor souls wandering the banks with lost, desperate expressions needed him more. And maybe he could help them find their loved ones.

"Excuse me, young man," an old man said to him, "can you tell me how it was that Rendum LaRock bestowed the drowning verdict on me and has now reversed my punishment? And who are all these other people who've come from the river? I'm afraid I'm rather mystified."

"This wet man's not among my victims. He must've been drowned by the tenth ruler of Mystic Steeples named Rendum," said

Falmoth, tugging the wrinkles out of his coat lapel.

Valor softened his voice. "I'm sorry to tell you, sir, but Rendum LaRock didn't reverse his verdict. You've been in the river for many, many years. Mahrata LaRock is the head vespercestor now, the thirteenth."

The man's face twitched, and he collapsed on a clump of weeds as though he had a disturbing vision inside his wrinkled forehead. A woman lifted her tattered dress, releasing a trapped fish, which landed beside her missing, left big toe. Valor offered his jacket to wrap around her bare shoulders.

"Thank you, young man. I am High Priestess Siouxanna Demollien, and I will see that you are rewarded for your duty." She handed a bouquet of waterlogged roses, she had been holding, to Aaron.

"No, thanks. It's the least anyone could do," said Valor, waving goodbye to Siouxanna as she trudged up the hill away from the river.

"I'm not so sure this was a good thing to do now. Who's going to tell her she's no longer the high priestess?" Valor said to Aaron before a man and woman, with sheets of river weeds and algae covering their arms, pressed in on him.

"Please tell us if you have seen any of our children; their names are Shadrach, Dash, and Stabbah?" asked the man, grabbing Valor's shirt.

"Don't tell me," gasped Valor, electrified with excitement. "You must be Horus and Mini Scarveda."

"Yes, yes, we are!" Mini began to cry with hope, cupping her hands under her chin. Horus put his arm around her as he awaited Valor's response.

"I'm not sure where Shadrach and Dash are," said Valor, "but Stab is living at Candlewicke Mansion. Please go to her. The address is—"

"Candlewicke on Spookum Alley? Yes, I know exactly, yes," said Mini Scarveda. Her eyes focused over the piers toward Mystic City. Her tears reflected her anticipation to reunite with her lost daughter. "Thank you!" She breathed in hard, hiked her wet dress, and Horus pulled her up the incline as fast as she could walk.

Valor turned in circles, soaking in the magnitude his spell had produced across the landscape. "We'll have to provide shelter for these people," he said to Aaron. "They don't even know what happened to them?"

"Hundreds of wet, muddy, strangers are not going to stay at Candlewicke, Valor McRaven. Do not entertain such an idea lest I slap you with a thorny bouquet," said Aaron shaking the soggy flowers at him.

"Gather around. Gather around," said Falmoth to the river people. He twirled his staff, drawing a warm wind across the landscape. Valor floated away from the river and stood with Aaron at Falmoth's side, while the Sorcerers came in closer.

"The not quite twelfth, not quite fourteenth hour is drawing near! You all have been in the river for many years. But I, Venerious Dyvonases Falmoth, have pulled you out by hand—saved you for my plan. We must infiltrate Mystic Steeples and remove the vespercestors and corrupt people." Falmoth reached into his conjure bag, removed fistfuls of candy, and flung it at the crowd.

"Certain members of Mystic Ministry have erased Sorcerer history. Today they call themselves the Sanguinati," yelled Valor. "Their magic is now carried out by ghosts, but they are unaware of this."

Falmoth's body jerked as if from shock. "All in attendance, hold on a minuscule minute," he said, before bending down and whispering to Valor, "I know we shouldn't linger, but my-my, where did you come up with that humdinger?"

"If you don't already know, I'm not sure I should tell you," said Valor. "But it's the truth. It must've happened after those remaining at Mystic Steeples lost their sorcery—after The Fall."

"Ghost magic? Why, that sounds enchantingly tragic. But the period after Urbanne had taken over was sour; even I, of course, lost my powers." Falmoth reared back and folded his arms while the crowd appeared to grow impatient. "If they're using ghost magic, why, that's just a form of sorcery mockery. For I became Noctivatian and gained wickedly wonderful warlockery."

"Good greetings, my fellow Sorcerers," Aaron shouted to the crowds. "We must use caution. The rulers of Severance, Hoopenfangia, have redefined us as wicked witches. Many of the current vespercestors wish to eradicate us. We must convince the entire Sanguinati of our heritage."

"We'll do more than convince them," someone in the crowd shouted, and the others agreed.

"Now, hush the chatter before things get all a-tatter," said Falmoth. "It's vital for nothing lesser than you all to reinstate me as head vespercestor!"

"Why should we help you?" a woman in the crowd shouted. "You shackled my daughter and me and tossed us in the river!"

Before Falmoth could answer, lightning bolts whipped across the sky. Several guardians, on Missile Thistle Bristles, soared from the skyline of Mystic Steeples. The muddy river people seemed confused at first, then dispersed fast.

"What? Stay and fight. Show them your might!" shouted Falmoth.

Some of the Sorcerers floated up into the clouds to engage in combat with the patrolling guardians, while Falmoth stayed on the ground, barking orders.

"No. They're too weak to fight right now," insisted Valor. "Besides, Aaron and I didn't set them free to fight battles for you."

Aaron dodged a ribbon of fire from a wand. He approached Falmoth and said, "It will take time to convince these people of all that has come to pass, but when it happens, they will be ready to defend. In the meantime, I'm certain the guardians think some sort of revolution is mounting."

"I don't give a moldy leaf of cabbage about their heritage," said Falmoth, before softening his approach. "Look, I know that sounded snobby, but we need to overthrow the Sanguinati."

Valor and Aaron ignored Falmoth and fled from the guardians. Keeping under the protective tree branches as much as possible, they soon reached the narrow side-alley of Candlewicke Mansion.

"Do you hear that?" asked Valor, bending his head toward the courtyard. "Someone's crying."

"'Tis sobs of a girl," said Aaron.

They eased toward the backside of the mansion and peeped through a round opening in the stone fence, where a low-lying oak limb had grown through for many years. There in the courtyard, in a black veil and matching collar, reclined Rose Decay, draped across the basin of the water fountain. The pearl drops she had glued near her tear ducts were white like her dove-feather eyelashes. While regally dressed ghosts waltzed around the courtyard, her black cat, Venus, walked the edge of the fountain, occasionally dipping its tiny boots in the water, splashing droplets onto its black leather skirt.

"We should go to her," whispered Aaron, bolting forward.

"Wait." Valor grabbed Aaron's coat and restrained him when Micha approached the fountain and sat beside Rose. Because of the swarm of bats and witches passing under the crescent moon, the night sky appeared to ripple.

"Hey . . . hey, Rose. Are you all right?" asked Micha, slipping his arm around her back.

Rose pushed her upper body away from the fountain and straightened her posture and dress. "Yeah," she mumbled with a quivering smile before shaking her big black coils of hair across her face and collapsing onto Micha's shoulder. Her tears left red streaks from her powdered eyelids, matching her deep-red lips.

"There-there now, Rosie," said Micha. "I know it must be tough losin' Creighton. We all miss 'im. You two were tight, but another guy'll come along, he will."

"We dance to relive the past," said the female ghost when her partner dipped her head over the fountain in a dance. "You dance to forget."

"Creighton was just a friend. We were each other's shields." Rose laughed as though she didn't see the ghosts before she wiped her eyes. "He understood me. I understood him. Even if I were pretty, I'd scare off a real boyfriend."

Micha removed his arm from her back and glanced around the courtyard. "Ah, c'mon Rose," he said. "Ya may style ya'self like a ferocious Sorceress, but I know underneath all that enchanted powder and leather, there's a girl—a girl that any guy'd still be happy ta have."

Venus raised a playful cat-eye at Micha and rubbed her black fur against his leg. Micha grinned with a blush.

"I'm not vulnerable," Rose said in her baby doll voice. She pivoted away from Micha and tore loose a ringlet of hair that had become stuck to her painted lips. "This is just—I'm just—sorry for Creighton, that's all."

Micha shrugged. "It's okay ta be a little vulnerable sometimes. That's all I'm sayin'."

"Purrrfectly fine," purred Venus, sitting on Micha's boot.

"Most guys are rotten. I like intimidating them," Rose said to Micha. "I like to give them a reason to taunt me, but they can't see my soul, they can't touch that. Creighton was all I needed, whatever that was. He taught me to live for the moment. We didn't need to be accepted by the stupid Sanguinati, or at least I thought *he* didn't. He wasn't happy, and he didn't tell me. Now I don't know what to think."

Micha gave a subtle nod. "Reminds me of my favorite comedian, Leadbelly Lofton."

Rose wiped the black streaks of eyeliner off her snow-white powdered cheek. "Oh yeah, the comedian who deliberately turned himself into a tussle bug in the middle of a stampede of hippogriffs. That was awful."

"Yeah," said Micha, "'cause we depended on 'em ta keep us laughin'. It helped us through the bad times. But when they're gone, it makes us feel alone—vulnerable somehow."

"I wanted Creighton to become immortal. I thought it might prevent him from ending his life. I never admitted that to him, but it didn't help," said Rose, dropping her head.

"Aw gee, Rose. Tell me that's not why ya wanted ta become immortal?" asked Micha.

"I don't know." Rose pivoted away from Micha, pulled her moon-shaped compact out of her conjure bag, and reapplied white powder on her tear-streaked face using a powder puff. "It's like I feel disassociated from who I really am. I know I experienced some sort of childhood trauma. But I think there is a tiny part of me that's trying to protect the rest of me—the part I fear might become unhinged, that craves danger and thrills."

"Taking care of yaself is a good thing, Rosie." Micha gave the softest of fisted punches to Rose's shoulder. "You'll learn ta look within ya'self and find inner strength that's way stronger than this outer you that ya created." He smiled bashfully.

CHAPTER EIGHTEEN

THE ABDUCTION DEDUCTION

BEFORE a day had passed, Valor got Aaron to agree that they should purchase two adjoining buildings on Charnel Alley since Aaron, Salazants, and Manning didn't want to house the river evacuees at Candlewicke Mansion. The buildings needed repair but were affordable and livable for the time being. Stabbah let her elf familiar, Ellfroy, and Ruza Renata run Thunder Plant while she moved her parents into her old home in Mystic City. Stabbah wanted to spend some time catching up with them, and all that had happened in the years since she had last seen them as a young girl.

Micha had skipped Spurgmulin practice to help catch the evacuees up on his favorite subject, Sanguinati History. Several of the Sorcerers had found their old homes now inhabited by their descendants, others were unable to convince their new families of what had happened to them, or so it seemed. Valor's heart warmed to see displaced immortal children finding new parents: men and women filling the emptiness from the loss of their own children after years of confinement in the bottom of the river. It had taken a few hours before the strange stirring had spread throughout all of Severance. The river people scurried about, pacing the floor.

"Must we continue this buzzing about like hillylippits," Aaron said to the river people, "'tis making me rather anxious."

"They can't help it, Aaron," whispered Valor. "You wouldn't sit still either if you'd been chained an inch from death at the bottom of a river for over a hundred years or more."

Summoner Eelias Mamahchi and a reporter with *The Daily Hazy Herald* barged inside the old cauldron factory on Charnel Alley without an invitation, and they inspected the new residents.

"Is there a problem, Summoner?" asked Valor, trembling inside.

Mamahchi wagged his finger scoldingly. "You violated the new *Questioning Regulation.*" He tore off a piece of parchment and handed it to Valor.

"A vespercestorial fine of seventy globulnugees? But that's not fair," said Valor, while the reporter went through the old factory asking questions to the new residents.

Aaron directed the furniture deliverers to place the mattresses in the front rooms so the workers wouldn't linger and snoop into their business. Rose had placed several *Controssuas* on the nightstands to make the rescued victims appear like compliant Sanguinati witches.

"You write violation tickets for pleasant greetings. The nerve," huffed Aaron, looking at the ticket in Valor's hand. "I know how to beat this game." Aaron strutted up to Mamahchi with his right hand braced under his pursed lips, as though he were sizing up the old witch. "Summoner, we should not receive a fine if we just happened to word our communications with the vespercestors with a bit of cunning. We possess the deed to this property and are abiding by the laws. Therefore, I would not imagine any problem here that would justify this intrusion upon us."

A female Sorcerer with tall gray hair began twitching and growling in her chair. She and the chair levitated four feet before the woman latched her muddy boots around Mamahchi's neck, choking him. Her eyeballs bulged wildly.

The Summoner aimed his blackthorn staff at the woman and chanted a spell. With a scream, she shriveled into a crumpled wad of skin and clothing before collapsing on the fallen chair.

Valor, Doomsy, Aaron, and the rest of Candlewicke Coven froze with shock. Booger Fay hid behind a wardrobe, except his golden tail remained on full display.

"You didn't have to kill her," said Valor. "She has been through a lot. I'm sure she was just frightened."

"I captured everything on my crystaleer, Summoner," said the news reporter. "Another victim of the Possessing."

Valor and his friends exchanged horrified eye contact. If that woman had really been possessed, then it could only mean the Grim Warlock was still alive.

"Mystic Ministry will not allow . . . any attacks," replied Mamahchi, while half the river people cowered in the back of the room, and the other half appeared ready to attack the summoner. "Very peculiar. I sense a formal investigation soon."

"Summoner, I can meet with you in private and explain—like you wanted me to," whispered Valor.

Mamahchi pulled away from Valor and examined a mud-covered dress someone had tossed on a dusty crate. "These *peasants* must stand before the vespercestors . . . explain where they've come from . . . so suddenly." Mamahchi motioned for the reporter to leave. "They must be brutally honest, McRaven, or the walls of Grossatete Sanatorium . . . will expand to accommodate them."

"I assure you, Summoner, these people have every right to be here," said Valor, snatching the door open for the reporter and him to leave.

"Remember," said Mamahchi with a slower tongue and cautioning glance under the floppy brim of his hat, "*brutally* . . . honest."

After the summoner left, Rose rushed behind Valor and turned the key, locking the front door tight, while a crowd began to form a circle outside chanting, "Surrender, surrender, the intruders from the river . . . ." Two of the river people scooped up the remains of the possessed woman and flew up a chimney to find a place to bury her.

"Oh, my gargoyles! What do they want to do—drown these poor people again?" squeaked Rose. She adjusted a fallen curl away from her squinched eyes and slid away from the door. "You don't think it's true, do you? You don't think the Grim Warlock is still alive?"

Valor nearly fell over from thinking about it. "It can't be true. I mean, O Enchantedness had to be the Grim Warlock."

"Try not ta panic, Val. That woman might not've been possessed, ya know? Maybe she just hated the summoner an' wanted ta attack him."

"I'm desperate to believe that, Micha. But the river people promised they would remain as peaceful as they could until we come up with a plan to explain their true history."

"O Enchantedness was just murdered. I cannot think about what this could mean for us." Aaron flung the vespercestorial fine onto a mattress and placed another red grape on the tip of his tongue, eating more delicately now that he had fangs.

"He was rotten—he murdered Mesthu. And Micha is right, that woman could sense that Mamahchi was rotten too. I should've put the whammy on him for what he did to her," said Doomsy, clutching her poppet more than usual. She inspected the river rescues.

Valor wondered if Doomsy were hoping any of them might be her parents: If she saw the right person, would it break the memory-loss spell? She didn't seem happy that Stabbah had reunited with her parents. After all, Stabbah had been like a mother to her before Doomsy became Valor's adopted sister.

"Until we know for sure that the Grim Warlock isn't dead, we mustn't panic," said Valor. "We need to work fast and come up with a plan to remove the Great Deception."

Rose stomped around the cluttered front room with her hands on her hips. "Well, I'm about to panic. The vespercestors are forcing strangers in Mystic City to explain their presence now. Ugh, I'm so angry! They don't harass Nizzertit tourists like this." She put a spell on the brooms to sweep up the tracked-in debris from the alley.

"The Nizzertits are paying to stay in Mystic hotels with month-long passes to tour Mystic Steeples," said Blade. "The Ministry rolls out the purple carpet for them."

"I don't think the Sanguinati care that Urbanne murdered Mesthu. They know Bohemia was a Sorcerer. They're going to be watching us because she helped Falmoth get revenge on Urbanne," said Valor. He unpacked a box of soap and toiletries, Ruza purchased from the nearest gift store for the river people.

"No surprise that they're watching us. Bohemia joined the Noctivatians—warlocks—vampires, mind you," hissed Blade. "And we've had three from Candlewicke Coven—*three* who have become the same disgusting thing!"

"I think we're all still upset over losing Creighton," said Valor. "He would have wanted us to move forward, to continue with our mission." Valor thumbed through his Mystic Memoir to refresh his memory. "Which I've been wondering. Does anyone have a clue what the message Creighton received from Spirit could mean? I wrote it down here: He said, 'One with the longest lifeline . . . half-born from an earthbound spirit . . . can shake the hand that holds the staff.'"

"So, someone is actually holding the Staff of Gleaning. No need to check out any more flagpoles," said Doomsy.

"Palm readers call the curved line between your index finger and the thumb 'a lifeline,'" said Rose. "The longer the curve, the longer the lifespan." She looked at her hand and frowned.

"Good thinking, Rose," said Valor. "Then, the prophecy must be referring to the oldest person in Hoopenfangia. But how can someone be half-born?"

Doomsy stuck out her bottom lip. "I wouldn't get worked up about anything Creighton said. People often hallucinate on their deathbed."

"Erm, what's a deathbed?" asked Booger Fay.

"It's these mattresses you call 'bouncy boxes,'" said Valor, pointing to the row of beds in the room. "Except they're called 'deathbeds' when people die on them."

"Does this mean I get to sleep on all these bouncy boxes?" Booger Fay bounced on the bedding, leaving stray feathers from his wings here and there. Valor couldn't respond then. He couldn't stop sniffing the vespercestor soaps, though the Fengurstaph bar reeked of moldy grapefruit.

"I apologize if this upsets anyone, but I have been wondering . . . if the guardians have made a Death Mask of Creighton, and if they are controlling his spirit as we speak?" asked Aaron, shooing Booger Fay off the mattress.

"I can't imagine Creighton would let anyone control him. You know how he was: Two weeks of anything, and he was ready to move on," said Rose, tying a black ribbon into a bow around Booger Fay's tail. "I'm surprised he kept me as a friend for so long."

"You gave Creighton no choice; you would hit him with that cat-o'-nine-tails of yours," said Blade with a smirk. He posted a "Private Residence. Go Away" sign on the front door of the old factory. "Blade doesn't enjoy being a killjoy, but how will we explain all these river people you and Aaron resurrected, Valor? It would be tragic to see them tossed back in the river."

"You underestimate their potential, my pet. They won't let the primitives toss them in the river ever again," said Doomsy, passing out bed sheets and blankets to some of the evacuees as they came into the front room. "But I'm teaching them a few choice spells, just in case."

"What if you were wrong about the Grim Warlock, huh?" Rose asked Valor and Aaron. "He may be running the Hermetic Order. We need to find a way to get those Mystic Keys out of your stomachs."

"Recklessness is the ruin of a Sorcerer. Even if Valor and Aaron swallowed the Mystic Key, they could still choose to do the right thing, although they may die in their choices." Blade patted Valor on his stomach. "We could use a ritual dagger and cut the keys out of you and Aaron. That is why they call me 'Blade,' if you didn't know."

"You will do no such thing," snorted Doomsy. She stood between them with her finger pointed at Blade.

"Oh, I wish we could bring Creighton back," said Rose, just as a loud series of knocks startled everyone.

"Erm, who is pounding on the door?" asked Booger Fay, emerging from behind the wardrobe.

"Valor, are you in there? It's me, Magister Crypting," yelled a man's voice from outside on the alley.

"MAGISTER CRYPTING?" everyone gasped.

"Yes-yes. Hurry and let me in!"

Valor cracked open the door to find a shriveled man concealed under a gray woolen cloak.

"Lock—lock the door before those dastardly nosy-bodies force their way in. Goodness-goodness me," stammered Magister Crypting. He pulled his cloak off, meaning to hang it on a broken wall lamp, but it fell to the floor. His messy bobbed hair resembled a skunk with its patches of black and silver waves.

"I cannot believe it's you! Everyone said you were dead," said Valor, hugging Crypting. The old magister's bony body appeared frail beneath his layers of clothing. "Where have you been since the pock-bellied dragon flew away with you?"

Crypting started to sit on the bed with Booger Fay but decided to sit on another mattress. "Frightful. A nightmare, a living nightmare. Those dastardly conniving beasts," said Crypting. He crossed his legs in a dignified manner and blinked his eyelids as though he were trying to erase flashbacks of monsters.

Everyone gathered around to hear his story except for Micha, who remained in the back of the building, impressing the river people with all that had happened since they'd been underwater, and showing them books he borrowed from Candlewicke's library.

Magister Crypting pushed up his spectacles, which magnified his tiny wrinkled eyes. "I'll never forget that fateful day," he said. "O Enchantedness wanted me to lecture at the sanatorium. I felt a certain sense of doom, especially after I, uh, received a request by somebody wanting to access the Chamber of Oracles. I had just stepped out of the Subju Gate of the sanatorium when the stranger approached me, claiming some ridiculous affiliation with Cryptic Chambers, but I knew he was an imposter. Naturally, I, uh, refused to allow him access until he could procure a key of admission from O Enchantedness. And dear, dear me, that's when a, uh, pock-bellied monster flew out of nowhere, grabbed my leg, and there I was hanging under the scaly, scaly beast. Next thing I know, it, uh, carried me off over Grossatete Grove."

"Yes, sir. And you lost your breeches in a tree," said Valor.

Magister Crypting glanced at Rose and Doomsy. His face turned red. "Oh, that's not appropriate to say in front of mixed company—not appropriate at all. Anyway, I, uh, must've passed out from all the blood rushing to my head. Voices—dastardly voices woke me up, and I realized I was, uh, being held captive by a bloody armchair."

"By an *armchair*?" Valor asked, in case he misheard him.

"Yes-yes, its cold wooden arms were, uh, covering my eyes, and its legs were gripping my wrists and ankles. See." Crypting held out his hands. "I still have splinters."

"Hold still. I can get the splinters out," said Doomsy. She held Crypting's right hand steady while she reached into her conjure bag, removed a swamp leech from a specimen jar, and placed it on his wrist. "There. You'll be your old self in no time."

Crypting' bellowed and flung the slimy leech on the floor. "N-now w-where was I?" he asked. "Oh, I h-heard a b-boiling cauldron behind me, and the whole time I, uh, suspected my abductors were going to cook me in some potion. And inquire, oh, how they relentlessly inquired how to get inside the Cruxvein Abyss. And their voices, something was recognizable about their voices. Then I, uh, realized they were drinking Tongues of Fun Tonic."

Valor started to mention drinking the tonic at the sanatorium until Crypting continued:

"Some sour rubbish mere imbeciles drink to change their voices. But what they didn't realize, as the master archivist, I'm, uh, well versed in cryptic codes and language pathology. The phonation of the leader's words and voice had an unmistakable resonance. It was none other than Urbanne LaRock, uh, telling the others that they needed to get the Clandestine Chamber before the Grim Warlock could."

"You must've been held captive awhile. O Enchantedness was killed about four days ago?" said Valor.

Magister Crypting held two fingers over his lips. "I have been in hiding in the most wretched places, but I heard about his murder. I recognized a fellow magister's voice and knew it was Calamus Tuberstooge by the, uh, variation of his vocal pitch. He assured O Enchantedness they were, uh, stockpiling enchanted weapons in the sanatorium in case their magic failed again."

"They have forgotten how to access the Cruxvein Abyss hidden under the Catacombs. We believe Mesthu Marsh from Shadowhaven Heights knew how to access it, but O Enchantedness murdered him," said Aaron, tapping his finger on his cheekbone in deep concentration.

Magister Crypting leaned forward on the edge of the mattress and said, "O Enchantedness may be dead, but Calamus and, uh, whoever else held me captive know you are the Knight of Night, Valor. They know you have the Crown of Chacodophilus and the, uh, Electricus Hexigus."

"Wouldn't they at least try and threaten us or something, you know, to get the things they want?" asked Rose.

"Probably not if they're waiting for you to lead them to the abyss," replied Magister Crypting. "There are others who were working for O Enchantedness, but you mustn't lead them to the abyss, even if you know how to get down there."

Valor realized something he needed to tell the magister: "Your understudy—"

"Bessbadora Breeches?"

"Yes," said Valor. "She knows we found something important in the Chamber of Oracles. She may be a part of the group that held you prisoner. She did a spell to try to get me to confess," said Valor.

"We used the Electricus Hexigus to make the talismans," added Doomsy.

Magister Crypting's eyes darted as if spying for eavesdroppers. "The talismans can, uh, render you invisible on command," he whispered. "You all are in danger. Remember this so the vespercestors won't see you."

"Invisible?" asked Blade, rubbing his hands together with pulsing eyes.

"Ugh," Rose moaned, giving him a look of disapproval. "You shouldn't have mentioned it in front of Blade. He'll find some need to spy in the Sanguinettes' changing room."

"The amazing and handsome Zagato skipped Magister Tripp's assembly to do charity work, Rose Decay. You must see the admirability in such a sacrifice," said Blade, puffing up his chest.

Rose clasped her hands against her cheeks and gave Blade a fake and fleeting look of adoration.

"But how did you escape, Magister Crypting?" asked Valor. He tried to ignore Blade and Rose, while Doomsy made kissy fingers at them with a weary expression. Micha started eyeing Rose and Blade from the back of the room, where he was still showing books to the river people.

"After I told them a hundred times that I, uh, didn't know how to access the Cruxvein Abyss, they threw me in a giant cage with gargoyles," answered Crypting. "Those horrid gargoyles ripped my clothes, bit me, and, if from sheer exhaustion I would get to sleep, I'd soon find gargoyle fingers in my nose and ears. I learned the creatures' ways of communicating, and, uh, using a banana, I taught them how to steal a wand out of the guard's pocket and hand it to me. I've been in hiding until I saw the headlines in the *Magic Ledger* this morning about the, uh, people coming out of the river, and how you had been suspected of resurrecting them," Crypting said to Valor and Aaron. "I had to warn you."

"How didja find us?" asked Rose.

"Another, uh, communication device I learned as an archivist and magister of *Controssua* Studies," said Crypting. "All a witch has to do to find a suspected coven dissenter is look for a gathering crowd— and there they were, out there on the alley."

"It'll be interesting to see if Mahrata mentions the Severance River situation to the public. I mean, everyone knows they used to drown people there," said Valor.

"Blade overheard Graven Dust bragging this morning. It seems Mahrata told the magisters of Toadflax Hall that the people from the river were tourists seeking sunken treasure. Don't know how she expected anyone to believe they were Nizzertits—the guardians had already reported them as floating out of the river," laughed Blade. He stacked boxes of clothes and necessities for the evacuees on old display shelves for cauldrons, ripping the corner of his lace sleeve on a ladle hook.

"The magisters of Toadflax Hall are smarter than Buckthorn Hall. They won't believe Mahrata," said Doomsy, peeping out the door's curtained window before stepping away.

"We'll have to explain it to everyone then," said Valor. "Perhaps they'll finally listen. They heard O Enchantedness himself admit they were all once Sorcerers."

"Valor, I wondered how long it would, uh, take you to figure out the truth about the origins of Mystic Steeples," said Crypting. "I've wanted to expose the truth in my assemblies for years, but as a magister, I must be very selective and discreet. I don't want to end up dead like Magister Kettles. He wasn't the only magister of Sanguinati History to mysteriously die after they learned too much."

"What do you suggest we do?" asked Valor.

"The vespercestors are having a meeting in half an hour. I, uh, must figure a way to hear what they'll discuss. I have a feeling something's about to trigger a ripple within the vespercestory." He put his cloak back on and prepared to exit the building.

"Let's stop by Candlewicke and get the talismans so we can sneak inside the meeting without them seeing us," suggested Valor.

"You read my mind," said Crypting with a thin-lipped smile. "You Sorcerers were always good with mental magic."

Valor and Magister Crypting left through a back door of the building on Charnel Alley. They dashed toward Candlewicke Mansion, where Valor removed one of the talismans that Stabbah had hidden under the loose floorboard in the butler's pantry.

"You go first," said Valor handing the talisman to Magister Crypting.

"Oh my, I've never done this before. I've always wanted to be invisible but not for anything naughty, of course," said Crypting, taking the talisman with thin, shaky hands. "Now, what command should I say for this to make me, uh, invisible?"

"Um, Magister Crypting, it already worked. I can't see you, well, except for your clothes," said Valor, as the talisman appeared to float from Crypting's invisible hands into his. "Make me invisible too!"

Valor almost dropped the talisman when his body vanished. He could feel his hands, though he somehow imagined he would not be able to feel his body at all.

"Oh dear, dear, dear. Now, why should I have expected it to make our clothing invisible?" asked Crypting.

Valor stripped off his clothes and boots and said, "Okay, your turn."

Crypting's cloak folded in midair and floated to a chair, followed by his boots, socks, shirt, and pants until just his underclothes covered his invisible body.

Valor laughed. "The only way it's going to work is if you get naked."

Magister Crypting wedged his underclothes deep inside his cloak, which he then folded ten times. "Now, now this is strictly for security reasons," he said. "Nothing—nothing more."

Even though Valor was invisible, he was sure his face had to be red. He covered himself with his hands as best he could. "I hope the spell doesn't wear off until I tell it to," he said, "or I'm going to have to move back to Diabolishire."

"We had, uh, better hurry to the meeting then," said Crypting. "Follow me."

Halfway down Spookum Alley, Valor said, "Wait; I can't see you." He bumped into Magister Crypting by accident.

"Oh dear, dear, dear. This could get very messy. Here, hold my hand," said Crypting.

Valor reached everywhere for the magister's hand, then froze in horror when someone whistled. Valor looked over his shoulder and breathed with relief: It was only an apprentice whistling for a carriage to stop.

"That's not my hand," squeaked Crypting.

"Aw!" groaned Valor.

"See the piece of chewing gum stuck on the bench arm there?" asked Crypting. "My hand is resting there."

"Okay, I think I found it," said Valor.

He couldn't believe it. There he was standing butt naked in the heart of Mystic City, holding hands with a naked older man. He swallowed the lump in his throat, wishing to goodness that the invisibility spell would last a long time. While Snuffinumbra marched through the halls of Mystic Steeples, humming a death anthem in honor of O Enchantedness, Valor hurried behind Magister Crypting into the Vespercestors' Vestibule, as the private meeting with Mahrata had begun. He and the magister stood between the warped mirrors and Mesmertector used to protect the head vespercestor from any harmful spells. Valor danced just to make sure he couldn't see his reflection in the glass. Six of the guardians secured the doors while the lesser vespercestors began consulting with Mahrata LaRock. Chief Counselor to the Covens Drucilla Drayn Hollapolk unveiled a crystaleer and projected its captured scene against the wall: the image of the Sorcerers rising out of the river.

"I'm afraid we have a big problem, O Captivatingness. These Sorcerers have invaded our city. Many of them are insisting they are apprentices at Mystic Steeples and members of Mystic Ministry," said Drucilla.

"More and more of our people are becoming convinced that these invaders are their dead family members," added Ortho Bisland.

"They are our ancestors. Hmmm, nevertheless, that secret stays within this room. Now hand me that crystaleer, haaa, any new moon now, Drucilla," sighed Mahrata.

Her fingers clawed at the crystaleer while her face broke out in purple splotches. Drucilla nodded her head, and her Familiar, a pheasant, bounced its feathers over the brim of her pointed hat where it rested, pecking seeds out of a sunflower, also adorning her hat. She handed the crystaleer to Mahrata.

"You may erase the capture, O Captivatingness. But others recorded the event on their crystaleers. The evidence has spread out of Severance to Toadvine Citadel. And, as we all know, the ministry at Toadvine has condemned Mystic Steeples because you—"

Mahrata snatched the crystaleer, interrupting Drucilla. "Hmmm, tell me something my tarot cards haven't. The, haaa, bad blood between Toadvine and Mystic Steeples is unfortunate."

Mahrata leaned back in her regal chair at the head of the table while several dwarves holding purple rags stood on each other's shoulders so they could wipe her sweaty forehead through her dragon headpiece.

Mumbazandie held up a copy of *The Daily Hazy Herald* for all to see. "Now, O Captivatingness," she said, "it looks like the bad blood's getting worse. Front-page headlines say: 'The LaRocks

Violate Regulations Yet Again In Unparalleled Effort To Build Their Empire.' It goes on to say, 'Toadvine Citadel will no longer allow the LaRocks further involvement in their policies or any further seats in the Hoopenfangia Sanguinati Convergences. And as some are calling an act of reprisal, Optimus Pearl has pardoned Braynard Mamahchi and appointed him as commander-in-chief of the Toadvine army.'"

"Hmmm, were you aware of this, Summoner Mamahchi?" asked Mahrata.

"I was not, O Captivatingness," he answered.

"Your own brother?" continued Mahrata, tightening her lips. "Somebody, haaa, must have notified you."

Mamahchi took the newspaper from Mumbazandie and glanced over it. "O Captivatingness," he said, clearing his throat, "Braynard and I've . . . never been close. Still, I do not believe he killed your father. The evidence now, as it was then, points to the workings of Noctivatians . . . perhaps even Sorcerers."

"And you, haaa, you have no ill feelings that O Enchantedness and I removed your brother from power?" Mahrata asked Summoner Mamahchi with one eyebrow steeply raised.

"None," replied Mamahchi without flinching. "I do not consider Braynard as my brother. I doubt he'll lead Toadvine's army . . . in any effective manner."

"We need to strengthen Mystic Military, O Captivatingness," said Scribe Fengurstaph, easing a copy of the *Magic Ledger* on the table. "Two of those who transvected out of the river are Ancients."

"Who?" asked Mahrata.

"Ancient High Priestess Siouxanna Demollien and Ancient High Priest Festavier Falmoth."

Mahrata scowled. "Haaa, I suppose it's too late to remove their statues in Usabelli's Square and portraits in the Passage of Prestige. Too many of my people have already identified them."

"Wearing his crown and medallion, Festavier was," said Scribe Fengurstaph. "Why they resurrected and were free-floating, that's what good folks demand to know. Public records recorded they drowned in the Severance." Fengurstaph leaned over the table. His waist-length white beard jingled from the little bells and charms woven throughout it. "And forthrightly, O Captivatingness," he cleared his throat. "I would like to know, too—since they seem to be Sorcerers and all."

Mahrata grabbed Scribe Fengurstaph's beard and jerked his head against the table. His long pointed cap fell in Tilta Crumpecker's lap. Crumpecker remained in the chair, wearing a coronet of burning candles on her head for the secret meeting.

"Hmmm, you'll know what we've already told you, which is sufficient. Haaa, can you think of anything better than keeping faith in my leadership, Fengurstaph?" asked Mahrata. She stood up like a soiled dove and perched hard against the edge of the table with her hands. "Haaa, Lesser Vespercestors, it is imperative that the Sanguinati love me. They worshiped Urbanne. Hmmm, you all would have put a stop to this for him. But you—you've upset me greatly with this news."

As if she had run out of words, Mahrata looked away and moistened her lips with downcast eyes that seemed more wrinkled now. Then she placed her hand over her chest and slunk back in her throne chair.

"My heart, haaa," she panted. "I need somebody loyal still to, hmmm, take me to Gitchi Patootie's Bewitching Beauties."

Scribe Fengurstaph and Ortho Bisland shot Mahrata a stunned look.

"If it's your heart, O Captivatingness, you should see the witchdoctor," said Yma Le Breton.

"Hmmm, of course; I meant the witchdoctor," said Mahrata. "You all have just upset me so. I might need to find replacements."

Valor kept his hands close by his sides, trying not to touch Thiery Crypting, but had no doubt the magister was chuckling as well.

"She did mean Gitchi Patootie's," whispered Valor. "There's a Spherical Portal of Reformation in the spa and in the sanatorium. But I don't know what the portals are for."

"Neither do I, Valor," whispered Crypting, brushing against his shoulder. "Mahrata probably has a bit acid reflux. It seems the river people have put a few doubts in her promising reign. Don't count on a major uprising yet. Her, uh, little act of royal heartburn just may garner her sympathy from the lesser vespercestors, but I, uh, have a feeling it'll be tough to silence the masses."

While Mahrata's dwarves escorted her to the witchdoctor, Summoner Mamahchi approached the table and propped his elbow on his magic staff. "O Captivatingness will need an energy infusion," he said. "If our people start believing these resurrected shadesters are our former leaders . . . trouble is coming."

"Toss that crap in a cauldron and boil the blasphemy out of it!" shouted Crumpecker. "They may be Sorcerers, but they can't have been leaders of our people!" Her head swung around, and candle wax dripped down her forehead.

"Continue this . . . grand illusion . . . forever?" asked Mamahchi. His head bobbed, trying to focus through the gathered folds of his eyelids. He placed two fingers across his chin and frowned at the room of vespercestors. "Time to be honest . . . even if it causes a revolt."

"Are you suggesting, Summoner Mamahchi, that the former leaders of the Sanguinati were indeed shadow tossers?" asked Scribe Fengurstaph. The wrinkles deepened around his dilated pupils.

High Priest Manoj loosened the ruffled collar around his throat and gazed at the candlelight on the ceiling. "Like butterflies, which alight for a moment," he said dreamily, "we must look for the flower with the most nectar and not linger in a field of parched daisies. Keep flying, little butterflies, until O Captivatingness spreads her petals again, and the nectar of her essence overflows our thirsty meadows."

Though Manoj seemed enraptured as he spoke, he began each sentence by tapping the edge of his *Controssua* on the table, as if the pages were coming loose from its leather binding.

"Lo, she has placed the plow in my hand, and *I* will prepare that field, cultivate its soil with the manure of the beasts that threaten to devour the cocoons of tomorrow's butterflies."

Summoner Mamahchi glared across the room, gripping the corners of the table like the gargoyles that perch on the roof and pinnacles of Mystic Steeples. "Uugggh, you might be the high priest, Manoj, but you can't foresee the . . . dark forces . . . at work here. The Ancients are calling us to battle. Ignore it . . . if you wish, but I won't be responsible for what might happen to you—to our country."

"Now, Mamahchi, as chief counselor to the covens, I do worry about what's happening to the apprentices—their fears, their unrest, the deterioration of their allegiance. But we must let O Captivatingness make these decisions," said Drucilla Hollapolk.

"Of course, because she's . . . your . . . grandmother," Mamahchi said to Drucilla, while Teddyus Manoj eased to his feet and lifted his magic staff. The feather on his buckled hat fluttered.

"For to risk a war," said Manoj, "is like a herdsman of goring rahfaluses who gathers his beasts behind a fence of bamboo on a mountain cliff. And when the troubled winds blow, and the sun sends forth solar flares, the hollow stems of bamboo crack so that—"

"Oh, go chew your bamboo on a mountain cliff, Manoj," groaned Mumbazandie, who had been sitting between Yma Le Breton and Ortho Bisland. She bolted up with her back to Manoj. "It seems we are divided."

"Divided?" asked Ortho Bisland with nervous amusement, stacking tarot cards into a complex structure on the table. "I'm just as confused as Scribe Fengurstaph. I don't know the reason for all this hot stone tossing." He studied their reaction through the windows and steeples of his grand building of cards. "But I sense it. Some of you are nervous, and the rest, overeager."

Valor could relate to Ortho Bisland and Scribe Fengurstaph, for he, too, had friends who often withheld things from him.

Crumpecker tapped her ring on the edge of the table four times, summoning ghosts to restrain everyone in their chairs.

"Now listen here, you numbskulls," gargled Crumpecker as the flames on her coronet shot up. "Stop all this gargoyle goop saying we're divided. O Captivatingness is in control, and if any of you stop paying your devotions, I'll make sure you spend the rest of your days in Grossatete Maximum Security, knitting stocking caps with nothing but broom straws!"

After the ghosts released the lesser vespercestors, Teddyus Manoj took a reflective breath and eased his cape back over his shoulder. "Vespercestors," he said, "somebody in this vestibule is a snake coiled among cactuses. And the cactuses grow, and their thorns pierce, knowing not that their fatal prick was fangs." He stroked the Vortex of Revealing mounted on the end of his magic staff and gazed into it. "That fatal prick is among us, for the Ancients have given me a vision of you."

Valor swallowed hard and bumped into the Mesmertector, knocking it two inches. Crumpecker bolted up from her chair and crept toward the Mesmertector, inches away from him and Magister Crypting. She poked her wand around the top and sides of the glass case, discharging threads of lightning. The brass witches' brooms turned like compass needles on top of the columns surrounding the magical contraption. Valor rubbed his eye where Crumpecker's wand had poked him.

"Mamahchi, I think the 'snake' is lurking over here," said Crumpecker, sniffing the air. "Lurking, lurking, lurking." She pulled a cloth pouch out of her charm bag and held it in front of her. "Whatever slime-footed little pestilence is hiding in this room; you won't get past me. Now, come here and get your reward!"

Valor began to will Crumpecker to take the reward herself, but Magister Crypting pulled him away from the Mesmertector and the high priestess.

"Well, tangy toad warts! We're shy, I see. I s'pose I'll have to hand you your reward in person," said Crumpecker. She reached into the sack labeled "Dotty Deke's Ident-a-Dust" and flung glittering powder onto the backsides of Valor and Magister Crypting. Most of the dust hit the warped mirrors, and some of it made Crypting's backside and Valor's shoulder blades visible. They scrambled out of the Vespercestors' Vestibule, past a crowd of tourists, and to the Front Atrium, where they hid between the lit arms of the enormous chandelier, which dangled just inches over the parquet floor. The earthly bodies of the Bound Order of the Zodiac Hexagram seemed to stare down at them with insight, while Magister Crypting brushed the revealing powder off Valor's shoulder blades.

"You have some Ident-a-Dust on your—well, you'll have to wipe it off yourself, sir," said Valor. Magister Crypting patted off the powder until a sparkling cloud of it formed over the chandelier. They froze there, the celestial candles burning close to their bare skin when Guardian Czerena Slain stopped Preston Fox while he passed through the hall with his hair combed high on top of his head like a blue-black flame.

"There you are, Dirge Diviner! So sorry about your wife. Here's the scroll recovered from the Necromanceropolis," said Czerena, slapping the scroll into Preston's hand. "This is what O Captivatingness wants—*you* to rearrange it—make it into a sappy song—a tune that'll have everybody ready to sacrifice their firstborn child to Mystic Military—know what I'm saying?" She snickered out of the corner of her mouth.

Preston clutched her arm. "Hmmm, something dribble-ish, something quiverish?" he asked.

Czerena nodded and said, "This has to be ready by the next Convocation and announced as a long-lost song. Use some of the particulars from the scroll and tell them Ancient Darbledevin wrote it just before a free-floater or warlock turned him into a toad while the poor man was fighting to protect our heritage."

"Oh, I see, something historical-ish as well. Hmmm, 'Darbledevin,' you say. What's the spelling?" asked Preston.

"That's up to you. Just make sure everybody cries," said Czerena, pushing back the hood of her dark-brown cloak.

"I'll conjure up something signature Preston Foxish, after much chanting and meditative reflection, of course. The orchestra and drummers will play the tune at heartbeat rhythm, as usual, to sedate their brainwaves. And with the resonant dolerite columns, Vespercestor Bisland added to Mystic Chantry, the rhythms will induce hypnosis better than all the megalithic ritual monuments of old."

"Yeah, it's even hard for me to resist sometimes," snorted Czerena.

CHAPTER EIGHTEEN

"Don't you love seeing all the glassy eyes during Convocation?"

"That's our secret, of course. We know what Mahrata's looking for," said Preston, watching over his shoulders while apprentices passed by them. "She doesn't need to be bogged down with any more silly doubts and questions."

"This is true," agreed Czerena with a wink. "We have to increase the confidence of the covens. Guardian Gereon—bless 'im—felt moved to bury a sculpted marble toad in the swamp to give it an antique look. He'll retrieve the statue and present Ancient Darbledevin on a pedestal right after you announce the song."

"It's as I suspected, Valor," whispered Magister Crypting while they returned to Candlewicke Mansion. "They have been counterfeiting much of their history."

"Who opened the door?" asked Salazants, looking around the front hall with wide eyes. "Who's there?"

"It's me—oh, and Magister Crypting," Valor said, as they changed back into their clothes.

"I hear your voice, but a ghost is putting on clothes just like yours, Master McRaven," said Salazants.

Valor ignored Salazants and ran to get the talisman. Once he made himself visible again, he brought it into the front hall and said, "Magister Crypting, here's the talisman. Unless you want to remain invisible?"

"Indeed no, it's far too drafty in this state," replied Crypting, startling Salazants once more, before saying the magic command, "O talisman of the Electricus Hexigus, render me visible once more." Happy to be his old self again, Crypting handed the talisman back to Valor, and they took comfort in the wizards' parlor with refreshments Manning had brought them.

"What do you think will happen now? I mean, obviously, the vespercestors are at odds with each other," said Valor. He held his head low, searching for answers, his mouth ajar from the shock of it all. "I'm worried about the river people and my friends. You don't think they'll try to drown them again, do you?"

"I don't know what'll happen." sighed Crypting. "But I'm certain they can't ignore the, uh, sudden influx of Sorcerers and new information."

Like centaur hooves over the cobblestone alleys, the swinging of the grandfather clock's pendulum tapped steadily, grating on Valor's nerves, so he willed the clock to stop.

"Do you remember my saying?" asked Crypting, starring at the clock while taking a sip of warm tonic.

"I know," said Valor. "'Never mess with the hands of time, unless you've got a minute to unwind.'"

"Ah, perceptive, my boy," said Crypting. "And it is no understatement. I fear we have limited time to unwind. You see, with each passing minute, the river people are telling their stories, trying to convince this city who they are—the real history. And it is going to be, uh, nearly impossible unless we make a paramount effort to help them. I've decided to attend the meeting tonight. Won't Cryptic Chambers be stunned to see me?"

"I should say!" Valor stood up with a surge of excitement. "That will shut their unruly mouths forever. Why, it's simply divine."

"What *are* you going on about, dear boy?" asked Crypting.

"Twila and Marston Diamone—they claimed they found clues in all the newspapers that Sorcerers murdered you and Ernest Diggs. They recently claimed I killed you."

"Me?" asked Crypting. He raised his bushy eyebrows over his spectacles. "Ernest Diggs?" The ends of his upturned mustache seemed to droop. "You? Sorcerers?" He loosened his knotted neckband in puzzled thought.

"They'll be shocked to see you," said Valor, as they made their plans for his reveal. "Won't you stay here at Candlewicke? We have plenty of room."

"Oh, I couldn't intrude," said Crypting, easing his empty cup on the table. He seemed disoriented behind his eyeglasses. "But I believe I should rest here before the meeting tonight. Who knows what might happen?"

"Salazants will show you to a room," said Valor, walking with him to the grand hall. "We have ghosts, so you might hear noises."

Hours later, Salazants parked the carriage in front of Cryptic Castle and held the door for Magister Crypting and Doomsy, while Aaron, Egg, and Valor got out of the coach on the opposite side, by the alley. Valor handed a box of magical goods that Stabbah had created and was selling at Thunder Plant, to Egg.

"When I give you the signal, start passing these out to all the Crypts."

Egg peered inside the box with a giggle, and they all marched straight into the auditorium where the Crypts had already gathered, listening to the conjoined triplets, Donny-Dale-Dharma, scoffing behind the podium while holding a goblet.

"Crypts, Cataragis Dather here claims to be a founding member of our coven," sneered Donny Thelastone.

"He just popped out of the Severance River like a hurinatse and made this outrageous claim," said Dharma Thelastone, trying to keep hold of the Elixir of Cryptic Brotherhood.

"Absurd," chuckled Dale Thelastone with a snide expression. The Crypts laughed at Cataragis, but he stood tall on the stage with his dark hair combed back in a ponytail, which appeared stark against his pale but youthful skin.

"'Tis true," insisted Cataragis. "For I was initiated by Sesepha himself, the one you all call an Ancient for whatever reason. Behold my coven pendant, forged before my eyes on this very altar with a globulnugee from each Crypt." Cataragis raised his pendant for Donny-Dale-Dharma to see.

"I think you mean 'forgery'—the work of a metallurgist," laughed Donny.

"Or common witchcraft, no doubt," said Dale.

"You fool. You'd have to be hundreds of years old to have known Ancient Sesepha," Dharma said to Cataragis.

"You are all so quick to doubt. But you are, uh, responding as you've been trained, I'm afraid," said Magister Crypting, walking onto the stage, followed by Valor and his friends.

Everyone in the auditorium gasped, "Magister Crypting!"

"Are you going to claim he is a forgery, too?" asked Valor.

Doomsy maintained a cautioning glare at Donny-Dale-Dharma, and they backed away from the podium. The Crypts huddled together as if witnessing an apparition.

"As, uh, many of you've heard, a dragon did abduct me, and it was most certainly not, as some would have you believe, the work of Sorcerers," said Crypting. "Truth is, uh, O Enchantedness and some of his henchmen held me captive in hopes of accessing the Cruxvein Abyss. The LaRocks are dangerous rulers. You all have been, uh, lied to by vespercestors and magisters alike."

"Watch what you're sayin', old man. Some of us are related to the LaRocks," Burdock Crowley shouted across the auditorium, over noisy exchanges. "How have we been lied to?"

"I, uh, I have proof," stammered Magister Crypting. "I discovered some scrolls in the, uh, Chamber of Oracles and decoded much of the language, written in the, uh, tongue of Sorcerers, mind you. The author of those scrolls documented that Urbanne and Mahrata LaRock, and several others had, uh, cast some spell, removing our magic powers so they could control us."

"Did the dragon drop you on your head, Crypting?" asked Dale Thelastone.

"Perhaps he has post-traumatic stress disorder," suggested Dharma.

"Or dementia," added Donny, interlocking arms with Dale and Dharma, bracing themselves as they bent over with laughter.

"This is rubbish. How are we doing magic then, with rubber bands and hidden wires?" asked Marston Diamone. "*Quattrobie Vacubie*," he chanted, firing his wand at Magister Crypting, and four ghosts sped around the magister, forming a breeze around him, disheveling his hair and clothing. How could Valor make his coven mates see the ghosts?

"S-stop it, young man. I am s-still a magister and former, uh, president of Cryptic Chambers, and I deserve respect," said Crypting, gripping the podium to keep the wind from blowing him across the stage.

Doomsy pointed both of her hands at Marston, who was still

summoning the ghosts around Magister Crypting with his wand. Her eyes squinted under her veiled hat. She mumbled something in a tone of determined anger, levitating Marston above the occupied chairs in the auditorium.

"Hey! Put me down," growled Marston, kicking his legs in the air.

"Huh? Marston's free-floating. He's in wickedness," said Delicia Jones, gazing up at Marston, her eyes full of fascination.

Doomsy crooked her fingers, guiding her spell to seize Marston's wand hand, redirecting the aim of his wand away from Magister Crypting and at his own butt.

"No. Oh, please, no!" cried Marston.

"Doomsy Gloomsy, you're not supposed to use magic on a fellow apprentice," Twila Diamone yelled over the Crypts' laughter. Twila gazed up at her brother, dangling above their head. Marston's cheeks flushed in his struggle to divert the wand away from his bottom.

"Tell that to your brother. He has no problem attacking others," said Doomsy, tapping her finger in the air until Marston's wand inched closer to him.

"As a magister, I demand you stop this," said Magister Crypting, gripping the podium while his feet shot out from under him.

"Stop what? Yo' saids we ain't haves no magic powers?" cackled Lolita LeCreme. Bouncing on her toes, she locked her eyes on Marston, who dangled over her head. Twila fired her wand at Doomsy, knocking her across the stage with such force she became as limp as a poppet doll.

"My butt! Is my butt okay?" asked Marston after falling on Lolita.

Doomsy lay unconscious on the floor, her tiny limbs twisted, broken from the crash against the wall.

"Oh, dear! Doomsy, can you hear me?" panted Valor before chanting, "*Custos Abolla*," putting a barrier of protection around them.

She lifted her eyebrows first. Then Doomsy's eyelids quivered open. "Straighten my legs," she whimpered.

Valor positioned her twisted legs where they should go, and Doomsy screamed in anguish.

"Twila b-broke your legs. We n-need to get you to Magister Kraneswaddle," said Egg Goodridge, reaching his hands out to help her.

"No, we can't leave," groaned Doomsy. "Magister Crypting needs our help. Tell them about the ghosts—how the ghosts respond to their chants."

Valor breathed into his fist. "You're right," he said. "We need to support Magister Crypting while we have the chance."

"Go ahead. I shall keep her safe," said Aaron.

Valor marched up to the podium beside Magister Crypting and said, "Crypts, it's bad enough that you disrespect your coven presidents, but how dare you mistreat Magister Crypting!" Valor paused and bent over to check on Doomsy.

"Why should we listen to you, McRaven?" asked Marston. "We all know the sparkle in your eyes is just the reflection of the moon—it's the mark of the Grim Warlock!"

Twila moved to the front row of the auditorium and caressed open her *Controssua*. "Now I don't mean to sound uncompassionate," she said, "but I'm sure Doomsy will be her ugly old self soon. The *Controssua* states in Alegeme-60 that unless a Sorcerer is dismembered or burned with flames, they can regenerate. It's the test for a real shadow tosser, or did you prefer we not know, McRaven?"

"May, I, uh, say something?" asked Magister Crypting.

Doomsy floated up from the stage and landed on her feet. Gasps echoed across the auditorium while the Crypts on the front rows scurried toward the back.

"Yes, I'm a Sorcerer, and so were your stupid ancestors," growled Doomsy.

"How else do you think your descendants like Cataragis Dather here survived being shackled under the river?" Valor asked the Crypts. "They're trying to tell you the truth. After your ancestors lost immortality and real magic, the LaRocks found a way to work your spells by controlling ghosts instead. Mystic Ministry erased this history."

"I knew I saw spirits moving around Magister Crypting," said

Delicia Jones, sitting on a bench by herself. "They was goin' like this." She waved her hand around the top of her head, making a whistling noise with her mouth. Magister Crypting seemed stunned at this information about the ghosts.

"Monkey pawed imps control your magic," Marston said to Valor. "Besides, we're not allowed to communicate with any spirits except for the Ancients."

"Ah," said Aaron. His regal shirtsleeve fluttered in the air as he gestured with his hand, "and do you know why the vespercestors forbid it, or no?" He moved to the edge of the stage to speak with Marston. "Because they are frightened you will communicate with the other spirits and discover the truth about this deception, your bogus pocus."

"Preposterous," said Donny.

"Absurd," added Dale.

"Lies," concluded Dharma, pointing her finger at Aaron in sequence with her conjoined siblings.

Valor stepped in front of the podium and spoke more forcefully: "Mystic Ministry has rewritten history by causing some sort of Great Deception. Somehow, they control the spirits of the Ancients with death masks. And they plan on doing the same with each of you after you die. Many of the monuments of the Ancients around here aren't that old. They're only made to look ancient."

"Are you saying they're fake?" asked young apprentice Seth Tuberstooge.

"Some of them, yes, perhaps," replied Valor. "And another thing: Mystic Ministry instructs the Dirge Diviner to play the music at heartbeat rhythm to brainwash us—make us more suggestible. You heard O Enchantedness confess that you were all once immortal Sorcerers before he killed Master Mesthu. Well, those ancestors have now returned from the Drowning Verdicts. Mahrata LaRock is worried about losing her rule over us, so she's going to try to erase all of this new information."

"What proof do you have?" asked Jama Slain, the cheercaster engaged to Enzo LaRock.

Valor paused and prepared to reveal the evidence he had anticipated while they were actually listening to him.

"During the next Convocation, they're going to present another false Ancient named 'Darbledevin' to portray the Sanguinati as a victim of Sorcerers," said Valor. "The music will be at heartbeat rhythm, and they're going to try to make you cry. In the meantime, Guardian Gereon is going to retrieve a sculpture of 'Darbledevin'—a toad he buried in the swamp to make it look antique. They're going to present the toad on a pedestal before the song. But you mustn't listen! It may be the only way you'll remember what I'm telling you."

Valor motioned for Egg to start distributing the magical goods from the box.

"That's why I'm giving out free Hypno-Filters, fabrication-filtering earplugs, compliments of Thunder Plant magic shop." For demonstration, Valor removed two spiraling, horn-shaped plugs from his pocket and stuffed them in his ears for a second. "If you don't want to use the filters, then I beg you to work some type of spell on your ears during Convocation."

"If there's any brainwashing going on, you filthy Sorcerers are behind it," said Marston, stomping on his Hypno-Filter. "Don't fall for it, Crypts; Valor and his friends are possessed—they're evil!"

"May I say something?" Magister Crypting asked again, but the Crypts' debate muffled his thin voice.

Vadableatus stood up and said, "Our presidents are just trying to poison us with their lies!" He swished his wand around. "Do you know what the Ancients say we should do with shadow tossers like you all? Go ahead, guess what they would have us do." He nodded with exasperation.

"I wouldn't know. I haven't visited with the Ancients as of late," said Aaron.

"I'd rather resort to using enchanted weapons than be a shadow tosser," hissed Marston. He lifted his wand from his pocket and chanted the Flame of Glory spell, which spiraled up his wand and shot down like lightning bolts at Aaron.

With his monoculous aimed at Marston, Valor chanted

"*Remordeo*," before the stunned onlookers, sending Marston's lightning spell back at him until he fled the auditorium with Twila and a few friends. Valor looked across the stage; Aaron had vanished. Only a sprawling scorch mark remained where he had been standing. The remaining Crypts scattered, knocking over their ritual objects on the brass tables near the exit door.

"Are you okay, Doomsy?" Valor asked, dropping to his knees and inspecting Doomsy for any permanent damage.

"I'm still sore—sore that I didn't hex those idiots," hissed Doomsy, before Aaron came out from behind the platform with Magister Crypting.

"Things cannot be the same after this," said Valor, with the worst chill bumps he ever had. "We need to prepare."

"Prepare for what?" asked Aaron, bent over and catching his breath.

"The worst," said Valor, slipping his hand on Doomsy's back, while his fangs buried into his tongue.

CHAPTER NINETEEN

THE THIRTEENTH HOUR BEGINS

TENSION filled the air as Cryptic Chambers gathered in their section of Mystic Chantry for the weekly Convocation. The Crypts had expressions of disbelief when Doomsy took her seat without casts on her legs, for they had healed fast. Valor's great-grandmother Lockie LaRock hurried past them, wearing a Graven Dust robe.

"Once again, so close to us but still so far. I don't know why Lockie has always been so indifferent toward us?" said Valor.

Doomsy flicked one hand dismissively. "First Lockie, then Genola, then Lithium—all weirder than thirsty flies in a rum cake. Get down on your knees, my pet, and thank your lucky stars that your mother didn't have those baby girls she wanted."

Aaron waved at Marston, who sat on the back bench with a few of his remaining but loyal friends. The Crypts glanced at Marston to see his reaction after he had tried to murder Aaron the previous night, but Marston locked his icy eyes straight ahead, avoiding everyone's gaze.

"I don't th-think he or Twila will dare tell on us s-since they attacked Doomsy and tried to kill you," said Egg, but Aaron didn't seem comforted.

"I imagine they told Mystic Ministry everything we said, so they're going to change their brainwashing plans to make us look like liars," said Valor.

"You mean they're going to abandon the heartbeat rhythm music and the fake toad idea?" asked Doomsy.

"Yes," replied Valor.

"I still think we should work a spell on the music, to keep everyone from being conditioned to their lies," whispered Aaron.

"Believe me I want to. But if we do that, the Crypts will think I made it all up," said Valor.

"Yeah, but if this stupid ceremony brainwashes them, they probably won't remember what you said either," added Doomsy.

"That's true, too," agreed Valor. "But just in case, we had better insert our Hypno-Filters."

He shoved a filter in each ear and looked around. Many eyes were cutting over at him, including the river people scattered throughout the Chantry. Preston Fox, the Dirge Diviner, sprung from his chair on the far end of the platform and approached the podium to speak. All across the Chantry, members of Candlewicke Coven inserted their Hypno-Filters, as well as Esoterica and a few members of Cryptic Chambers. Several apprentices from other covens placed their wands to their ears as unnoticeably as they could.

"As you know, Sanguinati, we all have received a terrible shock with the recent tragic events. But tonight, it brings me much honor to humble myself by presenting to you this ancient oracle, which no hands are worthy to touch," said Preston Fox. "I would like to commend High Priestess Tilta Crumpecker for recovering the oracle from the Chamber of Oracles."

"He's lying. That oracle came from the Necromanceropolis, and they've changed it," Valor said to Doomsy, Egg, and Aaron.

"This is a patriotic story of sorts, which should make you *all* appreciate the price our ancestors paid to keep the Sanguinati from falling into the hands of the Sorcerers—very clammy-ish hands I've been told." The apprentices laughed as Preston continued: "At first I determined I would play the ancient hymn on the organ, but this old windpipe organ isn't worthy of such a song unless somebody can do an organ transplant real quickish."

"He's trying to get everyone to relax. It's part of the brainwashing," said Valor, while the apprentices laughed again and gave Preston their full attention.

"The hymn is by Ancient . . . *Darbledevin*," said Preston. Again, he glanced down to read the name on the palm of his hand. "Just before the ruthless Sorcerers turned him into a toad for fighting to protect us. I dedicate this in memory of Darbledevin and O Enchantedness, who, if he were here, he would say, 'We must fight for our Destiny, Heredity, Ministry.' Can I hear everybody in Convocation repeat our motto with me?"

"Destiny, Heredity, Ministry," the covens chanted dutifully.

"Blessed be," Preston Fox whispered into the levitating magihorn, positioning his best soloist up front. With their wands lifted toward the uppermost balconies, the choir eased into a soulful song.

"They look a bunch of fork-tail puffers choking on air," said Doomsy, puffing her cheeks out like a fish.

The witches lowered their heads, so Valor elbowed Doomsy to quieten her. Guardian Gereon McMahon carried a stone toad atop a portable pedestal. He eased across the base of the platform and paused at the altar. With their heads low and faces somber, Mystic Ministry gathered around the pedestal to toss wreaths of flowers onto the toad. Before the song had concluded, the pantomagi mimed the heart-wrenching story of Darbledevin, while the guardians began passing around a purple handkerchief to collect everyone's tears.

"There is power in that tear-soaked handkerchief," said Tilta Crumpecker. "We will place it inside Darbledevin's grave monument as a pledge of our loyalty to show him that we care about this Sanguinati institution."

"This is ridiculous," said Egg, thumbing through his *Controssua*. "I've never even heard of D-Darbledevin before tonight." He passed the handkerchief to Doomsy, who blew her nose into it, attracting more head turns and frowns before she gave the cloth to Esoterica.

It took half an hour for O Captivatingness to descend the steps from the highest balcony. A globe of the earth levitated inches above her wand. Preston Fox struck a gong when Mahrata stepped behind the podium and nodded at the crowd as if she understood their tears.

"Hmmm, haaa, my people . . . can you feel this? Can you feel the Ancients' tears of sorrow pouring down on this Convocation? We have gone the ways of Falmoth and Banzalta . . . gone the ways of Mesthu. Hmmm, I could name countless others." Mahrata paused and glared with one lifted eyebrow at various members throughout the Chantry.

A dozen or more members in the Convocation screamed and growled, and then their contorting bodies shot up toward the chandeliers. Foggy apparitions poured from their mouths as they swam down through the air. Valor, Aaron, and Doomsy scooted low in the bench, narrowly avoiding a male apprentice who clawed at their heads.

"They're possessed. Bind 'em. Bind 'em!" ordered Tilta Crumpecker, spreading her arms to protect Mahrata, two inches behind her. While the guardians twirled their magic staffs, casting binding spells at the possessed victims, Mahrata swallowed and eased back into her speech.

". . . *Hingu Raysea Entia*," she chanted, making sticky wet noises with her mouth as her eyes rolled back in their sockets. "My people, judgment has come to Mystic Steeples, haaa, because you have tolerated those shadesters that came out of the river, claiming to belong in this city." Mahrata placed an hourglass on the podium, and huffin flies inside the glass began to swarm to the bottom section. "Hmmm. The Grim Warlock has invaded our region. The Twelve-plus Hour has begun!"

A wave of screams and startled movements rippled through the Sanguinati. Using their wands, a line of vespercestors passed the floating earth globe to one another, while the male voices in the choir droned, and the women shook rattlesnake tails.

"Hmmm, in a few minutes, haaa, Mystic Steeples and Mystic City will be in lockdown." Mahrata slammed her fist on the podium, then turned to face the high priest and priestess. "At this time, hmmm, I need Teddyus Manoj and Tilta Crumpecker to proceed to the Front Atrium and prepare to unleash the Bound Order of the Zodiac Hexagram."

Brahm Cadabranathy, the father of murdered Vespercestor Abner, stood up near the middle left section of the Chantry and said, "But, O Captivatingness, I have to meet with a book dealer in Squibthistle tomorrow. How—"

"You violated the new *Questioning Regulation*. You, hmmm, are in no position to ask anything," said Mahrata. She grimaced, flinging out her hand as though Brahm had disturbed her psychic connection to the astral plane. Two guardians on the platform cast a wand spell at Brahm, conjuring thick silver chains from the back of the Chantry. The chains looped around Brahm's head until just his eyes were visible, and a muffled moan was all he could speak.

"You are not our leader, Mahrata," cried Brahm's wife, Gilda, co-owner of the Lunar Nooner Library on Craft Street. She tried to pry the chains off her husband's head but was unsuccessful.

"Silence your tongue, Gilda." Mahrata lifted her magic staff. "Haaa, I assure each person in this room that every beast in Hoopenfangia will bow to me if you, hmmm, if you refuse."

The orchestra began to pound the bass drums in a rhythm of inevitable doom.

"What's h-happening? W-what's the, um, Bound Order of the Zodiac gonna do?" asked Egg, shifting higher on the bench so he could better see.

Valor tensed and dared not answer: Two benches in front of him, a stargazer stopped and leaned his bald head against a silver ear, similar to the Word Catcher that Venerious Falmoth used. Had the man overheard Egg asking a question?

"Yes, I agree, Egg; the bathrooms are too far in the back," Valor faked an answer, trying to confuse the stargazer. "I hope you don't soil your pants."

The stargazer cringed and walked away, much to Valor's relief.

Vespercestor Mumbazandie approached the podium and said, "Covens, open your *Controssuas* to 'Hasty Revelries 98-plus' and join in with the choir as they sing the countdown song, *Broomways to Oblivion*."

Valor opened his *Controssua* as everyone began to sing, counting down from ten at the end of each line:

"Join us, Sanguinati. Unite our noble cause.
The enemy seeks to destroy all our sacred laws.
Elite, rise up, charge your staffs and wands.
The signs are in our divination bowls, even on our palms.
Head Vespercestor, destroy all our enemies.
Make Nizzertits, Nockies, and Sorcerers pay the penalty.
Strengthen Mystic Military, build more shackles and jails.
For the Children of the Ancients, always shall prevail.
Flying broomways to oblivion, who knows what lies in store.
But at least the dark auras shall finally be no more."

The cloud of conjure seeped through the walls, and the whole Chantry grew silent and dim. Even the moonlight, which shone through the stained glass windows, went dark. Witches young and old dropped to the floor and huddled between the benches. Inarticulate chants melted into nervous cries. The air in Valor's lungs evaporated, leaving a frightful knot in his stomach before he regained a facade of composure. Egg tumbled from the bench to a safer spot between Valor and Aaron.

"W-wha's h-happenin'? Wha's happenin'?" Egg sputtered and panted, kicking Valor with his boots and head-butting Aaron in the ribcage as Mystic Chantry began to shake. A man fell out of a small balcony, screaming as he plunged to the floor.

"It's getting really bright outside, like a comet's coming at us," observed Doomsy.

The witches' Familiars began to cry out and throw themselves against the stained-glass windows. A wiggiwami burst into the Chantry, howling as if it had gone mad. The guardians blasted the wiggiwami with their magic staffs.

"Stay down," cautioned Valor. He pulled Doomsy back under the bench, watching the huddling fear from where he knelt.

"We summon thee, Bound Order. The Ancients of Judgments, we implore. Bring the Sanguinati protection and to our enemies what's in store," the stargazers began to chant.

As though the heavens had unveiled, the ceiling glowed darkest blue, constellations appeared and grew brighter, and planets coursed around the chandeliers.

"Whoa," panted Valor, peeking over the bench in front of him as hot sparks singed his face. "That's the unicorn constellation, Monoceros."

They all watched as it galloped right through the highest stained-glass window. Aaron held up his hand after a big glob of purple wax splattered on it.

"The constellations must be melting the candles in the chandeliers," he said.

Burning stardust fell like hot ashes on various witches in the Chantry. They screamed and dove under the benches. Out of the beauty and chaos, five human-like figures appeared, glowing like the stars. And from their hands, five elements manifested: Fire from one, Wind from another and, from the rest, Water, Earth, and Spirit. The Zodiac Being Spirit gently floated through the heated windstorm.

"Behold four-plus of the Six Ancients of Judgment!" said Mahrata. "Hmmm, when the Dark Hour reaches its pinnacle, haaa, Death, the last Being, will await my summoning."

The choir shook their rattlers, and the stargazers lifted their eyes to the ceiling.

"Haaa, they shall ensnare any of you who oppose my sovereignty, hmmm, and whisk you into the air with their celestial ropes and, haaa, deposit you in our new rooftop opening at Grossatete Sanatorium designed by Ortho Bisland." Mahrata motioned for Lesser Vespercestor Bisland to make his announcement.

"Thank you, O Captivatingness," said Ortho, sticking his fingers in his vest pockets in a confident pose. "Witches of the covens, don't let our kind and loving demeanor fool you. We—"

With a wrinkled grin, Summoner Mamahchi scooted to the edge of his throne chair on the platform. "And 'handsome,' Ortho. Don't forget 'handsome,'" laughed Mamahchi. He stretched his leg out on the platform, flaunting his shiny leather boots.

"And 'handsome,'" added Ortho, with a brief strut. "But seriously, as I began designing the new prisoner-deposit roof for the sanatorium, I said to myself, 'If it's the last thing you do, Ortho, don't forget for whom you are designing this criminal chute.'" Ortho gestured grandly at Mahrata LaRock. "And here I am. And I can't tell you how much I enjoyed completing this project."

Several apprentices emerged from under their benches and clapped dully. Mamahchi jumped up and, again, interrupted Ortho to address the Convocation.

"Any found allegiances to the Grim Warlock . . . or illicit free-floaters . . . will result in death and imprisonment . . . never before seen in Hoopenfangian history!" growled Mamahchi. He reached into his coat pocket, removed a bottle of Auravitamax, and placed it on the podium.

Many in the Chantry gasped while Harwin Hollapolk, and Marston and Twila Diamone joined others in applause, raising their wands and staffs. The stars and planets engulfing the ceiling emitted a unique sound, lovelier than any choir could hope to sing, but it was not enough to calm Valor's racing pulse, and he wasn't sure how much more he could take.

Sessions and Hilda Diamone sliced through the congregation, and with heads high, marched up the steps to the platform where they stood on either side of Summoner Mamahchi. Marston and Twila looked on with devious grins as their parents placed a Vortex of Revealing beside the bottle of aura tonic.

"Sanguinati," said Hilda, "as representatives of the Elite Auravitamax Company, you need not fear the coming dark times ahead—as long as you drink our special tonic." Hilda cut her eyes at Sessions, who lifted the bottle of Auravitamax with his knobby fingers. The rainbow-colored bottle quivered in his hands, but he gazed at it as though he had a massive diamond.

"Do you think we should show them what'll happen if they don't purchase Auravitamax, Hildy?" Sessions asked Hilda.

"We care about them, don't we, Sessions? It's the Sanguinati's right to know, is it not?" asked Hilda. She swirled the bottle of Auravitamax in her bejeweled fingers, removed the lid, and inhaled its aroma before taking a tantalizing swig with pursed lips.

"I'm afraid we must," added Summoner Mamahchi between them, before turning toward Mahrata LaRock. "May we show them the revealings . . . of the Ancients, O Captivatingness?"

With her dwarf assistant by her side, Mahrata swallowed and eyed every person in the Chantry with a look of grave disappointment. "Haaa. Just do it already," she replied. "Show my people the things that will *sadly* be."

A teenage apprentice bolted up from the Dragon's Mantle Coven section and ran toward the base of the podium with his arms flailing.

"You monsters! I had a vision. You have Death—a demon—chained up at your disposal," the apprentice said with wild eyes as drool rained from his mouth. "You won't kill it. Oh-no-no! You're feeding it so you can—"

Valor froze in disbelief when Mahrata rested her magic staff on her dwarf's head, angled it at the wild-eyed apprentice, and chanted, "*Diabolus Adnihilo!*"

Shadowy paws, claws, and sharp hooves stretched from the tip of her staff and overwhelmed the apprentice. In an instant, the boy became an unrecognizable tangle of flesh and clothing on the floor.

"Is this what has become of the Ministry?" gasped Esoterica Knowles, the secretary for Cryptic Chambers. Her glasses slid down her nose, and her mouth dropped. "That spell is highly prohibited."

"O Captivatingness," mumbled Summoner Mamahchi in his deep dry voice. "May I remind you . . . not even the head vespercestor is allowed to use . . . unpardonable curses!"

"You tell it, Summoner!" yelled a man from the Balcony of Elders as a few applauded.

"At least somebody has the gall to stand up to this lawlessness," shouted a woman from the Wormwood Philters section, while friends and loved ones of the murdered apprentice gathered tearfully around his remains.

"Summoner, hmmm, see me in my office later," said Mahrata with a raised eyebrow. Easing her head in the slowest turns, she brooded at select people in the Chantry again. "Sanguinati, haaa, that apprentice was clearly possessed by the Grim Warlock. These are dangerous times, and, hmmm, dangerous times call for leaders, such as myself, to use such defenses at our discretion. Summoner, haaa, perhaps now is the best time to show the Sanguinati the warning from the Ancients."

Mamahchi cleared his throat and said, "As you wish, O Captivatingness." He touched his magic wand to the Vortex of Revealing, and as the glass sphere lit up, it projected scenes of devastation in the churning conjure cloud that formed in the center of the Chantry between the chandeliers and the ground-floor benches.

"Witness the Grim Warlock's Dark Hour as it ravages your world. You have invited death and destruction into your lives by tolerating Sorcerers, Noctivatians, and Nizzertits, and all forms of unlawfulness." The vibrating voice in the projected prophecy rang ominously, burrowing into Valor's intestines and eardrums until he wanted to vomit.

Lilith's Lantern and many stores that Valor had often shopped had been closed. Many homes had been boarded up. Valor shuddered. The property owners slumped on their entry steps in tattered clothing—mere shadow figures, now, with grime-covered faces. On occasional moments, during the projected nightmare, the Sanguinati elite and several members of Mystic Ministry roamed through the city in dreamlike bliss, carrying their recent purchases of Auravitamax. Halos of light illuminated their bodies, as they stepped off the sidewalks and into the alleys to avoid the destitute owners.

"Don't go near those vagrants, Constance," said Magister Gorgia Mesmerthang to her sheep Familiar in the vision, while the irritating narration continued its warnings.

"Whyyy?" bellowed Constance, before licking a bit of grime off her dyed-pink wool sculpted to perfection.

"The Auravitamax proved their auras to be dark—all dark and wicked, that's why," replied Mesmerthang, pulling her sheep's leash. "Those vagrants will eat you, my little lambkins. They probably practice Grim magic."

The vision in the cloud changed: Tilta Crumpecker burst forth from the images with the Diamone family, followed by other witches as they led a death parade down Skullhead Street. Trailing behind the Diamones were bound and blindfolded witches, Nizzertits—anyone without a glowing aura. Many elite witches marching with the Diamones carried signs boycotting other businesses. Marston Diamone magicked a banner in the air that read, "Bring more light to Mystic City—Burn Candlewicke Mansion." Twila Diamone conjured another banner that read, "Bright auras erase Grim tomorrows."

Gripping their brooms, the guardians swarmed over the banners, casting spells that lassoed people with dull appearances, plucking them from the city by their arms or ankles. Valor watched in disbelief as the guardians carried people he recognized, up into the air, and dropped them into the rooftop opening of Grossatete Sanatorium.

Something grabbed Valor's ankles and pulled them apart.

"Delicia!" he gasped. "What are you doing under the bench?" He bent over with a start. His breath now surpassed his heart rate.

"Ho-ho-ho. Helping my friend out is what I'm doing," said Delicia. Her hair spread out over the floor so wide it dusted Doomsy's and Aaron's boots. "I overheard Marston saying he made a deal with a vespercestor to have you, Doomsy, Aaron, and Egg arrested before Convocation is over. Come with me; this way, nobody will see you leave." Delicia rolled over and disappeared under the bench while Valor and his friends followed her, crawling between boots in the dark sanctuary toward the Vespercestors' Vestibule, while the prophecy continued to hold the audience in frightened awe.

"Wait," whispered Doomsy. "My dress is caught under someone's boot; I think it's Marston's."

"Don't move," whispered Aaron. His head dropped to the floor as if he were resting his brain to think. With a devious smile, he wiggled his fingers, imitating a crawling spider. His shadow poured loose from his hand, took on the likeness of a tarantula, and crawled up the boy's leg.

"Eeeeeehh, a—a spider!" the boy screamed and kicked, swatting his legs.

"Yeah, t-that's Marston," said Egg.

Doomsy freed her dress, and they all scurried into the vestibule, then into the Atrium, where five of the Six Ancients of Judgment had come to life in their alcoves.

"Um, this way is not such a good idea," said Valor. "The Zodiac Beings are awake."

"We'd better take the exit to Ickylous Street," said Delicia, turning back down a side hall.

It was a surreal autumn night. Constellations now bobbled over the cityscape, stretching across the sky like apparitions holding lit jack-o'-lanterns. As if spying upon everyone, planets seemed very close to the land now; their eerie glow radiated through rows of columns that supported elaborate pavilions. The Sorcerers' Nocturne played in the distance, suffocating a miserable song by a nearby band. On the alleys, guardians were diverting carriages from the two exit roads leaving Mystic City. The carriages turned around, and the centaurs trotted back into the city over lawns and through gardens. A loud cracking sound and flash of white light preceded a yelp. Everyone jumped.

"Someone crashed into that tree," said Doomsy, pointing to the oak overhanging the fenced courtyard near where they were walking. They paused to see if the man had been hurt as he hung from a tree limb by his hands before he floated down to the sidewalk.

"It's me—Cat," said Cataragis Dather, one of the river rescues. He squatted down behind an iron urn with a shrub sculpted into a dragon topiary. "Alas, there's no escaping this city by air or by road. And to think, the joy I felt believing you all had given me a second chance, a new life. Doesn't seem I should ever plan for the future again."

"I don't know what's happening, Cat," said Valor. "If you want to leave, you might be able to escape at the old, abandoned boot factory on Dead Maudie Alley."

"You mean the Kitty's Kabootle is abandoned?" said Cataragis. He released his grip on the urn with a limp defeat. "My! I had been in the river for a long time."

Valor bent over and whispered, "There's a portal there in the broom closet."

"Much obliged, McRaven. I'll warn the others on Charnel Alley so they won't get swatted out of the air by a Zodiac Being," said Cataragis, showing the red lash mark on his forearm where the Being had charred his coat and shirt as well, then he dashed away in a blur.

"I haven't seen that manner of sorcery in a while," said Doomsy. "Cat has Hermes's Knees."

"Whose c-cat has herpes?" asked Egg, carrying a dead crow while he caught up with them.

"Never mind," said Doomsy. Aaron looked at the crow and turned his back to everyone.

"Um, okay," said Egg. "But I f-found him at the door of Mystic Steeples. Isn't this—"

"Yes, it is Switzer," Aaron said in a sad voice. "I saw the white marking on his left eye the minute you arrived. Poor Familiar, he must have tried to warn me when they unleashed the Bound Order of the Zodiac."

"Aw," sighed Valor. "I'm so sorry, Aaron." He placed his hand on Aaron's back to try to comfort him. Doomsy pulled Mr. Grudgings out of her dress pocket, petted his head, and slipped him back inside where he usually stayed.

"Uh, I'll go p-put Switzer in a shoebox so we can b-bury him later," said Egg, leaving for Candlewicke Mansion.

Aaron's smile appeared forced, while ashy embers of stardust trickled down from the sky and over his shoulder.

"Valor, please explain what we are supposed to do now and why you would bloody listen to Delicia," Aaron said bitterly.

"It's my fault," said Doomsy. "I told Cryptic Chambers I'm a Sorcerer. Now they'll hate us."

"Huh?" grunted Delicia with a confused tilt of her head.

"You know how they treated us at Cryptic Castle. You saw what happened tonight," said Valor, unloading on Delicia. He turned away to try to calm his anger, before pausing to admire a painting in an art gallery window.

Delicia shook her head. "I don't believe it's that bad. You gotta push that negativity outta the way."

"You're just like the Sanguinati. You think there's darkness in my life, and you are set on helping Genola rid my friends and me of it," said Valor.

"Not darkness in you," laughed Delicia. She positioned Valor's shoulders closer to his reflection in the gallery window. "You men always think us women are trying to change you. Look with your inner eye at the darkness around you, trying to get you. But it hasn't yet. It's a sign that you're the Knight of Night."

"Whatever you say *now*. But I know what I heard," said Valor. He ignored his reflection and admired the thick brushstrokes and color in the painting, the way the frame reclined on the fancy iron easel in the window.

Delicia pressed her face against the window above his face. "This is a sign," she said.

"What—you see *dark* colors oppressing the painting?" asked Doomsy while Aaron stepped back on the sidewalk. His golden waves began loosening from his ponytail.

"Your grandmother Genola showed me a vision of you, Valor. You had your little paintbrush, and you were going like this." Delicia's hand danced in the air. "And I said, 'That Valor, he's gonna be painting people's portraits.'" Delicia's face became long, and her shoulders drooped. "Genola seemed conflicted. She didn't like you doing that, Valor. No sir! She wanted me to stop you. Then I saw these oppressing auras, essences, or something dark absorb into a picture frame like that carved beauty there in the window." Her head snapped with a goofy smile. "What do you think about that sign?"

Trying to think of a response that wouldn't be too harsh, Valor examined the painting in the frame once again and shrugged his shoulders in silence.

"It's called spirit capture," responded Doomsy. "Stab told me about it. Not many have the gift, but if they destroy the painting of anyone they capture their spirit on, it blocks the person from harming others. The painting has to be visible to many eyes for it to absorb their spirit."

"I don't believe in stopping people from using their gifts now," said Delicia, shaking her head. She took out her magic wand and used it to scratch her back, exposing a few remaining warts on her forearm. "Falmoth told me I hadn't been using my gifts, you know, when he rescued me from the swamps."

"Do pardon my friends for turning you into a toad," said Valor.

Aaron's hair seemed to dishevel by itself as his new wilder Noctivatian appearance, he had tried hard to groom away, overtook his refined nature. "Yes, do pardon me," said Aaron. "I think an imp would've been more suited to your personality."

"Ho-ho-ho," laughed Delicia. "I already chanted those negative imps away. You men are always afraid of my special gifts and bewitching eyes. But you have to say, 'BE GONE FEAR,'" Delicia shouted with a guttural chant, as she leaned over and shook her enormous curly mane of hair. Then she stood back up, letting her hair fall around her thin frame. "I'm in the Hermetic Order of the Mystic Key now. That Falmoth, he's sneaking me out by a portal to Diabolishire. He believes in my special powers. And we're gonna show the Sorcerers at Shadowhaven Heights evidence that the vespercestors plotted Mesthu's death. That's what everybody needs to do is be honest."

"Venerious Falmoth? Talk about dark oppression! Obviously, your tarot cards haven't revealed what type of man with whom you have aligned yourself, woman," yelled Aaron, flinging his arm toward the western wing of Mystic Steeples as if sending a foul smell on its way. "You don't think being a vampire is dark? Or has your academy of metaphysics cured your desire to drink blood?"

Delicia's eyes bulged over the rim of her glasses. "Ho-ho-ho! I *have* been craving blood lately. You mean Venerious turned me into a vampire? I thought it was some of Valor's darkness trying to oppress me too."

"Yes, Delicia dear, you have been royally deceived," said Valor. "Your blood hunger will only get worse. And if you disobey the Hermetic Order, you'll end up dead like Creighton."

Delicia crossed her arms with a frown. "Valor McRaven, I thought you were my friend. You should've told me about those Hypno-Filters before I became a vampire."

"You mean the earplugs worked? You mean they helped you tell that Mystic Ministry was lying tonight?" asked Valor.

"Yeah." Delicia wrinkled her forehead. "Especially about that toad statue. I'll bet everybody who wore those earplugs could see through all of that."

"That's promising. Maybe Cryptic Chambers will start believing us," said Valor, desperate for a crumb of hope.

"I was wearing the earplugs when Marston claimed he made a deal with a vespercestor to have you all arrested. I didn't feel he was telling no story," said Delicia.

"We need more time to convince the Sanguinati. After all that happened tonight, we are obviously in danger," said Valor.

Doomsy stomped her little boot. "I don't know who's being more dishonest these days, Falmoth or Mahrata."

"For what it's worth, I can forgive Falmoth and the Noctivatians easier than Mahrata and the Sanguinati. If either one of them is going to kill us, at least the Noctivatians don't claim to be morally superior for doing so."

Much of the residents of Mystic City remained locked in their homes the next day, peeking out their windows at the invasion of the Zodiac Beings, who conjured down a giant dark bubble over Severance. Valor used this time to practice portrait painting in the drawing-room. He applied each brushstroke more determinedly than ever. Magister Crypting sat on the steps of a small stage, which former residents of Candlewicke Mansion had once used to perform intimate plays for entertainment—if anyone could find fun behind the walls of such a dark, infamous mansion.

"Indeed, Valor, I, uh, don't know how you could bring yourself to take up painting at a, uh, time like this?" said Magister Crypting.

"It's not ordinary painting, Magister Crypting; it's Spirit Capture. I'm using Pox Pigments—Stab brought me some from her magic shop in the Underground." Valor laughed, tapping, with the tip of his brush, the wooden crate where the paint bottles rested in colorful rows. "See, the slogan says, 'When someone is frustrating your imagination, Pox Pigments are not a figment.'" He added the final brushstroke on the painting of O Captivatingness. "It's supposed to be Mahrata LaRock," he said, turning the canvas around to a few of his friends who had gathered in the drawing-room.

Aaron kept his eye on the painting as he gazed at it from different angles. "Verily," he said, "if one moves around the painting, Mah's nastiness seems to emerge. I do believe you've captured her true essence."

"Oh, now I'm sad," said Rose, emerging from behind the stage curtain in a new gown she and Blade had found, along with an assortment of dark but fancy old costumes in the dressing room.

"Indeed, it's simply awful," said Valor. "I'll repaint—"

"No. I'm sad 'cause Aaron called Mahrata 'Mah,' like Creighton always did," sighed Rose before grabbing up Valor's painting. "It makes me miss him. And, no, I think your paintings are about as good as mine. You captured the old crone—I hope. But why didja paint her in shades of red?"

Valor wiped the paint from his brush onto a towel and placed the lid on the jar of Emulation Crimson. "Stab said this color would ensnare Mahrata best, my dear," answered Valor, realizing his fangs were showing when he smiled.

Everyone did a double glance at the painting and Valor.

"Oh, wait—no! This isn't Mah's blood," said Valor. "It's just paint—red Pox Paint."

"One never knows. Those Pox ingredients can get rather complicated," said Aaron. With a mischievous sparkle in his eyes, he pursed his lips, running his finger around his mouth, concealing his fangs.

Magister Crypting frowned and walked over to a wall adorned with ancient weapons.

"Mahrata has, uh, certainly ensnared everyone," said Crypting. "All of the roads to and from Mystic City are blocked. I won't be able to go to my sister in Wayova Yanda any time soon, I'm afraid. Guardians are, uh, positioned on the steeples in case anybody tries to leave broomways." Crypting pulled at his face while gazing at his reflection in the silvery armor on the wall. His eyes lit at first, then drooped with disappointment. "Despite the recent revelations and events, there seems to be little resistance to Mahrata. And I, uh, never expected apathy from the river people." Crypting shuffled over to look out the third-floor window.

"In Zagato's day, indifference to greed and corruption equaled approval. It's the last stage before destruction," said Blade.

"'In your day,' laughed Rose. For someone who still gets pimples, you act as though you're a living Ancient or something."

"I, uh, wish I were young and immortal like you kids," said Magister Crypting. "I'd go out there and, uh, 'really shake things up' as you say."

Valor heard Blade's projection of thought in two words: "Wish granted."

Rose and Blade glanced at each other with devious enthusiasm. "Oh yeah," they chorused, before seizing Magister Crypting, pulling him up on the stage, and placing him in a chair. Rose flung a cape over him while Blade started pulling out more men's costumes.

"I shall get the Athanasia Wand," said Aaron, while dashing out of the room.

"I'll see what Stab has in her apothecary room," added Doomsy, following behind Aaron.

Valor almost dropped his new painting when Rose first removed Crypting's spectacles before shaving his mustache and cutting his graying locks.

"Oh, dear! Oh, my!" Crypting feebly protested, while Rose applied enchanted powder on his face. His fragile eyes flinched with each smudge of the brush.

"Drink this, Magister Crypting," said Doomsy, after returning with Aaron to assist in Thiery's transformation project. "It's one of Stab's concoctions called Boost of Youth."

"I'm trying to do his lips," said Rose; "they're gonna be wicked."

Magister Crypting waved his arms as Doomsy forced more Boost of Youth down his throat. "Now, Doomsy," he stammered. "Now let's, uh, let's don't get too—"

"Stand up straight. Lift your chin," Aaron said to Crypting. "We're about to begin the Athanasia Mutatious incantation."

"Uh, you mean *immortality*?" asked Crypting, holding his arms out so Blade could put a black-velvet coat on him. "But, I'm not a Sorcerer."

"I should say it worked for Egg," said Valor. "Since the Sanguinati were once Sorcerers, before 'The Fall' and Great Deception, making them immortal seems to work as a catalyst in restoring their sorcery."

"I, uh, don't see how because Egg was born long after The Fall," said Crypting.

"Then sorcery must be 'in their blood' as the saying goes—only it sometimes remains dormant," concluded Valor. He wouldn't have dared offer Crypting the curse of immortality, the gift of eternal persecution, but it had not been his decision. Wouldn't Crypting want to retain some sense of Sanguinati allegiance since he had been a magister for so many years? But he had already proven himself daring to go against his employers.

While Crypting was passed out, becoming immortal, Rose, Blade, and the others remained behind the curtain, adjusting Crypting's clothing, posture, and appearance, in preparation for his permanent transformation. Minutes later, Magister Crypting emerged with closed eyes and no eyeglasses. Aaron and Blade supported Crypting's arms to keep him from falling down the steps as they escorted him over to a tall mirror to see the results.

"Okay, open your eyes to the hot new Crypting!" said Rose, dancing on the tips of her boots. "You're officially a Sorcerer now—you're immortal!"

"No," Crypting gasped. "This can't be." He touched his much younger-looking face and the tips of his straightened bangs but withdrew his hand as if the textured points of his new hairstyle might cut his fingers. "I, uh, do look like a creature to be reckoned with, don't I?"

Valor shook his head in amazement and laughed. "I promise I'll never mention you once had to wear spectacles and ride a broom."

"Incredible!" Crypting laughed as well, but no phlegm gurgled in his chest the way it always did. "Cell upon sloughing cell. With a wave of Aaron's wand, the, uh, years that had begun to enshroud me have been erased." He bounced with excitement and found himself floating above their heads. "Hoo-boy!"

Rose picked up Magister Crypting's old pants and jacket from the floor. "We need to toss these old fogey clothes in the fireplace," she said before Doomsy lit the logs for her to burn the garments.

"Burn my coven robe, too. My time was up anyway," said Crypting. He floated to the arched ceiling, where the flames highlighted specks on the gold covering the intricate moldings.

"Whaddaya mean?" asked Rose, lifting the black-velvet folds on the back of her dress and sitting in the chair to tend the fire. Her pale back peeked through the red ribbons lacing all the way to her waist.

"How did I ever imagine I could come back to Mystic Steeples and, uh, regain my magister's position after what O Enchantedness did to me?" Crypting floated back to the floor. "Now time has dictated a change, so no more 'Magister Crypting;' I wish to be called Thiery."

"Here's to Thiery, the newest member of Candlewicke Coven," said Doomsy. She plucked ambrosial red petals from a funeral wreath she had made for Creighton and tossed them over Thiery's head. The petals floated to the ground like drops of blood. Valor had to look away, for it had kindled his hunger. A pain quaked in his stomach.

"Now, Thiery, toss your hair more. And you just need to work on your words, they're a bit oldie moldy," said Rose. "Try adding a few trendy words like kapow, super-sonic, dazzle, and witchin'."

Thiery forced his hips to loosen into an unreasonable lean and tossed his bangs as if he were having neck spasms.

"I think I've got this, ya know? Like, KAPOW! I feel like a zinger-fingered part of this transvection generation with my, um, super-sonic new look. I'm gonna walk up in the Steeples and toss a little shadow and be like, 'don't let my, uh, dazzle frazzle you primitives!'" said Crypting, snapping his fingers with attitude.

"I know you miss Creighton, Rose, but this thing you've done with Thiery is only creating another monster," said Doomsy, looking as though she had swallowed spiders.

"I agree," said Valor. "Let him retain a fraction of his former self."

"Nah," said Blade. "Now that old Thiery's immortal, he'll have to get used to reinventing himself. You either metamorphosize in a big way, or you collect cobwebs." Blade's eyes settled on Aaron with intent.

"Easy for you to say," Doomsy hissed at Blade, while Thiery continued to swagger around, uttering slang words. "You probably tossed your mother out of the house as soon as you could feed yourself."

"A truly extraordinary witch can go from the bib to the pub," laughed Blade. "But my mother, well, Blade did try to pacify her."

"Oh, do pardon me for intruding. I didn't know you were receiving visitors today," said Salazants after seeing Crypting. Salazants gave the magister a strange look and placed a box full of crystaleers on the writing desk by the door.

Valor laughed and said, "He's not a visitor; he's the new Magister Thiery!"

"My new look is witchin', huh?" asked Crypting.

Again, Salazants gaped at the transformation in the man he had just seen hours earlier, the man who now appeared thirty years younger. Magister Crypting tested his new body, stretching and flexing in odd positions until he ripped a hole in his pants.

"Well, peel the pine overcoat! The new me is, like, going to take some, uh, acclimating," continued Crypting.

"Right, sir, but I'm afraid we're all going to have to do some acclimating," said Salazants. "Vespercestor Yma Le Breton is at the door. She said by the new *Communication Device Recall*, otherwise known as *Implementus Correctus 932*," (Salazants unfurled an Implementus scroll in front of them) "every witch in Severance is to hand over their crystaleers and receive these replacements." He pointed to the box of crystaleers on the writing desk, and his expression dimmed. "She tried to send in a crew to collect our old crystaleers, but I insisted I'd get your permission first."

"They can't take our crystaleers!" snapped Rose. Her anger vibrated the theater seats. "They're like extensions of ourselves."

"That buzzard-gizzard Twila Diamone is behind this; she threatened to get new regulated implements," said Doomsy. "So, I hid mine."

"Of course. Her parents oversee the ritual implements inventory department," said Valor.

Blade jumped off the stage, landing just inches from Salazants. "We can't expect any old crystaleer to give us accurate communications," said Blade. He bewitched a chair to fly against the door. "Do they think we're stupid enough to use those new crystaleers? They are using them to spy on everyone. Blade would bet his Rexella." He reached up and tickled the throat of his chameleon Familiar, and Rexella shot its long tongue in his ear.

"Mister Zagato, do not scuff the floors," said Salazants, removing the chair that was blocking the door.

"No telling what residual information they'll find on our crystaleers," said Valor, with a rush of panic while Blade stomped toward the door and stopped; his bronzed skin had flushed, and his lips pressed inward as if he were gnawing on them.

"We'd better get our wands a-whirlin', Merlin! Those zing zappers may view all of the crystaleers in a public screening," said Thiery, swinging his new bangs over his left eye. "According to Aves Treacle, there's a lot of, uh, information they can gather from those implements."

"The magister of Divinatory Arts should know," added Aaron.

"You're all owled out over there, Blade. Are you all right?" asked Rose, while Blade remained wide-eyed and immobile, as though gazing at invisible monsters.

"Zagato is just wondering if he remembered to erase some *things*," said Blade. "He tends to leave his crystaleer in record mode."

"We have to hand our crystaleers over. I shan't have them snooping around Candlewicke," said Aaron stiffly. "You may count on me to help you collect everything, Salazants."

"It'll take a while," agreed Valor. "We'd all better help."

Downstairs at the front door, Manning had been keeping watch of Vespercestor Yma Le Breton and her collectors, when Candlewicke Coven dumped their crystaleers in a two-foot crate marked "Under-14 Spookum Alley, Crescent Moon Quarter." Blade stormed back upstairs, muttering something under his breath.

"Good. There ya go. Put all of the crystaleers in the collection box," said Yma with a smirk just outside the door. She looked down a long list on her scroll. "He-he-he. Some of you fine Candlewickers have been missing assemblies lately." She pressed her head through the doorway, like a curious monkey, eyeing as much as she could.

"Aaron and I won the Golden Hooky Award for winning Spurgy. And I gave my spare award to Rose," said Valor. "As long as we pass our final exams, we're allowed to miss assemblies."

"For half of each apprentice level," added Rose. "Or has that changed, too?"

"Not yet," said Yma with another smirk. "Perhaps your new implements will help the rest of you get your schedules synchronized."

Doomsy eased her black-lace veil from her face and glanced out of the doorway at the darkness looming over Spookum Alley. The others followed her odd reaction and peeked up at the ominous sky, where it now appeared as if they were living in outer space. A ghostly face and hand manifested in the darkened atmosphere and pointed down at the Crescent Moon District.

"I didn't know spirits got that big," said Doomsy. "Why is he winking at us?"

"He's not winking," said Valor; "the clouds are moving behind him."

"It's still c-creepy—spying on us like that," said Egg, dropping his crystaleer in the collection box followed by Stabbah.

Yma waved up at the figure, which overshadowed the Crescent Moon District. "It's only spying if you have something to hide. Do you?" asked Yma in a songlike voice. "It's just an Ancient. They have been appearing over Severance now that the Dark Hour has begun. So, we must all be mindful of our loyalties to the vespercestory, and the devotional bowl is a good place to start." With a demeaning glint in her eye, Yma held out a bowl smaller than the one in Mystic Chantry. "O Captivatingness suggested you would like to purchase some indulgences. I mean, you wouldn't want the stargazers to conduct any investigations after what your late friend Creighton told us about you?"

"What did he tell you?" asked Rose, pushing her way toward Yma.

"Ah-ah-ahhh," said Yma, shaking her finger. "You just asked a question. You'll have to pay a fine."

"Here," said Valor. He grabbed a bunch of globulnugees from his pocket and dropped them into the bowl. "We don't believe Creighton would've told any lies. Well, uh, what did he say about us?"

"Another question," said Yma, holding out her hand, while the painted black heart on her cheek twitched under the brim of her shifted hat. "Your dear but dead friend, Creighton, informed us that you all knew the Grim Warlock was trying to channel us vespercestors against our will," said Yma before shuffling through an armful of file folders in her arms.

"Preposterous. I've never even heard of channeling the living. But Creighton's no longer alive to defend himself against that accusation. Please respect his memory," said Valor. He tossed more money at Yma. While she began scooping up the scattered globulnugees, the wind blew a sheet of paper out of her arms, and it drifted to the floor at Valor's feet, just before he slammed the door and locked it.

"Golly gremlins!" said Rose. "This is Blade's latest *Progress Gauge Report*. Should we have a look?" Her eyes squinched with mischief.

"Heck, yes!" agreed Egg while they gathered around to read the report.

PROGRESS GAUGE REPORT

Seat of the Assembly of stargazers

Case No.:176,058-plus Blade Dean Zagato

Individual's Test No.: 26

ASSESSMENT PROCEDURES: Blade Dean Zagato has thus far participated in 11,374-plus hours of Sanguinati apprenticeship, 22 hours of PGMI-24 testing, and a seven-hour diagnostic interview. Latest tests were administered by Dayonis Augusta, S.G., and witnessed by Scire Stoker, S.G.

Arithmancy Multiphasic Inventory-34-plus (AMI-34-plus) <u>Character Number</u>: Under-2D. Subject's latest readings have worsened. He has become tenacious, contrary, vicious, unpredictable, dispassionate, and dangerously detached. Blade's cogent and magical tendencies may prove dangerous being they can compel him into a delusional lifestyle where his psychic perceptions become his reality. He convinces himself that nothing in Severance would exist if he had never been born. <u>Heart Number</u>: 2D. Subject indicates the need to sever friendships, become self-governing, thereby disobeying authority. He becomes condescending of all forms of constructive intervention unless he feels ignored. <u>Personality Number</u>: Under-4D. Blade is narcissistic and sometimes emotionally disillusioned because the buried expectations he places on others never satisfies him, although, he is a master at hiding the rage this brings him. Subject craves positive reinforcement despite the appearance of lacking interest. This is a deception. Despite his simulation of apathy, subject is now prone to clever and sporadic stealth, deceit, violence, and spitefulness, which can manifest from an unrelenting abhorrence for those he perceives as unwilling to indulge him.

Belt Knots Accumulation: Subject has thus far achieved a belt of 6 x 2+ with Sorcerous bamboo beading and crow feathers disturbingly integrated with Noctivatian black bat bones but failed to attempt any knotting conducive of successful Sanguinati spell casting.

Past Life Memory Erasing: Inconclusive. Subject has thus far been resistant to mesmerists' procedures. His subconscious holds false beliefs that he attended Mystic Steeples in the year 1805 as the apprentice documented as Colbin Antedgio. Mesmerists also extracted false memories where Blade Dean Zagato has convinced himself that he rescued and married a girl named Swarmi Diamone, an 18-year-old girl the vespercestors handed a drowning sentence for an undisclosed offense. However, records in the offices of Mystic Ministry for Swarmi Diamone are from the year 1657 and show that she did escape her execution. In 1805, 148 years later, records indicate that the vespercestors discovered a murdered female vampire in the Den of the Doubter Sacrifice located in the Necromanceropolis. Upon viewing an old Diamone family portrait, the vampire appeared identical to Swarmi. The vampire was also wearing a necklace with the Diamone crest, as well as a wedding ring.

Practice of Perception: Utilizing Vision Rewind Gloves on Blade proved futile; subject scored criminally high on blocking and deception. He exhibits Magister Level skill in foreshadowing others' motives through Scrying.

Metaphysical Records: Aura Interpretation indicated a murky blending of yellow and black around subject's head, signifying wicked intentions radiating from his mind. Blade shows signs of having lost many things dear and possibly has the ability to cheat death itself. A murky blending of green and black around subject's body indicates subject is prone to bitterness and distrust. Palm Readings and Physiognomy Analysis, however, failed to support these conclusions as well as previous documentation, which could make subject more of a danger to society. Phrenology Exam (to be utilized for final Death Mask fitting and final Ceroscopy.) Subject had a knot on his temporal lobe that he claimed his sisters, Bess, Tess, and Tundrah, inflicted on him when he was a toddler. Upon investigation, we could find no records of his alleged sisters or his parents, Miraje and Neptune. Blade displayed Touch of Hercules magic during conversion therapy, giving him the strength to knock a hole through the Converts' Grotto wall into the Persuasion Gallows. Subject's brain wave activities suggest that of a primeval witch. He tested above average in vision and hearing tests. Blade is erratic. Mystic Ministry cannot depend on consistent results from him.

Extended Control Factor: He is not controllable. His fears seem to be any actions that do not involve his planning or input.

Eavesdrop Reveries and Oneiromancy review: Oneiromancy sessions have proved inconclusive and obscene at best. Aves Treacle, Magister of Divinatory Arts, entered subject's dreams on less than four occasions. Blade has vivid nightmares where he is fighting guilt of allegiances, trying to take care of some child hiding in Mystic City as well as his wife, Swarmi, hiding in the Necromanceropolis. He is also struggling to maintain an apprenticeship at Mystic Steeples while spying on the Sanguinati. In a recurring dream, Blade goes to the Necromanceropolis to check on Swarmi and finds two cloaked Noctivatians bowing down before another cloaked figure he believes to be the Grim Warlock. Blade's night sweats worsen when he dreams the Noctivatians have turned his wife, Swarmi, into a vampire, and she has drunk his daughter-in-law's blood, a woman known as Battista McRaven. Blade watches as Swarmi places *The Book of Chacodophilus* over Battista's heart as it beats its last beat. Swarmi drives a dagger through the legendary book, killing Battista. Blade tries to stop Swarmi and, in defense, kills her. But the book, made of flesh, now has a spirit. And, in its spirit form, it levitates and enters into the hands of the Grim Warlock. In each dream, Blade flees from the underground city of Noctivatians.

Mystic Ministry never found the body of Battista McRaven, and all records of her are missing. Subject is suspected of incorporating coded imagery during dream interpretations. Instability could lead subject to act upon his bitter impulses.

Graphology Analysis: Psychography indicated that subject shows an intense preoccupation with unleashing revenge, while his use of minor symbolism indicated that he is prone to dry humor to conceal his perilous nature.

Blade's ego intensifies when he manipulates others, as discovered during Unconscious Calligraphy exercises administered by the scribes. After evaluation of his graphic strokes, including cryptic pattern, freeform feather floating, and rhythm command. Results showed significant social deterioration.

Spectral Assignment: Upon subject's death and successful crossing over, his spirit could prove unreliable if not fatal in the reinforcement of Mystic Ministry. Blade's spirit might be utilized to assist with spells for his alleged cousin, Anasircea Zagato, should she not rely on sorcery. His spirit might prove obedient in magic staff spells in which he could fool others into thinking their enemy had been turned into a reptile. His spirit might also prove willing to perform tasks for Candlewicke Coven and pretty girls. Blade's spirit could be prone to materialize if summoned or during True Name Spells, if we could discern his actual name.

Doomsy slumped forward with a crease between her searching eyes. Her breathing became noticeable, and she didn't respond to concerns from Rose.

"No way," said Valor, still dizzy with shock. "It couldn't be the same Battista McRaven as one of my distant relatives."

"'Tis a unique name," said Aaron. "How many others might there have been in Hoopenfangia, pray tell?"

"If it's the same Battista McRaven, then her brother, Balmy, is my great grandfather," said Valor. He tried to imagine Battista being Blade's daughter-in-law. "My father never admitted to knowing Battista. Someone had erased her name on the McRaven family tree. But I used Saving Face Erase Retracer and found it. My father tore the rest of the names off, so I don't know who they are."

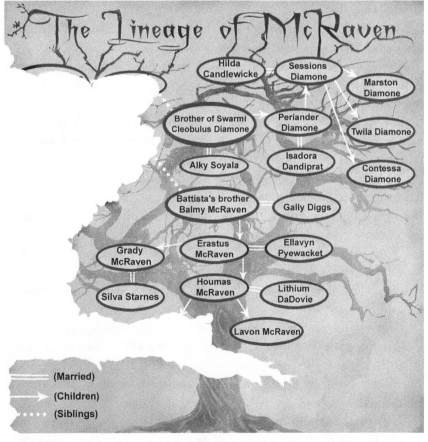

"Guys, that means Blade has a son who married Valor's great-grandaunt," said Rose.

"That's ridiculous. Blade would have to b-be ancient if that's true," said Egg.

"He didn't tell us any of this," said Rose, rubbing her arms as though she had chill bumps. "This is unnerving. We could be living with a killer for all we know!"

"But was Blade's real name Colbin Antedgio?" asked Valor.

Doomsy shrugged her shoulders. "Who knows?" she croaked. "He used that name when he was supposed to be looking after me in 1806." She shook her head. "And to think I helped that snake become an apprentice."

"Dahhhlings, after all these years, it wasn't safe for Colbin to return to Mystic Steeples using his real name—him being on their list of suspected Sorcerers and all," said Stabbah. "I used my real name. That's why they arrested me."

Aaron folded the parchment and shoved it in his pocket. "We had best not let Blade know we read his report."

"Blade wouldn't m-murder anybody," said Egg. "You can't, um, trust those *P-progress Reports*. The g-guardians said my last report showed, um, I was secretly a m-master of four different languages."

Rose crossed her boots and leaned against the hall wall. "I can't vouch for Blade," she said. "But I just can't let myself believe Creighton would've told the vespercestors anything to harm us."

Blade entered the hall, and everyone jerked from their huddled position. Thiery grabbed Valor and Aaron by their arms. "No need to focus on might-haves and might-bes now. We must get rid of these new crystaleers. I'd, uh, throw them in the swamp, but I'm afraid of water."

"You're an immortal now. Water shouldn't frighten you. Nothing should frighten you," laughed Blade. "But Zagato will toss them in the swamp unless you all think disposing of them underground would be better?"

"Um, no; the swamp should do," said Aaron, and everyone agreed.

"Your good opinion counts. The swamp it is," said Blade, patting Aaron on his chest right where the parchment remained hidden in his coat pocket. Then Blade hurried up the stairs to the drawing-room where Salazants had left the new crystaleers.

They peered around the wizards' parlor. "That was rather strange," said Valor. "Do you think Blade knows we were looking at his *Progress Report*?"

"Does a snake have eyes?" asked Doomsy.

Valor conjured the painting of Mahrata from the drawing-room, down the stairs, and into his hands. "I'm supposed to display this in a public place where most people can see it. Isn't that right, Stabbah?"

"Yes," said Stabbah.

"Why in a public place?" asked Thiery. "It would be safer to do it secretly."

"For every person who sees her portrait, they'll drain her energy unconsciously," said Stabbah. "The special paint Valor used will extract their secrets and memories of Mah and hopefully bind her from harming us."

"You didn't sign it, didja?" asked Rose.

Valor's eyelids lifted in a mock of revulsion. "Goodness, no," he said. "But where should I put her?"

"How about on the floor of the men's restroom or some centaur barn," suggested Doomsy.

"He-he-he," giggled Rose. "You should replace her old portrait in the Vespercestors' Vestibule. Plenty of people pass through there."

"Good idea, but what about the Bound Order of the Zodiac, their corpses are in the Atrium. You think I can slip past them with this?" Valor gestured to the painting. Would they think he had painted it with her blood?

"Truly, you might try holding it over your head. Perchance the Bound Order will mistake you for O Captivatingness," said Aaron.

"Wanna pass as Mahrata? Just raise one eyebrow and waddle straight to the vestibule," said Ruza Renata, stomping through the hall.

Valor held the painting in front of his head. "Hmmm, hello, you peons, I'm O Captivatingness . . . just passing through my domain." He tried to imitate Mahrata's voice while wobbling to the hall mirror to see what he looked like, but he bumped a statue off the table instead. "Why am I not convinced it'll work?"

Hours later, with the moon glowing over the tallest steeples, and only the bats and Zodiac Beings flying over the city, Salazants dropped Valor and Doomsy off at the closest entry to the Vespercestors' Vestibule on Ickylous

Street.

"Mistress Doomsy, I fear it's obvious you have the painting under your dress," said Salazants.

"It's not the painting. I often wear a wire bustle to fluff out the back of my dress," said Doomsy. "Valor has the painting under his cloak. I'm just here as his bodyguard."

"Oh. Well, here's wishing you success," said Salazants, handing her a lucky little totem, then he signaled the centaurs to return to Candlewicke Mansion.

"Why didn't we use the talismans of the Electricus Hexigus to turn invisible?" asked Doomsy, climbing a few steps to the interior entry of Mystic Steeples.

"Stab said we can't touch them for a few days until the Voo-Dew finishes curing," said Valor.

"What is Voo-Dew, my pet?"

"Some enchanted glue she used to attach the talismans to the Crown of Chacodophilus."

"Oh." Doomsy nodded.

"Thiery thinks we might be able to access the Cruxvein Abyss using the restored crown," said Valor.

"I don't think so," said Doomsy. "Even if we ever find the Abyss, the only way we'll get down there is by channeling Chacodophilus. Besides, we don't even have the gemstones for the talismans."

"You're wrong there, my dear. Aaron has had an excuse for gem shopping ever since we got the scroll. Stab is gluing the stones on the talismans as well."

When they reached the hall between the Front Atrium and the Vespercestors' Vestibule, they were sure they were alone except for the strange statue that moved past the doorway.

"Did you see it?" asked Valor.

"Yes," said Doomsy. "Was it Booger Fay?"

"No. Booger Fay's at home, playing Specter Checkers with Fleabane," said Valor. He clung to the wall as they eased toward the vestibule. On the high-arched ceilings, the soft musical hum of the constellations continued to drone. After they turned a corner, Gereon McMahon stood before them with his lantern.

"What are you two doing wandering around this area, and at this time of night?" asked the guardian.

"We—" Valor's heartbeat galloped. What should he say?

"I'm not feeling worth a toad's croak," said Doomsy. "Valor's taking me to see the witchdoctor. I'm getting strange spots on my—on my . . . *bottom*." Doomsy began lifting the back of her bustle. "You should have a look."

"No!" said Gereon. His eyebrows lifted like batwings, and his eyes became paler than usual. "However, I've sufficient reason to doubt your spots." Gereon's teeth clenched as he hissed. "Everybody knows Mystic Medicinary is on the tenth floor . . . on the eastern wing."

Doomsy gagged in her cupped hands and groaned. "So sorry," she said. "My sudden illness has caused us to become dis-displaced. Why are we upside-down?" Pretending to be hallucinating, Doomsy wobbled her head and looked up at the ceiling with a pitiful expression.

"Actually, guardian, I was taking her to the vestibule first. Last time she was feeling ill, she stood before O Captivatingness' portrait and it—well—it did the trick, sir," Valor said, fearing he was blushing.

"Did the trick? Humph," growled Gereon, showing more teeth. "You can't possibly make me believe O Captivatingness' portrait cured your disease?"

"Hmmm, you don't, haaa, think my beauty has a therapeutic effect on my people, Gereon?" asked Mahrata, stepping out of the vestibule in her regal nightgown and robe, applying half a jar of stardust on her face. Had she been collecting the glowing dust that the traveling constellations had been shedding throughout Mystic Steeples?

"Your, uh, beauty could cure anything, O Captivatingness. It's just these two are liars as we well know. Check her spotless bottom if you don't believe me," said Gereon. His head sank under his hooded cloak as Mahrata raised her left eyebrow at him.

"You have no business checking bottoms, Guardian," said Mahrata. "Besides, hmmm, I'm inclined to believe this poor child. I've, haaa, been told my portrait is quite enchanting, Gereon." Mahrata invited them into the vestibule, but she kept seven feet away from Doomsy. "Haaa, there now! You just feel free to stand under my, hmmm, portrait all you want, child." She motioned from a distance.

Doomsy stood underneath the painting, glancing sideways at Valor, who fidgeted as he clung to Mahrata's poxed portrait under his cloak.

"Hmmm, feeling better yet?" asked Mahrata. Her smile cracked the dust on her cheeks.

"Not so bad. I think we can all go home now," said Doomsy, moving away from the portrait.

Mahrata removed a dragon pendant from her robe and tossed it near the door. A small but fierce dragon manifested. Valor jumped away from the door when the dragon prepared to shoot flames.

"It's all right," said Mahrata. "We just need to, haaa, verify this for our records. Go ahead, child, bask a while longer under my, hmmm, soothing portrait."

"I was wrong. I'm still sick, *eeeuuuwwhhuugg*." Doomsy gagged in her hands. "I think I should just go home and read my *Controssua—*"

Mahrata aimed her wand at Doomsy, and she stood back under the portrait. "You're just heal-shy. Hmmm, just pretend we're not here and gaze at my portrait. Haaa, you had your back to it earlier."

With a shaky head, Doomsy looked up at Mahrata's portrait. She scratched her bottom through her bustle for effect.

Mahrata lowered her wand and said, "Hmmm, don't you, haaa, just feel the disease leaving your body, child?"

"I . . . I feel like something's going on in the pit of my stomach," said Doomsy.

"Haaa, why, of course," said Mahrata. "The magic's happening. Everybody, stretch your hands toward my painting and feel my power flowing over this child, hmmm."

Valor lifted his right hand but gripped the painting with his left hand. Mahrata took a deep breath as if soaking in the energy of her portrait before she noticed him. "Both hands, young man. Hmmm."

Valor swallowed hard and raised his left hand, dropping his portrait of her, which slid from behind his cloak to the floor.

Doomsy shot Valor a glance of horror over her shoulder, then tried to distract Mahrata and Gereon. "Oh look, O Captivatingness," Doomsy said in the perkiest voice she could force through her perpetual pout. "Your portrait cured me!"

Valor tried to retrieve the fallen painting, but it was too late.

"What were you hiding under your cloak, McRaven?" growled Gereon, reaching down and snatching the painting from the ground.

"Look, I'm cured. I'll show you my bottom," said Doomsy. She began to lift her dress to distract Mahrata.

"Hmmm, how sweet. You painted my portrait!" said Mahrata, taking the painting from Gereon and admiring it. "Haaa, you two have become obsessed with me. I can't tell you how relieved I am, haaa, to see you've come to admire my authority. Gereon, I have decided I want a special hall erected for this, hmmm, stunning portrait of me, and I want the new hall painted red to match my painting. Haaa, go straightaway and make it happen." Mahrata waved her wand, and the dragon dissolved back into a pendant, and a limber young ghost ran with it to place in her hand so that the pendant appeared to have levitated on its own.

"Yes, O Captivatingness," said Gereon, bowing to her while scowling at Valor.

"And, Doomsy," said Mahrata. "Hmmm, this old, and I dare say, not-so-flattering portrait of me has transformed you. I've, haaa, never seen so much color in your cheeks." From a distance, Mahrata floated her hands through the air as if she were brushing a frame of healing energy over Doomsy's head.

"But—"

"No need to thank me, child," said Mahrata. "Nevertheless, I do want you to testify at Convocation tomorrow night. Haaa, tell the covens how my portrait saved you from that, hmmm, deadly disease. It will be a grand celebration with a special preview of my new painting. Haaa, the perfect opportunity for Valor to apologize to the Sanguinati for all those lies he told Cryptic Chambers about the vespercestors and, hmmm, denounce all that silly Sorcerer nonsense."

Valor could keep silent no longer. "But you heard O Enchantedness admit that the Sanguinati used to be Sorcerers before he killed Mesthu. Everybody heard him admit it."

"You foolish boy," laughed Mahrata. "My, hmmm, husband was possessed by the Grim Warlock when that happened. He didn't know what he was saying or doing. You two will be at my party and, haaa, do the right thing."

409

Pumpaninny Magister & Sent Packing

Hiccius Doolally has been the Magister of Magical Multimedia Manipulation at Mystic Steeples for years. He also happens to be a pumpaninny. Under what many are calling a ministerial purging, with testing conducted by the new Aura Analysts, Head Vespercestor Mahrata LaRock recently fired Doolally suddenly when his aura failed to impress the team after Doolally drank four-plus bottles of Auravitamax and had to be rushed to Mystic Infirmary.

"Magister Doolally never really belonged in a position of prominence in the Sanguinati," said Sessions Diamone, an honorary noble who runs the Ritual Implements Department of Mystic Ministry. "We cannot allow the fragile minds of our young people to be influenced by such types as Doolally. The next thing you know, a cockroach will be made high priest."

MINISTRY MISCHIEF

VALOR and Doomsy slouched on top of Aaron's coffin in a secret passageway on the third floor of Candlewicke Mansion. Doomsy hid her face under a lace veil. Valor's arms remained folded, lips pouty, focusing on anything as long as it was far away and calm. The torchlights, too perky in their flickering dance, bothered him, so he willed the flames to cower down, and if he had to hear Doomsy sigh through her nose again, he would wrap her stupid veil around her nostrils.

"I don't know why you insisted on putting Mahrata's painting in the Vespercestors' Vestibule. Might as well walked right inside her bedchamber," hissed Doomsy.

"That was Rose's idea," said Valor. "Besides, you were the one who got all excited over Delicia's stupid vision of me painting. Don't you remember? You suggested it was 'the gift of spirit capture,' and you agreed I should put the painting in a very public place."

"I was just telling you what Stab told me about spirit capture. You should know by now not to trust Delicia Jones," said Doomsy. She jumped off the coffin and stomped to the secret exit behind a reversible oil painting of the Marbois family, who had died years earlier inside Candlewicke Mansion.

"There you two are, hiding like two bashful moths in your cocoons," said Aaron, entering the passage while Doomsy skirted past him to leave.

"I'm not bashful; I just hate people," she said.

"What, I dare ask, is the quandary?" asked Aaron. He stood in front of them with a curious glance, picking up a shredded piece of ribbon Doomsy had torn from her dress.

"Shadowhaven Heights is a much more fitting home for witches like us," said Valor, reclining on top of Aaron's coffin like a corpse. "Do you ever wish you had stayed there?"

"You never believed that, Valor," said Aaron. "You are avoiding my question." He propped the elbow of his olive velvet coat on a brick alcove, resting his chin in his hand in a theatrical gesture of attentive apprehension. "Now . . . the earth has paused on its axis, and my focus is clear; something is troubling you." His raised eyebrows formed a serious furl underneath his wavy golden bangs.

With a snap, Valor sat up and said, "We tried to display Mahrata's painting, but everything backfired. She wants Doomsy to claim her hideous old portrait healed her, and she wants me to apologize in front of the entire Convocation tonight—tell them I was lying about the vespercestors—lying about the Sanguinati all being Sorcerers originally!"

"And you agreed to this?" asked Aaron. With a hint of fear, his eyes searched deep into Valor's.

"No. I didn't say anything; neither could Doomsy. But if we do what Mahrata wants us to do, I'm afraid it will destroy everything we've worked for," sighed Valor. "She claims all that about O Enchantedness killing Mesthu, and saying they were all once immortals, was because the Grim Warlock possessed her husband. I guess the Sanguinati is buying it as usual."

"I don't mean to be disloyal, but I can't imagine what will happen if you don't do what she requested," said Aaron. He sat on the edge of his coffin, scratching his worried brow. "To the River Styx with it! We are turning into witches with conflicting compassions. Only puppets survive around here, and that is what we are going to do—survive. Even if we have to drink gallons of Auravitamax." Aaron folded his arms with a swift nod.

"As much as I'm tired of fighting to exist, I don't think I can bring myself to lie," said Valor. "Think of all those who are hungry for truth—struggling to fit in—to be themselves. And think of what the Mystic Key might do to us. We might end up like Creighton!"

Aaron seemed on the verge of surrendering to some inner struggle. He busied himself with arranging some of his favorite belongings on a shelf in the hidden chamber, their "substandard bedroom," as he called it since he couldn't bring himself to say, "coffin chamber."

"Think of what might happen to us if you *don't* give in to Mahrata. She knows what she's doing—just where to jab the knife," said Aaron, taking the ritual knife he had earlier pulled out of a box and stabbing it into a wooden support beam. "I suppose now is an appropriate time to confess since we have fallen deeper into this abyss. I've had all the mirrors in the mansion covered while you and Doomsy were hibernating in here."

"Tell me you didn't stop the clocks as well? Never mind, I don't want to know," said Valor, catching the glare from Doomsy's porcelain toad figurine she had left on the edge of his coffin.

"The clocks still tick," said Aaron, leafing through a book on the origins of wiggiwamis.

Valor's mind raced. What reason would Aaron have to cover the mirrors in the mansion? Aaron peeked over the edge of his book. Did he know Valor was contemplating the news?

"If you must know," said Aaron, "last night, the spirits were very active while you and Doomsy were trying to sneak inside the Vespercestors' Vestibule. Something peculiar came over me in the wizards' parlor, and I threw a cast-iron statue of Nefertiti at Ambergis's spirit, emerging in the mantel mirror. I felt awful for smashing the glass. Nevertheless, as I was picking up the loose shards, I saw the spirit of a veiled woman. I'm not certain, but I think she could've been Genola, the same ghostly image in this archival photo of Candlewicke Mansion." Aaron picked up the photo on the old bookshelf covered in various parchments.

"The reoccurrence was all too much. I don't think it would've happened if we had not encountered Delicia in the alley—if you had not accused Delicia of working with Genola to rid the darkness in you, or around you, or whatever. The point is, neither you nor I know for sure that the mirror manifestations aren't any old phantom menace who's developed a sick interest in the art of mimicry."

"Perhaps, my dear," said Valor. "But right now, I'm more concerned about menaces on platforms than in mirrors. Convocation starts in half an hour. We should sell all the mirrors and buy a boat to sail out of Hoopenfangia. If we can get through the enchanted barrier of mist."

Aaron lifted an amethyst lid from the cologne bottle and held it to his nose. "Verily," he agreed. "We could leave—just abandon this beautiful jewel of a mansion. That would make Marston and Twila Diamone, and a few others tingle with excitement."

Doomsy remained sullen and quiet, arms folded, levitating her *Controssua* a few feet behind her as they walked down Envisage toward Mystic Chantry. They refused a carriage ride so they would have time to converse. The shifted cobblestones made for a bumpy stroll. Aaron loved the warm evening air blowing on him to warm his cold body. Stabbah wrapped Ruza's lace sash over her hair so it would stay out of her eyes. Micha seemed to enjoy sending his shadow to rattle every spirit catcher, hanging plant, and wind chime, which hung from the endless galleries of the homes and businesses down the alley.

"So, I, uh, hear you and Valor have become Noctivatians. How are you adjusting to nocturnal living?" Thiery asked Aaron as if trying to stir the conversation.

"We are both tolerating those uncivilized coffins," replied Aaron.

"So far, the sun hasn't affected us," added Valor. "But with the Bound Order of the Zodiac taking over Mystic City, I do wonder if we'll ever see much sun again."

He looked at the midnight-blue sky and the Zodiac Beings shooting over the city like exploding comets, flinging whips of flashing stardust as air-travel precautions. The planets seemed to hover just over the tallest buildings now. Valor wasn't so sure the tallest steeple of Mahrata LaRock's office wasn't supporting Saturn.

"I would miss the sun if I were, uh, Noctivatian. Though I rarely ever stayed outside unless on an archeological dig. Always behind a desk," said Thiery, strutting lean, mean, and virile down the alley compared to the former magister they remembered. "I believe those days have ceased."

Valor felt as though he were walking to his execution and didn't want to make small talk, but he needed to appear friendly.

"Venerious Falmoth told me he's lived so many sunless years that he actually prefers ebony air," said Valor.

Doomsy spoke at last: "Falmoth is also of the Sanguinati belief that embracing one's fate is better than fighting it."

"Embracing? He thinks his fate is to retake Mystic Steeples. He's loving all over that fate," said Ruza.

"And a point for Ruza," said Blade, conjuring her name in the air with a feathery checkmark under it.

Doomsy paused to look inside a doll maker's shop window. "Sometimes," she said, "sometimes I think it would be less painful to kiss fate smack on its twisted little mitts."

"And a point for the little one," said Blade, conjuring Doomsy's name along with another checkmark in the air.

"You say that as though you're giving up," said Valor, still unsure what Doomsy would say or do when Mahrata called on her to confirm her phony healing.

"Uncertainties have roamed too long over our weary existence," said Doomsy with a vacant expression. She plucked the feathers out of her witch's ladder and let them float where they may. "It seems, behind every turn, a death shrine awaits us."

"Two points for Doomsy," continued Blade, while she grimaced at him.

"But we can't just give up and go rest on some shady park bench and, and watch another new statue replacing the old landmarks that used to stand throughout Mystic City," said Valor.

"And a hundred points for Valor," said Blade, conjuring so many checkmarks under his name it looked like a flock of crows following them. The Skeletons of Sorrow sign lit up on a theater marquee, while Blade and Egg lifted their heads to watch the skeletons dance.

"I agree with Dooms. The vespercestors are startin' ta hold trial over people who speak of—things. But we don't have ta say nothin' about nothin'," said Micha, as if unaware of the new crystaleers and Vortexes of Revealing swarming over their heads on occasion.

"Oh, all of this has me so worried," said Nalini, walking beside Stabbah as they turned onto Ickylous. Her long hair billowed like a silky black tablecloth behind her.

"I'm with Valor, guys. We have to keep fighting—now more than ever. But whatever you guys decide to do, I guess I'll understand," said Rose, grinding her boots into the flagstone harder than ever as she marched toward Mystic Steeples.

"Candlewicke Coven. Ha!" laughed Ruza. "What a joke. We're not a coven. We're as divided as Severance is from bloody Diabolishire."

"One is free to do what one must. As for me—though I may regret my decisions tomorrow—I shall never surrender to the misery of indifference and neglected possibilities," Aaron said while nudging Valor.

"Try not to worry, dahhhlings," cooed Stabbah. "*I've* brought some back-up." She shook the conjure bag around her neck with a wink and stretched her legs up the steps to Mystic Steeples as though she were going to battle.

Mistress Bessbadora Breaches met them in the Atrium and cornered Valor. "McRaven," she called out, "I hear you were right after all the fussing, crying, puffing up like a gassy dragon you did. Old Thiery Crypting's not dead. No, he is not. But where has he been hiding?" The pyramids of hair bounced on each side of her head, poking Aaron and Rose in their eyes.

"It is still Magister Crypting to you, Mistress Breaches," Thiery said, stomping forward in the group.

Bessbadora froze with her hands in midair and mouth open. "I would never have recognized you—wouldn't have known you from any boy on the streets if you weren't wearing your magister's pendant, oh, wearing it so loyally." Bessbadora formed an insane smirk on her face as if she had read Thiery's darkest secrets. "Mistress? You must think I'm still your understudy, your subordinate, your measly assistant. And even after your long holiday, vacation—wherever you went for this new beauty makeover, youth spell of yours. No, it's *Magister* Bessbadora now. The vespercestors have given me your position. *I'm* magister of Controssua Studies— the official archivist. *I* hold the keys to the Chamber of Oracles."

Thiery snarled his lips and said, "On holiday? I was abducted by O Enchantedness and his henchmen."

"My-my," said Bessbadora. "More than just a makeover; you even sling a little attitude now—dangerous attitude. This makes me think . . . not a makeover, no, more like sorcery—dark magic. Dare I say immortality?"

Thiery slung his bangs and simpered at her. "Think what you will but—"

"Oh, don't worry, Thiery," said Bessbadora. "I'll allow Valor, Doomsy, and Aaron access to the Chamber of Oracles. But next time they visit down there, I had better know which scrolls they take and what they intend to do with them. Tread lightly, all of you; Mystic Ministry doesn't like immortality—no happily ever after. And they don't like thieves. *Mmph*, I need to spit out this lozenge; they just last forever—not a good thing when I'm about to go to Convocation." Bessbadora spat out the candy into a piece of paper and slapped the paper into Valor's hand before she paraded into the Vespercestors' Vestibule.

"Hey," said Valor, examining the candy. "This is a Luminous Lulling Lozenge."

"Indeed, it is. And we know the supplier of that particular candy," said Aaron, sticking out his tongue to reveal a lozenge of his own. "It curbs one's bloodthirst rather well."

"Let me see that, my pet," said Doomsy, pulling the wadded paper from Valor's hand, then snatching the edges loose from the sticky candy. "Where did she get this? It's the last page of a children's book. No children's books around here have last pages."

Valor had a realization. "Bessbadora found one of the last pages from the books in the hidden room of the Chamber of Oracles. I'll bet we led her there," he said.

"But why?" asked Rose. "Why wouldja find whole books in the Chamber, but in all the libraries, all the old books have the last pages torn out?"

"Bessbadora knows. We heard her say it," said Thiery. "In their efforts to, uh, stamp out the history of sorcery, Mystic Ministry removed the pages that read 'And they all lived happily ever after,' because those words represent immortality."

"Now I understand . . . kinda," said Nalini Lusion. "I started working at the Lunar Nooner Library. I thought the missing pages were just some random act of vandalism. My boss has a grab-bag of bookmarkers with different little story endings so the kids will stop bugging him about the missing pages."

"Yeah," said Egg. "I, um, s-started working there and t-those bookmarker endings are like fortune cookies. Sometimes even old people grab them without even c-checking out a book."

"Say that this is all true; why would Bessbadora give us this clue? It seems rather unlike her to want to help us," said Aaron.

Feeling a bit dazed, Valor took the paper back from Doomsy and said, "Falmoth did promise that someone at Mystic Steeples would make a huge change in the way they treated me. I guess that was a rather large improvement for her."

Thiery's smile seemed disheartened. He walked between Aaron and Doomsy into Mystic Chantry as the choir's voices warbled in a strange chant. The orchestra's drumbeats vibrated in Valor's chest, overpowering his heartbeat, while Candlewicke Coven parted ways and went to their coven sections.

"I do not recall inducting you into the Crypts. How did you acquire your pendant and robe?" Esoterica asked Thiery as she edged past them to her seat.

"I am Magister Crypting, and I, uh, had my pendant since before you were born, dear girl."

Esoterica studied Thiery's face then her mouth dropped. "Um, I um," she stammered. Dropping her *Controssua*, she tried to say something else but ended up giving him a hand signal of approval, which made him blush as well.

Valor squeezed past Aaron and Egg in between the benches, and Donny-Dale-Dharma Thelastone's hair stood on end when Valor's hand passed over their heads.

"Watch it McRaven," the Thelastone triplets said in unison, scowling over their conjoined shoulders.

"Um, sorry," said Valor. His fingers twitched while sparks emitted from his fingers. He turned to Doomsy, and she, too, had sparks shooting from her fingertips.

"What is happening to us?" asked Thiery, trying to place his *Controssua* in the nook on the back of the bench, but it drew back in his hand. "It's like someone cast a Magne-Marrow spell on my fingers."

"Mine t-too," said Egg. He passed his hand over his boots, and the silver buckles popped off and clung to his fingers. "Oh, wow; I got the power!"

"The Bound Order of the Zodiac must be causing this," whispered Aaron. "Ever since I entered Mystic Steeple, I have had a strange sensation throughout my body." Aaron began rocking on the bench. Gripping the seat, he moaned and hissed through his teeth.

"Hmmm, haaa, thank you, Preston, for that special Invocation of the Zodiac," said Mahrata while the choir sat down, holding candles in the much darker sanctuary. "Haaa, I can almost see a charge of anticipation building in some of your faces. Hmmm, for this is a very special night indeed." Mahrata braced against the podium as two guardians brought in an easel covered in a purple velvet drape and placed it on the platform beside her.

Before Mahrata could continue, a man and woman, river evacuees perhaps, stood up from their benches and a woman amongst the group yelled, "Mahrata LaRock, we demand you acknowledge who we are; acknowledge the crimes committed against us."

"She'll never admit it. She's not even fit to be our leader," yelled a man from the group, shaking his finger at Mahrata.

Six shrieks discharged from the guardians' magic staffs and knocked the man and woman several feet in the air before the two landed in the Dragon's Mantle section unconscious in a nest of green robes. Hensle Centaury, a young apprentice with Dragon's Mantle, screamed and dove over Micha DeMise. The guardians carried the burned and battered protestors out through the side exit. Aaron was now growling through clenched teeth, and claw-like rips began to appear on his pants.

"Aaron, what's wrong? Do we need to leave?" asked Valor, but Aaron didn't seem to hear a word of his concern.

"May I say something, O Captivatingness?" asked Tilta Crumpecker, arising from the throne chair behind her. Mahrata moved to the side of the podium, allowing her to speak to the mass assembly.

"I was in meditation this afternoon, preparing me some rabbit stew," said Crumpecker. "I laid that critter on my kitchen counter and decided to use some of your special seasonings." Crumpecker held up a glass bottle filled with crushed herbs. "I sprinkled the rabbit good and, next thing I know, that critter sprang to life and bounced all over my kitchen."

Many in the Chantry laughed and smiled up at Crumpecker, as she continued speaking:

"It was all the confirmation I needed," she said, placing her hand behind Mahrata's back. "This woman is the leader you bunch of whippersnappers need."

"I need to borrow some of O Captivatingness' special seasoning," said Scribe Fengurstaph, rubbing the top of his head, while many applauded. "Maybe it'll resurrect these dead hairs."

"Hmmm, thank you, High Priestess, for you have truly been in communication with the Ancients," said Mahrata, taking over the podium again. "Haaa, tonight I have a very special unveiling. But before doing so, I need Valor McRaven and Doomsy Gloomsy to join me up here on the platform." Mahrata motioned to the back of the Chantry. "Haaa, chop-chop," she said, snapping her fingers, motioning for them to hurry.

Valor tensed his muscles while he inched toward the platform with Doomsy. As they moved past the apprentices sitting near the aisle, their magnetic pull caused the apprentices' clothing, hair, necklaces, and *Controssuas* to stir with a gusty trail of debris behind them. The vespercestors exchanged questioning glances as Valor and Doomsy strode past them to the podium. Valor tried to hide behind the cloaked easel, but Mahrata pulled him closer to her and in full view of the entire Convocation.

"Hmmm, before these two young apprentices here, haaa, testify to the overwhelming effect I have had on them, and may I add, so profound they, hmmm, insisted on publically denouncing the terrible influence the practitioners of darkness have tried to place on them. Haaa, I want to reveal a special portrait my newest little fan, Valor McRaven, painted in honor of me."

The guardians lifted the purple veil on the easel, revealing Valor's portrait of Mahrata in a red frame so enormous it made the painting look like a pea on a mattress. Mahrata began clapping, followed by a sea of applause. Twila and Marston covered their mouths and booed in the Cryptic Chambers' section. In the Balcony of Elders, Lockie Pomeroy LaRock clasped her hands in a look of triumph. Would Lockie now love Valor and be his grandmother?

A peculiar yearning softened his rage, and he wanted more than ever to continue this acceptance, to give up what he was to end the harassment and, then again, maybe Doomsy would do the same. She seemed torn unlike he had ever seen her. After all, neither of them had made a pact to deny their support for Mahrata. Rose sat on the edge of her seat with Warlocks' Bane Coven. Micha in Dragon's Mantle. Stabbah and Ruza in Wormwood Philters. Blade in Graven Dust. Thiery, Egg, and Aaron in Cryptic Chambers. Their fretful faces made Valor ache. For a moment, he saw the ghost of Creighton sitting near Nalini with Snuffinumbra Coven.

"Don't deny who you are, Valor," Creighton seemed to say with sad eyes as he shook his head.

"Hmmm, yes," continued Mahrata. "Guardian Gereon McMahon will mount this lovely painting in the new Gallery of Captivation beside the Chanting Arena for anybody wishing to view it. Haaa, and speaking of paintings of me, Miss Doomsy Gloomsy here claims my original portrait in the Vespercestors' Vestibule has healed her of a very deadly disease." Mahrata snapped her fingers, and some dwarves rolled out a small step stool so Doomsy could reach the podium. "But I want her to tell you of her life-changing experience with her own little transformed mouth. Hmmm, Chop-chop, Doomsy."

Gereon McMahon stood on the platform, keeping a hard eye on Doomsy while she crept up the stepstool until her head peered over the top. She avoided eye contact with Valor; instead, she blinked dully at whatever she had been looking at most of the evening.

"Hello," said Doomsy, wiping the mouthpiece of the levitating magihorn with a cloth from her conjure bag. "I guess it is time to put an end to all these rotten rumors—all these big bulbous noses sniffing around my friends and me as if something crawled in our bellies and died." Doomsy seemed immune to Gereon, who made muffled noises as if reminding her of his presence. "I was in the Vespercestors' Vestibule with my brother standing over there," continued Doomsy, jerking her head sideways. "It's true, I said I was ill, and Guardian Gereon seemed awfully eager to examine my bottom, but I suggested that O Captivatingness' portrait would probably do the trick, and—"

As a mix of shock, anger, and laughs traveled through the Chantry, Gereon's pale face turned even paler under his hooded robe.

Growling, Aaron ran to the front of the Chantry with glassy eyes and flushed cheeks. "Argh! I'm a Sorcerer! I'm the one who's been causing all the trouble among your people. Valor and Doomsy never wanted to be a part of my coven though I tried, oh, I tried."

Valor gestured for Aaron to stop, but Mahrata lifted her wand to one of the members of the Bound Order of the Zodiac, circling the ceiling.

"Spirit," she said, "take Aaron to the sanatorium!"

Spirit shot down a zap of energy resembling a celestial web, binding Aaron from head to feet and snatching him up to the ceiling before disappearing with him out of the highest stained glass window accompanied by a loud crash.

"No!" yelled Valor, running straight off the platform before the guardians restrained him and heaved him to the floor. As Valor continued to call after Aaron, the guardians put all of their body weight on him to the point he couldn't breathe. Everything dissolved in quiet blackness.

"Oh, honey, ya had me worried ya'd taken a permanent trip to the Astral Plane," said Witchdoctor Kraneswaddle in her rasping voice. "I was going like this: gooble-gooble-gooble." She shook like a wet dog, peering down over Valor as he reclined on a table in Mystic Medicinary. He bolted off the table and ran for the door, but Kraneswaddle leaped in front of him, flapping her spread arms.

"I have to go! I have to know what they've done with Aaron," panted Valor.

Kraneswaddle jingled little bells on the tips of her fingers and chanted, "*Nooga Sanga Wooga.*" Valor slid to the floor, feeling paralyzed and sleepy. "Oh, honey, now ya're gonna hafta listen to old Minty. I've watched yas ever since ya was a baby, and I've been very persuasive in getting the stargazers to raise ya progress gauge scores. There ain't nothing you can do for Aaron; he's gone. And I'm not about to let ya go and destroy yaself, too. What good would it do? Ya need to be here for Doomsy."

With visions of trying to save Aaron, and Magister Kraneswaddle yapping unintelligible words at him and snapping her crazy little finger-bells in his face, Valor screamed inside. His body quivered as he used every bit of strength to stand up from the floor, but his vision became like a smoke-filled tunnel, and he passed out again.

With a jolt, Valor awoke on the floor with his head propped against the door, salty crust in the corners of his eyes, and vines of ivy binding his hands and feet. Had his nightmares become a carnival? Kraneswaddle backed her rear end near the flames in the fireplace against the wall bordering her private quarters. Flowers swayed across the bottom of her sleeping gown, exposing her furry slippers and striped stockings.

"There ya are! Oh, honey, you'll never be able to get this outta ya head. Old Minty knows—she knows," gurgled Kraneswaddle. After the back of her gown started smoking, she shuffled her furry slippers over the floor and pulled down a long feeding tube from an overhanging bottle of bubbling goop. She shoved it into his mouth as he, again, tried to protest.

"Now, eat ya din-din before ya get cold," she said in a more baby-like voice.

Valor spat out the feeding tube, dribbling purple goop down his neck. He had bitten the inside of his mouth until it felt like sandpaper. "What have they done with Aaron?" he wheezed, ripping at the ivy bindings. "Aw, please let me go."

"Hun, now, you have to calm yaself and listen to me. Ya're lucky old Minty here has ya and not them star monkeys—them Zodiac thingies."

Horrific scenarios played in Valor's head. Had the Possessing taken Aaron as its next victim, or did Aaron deliberately cause a strange disruption to save Valor and Doomsy from Mahrata? How could Valor calm himself? All his friends might be dead by now. Every exhausted cell in his body wanted to run after them.

"Young man, I could just whup ya with the bristly end of a broom. Ya've done gone and become vampire since I last examined ya. Now I kept ya being a Sorcerer secret, but—"

"You knew?" asked Valor. He stopped tugging against the ivy bindings. Why hadn't she reported him?

Kraneswaddle squished her face then resumed ranting. "Yes, honey, but this is just too much. Old Minty here warned ya about those grimbots. What in the puddle gravy are ya trying to do, turn yourself into a Mystic Menagerie exhibit? 'Cause lemme tell ya, hun: the zoo is best experienced from outside the cage."

Valor pressed his lips together and tried to squelch any angry words. His eyes raised from his ivy bindings to Kraneswaddle's concerned face.

"Oh, honey, you don't have a clue what sorta havoc ya caused in Mystic Chantry tonight, do ya?" she asked.

Valor's eyeballs stiffened, and his breathing slowed to a near halt. *What had he done?* His mind screamed.

"You and all ya friends parted the Sanguinati worse than Bessbadora Breaches's hair," said Kraneswaddle. "Now I ain't endorsing ya behavior or nothin', but a doozy of a revolt occurred during Convocation."

Valor raised up and blinked to see if he was dreaming. "It did?"

Kraneswaddle frowned with a sympathetic head-tilt and said, "Oh, honey, now Aaron is gone, but some of the lesser vespercestors and magisters stood up to old Mahrata and forbade her to punish you and Doomsy." Her mouth gaped with a squelched laugh. "Ya friends and those Sorcerers from the river tore up the Convocation. I was holding my breath worse than that time I got caught in a swarm of unda gnats." Kraneswaddle bent over with a snort, but Valor found it a horrible thing to do, considering he lost his best friend . . . his Aaron.

"Untie me," growled Valor. Helping Falmoth defeat Mystic Ministry mattered more than anything else now. He concentrated and willed a knife to levitate off a high shelf and float toward the ivy bindings around his feet.

Kraneswaddle flung a patchwork veil over the knife, trapping it to the floor. "Gosh," she said, "how former High Priestess Siouxanna Demollien brought a hush over everybody in that Chantry. She approached old Mah and held up the severed stone toe from her statue to prove who she was. I thought old Tilta Crumpecker was gonna combust." Kraneswaddle shoved her hands in her gown pockets, and her posture deflated when Valor remained unresponsive.

"Ya're not happy, are ya, hun?" she sighed. She put a charm necklace around her head and began to unwind the ivy bindings around his feet and hands.

Valor rubbed his wrists and brushed off a few ivy leaves from his clothing. His eyes darted between her and the door. With a disappointed smile, she motioned toward the door with her head, letting him know he could leave.

With that confirmation, Valor shot out of the medicinary like a wand zap. He ran ten whole stories down winding halls, circling corridors, and steep staircases. Strangely, a black cat ran in front of him as though leading the way. Valor found the white patch over the cat's eyes rather odd, for it formed the shape of a woman's head. He turned through the east wing of Buckthorn Hall. But as he exited onto Ancient Alley, Summoner Eelias Mamahchi blocked his path with his blackthorn staff, and the cat ran away.

"Ah, I was on my way to gather crow milk and a large thick worm . . . for a confessional concoction," said Mamahchi, aiming his magic staff at Valor. "Confession is therapeutic . . . wouldn't you say, McRaven?"

"What have they done with my friends?" wheezed Valor, aiming his monoculous at Mamahchi. "Where are they?"

"How dare you aim your wand . . . at a vespercestor?" growled Mamahchi.

As Valor prepared to respond, Venerious Falmoth appeared at the Salty Charm Avenue end of Ancient Alley.

"He-he-ha-he-ho. Great show you gave in the Chantry, McRaven. Way to go!" sang Falmoth, dancing up the walls of the alley, twirling and tapping his skull-tipped wand.

"If it isn't Venerious Falmoth . . . our former head . . . *jester*," said Mamahchi, aiming his magic staff between Valor and Falmoth now. "Fancy seeing you here at such a . . . *tumultuous* time."

"Always dependable, but sadly expendable," giggled Falmoth.

"You will leave Mystic City . . . this minute, Venerious," growled Mamahchi through his bushy gray beard.

"Right, I will! But not without my little hero there, who the Ministry wants to kill," said Falmoth, beckoning Valor to come with him.

Which direction should he run? Valor wondered, as the summoner's magic staff aimed at him again. He didn't trust either of the men who stood at opposite ends of the alley.

"Why can't you do . . . what you're told, Venerious?" asked Mamahchi, while Falmoth continued easing his way toward them.

Valor wasn't sure he had the strength to float, so he aimed his monoculous at Summoner Mamahchi and prepared to knock him out of his path, but just before his wand zeroed in on the summoner, Mamahchi cast a spell that sent Valor spinning through the air.

"Eeli, meanie to our hope, try not to choke on my Nockie smoke," chanted Falmoth, releasing a spell from his wand until a fog of phantoms filled the entire alley. Valor collapsed at Falmoth's feet; the ghosts blinded him until everything became quiet and black, and his body surrendered.

CHAPTER TWENTY-ONE

VALOR'S GRIM INITIATION

S OFT ruched fabric greeted Valor's fingertips in the dark with
no room to stretch his arms. He was on his back in a strange
coffin with a lining of velvet. This was no time to sleep. He had
to find his friends. He shoved the lid aside and climbed out,
smacking his head on the stone ceiling in a coffin cubicle.
Candlelight illuminated the catacomb passage, where he floated down
to the floor. A six-foot cape of black fabric lowered to expose a pale,
familiar face. Janus Duperie looked as glum as he had at
Shadowhaven Heights. Only his thick mustache had a spirited
upturn.

"At last, he crawls from his bed. I thought we were going to have
to find a resurrectionist. You've been asleep for a whole day, haven't
you?" asked Duperie, peering through his mane of dark waves.

"You said I would never evolve. And you're afraid of fire," said

Valor.

Duperie recoiled behind his cape again. "Don't say that word, McRaven. Have you no decency?"

"Right now, I don't know what I have, what happened, or how I got here. I just hope my friends are still alive," said Valor. He despised Duperie, the dreary catacombs, everything.

"I sneaked inside Convocation long enough to tell you this." Duperie paused to feel the carvings on a coffin in the middle of the room. "After the guardians carried you out of the Chantry, Mahrata became enraged and expected Doomsy to deny her heritage and the lies you all were spreading."

Valor's heart threatened to punch through his chest. "What did she do? What happened?"

"Doomsy refused, so Mahrata used her Mystic Needles on her until she began to scream and cry. Then a revolt tore through the Chantry, unlike any revolt I had seen in recent years."

Valor slammed his fist through a vacant coffin lid. With his head filled with images of his friends tortured and dead, he bolted through the catacomb. "Where's the bloody exit? Mystic Ministry will suffer for this."

Duperie's chilling cough rang like a roomful of buzzards, a loud cackle that lifted Valor off the ground and snatched him back where he last stood. Shadows fluttered around him.

"But you *are* unevolved, McRaven. You are weak; can't you see? You will have no legend to strike from the tablets of time. I have. The evolved are heirs of Chacodophilus, which is why Sorcerers offer him reverence and lift him high."

Valor dodged the cackling shadows and tried to run again, but Duperie coughed out snakes, a hissing of shadows that slithered around Valor's ankles, binding his feet together.

"Let me go, Duperie! Mesthu didn't regard you as a legend from what I remember. Is that why you betrayed him, or do you prefer the stone coffins here?"

"I left Shadowhaven Heights because I am a living legend, McRaven. Legends are not complacent, but the Sorcerers, namely

Master Mesthu, had become thus. And, yes, I do like stone coffins. Can you believe the Sanguinati excavated their elite members and reburied the rest outside of Mystic Steeples?" Duperie filled an empty vial with blood spewing from a wall fountain constructed with bones. "Would you care for a drink, McRaven?"

Valor gazed at the vial Duperie shoved in front of his eager mouth until his intestines churned. "No," he said, forcing himself to look Duperie in the eyes and not at the tempting offer. "Why did they excavate the elite?"

"Why? Because after Chacodophilus's death, the vespercestors discover his body was not in his tomb," said Duperie. "They panicked, excavated all the corpses, and kept the elite on display. All the other dead, they reburied outside of Mystic Steeples. The vespercestors deemed the elite 'the Ancients' and wanted them kept on exhibit so the simple folks would see them as protectors. Or maybe the vespercestors wanted to make sure they could keep an eye on the corpses—make sure they didn't come back to life. Then, when *The Book of Chacodophilus* was reportedly found in the empty tomb, Fridline Sibyl went so far as to commission architectural wizards to secure Chacodophilus's tomb somewhere around 1703."

"Who found the book exactly, and what happened to it?" asked Valor to test Duperie. Valor wouldn't disclose that he had traveled back in time through the book and had seen much of its history. He remembered the spirits of the dead telling Chacodophilus that the only thing that would bring the legendary book to life would be a heart sacrifice from a person who didn't deserve to die. Chacodophilus vowed that before he would leave this world in death, he would sacrifice his own heart; that way, he alone could control the book from the beyond. But if Blade Zagato's *Progress Gauge Report* was accurate, then years ago, the Noctivatians had turned Blade's wife, Swarmi Diamone, into a vampire. Swarmi killed Valor's great-grandaunt, Battista McRaven, sacrificing Battista's heart, instead. And this replacement activated *The Book of Chacodophilus*. Worst of all, the Grim Warlock stole the book before Blade fled the underground city. If this were all true, then it seemed the Grim

Warlock might be more affiliated with the Noctivatians than the Sanguinati or Sorcerers. Did Janus Duperie, the self-titled "living legend" standing before Valor, know this?

"Who found the book? Ah, that question has been debated for years, McRaven," replied Duperie. "*The Book of Chacodophilus*—the physical copy itself—went through Noctivatian and Sanguinati hands, namely Head Vespercestor Cobbratz until somebody, thankfully, rescued the book from him. Nobody knows who has it now. Allegedly, some Sorcerer managed to conjure the spirit form of the book. Master Mesthu claimed the spirit form of the book was the only incorruptible version. But how can anybody prove anything invisible—anything only a few claimed to have seen—like corrupt leaders, who have used the invisible to assert their authority? Another reason I grew to distrust Mesthu."

"The current vespercestors have never acknowledged Chacodophilus or any missing book of his legend," said Valor, still unsure if he should trust Duperie.

"Precisely how history gets rewritten . . . a monarchy at a time," said Duperie, savoring the contents of the vial. "Now that you have lost friends, like I lost my girlfriend, Hertrand, you will see the betrayal of your own people."

"You blamed Doomsy and me for her death because you thought we led Falmoth and Banzalta to the tower. So why did you change allegiance to Falmoth and Banzalta right after that?"

Duperie's face pinched with bitterness. "I learned the truth. Bohemia killed my girlfriend. Master Mesthu could have stopped her earlier; he knew she had been a spy for O Enchantedness, but he was bewitched by her beauty. He also knew we wanted to leave the tower. You see, both Mesthu and O Enchantedness knew deception was occurring, and they did nothing about it. And the people under their rule don't care as long as they benefit, do they?" Duperie grinned as though he had triumphed with his point. "Monarchy and complacency of the unevolved."

"I don't care if I become a legend," said Valor. He pulled and wiggled his legs, trying to break free from the phantom serpents.

"Because of Falmoth I have a long way back to Severance and—and I just hope my friends are—"

Duperie grabbed Valor by his coat. "Falmoth brought you here so you can get revenge for your friends, McRaven. The Bound Order of the Zodiac is not something we can easily do battle with. Precisely why we'll put you through intense initiation—understand? You have no clue how to use Noctivatian powers, but you're going to learn. Everybody here has to learn. If you survive, you may just be on your path to becoming evolved."

"I don't care if I survive," said Valor. His head ached so much he could hardly think.

Duperie gave a grim smile and released the snake spell on Valor's feet. He clasped him in an aggressive hold and walked him out of the chamber past the window of amber. Valor looked back at the window: Arpad wasn't frozen in agony, and his flesh wasn't dead or burnt, which meant the sun was not shining through the resin, and the Noctivatians could safely go outside.

"Postpone your plans for revenge, for now, McRaven," said Duperie, as if knowing Valor was thinking of escaping. "You will not be leaving here until you are ready."

Disbelief and sadness numbed Valor while they moved through the catacombs where ivy had carpeted many of the neglected passages. They exited a mausoleum into a large clearing in the Tombstone Forest. Walls of enormous twisted vines now surrounded them like a prison cell. Sprites lounged in the holes of the vines, while imps carried sugared fruits through the latticed openings. A crowd of Noctivatians wearing horrible masks surrounded Valor and Duperie, while a roaring bone-fire lit up the night sky, revealing circling bats. The Noctivatians spread what appeared to be sheets of moist human skin over a wiggiwami's body as he reclined inside a coffin. The Noctivatians then covered the skins with a preparation of herbs or dirt; Valor wasn't sure.

"What was that . . . human flesh?" asked Valor, while three toddlers, which looked half human and half wiggiwami, chased each other around the bonfire, giggling.

"Yes. But we prefer to call it 'a perfection poultice,'" replied Duperie. "It begins the wiggiwamis' transformations . . . affects their metamorphosis into Noctivatians. Other transformations occur more naturally as when you became a Noctivatian, McRaven, or when Noctivatian women mate with wiggiwami men, like Widow Coren's two girls and boy playing over there."

"You mean that's Branwen Petrova's triplets," asked Valor. The last time he had seen the former magister was in Genevieve and Morty's cabin in Diabolishire. Branwen was pregnant then and in hiding, after the progress gauge had cut off her tongue for speaking bad things about Mystic Ministry.

"That they are," said Duperie.

Soon the transforming wiggiwami rose out of the coffin before writhing around on the ground. The crowd began to engage in similar lethargic movements as if stomping on insects. Others slapped animal-skin drums and made nocturnal animal calls, shaking skull rattlers, and stepping trancelike over crossed swords and leg bones on the ground.

"You must understand, McRaven, there are some Noctivatians Falmoth uses who were once wiggiwamis. After this ritual, he will lose his animal nature and his taste for meat and progress to only blood, before he will prepare to learn his craft, understand?" asked Duperie.

"Why are they holding animals over their heads?" asked Valor. He watched in horror at the vampires as they made strange creature noises with their mouths, held owls by their feet, and allowed them to peck the wiggiwami's head.

"They are syncing with their Familiars, and the Familiars are communicating with the initiate," said Duperie, plucking a sugared apple from Briny Cadabranathy's gaping mouth with his fangs.

"My casket's your casket, Duperie," said Briny Belfries, the widow of murdered Vespercestor Abner Cadabranathy. She put another sugared apple in her mouth and danced deeper into the gathering.

"Ghastly," said Valor. "It looks like their spreading ticks and mites." Had he made the worst mistake of his life by joining the

Noctivatians? What could he do now? If he tried to break from the Hermetic Order, he would surely die as well. "This is what some Noctivatians are—wiggiwamis?" asked Valor. He swallowed and tried to look calm.

Duperie pulled Valor farther away from the roaring fire. They found themselves amid two lines of women who were clutching their skirts, mirroring each other's movements as they slithered to the drum rhythms with small but lush willow trees cascading over their heads like hats.

"You're still thinking with your primitive brain," said Duperie. "We all require blood to grow in power. At the very least, Falmoth's candies will sustain us—precisely what you've been doing."

"So Noctivatians are of the same rank as the wiggiwamis?" Valor sighed, then jumped when an armadillo ran over his boots.

"Don't be alarmed. This is just my Familiar," said Duperie, picking the armadillo up by its hard shell. "His name's Dillan." He spoke to the animal in a babyish tone: "Calm down, Dillan. McRaven's not used to seeing Familiars participate in rituals. Those old vespercestors he's accustomed to don't permit it inside Mystic Steeples." Duperie put the armadillo on the ground, and it ran to inspect a piece of dropped candy. "But to answer your question: we're back to that greedy discussion of monarchies and ranks." Duperie blocked out the glow of the fire with his cape. "We're vampires if that term makes you feel any better."

Valor got a sick chill; he was a monster now. "Falmoth wants to overtake Mystic Steeples, so a dictatorship by him isn't a 'greedy rank' in your mind, I presume?" he asked.

Duperie shut his eyes and breathed hard, then lowered his voice to a whisper. "Whether anyone likes Falmoth's judgments or not, you know where you stand with him—even if he hates you. The primitives betrayed him, disfigured his face, and deprived his followers of crystals even though they had them in abundance—crystals that can save their lives."

The Noctivatians dismembered a life-sized figure of a man made of candy. Valor cringed and asked, "So, is this why the Sanguinati calls Noctivatian magic 'Grim magic' because the Familiars participate in their rituals?"

"Grim . . . dark . . . black," said Duperie. "Those terms came about because we do our rituals at night and for the symbolism, you see? The warlock priest inscribes a symbolic pattern on the ground like Sorcerers, who do Execration Rituals with images inscribed on the bottom of their shoes. The candy man they're ripping apart over there is symbolic of the vespercestorial forces they're up against. They are jinxing and breaking the vespercestors so they cannot harm others."

"And eating them," gasped Valor.

The Noctivatians bit into the candied pieces as if eating a shattered gingerbread man, while others wearing masks poured libations into skulls.

"Ha-ware-ye, McRaven?" asked Ratzy Pummels, dancing up to him, holding a piece of the candy man's elbow he had been chewing.

Valor scowled at Ratzy. He would enjoy shattering a candy replica of Mahrata at this moment, maybe even biting off her head . . . anybody's head, he feared.

"Okay," said Ratzy. "So basically it's, like, sweet and hard to chew, but ye're gonna hafta eat some." Ratzy offered him a bite of his candy, but as Valor declined, Orby Underkofler danced up to Valor and pushed him between the dancers all the way to the remnants of the candy man. Ratzy shoved his candy at them and said, "Valor coulda had some o' mine, okay? I didn't put no fang marks on it."

"McRaven, if you're in the Order, you have to take a bite at least. C'mon, McRaven, c'mon!" insisted Orby, forcing Valor's head down to a big gumdrop kneecap, which glistened with multicolored sprinkles. Valor imagined it was Mahrata LaRock and took a small but vengeful nibble—lemony: his favorite flavor.

"Whoa! You chewed up the foe like a pro. A few more bites and the foe will be no mo," said a costumed man bending over with a creepy mask on top of his head. When the man raised his head, Valor could see it was Venerious Falmoth with a python wrapped around his neck and two black panthers at his side. Falmoth stood up and twirled wands and bones in the air.

With his cape over his face, blocking the heat of the bone fire, Duperie came to stand beside Valor and Orby. He chewed off a chunk of the candy man and said, "Around the remains of the candy man, McRaven, you'll notice the foot-track magic. Those swords and bones are jinxed objects surrounding our foe. When walked over, they are activated, and summon an evolved wiggiwami to his mission."

"So, I'm not evolved, but that wiggiwamis is?" asked Valor. He wiped his sticky mouth on his coat sleeve. The whole ritual was animalistic. The Noctivatians began blowing whistles, and the wiggiwami ceased his convulsions and appeared to look right through the crowd with fearsome eyes rolled back into his head.

"For a wiggiwami, yes," replied Duperie. "But they are impracticable, see, and do not take orders from Noctivatians very well. But with the infusion ritual—once the exchange of our blood affects them—they will grow ears, be able to speak better, and acquire the proper diet of vampires. But they will not have powers as formidable as you or I, understand? We can access ancestor spirits and higher planes of existence."

The dancers stopped dancing as though a refreshing perfume had fragranced the air. Falmoth inched through the crowd with a blindfold over his eyes, holding his eyeball-ringed fingers out, searching his path toward the remnants of the candy man. He dropped to the ground like a dog and took the last bite of the candy foe—the pieces of a licorice boot, resting over candy crumbles. He spat out the chewed candy over a torch, held low by Ratzy, igniting the drawings on the ground all the way to the perimeter lined with moonflowers.

"Gather 'round, Children of the Gloaming. It is time for Valor McRaven to start his trainin'," Falmoth said to the Noctivatians who were moonbathing on the snowy ground like enraptured corpses under the blue moon. The wolves howled as if they were frightened of something sinister. Valor fidgeted, grasping for his wand, as the appalling vampires formed a large circle around him.

"I'll do the training," agreed Valor. "But please, can't I at least go check on my friends first? I just need to know they're okay."

Falmoth placed his gnarled fingers over his head and walked, doubled over, around a cauldron. His fingers slid down his face as he mused poetically: "I must bleakly say that day after day, Sanguinati dishonesty, masquerading as reality, is tainting all our hopes of rescuing anybody. And this is true. You must become twice as astute before you can seek retribution. But I'll see what I can do. So, for now, I must bid you toodle-oo," said Falmoth, waving goodbye to Valor, before a swarm of bats dove from the night sky and encircled him in a dense flurry. When the squeaking bats dispersed, Falmoth was nowhere in sight.

Humming a quiet melody, Duperie came from the circle while eating a Gooey Grape Gremlin. His armadillo followed behind him until they stood in front of Valor.

"Your first test will be working a True Name Spell, McRaven. We will begin with somebody you know, all right?" asked Duperie. He lifted his arm out toward the circle. A woman in a wombat mask and green velvet cloak came to the center and stepped in an iron cauldron. She lifted her mask, and her short graying curls dropped around her smiling cheekbones. The sockets of her eyes appeared hollow with black shadows around her grandmotherly face. It was Genevieve Sukles, the woman who helped Valor escape his parents in Diabolishire.

"Ms. Sukles! Oh, it's so good to see you," said Valor, feeling a little more hopeful, but it had been a while since he had last seen her. What was about to happen?

"Good to see you, sweetheart," said Genevieve. Her focus shifted with jerky head movements. "Now, don't you worry about hurting me. You just remember how I handled old Mike Busby and do your best."

What awful test would Duperie have him do to risk harming such a kind woman, Valor wondered? "Aw! I'll not risk hurting you, Ms. Sukles."

"Let's hope not," said Duperie. "You see? By learning to work this

True Name Spell on Genevieve, you'll, therefore, learn to control or free a person. You will need to employ mind control and hypnosis to alter her psyche, emotions—even her actions. Do you understand?"

"Aw! This is cruel to do to her. I won't," said Valor, licking his lips and crinkling his eyes.

"Oooh, hold on. I volunteered, and you will," said Genevieve, smiling. "This will make us all stronger and save your friends and mine." She pushed her cloak behind her shoulders, revealing her white-cotton skirt and black blouse before putting her mask back on and turning her back to him. Ratzy placed extra bones around the cauldron while Orby held a skull-headed staff to the ground and, out of its mouth, a powdery black line formed as he dragged the skull to the tip of Valor's boots.

Duperie whispered in Valor's ear, "Your first test is to make Genevieve say how old she is."

Valor took a breath of courage into his lungs and concentrated, willing Genevieve to state her age, but nothing happened. The powdered line ignited and began to burn toward the cauldron. Using his mind, Duperie urged Valor to press forward and sway her to do his will.

Say your age . . . , Valor thought, as the fire ignited the bones and began to rise up the sides of the cauldron. Genevieve began to squirm after two more minutes and whimper through her mask. Valor knocked his knuckles together under his chin. *Genevieve Sukles, I command you to state your age!*

"I'm sixty-two-plus!" she yelled, and the flames vanished, but not before she collapsed over the edge of the cauldron and onto the ground.

Valor ran toward Genevieve. "Are you hurt, Ms. Sukles?" He held her large bony hand, while her boyfriend, Morty Hestia, ran to her side and placed his healing cerebrabones on her legs and head.

"Oh now, Nutmeg," Genevieve called Morty in her breathy, raspy voice. She brushed a cerebrabone off her head. "I'm as fit as a fipinfeter."

Duperie pulled off Genevieve's mask, and she opened her eyes with dizzy blinks while steam radiated off her legs.

"I don't need any healing," she groaned and sputtered. "But I will need some cookies iced with promise—lots of promise."

"Let me be the mojo cavy," said Morty, while the jumbies around the clearing engaged in puppetry fun with the jaws from animal skulls.

"I will not," snorted Genevieve, knocking the cerebrabones off her legs and stomping to her feet. "Pretty good for a beginner, Valor." She pinched his cheek while panting. "Now, True Name mastery is going to get harder because you'll be dealing with spirits of the Bound Order of the Zodiac. So, you'll have to build you up some necromantic skills."

"Necromancy?" asked Valor, feeling as though a cold blanket of dread had enfolded him.

Duperie held up three fingers and said, "Will manipulation, illusion diffusion, and knowledge extraction. Things your shadow cannot control with sorcery alone, understand?"

Valor gave a skeptical nod, but he would rather someone else serve as the magic test target or "mojo cavy" as the Noctivatians called it.

Duperie scoped out the area for any eavesdroppers and said, "You just had a taste of will manipulation but not on a spirit being, understand? Ghosts are on another plane and can drive you insane— affect your emotions, reverse your spell command to manipulate you. They are tricksters, so you must learn to discern reality from illusions. The moment when you peel back these ethereal layers, you can begin to uncover their secrets." Duperie motioned Valor away from Genevieve as she pulled her mask back over her face. "Now, when you use True Name Spells on spirits, you can speak out loud, but we don't want Genevieve to hear, because you are practicing, understand?"

"I see."

"I hope so," said Duperie, "because the repercussions will be on you now, see?" Duperie and Orby tied Valor to a tall pole with many gauzy ribbons streaming down from its skull-tipped top. The ribbons draped over the ground and attached to more skulls, which the

Noctivatians grabbed before reforming in a circle around the pole. "This is a Maypole of Madness, McRaven, and unless you mentally will Genevieve to cluck like a chicken and peck the boots of four Children of the Gloaming, we will enshroud you with these mummy wrappings hanging down the pole." Duperie tugged a ribbon for emphasis. "This grim gauze is from a warlock who died from dementia, understand?"

Valor's hair fell over his face as his head rolled against the pole. How had he become trapped in this nightmare? He didn't like manipulating people, but why couldn't he move past this? People manipulate others all the time, just not with mental commands. Accordions began whining, and drums started pounding as the Noctivatians held their skulls and began to dance around the pole screaming, "Soon, soon . . . ," while the others sang a spirited song:

> *"Maypole towering with ribbons loose,*
> *Let folly befall Valor as we weave a hangman's noose.*
> *As lunacy lilies bloom, we'll spread death's dark petals under the moon.*
> *Soon, soon, madness shall enshroud him in this untimely tomb."*

Valor's head ached, trying to will Genevieve to cluck like a chicken and peck at the dancers' boots as they wove their ribbons of gauze farther down the pole, screaming the song full of rage.

Genevieve, you must cluck like a chicken; I command you! Valor mentally ordered her again. The gauze coiled over his eyes and then his nose. He resisted sneezing on the dusty scent of death. *Genevieve, imitate a chicken!*

Only a hacking cough, not a chicken clucking, resonated over the maddening noise of the ritual until the ribbons of gauze thickened down Valor's body, suffocating him, locking him to the pole until he felt like a mummy.

Valor awoke to something fuzzy wiggling over his eyes: a black bat with a wire cage over its face and gnashing teeth.

"Ugh," hollered Valor, jumping off the coffin lid. "Why were you holding a b-bat on my face?" he asked Briny Belfries Cadabranathy.

Briny glided away from him, eased the bat in a cage, then made a note in her grimoire. Her appearance seemed darker and more organic now, with knitted rosettes and other odd material on her dress and in her untamed hair.

"Trying to cure your madness," replied Briny. She inspected Valor with her golden-yellow eyes, and then pulled her black-lace shawl over her shoulders and sat in a chair beside the coffin. The black-painted room had an assortment of glass jars full of blood, some with peppermints floating in them.

"Tell me your name again and where you were born," she asked, holding an ink-tipped bone over a page of her grimoire. Above their heads swung skeleton arms, clutching bouquets of dried herbs and flowers, while a hooded man with a broad ax stood guard by the door.

"You must be mad, my dear. I know who I am, but you've obviously forgotten," answered Valor. He looked down at his arms, now covered in scratches and scabs. Necklaces with amber amulets rattled around his neck.

"We had to put those charms on you to protect you from yourself—the nightmares you called them—the hexes you accused us of putting on you," said Briny. "But tell me who you are just for our records?"

"I'm Valor Ulysses McRaven, and I was born in Mystic Steeples, in Severance, Hoopenfangia," he lisped, as he spat out brittle pieces of a translucent amber stone, which he must have chewed at some point during his recovery.

"You thought your name was Thoth; at least that's what you kept mumbling. After two whole weeks, we have cured your madness," said Briny, though her frown remained the same. "Two weeks spent on you in which you now owe me."

"Two weeks? You mean I've spent two weeks here with rodents on my face because of the stupid maypole test you all subjected me to?"

growled Valor. "I could've been looking for my friends!" He spun through the room until the hooded guard raised his ax, and Valor calmed himself.

"You owe me," continued Briny. "I am seeking my husband's killer, and the scrying bones told me you know something about his murder."

"The killer was wearing a hooded cloak like the man over there. My friends and I saw nothing of his face," said Valor pointing at the guard. "If everything I saw is to be trusted, he killed Abner because he refused to obey Urbanne LaRock—refused to do something awful."

"He wanted my Abner to do what?" asked Briny.

"Urbanne LaRock wanted Abner to make Kingston Crowley unable to have a Seventh Son using some toxin in his Wormwood Philters potions," said Valor. "And Abner wouldn't do it."

"But Urbanne seemed happy when baby Thiolahfuh was born," said Briny. "What else did you see? Are you sure you don't know who murdered him?"

"No. The killer just pressed a box over Abner's face, cast a spell, and then—then put him in the swamp." Valor didn't wish to tell her about the death mask they had found with Abner's *Progress Gauge Report*. Could he trust her with this information?

"You should have told me sooner." Briny scowled. "I have the power to make you very ill, you know?"

"If it helps any, Urbanne, the one who ordered the execution of Abner, was murdered—avenged for killing Mesthu Marsh," said Valor, as she scowled at him.

"Nobody can be trusted," said Briny. "But we have to get along regardless. Guard, take Valor to Janus Duperie. Valor will be expected to continue his training as soon as possible."

Two nights later, Valor had completed his True Name Spells. He successfully conjured up a spirit in the Tombstone Forrest and forced him to reveal his secrets, which amounted to little except that, when the spirit had once been a living boy, he had wet his bed until the age of twelve. The boy's schoolmates had also made fun of him for having a potbelly, so the boy confessed he later got caught wearing his granny's corset to try to slim his waist.

"No need to be embarrassed," Valor had told the ghost boy. "I once went all over Stonevengeance Mountain, collecting animal droppings in a lunch basket for my father to use as fertilizer for his garden because the soil was cursed. So, see, if you had been in Stonevengeance, you could've just peed . . . on . . . everything." Valor's throat locked. The ghost seemed to feel the Noctivatians' amused expressions. Valor tried to offer a comforting pat on the boy's elbow, but his hand had passed through him, and the boy had vanished.

Duperie squeezed his eyes shut, exhaling with a grunt. "McRaven, please tell me you won't be so tenderhearted with the Bound Order of the Zodiac. Of course, you could always embarrass them to death."

The licorice lanterns in the trees illuminated the Noctivatians' faces as they sniggered and laughed. Valor moved a bit lighter now. Would the spell work on the Bound Order of the Zodiac, the Star Beings that had snatched Aaron out of Convocation? At times, the Noctivatians in the circle around him appeared as his beloved Candlewicke Coven. Had he been gone so long that a coven of vampires reminded him of his true friends? Valor had to leave and find Doomsy, Aaron, and the others before he lost touch with reality.

"So, t'at's like da funniest True Name Spell I ever saw," said Ratzy, rattling his head.

Clenching his fists, Valor blew at the forest leaves around Ratzy's feet, sending them curling over him like an ocean wave.

Banzalta Drayn, Falmoth's bald partner and co-ruler, prowled from the circle's perimeter, cradling an active hornet's nest as though it was a nest of baby birds. Her presence silenced everyone as she convulsed in her stride toward Valor and Duperie. The bottom of her dress so tattered and trailing, she appeared to be rising from cracks in the earth beneath her. She lifted her animal horn and puffed out a vibrating roar through the curved antler. Within a minute, a sphinx emerged from the dark forest. Three panthers growled at the catlike sphinx before it came to a stop inside the circle of Noctivatians. The sphinx's white with black spots covered its curvy but muscular body, but not its humanlike head, beautiful and soft, like the head of a young woman.

"Grrr. I hearrr the mission hornnn. I smell the aroma of justice," growled the sphinx.

"Justice?" mocked a female Noctivatian before howling with laughter, sending chills over Valor. "The Ancients can no longer play the game of chance unless they do it with sphinxes and sympathetic shadow tossers like Valor McRaven."

"Silence," ordered Duperie, while Banzalta clawed and wiggled back to the circle of vampires, eyeing them with her usual anguished expression. Valor couldn't believe the swarming hornets had not attacked the Noctivatians.

"McRaven, your next skill to learn is shapeshifting," said Duperie with a doubtful smile. "Whatever nocturnal creature you've found a connection with, you can shift into it. For me, of course, my armadillo, Dillan." Duperie glanced down at his Familiar, which clung near his feet in its ridged shell. "We activate the change by saying, 'I shall go into an armadillo or whatever.'"

Duperie fell to the ground and appeared as an armadillo. Dillan sniffed him first then played pat-a-cake with him until Duperie returned to his true form. "See?" he asked. "With practice, we can transform all or parts of our bodies into bats, nocturnal insects, snakes, hellhounds, even other human forms. You can even shift another person into the same animal as you by touching them when you say the command."

"Okay, watch us change, and I'll name 'em off," said Ratzy. He pointed at Orby Underkofler and went counterclockwise around the circle, naming off the various animals, which signaled for the Noctivatians to change form. Ratzy changed his appearance last, but Banzalta had not changed her appearance, along with two others who had attended his training. Was it true? Could Banzalta and other Noctivatians with wiggiwami DNA not perform magic? Was this why many of them relied on enchanted weapons?

Duperie positioned Valor in front of the sphinx that Banzalta had conjured. "If you fail this challenge," he warned, "the sphinx will attack you."

Valor froze. "Don't I get to practice first?"

The sphinx's oval pupils dilated as it glared at him. Valor tried to think of a nocturnal creature but couldn't think of any he had ever come close to feeling a connection. Two things he hated were snakes and spiders, so those were out of the question.

"You'll learn fast this way, see? Because we often need to change form when under surprise attack. Now, give us something—change, McRaven—understand?" asked Duperie. "Give us something other than a shadow mass the Sorcerers sadly depend on all too readily. Now!"

"I, um—I shall go into a griffin," said Valor. He loved his Elusive Griffin, Booger Fay, more than any other animal.

The sphinx lunged on Valor, digging its front claws deep into his chest. "Oooh!" Valor cried. The creature lept over Valor's face and hands. Its human skin smelled like perfume, and its lion fur stank. Duperie called the sphinx back to his side.

"A griffin isn't nocturnal, McRaven. You didn't change. Now try again."

Valor pushed against the ground, trying to stand on his feet.

"Now!" commanded Duperie, releasing the sphinx.

"I . . . go in a cougar," stammered Valor. This time the claws of the sphinx slapped into his legs and arms, while its teeth sank into the side of his head.

"Back away, Sphinx!" ordered Duperie. He threw a bone six yards away, and the sphinx lunged after it. The Children of the Gloaming drooled at Valor while leaves and debris stuck to his bloody clothes and skin. Did pale blood trigger their thirst as well?

"You either have no affinity toward a cougar, or you need to visualize harder, McRaven," huffed Duperie. "Visualize yourself becoming the animal, breathing its breath, thinking its thoughts. Now stand up and try again."

Valor whimpered and wiped the blood from his eyelids. His body burned from the deep scratches as he stood up, wobbling.

"Now on the count of six, shift. Two, four, six," counted Duperie.

The Noctivatians watched in disbelief as Valor turned himself into a webbed toed, bushy-tailed, mink. The sphinx leaped high in the air and squashed him in its razor-sharp paws, sending tufts of shiny brown fur floating to the forest floor.

Valor's body cycled from achy to numb. His stiff arm reached up, trying to feel anything in the blackness. Was he in a nightmare, trapped in outer space for eternity, or had he died? His fingertips grazed a padded barrier, and it moved. He was in a coffin again. For the first time, the softest candlelight in the room seemed like harsh sunshine to his eyes. He sat up with the lid ajar, squinting at a room lined with skulls. He inspected the ceiling paneled with spirit boards and a curtain of vulture wings over what seemed to be a stone window.

Orby Underkofler jolted up from a chair, dropping the enchanted tool he had been twiddling with his fingers. His broad young face docile and lost as usual. The energy around him blew long strands of his hair across his white shirt and dark-velvet vest.

"McRaven, you nutty plonker. What made you think shifting into a mink could give you power over a sphinx, huh? Look, I don't know what Falmoth saw in you, but you ain't gonna survive unless you get mean. I'm telling you, MEAN!"

Valor shivered, clutching his arms around his tender ribcage. A tuft of loose mink fur fell off his elbow. "Duperie told me to turn into a nocturnal animal I could relate to," said Valor. "When I was little, Grandmother McRaven had a mink stole she always put over me when I took naps at her home. He should've told me it had to be an animal stronger than a sphinx."

Orby picked up a contraption resembling a boomerang, and both ends of it grew smaller offshoots.

"Falmoth shouldn't've left Duperie in charge of you, McRaven. If you want the truth, Duperie probably placed a bet that you wouldn't beat the sphinx."

Valor stiffened with shock. "You mean he used me as a betting dragon?"

"You gotta lot to learn, McRaven, but I like you," said Orby, flinging the boomerang contraption, and it spun in suspended animation before separating into three parts. "I remember when your friends captured me and Ratzy; you didn't want them to hurt us, I could tell. I'm gonna give you some tips. My brother was a guardian at Mystic Steeples. You remember Iliad Underkofler?"

"Yes. Sorry about what happened to him," said Valor, hoping Orby wouldn't blame him for his death.

"Iliad was a pushover like you," said Orby. "Like the rest of my family, he never got an apprenticeship. We didn't have money like you do—like half of the Sanguinati who get those high positions. They treated us like dirt, McRaven—like dirt. I wanted us to leave Mystic City, but my parents had dreams for us to be somebody."

Orby gave a timid smile and peeped out the door to see if anyone was near the room, then eased the door shut.

"My family don't know I hooked up with the Hermetic Order of the Mystic Key, all right, McRaven?" He took another long gulp from a stone goblet and licked his reddening lips. "I just know my father will say 'I toldja so, Orby,' if anything happens to me now that I'm Noctivatian. But not Iliad. No, Iliad could do no wrong since he kissed up to the vespercestors to get where he was, which doesn't say a lot." Orby grabbed the floating contraption, and the smaller pieces reattached to it. "I can figure out how enchanted weapons work just by touching them, McRaven. I can make people say anything I want them to, as well, so I found out my brother was part of something terrible before he died."

"Was he part of the Hermetic Order, too?" asked Valor.

"Noooo," replied Orby, looking as if he had tasted something sour. "D'ya know *why* the vespercestors haven't released Death, the sixth in the Bound Order of the Zodiac Hexagram?"

Valor raised his shoulders and made a guess: "I imagine they're saving the sixth Being for some awful time at the end of the Thirteenth Hour—the Vespercestors' Verdict perhaps—to punish those who oppose Mahrata."

Again, Orby checked to see if anyone lingered outside the room, then he sat on the edge of the coffin beside him. "That could be their plan, but my brother admitted the sixth Zodiac corpse in the front Atrium was a fake—it's not Death's body, McRaven. Before the Possessing killed Iliad, he said the vespercestors admitted they should never have tried to harness such a dangerous star monster inside Mystic Steeples."

"What do you mean? Do they have the sixth Zodiac Being or not?" asked Valor. He peeled back a bandage on his arm. The claw marks were healing fast.

"I got Iliad to confess what he and the other guardians were doing in the room under the choir loft in Mystic Chantry, McRaven. He told me that room lay over a hidden room, and every day the guardians inject Death with Squibthistle tree-frog poison to sedate it."

"Oh, so that's what we saw in the Shrine of Chacodophilus," admitted Valor.

"The Shrine of Chacodophilus? You've seen such a place?" asked Orby.

"That we did," said Valor. "My friends and I found it in the Necromanceropolis. The *Braggadocio* is directly over it as well."

"*The Tablet of Sanguinati Successes*? Hmmm." Orby stood up and grabbed Valor's shoulders. "So, you saw Death, then?"

"We saw a creature in a crystal capsule thing. Oh, it was too awful to describe."

"Must be *it* then, McRaven! Iliad said the guardians are keeping Death on artificial respiration in a vacuum-sealed, plasma pressurized iron lung."

"You mean they keep that thing sedated, then try to resuscitate it?" asked Valor, cocking his head. "That's rather daft."

"I know," said Orby. "The vespercestors realize they should've never tried to contain such an unstable monster. They're now forced to care for Death since they have to keep it sedated. They have to record accurate measurements of everything they feed it, everything it does."

Valor braced his hand on the back of his head, visualizing all manner of horrible things. "Why don't they just let Death die?"

"Ah, now you see the problem," said Orby without blinking. "It'd upset the balance of the entire Zodiac if they killed it. Can you just imagine the heavens erupting, McRaven?" Orby made a grim face. "They may have harnessed Death somehow—bound him on this planet—but the guardians have to take shifts just so they can increase and decrease the iron lung's pressure using pistons and tubes."

"So, they do this from the hidden room under the choir loft?" asked Valor.

"Every day." Orby nodded grimly. "That Zodiac monster requires a certain amount of luminiferous aether and hydrogen and helium atoms to keep its nuclear fusion from going out." He swallowed.

Valor exhaled deeply. "All this time, this has been going on under the choir loft? Unbelievable." Valor wondered: did the Grim Warlock possess and kill Orby's brother and Helios Hollapolk to keep the two guardians from sedating Death?

"Sometimes that helium gas escapes, McRaven. I've actually seen gas escape up between the choir benches, kinda like I've been seeing pulsing energy escaping between the fingers in the giant hand at the Palm Readers' Palace."

"No wonder the choir gets loopy sometimes." Valor laughed. "I assumed Preston Fox had acquired an unusual number of soprano singers."

They both sang in mousy voices, before the door swung open, plugging the knob into a skull's mouth on the wall.

"McRaven has finally recovered, and you two are in here singing?" asked Janus Duperie.

"Uh, yeah, Jay," said Orby. "Just testing McRaven's voice; he still sounded a little like a mink, but I think he's okay now."

"Has Falmoth returned? Oh, I have to know if my friends are all right." Valor asked.

"No, he hasn't returned," replied Duperie, motioning with his finger. "Come along then. You still haven't mastered shapeshifting."

With the moon overhead, they returned to the forest. Banzalta conjured the sphinx once more. This time, Valor would get revenge on Duperie for not being honest with him, and more so, he wasn't going to let the sphinx attack him again. Duperie gave the signal.

Valor held his breath and said, "I will go into a lion."

Dropping to his hands and feet, Valor saw claws emerge from his fingertips and golden hair growing on his skin. He roared at the sphinx as it charged at him, but the sphinx retreated before Valor could dig his front claws into the creature. Duperie fell backward on his hands with one fang over his bottom lip and a jagged row of creases over his widened eyes.

"Enough!" cried Duperie, and Valor shifted back to his own body. "You—from a mink to a lion—how?"

Many of the Noctivatians cheered, and Valor smiled. The sphinx hadn't injured him, except for a raised bump on his wrist, which he tried to conceal with his coat sleeve.

"What are you hiding there, McRaven?" asked Duperie, grabbing Valor's arm and sliding his sleeve back.

"Oh, just an old scab from the last shifting."

"It's no scab," said Duperie. "You have received the mark of the undead."

Valor's arm recoiled. "The mark of the what?"

"The mark of the undead, see? It is your warlock's teat . . . what Nizzertits call a third nipple," said Duperie. Everyone cackled.

"That's our Valor. He's quite a man now!" laughed Vanitas Moriendi, running her long fingernails over her sharp widow's peak.

Duperie tweaked the teat until a spot of blood dribbled onto Valor's wrist.

"It's nearly ripe, though the mark is usually in a hidden area. This is a sign, see? You should be on the lookout. Your nocturnal Familiar's about to claim you, McRaven. And when you meet your Familiar, you must feed it blood from this teat."

"Aw, I already have a Familiar. I don't need another one," said Valor. Though he tried to keep a confident posture, his bottom lip pulled down in a side pout when he spoke of things that made him unhappy.

Duperie flung his cape over his shoulder, revealing his armadillo at his feet. "You may have no choice, McRaven. All Noctivatians thrive with a nocturnal Familiar. They warn of danger and let us know when the sun is up, understand? Besides, if your other Familiar were of any use, it would be here with you now. Do not be quick to judge when your Familiar finds you. Whether a bird of the air or creature of the water, its size does not indicate its power. A potent Familiar can often be the smallest of insects. Its revealing will be uncanny. Take my Dillan here." Duperie patted his boot on his armadillo's back. "He came up to me in the dead of winter two-plus times and sat on my boot."

"But seeing a nocturnal animal is not the receiving, understand?" said Duperie, keeping his head low, filtering his gaze through his bushy eyebrows. "You may not become aware of your Familiar until prolonged periods of hibernation where your spirits unite on the threshold of consciousness when your body is on the border of blood dehydration."

"I got my Booger Fay just by reading about his species in a book."

Valor wanted to be back at Candlewicke with his friends and his own Familiar. With each passing day, the reminders of death strangled him, but the Children of the Gloaming celebrated these things. Even as he tried to conceal the unwanted mark on his wrist, Ratzy, Orby, and two other Noctivatians carried a coffin on their shoulders and placed it on a stand beside him. The wiggiwamis prowled in the bushes, watching the ritual with eyes of fascination, in particular, the one that had recently become a Noctivatian. Was this the Noctivatians' goal, to make the wiggiwamis look and speak more like humans with each passing night?

"You get what you offer, McRaven," said Duperie. "And now, with the morning sun on the horizon, we have come to a most detrimental challenge . . . Channeling. You see, in the coming days, the Hermetic Order will begin attempts to invade the vespercestors' minds and control them. We channel the living." Duperie placed a grim doll in Valor's hand. "You'll learn to gather your own materials for these dolls, but just know . . . that's the easy part. This particular doll contains articles of hair and clothing from Mahrata LaRock. You'll take her effigy with you in your coffin when you sleep, and this will allow you to channel her." He lifted the lid and motioned for Valor to climb inside the coffin.

Valor looked back over his shoulder for affirmation before climbing in, and when he had reclined his head on the little bone pillow, Duperie positioned the grim doll on his abdomen. His curly dark hair blew over his drooping mustache before shutting the lid.

"I am now placing a quill and scroll on the coffin lid," continued Duperie. "Before the sun goes down tonight, you must enter a cataleptic state, keeping Mahrata's effigy over your solar plexus at all times. Call Mahrata LaRock's name until you fall asleep, understand?"

"Call her name until I fall asleep," Valor reminded himself. But was Duperie placing another bet on him?

"Good. This will allow you to summon her spirit," said Duperie. "When the conjuring happens, your spirit must ask her spirit what her plans are with the Vespercestors' Verdict. Have her write her answers on the scroll, understand?"

"Yes," said Valor.

"You must stay in your coffin and not let her spirit see you or know who you are. Neither must she know where she is," warned Duperie. "Children of the Gloaming, return to your coffin chamber. The sun will rise soon."

The clanking sounds of drums, skull rattlers, and other ritual tools faded after a few minutes, assuring Valor he was now alone in the forest clearing. His heart raced, feeling vulnerable in a box in the middle of the wild. What would happen if the wiggiwamis took off with him, or a dragon, or ogre, or any number of the wild beasts? And what did Duperie mean by Valor's most detrimental challenge? Only death could be worse than what he had already endured.

When he got his mind to relax, he had grown sleepy. He had better start calling out to Mahrata before he lost consciousness.

"Mahrata LaRock, I conjure your spirit to me. Come to me, Mahrata LaRock."

After a few minutes of sensing nothing, he repeated the command louder and louder, but it was not enough to keep his heavy eyelids from closing. He jumped with a start when something bumped against his coffin.

"Who's there?"

He forgot to keep the grim doll over his solar plexus, and the coffin lid flung open with a snap. He covered his eyes, expecting the sunlight to beam down on him, but soothing night air and fog poured over him. Duperie appeared between the coffin slats, holding the scroll and pen with a strange look on his face. The Noctivatians gathered around the coffin with similar expressions.

"What's wrong? Why is everyone looking at me like that?" asked Valor.

"I think you had better step out of the coffin," insisted Duperie. Orby looked at Valor with a frightened expression.

"Why? What have I done?" Valor planted his boots on the ground, accidentally dropping the grim doll.

"I have some terrible news, McRaven," answered Duperie. "Very bad news, indeed."

Valor's tongue passed under his top lip then over his bottom lip with a swipe. He gazed with sleepy eyes between the scroll and Duperie's face, expecting everyone to pounce on him.

"You are not aware? You made contact with Mahrata last day," said Duperie, tapping his temple with his finger. "Maybe I should just read Mahrata's message." Duperie held the scroll and cleared his throat. "My Vespercestors' Verdict has already begun and will show its might. At my command, the guardians have executed the ringleader of rebellion, Aaron Hutton. They are retaining the Coven of Candlewicke until I decide if there are any more appropriate verdicts for these rebels who threaten to undermine my rule. My rule, the way the Ancients have always intended."

Genevieve Sukles approached Valor with outstretched arms and a sympathetic gaze, but a volcano of emotions threatened to erupt from the core of Valor's entire being. He pushed past her, broke through the circle of Noctivatians, and headed for the forest.

"Grrr," growled a wiggiwami, grabbing Valor by his chest, before it began dragging him back to the circle.

"Get your dirty hands off me!" Valor shouted and kicked.

"Let him go, Tohsha," Duperie said to the wiggiwami. "Let him go."

Valor jumped out of Tohsha's arms and sped into the dark woods. The Tombstone Forest echoed with laughter as he passed a coffin boat filled with blood. Owls perched on its edges, turning their heads from their red reflections. For a long way, the slapping tree limbs swabbed Valor's tears before he collapsed against the rough bark of a porky-pine tree.

"I'll kill you, Mahrata, if it's the last thing I do!" Valor swore. His fingers dug into the pine bark, ripping out chunks in his anguish. He could never find the Noctivatians' portal in the darkness, so he proceeded to leave Bogamuckla the way he knew best—the long way. He floated straight up through the trees, snapping any limbs in his way. Something massive caught him in midair and squeezed its giant fingers around him.

"Mama?" said the giant, Sweeturnips, lifting Valor in front of his face, which the overhead moon illuminated in all its frightening detail.

"No, it's me, Valor; the boy who rescued you from the ice hole. Now, kindly unhand me."

The giant lowered Valor to the ground. "Mama?" he roared again.

"No, I'm not your mother. Your mother was Ambergis LaRock. She's dead."

"Momma . . . dead?" The giant collapsed on the ground, squashing a tree. He then covered his eyes and sobbed.

"I'm sorry," said Valor. In his rage, he had been insensitive. He had said too much.

Sweeturnips lowered his hand and looked at the tears pooling in his palm. Tingles prickled the back of Valor's neck and head. He looked at the giant's palm and remembered Creighton's prophecy: "One with the longest lifeline . . . half-born from an earthbound spirit . . . can shake the hand that holds the staff." What if the prophecy didn't mean someone who had lived the longest but, it meant someone with the lengthiest lifeline in measurement?

The tingles travel down Valor's spine now. The giant wasn't fully born from his mother. Banzalta's curse had caused baby Sweeturnips to grow so fast in Ambergis's stomach, Sweeturnips had ripped her in half. Ambergis died shortly after this and became an earthbound spirit. If this were so, then Sweeturnips needed to shake the hand that held the Staff of Gleaning. But who had a hand big enough for Sweeturnips to shake? Suddenly, Valor got a vision of the giant hand in front of Palm Readers' Palace and remembered Orby mentioning the pulsing energy escaping between its fingers.

"Say! I need a favor," said Valor. "I know a hand as big as yours, and I need you to shake it."

The giant stopped crying at looked down at Valor with enlarged eyes.

"Yes, it's in a city where I've seen your mother's spirit wandering around. Who knows, you might get to meet her while you're there."

Sweeturnips stood up and said, "Mama?"

Valor pointed toward the region of Severance, and the giant picked him up and put him on top of his head. Valor held on to a patch of his hair as Sweeturnips took off running toward Mystic City. With Valor directing the way, they soon crossed over the Ambergis Divide on the outskirts of Diabolishire.

After miles, the landscape of snow-capped mountains changed. Cypress trees, dead and silvery from their sun-bleached years, dripped with mopey moss. Below them, the familiar sight of rippled swamps, riddled with blackened algae, seemed to strangle the patches of whipping podgrass and kittentails. Reptiles slithered under canopies of willows, waiting for snowy egrets or a falling witch to stir the marsh.

At last, Valor saw the Bound Order of the Zodiac protecting the sky above Mystic City, and the guardians defending the entries to the Sanguinati kingdom. He paused the giant by a tree at the west Riverwalk entry to Mystic City and waited for a cargo carriage to gain access into the city, which took over an hour. While the guardians checked the driver's identity and freight, Valor shapeshifted into a mink, and just as Duperie had said, the giant also tuned into a mink, because Valor had been touching him when he said the command.

They scurried beneath the carriage wheels, past the guardians, and under the centaurs' hooves, before they scuttled down Crumrod Crawl and hid in the shadowy entry of a closed gift store. Upon entering the Crescent Moon district, Valor's repressed anxiety began swelling. As much as he wanted to check on his friends, he first needed to get Sweeturnips to the Palm Readers' Palace and rescue the Staff of Gleaning to stop the Possessing—if Mahrata hadn't killed Aaron already.

The usual vapors hung on the soft breeze while Valor and Sweeturnips darted in and out of shadows in their mink bodies still. Lush ivy, once contained in sculpted designs, now strangled the ancient brick walls. The snapping of centaur hooves on the cobblestone alleys, and the crackling sparks from the patrolling Zodiac, kept time with the intense rhythm of Valor's heart. Sweeturnips drank from the rainwater accumulating in the cragged architecture, dripping out of stone holes as if weeping now. Courtyard walls, concealing bygone mysteries, disappeared behind them, as they interweaved between magic shops and vile dens. Finally, they had reached the Palm Readers' Palace. When no one was looking, Valor touched Sweeturnips with his little paw, and they shifted back to their natural forms.

"This is it," said Valor looking straight ahead at the giant fist of stone that served as the entry into the towering palace. "Go ahead, Sweeturnips, try to shake hands with . . . the hand."

Valor pointed at the fist and simulated a handshake. If the Staff was hidden somewhere inside the palace, he would have to resume his mink form to avoid detection.

Sweeturnips held out his massive hand and chopped into the stone hand, causing a crack to form across three of its fingers.

"No, shake the hand; don't chop it," said Valor.

"Shake?" grunted the giant.

"Yes, 'shake'"

A sinking feeling made Valor weak in the knees when Sweeturnips brought both hands down on the stone fist using his full body weight. He shook the whole stone entry until the entire hand crumbled. After the dust and rubble settled, a shiny metallic staff covered in jewels lay at Valor's feet. But above his head, a Zodiac being came swooping down toward them.

"Run back home, Sweeturnips!" said Valor, grabbing the Staff and dashing toward Spookum Alley, where the gas-lit signs and flickering lamps faded into darkness, offering him safety. With a swarm of bats, owls, and insects chasing him, Valor ran up to the doors of Candlewicke Mansion, but someone had nailed large boards over the entrance, blocking any access. The sign on the door read, "Vacant pending Vespercestors' Verdict."

"No! No, they can't do this!" wheezed Valor, getting bugs in his mouth. The magic Staff was somehow upsetting the animals in the area. When no eyes were on him, he floated up to a second-story balcony, broke the glass to a window, and entered the room. Dried blood on the picture frames added color to the sepia-toned photos on the table. He ran through the mansion calling his friends, but nobody answered except a man's wicked voice, which seemed to come from the walls around him:

"Argh! You think you are so clever, Knight of Night. You think you have suffered loss? You will beg for the days to be as kind as when your only loss was your twin, your grandmother, and Creighton."

The grand hall seemed like a faded memory now, as lunatic ghosts came at Valor, brushing against every surface, tainting them. In Doomsy's bedroom, her poppet doll lay under a toppled nightstand. Valor's heart sank even lower. He held the doll to his nose to smell her scent. Why were the initials C.C.H stamped on the back of the doll's leg? Why hadn't he paid more attention to her—to these important things?

Ambergis's spirit cackled, sending shocks over every one of Valor's nerve endings. He wrapped the Staff of Gleaning in one of Doomsy's lace veils and charged out of the mansion, down the alley, and through the scorched remains of Bootjack Square straight for Mystic Steeples. He would punish Mahrata for Aaron's murder. But he feared that, if he did, all his friends might die . . . if they were still alive. Rounding the corner of Skullhead Street, someone grabbed Valor and pulled him into one of the dim, iron-gated alcoves of Bootjack Square.

"There you are, McRaven," said Orby Underkofler.

"Let go of me. I've got things I have to do!" demanded Valor, pulling free from Orby's grip.

"What do you have wrapped up there?" asked Orby.

"A weapon—to kill Mahrata," hissed Valor.

"Listen here, you bampot. I tried to tell you before you ran away. But the scroll Duperie read to you—pure rubbish. I suspected he was up to something when I heard him mumbling angrily about the Knight of Night being a big joke. I knew he was going on about you, so I snuck out of the catacombs and caught him, or somebody, beside your coffin. They were hiding under a cloak. He wrote that stuff on the scroll, not Mahrata; I watched him, McRaven."

Valor's heart raced with promise, so much so, he didn't consider being angry with Duperie. "Aw, why would he do such an awful thing to me?"

"Duh," spat Orby. "Duperie wants Mahrata dead. I think he wanted to make you angry enough to do the job for the Hermetic Order. But it doesn't guarantee Mahrata didn't do anything to your friends, though."

"No," sighed Valor. "The Bound Order took Aaron—I know— and I'm sure Mystic Ministry has my sister, also. I just came from Candlewicke; it was boarded up, and nobody was there. Something awful happened, though."

"I know Duperie's been hard on you. But you need to return to the Order. Don't tell anybody I said this: You and Duperie have

Sorcerer blood. You're the only two who can use your minds to manipulate the Bound Order of the Zodiac. Noctivatian blood alone cannot work mental magic."

Valor gnashed his teeth. Had Duperie been truthful with him, or was he being mean because he wanted to be the only Noctivatian capable of working mental magic? Either way, people were still manipulating Valor.

"I need to get back to the portal, but I hope you find your friends, McRaven," said Orby. He peered around the fence and left.

"Thanks," said Valor.

He moved back behind the fence when two stargazers escorted Mahrata as she reclined on a flying carpet while moaning. The stargazers directed the carpet down the steps of Mystic Steeples before turning right onto Skullhead Street. Valor remained in the shadows behind them. Two little glowing eyes looked up at him in the tangling hexteria growing behind the iron fence. Valor walked up Skullhead Street, but when he looked back, an opossum with dingy fur, a long snout, and a pink tail was following him. Valor circled back, clinging to the Bootjack fence line, hoping the opossum would stop following him, but it scampered along on his heels.

"Go away," said Valor, and the opossum rolled over on its furry back and became stiff; even its little feet stopped moving. "Aw, I didn't mean to scare you to death, little fellow." Valor leaned over the animal, feeling sorry for it, and it flipped back on its feet and hissed. "That's not very nice, you know? You shouldn't fool someone with death."

Valor walked away fast, but the creature kept stride behind him.

"All right now," groaned Valor. "I can't have a nocturnal animal following me." He trapped the opossum's tail under a flaming garbage urn at the curb. "Sorry about that, but I have to see where they're taking Mahrata. And I think I know a way to follow them." He hid the Staff deep in the boxwood hedges growing along the perimeter of Bootjack Square and said, "I will go into a mink."

He shapeshifted into the furry mink again and scurried behind the stargazers who paused in the back alley of Gitchi Patootie's

Bewitching Beauties. The stargazers inserted the crest of Mahrata's magic staff into an indentation in the elaborate pink iron door, and it opened, allowing them to carry Mahrata inside the beauty spa. Just before Stargazer Scire Stoker closed the door, Valor leaped onto the back of Scire's robe, clinging to him with his mink claws.

Valor took refuge under the giant turning gears on the lower right of the Spherical Portal of Reformation. He peeped out through the grinding steel cogs and copper tubing. A male prisoner from the sanatorium stood strapped to an upright, pink-padded table in front of the portal. It was Egg Goodridge, Valor's friend.

"I think it'll work this time; we have a younger convict. You all right, O Captivatingness?" asked Scire in a ghostlike groan.

Egg had a metal ring stuck in his mouth, held by straps fastened to the table. Valor's whiskers twitched under his beady mink eyes. What were they going to do to his friend? There was no one else in the spa to help him.

"Ye-ye-yes," sputtered Mahrata, standing under the spherical portal's glowing rings, which rotated above her head. "But, haaa, hurry up with it be-before I waste away here."

Stargazer Dayonis Augusta placed a Vortex of Reveling in a slot over Egg's mouth. Then he inserted a key in the atomic clock midpoint in the wall of clocks. The hands of time sped backward. Egg whimpered before the mist in the Vortex calmed, and the portal's gears ground to a stop. Glowing shafts of light spat out from the Vortex onto the mirrors, which shot over Mahrata before fading dark again.

Dayonis tugged his beard. Something had gone wrong. Mahrata pulled a pink framed mirror down from over her head to inspect her face. "Hmmm," she moaned. "Ga-give it another ga-go; it's not working."

"But, O Captivatingness, it will kill him," said Scire, wiping the sweat off his face with his white ruff collar. "We tried this two days ago. Whatever you have is not responding to the treatments."

"These treatments have, cah-cah-cah, kept me from withering away ever since I lost immortality. Haaa, you and Dayonis as well.

CHAPTER TWENTY-ONE

Now, who de-deserves to die, him or us? Cah-cah-cah," Mahrata coughed.

"As you wish," said Scire, motioning for Dayonis to reset the atomic clock.

Valor scurried under the portal. He had to do something to stop them from murdering Egg. But if Valor changed into his regular form, they would see him. What should he do? Mahrata's magic staff leaned against the portal. If Valor could knock it a few more inches to the left, it might fall into the portal and jam the gears. He reached his little mink paws up and pushed the staff, as the portal began to reactivate.

The staff's crest hit the spinning gear, but instead of jamming it, the staff flipped through the air and smashed Scire in the face. Scire fell back against the portal, where his robe caught between the gears, slowing the cogs to a groaning struggle. Dayonis rushed across the room, giving Valor time to scurry up Egg and knock the Vortex out of his mouth. The Vortex fell to the pink marble floor and shattered.

"Get that mink," ordered Scire, tearing his robe free from the portal.

Dayonis fired his magic staff, and the spinning likeness of Saturn, on the staff's tip, spun off and soared through the air. Valor squealed as its rings sawed into his furry behind, so he scooted through the pink spa, knocking over beauty potions and instruments. If he could just make it to the hand-mirror-shaped door, maybe he could get out of the spa alive. He looked over his furry back, at the Saturn medallion spinning at him, emitting colorful gasses now. Choking, Valor ducked, and the medallion crashed through the glass door, just as a witch was flying low over the alley. Yes! This was Valor's chance to escape. He jumped onto the witch's broom bristles, then dived onto the roof of a passing carriage, losing the Saturn medallion somewhere along the way.

In the distance, lights shone through Mystic Chantry's windows. Were the vespercestors holding Convocation? Valor had to see what was happening. He jumped off the carriage and darted to the gardens flanking Mystic Chantry, where scores of Familiars peered through the stained glass windows. Were the animals trying to get to their owners or escape the Zodiac Beings? Valor scurried up a stone rain gutter on the corner of the Chantry. He then scurried across the first ledge of windows that he could access from the gutter. His little mink eyes settled on a hole in a glass windowpane where he shimmied through with much difficulty. It proved a tight squeeze, shaving off a long strip of fur down his back. He crawled onto the inside ledge and found himself looking down from the first row of balcony windows. He scanned the Chantry looking for his friends. Where were they? At least Egg was alive, barely.

Magisters Calamus Tuberstooge and Bessbadora Breaches moved across the platform to the podium, and Calamus addressed the covens who sat on the edge of their benches, not in their usual places, but in segregated groups. Even the Balcony of Elders seemed to have their backs to each other. On the ground floor, Twila and Marston Diamone were sitting in a section with many of the LaRocks, waving their wands, manipulating a transparent banner with Mahrata's image to rise in midair.

Calamus embraced the podium and said, "Uh, as most of you know, my wife, Toonya Tuberstooge, left me a few years ago to raise my son, Seth, by myself. My, uh, sense of humor is old-fashioned, I reckon. But I am not distrusting of the lady folks. Enchanted weapons are my specialty—not politics." Calamus belched into the magihorn as if expecting the covens to laugh. "But, uh, even if you're like me and you've been living under a LaRock, you gotta see the grim situation we're in."

"I'll say it for you, Calamus," said Bessbadora. "O Captivatingness is in intensive care and not expected to live much longer."

"Get your stinkin' hides off this platform," yelled Tilta Crumpecker, rising from her throne chair as smoke billowed from the coronet of candles on her head. "O Captivatingness ain't dead yet! How dare you all try to replace her? How dare you try to divide the Sanguinati as you have?"

"High Priestess, if we're divided . . . split . . . at odds with each other . . . it is not because of me or Calamus," hissed Bessbadora.

"The LaRocks have corrupted everything. They have destroyed Severance with their rule. And, with that needful declaration, I've invited a couple of former members you all will remember."

Bessbadora motioned to the side of the platform, and Valor slipped on the window ledge when his parents, Houmas and Lithium McRaven, walked up the steps toward the podium, wearing their weatherworn wilderness clothes. Valor hooked his little mink claws on the ledge and pulled himself back under the window. Had his parents come straight from the Bumbling Boonies? Lithium's auburn hair had grown long again but hung stringy around her face. Houmas had lost more hair and gained more hard-life wrinkles.

"That's right, you two," continued Bessbadora. "Just step on up here and tell it. Say your peace. Now's your time to set things straight."

Houmas frowned at the magihorn, which Bessbadora had lowered to his thin, leathery lips. With his mouth open, he squinted unhappily across the Chantry as if everyone were wearing ridiculous pantomage outfits.

"Git this thang outta my face," grunted Houmas, punching the magihorn, causing it to float to his left. "Don't need no highfalutin gadgets when ya got a manly set of lungs." Houmas grimaced and slammed his fists on the podium, showing his severed finger the troll had bitten off with its jagged teeth. "Now, anybody who knows me knows I'm of the upbringin' to respect authority."

Several witches from various coven sections snorted with laughter. Houmas grimaced at them before continuing his speech.

"That's a'ight ifin some of you don't respect me. My old man never told me he loved me, but I knew it by the look in his eyes. And that's what y'all need—some tough love," said Houmas, appearing so alone on the platform, so uneasy. Lithium stood beside him with a dejected expression. "Take my pert-near purty wife here; she can tell ya what sorta fellah I am." Houmas held his neck stiff and didn't look at her timid reaction. "My knowledge of the *Controssua*—my integrity's all a man needs. If'n I want something done, I just do it. I might look short to you, but the Ancients have given me some mighty tall shoes to fill."

"It's true," sighed Lithium, "We're both very long-suffering. Anybody who knows me will tell you, I tried to be the best wife and mother I could, but what good did it do?"

Some in the Chantry rolled their eyes at Lithium's comment.

Houmas cleared his throat. "We both tried, Lithium. We wanted to do better things with our lives, but we couldn't, in all integrity, be part of the, uh, whatchamacallit?" Houmas asked Lithium while scratching his head.

"'The corrupt system,'" replied Lithium. Her cushy chin pressed against her collarbone. "Remember? You said—"

"Dadburnit now, Lithium! Don't go a-interrupting me." Houmas's voice raised two octaves. "I can honestly say, I've kept these here boots of mine on the old paths and ain't compromised my values the way many have gone a-doing."

Many witches appeared to grow impatient and shifted around in their seats. The LaRock supporters took turns keeping Mahrata's banner in the air.

"It's true, Houmas," Lithium said in a sad tone. "Your father approved of you. We both saw the glint in his eye just before he died."

"I know—I know, Lithium," sighed Houmas. "I jes' woulda liked to hadda chance to of been the dog-tootin' high priest . . . lead these here covens in the right path. But the LaRocks put us in that bum-burnin' sanatorium."

Calamus stood in front of the magihorn and said, "And you could've been the high priest, Houmas, had certain shady politics not been established at Mystic Steeples. And we all know how I feel about politics."

Again, Crumpecker sprang from her seat. "Houmas and Lithium are just a coupla sanatoribums who've escaped the sanatorium without permission," she screeched. "I'll not stand for this Convocation to be turned into a rally against O Captivatingness!"

The covens responded with a mixture of cheers and jeers. Crumpecker looked over her shoulder at Teddyus Manoj, who seemed extra mellow in his throne chair.

"High Priest, back me up over here," demanded Crumpecker.

Manoj turned his head toward the choir loft, took a deep breath, then drifted over to the podium. His head tilted back as though communicating with the Bound Order of the Zodiac, which patrolled under the ceiling. He extended his hands and said, "He who laboureth to put a rooster in a den of pregnant hens, shall forthwith expect perturbed poultry." Manoj turned and drifted back to his seat while Crumpecker's face convulsed.

Lithium took the magihorn from Calamus and lifted her misty eyes toward the seated covens. "It kills me to say this, but I have no choice because Houmas and I are led to obey the Ancients," she said, lifting her *Controssua*. Her eyes dulled with scheming vindictiveness, though her posture seemed broken. "Our son, Valor, is the Grim Warlock. And I would think you all would want to stop him—stop him at all costs."

Valor felt as though a bolt of lightning had pierced through him. His furry back collapsed against the window, and his whiskers twitched under his bulging eyes.

"Houmas and I can only be a part of traditional Sanguinati leadership, so we can only lend our support to Venerious Falmoth," continued Lithium, squeezing her lips tight with a forlorn nod.

Mistress Bessbadora prowled to the edge of the platform and motioned toward the back of the Chantry. "Yes, that's right," she said. "Falmoth Most Fortuned, come up here and vie for your rightful position as head vespercestor."

Venerious Falmoth skipped down the aisle, flinging candy at everyone. "Yup, really, you can have it. Eat up, eat up!" he giggled. "Aren't I generous to give you some of my most magnifiskull confections and bonerrific sweets? Soon, Mahrata LaRock's chubby cheeks will be resting beneath roots of weeds and mourners' feet." Falmoth danced up the steps to the platform as several coven members and magisters tore out of the Chantry.

"Over my dead body, you'll step on this platform!" growled Crumpecker. She fired her wand at Falmoth, knocking him off the platform several yards. The Bound Order of the Zodiac made an awful noise and swooshed down over the Convocation, which erupted in chaos. Valor jumped through the hole in the window, narrowly missing a wand zap, before scurrying across the ledge and down the rain gutter.

CHAPTER TWENTY-TWO

Anasircea

THE MYSTIC MEDICINARY

THE moon shone over the gardens outside Mystic Chantry, where Anasircea Zagato knelt under a bleeding madgollia, pulling up handfuls of lilacs and placing them in a leather pouch. Still, in the form of a mink, Valor crawled under the shrubs before shifting back into his real appearance.

"You startled me," gasped Anasircea. "Did you escape the sanatorium again?"

"No, Ms. Anasircea, but you are related to Blade Zagato. Please, do you know if my friends are all okay?" asked Valor. He drew close to her with pleading hands and eyes.

Anasircea placed the flowers in her bag and wiped her hands on a large madgollia leaf. "I knew we would have a private talk, Son of the McRavens," said Anasircea. "I do not know where Blade finds any relation to my family. And I do not know the state of your friends. That mystic revelation has not come to me."

Valor found himself fidgeting with fear. "Are you sure? I mean, are you certain Mahrata didn't kill any of them?"

"O Captivatingness is very ill. She hasn't felt like talking. I don't think she'll live much longer. Magister Kraneswaddle has proved unable to cure her, so I have spent all my time and energy trying to save her."

"I wouldn't doubt she did something to my friends. You know what she's capable of—Blade said you were like us, and the Ministry uses you when all else fails," said Valor. "Was that just a lie, too?"

She remained serene, beautiful, as pale as the moon. Could she see his chest heaving?

"Some things must remain our shared secrets, mustn't they?" she said with a smile.

"Yes, 'our shared secrets,'" Valor agreed, relaxing from his tense position.

"I don't want to heal O Captivatingness, but if I fail, I know my fate will be that of your friends." Anasircea gazed at him as though awaiting a confession. "I sense something else is bothering you, Valor."

"I know you couldn't cure Creighton, but I, um, think I know what's wrong with Mahrata." He moistened his lips and lowered his head. "The, um, the painting I did of Mahrata was hexed, but I didn't know it could kill her."

Anasircea rubbed a violet blossom on her cheeks, and her expression came alive. "That painting may be our chance," she said, "our only chance to save your friends. In fact, I believe it might just change everything."

"I don't understand. It's a good thing I did?" asked Valor.

"Have faith for it to be so. I'm certain I can cure Mahrata, but she will owe me this time."

"That will be hard to do. She nearly killed my friend Egg earlier tonight. This plan of yours had better bring a big change in that awful woman." Valor confessed that he had found Spirit's Staff of Gleaning. "It's hidden in Bootjack Square. I can return it to Spirit since you can get me inside Mystic Steeples."

"That is the best news I've heard in months. At least thirty-four people have been possessed and died in the past two days. Hurry and get the Staff, Valor! But promise me you'll back me no matter what I say to O Captivatingness. She is awaiting me now. These violets are for her pain tonics."

Anasircea awaited Valor's return with the Staff, and together they dashed through the interior entry of Mystic Steeples.

Guardian Czerena Slain blocked them at the door with her magic staff. "Hold on. What are you concealing there—a weapon?" she asked, while ghosts, flying animals, and Zodiac Beings began to swoop down from the sky toward them.

Valor unveiled the Staff of Gleaning, and Czerena's hood fell back on her robe. "You don't say! Valor found another stolen instrument?"

"Curse you, Valor McRaven! Those Zodiac Instruments belong to me. Everyone will pay for these foolish acts you are committing." The same wicked man's voice Valor had heard in Candlewicke Mansion rattled Mystic Steeples.

Czerena scooted aside, letting them inside the hall where Valor ran and placed it in the hand of the Zodiac Being known as Spirit. Several apprentices and members of Mystic Ministry ran out of Mystic Chantry and cheered when they saw what Valor had done. A smoky black mass screamed and shot through the walls. It passed through Twila Diamone, knocking her to the floor before pouring out the doors into the city. Twila remained sprawled on her back, convulsing next to a crystaleer she had intentionally knocked out of Hanzabuh Cuddy's hands.

"Guardian, make sure nobody steals the Staff again," ordered Anasircea, while cameras flashed, and more crystaleers recorded the event. "We have to go and save O Captivatingness."

When Valor and Anasircea made it to the tenth floor of the

eastern wing, Ulysses LaRock, Mahrata's brother-in-law, was standing in the hall, comforting Vespercestor Mumbazandie after she emerged from the medicinary, swabbing her tears with a lace handkerchief.

"We should get the immediate family here," said Ulysses. "Mahrata will be joining Urbanne on the astral plane soon."

"I think I can cure O Captivatingness now, but Valor and I will need to be alone with her," Anasircea said to Ulysses.

"With that boy?" snorted Ulysses, while pointing his wand between Valor's eyes. "Absolutely out of the question."

"By 'boy,' do you mean the Knight of Night who just found and returned the Staff of Gleaning? Then, yes! Or do you *want* O Captivatingness to die?" asked Anasircea.

"Of course not," said Ulysses, withdrawing his wand with a drooping jaw.

Mumbazandie peeped over her handkerchief with surprise as Ulysses cleared Mahrata's dwarves out of Mystic Medicinary, allowing Valor and Anasircea to enter the room. Mahrata reclined on a majestic bed in the back with purple-fringed pillows propped all around her. A harp stood beside her bed near a table crowded with half-full potion bottles. Someone had applied layers of enchanted powder all over her puffy face and wrapped a purple turban around her hair. She made a *"cah-cah-cah"* sound every time she exhaled. The aroma of violets sweetened the room. A Mesmerist's wheel continued to spin at the foot of her bed, and a dragon statue at the head of her bed exhaled a fine mist. Could it be magnetic water?

"Hmmm, haaa. What form of death do you have planned for me, Valor?" said Mahrata, leaning back on her velvet pillows with a bit of dribble across her chin. "You, cah-cah-cah, are tempted aren't you . . . to finish me off?" She leaned forward with her probing, beady eyes drooling over the top of a tissue now. Her dwarves remained pressed against the medicinary door.

Valor looked away from her and said, "Let's just say it's tempting *not* to help you, O Captivatingness."

"Hmmm, how about you, Anasircea? Do you have my cure?" Mahrata asked with a puny breath.

Anasircea placed the violets on the potion table. "Yes, O Captivatingness," she said. "Once again, I can cure you when others fail. But you must know I am a Sorcerer."

Mahrata nodded and sputtered, "Don't come any, cah-cah-cah, closer. Your shadow might get on me."

"O Captivatingness, can't you see?" asked Valor. "Your only real hope of retaining your rule over Mystic Steeples is to stop persecuting the Sorcerers and break this cover-up you and the vespercestors have placed over the Sanguinati. No matter how much you keep fighting it, eventually, they will learn the truth of their heritage."

"Never cah-cah-cah! And you have, haaa, broken the *Questioning Regulation*, I will send you the invoice," wheezed Mahrata, while Anasircea began rummaging through her medical bag.

"Wait," said Valor, backing away from her bed. "I can't help her if she has harmed my friends; I'm sorry, I just can't."

Anasircea flashed him a displeased look. "O Captivatingness, are Valor's friends alive?" she asked.

"Hmmm, cure me before I answer that, or you will join them. Cah-cah-cah."

"How could you harm Doomsy; she's just eight years old, you know?" he asked the head vespercestor.

Mahrata wiped her drool again. "Haaa, yes," she said. "And Venerious Falmoth was eight once. Cah-cah-cah. Another invoice coming your way."

Valor found himself leaning forward, desperate to sink his fangs into Mahrata. He slammed his hands on the footboard of her bed and dug his nails into the wood.

"Now listen here, Mahrata," he growled. "I saw you at Gitchi Patootie's. You admitted you lost immortality. How dare you kill innocent people to preserve your youth! Severance is in an upheaval right now. I don't care what rosy little lies your servants are under obligation to tell you; the Sanguinati is planning to replace you. Falmoth has many supporters, and so does High Priest Manoj. Toadvine Citadel has turned against you. For once, you don't have time or room to make the rules."

A loud explosion echoed through the walls. Mahrata held up her hand to stop Valor from leaving. "Your friends are, cah-cah-cah, all alive," she said. "They're being held in maximum security. Please, cah-cah-cah, help me."

"We will cure you, O Captivatingness, but here are the terms: You will confess the truth of everyone's heritage and allow Sorcerers to attend Mystic Steeples and allow them positions in the Ministry," said Valor.

"And remove the *Questioning Regulation*," added Anasircea, sprinkling a few violets over Mahrata's bed. She waved her wand, conjuring up a glittering square slab of what appeared to be pure gold. "This is a testament tablet. Sign it and seal your word."

"So, mote it be," coughed Mahrata, pressing her insignia ring into the tablet. "Hmmm, now hand me my Crystaleer over, cah-cah-cah, there." She pointed to the potion table.

Cauldrons of flowers turned their wilting heads, while other flowers drooped when Valor grabbed the crystal sphere and handed it to her. Mahrata held the crystaleer in front of her face. The bags under her eyes sagged to match her droopy jowls.

"Summoner Mamahchi," she said into the crystaleer, "cah-cah-cah, release Candlewicke Coven, and lift the *Questioning Regulation* for them. Haaa, also, release all the Sorcerers from the sanatorium and tell them—cah-cah-cah—tell them they are now proper citizens from this day forward. And, hmmm, Summoner, this is a command."

The crystaleer turned into a ball of white light and passed through the wall on its way. A surge of hope mounted in Valor's heart before Mumbazandie and Ulysses walked into the room.

"Everything all right, O Captivatingness?" asked Ulysses.

Mahrata nodded.

"I will prepare your cure," Anasircea said to Mahrata before leaving the room with Valor.

When they reached the front Atrium, Anasircea turned to him and whispered, "I will remove the hex on Mahrata's portrait, and you go check on your friends." She smiled as he ran out the door.

And run he did, out of Mystic Steeples and down winding alleys of the city. Objects along the way seemed as glittery as the gold tablet Mahrata had just signed. The Bound Order of the Zodiac still patrolled the night sky over Mystic City, so Valor retreated inside a business entryway on Mystic Circle near Charnel Alley. His heartbeat became a steady thump, and he had trouble thinking. He had to see Doomsy and his friends, so he continued running toward the long roads leading to the sanatorium, thinking he might find them there. He paused again. Would the guards let him through the gates? He jumped forward when someone tapped him on his shoulder.

"This is tragic. You're supposed to be in Bogamuckla learning Noctivatian magic," said Venerious Falmoth.

Valor pointed his monoculous at Falmoth. "I tried—no thanks to Janus Duperie, who'd rather play cruel jokes than teach me anything," he said. "And you, you were supposed to be here trying to rescue my friends, not putting yourself on the Sanguinati throne. And, and how dare you recruit my parents to turn on me the way they did just to help you!"

Falmoth dove inside a fortuneteller booth and fired a wand blast at a Zodiac Being, ignoring Valor who, to avoid the Being's wrath, jumped under a hotel awning dripping with kudzu vines. The phantoms from Falmoth's wand engulfed the crablike Zodiac Being in a cloud of screaming faces, which then turned to ash when the Being clamped its claws together and lit up like a comet. Falmoth lifted his hat and began to sing and dance around the sidewalk, letting the ashes from his magic spell fall over him:

"Oops—soot. I got ashes on my suit while McRaven wanders and whines. All through the night, the Zodiac tries to bite as Valor stands here, squalling 'neath vines of kudzu creeping and crawling."

"There's no need to mock the Song of the Sanguinati," said Valor. He couldn't stand to look at Falmoth, so he walked away, not wanting him to be around when he saw his friends—if Valor ever saw them again.

"Don't walk off into oblivion! I didn't recruit Houmas and Lithium. Perhaps it was my fauns; after all, the Bumbling Boonies is their home." Falmoth danced in circles until he caught up with Valor to block him with a bouquet of candy. "Whether in words or with a song, I do appreciate their noble effort to put me back on the throne."

Valor pushed the candy out of his way. "My parents accused me of being the Grim Warlock. I suppose your faun pawns gave them that notion, too?" he asked, lifting his eyebrows. Did Falmoth take him for an idiot?

"Your skin's too thin, my friend. You *are* a warlock now, and they do call our magic Grim, understand?" replied Falmoth. He picked up some of the broken candy on the sidewalk and shoved it into his mouth with a syrupy, sympathetic face. "We're all Gwim, Gwim, Gwim." He crunched the candy between his teeth and gave a toothy smile with rainbow-colored speckles.

"Well, someone failed to mention 'Grim' to my parents, or they wouldn't be supporting you, now would they?" asked Valor. He walked around Falmoth, watching for his friends out of the corner of his eye.

"No need to worry about your father and mother. I'll not invite them in our Order. All they do is gripe and gripe, spewing their tripe while everybody hurls and heaves," said Falmoth with a goofy, woozy face, appearing as if he would vomit. "Oh, please. Houmas and Lithium will soon split—go back to their dusty cliffs. While I remain breaking my back to thwart these attacks."

Should Valor tell Falmoth that he had just worked a deal with Mahrata against him? Were there any guarantees he could trust anyone? He decided to keep his dealings quiet, which was very hard for him because he was a McRaven after all.

An alley parade marched past them. The marchers carried signs reading, "Return Falmoth to the Big House." The marchers hurled garlands of candy, with images of Falmoth's face, at the spectators on the alley.

"Magnifiskull!" cheered Falmoth. "They need me to march among them. See you back in Bogamuckla, my *Grim* little brother."

Valor didn't bother with any goodbyes; he headed toward the Crescent Moon District to wait for his friends at his home. He lingered on Spookum Alley, remembering the first time Aaron had seen Candlewicke Mansion, how he couldn't stop making plans. The mansion appeared now as it did then, a deserted hotel, like the peeling-bricked storefronts that sheltered once but now frightened people away. He sat across the alley on a bench by the fence line of Shickbone Cathedral, fearing the sun would come up before he would see his friends. A clap of thunder broke the silence, accompanied by a bolt of lightning somewhere in the city. Rings of smoke lifted through the trees, the aftermath of the thunderbolt.

A distant voice cried, "CURSE YOU, MAHRATA. The Grim Hour can't be worse than this ruling you have given!"

Valor remembered the Grim Warlock's warning that he, Valor, would experience so much more death that he would beg for the days that his only loss was his twin, grandmother, and Creighton.

A whisper from the wind passed over Valor's ears: "You are still the Knight of Night, Valor. You must discipline yourself and lead the people through the dark hour. If you succeed, a new dawn will arrive for those who survive."

How much darker could it get? Valor still had to find two more stolen Zodiac instruments: the Winged Staff of Iris and the Vial of Mortal Plague from Death. Valor trembled. How in the turbulent heavens could he even get near Death—the sixth and final Zodiac Being the vespercestors kept inside an iron-lung feeding tube? And how much longer could Valor go without blood? He was growing weaker by the day, and more impulsive. His heart overturned in his chest when a shadow stirred, passing through the intersection.

"Aw, just another stupid carriage," mumbled Valor. He sank on the bench, resting his chin on his chest, watching a little bird peck at trash on the cobblestone under a gas lamp. By the time the fifth shadow passed down the alley, he couldn't get his hopes up. He would just wait until something came closer.

Under the amber glow of the flickering gas lamps, before the morning sun cast its first ray on the depth of twilight, Valor turned his head. Moving out of the shadows of an old abandoned restaurant filled with dust-covered china and carved chairs was the most glorious sight he had ever seen:

"Doomsy! Aaron!" It was Valor's entire, glorious coven along with Booger Fay. He jumped up, and his chest swelled in gasps. He tried to call out to the others but choked on his tears, so he ran as fast as his short legs would allow until he crashed into the middle of Candlewicke 13.

Doomsy climbed out of the pile and steadied herself.

"Sorry, dear. I didn't squash Mr. Grudgings, did I?" asked Valor, bracing her with his arms and worrying about her pet snake.

Doomsy shifted her hands behind her dress and said, "I don't think so, my pet. Either he's still slithering around, or there's a wire loose in my bustle."

The End of Book Four

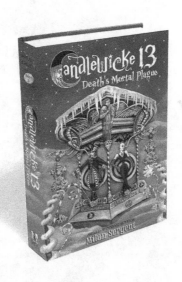

BOOK FIVE (Series Finale)

Candlewicke 13: Death's Mortal Plague

Available Soon!

Broad Map of Hoopenfangia

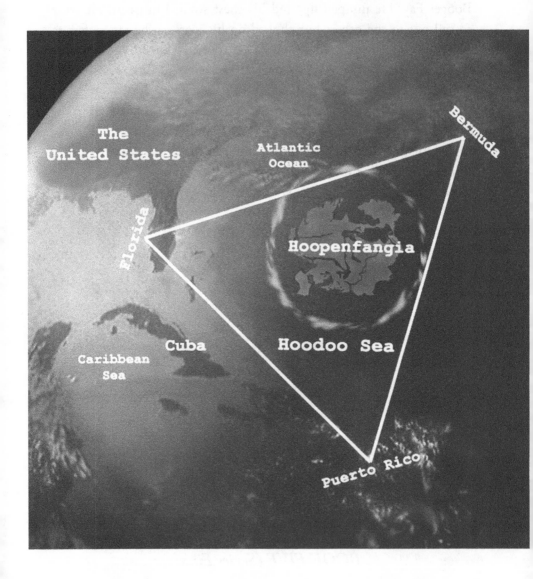

Detailed Map of Hoopenfangia

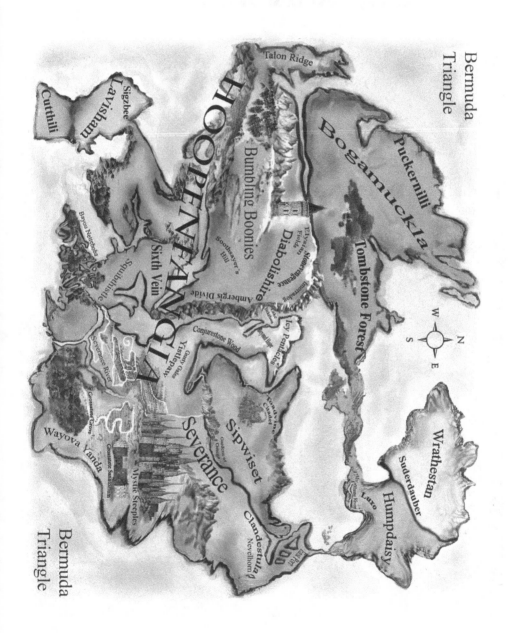

Broad Map of Mystic Steeples, Mystic City, and the Sanatorium

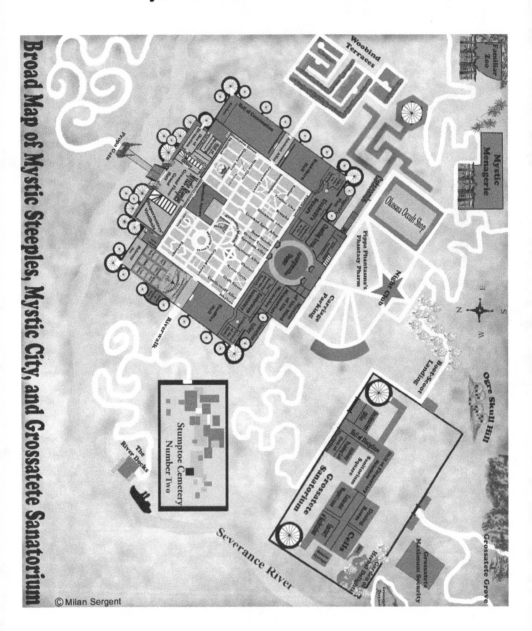

478

Detailed Map of Mystic City and Mystic Steeples

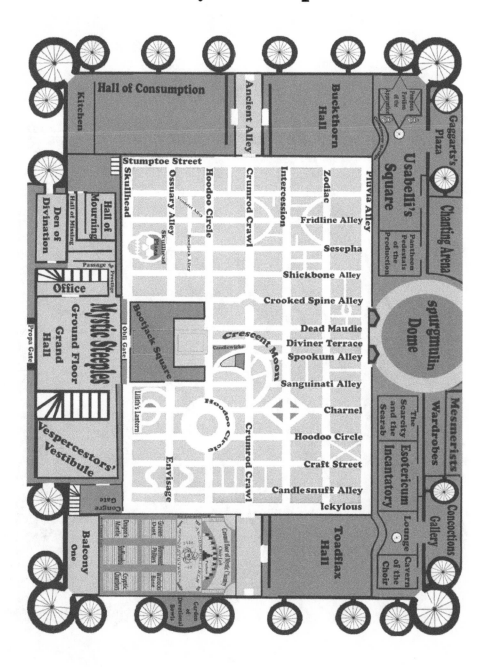

Detailed Map of Grossatete Sanatorium

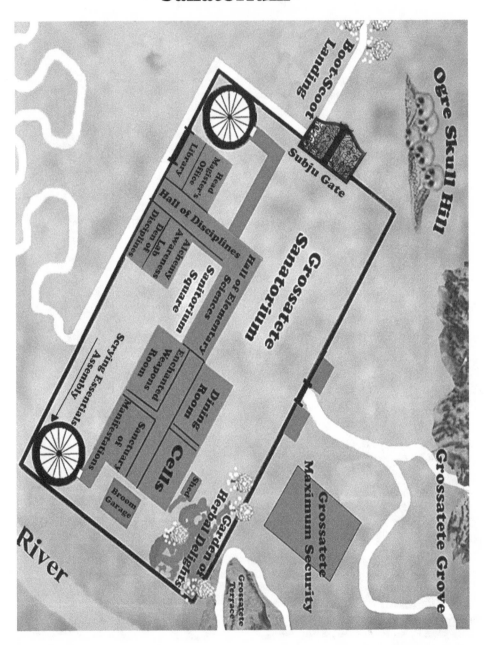

ABOUT THE AUTHOR

Milan Sergent studied creative writing in college and began writing the Candlewicke 13 novel series in 2007, a year after featuring some of the series' characters in his solo art exhibition, *Outsiders and Apparitions*, near Rockefeller Center in New York City.

Sergent's *Candlewicke 13 and the Tombstone Forest* won the Readers' Favorite Finalist Award in the Children - Fantasy/Sci-Fi category as well as the Book Excellence Award Finalist – Fantasy.

An artist and poet since adolescence, a few of Sergent's poetic works were published in *Scarlet Literary Magazine*.

To learn more about the author or view the illustrated companion guide to the Candlewicke 13 series visit **www.milansergent.com**. While there, join the mailing list for important news updates and notifications about future novel releases.

CPSIA information can be obtained
at www.ICGtesting.com
Printed in the USA
LVHW111649180520
655943LV00011B/68/J